CW01102886

THE FAT MAN CAN'T SWIM

THE FAT MAN CAN'T SWIM

RICHARD H. A. BLUM

Creative Arts Book Company
Berkeley • California

Copyright © 2001 by Richard H. A. Blum

No part of this book may be reproduced in any manner without the written permission of the publisher, except in brief quotations used in articles or reviews.

For information contact:
Creative Arts Book Company
833 Bancroft Way
Berkeley, California 94710
(800) 848-7789

ISBN 0-88739-309-8
Library of Congress Catalog Number 99-65729

Printed in the United States of America

THE FAT MAN CAN'T SWIM

1

He'd been on this United flight many times, but that was long ago. He'd flown to Washington many times, but those were different times. He'd done his millions of government-dutiful miles, sleepless and jet-lagged, to Europe, Asia, the Middle East, and—what was always the worst for him—Mexico. Corruption and sometimes corpses.

By now, after so many others faring just as he had and must, even the air was tired from so much human movement; polluted and retaliating. Worn travellers, their planes circling darkening cities, might well wonder whether there could ever be fortunes made large enough to provide repair for this turbulent and damaged world. But some of those making fortunes were themselves a curse. Money was by no means always that, but the people with whom he dealt were irredeemably so.

The traveller was bound now for further struggle in this black game of curses. Wherever he went—on this trip, Western capitals, Eastern and Central Europe—would be the black game: zero sum and few gains at the end of it. If he won, yes, the small triumphs of laws. If he lost? Commerce and struggling nations would become more savage. Whole peoples harmed, cheated and dismayed. Not civilization completely lost, but further entropy, of which deaths were one form. He had become too tired, too wise over time to expect it otherwise. Amazing then, that Lee Barbour was still an idealist, albeit one who carried a gun.

Barbour, ignoring the bump and bustle of late boarders wrestling their way down the other business class aisle, was concentrating on page proofs when he became conscious of eyes and intentions focusing on him, for he had much animal learning as to slight significances. He looked up. It was the stewardess with her tray of glasses. She wore her airline-issue plastic and brittle smile.

"Champagne, Mr. Barbour?"

She'd flown many times too, beginning younger, thinner, kinder years ago.

Soldiering on with the rest of them, not yet over the hill, indeed if relaxed probably a rather attractive forty-five or fifty or what the hell; Lee Barbour was not a good judge and had no intention of Gilbert and Sullivanizing, "I can always tell a woman's age and I do." Her cabin serving partner, young enough, pretty enough, tits enough, but too uniformed straight and sterile in the ham to be provocative, looked every bit as weary and even harder. Unforgiving of unknown sins, hers or others'. These days youth begins with fighting and learns to armor itself quickly. Not all those in armor are chivalrous knights; too many wound others as themselves, preferring their own version of the Golden Rule, "do unto others first." Some of the young toughs and savages, disciplined only enough to qualify as runners, enforcers and slayers for their richer masters, killed, raped and maimed only for the fun of it, to relieve, say, the boredom of burglary. Trouble enough though for investigators; for these would be the ambushers behind silk curtains in the palaces of the criminal rich, those international economic entrepreneurs with corroded souls whom, once again, Barbour must pursue. The rustling of any palace silk could be a deadly matter.

What the hell, he was so tired, unwilling to face ambush that could come in so many forms, more often an office intrigue or an angry woman than an Uzi's bullets, but presumably, though he could not really be sure, the Vienna worry would be the latter. It was, after all, a city of palaces. What was there waiting? IFFY had furnished little help but the slim packet, sent by ordinary express mail to his Montreal hotel. The packet was an unlettered guide for a Snark hunt, a map for a wild goose chase, a satire on background briefs for investigators; it was Baron Munchausen's notes on becoming a detective. "Schlamperei," Barbour believed would be the Viennese word for the uncharted swamp implied. What could IFFY be about on this one? And to take the cake, an inexperienced new woman hire, one Claire Dubois was waiting for him. They seemed to expect him to be her new kindergarten teacher.

Sofia was his next detour stop on the way. His first had been California, to visit his beloved Adams Napa Valley vineyard-keeping kin and have dinner with close friend Markowitz who was licking his GI wounds, playing at cop in an ugly, ugly town. Markowitz was happy in its simple violence and squalor because it was all better than the Mexico or Washington, D.C. they had shared. As for upcoming Sofia, Barbour had scheduled it because of a friend and onetime enemy there, Vassili, and his promise of "some interesting information, not over the telephone thank you," about "some missing items." Barbour had no idea whose items they were, but Vassili would not have suggested his "stopping by in Sofia" unless the items were in the high dollar range. What items might they be, and whose? Barbour had no idea; in his line of work so many billions of dollars went missing.

Sofia had no palaces at all, no silk curtains about which to worry. But the secret service of Bulgaria, and its history as drawers of water and hewers of wood—the "wet affairs" choreboys—for the KGB had made Sofia during cold war days into a grim, gray tumbledown garden of *hashashins*, new men of that old mountain, assassins. There was always some new old man of that mountain, a new Hassan ben Sabbah, always new recruits to his bloody labor: an influx of Russians, Chechens, Armenians, Azeris, Georgians, *mafiya* now and well dressed by their Sofia tailors, some of these excellent. His thoughts wandered to Sonya in Sofia, as splendid a cutter and costumier as she was in bed. Barbour had worn, and would soon wear again with equal pleasure, sport coats she had tailored, silk ascots she had designed, and hickies she had very personally planted, accompanied by a beaming morning-after smile.

In Sofia, not against Sonya but the likes of her clients, one would be on guard. Barbour's line of work required the capacity for appreciation of the enemy's cunning, if not its results. Admire the very artfulness of the devil, never doubt his presence. Ever. Without this appraising gift one was defeated without battle, or moved in too quickly to too-close combat, only to be surprised at one's own stupidity as one died. The devil had enthusiastic princes and gangster soldiers. Screwtapes often won by default.

"Oh my," he startled himself to halt his mind's meandering, to return to the question, for the stewardess was still waiting for his reply.

"Wear and tear gets to us, doesn't it?" He put the question idly, without reference to champagne—he hadn't decided on that or orange juice.

She looked at him hard, appearing once again offended by a nasty world and, as with most, despite their appearance of competence, helpless before it. Lee, sensing that she took him for an adversary, not just one more worldly comrade among the too wise and walking wounded, felt a rush of remorse. Another of those careless slips of his, even after so long: assuming casual human sharing when all the lessons were of dogs eating one another. He'd read terrier pups were the worst, he thought irrelevantly. An English breed those; so much for inbreeding high civilization.

He interrupted her just-forming response, "Sorry, I intended it sympathetically, but I had no reason to assume you'd know that. One more idiot on your watch, I guess."

Her hard look turned quizzical then reassured. "No, my fault." she said. "Too short a layover, too many overtime hours, and too few philosophers joining me on my watches. Will the champagne get you into the air bubbling? It's California but I can sneak you a Roederer from first cabin if you prefer it to Mumms." She was smiling, genuinely.

"Don't usually at lunchtime, but sure," he replied. "One glass of the Roederer and then the discipline to get through this." He waved at page proofs in their manila folder, marked *Journal of Financial Crime*, and beside him, on the empty window seat an unstable pile of his books, the overflow from his well-worn, soft leather brief case. The IFFY Vienna pages lay behind the page proofs, standing out because red ink from the *SECRET* stamping, too moist a pad and badly aimed, had colored the upper edges of the paper.

She fetched the drink from the front cabin, a few aisles up from his Connoisseur class seat and returned, enjoying looking at this man. Graying hair, North Sea gray-blue eyes, trim, "well faced"—an odd and private term her mother would have applied, perhaps five-eleven, in his fifties, correcting journal pages. An economist? A professor? No, his eyes were too hard, and yet much worldly amusement, and complexity spoke from the wrinkles near them. His appearance brought questions, not certainties. Well-traveled Nancy, who knew her London, recognized a red Liberty necktie, a black cashmere Savile Row sport coat, and, somewhat incongruously, badly scuffed old brown shoes.

Nancy did look at a man's shoes, even if as now she had to strain her neck a bit to do so. When she thought she might like the man she also looked at his hands, for wedding rings for instance, or the wrists, for something Rolex-y, gaudy and expensive. Both were her exit cues. Neither were visible on Mr. Barbour here, who seemed old school of a sort; damn few people dressed decently these days to travel. First cabin passengers on this flight looked like a workout class in an expensive gym: tasteless, conformist yuppies, not classy, not even stylishly eccentric, even flying out of San Francisco, which was the last classy town in the country, New York excepted. Some—were probably movie producers or Silicon Valley billionaires—badly needed, though they probably prided themselves on their raffish stubble, a shave.

"Rastafarians by the Bay" her private term, no racial overtones implied. Mr. Barbour, if that was really his name, was not one of them. His accent, easy San Francisco out of New England (how many generations ago?) affirmed some style. Why did one wonder about him at all? Nancy mused.

It was halfway the five-hour-plus flight, sixish Eastern time; Barbour had been diligent in drinking water, restrained in eating, and abstinent with respect to alcohol but for the glass of Roederer. Nancy had more to do, even in a half-booked flight, than observe, but in his case she did.

"Scholarship is served?" she asked, making a special trip down the aisle to refill water-glasses, "I mean your page correcting."

"A bore," he nodded, "a crashing bore. I can be so pleased with what I write until I read it soberly, months later."

"May I ask what it's about?"

"Crime sometimes, money crimes mostly, and thus, to put it cynically, the normal business of modern life."

"That bad, are we?"

"Maybe not us—the poor, honest and overworked, who know our unstriving place," Barbour offered a wry grin.

"And your place?" she asked, her face and voice neutral to allow for a range of interpretive response.

The cold ocean of his eyes washed over her face, lively, and pleasing in its "I have been there too," maturity. She was, he decided, bright, impish, probably honest, and—too infrequently encouraged these days, attractively provocative. He grinned, "I will, as the lady at dinner said to old George the Shaw, 'give you tit for tat.'"

She laughed. "As GBS replied, 'I have tat.' As for the other, well a proper maiden of forty-eight makes no promises, but you can buy me a cup of tea, light on the scones, in Washington. As to 'my place,' not yours either please, and so do you have a favorite coffee shop?"

They both laughed. It was no shipboard romance in the offing, only a blessed relief to be enjoying someone's flirtatious good-natured company on a tedious flight. He was grateful, and as men must be, flattered. Nevertheless he had been, was, and would be tense—those conjugated tenses, he realized, of his life past, present and likely future. He replied gently.

"I'll be busy as hell, and jet-lagged as always, thanks to compulsory visits to numerous bureaucratic jerks, with maybe, if I'm in luck one or two honorable men among them." Barbour well remembered that that was the title of his now dead old friend Bill Colby's book, an inscribed copy on his shelf of favorite books. Too many ghosts. She noted the pause. He resumed, "Maybe a few honorable men have survived the carnage of democracy as we know it. If you saw the old Hoffman and DeNiro movie *Wag the Dog*, you know what I mean, spoof as humor as spin as reality as prognosis as horrifying."

"I remember the movie. I know about politics." She was only a bit wistful. Men and women when making advances learn early, as do generals, to retreat intact and take as few casualties to the ego as possible. "And so, no tea?"

Jesus, he thought, do I never have sense, must I always take time I don't have to be with people I don't know just because they ask me? "Sure, tea. The Jockey Club at the Ritz Carlton on Mass Ave, five-thirty, and allow me to be on California time? If I don't show by 6 o'clock, cuss me out but know I am trapped in Godzilla's cave, or more likely Cyclops', and that I wasn't worth waiting for. I really can't promise better, tomorrow is likely to be a difficult day."

And it would be, and tomorrow and tomorrow.

"All is forgiven," she said quietly, almost maternally. He could imagine her; there was a goodness there in this seemingly ordinary middle-aged stewardess whom he knew he would not see again after tea. Forgiveness indeed. Too little of that about. She offered it as grace, as might an Episcopalian or Lutheran woman pastor sure of God as good. Given the tomorrows that might occur, Barbour could use some of that. Particularly since he had, however religiously needy, always been of two minds as to God. Well, the Balkans of his tomorrow were also religious. Barbour had been there, collected chants on discs and ikons for his chapel, knew those Balkans tolerably well. He had found some blood, much conspiracy, always dolls within dolls, trust as rare as saints' bones, and no certainty ever about his own tomorrows. But, in a cathedral perhaps and praying, no Thomas à Becket be him, he also would pray. A chill ran through him. He brought his thoughts to heel, to the here and now. He was embarrassed by what he feared this woman might have heard as self-important brusqueness. He must put that right with her.

"Look," he paused, "I don't know your name, but…"

"Nancy" she said, "Nancy Cranmer, with only a bragging relationship to English archbishops of the same name."

"Nancy, I' m sorry if I put it badly, do forgive me. I'm not one of those very busy businessmen, all self and thousand-dollar bills. Of course I'd like tea with you, or a real drink if you like, but it just can't be for more than forty-five minutes. And please, I intend no rudeness, but beyond the scones, that's it. I am, for lots of reasons not all good and some not avoidable this trip, no investment beyond tea for a woman."

He paused, waiting for her to sense some insult.

"Fine." Her expression was unperturbed, thoughtful. She was examining him but her initial words were lightly spoken. "I'm too old for hopes and too young not to enjoy company. But, what I really shall want from you is satisfaction for my curiosity. You see, I think I met you years ago on some of these flights. And maybe others. I'm wondering about something. I have to go aisle-walking now, so just think about it, not me, but *it*, where 'it' in particular could have been Senator Royston Cranmer."

"Cranmer?" It was Barbour's turn for surprise. He began to respond, "Of course I knew…" but she was already picking up glasses, chatting with passengers. Cranmer indeed.

The senator's name was appended in a confidential note from Dolan, an old friend and one of the good guys at IFFY, who had written the cover letter for the packet expressed from Washington. Dolan, no new kid in that cutthroat town, warned of a potent Senatorial interest in the current phase of IFFY's Eastern European work. Budgets and heads could be at stake, headlines of course. Leading the charge was Senator Royston Cranmer, head of the Senate Crime Committee, member of the Banking Committee, a force on the Hill and even more powerful off it. One of his nicknames, was "the Chummer," one who threw bloody fishbait to frenzied sharks; his invited maneaters, of course, being his righteous colleagues and the sensationalist press. "But," Dolan had written, maybe more to this than meets the eye. Who on the Hill doesn't have hidden agendas? Buddy, look out for the Chummer." Apt indeed. Cranmer the chummer; sharkmaster Cranmer, much changed over the years from good to bad, could feed the unwary to these sharks as well.

So, Cranmer again and politics as usual. Barbour might learn more tomorrow. Quid pro quo, so would Nancy. She was right. He had been on these flights, first class in the good old days, with his once-upon-a-time (and long it had been) friend, Royston Cranmer. Before the good Senator had, against Barbour's and many others' advice, run for President, turned bitter in that predicted and stunning defeat and, according to those inside the loop—Barbour was no longer one of these—did indeed have his own still-ambitious agenda, in which needy constituents did not figure much at all.

Later, as Barbour returned from the lavatory, there came forward, passing too slowly by Barbour's empty seat, a puffy-faced, oyster-complexioned chap, perhaps thirty, dressed in an elegant lambswool maroon sweater sloping down over baggy gray trousers. He wore glasses with lenses thick as coke bottles, behind which his colorless eyes wavered, distorted as if by Funhouse mirrors. He sported straggly, shoulder-length hippie hair. Around his neck hung one of those cultish voodoo-inspiriting crystals, this one an inch across, gold chain dangling. Could even a mother kiss such a maldeveloped offspring of Berkeley's Telegraph Avenue, Barbour wondered?

As Crystal Man reached Barbour's row his foot hit a seat mount and he stumbled, flailing sideways toward Barbour's seat. The man protectively extended his thin arm to the empty window seat at his right, his hand landing flat on the manila folder Barbour had set there, tumbling a book near it. Once capsized, Crystal Man, head down, peering, but thrashing as if to get up, splayed open the folder. We all, Barbour knew, can be curious about what our fellow passenger may be reading, but this was a bit much: intent and the fact of it. These are elements for criminal conviction anywhere. Punishment was on the way. Half clown, half acrobat, Crystal Man jerked in surprised pain at the fiercely angry, shoulder-locking backwards, upwards pull by which Barbour roughly righted him.

"My God, man, what are you doing to me?" cried the fellow, trying to loosen Barbour's grip. Obviously he did not know the correct response to break the hold, although Barbour had, arching, braced himself for it. Struggling hopelessly, Crystal Man's other hand swept page proofs to the floor. One page, red-stamped *SECRET*, was face up. "Damn you, what are you trying to do?" shouted Crystal Man, shocked and strident.

"Giving you hurt?"

"You shit," snarled Crystal Man.

Barbour said nothing, but keeping his chest close to the man's back and thus shielding himself from view, he hoisted his wrist another notch upward toward the neck while twisting his wrist crushingly inward. Crystal Man yelped in pain.

"You *shit*!" This time Crystal Man's angry shriek penetrated the whole of the cabin.

"I'm so sorry you hurt yourself falling," said Barbour calmly, loud enough to be heard by others, as he released the arm from the conventional police torture hold, adding solicitously, "You must have lost your footing, you had a bad fall. Perhaps the crew can get you an ice pack." He paused. "And now, if you will allow me to sit in my seat?"

Crystal Man stumbled again, turning in the aisle to face alarmed, puzzled passengers in the rows to the rear.

"You fucking, fucking shit!" he yelled wildly, his pale, sweating face mottled with irregular patches of red.

Public vulgarity, excess verging on madness, interruption of their space, the man a scary weirdo to boot: there was no sympathy for Crystal Man to be found in the disgusted faces of passengers, mostly businessmen, a self-disciplined and conventional lot whose work had been disturbed by this drama. Their version: a dirty hippie—out of place in business class in any event—stumbles, probably on drugs. He's helped back up by a perfectly respectable, cordial man, one of us, and in thanks the hippie makes this appalling scene. What are these times coming to anyway? Passengers turn their eyes downward, back to laptops, papers and charts. Romans at the Circus would have turned down their thumbs. One more deviant dispatched.

Barbour, on the other hand, wondered two things. Had Crystal Man been able to see what was on that page stamped *SECRET*? A glance at it on the floor had told Barbour that only two, maybe, identities in the lousy packet were, with some luck and eyes more acute than Crystal Man's thick glasses suggested, readable; one Brody, the other "Mr. C." One was in Vienna, and the other had last been heard of in that miserable, deadly town in California where, coincidentally, Barbour's good friend and former partner-in-crime, Markowitz, was now hiding out from the big world, playing detective, and getting his ass shot at for (too often) real.

The other question, much more important: who had hired Crystal Man? The Montreal-to-Jersey-to-Geneva reinsurers of his recent interest, or other entrepreneurs, the only hint of which was the name Brody in Vienna? In any event they were "princes of the new class." Barbour had borrowed the term, finding it more appropriate than the common "mafia," or Russian "*mafiya,*" which diminished predators whom it was dangerous to underestimate. These princes had hardly gone for class in this hire: Crystal Man was a scumball. Like many honest people who had come up the hard way to riches, like more who had done it through crime, then stayed alive and prospered, the princes and their paymasters tended to be tight. Especially when hiring short-term foreign help. Such princes—the new new class to be sure, but bejeweled and profligate—once again held historical sway over Muscovy, Kiev, Vilnius, and Tallinn. With their wolf-spider kind in every other European capital, they had expanded now to North America as well. Such princes, happily, made tactical mistakes.

Barbour was to be reminded that he made doozies of mistakes as well when, leaving the plane at Dulles Airport, to enter the levitating lounge/bus to the main terminal, a whizzing knife imbedded itself in his upper left arm. Crystal Man might be a scumball, stupid, even ridiculous, but good enough at throwing from twenty feet away to wreck a perfectly good Henry Poole's (Savile Row, "Tailors to Royalty") jacket, and thereby cause a good deal of commotion as the blood flowed. Barbour later learned the knife was made of specially hardened plastic parts—the shaft weighted with a balancing lead ball—capable of disassembly, and undetectable as such by security cameras.

"Specially made," said the appreciative airport security officer interviewing a not fully candid victim Barbour in the airport clinic, "for the unpleasant passenger trade."

Nancy, after bandaging the wound, wheeled him to the clinic amid a flutter of staff, police and clucking onlookers. He insisted he could walk and yet felt it might not be too bad an idea, so he made only a nominal fuss about being wheeled. In the clinic he was relatively pleased to learn it was a lucky wound; no artery damage and only scraping the humerus. He was not pleased, however, by his utter carelessness. Coming back after so many years away from the ugliness, if a wimpy scumball could do this to him in a security-surveyed American airport, what would they do when he got to Orson Welles' still *Third Man*-zithering Vienna, or the princes' very own Sofia?

"Dead meat," he said absently, "getting old and stupid. I'm dead meat."

Nancy heard only muttering. She was so relieved that she could now tease, her hand on his shoulder, "Lee, if you really are a 'reforming social philosopher,'" as he had earlier told her was as close a name for his calling as any, "why didn't they offer you hemlock, like Socrates, instead of throwing a knife?"

He pondered his reply. "The people I deal with are not conservative Athenians."

In the distance all could hear Crystal Man yelping, screaming obscenities. He had finally been subdued by a host of guards during an attempted lunatic chase by Barbour in his stewardess-propelled racing wheelchair. It was a scene out of a hardly-silent slapstick comedy—Buster Keaton, Laurel and Hardy, although Woody Allen could have directed it. Barbour would have laughed more heartily but for his real worry Nancy might tip the speeding chair over as she careened around an outside turn.

She nodded belatedly, "I believe you're right."

The kiss she bestowed on the top of his head was, she said, "for a civilized man in a still uncivilized world." And yes, the doctor agreed they could still have tea at six the next day.

2

Stanley Markowitz used to be in the drug business in the good old days. A specialist, you could say. What was he doing thinking about them? But harking back to the good old days had, he knew, itself a long history, and a fundamental appeal. He really liked to imagine himself in, the "golden days" of which Hesiod wrote in the seventh century BC, himself harking back to Homer, Troy, Achilles, the lovely Helen and all that. "Yes, I know," he was saying to Andy, Officer Stein, sitting on the bar stool next to him, "a whole bunch more folks care about doing drugs than about Hesiod, or Virgil for that matter. So much for the good life sought through chemistry, and associated dead bodies."

Markowitz was a stocky five-ten and 185 pounds of football muscle, heavy-boned, with hints of battle-smeared nose, and facial scars to match, all in all a formidable warrior. In another setting he might have been more combative about—well in this instance, poetry. But not here; not here in a black bar in an impoverished town, half the patrons low-lifes, most of the others simply thugs, and himself sitting next to the biggest cop in California. That cop, Andy Stein, cast a daunting shadow over crime from a hundred yards away, and was sharpshooter enough to enforce control if need be. And hereabouts, "need be" often was.

Tonight's bar-hopping was a social call, sort of, keeping the peace by showing the flag; with just enough intimidation to prevent, or Lord be praised, be present at, a third armed robbery attempt this week. Not that Robbie, founder and chief barkeep of Robbie's Club, didn't do everybody a favor by having shot one dead and badly hollowed out the other. Every cop in town applauded. But to keep that jolly executioner's Robbie's luck running just in case some faster draw, one not drunk or strung out on coke, was the next entrepreneur to stick up the place, one showed police presence. Drinking on duty was forbidden, but in this town, for such purposes, the rules were vague. And who could fault a good beer?

Markowitz was nursing an Anchor Steam, keeping at the ready his open eyes, his detective's 9mm, that reinsuring wee bit of a .32 in his ankle holster, and the officially definitive wallet badge, thus his good nature all intact. He was as off-duty as a cop can be in a 24-hour murdering town. "Fact is," he announced, addressing both Andy and the barkeep, "poetry is good for you, 'passion not a purpose' as Edgar Allen Poe said of it for himself, and yes, I know, one can't make as much money at it as dealing dope, guns, stolen electronics or, top of the line, dealing the dirty money itself."

Officer Andy Stein nodded tolerantly. "I know a few dirty limericks, that's it. There's the one begins 'On Thursday at tea with the vicar, Maud's maidenhood disappeared quicker…'"

Markowitz curled down his lips, "Jesus, and to think it was you not me majored in English in college. I'd rather talk about wily Ulysses, we need him out here."

Office Stein grinned, "You Homer, me no get to first base."

Robbie joined in the chuckling. Stein downed a stein of St. Pauli Girl. On a dose-per-pound basis it would take a keg to get him drunk. Stein was curious about his new friend Markowitz, who had indeed been "big" in The Department of Justice, DOJ it was called, in Washington, D.C. and elsewhere. The scuttlebutt was that Markowitz had "retired" to this crummy town to take a detective's job. It made no sense to Stein why a Federal Justice official, or it was rumor maybe even something more interesting than that, but a "big man" was the rumor, a top dog, would leave that to work in a miserable, low-life little town, once before and probably again the per-capita murder capital of the country, to drudge away at street-level crime. Uneducated thugs, a city council nearly as bad, a department that couldn't afford to keep its patrol cars all running, a chief who couldn't find his ass with both hands and the light on, who'd want it?

"What the hell, sir, why did you leave the high life? Power on the Potomac, springtime in Paris, mariachis in Mexico, king of the press conferences in Mendacity, D.C., whatever?"

Markowitz shrugged. "Better climate in California. Besides, I grew up near here."

"But sir, you could be a chief mucky-muck, a *jefe* somewhere, or sipping Chardonnay on the beach."

"People get tired of the pressure."

That ticked off the younger man. "For God's sake, we got more pressure here than any ten departments in the country put together. No manpower, lousy management, some of our own guys on the take, brutality, lieutenants screwing the lady cops, a hundred emergency calls a day, and most of them out there got guns. What are you talking about, chief? This ain't no retirement center, it's a hellhole. This town is mother to poverty, father to sin, twin sister to misery. It invented corruption, feeds on blacks hating Hispanics killing eensy-teensy chillun in drive-bys, and showcases horror and filth. The town has only two industries besides us: making money and life's deep meanings out of crime, and off getting poverty grants as handouts. Makes do-gooders happy, makes the locals happy, and yet nothing changes. If anyone could count all that cash coming in, this place would have the average family income of Belgravia Square, Westchester County, Atherton, or Neuilly-next-to-Paris, excepting us poor bastard cops and the dope fiends who are the town's genuine poor."

Markowitz could only nod in agreement.

"And so?" pursued Andy Stein, passionate but not about poetry, one-time Bachelor of Arts in literature and now streetmeister—only for the moment they were in sight—of all the scumbags, gangsters and unrein unmaidens his Siegfriedian eye might survey.

"And so, sir, why did you leave the good life for the low life here?"

"Political pressure," said Markowitz, voice soft with hard memories.

"You sir? I can't believe it." His respectful companion's voice raised with astonished disbelief, the "sir" was constant and genuine. "You're so tough they feed you rolling steel and you spit out finish nails. Come on, Detective, I know a little something. You harden under pressure. I've heard your reputation on the streets, how the real fire-fights begin and end once you are on the scene. Everybody knows it. *I* know it."

"Well, let's say the food in those ritzy places in Zurich, Vienna—even conch in Nassau; I must admit never Panama City—was too rich."

"Who was paying?"

"The bankers, of course."

"They were rich, so was the food, so what?" Andy, who was some pounds overwieght, but not yet a sumo wrestler, could not imagine food too rich.

"They thought they could afford me too," was the wry reply.

"Ah, I got it. Just like River City here, a little silver across the palm, 'But for you my friend,' as the gypsy foretells, 'maybe a secret bank account in Switzerland.'"

"That would have been the earlier days. I helped negotiate one of the treaties that made the Swiss almost honest—mind you, I said 'almost.' Maybe I should qualify that and say, 'after enough bad world press made the Swiss establishment want very much to appear honest.'"

"And so?" Andy was so young, and interested, that he was not conscious of prying; he was simply immensely pleased to glimpse the celebrity life beyond these trash-strewn, ghetto confines.

Markowitz understood his young friend, took no offense, and like most, appreciated the other's admiring interest, up to a point. "So, sir, why not enjoy their expense account, do your business, stay straight, once again, why aren't you dining?"

"I told you, young'un, I don't bribe good, even get testy about it if it's clumsily done, and I get a stomach ache if the food is too rich. Besides, some things happened."

"Like?"

"To tell you true, my new young friend, like getting my ass fired. But nobly, Andy, nobly. The President and his new bureau heads did me the courtesy personally."

Andy pursed his lips, "Nice touch, sir. You must have been dynamite."

"Yeah, and they lit it and put the stick up my ass."

"Just realizing your potential, sir. Get up high enough and the bigger boys will blow you sky-higher, unless of course you're as expedient, or maybe dirty, as they are." Andy had a problem with the cold-eyed bosses, and their abuse of power. His current problem was the police chief. He remembered from Conrad, "'To be a great autocrat, you must be a great barbarian.' I always liked Conrad. So did my uncle; he named my cousin after him. Bastard turned out to be a banker. Like you say, bastards."

"Your Conrad is fabulous, mysterious and legend-building, with central characters as doomed as Achilles, though more profound. What I miss in Conrad is the glory; he's too modern, intricate, and thoroughly depressed. For me the golden days are the imagination of glory, the being there. Bright armor, myths come alive, every man a poet, hero, or Plato or Praxiteles. I never found any beauty or splendor near the top, Andy, never, just cocktails, scurrying, scheming, and the idealists either smartened up or down in the dumps. My favorite senators and I worked with some, all quit out of disgust and frustration. The bums thrived. For me, I didn't find my glory—importance, yes, but nothing burnished, bright and glowing. Out here I don't expect it. And I tell you, some of those black gangster homeboys sitting out there, and sure the Hispanics too," he nodded toward the tables, "are closer in their hearts to Achilles, to that prideful honor, saving it, killing over it—the old omerta—than the bastards I worked for in Government. Salvation for the polity coming out of Washington? Save me." His tone was bitter.

Andy Stein was a Wagnerian character: six feet four, 290 pounds, shaved head on a 24-inch neck connecting to a bullhorn voice, and all young enough to seem still to be a growing boy. He could not control the emotional tone of his voice, complex with awe and sympathy, "Give me an instance of what it was really like, back then, the first battles of this stupid drug war. Hey sir, I sound like a junior officer coming on board the Starship Enterprise, don't I?"

"Okay, I'll give you a simple one. I was...call it Justice liaison with Mexico, an office with their Attorney General and in our Embassy in the Zona Rosa, big stuff as I thought back then. There was that weekend I got the blood on my hands from eighteen guys whose very dead heads got chopped off down Sinaloa way just to please me, to show Washington my Mexican government associates were serious about cooperation. You see I'd demanded on behalf of our executive office that the Mexicans show us some progress in narcotics enforcement. What did I get but eighteen heads shipped personally to me at the Reforma, Ciudad Mexico, in a couple of wooden boxes. Old truck rolled up, new boxes dropped off with new heads inside, the same old hopeless bullshit when you come down to it.

"It was a serious message, you'll grant that, eh? But you've got to know how to read it. 'More heads coming whenever you ask, Señor Ambassador'? or 'Make our day again, Gringo'? Or maybe, 'Your head can be in this funhouse picture, too.'"

"It was a lousy job of butchering though, tag ends of meat hanging out everywhere and blood still dripping from behind those giant arterial clots. Veinous stuff sticks harder. They didn't know to cut through the gristle, the bone, on neck jobs. Handling them wrecked my suit and damn near—well, I exaggerate, I do like a good meal and a skirt to go with it—my dinner. "Damn spics," he said, by now half amused at the *grand guignol* of it, and himself as teller of the tale. Cynically then, "There's a story for you! Know any lyre-playing Homer who can make a ballad worth singing out of that? Any nobility anywhere, them or me or my various attorneys general, in that? Priam maybe, crying over his son, if anyone ever knew what had happened to his son down Mexico way."

Stein, born unsympathetic to bad guys, at least knew how to think cop. He downed another beer, self armoring and chuckling, "Just plain folks, sir. Sorry I wasn't there to mount those heads on pikes. My ancestors did that to three Roman legions, can you imagine that? Three legions, three eagles and we got them all, 'Remember Teutoburger Wald and jump on Quinctilius Varus' grave,' my old granddaddy used to say, 'and screw those Wops.' Granddaddy had a foul mouth. I tell you a fact, us Teutonic types are good at pitting heads on pikes, ask Caesar, Drusus, Tacitus, Augustus, I mean, Komrades, I love violence. Legal of course, and all in the spirit of community, yes? Vlad the Impaler lives on."

Stein's now raucous laugh roared through the bar. A few grizzled elders playing cards, a few younger blades too, but no one, however blooded in shootings or toughened in prison, smirked. Certainly none thought to challenge. Whites in black bars in this town were rare, and wisely so. Cops coming in for an apparently off-duty drink, well for any other cops not likely, but these two at the bar were unlikely characters. A cop who had been seen to lift two six foot 180-pound street toughs three feet off the ground, one in each arm, the strapado of a grip under their handcuffs set very tight to assure real pain, and to throw them into the street, begging and sprawling, deserved respect. Stein got it. Some gang graffiti showed him doing just that—Superman stuff. Stein was a legend. A scumbag grew larger in his own esteem when his opponent was an invincible, sometimes even good-humored, giant of a god. "Wodin" Stein might remind them of it, and indeed sometimes wore in play in parades for example a horned Viking helmet. Not all police work in this town was done by the books. But then not every officer was good at reading. Cops like nothing better than heroics-splashed quasi-criminality on the side of the right and the true. Once in a while the good guys had to win, by fair means or just expedient ones.

Andy turned to the barkeep, a black man almost as big as he though more of it was paunch, and deadly in his own way, as seven dead or wounded would-be armed robbers of his over the last two years bar could—well, not if dead—attest. "Robbie," Officer Stein asked with respect, "What do you think of this? Any African Americans making enough money out here to launder it big time? Before asking the question, the officer had lowered his head a bit before his companion; deference was due the detective in a patrolman-dick relationship, and Andy would be sure Markowitz felt no infringement on his rightful status. Whatever the camaraderie, indeed consistent with it, cops were a hierarchically military bunch.

Robbie boomed out, "What do you mean, man, 'African American'? That's PC shit, man. If we have to change our name every year who the hell are we? And what cute-assed trendy columnist tells me what I call my color? *African American*," Robbie spit out. "Officer Andy, you ever read about Africa? Oh yeah, you read, man. And you ever read about your own sweet mother Germany, do you? Yeah, gas chambers. Jew killers, cannibals, whitey, the injun-killin slave owners—everybody, when you play that ethnic card, s'got his bad side. You white, me black, you Jane, me Tarzan."

Stein's eyebrows went up "Me Jane? Now Robbie..." Stein was going to make an adverse point there, but Robbie was blasting on. "You 'Germano American, is that it? and me stuck with being next 'Ghana American'? Get hung up on labels and we end up mean-mouthed, me nigger and you Nazi, that's what. Fuck the labels, fuck the differences. We're here, man, whatever this place is like. Don't unload that 'old country' shit on Robbie. Got that?"

Nobody within earshot failed to get it. Or take issue. Robbie was one furious son of a bitch. And big, and after all easy, for with a glorious smile he said, "Here, have a St. Pauli whore on the house." He slid a frosted bottle over to Officer Stein.

"I'm with you, Robbie," said Officer Stein. "Screw the differences. And ain't no one here to argue the niceties but the pansy liberals, and none of them got the guts to come here to quibble since that liberal lawyer Association fellow got himself killed at the stop sign robbery here last year."

Markowitz, sometimes feeling more jaded than an eighty-year-old, still-working whorehouse madame, was generally careful of what he said. But perhaps even the one beer, the late hour and those aroused dark memories, all those defeats contributed to his sudden, slightly inebriated sense that here was one of those moments of general brotherhood. Exhilaration. There was hope for democracy, down here with the unwashed, and himself sure as hell one of them. Thomas Paine and Zapata live! The rest off in the tumbrels. Markowitz lifted his glass and toasted loudly, "To all of us poor spics, niggers, honkies, slant-eyes and other universal defectives. It's our town and fuck all the differences!"

Except for the deafer old men playing board games, all heard and surprised their ordinarily reined-in cynical, macho, deeply suspicious, racially self-conscious inner selves with spontaneous, "Jesus, that cop said *that*?" Lapping liquor blown waves of chortling approval, most downright startled but all expressive. "Yeah, fuck em!" "Right on!" and "motherfuckin all right, bro!" Drunkenness was rare for most who were young, tough, and smart enough to be accepted enough to drink and stay alive at Robbie's, and thus held their liquor as they did their correlated lives—carefully. But one drunk was restrained from hoisting a sawed-off shotgun from the strapping underneath his trousers so as to blast a, "Hey man, I'm with you man. Don't fuck with me, man," explosion into the ceiling. Had that been done, perhaps an overly enthusiastic gesture, it would have chilled the whole affair: people hitting the floor and possibly firing back, that sort of thing.

As it was, just a few cheers and no uglies at all, it was the most cordial moment seen in years, as the town was rising in numbers once again to take its rightfully sensational place as per-capita murder capital of the country. The latter, like a dark side of the Super Bowl or soccer championship match won, found the body count going up. For the press, who dined on sensation, and the city council which always looked for a reason to demand more money from government to waste and embezzle, numbers going up meant things looking up. As for the long-coated shooter with the sawed-off shotgun, upon a call from Stein, a bustling rough crew of patrol cops would pour in here to bust the drunk and probably slap a few other people around as well. Back to normal in police-community relations. But the reason, concealed sawed-off shotguns—was hard to fault.

Markowitz's beeper went off. Unlike a patrolman on duty he had no cell phone. "Use your phone?" he asked Robbie. The big man nodded toward one on the wall inside the bar. A few minutes later Markowitz returned shaking his head, "Who and what, sir, might I ask?" Andy put the query.

"San Francisco DEA. A while back, Washington headquarters asked them to ask us if we had anything on a supposedly local guy, moniker 'Mr. C,' standing for who knows; cocaine, capo, century note? Anyway an inter-government outfit—International Financial Crimes Investigative Group, most of us call them IFFY for short, Brits say 'the Network,' they're economic crime—were given his name by central bank people. They were out of somewhere in central Europe when a couple of commercial banks were rolled up, caught too dirty for even them. Some paper with very large numbers on it was a local law partnership's transaction, caught just before it hit the bank transmittal wires. Or at least that's their story. You can be damn sure it isn't *the* story."

All cops are suspicious of all stories, not least from officials anywhere higher up than were they. Officer Stein asked, "What's IFFY got to do with this Mr. C character?"

"Seems the lawyers hadn't kept up their juice payments, so they gave away to IFFY some of their client list, or at least the small potatoes who wouldn't have clout enough to set up contract killings for snitchings. Out there that means really small fry. Anyway Mr. C was a name the finks gave up, and IFFY blesses DEA with it, no doubt in return for some favor they have in mind. DEA wants to run with it because it looks on its face like drugs, money laundering and international game time, but mostly—I know those guys—because we are conveniently here to do the groundwork for them. What have they to lose?"

Stein had no difficulty answering that one. "Being caught with one more bum steer. This Department knows, in fact, *I* know, every shooter, dealer, burglar, car chopper, thief, whore, and gambler over twelve years old in town, all thousands of them, even if we can't get them sent up. A guy like that would be right in our faces," said Andy confidently. "We'd know about him. He *can't* be here. DEA's got it wrong."

Robbie had heard their conversation; he looked around so as to be sure not overheard, riveting their eyes with an I-have-something-for-you-look. "The world can be full of surprise, Officer Stein, just full. You listen up softly now, there's a Mr. C around all right. He just invisible and he like it that way." Robbie's conspiratorial look was full of possibilities, portents, warnings. Or alternatively—as any cop wise to the world knows—equally full of hogshit. Robbie, having had his theatrical moment, exited stage right to wash glasses.

Andy, in a good mood from all this barroom fellowship and the surprising snitch out of ordinarily taciturn Robbie, was feeling rosy. He announced to all who could hear, and none could fail that. "I'm off duty, I hate this town, I hate you thugs, beer for all of you on me."

The thugs, and indeed some that were not by any outside standard, grinned and as Robbie served all around, drank up. One hoodlum, Hard Ass Ervin, a two-time convicted killer, but only as a juvenile and thus expunged for the drive-by stuff, no justice system paper on him for his serious current business since he had graduated to nonviolent non-drug crime about which a press-sensitive, otherwise preoccupied police department could not take time to care. In a town where police didn't bother to answer burglary calls, big-time fencing was considered practically an honest living. It was also safe, lucrative and respected by the locals, almost all of whom, Christian families or other, were customers. Hard Ass stood up, looked grave, took the floor.

"Officer Stein, you are a fuckin honky oppressor and I shit on your mother's grave, God praise her soul." He paused, public-speaker like, "and I respectfully thank you for the beer, brother. As cops go you are a righteous motherfucking real bad dude. I was never so proud as the night you collared me for that mugging, dropped me on my head, broke my arm, never read me no rights, and done told me, just like Pastor MacKenzie do, 'Go forth and sin your shiny black ass no more my child.' I ain't done any time since, and you, Officer Stein, are to thank. I am re-ha-bil-i-ta-ted," he said, each syllable standing by itself. "You, brother, you are an all right big man and I thank you again."

No higher praise was possible. The patrons murmured approval, Andy damn near sobbed while a five-pound tear ran down over some of his 290 pounds threatening to rust the shiny 9mm Walther stuck in his waist, and Markowitz, who was without sentimentality but tonight had somehow been launched on a communitarian jag, allowed that not all nights in California's murder capital were without tenderness.

Even so, love is not enough. Andy and Detective Markowitz independently made a note to put Hard Ass away when they had time. That's what comes of making yourself a public figure.

The barroom theater of good will returned to private murmurings; only for a moment had the underlying tension of carpetbagging white cop and black plantation gangster dissipated with only the gray haired elders indifferent. Andy once again turned his attention to his for the first time personally forthcoming superior. "What else, sir, since obviously there was something else?"

Markowitz was surprising himself this confessional night, but what the hell, he realized, there have got to be a few young colleagues in whom you confide, for their sakes if not your own. Coaching. "I'd done some things, Andy, turned some people down on things they wanted, offended some very important folks. In Washington if you stop being useful you're dead meat. No impotent man is forgiven, Andy, never. And I also caught some of the wrong people dirty." Markowitz, reflecting, cupped his prize-fighter hand against his roughhewn chin, his stubbly face rough enough to appear almost pocked, and yet there was poise, deliberation. However impotent at self-appraisal, to Andy as to others, Markowitz breathed the potency of a sage old tiger's calm, grace and calculating potential menace.

Andy needed no psychology 101 course to tell him the truth of every man's sometimes actual impotency. It was not a truth generally shared among cops but one of private pain over a solitary bottle of booze. As with many men.

Andy was presuming more than most men however man to man dare, and with his youth he knew he would get beyond his depth. But Markowitz needed reassurance. "Most guys know what it is to be impotent, at least sometimes, in any job, any sport, probably more than one woman's bed. And so you add politics; what the hell, that's just guys wanting, trading, lying, promising, maybe sometimes working. I don't see that it's special. Hells' bells, three surprised, you'd think politically-savvy police chiefs in this Department were flushed down the drain in the last six years. Musical chairs; city council does the conducting. We all got problems, sir," said Andy. "And whether it's me or those chiefs, this town is trouble."

"Yes and no," replied Markowitz. "Oddly enough I like working here. It's kind of a bug-size Mexico, only simpler and more stupid. They're lousier shots here, that's real good, a whole lot poorer, and a big conspiracy here is when three guys plan to steal a car or trade some crack for pussy. That's why I'm surprised to hear from DEA that we've missed somebody big enough to operate anywhere very far out of town, and move the cash abroad no less, even if it likely is for someone else. Nobody moves that many millions worth of narcotics, that many chopped car receipts on these streets. You know how I feel about narcotics anyway, Stein, overhooted. The real money for the real players doesn't accumulate from nickel and dime bags, not even a million of them. Politicians use drugs as the new devil who, as a powder of chemicals, is only that. Have to look to people for evil, Stein, not to chemistry. And as to drugs, it's no war because we lost it. Let the doctor boys with white coats take over. Treatment is cheaper and better."

"Yes, sir. I hate to, but I have to agree, sir. But it's not PC."

Markowitz nodded no, it was not politically correct. He went on, "So with respect to Mr. C, whoever he is, he's fancier than I figured for around here. And I wonder, who's he paying off and how high up? Nobody lasts in that business without a very large shade tree, and some savvy financial pros."

"Shade tree?"

Markowitz once again felt old. Slang marks one generation from another. He explained, "Old term for protection, umbrella, juice, mesa, influence, connections. You buy it, you buy one with kumshaw, bzyatka, guanxi, mesa, podkoop, payoffs. Got it?"

Andy had no problem getting it. It was the way the world moved. Certainly this town's city council. Like they invented graft. Andy persevered. Mr. C didn't interest him nearly as much as did this enigmatic detective who had so clearly once been much more and other than that. "So you don't miss the big time, all that travel, money, juice, fancy eating?"

"Not much, maybe, who knows, sometimes, yes and no, like most things." But Markowitz was thinking not of ambivalence, but the puzzle. "Just doesn't make sense that it's a local boy, does it? I mean no homeboy here is that connected, worldly wise, cosmopolitan. These local scumbags fly to Reno and think they've done the world tour."

Andy smiled benevolently. Beer greased understanding. Sympathetic Andy was flattered to know Markowitz, the eccentric, brain-overloaded, more-than-detective. Andy, whose work was answering daily calls to killings, fights, robberies, with no time for burglaries, not even in progress, would never have an interest in politics outside the Department or city council, nor be but bored with the intricacies of finance.

Although an intimidating giant, Andy was in fact a gentle and sensitive man, had been known to send anonymous flowers to the mother of some gangster kid ("they're all assholes" was his tougher public posture) shot down in a gang fight. Few cops can admit to tenderness, but a couple of his buddies had seen him cry after leaving a particularly brutal scene. His sergeants worried about kindness in any cop on these streets. Citizens and even scumbags respected him, but his superiors wrote bad personnel reports. There's not much room to be a person in a real tight department.

"Time to leave. I do personal questions better in private, if at all."

"Yes, sir. I should have known better."

They both got up to leave, nodding and smiling goodbye to Robbie. In this town a smile was as near to community policing as it would ever get. They nodded to Hard Ass, who actually half stood in his chair to show respect. Never ever had that happened before; nowhere and by nobody in this town. Hard Ass must have read a book.

At the end of the bar near the street door, talking quietly with a man in a clean white shirt, was a short, wiry, tense-postured light colored black man in his early twenties, fine-featured as if with Ethiopian blood. He acknowledged Officer Stein with a scowl and a curt, at best ambivalent hand gesture. Stein nodded, with a no more community policing glare.

"Who's that?" asked the detective, for it had been an oddly ambiguous interaction on both sides.

"Little punk, street name of Rooster. I'll tell you about him, what I think and what I know, someday. But if you will allow me, sir, I really am interested in you and the big time. Please, no intrusion intended, but I'm a small-town cop who's only read a lot; why did you, how could anyone high up as you were, really leave the big time?"

Markowitz paused and gave some thought to whether to answer at all. But for all the murders he'd attended, this Officer Stein was so damned innocent. "Okay. First off I told you, I was fired. Didn't respond to some requests, was worrying people about what I knew."

"And?" Stein, an eager student of any other kind of police world, pressed. "Was it because they were leaning on you? Keep the dirty hidden? And I know what pressure there is not to report when a fellow officer is dirty."

"Something like that."

"But more, maybe. For instance the best of cops can get in real trouble with a woman."

"Jesu Christi, Stein, there's always going to be a trouble with a woman."

"And so?"

"No way, Jose. A friend of mine and I, you must realize we were considered pretty effective in a lot of things in the business, turned down an Executive request. That was while I was preparing a report on some large-scale official misuse of funds."

"Wow. But what was the Executive request?"

Markowitz stared through Stein at another world. It was a low voice that replied, "Run an assassination team."

"Oh."

"Yeah, me too, my friend Lee. Lots of 'ohs'."

Stein was silent driving the rest of the way to the station. The steel gate for the squad car parking area opened for them. As they always would, both made a last-minute check of their message boxes before heading home; it was already ten P.M. One more fourteen-hour day.

"Well, well," murmured Markowitz as he read a message, "what do you know?"

"What?" asked Stein, always curious.

"Before the DEA called me on that C report, a call came in for me from the Senate Crime Committee, from the personal assistant to that famous chairman of theirs. The note here says 'under the chairman's request.' They want to know what's happening on the C case. I read the time log and see the Senator called me before DEA. Can you imagine?"

Andy shrugged; Senate business, even DEA business, was way beyond his level. "Doesn't mean anything to me, but maybe they think it's a yummy news article."

Markowitz' face was grave. "No, buddy. The Senate Committee does investigations, not newspapers, and 'they' are the staff. The chairman, the Senator has so much seniority he qualifies for a founder of the Cincinnati, never gets involved but for policy decisions, log rolling, and getting his name on the most carefully crafted banker-safe legislation he can pretend is anti-crime. By rights he shouldn't even know about this case and he certainly has no right to intrude on an ongoing DEA or IFFY investigation, let alone make a telephone demand to a junior nobody like me. He doesn't fool with anything less than earthshaking publicity, never, and until now this town only shook the national murder statistics. Think about it. His aide made this call at eight o'clock Washington time. That's cocktail hour on the Potomac, buddy, or speech-making time at the Press Club. There's no way this thing at bottom is about drugs. The Senator knows the difference between public hype and what's really important. It's called publicity. Or for Senators not setting type for the front page, it's all power and money and connections and again the next election. Somehow this Mr. C looks big to somebody on the Potomac."

"Oh."

"And if it's not to get public first on some big case, some suit in Washington figures I—now, man, that is you and I—can dig some useful dirt, or hide it. Get some other suit, or higher than a suit, like maybe a Cabinet secretary out of deep doodoo on the QT. After all, DEA has an office nearby in the City, and this must be mighty consequential for them to overlook all those vulgar words I used when my friend Lee Barbour and I got fired."

"Oh!" Stein liked the looming sense of the big time. Drama is any good cop's natural flair. But first he had to ask, "What's a 'suit'?"

"Any official who doesn't know his ass from a pothole. Somebody miserably powerful, narrow-minded, lazy, and ambitious, who doesn't know the streets. In other words, most managers in Wonderland by the Potomac."

Stein went to his original question, "Who is the big-man Senator who runs the Crime Committee?"

"Cranmer—ever so smooth, ever so handsome, ever so shitty Senator Royston Cranmer."

Stein shrugged as they headed out the door. "Never heard of him, but then I don't read any but the local paper."

"I have." His was a low voice, suggesting anger and regret. "I suspect him of, as melodramas used to have it, 'deeds most foul,' and I guarantee all of them profitable. Don't have a damn thing on him, never did, and the only people who might are the ever so rich and mighty just like him," Markowitz paused. "But then if C is any kind of homeboy here, he won't likely be elegant, will he? Which means, if I stretch my imagination to the limit, somebody worries that Mr. C might not be very good at keeping world-class dirty secrets. What do you think?"

"Can't prove it by me, a snitch is a snitch is a rat to be tamed in my book. When I find a candidate I turn him upside down, hold his itsy-bitsy ankles and I shake him, head stopping in jolts real near the concrete floor, until gravity brings those little goodies flapping out of his mouth."

The detective smiled. He had seen Stein doing just that.

"You're a good man, Office Stein. I admire your humor."

"I admire you, sir, but I still think you're nuts, if you will excuse me for saying so, to be in this town."

Markowitz swept his arm out in an airy arc, indicating the town surrounded by the dark parking lot. In the distance could be heard shots and sirens. "Paradise is in any event but our fancy. If you remember your *Rubaiyat*,

'And that inverted bowl they call the sky, where under crawling cooped we live and die/Lift not your hands to It for help—for It/As impotently moves as you or I'."

"Yes, sir, but this town is not to my fancy, and it's no one's paradise." Stein was deeply serious. "This town is what is left behind when Purgatory is cleansed and the Devil has taken away the best of Hell. This is the snakeshit left over after the serpent wrecked Eden. This, sir, is one of those places where evil begins, and ripples ever outward."

Markowitz put his hands on his hips and leaned back against the hood of his blue Buick, "Nicely said, Officer Stein. If you are right, and I personally know there are centers of evil and ripplings out of its contagion, then this Mr. C must become of interest to us. Who knows, right here in River City may be more than scumbags, dead bodies, and a dirty city council—Mr. big ripple C himself."

"I only know, sir, whatever he is, if he is, I don't want to have decent people hurt. That's why I'm a cop."

And that indeed was the case. Markowitz wished his own personality, motives were that pure and simple. The two men bid each other a thoughtful, mutually respectful good night.

3

She did not know where she was, or who had put her there or why. Or what would happen, except that it was likely to be quite unpleasant. Happily she was good coolheaded, in crises. Would that help this time?

A dark room somewhere, the dim outlines suggested the almost palatial in, probably, Vienna. As kidnappings go, and Claire was glad she had no earlier experience, this one seemed upscale. Automatic weapons, but discreetly concealed. What would she tell her best friend Beulah about the adventure when they met for their London lunch next month?

"I was just window shopping. You know how I love clothes, really do, and why not? I know, it's an indulgence. I was in front of Aldmuller's on Karnter Strasse—you know, right down the street from Silhouette, and Harnerrer's. You know me, Beulah; of course the first thing I do in an attractive city is go look at the stores. And then suddenly there was this car pulling up. Two men got out, well dressed, I mean they didn't strike me as dangerous that first second. One greeted me, 'Hello Madame,' something like that, and then it was so quick, one on each side of me, holding my arms, but just before they touched me one of them showed me the gun cloaked by his coat that was pointing right at my heart. 'Be quiet, Madame, or I shall kill you.' Oh, I suppose I should have screamed, but the look on his face told me he really meant it. 'I don't care, Miss Dubois, alive or dead. It's up to you.' Calling me by name, what was this? I was just stunned by it all."

"I tell you, Beulah, it was done so coolly. No swear words. Both men were about thirty, really well dressed, Russian accents, dark glasses but not otherwise even trying to hide their dark hair. One had a blue necktie showing at the collar underneath his black coat. The other of course was the one with the gun and his coat was over his arm. Nobody passing by would see it at all, but I could, and then, painfully hard, it was pushed into my side. I think that's when I became frightened. It took a bit. But, Beulah, they looked so bored, but I knew they weren't, I mean every muscle on their faces was taut, and they moved so quickly."

"Thank God, after we were in the car they weren't physical, improperly I mean, not that forcing me off the sidewalk into a car in Vienna is proper, but *you* know what I mean, not even a hint of sexual interest. And you know, it sounds corny, but without hysterics or acting the pure maiden in a Gothic novel, I think I'd rather be killed than raped. Before they shoved the needle in my arm I saw we were in a big black Mercedes with, naturally, opaque glass windows. The man using the needle was quite professional, I must say. He wore expensive gray kid leather gloves; quite unusual, with a rosette design on the back. Anyway, it was quite smoothly done. But all in all the kind of car and people that you'd cast for a B gangster film."

Beulah would be so interested; she always was. She would insist on details. Good-humored and sensible, her own life as a public health doctor in Scotland was so conventional, her marriage so solid, she loved other people's adventures.

"Beulah, I can tell you it wasn't the kind of car you'd hire if you were worried about witnesses or police investigations. The person responsible had to be confident about that—well, not entirely, or why hire men with guns? Still, it wasn't entirely a mystery; after all I'm working on this big case. Big-financial crime. Inevitably, I expected to hit some sore spots, like seizing someone's billion dollars under forfeiture statutes, for example, or finding the premier's wife was the secret mistress of the biggest Arab mobster in three continents, or maybe the parliamentary speakers' sweet deal with five ethnic mobs to cover their contraband transport. The best bet is always the most respectable banker in country *X* being paid off in girls, cars, millions and more to grant what was called in the trade, 'a banking facility.' Oh yes, some facility! But I tell you, Beulah, if my hunch on this one is right, this could be scandalous back home in River City—that is, Washington, D.C."

And Beulah, who was always so no-nonsense sensible, would grip her hand and say, "But Claire, if they had killed you, there might never have been a ripple; after all, aren't you the very first one on the job to organize the leads and I, presume, those telltale pieces of paper?"

If she ever got to see Beulah again, that's how the luncheon would go.

How indeed had she arrived in such a situation? She was drowsing off again. What drugs had they used? Prescription no doubt. God, how funny. These kinds of men don't need prescriptions, they probably rob pharmaceutical warehouses. She began to giggle and recollect, the bits and pieces of herself, how she had got here. Here, wherever it was, in the dark, locked up, guarded by sophisticated thugs with guns. How *did* she get here? Courtesy of her new job with IFinCIG, or IFFY—a mostly affectionate acronym for International Financial Crimes Investigative Group. It was a multi-governmental organization, but its initial push had come from the Americans following the work of their Senate investigators on money laundering. The Brits and Germans, Benelux, Scandinavia had signed on quickly enough. The French? The French always held back; "*le rêve de la gloire passée de la belle France*." The Italians weren't trusted as members until late; she so admired judges and prosecutors with the *mani pulite* who had worked to break the back of the Mafia, and half of Parliament, the industrial elite, some prime ministers in the process. A pity that the *toghe spoche*, the dirty gowns, kept dogging the country as finance and image.

She felt alternately giggly, scared to death, drowsy, in and out of mental clarity until this moment, what had her life been? What had Pavlov called the brain that observed the brain? Oh yes, the second signal system. Did Pavlov have a beard? The second system told her she was slipping her moorings. But it should be easy to recall the critical transitions. Why did she care? Why did she like her homemade fudge? Why look forward to seeing Gavin again? Why was her brain not working? Force it, the second system told the first. She would. Think hard, damn you Claire; *concentrate*. Well, when she was twenty, fifteen years ago, she had wanted to read archaeology, but had done history instead, which was near enough. She had enjoyed reading theology, but majored in political science, which was only sometimes close. She would have stayed at Cambridge beyond her junior year abroad because the old buildings were so beautiful, and the Fitzwilliam had medieval art almost worth stealing—she seriously considered doing that; there was one Simone Martini that…oh never mind, you can't really steal from your University museum. Best of all, at Cambridge the people were so astonishingly bright and witty. She had learned to like ale, several kinds of it.

And there were a few attractive English students there, misleading as men because they were not as sophisticated as they pretended or as those clipped accents implied, at least to an American, but good hearts in fact. Damn good conversations about their subjects, and once she'd "broken them in," as she said lightly of her amateur lovers, after having had "that charming lecturer break, well sweeten me in," quite good in bed. "But then, when they're young, boys are so hot they don't know sex from pleasure anyway," as she had told her then and her still best friend, Beulah. When she told her how she really felt, that was their first really close moment as friends. From then on, with Beulah more than anyone, she was not the always light-earted Claire, but the real one of normal human pain and no pretending.

"Fact is, I was totally in love with him, he could have taken me to Siberia with him if he wanted. But Irish lecturers in economics at Cambridge, however wild in bars and bed, have mostly a sober side. He was an expert on Eastern European commerce; that fascinated me too. He went there a lot, that was pre-*Perestroika, Glasnost* when we were together. He knew some heavyweight people. He told me they could see what was coming, and he gave them advice. He never said what about, but I don't suppose he ever made a nickel on it, for what he called 'insights.' Said that soon he'd need bodyguards in Moscow. He talked a lot about banking, the old apparatchiks taking over commerce, about 'brass plate' banks, that sort of thing. It was really educational. He was so light-hearted about almost everything, but when he talked about Eastern Europe he was grim. That was a streak in him I never understood, nor was he ever that hard, cold way to me. What broke us up was his wife. Beulah, you remember how I cried for a few days and then wanted, really, to kill him because he didn't have the guts to deal with her, leave her for me? New mistresses, I suppose, always believe their married man is going to leave his wife for them. What idiots! But I did hate him for a minute and could have killed him. But like stealing those pre-Renaissance paintings from the Fitzwilliam, or the Uffizi Gallery—you just don't.

"I'm just spoiled I suppose. Got most everything I wanted. I really did think about killing him. I had no idea I had such a dark and angry side. Maybe it matched his. It wasn't morality that stopped me; maybe conventionality. In a way I still feel that when love is inflamed enough to kill, it's somehow all right. You can be sure I never for a minute thought I'd get caught. How's that for self-confidence, eh? When I think about why I didn't—well, other than time passing...I bet Nietzsche would have said mine was 'incapacitation of the Will,' though Freud would have said, 'following the reality principle her ego at last had common sense.'

"Great minds always have a different take on things," Claire continued. "Calvin, I suppose, would have said that God showers no rewards on those immoral. Sam Spade in those detective stories would have a tough guy say, 'who cares?' But do you ever ask yourself, Beulah, if killing when you really want to, or really gain from it, no matter if it's illegal, and usually immoral in the abstract, isn't always personally wrong? You see, when I think about wars where there is so much reason to hate, or if someone raped me, or when I have road rage sometimes, not to say my believing in capital punishment—and as to Gavin, I'm still a little in love, enough to be angry at him, and there's something in him I don't know and really don't like. So you see I'm really not against *all* killing. I could actually do it, you see." Claire gave Beulah an intensely quizzical look.

Beulah had come to Vienna just to see her old friend, but then who wouldn't enjoy a trip to the new opera house and pastries like this? She replied without a moment's hesitation,

"I don't think I ever wanted to kill anybody. I hate blood. Faked as much of my training surgery as I could. I do public health. Just nice clinics and statistics. You're tougher than I am, Claire, always have been, and more ambitious even though you pretend not. Look at you, that master's degree you took in political economics. I know, it was Gavin's influence, and then you gave up that good first job in publishing in New York, you could have gone places because you're so scintillating and read everything, and then you took whatever that last government job was..." Beulah paused, hoping to be told at last what that mysterious job had been. Claire began to interrupt, but Beulah insisted on going on—an interruption contest between two women goes bump bump bump, like jousting locomotives, they don't even notice, "...and so you have this job now, whatever *it* is, but I gather you see Gavin from time to time."

Query, needle, barb, score, and satisfaction. Old friends among girls do it best. Claire blushed. Beulah said simply, "Good thing you didn't kill him, righto?"

It seemed just a few weeks ago that Claire and Beulah were having the world's richest coffee and tarts, *mit schlag* in whipped-cream Alpine heaps, and here, fifteen years later, she and Beulah were still reflecting on loves, Gavin obviously not entirely forgotten. Although it was now just friendship, sometimes she thought that he had changed very little, and she gained very interesting insights from him about their work. She just had to talk about those Cambridge days with him.

"He was passionate about me, said he would leave his wife and kids. Fat chance!" Claire tensed. "Fat" was a sore spot with her. She was plump and no matter how much weight she lost, she felt overweight—"pleasingly plump," her men friends might say. She knew she had a nice face, and not a bad figure in some ways, or so at least she was told. But ever since she was a girl she had felt horribly fat no matter what people said. Fashion was coming to the place where the only acceptable form for a woman was a skeleton, and the beauty treatment was anorexia. Having to look perfect was a terrible burden for women, especially if you were even a little bit on the heavy side. She just couldn't get over feeling that way. She knew her face was nice, was sure she had a pleasing personality. Strong, yes, but she knew people were telling the truth about her sense of humor, and she knew she was bright, and most men told her she was pretty.

"Anyway, 'fat chance' and no pun intended, Beulah. The only one of the three of us who wasn't silly was his wife. Caucasian Georgian and gorgeous, but deadly jealous. She told him she'd cut his balls off, shoot them out a 10-gauge shotgun into his face, kill the kids, and roast pieces of them all for dinner. Remember Jason, commander of the Argonauts, and his wife Medea? Medea, who slaughtered their kids when Jason was unfaithful? And, one legend has it, *did* roast their butchered pieces? That's what a history major, tripos, does for you. Guess what, my wild Irish rover's wife's name was Medea, get that! The two came from the same home county, Colchis then, but it's Caucasian Georgia now, and no surprise. It's not so far from Chechnya." She finished telling her, "No surprise we scrambled out of the sack before an Irishman could say 'Sodom and Begorrah,' or whatever."

Her first job after Pomona, Cambridge and taking a fifth year to finish, doing that masters in economics—yes, Gavin had influenced her—was in New York, working in publishing. Her dad had a friend who headed a big house; Claire remembered the interview.

"Lordy, Claire, am I glad to see you!" Frank Gardner was beaming. "Oh, what a sight you are for sore eyes. Lovely, absolutely lovely." They hugged each other warmly.

"I'm overweight, Frank, fat. I just can't lose it."

"What matters that, my little chickadee? My wife Mary thinks she's fat too. I think she's beautiful. A man likes something there to hug. Plump is pulchritude is pneumatic is great. Women are obsessed with pounds. Bulimia is the national pastime. Claire, if you don't realize that you are gorgeous, vibrant, exciting, attractive, I'd say 'sexy' but Mary would strangle me, you're crazy."

She knew he meant it. She grinned.

"But what maybe is nuts is coming here wanting to start a career in publishing." Frank Gardner had asked that question much later, after coffee and catching up on the news of her father, a famous career ambassador. Claire's dad, famous in his way, got some of Foggy Bottom's most ticklish assignments. Some of the assistant state secretaries charged with postings chose him for the hot spots because of his excellence; "Old Smoothie" was the nickname he'd earned. Others, envious of his success, gave him hot spots because they wanted him to fail. They called him the "Crocodile." Sure enough, the cunning old crock had in due time made meals of them: secretaries, assistants, under, assistant under-over, deputy over-under, et cetera. Thinking about those picayune niceties of hierarchy, talking to Frank about her Dad, made Claire think of a novel, one of her father's favorites. After all, in a publisher's office, asking for a job, one *should* be thinking about novels.

"Frank, did you read *The Augean Stables* by Durenmatt? He was the Swiss writer whose book was made into that Ingrid Bergman film, *The Visit of the Old Lady*. Like Daddy, Durenmatt is right. Don't you think, Frank, that government bureaucracies are piles of neatly stacked aging manure?"

The President of this very lean and clean-smelling publishing house could only agree. And since they were being tangential, and the serious topic of her coming to work for him took some warming up, he replied in kind,

"I have a friend who sent me his newest common-place book, *Winter Rules.* In it he quotes a satirical poem by Sir Francis Lindley, British Ambassador to Japan in the '30s. It begins, 'Oh Thou who seest all things below, Grant that Thy Servants may go slow, That they may study to comply, With regulations til they die.' You ought to read it. I'll ask George to send you a copy. But now, Claire, preliminaries over, I asked you why I should hire you."

Claire, looking quite dramatic with her shining blonde hair framed in a large hat, floppy, blue and unmistakably English, wearing a blue paisley scarf above a cranberry-hued raw silk blouse, deep blue suit completing the ensemble, well dressed enough to make any woman confident. She responded blithely, offering her most winsome smile.

"I want to live here in glamorous New York, the Big Apple itself, in Manhattan and only in an excitingly complex, elegant neighborhood. Obviously I intend to grab a brass ring or two while I'm here. From your standpoint, you know I'm one of the few recent graduates you can count on who knows how to read and in several languages, who knows literature did not begin and end with *The Seagull or The Cardinal's Hippopotamus*..."

"*The Pope's Rhinoceros*," corrected the publisher, whereby Claire gave an indifferent brush of her hand to indicate what she thought of it, continuing. "I do know good writing even if there's not much of it published. The lucky side for a publisher is that I'm young and *au courant* enough to know which truly bad writing is mod enough, really reprehensively stupid enough to sell millions."

She set her impressive jaw sternly. "I work hard, very hard. Because you and I are family friends, you know my character. You know you can trust me to watch the shop for you behind your back. I learned about that growing up with

Daddy. I work for you on the relatively cheap the first two years, I have some independent income, and won't fuss to Daddy if you fire me. But I will bitch like the dickens to him on the phone tonight when I call him in Kiev if you don't give me a chance. The Ukraine, as you know, is going down the tubes. That's why he's there. And about his work, I know he has a big new book coming out next year and you two haven't signed any contract yet. You'll make more off it if he signs with you—which he no doubt intends to if out of pique I don't queer the deal—than my salary would ever cost you. Blackmail of course, but keep in mind high gain, low cost." She grinned at him. She had an absolutely lovely, mischievously sweet grin; it conveyed essences of the beauty of her character and, in fact, extremely attractive features, a bit overweight be damned. "Besides, I'll buy you lunch." She gave her little speech with such good-natured cheer that for all its confident presumption there was no hint of arrogance or obnoxiousness. "And just think, I may even write a book one day, and I promise not to submit it to our company. Not one manipulating tear for trash. Now isn't that a relief?"

"Maybe not," he smiled warily. "It might be one of those miserably good first novels. The sort we turn down and watch Scribner's buy, only to see it climb to the best-seller list. I hate first novels."

Claire broke in, "Oh no, not a novel; I'm going to do serious work on money and politics, do muckraking. Lincoln Steffens is still my hero; wait until I find my own Deep Throat source! The real story behind something or other, the waiting murderer of a nation revealed—you know, something like that."

"Not on this company's time you won't. You work here and learn the ropes fourteen hours a day. The demands get worse when you get promoted."

"Daddy says publishers drink a lot of champagne and eat very well on each other's expense accounts."

"Your Daddy has to live the same exhausting life himself, and we both hate it."

"Let me be your personal assistant and I'll do the champagne work for you. Besides, sooner or later maybe I'll uncover the right scandal, right there over your expense account. Let's call it 'Grousegate'; Daddy loves wild grouse. I imagine you do. The acknowledgements will read, 'To the occasion of the grouse and the dear friend and boss whose expense account made this investigative writing possible.' Or 'Start Grousing' for short."

"Claire, that's enough. Stop teasing. Of course we both knew I'd hire you. I even want to hire you, I'd even bid on you like a manuscript up for auction. But please, I know you have a light heart and good, so don't do anything foolish to make either of us sorry. You have to be serious, learn some distrust. For starters, in this town assume a promise of business friendship is an invitation to a killing—your own."

Over the next few years, Claire had been serious, albeit not losing her whimsy or her, well, way. She had learned more than a bit about the world of business, to her surprise rather liking it. But her genuine interest in describing the concealed underside of the business world was frustrated. She saw one kind of book, those her company published; not the other set of ledgers, the ones she knew were the private accountings of major corporate, and political movers on the world scene. At one *intime* dinner with a devilishly handsome, successful Wall Street man who turned out, charming rat that he was, to be married, she had been pumping him about his firm. "I thirst after the insidious, what's hidden that we all suspect is there. At heart I'm still a Lincoln Steffens reformer with a detective streak to give it dark romance. Tell me, Jeffrey, what do you know about it?"

Her date's aim was hardly to teach criminology, or provide grand jury material for his own indictment should this sexy woman be wired. He was an ordinary rogue male. Weren't most of them? she asked herself. But one need not dislike a handsome rogue, to the contrary. For the moment he was diverting. After a couple of drinks, he poured more for her than for himself but could not anticipate her immense capacity for liquor; to others who partied with her, her liver seemed a perfect chemical plant by Glaxo Wellcome. Her debonair brokerage house manager did allow that, "Yes, money games were played, a few hundred millions this last week were made out the back door by one firm, I won't say which. And yesterday another firm, I won't say which,"—his grin told her it was his—"with an inside line to bribed tenders for some big, honey I do mean big, China construction project earned itself some hefty pre-award public announcement profits on the bid-winning bidding company's stock. Honey, you would be surprised how the money flows in. Have to be clever, that's all, nothing special, Claire; I mean that's the way the Street works. The idea of the Street is to make money, isn't it? Nobody's really criminal. I mean Boesky was a bit flagrant, that was all, or Insul in the old pre-SEC days. What the hell, think of Gould or the South Sea Bubble for that matter, but it's business, darling; it's the way the world works. And now, here." He leaned very close, made sure his knee glued to hers under the table, and began his night's personal business, and hers. "First" he winked confidently, "let me hold your hand."

She did, and he moved quickly to his current business, which was more than hands. "My darling, all mysteries of consequence are those perfumes that the sensing woman's and man's bodies arouse to love." Such mysteries could jointly be appreciated, resolved by him in bed. Jeffrey was a charmer, and a normal girl in her twenties likes essence of handsome man uncorked, unbottled. Afterwards, thank God, no Bogart scene with his turning over for a cigarette, but he had not been as good a lover as his line had promised. Yet she, like any woman freshly loved, wanted to call him the next day. He was unable to tell her his home phone number. Jeffrey explained, ever so reasonably, "I'm moving apartments, darling, there's no phone at the moment but through the office." Noonish, breathless after all with a new love, she called the office asking for him. A receptionist, obviously untrained and making her first and probably last mistake, said, "Oh yes, Mrs. Cochin, your husband Jeffrey is in conference. I'll have him call you."

The immediate unsolved mystery to Claire was not whom and of how much Jeffrey might have defrauded last week, but how could she have been so easily fooled. Sophistication in a big city takes a while to learn. Heel marks from kicking one's own behind are a sign—black and blue, to be sure, with tears on it—that one is learning.

In a griping mood, very unusual for her, she told an office colleague over spinach and goat cheese salad a few days later, "I've been here four years, read a mountain of manuscripts, gone to six meetings a day, been involved in promotional planning to the point that I could sell Bluebeard's memoirs as nursery tales; I've had several affairs and only one almost-true love, two bad judgments about handsome devils who turned out to be ambidextrous, by which I mean half or more gay, 'amphibious' as the French say, and a good way to get both AIDS and disappointed. All in all, nothing exciting to stir me beyond myself. After being promoted to the serious champagne circuit last year I am doing some of Frank's top-level stuff for him, and I've come to the point where I prefer orange juice and more sleep. Frank Gardner is wonderful to me. I love him. No better boss in the world. But what's missing is a love for my heart, not just a peach of a boss."

Her companion, wedded to the world of publishing and a very good husband, protested, "Claire dear, it will all work out. You'll be a Vice President, get married, think about children in your thirties, it will all be perfect."

"No!" Claire surprised herself with her emphasis. "What I need is a project that's really my own, start to finish. What I'm ready for is something extraordinary. I want to leap out of myself; it's romantic, I know, but I long for zesty revelations of dark and secret world-shaking doings. That would mean elixirs at the top. Professionally I won't know anything about practical economics unless I learn what's going on under the table. I read the papers; I know the schemes are there. I just don't know where to look. Teapot Dome, Insul and the Inland Empire of years ago, Watergate, Keating and the Savings and Loan affair, Dreyfus for that matter, the Jackal himself, none come shouting, 'Claire, hello, here I am, come look!' And what's more, I'm coming into responsible citizenship. I actually believe a world society can only prosper if it is trustworthy. Civilization requires it. So there!" She had embarrassed herself with her hard new idealism. She really believed it!

Claire stared suddenly at her luncheon friend, one or another Sally from the office. She pushed back her chair, stood up and affirmed, "You know what? I'm going to tell Frank I'm quitting! Books are wonderful. Money isn't enough. I have now lived in Manhattan—and so what?" So announcing, she scurried off to her paper-stacked office and called Frank's secretary to invite him to an I've-decided dinner. Without serious inquiry: in fact she did not want to know negatives; one never does at times of impulse. She was after all only twenty-seven, still allowed to be an impressionable, romantic, patriotic, and idealistic adventurer amid those "wider shores of being" as she called them, having in mind a book she had admired: she decided to join the CIA. It had been in her mind's imagination for some time.

Before going to sleep that evening she was immersed in dreams of superspies and the insider's world, of knowing more about events than do the people who are part of them. All secret and so oneself, one's colleagues in the very cell, the central energy source, of the inner world—why did the word mitochondria come to mind from school? Oh yes, energy makers in the human body cell. Insiders and in charge in a way, as a superspy might be; he or *she* might be noble and patriotic but yet righteously diabolical if need be, masterful spiders at the center of the world's web. No, she would be the patriotic spider helping a great nation to do its work in the world. Ah, the glory of it—and yes, she told herself, however foolish, totally romantic and wrong, that's what she nevertheless expected.

Her academic credentials, Gardner's glowing recommendations to some old friends of his from earlier days, her professors, her daddy's friends—including of course a host of station chiefs who had served in his embassies, a deputy director or two with whom awkward problems had been solved quietly with smooth ambassadorial help, a feminist affirmative-action requirement, and superb scores on oral interviews got her into the Agency with no trouble at all. The field training at the Virginia farm was great fun, but being a Green Beret was not what had brought her to intelligence. Nor was there that much of it generically in the "community" these days.

Beulah, whether they met in London, New York, Paris, or even once Cairo, was too smart to believe Claire could ever be working for the Department of Commerce. And when accidentally Claire's purse dropped to spill a Canadian passport with her own photograph under the name of Ruth Spiller, Beulah would have none of it.

"All right, lie to me as much as you want and make yourself look the idiot. Even Mossad has given up Canadian passports. Any woman knows enough about deceiving not to do it stupidly. Shame on—what did my father call your people? Yes, 'the cigar factory,' that's what MI6 called them. I've no idea why."

Claire was flustered; the people providing cover, a poor joke whenever she was so saddled, were constantly making a botch of it. The Cambridge Economic Crime Symposium last year had been worst of all. They gave her State Department cover, passport and the like under the name of Leona Gramptom; how uneuphonic. And just after registering as Leona she ran into a distinguished Norwegian economist, Lars Dahl, who knew her father and had met Claire long ago.

During it all the delegates had a hoot at her and the Company's expense. Her cover story was something for a TV sitcom, utterly ridiculous, and perceived to be so by everyone right away. She was deeply embarrassed and hated the Agency for being so stupid, and making her look and be so stupid. Next time, she thought, I'll wear a beard and moustache. She had called Gavin to say she was coming and, how was that for being clandestine, told him some silly story about writing a novel and trying out how it felt to use an alias. Gavin had almost been unkind in his response. No, truth was, he was unkind. He would, he said, "have none of your filthy American imperial politics. I'm ashamed of you, Claire, and I loathe your meddling superpower CIA." This was a new Gavin, or the old Gavin with a different face. She didn't know. She didn't even suggest they have coffee. He had made her deeply sad.

Lars of course had known from the start, how could he, like Gavin, not? But he was embarrassed for her and was deeply sympathetic. His response struck a deep chord. "Why in heavens name would you want to work for them anyway?" asked Lars. "Look how they've botched this. And no, by no means do I believe they were incompetent in what they did wonderfully well for all of us during the Cold War. Wonderful work. But now, well, is it right for you in terms of your future? Sure, learn to read the Arabic and Parsi press of course, and Eastern European economic journals, suborn Algerian generals, pay for the humvees for the Cambodian army, whichever army it is that day. Scan intelligence analyses of Middle Eastern targeted satellites to your heart's content, but there's no

Paris in any of that for you. No spying games by any of us can ever hope to get the French to come clean. They've got their industrial espionage bugs in every high-cost Air France seat, and pity us in the rest of the West, for we still can't duplicate the lobster sauce at L'Arbuci. Don't even want to. You're an adventurer, Claire, and a bright and very attractive one. Don't get sidetracked." Lars' words—he was very handsome, older, once a diplomat himself, now professor at Oxford—hit home.

Claire had her last, tedious, pointless humiliation as "Leona." She was furious at the little men doing little things with phony names, and while there was no doubt major confrontational action in the future, its name was China.

"Lars," she said grimly, "you're absolutely right. Past glory does not a present make, and since I'm neither an East Asian or Middle Eastern specialist, in fact damn near no kind of specialist at all, I think maybe I'll sit out this stage of the Little Men's Chowder and Marching Society theater. It's absurd. What's simmering in Eastern Europe, spilling over westward, is the boilover of old fashioned ethnic crime: Russian, Italian, Colombian, Azari, Kurd, whatever, and in the U.S., Britain, France too—now partners with every color and language who hatch ruthless young."

Lars was thoughtful. "Don't forget the new reach of being a crooked cosmopolitan; those master entrepreneurs are utterly without loyalty. Whatever their passport, the nation they are in at any given moment is just their banking facility. Or maybe where a girlfriend lives."

"What do I do?" she asked him, no whimsy in her manner these days. A woman at work professionally in this world can grow older faster than the calendar days provide. Claire, a delight always to her friends, had been battered enough in government work to have a line or two of permanent pain on her face. Makeup could cover the outside, not the experience. More than ever she appreciated the genius of her father in mastering it all without losing his ability to smile.

"Your DEA is quite good," continued Lars, "badly run but good cops, yet drugs are a crashing bore and too much a politician's invention of a convenient devil. They're the modern equivalent of the Roman circus, albeit one grants no ordinary brain gets better narrowed chemically. For really interesting work on the world scene, the sort you seem cut out for, there's the German Wissenschaftlichekriminalamnt, which is tops, but you'd need to be a German national and a criminal lawyer to boot. Our own Norwegian intelligence concentrates on maritime piracy and terrorist threats. After all, we are a petroleum power and there are a hundred threats, from bombs to tanker hijackers, to guard against. But we too are provincial about employment. So how about that outfit I've been watching grow, the one recommended by your Senate back in the 1980s by the Permanent Crime Committee, before that—" he paused, "before that abominable Senator Cranmer took it over. It's the International Financial Crimes Investigation Group, IFinCIG. Insiders call it IFFY; the Brits and the EU call it the Network. I have a Norwegian friend who is liaison. Shall I call him?"

Then and there it was. "Yes, call him." She stayed on at the symposia, indeed having lunches at the old Eagle Pub, learned a lot, met some important contacts, and swore, "Ill never again pretend to be Leona anybody." One of the after-dinner speakers at this elegant and the worldly assembly in Jesus College, Cambridge, was, of all people, the famous Senator Royston Cranmer. But was he really "abominable?" She had heard rumors, but what silver-haired, golden-tongued senatorial patrician, a power in banking and crime legislation, wasn't a target for a gossipy press?

Gavin, who was attending, naturally, as a star speaker, seemed to know the senator well. She and Gavin met almost accidentally. She certainly wasn't going to pursue him. But this time he smiled, seemed pleased to see her. And she was a woman who knew what she wanted. So she asked him point-blank, "Will you introduce me to the senator? And please use my real name. The devil take those idiot spooks." That did seem to please him. Gavin would be more than happy to introduce her to the great man. Ah, the Gavin smile. A nascent thrill arose within her. Much better than after that awful telephone conversation. But really, it had been too much for her to ask anybody to overlook such Agency stupidity. She was glad her heart beat just a little faster. First loves revisited should be like that always, even when outgrown. As she expected, he was still handsome and yes, she was a sexual woman, still easily aroused. She remembered how it had been with them at first, as he teased when she would get all hot and bothered in foreplay, "Your pussy feathers are flying." Bawdy and great fun. This evening Gavin looked careworn, not his cheery and flirtatious Irish self. Regrettably, there would be no standing on the bar reciting as he used to do from the Irish epic, the *Tain*. Maybe his shrewish wife Medea had worn him down.

The Senator had been glad to join them after dinner in the College bar. Claire was surrounded by charming men; that was her nightly fate and she loved it, while Gavin and the senator talked at a corner table. She joined them. Never a shrinking violet but nevertheless gracious when coming to her point, she told them both that Lars Dahl had suggested IFinCIG would be a good place for her to work.

"Your recommendation, Senator, if Gavin here will be kind enough to tell you a good word about me, would be much appreciated."

"Of course, I'd be happy to," the senator said.

Gavin was somewhat hesitantly. She had never before known him to lack confidence; perhaps it was his fear of Medea. He asked if she would like his recommendation as well: "I think the people at the Network will have read my studies on Eastern European economics. A good word from an academic can't hurt." How right he was. "Yes, of course" and "thank you very much, Gavin," she responded, then leaned over and kissed him—not quite like the old days, but more than perfunctory. There was no emotional response. The Gavin she had loved, to whom she had lost her virginity—odd, she had often mused, how a supposedly modern woman cares so much about that—was simply not there. Careworn and angry and sweet he was, but her lover was gone.

She was hired by IFFY more impersonally, but as quickly, as by Frank Gardner. How she longed for that kind of family setting and personal warmth! But IFFY needed its female affirmative-action hire, who it was be damned. Claire was worldly wise enough to know that IFFY would be pleased to get a connected woman. State was their primary sponsor, along with Treasury and DEA, so they must require an educated woman who knew some business and economics. Claire had Pomona and Cambridge, and the qualifications requirement for languages was met by her German and French. That she had been with the Agency even for a short time, leaving with no blemish and current clearances, was for them perfect; she could fill a slot immediately. Such was government.

From day one, the personnel people at IFFY seemed to care no more about Claire as a person than they would for hired window cleaners, or window dressers for that matter. She was, they told her, to be sent to IFFY's version of an academy; no independent school, only internal seminars. The first disorganized day of these found a small mixed group of newly hired secretaries, accountants, file clerks, and one lawyer. There were no other investigators. It was a bore but for two items. One was an introduction to organizational intelligence computer software programs. Filling in the blanks, naming names of people and institutions that were the underground railway for networks, that was going to be exciting. That would be her job. The other was *Offshore Haven Banks, Trusts and Companies*, a book about international money laundering. It was on the required reading list. Claire, who treasured books, called her bookstore to learn it was out of print. IFFY had a one-half room library. She went there, introducing herself to the secretary *cum* librarian. The library's copy was missing. So far IFFY was batting zero.

"Thieves within," Claire commented a bit acidly. But she was surprised at theft within a quasi-police agency.

"Try the Library of Congress," replied the grim woman curtly.

As Claire walked away, low dudgeon moving into high gear, she could not but be aware of how intensely the woman stared after her.

She was given a temporary office filled with loose files, with no room to actually work, much less feel at home. That was further guaranteed when she was told it was to be shared by another new hire who had yet to arrive. Followed a week spent mostly reading, punctuated by casual introductions to superficially smiling people who scurried off. She did not need to be an organizational psychologist to tell these were unhappy folk protecting themselves as best they could. Morale was low, and hers was sinking. A clerk carried the message to the ambassador's daughter that headquarters staff was "too busy" for coffee. It was demeaning. Humiliating. Worse than the Company. If it went on she would not last long at all. So much for her dreams of adventure, her genuine patriotism, (albeit these days an unfashionable sentiment), and, equally genuine, her desire to *know*, to be in the midst of driving world forces: power, politics, and money. To be there *alive* but as a force for the good, not simply for adventure's sake. Her emotions swirled around in that messy space between disappointment, fury and despair when the emergency arose. It was her third day at IFFY.

Jones, the deputy assistant director, was her boss, as she had been told by a nonentity of a guide on the first day. She knew little more but that he was on long loan from her father's own Department of State. He called her in.

"You are," he said, as Claire walked in to his quite comfortable office with its American flag next to the desk and mandatory pictures of the President, Vice-President, and Secretary of the Treasury on the wall, "my only option. As they say in the Army, warm bodies are to be supplied as needed on the front. As with police trainees, they learn what they really have to know on the street."

He had not even said "Hello." Or "Please take a seat." Or "My name is Jones." Nor did he stand when she entered. Jones was a jerk.

She walked directly to his desk and held out her hand aggressively across it. If it had been a pistol it would have been aimed at his nose. With her eyes she dared him to further rudeness. He was more than annoyed to be forced to rise and extend his hand, one-upped at the very beginning. Not Jonesy's cup of tea. He spoke with evident irritation, enunciating precisely.

"Miss Dubois, I regret we've no time for introductory formalities, or indeed for training or settling you in. An emergency has arisen. I'm dispatching you to Vienna on Friday."

When he sat down, she did, intentionally staring, her square jaw set in its "you worm" clench, at this tall, skinny, blade-nosed, pale-eyed, pin-stripe-clad, supercilious, self-important man. A faint smell clung to him of what? stale roses and a dash of vinegar? Ugh. And no friend anywhere in IFFY to give her a clue. Who was he? What was this outfit? Vienna in two days? That was great, anything to get out of here, but what did she know enough to do? She was so new she couldn't even find Jones' office in the Treasury Annex which provisionally housed IFFY. The building was an outcast place on Indiana Avenue, perilously close to the you-don't-walk-ever Northeast. Signs warning essentially, "Watch your everything" hung on the composition walls, in spite of the obligatory guard and sign-in book in the front hall. She wondered. If the wallets of these chase-the-money cops weren't safe in their own offices, what was the field work like? The building gave off a sense of squatters about to be rousted, with cardboard files stacked in the halls and temporary partitions in warehouse-like rooms to separate clickety-clack computer keyboard clerks. Who hardly ever spoke to each other.

Claire well knew that in Washington some agencies are loved and some are barely tolerated. The Executive and Congressional attitudes may have nothing to do with need or competence. What counted was the power held by sponsors of the bill creating the agency—that, and what politicians thought they had to show the public they were doing, even when intent upon not doing it. She well knew that controls on money laundering imposed costs on banks. Banks had fought IFFY from the start. Even now it was mandated to deal primarily with money flows involving drugs and organized crime, not the tax evasion of major corporations using transfer pricing, export-import bunco to save billions. Claire said to herself, "So here I am on our side of the war against international economic crime. I wonder if the criminal side might not be a bit more jolly. It will certainly be more luxurious." Jones, indifferent to her thoughts, droned on.

"One of our teams working in Poland and Estonia serendipitously picked up some information on what they think may be a laundering operation involving some U.S. nationals along with Eastern Europeans, Austrians, who knows what else? They stumbled over it in the course of another case which they simply can't drop now; their case is *big*." Jones emphasized the word to show his own linked importance. "*Their* case," he repeated, stressing "their" to indicate that her upcoming Vienna project was small potatoes, "has to do with hundreds of millions of dollars, perhaps billions, of illegal—if you can even use that word for any Russian business, and what the Russians hopelessly call their 'near abroad' business, since there is almost no other kind—Russian metals export through the Baltics, involving particularly bad mafiya types. And unsupervised banks in several jurisdictions. These mafiya, the word comes from our Italian M-A-F-I-A, a mongrel bunch, a dozen ethnicity's. IFinCIG's business isn't Russian iron or industrial rare metals theft and export, or gas or oil exports, or timber or gold or chemicals, whatever—let the Kremlin worry about them. Our interest is in the financial networks these people constitute in their commerce in commodities that are illegal when they get to the West, or are prohibited to rogue countries. Arms smuggling, drugs, contraband art and national treasures, wild animals, furs, prostitutes, undocumented immigrants, dangerous pharmaceuticals carrying Western brand labels, and, always, the rumor of weapons-grade plutonium or armed missiles themselves. These latter are probably journalists' exaggerations. Sensationalism keeps our budget going here, but it has to be titrated; too much fuss and Congress becomes unpleasant about any agency's performance."

Jones, having delivered his opinion on the role of the fourth estate vis-à-vis his job, seemed pleased, tapping his well-manicured fingers together.

"In any event the bunch we're chasing down now is but one of dozens. Every one of them is bad for the originating economy, since such profits don't get taxed. All of Eastern Europe is black economy; national collections are low, and they're all desperate for tax income. Poor economies mean unstable governments, and thus the return of dictators and wars. Well, more likely starvation and riots. Let the Cassandras worry about all that. Our job is the dirty money networks. And so to your job."

"Assume, Miss Dubois, that your case—if there is one, and right now there are hardly even allegations—will be typical. It will involve Russian *vory*, who are rather like our mafia godfathers. Looming large are the authorities, *avtoritet*, who may be crime bosses but are, at the same time, big men in business and government. I know I am giving you a short course on Russian criminal vocabulary, but you'll hear these terms and even meet these people when you work in the East. For example, you'll meet "whites," which is another name for the new Eastern European breed of criminally involved business, military, and political leaders, as opposed to the "blues," or old-style of tattooed career gangsters.

"Lump these scum together with the apparatchiks, who are the old bureaucrats turned capitalists; KGB turned hit men; bodyguards and palm-greasing extortionist entrepreneurs, and indeed other entrepreneurs and their paid politician friends, and there you have the scene. Mafia, or as the Russians spell it, *mafiya* is a general word, derived as I explained, meaningless except to imply corruption and lawlessness, and applicable to probably most big business in what was the USSR, and now, well, it's a giant political conglomerate. I tell you all this because you will probably come across the same kind of Slavic and Austro-Hungarian scum in your Vienna assignment." He paused. "Forgive me my frankness, Miss Dubois, but the 'one world' we live in might better partition off the scum."

Claire decided to be calculatingly bitchy. "I understand your meaning, sir. The term, if I recall, was Wendell Wilkie's, in the Presidential elections of 1940."

He looked at her quizzically. "What term?"

"'One world,' sir"

"Oh, for heaven's sake, woman, don't show off in front of me."

Claire, who had rarely said "sir" to anyone since boot camp in the Agency, was burning. She offered an icy smile, with a knife in her voice.

"Sir?"

"Yes?" Jones radiated impatience.

"Your Russian word list might have included *kriok* for crook or criminal, *kriminalnee* or *oogolovnnui*. I apologize for my pronunciation, but I have only been looking at Russian for a few weeks. More importantly, sir," her voice dripping ice enough, as one of her college boy friends used to say, to freeze the balls off a brass monkey, *oligarch* is the term in current use for those powerful in Russia of whom the majority are, according to a recent Georgetown study, sir, *krioks*. In any event, Sir, from my point of view…"

Jones interrupted, "I have no interest in your point of…"

Claire raised her voice to continue. "I think we might as well avoid the distinctions and call them all, keeping in mind the Djilas' famous book, *The New Class*. I remember my father telling me about Djilas, a great man. He told my father he was like Lady Macbeth because he could never wash the blood from his hands. His *New Class* was the first postwar exposé about the crooked Yugoslavian Communist *nomenklatura*. Since Djilas was Deputy Premier at the time, it was quite a scandal. He went to prison, of course. But I do think rather than all the Russian entrepreneurial crime details, why don't we just all call them the 'new new class'? Isn't that easier, Mr. Jones?"

He sputtered. "I mark your impertinence, Miss Dubois. You will regret it."

"If you please, Mr. Jones, I shall take careful notes of this meeting; you are the one out of line. These days a man, even half a man, has to be so careful about sexual harassment, don't you agree?"

Jones was livid, sputtering. Claire was delighted. But she realized she would pay dearly for her triumph. Jonesy-boy would get his revenge. People like him do.

"About Vienna, sir. What shall I do there?"

Jones had regained control of himself, shifted into a neutral persona.

"Yes, of course. First, realize the whole of it is insubstantial. Most unlikely that any U.S. citizens are involved at all. Like the time the Nassau Bank showed President Nixon's name on the secret depositor list; they thought they'd buy protection with a lie. And our cable was garbled, our computer went down so we couldn't even get at any original message, and the Polish team just sent a scribble to the Embassy. We know, because we just asked. Warsaw can't find the scribble or their cable copy. Some of our embassies over there are not what they should be, Miss Dubois."

Jones had just taken a gratuitous shot at her father running the U.S. Ukrainian Embassy, thus at her. Well, it was at least evidence of some jealousy. Good. Jones went on, ever so calmly.

"Before you get there you'll read what little we have on Vienna. One name, as I recall, and some alleged transit points. I'd ignore it myself but one dare not; Washington is a boiling stewpot full of ill will waiting to find a lap to dump in. My instructions are to pursue whatever hints we get of this sort; and so, Miss Dubois, you are set on the pointless path of pursuit. Taxpayers' money wasted but," Jones seemed amused by the thought, "who are we to care? When you get to Vienna, wait for Lee Barbour. He's your field boss and team leader. He's on his way from Montreal. No doubt," Jones sneered, "playing some hooky on the way. Presumably he's been looking into some nasty business routed via Panama, Mexico, a European rumor of a Vanuatu company, that would have to be a French interest; it's some reinsurance fraud out of the Channel Islands, I think. Somewhere behind it are the Swiss of course, and a few billion dollars' worth of fraud. On his way to Vienna, he's been told to report here, not that I can count on his doing that. He tells us, not me mind you, that he has a short Sofia stop; his itinerary not mine, I can assure you. He'll meet you at the Intercontinental in Vienna in a few days. Now…

"Not my call, Miss Dubois, against my advice. But some people," Jones raised his manicured eyebrows ceiling-ward, "will not listen. He has friends, Lord knows how or why, in high places. Congress, the press particularly. He's famous you see; someone wrote a *roman-à-clef* about him; oh yes, a philosopher, adventurer, savior of maidens and policies gone wrong, noble bandit and possible assassin, that sort of nonsense. What he will probably expect of you, Miss Dubois is a drunken debauch, a roll in the hay. Never mind. They say economic crime is rampant. They say this institution needs help. They say we need any kind of help we can get. Simon says, Give project contracts to Barbour. Simon would probably say, Get Markowitz too, but that I won't do. Now," Jones was glaring again, "this Simon says to you, Miss Dubois, Get out of here."

Claire had experienced others' rudeness enough, but Jones' took the cake. In this she was outclassed. She could only summon a disapproving, "Now, really!"

"Yes, really. Get out. Go to the commo room and get your packet—it's highly classified, 'eyes only' stuff, all those gobbled, unauthenticated, hard-drive lost and otherwise unrecoverable pointless few pages of it. A packet of nonsense, and the people who sent it can't find their full copy or remember it. That's how important it is. Even so, as a matter of regulation it will be your career, Miss Dubois, if you leak a silly word of it. In any event, study it on your way over. For your own sake keep all of its virtual nothingness secure. Chain your briefcase to your wrist or something. Go to Vienna, eat linzertorte, and wait. Now, I know you've been with the Agency and are used to lots of spooky hocus-pocus. We don't do those silly things. We sometimes have real work to do. We use true names here, no clandestine anything except absolute commitment to confidentiality, even when it's about nothing, on any investigative matter."

"Have you yourself seen the material, Mr. Jones?" She swore she would never again "sir" this stuffed-shirted, essence-of-idiot barbarian, and so swearing she remembered lines from Gabriel Garcia Marquez on Bolivar: "lost in the solitude of his immense power, he began to lose direction." Poor Jones, Claire thought, no greatness and no immensity, just a savage in herringbone tweed, and quite possibly over his head, lost but beastly. His response interrupted her thought.

"No, can't say I've had time but for a glance. The essence, you'll read for yourself, names a Vienna 'fiduciary,' no idea what that implies; one Brody, who is said to be a banker of some sort, agricultural export financing perhaps, health insurance and pension funds, nationality and role not clear. His name came up because the Polish law firm, Balinski and Konopnika, that our team was investigating for its role in a very big Russia-via-the-Baltics west import-export contraband business, was pretending to give away the store to avoid serious prosecution. That law firm gave away nothing. There was some silly reference to child prostitution rings exporting from Eastern Europe to the West and onward via Austria to Arabia, and Israel, which can be no serious business at all. That's for the morals squad, not us. We are interested in the big money."

Claire gave him a hard-eyed, disapproving look, "Oh?"

"Not big business, Miss Dubois, not at all. Unpleasant of course, but not very grand. Don't get sentimental on us."

She was too shocked to speak.

Jones went on, "If I know the game, they plied us with red herrings. The only other ID, and a place even, California no less. They're reading comic books to get this one, a client nicknamed 'Mr. C.' Can you imagine? Anything to do with drugs in California the DEA will know about. We passed it on anyway, but if there is a Mr. C, DEA's BSI will have it in their computer. These Poles have third-rate imaginations, Miss Dubois. Third rate. They could have picked the names to give up out of a phone book; after all, they know the drug tip is bogus or inconsequential, and if there were anything important in Vienna it will take us, or rather you, Miss Dubois, months to verify."

Jones took obvious pleasure in negativism. No wonder, Claire realized, even the State Department with its penchant for due and deliberate non-haste had transferred him elsewhere.

He went on. "But then, unless there's pressure there's never any hurry, is there now?" Jones paused, polished his manicured fingernails on the gray of his well-tailored suit, and looked up again. "No, one shouldn't hurry these things. We have some precipitous people about, that Barbour for example, or Markowitz, but both had something to do with law enforcement and we all know cops are never very bright. I myself am from State. State trains their people. Patience, discretion, negotiation, accommodation. The civilized rules. Pity so few understand them. We even have ambassadors who don't." Jones, letting the innuendo linger; finger-polishing his lapel, he studied the ceiling. Claire was wondering how best to kill him.

"And so mind you, Miss Dubois, there is always plenty of time once you've put in an appearance, shown the flag so to speak. That's the Vienna case in a nutshell. Perhaps we'll get better acquainted when you're back, who knows? Maybe you and Barbour will score a coup." Jones laughed deprecatingly, scanty in humor. "That's it, trundle off now. But do be careful, Miss Dubois. Some of these people over there are killers. My oh my. Who knows what Mr. Brody is like, or indeed if he exists, who his patrons are? Such people always have powerful patrons. Well then, so do we here, if you think about it, no? You must be careful about that, very careful. Patrons matter, don't they? Like your father, for instance, or that dreadful Norwegian Minister Dahl who foisted you off on us. You see, we must all pay attention to the geography of patronage—where a patron is when you need him, what new patrons might better serve, that sort of thing, eh?"

Claire reviewed it all: Jones' patronizing, Jones' warning, Jones' advising,

Jones' threatening. Be he Jones the precious, the disparaging and rude, the envious, the liar, Jones was just plain bitchy. But underlying this lay, not her intuition but his message, ready hatred and menace—whatever the Vienna job is, don't do it. Here, Vienna, landmines all about. Triggered for what? And ubiquitous, the play of bureaucratic sloth and power. There came to mind the closing refrain of that same Sir Francis Lindley's whimsical poem, which Frank Gardner had first quoted to her. Frank had sent her his friend George's commonplace book, just as promised. Claire, a State Department brat who knew the workings, who could memorize almost anything interesting immediately, delighted in quoting Lindley's ambassadorial ode about bureaucrats. Jones the epitome. Claire read it over in her mind.

Teach us, Lord, to reverence
Committees more than common sense,
Impress our minds to make no plan
But pass the baby when we can.
Or when alone we go too far,
Chastise us with a circular.
'Mid war and tumult, fire and storms,
Strengthen us, we pray, with forms.
Thus will thy servants ever be
A flock of perfect sheep for thee.

But Jones seemed a Red Riding Hood's grandmother sort of sheep. She realized she might have made the first real enemy of her life.

Claire had an ID badge, an electronic card key, for IFFY's Annex. Otherwise unknown, unknowing and obviously not welcome (perhaps Jones had accounted for the general chill of her reception), she had to ask Jonesy's secretary the way to the Support Office where she would get a new, one-day rush-order official passport and more shots if her Agency ones were insufficient. Not that a girl pleasingly plump in others' eyes, still just fat in her own, would find a vaccine against Viennese sachertorte, wienerschnitzl, pfannekuchen, schlag and more schlag, that so-thick whipped cream. And yes, she would get a coach air ticket which she would upgrade with her own funds. In Claire's view no civilized woman traveled long distances in airline steerage. As she completed these support chores before going home—she had no intention of returning except to check her pigeonhole—she had been overcome by the loneliness; walking strange halls, knowing no one, known personally by no one here but Jones. Once out the door she began to cry.

And now again, remembering the long beginnings, her captive reality in

Vienna, she was trying the locked heavy, carved panel door, testing the closed-down steel very nineteenth-century European shutters on her richly draped windows, her mind was no longer the sedative's captive but clear enough now to acknowledge that she was a prisoner, velvet cage or no. Ever so contrary to her image of herself as 007 Joanna Bond, she sobbed.

4

Some distance from Austria, serious men in white lab coats, black ties askew, most smoking, bustled in near silence about a white-painted, spacious, sterile office—no hint of poster, painting, family photographs anywhere. A squarish 100 feet across, windowless, cork-floored, insulated high ceilings holding bright florescent lamps, the space contained computers, transmitters, specialty presses, files and the gray cubicles. It might have been any major company's electronics center unless one knew its special business. It was not the kind of business these men would talk to outsiders about. The location was both secret and carefully chosen, away from the hustle and bustle of nerve-center Moscow, even Russia itself. A friendly capital city, a compatible Slavic society, little of the violence or daily tension of Moscow, here secretly situated inside a friendly bank building, a few of the staff in this forbidding complex of rooms easily posed as bank employees which, in a way, given the actual ownership of the bank, was correct. It was simply that the public, or democratic authorities, did not know they were there. Genuine bank employees who might wonder about an off-limits area, for there was but one access door and that seen to be used by only one or two men dressed in worker's coveralls, must think it was a warehouse, for janitorial supplies, that sort of thing. To think about it in any other way would be bad for the health. Entrance for most staff was gained through two other buildings, each adjacent, each owned and designed by the UST&D. The situation was perfect cover, provided perfect safety, allowed perfidy and profit. These were the essence of their business.

"The IFinCIG woman. How long to reproduce the genuine paper, U.S. Civil Service personnel stationery, forms, all that we need?" The question was peremptory. The habitually nervous dark-complexioned man, fifty perhaps, highly polished black alligator shoes but black-bearded stubble on his face who had asked it paced about in anger. He chain-smoked, snarled.

"Sir, we have most of what we need in the ready supplies file." The technician in charge, businesslike, had a reassuring voice.

"And her photograph? We have it?"

"Yes, sir. The partner there has been very helpful. Notified us about the woman. The man comes soon after her to Vienna. Sending on their file document copies. The partner has reliable help."

"Yes sir, quite true."

"Do we need her fingerprints?" The voice of a detail-attentive man.

"No, we dare not use them, sir; they would be validated and prove one woman, not two."

"Of course, of course. What an idiot I am." The voice lapsing into rare but genuine self-criticism.

"No, sir, the staff have been through this drill before. It's a new thing for you. You've just arrived in Sofia. Takes a bit of getting used to. Our procedures, we do the best we can, reflect a less highly technical support environment than you are used to at home, sir. We apologize."

"No, no, carry on. What you say about the fingerprints was of course quite right. I shame myself. But I worry of course. It is a very important, very difficult, quite technical operation to insert full correspondence, delete entire files in secure U.S. government computers."

"Sir, our branch has had that assignment for years, but it's only recently we have had the equipment, financing, cooperation in the U.S. itself to allow us efficiency, reasonable success. No cold war sir, simply capitalists cooperating across frontiers. The kind of thing they taught us in Komsomol that Communism would do. And now, here we are, sir, all getting rich, and we are able to do it. No frontiers for money, Sir, isn't that true? No confronting ideologies, either—a rich agreeability, so to speak. Would you yourself not agree?"

"Yes, it's true. But damn the ideologies, I worry about the details that make or break us. Do we have a PIN number for computer access for red emergency personnel notifications to Treasury? Can we mimic Civil Service computer transmissions intra-agency perfectly, I mean absolutely perfectly? A lot depends on this, you know. What I am saying is that it all depends on your staff here." A no-nonsense voice of command.

"Yes, sir, we know, sir. We have done it on a trial and we can do it now, sir."

"Can we really breach a Treasury Department personnel computer system? I find it hard to believe, that kind of luck on our side. Dubois disappears from IFinCIG and a warning that she was really Liebowitz appears instead. And in Langley, now *that* is a trick, to alter all personnel and security entries with Dubois photographs, substituting the new photo on them in all of those sector-independent blocked computer systems there. Truly?" The voice was uneasy.

"Not really that bad, sir. We have had computer access to Langley for some years. No moles indeed, the Americans used to say, and how wrong they were, how wrong they are! Profit sharing makes recruitment so much easier, and Langley morale is so low now they are what KGB used to be toward the end. No, we have a computer scan photo match that deletes Dubois' picture and her physical appearance description; and thanks to our mole, it is handwork of a sort, Liebowitz appears in her stead. Dubois left the Agency, no one will think to look. If they do—well yes, they could find other inconsistencies, but they will never look. The people who knew her after all are in their clandestine service; no one in personnel but the routine processing, lie detector people, that sort of thing. You remember how impersonal it all was with us, don't you, sir?"

A tightened voice subject to the memory of bitter horizons, "Oh yes, impersonal."

"Difficult of course, sir, but don't forget that our own Sergei's KGB section specialized on that access. And Sergei's group has more people inside now than they did before. Much easier these days, as I said, sir."

"Yes, yes, I can understand that. Still amazing good fortune to have Sergei available." A careful listener to the voice might have detected doubt.

"He's made himself available, sir. Stakes are high for all the Partners on this. They are all in a state of shock themselves after the Warsaw catastrophe. Unforeseen. One stupid fearful man, one lucky American team on an entirely unrelated case. One piece of bad luck on the cable transmission documents. More bad luck on a deletion command failure that led Warsaw Interior Ministry people, unfortunately not ones on our payroll, to their Finance, Central Bank people; it's almost unbelievable sir, all of it coming up with a true name trace to Brody in Vienna. A most unlikely accident chain, those gutless Warsaw banking attorneys crying their hearts out to appease, get themselves off the hook, bargain their clients away to get off the hook. So we know they rolled over on Brody."

A tension-filled voice: "If only we knew that was all the lawyers knew and told. If only we knew what other documents accidentally came into their hands when they began the new layering, the new transit banks, the new front companies, the new straw men as protection when our red government here fell. Sooner or later the new government will begin to look for the money. One can never be too cautious. What idiot hired Warsaw? What did they see that we don't know about, that IFinCIG does know?"

Always deferential: "Yes, sir, what we don't know is the worry. I should think Brody is no problem."

An emphatic voice: "No, Brody is no problem. If only the monitoring of the embassy transmission hadn't garbled. The critical moment—and a sun spot, or tape flaw, or whatever goes wrong with these damn gadgets."

Sympathetically: "Yes, sir, technology can be frustrating."

Angrily: "That's putting it mildly! So all we know is that IFinCIG, and that means their interagency colleagues in DEA and FBI, know Brody's name, and about the C. But is there anything else the Warsaw lawyers knew and told? That's why this damn woman is so important."

Reassuringly: "Yes sir, but she's as good as ours now, Sir. Whatever she knows our Vienna partners will know. Still, bad luck that IFinCIG would move so quickly.

On the other hand, with the Partner's information from Washington, it puts her in our hands as soon as we've finished this work here. And in Vienna."

Doubting voice: "The embassy monitoring screwed up on the garble. Are you sure the records replacement will work?"

Always reassuring: "Quite sure. We still enjoy the worldwide electronic surveillance capabilities of GRU. That little war goes on still, sir, GRU and the new State Security Section. It's money at stake now. Competition makes them all keener."

"Indeed, indeed. Capitalism turns out rather nicely."

Admiringly: "I know General Bratislav is one of your Partners, sir. We all here appreciate the wisdom of that, sir. His group's cryptographers are splendid on U.S. embassy, DEA, IFinCIG material. Don't do so well with the CIA, never did, but it's all right as long as embassy DEA feeds to Washington via embassy, not CIA, code—but for the garble this last time from Warsaw. As far as penetrating their internal computers, hacking I suppose, there's no question that with General Bratislav in charge we penetrate them more easily than they could penetrate us. I find it exciting, being a capitalist now, with incentives I can understand. Our assets are much bigger than IFinCIG's, everyone knows that. IFinCIG doesn't have much of a staff. Our business is low priority for them. Capitalist bankers see to that. So much is gray area, isn't it, Sir?"

A sigh: "Business is not a moral nor ideological area. It's a matter of colors; gold is the nice color, red is the bad one. Commerce as color sensitivity. All business will do what it can to turn gold. Ours after perestroika is just newer, more experimental, freer; we have unusual opportunities that the Partners comprehend. As for "gray," that is a color only philosophers should use."

Affably: "Yes, sir, I stand corrected. But it is excellent, is it not, sir, that you, the other Partners have internationalized so quickly? Brilliant, I should say, Sir. Organizing a Partner in Washington, D.C. is rather a coup. For this job, I know he, or they—I appreciate we are all on a 'need to know' basis—are being exceedingly helpful in this matter."

Preoccupied, a worried tone still: "But who could have foreseen such a chain of events? The wrong layering documents to Warsaw potentially exposing so much? Exposing Brody is already quite enough. The Partner who works most closely with him could be at considerable risk. If only we knew. We must get that Dubois to ourselves with no blowback risk. She must cease to have existed before appearing in IFinCIG."

Mollifying: "Exactly, sir. Exactly what we are doing here now, in the Washington files, surely in Vienna."

"The Warsaw lawyers have been terminated, of course?"

"So I understand, sir, even as we speak."

"The Warsaw Partner is in action then, fully?"

Deferential but confident: "You know the Partners personally, sir. We at this level only know *of* them. But we're told the lawyers will be working late, an unfortunate electrical fire will consume their small office building, dead lawyers, the files in ashes."

Musing: "For this sort of thing we usually bring in an arsonist from abroad. The Czechs are excellent. In the old days defenestration, now arson. Perhaps the Partnership should look into it as a diversification. Small, elegant, high-paying work."

"Yes, sir, I should think you might."

Brightening: "Well, Warsaw is not our business here. I'm pleased to see your staff are all so competent." The voice of almost friendly management practicing newly learned Western human-resources psychology.

"Thank you, sir."

"The stakes are very high. Billions. A definite Kremlin, Bankers High Council and Duma interest here, Tallinn, the Western Partners of ours. Yes, a major corporation, multinational, yes, billions and some important connections at risk. Failure would be intolerable. You understand?"

Staff understood quite well. Firing certainly, a death sentence possibly. Capitalism was rather like the previous regime: many of the same people doing the same things but making much more money and, the remarkable difference, no State control at all. The partners and the State were functionally one. Initiative, capitalizing on opportunity had become everything.

Reflecting: "Great Russian minds that would have been mathematicians can now be creative entrepreneurs. Yes, glorious is the freedom to compete without any restraint, no holds barred—the religion of rational economics freed of moral taint. All one needs is the stomach for it. The color gold is the carminative. 'Plus ça change, plus c'est la même chose.' And we arrive thereby at disincentives rather surprisingly akin to those wielded by Comrades Stalin, Beria, Andropov. Fewer casualties of course, and that all for the good."

"Yes, sir."

"Efficiency, coloring things gold demands least cost, greatest speed, most impact. Thus no gulags nor torture in psychiatric hospitals but simple assassination, kidnapping, hostage taking. Efficient, no capital or administrative costs. It's the free enterprise way. We Oligarchs are the Furies now, we impose fates."

Yes, staff were indeed motivated to be highly efficient, nothing of the old Oblomovian paralysis, that helpless earlier Russian refrain that forced even Lenin once to cry out, "What is to be done?" No, staff and Partners understood exactly what was to be done and whence Fate came.

"Report to me when you have completed the Washington document erasures and replacements."

"Yes, sir."

"How's the work going?" A new voice, no-nonsense and commanding; husky, comradely asides as he shook hands with the Partner already there.

"General, sir. Another two hours. With that on site assistance we've hacked into their central computers. Their personnel departments have always been their weak point in computer security. Americans are action-, not people-oriented, and it does cost them dear. Personnel files are all we care about this time. No monitoring to detect us, sir. Their counter-intelligence people have their ears to the wrong wind. And Treasury doesn't even *have* a capability. We'll insert the changes, sir, never fear."

"Good. You understand that once the personnel files are dubbed, it's urgent that we insert, and get into the right hands the red alert warning from their Civil Service Personnel Security section."

"Oh yes, sir, no question, it's scheduled."

"Again good. Essential that it be perfect. Claire Dubois, as they have known her, is an impostor, true name: Greta Liebowitz, a Jewess. That racial touch should resonate with a few of those hypocritical egalitarians. And so they come to learn the real name of the woman they have foolishly hired at the Network. Her CIA and other references all contrived to get her into IFinCIG, yet she is a mafiya mole. Delicious, eh?"

"Yes, sir, absolutely delicious."

"The action-urgent advisory tells them that Liebowitz is a high-level computer data thief, until now also paid to run a Ukrainian prostitute export ring as a side business, herself once a common whore but now a highly educated, well placed one. Very clever. Much too embarrassing for U.S. authorities ever to admit. Greta Liebowitz, no less! They know their heads are on the block for a grotesque security lapse. They have hired a U.S. Civil Service-certified, mafiya-inserted security risk—and a whore! The Dubois 201 files everywhere now will have the photograph of a slightly different woman, not much different and just a bit blurry, so they'll understand someone on this side set them up, decieved them with a look-alike mole. There's our beguilingly indistinguishable girl Liebowitz, staring out at them from Civil Service, the Agency, FBI and Network/Treasury, with the personnel red alert notification to all of them." Yes, indeed. It was the voice of a man who wishes it known he is dangerously attentive to every detail.

"Yes, sir, most thoroughly planned."

"How have you handled the problem of the originating Civil Service Personnel Security sender? A real man, senior, whom obviously no one can get back to once he, has so to speak, sent out the red-flag message."

"Quite right, sir, as you say. Japanese-American fellow, Hashimoto is their Deputy Director. Highly respected, methodical, cautious. Never wrong so far. His signature out of his computer station, hacked in of course."

"And the man himself?" The voice of a careful administrator.

"A boating accident very soon, sir—the next time he takes an evening or morning trip on his boat moored near Arlington. They have so many accidents on the Potomac. Why, even the CIA director drowned off his own boat, not counting several whom the Sea Scouts assisted. Never a trace of the Sea Scouts, sir. Hashimoto will be dead within a few hours of the red-flag dissemination."

"Sea Scouts?" the General and the Partner asked in unison.

There was a brief smile, the first. "Ah yes, a bit of levity. The real name of a branch of the English and American Boy Scouts. The Bulgarian service Special Section has adopted it. Their wet affairs unit has made a kind of specialty of boating deaths, along with umbrella tips and limu. Limu, sir, that's one of the most potent polytoxins known, from coral-contaminated Hawaiian seaweed, sir. Of course the most spectacular toxin, brevetoxin B is from an algae, even more deadly than frog skin bufotenines or puffer fish. The Bulgarians just add a microgram of the seaweed—Orientals typically use seaweed as food—to a target's soup. Their biochemists synthesized the toxin; thirty-three man-years of labor, I'm told. Took them a dozen years. The Service is very proud of it.

Wouldn't share it with the KGB. Pride of synthesis, sir. Toxicologists never detect it. I know—because before I went into computers I did biochemistry, the secondary metabolites. Worked on the team. Thought poisoning would be a career, but this, sir, is much better."

Disapproval in General's voice. "I'm not interested in your personal life, but I still don't understand 'sea scouts.'"

"Bit of a joke, sir. Not that the Bulgarians have an ocean, but there is the Black Sea. The West sometimes landed spies by submarine on our coastlines, their naval patrol people there amused themselves by copying the U.S. Navy Seals; they generated quite a competent group. They used to do mock wargame penetrations of the Russian Crimean Sevastopol facilities. The Russians made it more realistic by killing those they detected. Bulgarian Seals countered by killing as many as they could of the Russians assigned to the mock defense. Officers on both sides had a grand time: bet on the casualty numbers, paid off over drinks at the Sevastopol Naval Officer Club I was told. The officers brawled of course sometimes; you know how Russians can despise Bulgarians. Hushed up a Bulgarian commander getting killed. But running the games like that gave real incentives for enlisted men on both sides, sir—rather like capitalism."

"And so?" The Partner's voice was impatient.

"Sorry, sir, I was carrying on, but you see my uncle—I apologize for the personal reference, I'll be brief—was a naval officer stationed in Sevastopol; those games and the officers brawling lent themselves to some family jokes and all that. But be assured, sir, the Sea Scouts will see to it that Hashimoto falls off his boat on time, and no coroner or pathologist will be the wiser. The Bulgarians are old hands at that."

The voice was relaxed. "It should go well. The impostor doubling for Claire Dubois is unmasked. Network's Personnel Department own personal memories will now fix the one they met as a dangerous fraud. No doubt they will all recall their own deep suspicions of the woman they saw. Everyone will cover their own ass. We can be sure there will be no news releases on this lapse, not after the last few years of CIA and FBI screw-ups, DEA and Customs corruption. American intelligence and law enforcement, let alone the President, are not looking good to their public."

"And the Dubois woman herself, sir?"

"On vacation or an assignment, but in any event unavailable. I've seen to that myself, I don't mind telling you."

"I'm gratified, sir. All the staff are amazed at the planning details. Your

Plans committee, is a very effective group, sirs."

The General, affirmative, proud. "Quite so. The software scriptgraphics replicating program is superb. The mail cover in Washington, and to her lady doctor friend in Scotland, yielded dozens of letters. We even managed a few out of the U.S. Embassy in Kiev. Her own father's mail. Gratifying. It reproduces her handwriting to perfection; the only risk is that there is no new variant to her script. We have reproduced her stationery of course. The letters are going off as soon as she leaves Washington, posted from Paris—the Montmartre post office, since she favors the district. They will counteract anything she may have written before, or telephoned about. In these letters there's drama, something sudden has arisen.

"She writes a bit indiscreetly, hinting at her secret assignment, telling her father and friends—a bit of housebreaking produced her correspondence list—how happy she is with her work and, a nice touch, a designer dress from Rue Faubourg St. Honoré. She dines nearby at the exclusive Cercle l'Union Interalliée. The Paris Partner's group sent a double in to buy an expensive frock and then, dining, to make herself known to a waiter there in the company of one of the Club's members, with false documents of course, while dining. As for the nine-thousand-dollar dress, one of the Paris partners has a lady friend who will enjoy that. Moreover the 'Plans' committee has given Dubois a new romantic interest. First name only. Harry. Appropriate for an American in Paris, there is the American 'Harry's Bar' there, although 'Ernest' would have done as well."

Clearly not understood by either staff or the Partner: "Your meaning, General?"

A condescending response: "Amusing. One must have read Hemingway to appreciate it. Well, it's not the CIA she once worked for who gives her a legend of the documented life that was not, but our Plans Committee. Your graphology group here did the mechanics, and we created her busy ghost. She has written briefly to her best friend Beulah, a quick card to her father, from Paris then Cyprus, for there's very active terrorist-related banking there, which everyone knows. She'll then be sending casual cards to others, all saying they are not to expect to hear from her for some time. A nice touch I think—she tells them they can inquire of IFinCIG—the British, Brussels, and Interpol all call it the Network—so, yes, they can ask Network Headquarters should they want to know anything about dear Claire." The voice was purring.

"The last touch, yes indeed, sir, is genius. Network, as you say, will deny any comment as they cover up. I can see that, sirs. That will support family and friends' appreciation of just how clandestine is her assignment. Or what a liar she is, off with her Harry on some romance. Sirs, the staff all commend you and the Plans committee. Imagine her father being told by Network that Network never employed her as they try to cover themselves! That will give the old devil a start. His romantically delinquent daughter! Oh sirs, what a sense of humor in the service of the credible you all have. Network will be consistent with routine denial, more than believable for those who like melodramatic spy stories—or know how impulsive a woman in love can be."

"Yes, sir. I hope, sirs, you will allow all of us on the staff to congratulate Plans, you General, you sir, all the Partners, sir."

Dismissive, peremptory: "Yes, yes, see to it that staff gets on with their work. Keep us informed."

As the two executives walked away, the one who was nervous by nature remained agitated. "This damage control *must* succeed."

5

Vasil was walking west from Vilosha Boulevard toward his office, feeling uneasy. He didn't trust his boss, nor like him, and it was mutual. "Son of a bitch," Vassili muttered. Vasil, well brought up in a historically honored family, did not ordinarily swear. When he did, he meant what he said: the vulgarity, intensity, still a bit of bad-little-boy shock to it, and yes, the child's sincerity. "Son of a bitch," he repeated.

Vasil clasped his hands behind his back, the movement and his stride as casual as he could make them. He needed to feel the reassuring steel and leather touch of the Smith and Wesson police special in its holster on his belt in the small of his back. It wasn't as good a gun as, say, the Austrian Glock .45, but the gun was his statement. Vassili was pro-American, pro-English. He was a member of the local Atlantic Alliance Club. No mealy-mouth, play-both-sides-of-the-street, waiting to see if the Reds, the mafiya, would take over for him. Stand straight, stand tall, back to the wall. But still, this was Sofia. Vasil's own work was not without complexity. In the meantime he whispered, lips pressed together. A fellow didn't want to be seen talking to himself on the street. But his words were prayer as well as oath: "By Saint Rilski!" One of these days, on some dark street, maybe in some well tinkered-with exploding car—a local signature of displeasure—some very personal ugliness would hit some highly personal fan.

The newly painted sign hanging over one of mans dirty, dreary, gray, smallish buildings on Count Ignatiev Street, not too far from McDonald's or a convenient lunch at the upscale Restaurant Crimea, read "International Translation Services." A clothing shop, that carried high-priced blue jeans, plaid shirts, and bargain running shoes was on the ground floor. On the wall of the foyer *cum* stairwell a smudged directory listed "International Translation Services (ITS)" on the third floor. The foyer, its glass street door unwashed for decades, was no darker, grimmer, or dirtier than most foyers in the short block of endlessly same similar streetsfilled with buildings constructed from the 1880s through 1950s in downtown Sofia. Down the same street was General Parensov Park. Standing in it, bearing shabby witness to poverty and Communist decay, was the basilica Sedmochislenitsi. The church was in the same neglected state as his office foyer.

Walking further, a few corners away, on September the Sixth Street was the Interior Ministry. In the opposite direction, via Czar Kaloyan Street to Saborna Street, stood the U.S. Embassy. It was a small, dingy building, and if any of that fabled American optimism resided there it was certainly concealed by contrary externalities. The embassy was guarded by one of a squad of depressed-looking young soldiers who spent bored hours, not always vigilant in the armored guard house, but instead sitting on auto bumpers under signs reading "diplomatic parking only" in two languages, talking with friends. One might see a guard and his visiting friends eating piroushki (5 cents equivalent each, and tasty), his automatic weapon swinging on its shoulder sling, taking a bite or two of greasy pastry in its muzzle. A sign of peace or the hunger of guns?

Likewise on Saborna, on a corner, was the Ukrainian-Sofia Trust and Development Bank (UST&D). Fine quarters, new and marble. Two serious armed guards inside the locked bulletproof glass doors ate no piroushki. "Trust," in the case of the UST&D, was, as with much in the Balkans, conditional upon many things, most of them carefully, often guilefully, concealed from those whose interests were at stake. "Non-transparency" was the word. Nearby, another of the few fine buildings downtown, this one facing Vilosha Boulevard, the quite grand Sheraton. Its smiling doormen, husky body-builders in dramatic black frock coats, had no guns visible. A wise man made no bets about that. Where there was money in Sofia, one either fought for it or stood to lose it. As for Vilosha Boulevard of the many shops, many proud locals would say it was the Champs d'Elysées of Sofia. The courteous visitor would not respond with a sour comparison to Sheffield, the old East German Leipzig, or American coal and steel cities in their down-and-out days of the Depression. For the locals, the new presence of consumer goods in the capital city was a joy. For the vendors the absence of a mass clientele strictly limited an honest income. On the outskirts of Sofia a new and richer city was growing, but downtown the Vilosha shops, the Sheraton, and the UST&D were staging paradise. Like the other Paradise, assuming God to be like a secular Bulgarian, harsh and arbitrary, only a few elect might enter.

The same was true for the office of the International Translation Service, where Vasil worked. Its newly furnished rooms were tolerable if one ignored bilge-beige walls unpainted since King Boris' time (1918-1943), posters of Black Sea resorts more pleasant to the eye than to actual tourist experience, and two paper icons. ITS, for more profound reasons no paradise, nevertheless enjoyed a locked heavy steel entrance door. Here too then was reflected the mood of buildings, the mood of the place: a highly selective hospitality. The reciprocal of Sofia hospitality was distrust, and fear, of risk to persons and assets—including sometimes ones as precious as little girls.

And the mood of the people? Who can say what really was in the minds of those surly, suspicious, dark-countenanced passers-by, no greeting returned even to a happy child? A Continental heritage in part; the people of northern and central Europe were, before mid-century, the same.

Politically sophisticated Bulgaria is post Communism's unwilling laggard, some complain a millenia and a half of historical delay. The work of ITS on Graf Ignatiev Street and its parent elsewhere cannot be understood out of that context, for interests, cunning, treachery, and murder, like man's sin arising out of Adam, even viewed irreligiously and perhaps more painful when so viewed, derive from the compulsion of history. ITS and its, until recent, owners' grandparents may be determining. Its "ownership" as attitude and ideology remains in doubt. The Bulgarian fat woman has yet to sing. Some of her predecessors having been murdered in mid song. Such interruptions serve to delay conclusions. But ancestry is significant. The apologist for history reminds us that to know where we are today, at all to comprehend cultures whether of rampant theft, sterling glory, the democratic achievement of simple voting or businesslike murder, one begins with history. In more isolated Bulgaria, in its isolated security services, the moreso.

Consider: Roman invasion and Christian exposure not long after Constantine's death in the mid 300s. Constantine himself was born in "Bulgaria" then Moesia and in his own life provided a kind of Balkan model. Religious, he was brilliant, imperial, generous and bloody, for he did after all execute his own son Cristus and his wife Fausta, and Licinius an honorable military foe, if by then in the Eastern Roman world much of honor was known. Bulgaria defined itself early (780), as a nation state, and inconsistent then as now ideologically, had its earlier vague Roman and southern Christianity reimposed by Boris I (864). Hermitism was important early on. There was much about the real world to denounce and desert. St John of Rila who was a hermit was, is the national saint. The greatest monastery, Rila, bears his name. From hermitism Bulgaria became preoccupied with evil through the bogomils about 950. Bogomils, themselves monks, were formidable. They asserted that all the world, mankind included, were the Devil's creation. Theirs was a Gnostic doctrine, elsewhere lost as Christian heresy but evident this day in ITS's own hidden domains.

Consider that "Sofia" was the Gnostic's name for wisdom, the female partnership in and as God, but Sofia's and the bogomil wisdom dictated that as quickly as possible, and through the wisdom of secret knowledge, as heavenly aspiring aescetic one denounced this world, accepted poverty, and through death fled to the presumed godliness of one's soul. Hermitism as simply turning inward was, compared to the assertion of evil by the bogomils, a halfway measure.

If Evil is autonomously strong and God is no sure winner, or indeed as with the Gnostics there are two gods, the bad guy who runs this place and the nearly unreachable One ever so high away, there is double Manicheism. As with Faust, you get to choose sides.

Never underestimate the importance of citizen's choosing Evil as the likely winner when seeking to comprehend the theology of Balkan politics.

Perhaps that is why the Interior Ministry's Sixth Department's Special Services "wet affairs" unit, arcane also in its knowledge in its secret nest in Sofia, was so enthusiastic in its assassin's partnership with, first the Nazis and the KGB until 1989. Killing was after all, as with a Muslim warrior dying slaying infidels in Jihad, doing you a favor. But credit even to the fathers of ITS, Bulgarians are stubborn and survive that way, and they know who they are. In spite of the Nazis the Bulgarians did not export their Jews to the camps. Their own people yes, to gulags, regardless of ethnicity, but not for being what they were but for thinking as they did or, as with Stalin, for what they *might* be thinking.

The bogomil bequest remains realistic. Their conviction that mankind and all of its institutions are evil has been a too realistic appraisal, dramatized from time to time even beyond the daily grimness of the oppressed life of a people potentially flowering with literature, music, art, crafts, powerful religiosity and mathematics. One drama, (1014) Constantine's Basil the First, who in defeating Bulgaria's army thus it as a kingdom, became an epiphany of horror. Basil "Bulgar Slayer" blinded 99 out of 100 troops captured, the odd one out led the straggling rest home. One is reminded in this bloodiness of the later, more northerly neighbor Vlad the Impaler who skewered on poles, strong pointed saplings thrust through the anus and viscera; the poles then hoisted as standards. This decorative scheme was probably borrowed from the Roman practice of attention getting urban way crucifixions. Recall that Nero sometimes doused and lit Christians so impaled as a kind of pre modern street lighting—to line the roads to his capital. Vlad's was a presentation to visitors, or their armies, of the kind of hospitality to expect. Bulgarians do not, dare not forget examples such as these.

After Byzantium's domination came later Serbs and vanquishing Ottomans (1396), the latter overthrown by a liberating Russian army with freedom memorialized in the Treaty of Berlin (1878). A sense of national revival had begun much earlier with the monk Paiisi from Mt Athos, a kind of Slavic Tom Paine writing just at Tom's American revolutionary time, the mid 1700s. Revolution, rights and romanticism. The Germans giveth and the Germans taketh away. The Berlin Treaty 1878, first by losing WW in which Bulgaria had been allied with German and Austro-Hungaria, suffering in consequence starvation and Allied occupation. There had been earlier national liberating ferment and example. One of the heroes of these, Rakovski, established the Secret Central Committee in 1866. However nationalistic, idealistically revolutionary in conception the nomenclature "secret" is mindful. Beholden to the Byzantine mind, to Richelier's master spy, de Tremblay, anticipating likewise revolutionary Bakunins, Bukharins, anticipating bands of Dzerzhinskys, Trotskys and Lenins whose institutionalized practice was, shall we say? of unkindness, secrecy is sacred. Such goals and methods were beholden in turn to Rakovski of whom historial Crampton writes, "Rakovski's greatest achievement was to establish the practice of conspiracy for political objectives."

The Turks, no slouches in the violence game then or now, were hard on patriots. Levski for example, intent upon liberation, was hung by Turks in downtown Sofia in 1873, and those peasants heeding the call to uprising, including perhaps 4000 women and children near Plovdiv in Batak, were assembled in churches by other Bulgarians, albeit Muslim ones deployed by Turks, there to be burned alive. Once liberated during the 1890s, while bolshevism and World War II were a-brewing, finance ministers and Bulgarian foreign emissaries were handily assassinated, and in 1894 the reforming strong man himself, Stambolov while being murdered, had his hands cut off. They are still at least pictographically on display in books.

Burning was not a strictly Ottoman device. In 1925 in Sofia the communists sought to kill the king by a bomb placed at Sveta Nedelya Cathedral, the decrepit building in front of the Sheraton Hotel. One hundred and twenty died but the king survived. Among thousands of left wingers arrested some to be burned alive in the furnaces of Sofia's police ministry. Yes, furnaces and in the police headquarters. Prescient was it? By 1935 Hermann Goring visited and was feted, by 1940 Bulgaria had become an Axis power. But, World War II lost by the Axis, the Bulgarians as a result of their various clever twists and turns, by war's end were technically at war with every nation Allied and Axis (excepting far away Japan). This is sometime referred to as "Bulgarian luck." It continued. The Russians, having given freedom from the Turks through war ending in 1878 did, like the Germans also taketh away.

At the end of World War II Bulgaria became a Soviet satellite, considered as one of the most loyal of Soviet provinces and enjoying all the perks—primarily equality in poverty, pain and oppression—of communism and Russian hegemony. But revolutions are of many kinds, and Bulgarian efforts to accommodate continued. Capitalism was announced again in 1997. But except for a supportive Thomas Paine elite and some citizens' prayers (opinion polls gave free market democracy no more than 50% support), well mirabile dictu, down there in the alleys, it turned out not always to be so different from what had preceded it. Crime, the cops, those ex-spies still on the payroll, the *mafiya*, national self-confidence, not knowing the how of self-government have remained problems. It is the luck of the Bulgarians not to suffer more harm than they have. It is their luck also to have had as neighbors some remarkably unpleasant muscle-man regimes, contemporary Serbia has been until recently a reminder, and to which militant body-building no one can yet be sure the Russians will not return. Distances are small in this part of the world. An Arab missile aimed at Tel Aviv, or another outbreak of Balkan war, a serious beef over Macedonia, in Kosovo—and some say that European gutlessness, French cunning, and Russian scheming, among other things, guarantee that there will yet be explosions on Sofia streets.

It was this hapless "luck" of the Bulgarians that ITS had been formed to prevent striking again. Its staff, as that of the parent and predecessors, had as a family heritage memories that could either be protectively warning, or followed as examples to bring more pain. Consider: Bulgaria, a small country, was governed by a smaller, radically discontinued elite, all of whose descendants have family memories. These are names which others recognize, carrying stigma or glory. Vasil of ITS was a descendant of monarchical, nation-building and anti-ecclesiastical murdered Stombolov. Vanya, young, pretty, very bright, newly hired at ITS, was kin to once Premier Tsankov, who had hosted Nazi Hermann Göring in 1935. Tsankov had ordered that communists be fed, some alive it was said, into police-station furnaces following an assassination attempt on the life of the king in 1925.

Giorgi, Vasil's boss, at ITS, was nephew to a proletarian who rose to become a KGB favorite in the Bulgarian services. Uncle had brought Giorgi into the secret police,and tucked Giorgi comfortably into a promotion-track rung of the ladder. He was still rising. Peter, a bright new hire, had a mother whose family bore Stomboliski's name. He was the populist-agrarian premier (1920-1923) until he was tortured to death. The king had been told of his fate in advance and approved.

In the educated class, and Bulgarians prize education, everyone is some important person's kin. One Balkan lesson: rely on kin, keep family memories proud, and never forget vengeance due. Gentle-faced new hire Peter, for example. How could one know that when he had a truncheon in his hand, any heir to peasant Stomboliski's murdering alliance of military officers, Macedonians, or senior academics would be lucky to emerge from an interrogation unconcussed, or indeed alive.

Everyone's Balkan lesson: power is necessary. It is also ephemeral. This century, from king to Nazi to Communist to capitalist and democrat, and free-market mafiya married to elite corruption. Today money is power is politics. Democracy nevertheless is doing its best. But positions and ideologies change quickly and violently. When an underling, seek patrons; be cunning, be a toady, be ready to denounce and betray. Lie. Be astonished at honorable men. You can identify them as such because they announce themselves as such idealistic fools. These days, when wealth is vast and expanding, movable and fungible, every man's tool to power, protection and pleasure equal money. Crime is the alchemy for its easy and secret attainment. Giorgi and his junior colleague Mustafa knew their Balkan history, and its imperatives.

Giorgi was portly, healthy, not handsome and he did not care. He was well armed—a German 9mm Sig Sauer P226 was holstered beneath his arm. No self-respecting Bulgarian would be seen today—tomorrow, who knows?—with a Russian weapon. Immediate correctness as well as better fire power, was why his venerable 9mm Makarov SL and some 10/8 round boxes of shells were in the file cabinet. Giorgi was content. He was grinning while playing solitaire. He was not due for work at the—which embassy was it? for another hour, and last night had been pleasurable. He had indulged himself at some cost, but reasonable for what he got. Near the railroad station, down Maria Luitza Boulevard near the abandoned, decaying St. Nedelia Orthodox Cathedral, one could buy young girls. Whores abounded, many charming, all willing. But the pimps who ran the little girls, aged maybe eight to fourteen, after which if they had been in use they were too old and ill or dangerously diseased for pleasure, were protective of their stable. Not for the girls' sake, but for the income. German, Austrian tourists especially paid exceedingly well. Some elegant gentlemen, Giorgi knew from the pimps and his own surveillance—who, for God's sake, would rely on a gypsy pimp for social information?—were regulars. Nabokov's *Lolita*, all of them Lolita. She, oh he loved her, had been translated into German, and into Bulgarian. He smiled to himself, for he loved reading. Very, very nice.

Were you to see some sweet little girl in her schoolyard or on the street—not in better neighborhoods where parents or servants had time to be watchful—one could negotiate her purchase for a good sum of money. Kidnapping and as many first nights in her new pimp-locked room as you might like and afford. Giorgi liked. Giorgi afforded. And last night, her first kidnapped night, God how that child had screamed. [passage omitted] How, he mused to himself, could he not be happy? He was so happy he had not even gone out to lunch. Some soup, meat, pilaf, sweets, wine, a bit of raki, brought up from the restaurant next door. He had had a particularly satisfying bowel movement this morning as well. God smiled. All of the bodily pleasures.

Time now to think about, not hurry about, work. The afternoon schedule called for work with the Turkish commercial attaché. Mustafa, among five translators working for Giorgi, did all the Turkish work, mostly for Germans who ran the biggest transport services. Mustafa could handle English, Dutch, Greek, French if need be, English not so smoothly. Mustafa purposely butchered Greek as he would, if allowed, the Greeks themselves. The Balkans are a region of inherited hard feelings.

Giorgi had no Turkish. But most representatives of the land transport companies could use English, and insofar as transport and customs agreements were canned, boilerplate, only the bills of lading, insurance, truck and driver ID, and particular charges required special translation efforts, as the great trucking lines which ran from Western Europe through Turkey as far as Syria and Iraq, sometimes branching to the Lebanon, made their export-import way through the Balkans. A billion-dollar business but in itself worth knowing about, for there were always special shipments. Intermixed with food, textiles, furniture, building supplies, pharmaceuticals, chemicals, refrigerated produce, wines and liquor, might be women, drugs, contraband munitions, and other sealed cargoes unknown. The "unknown" guaranteed transit by concealment or bribe were the best, for everyone along the way made money. Hundred of tons of the licit cargo, and a few tons of the other kind, going through Bulgaria every month. Such was the privatized business of ITS, much of it done with foreign consulates, but by no means its major thrust.

A great deal of responsibility fell on ITS, on Giorgi who was himself an excellent linguist. Or, as he reflected smiling on last night, cunnilinguist. Yes, things were going well. Business for example was good. All embassies, even the Russian, needed their services, these for much more than commercial transactions, for few foreign embassies had Bulgarian speakers and most Bulgarians with whom they dealt had a language in common: English, German, French or, for those Eastern, the now officially despised Russian. Wily Giorgi and his superiors had seen to it that Bulgarians who might be fluent in one of the international tongues were instructed by higher authority not to use it. This assured that ITS would serve as many embassy transactions as possible. The six translators in ITS could handle most foreign-Bulgarian transactions, Oriental languages excepted. The few Japanese who invested or arranged tourism spoke what they called English. ITS saw nothing to justify a Japanese translator. Companies could provide their own.

The reasons for ITS being in as many embassies doing as much as possible were for more than profit. ITS was part of the Ministry of Interior's Secret Service, part of the new major division, Commercial and Political Intelligence group (C&PI), a special branch of which was the Central Service for Combating Organized Crime (CSCOC). Other directorates of Interior handled local and national policing, border guards, and internal surveillance, in spite of sincere but impotent political promises to discontinue near-universal telephone tapping. Nevertheless most of what had been "spying" as the Sixth Department special services was dismantled; assassins assigned to and by Russians as "wet affairs" were retired, reassigned, or privatized themselves as mafiya help. Counter-intelligence however, branching now into economic crime and mafiya control, had expanded. Heretofore, before capitalism, "Commercial" had hardly been on the mind of the democratic successors to the special branch.

Knowledge of ITS's innovative parenthood was closely held. The new President for example did not know, nor did the Council of Ministers. Layers of the onion, wooden dolls within wooden dolls. Those so-familiar Russian *kraseevuye korotkee kooklas*, beautiful little dolls. Secrets within secrets. Giorgi reflected on his world, on his prior evening. That little doll, his secret. She would remember her whole life what a real man was like.

Mustafa, who was one of the three staff who had the electronic entrance key code, came in. He burped.

"Good lunch, eh?"

"Yeah."

"You have," Giorgi looked at the master appointments schedule, "you have the Hansa people to see about next month's shipments to Syria."

Mustafa yawned. "The usual. No money in it. Plumbing and car parts no doubt. No contraband."

"Take the bad with the good."

"I don't like Vasil," Mustafa said irritably.

"Neither do I. But there he is. The Ministry likes him, C&PI likes him. His father was in the old bunch. He's good, so the embassies like him. What can I do?"

"You're his boss. Set him up. Fix him. Get him run over. Hire a hit."

"We don't do that any more, not officially. They'd have my ass."

"If they found out."

Giorgi shook his head glumly. "The Minister has had forty years in this business. He'd know a hit instinctively. So would Dimitri, the new man these democrats have appointed to clean up counter-intelligence and internal affairs. He used to be in wet affairs, those good old days when we had some muscle in this country. Vasil's old man was with Dimitri in clandestine services for years. Worked with some of Andropov's boys abroad. Dimitri is as smart as Vasil which you, Mustafa, are not. In the old days the bosses were clever, but not smart. Nowadays they're too smart. Dimitri can tell a removal, termination, hit job, whatever these bright-eyed democrats want to call what we don't do anymore—Dimitri can smell one of those just by reading the obituary. He's got the mafiya people scared. Bad news all around. Lucky we can make money without them. Not like Russia. Count yourself lucky, Mustafa, you son of the Prophet out of the wrong side of the bed. Vasil can't be fired and he's a dangerous man to kill."

Mustafa was not persuaded. "I'll off him myself. Robbery gone wrong. Dark street, they all are anyway, on his way home. Maybe let his wife and kids watch it. Nothing special. I tell you, Boss, Vasil is a problem. I want to fix the problem."

"You're just a translator. Don't let your Ministry ID and gun permit go to your head. Don't believe what you tell your girl friends. You couldn't off an ant on the pavement with both heels stomping."

Mustafa was young, handsome, spoiled by his mother. He enjoyed a rare trust in having a secret and profitable government job, for Turks in Bulgaria had not always been an accepted minority. He made money on the side with deals with smugglers, over and above the usual customs shared, and no one but those Ministry bosses on the take with him the wiser. He was nevertheless pouting. "I don't trust him, Vassili."

"Neither do I. How can anybody trust a democrat, an honest democrat? But he does his job and no fuss."

"He doesn't like us. I think he's screwing Vanya, that new translator you hired. What does she see in him?"

"Money. What does anybody see in anybody? But you're wrong; he's happily married, has young kids, and doesn't have the imagination to play."

Mustafa looked at his boss. "Biology or weird taste, not imagination, Giorgi. Now in your case, I'd say it takes imagination."

Giorgi was startled. "What do you mean 'my case'?"

"Enough to make sure you want me happy here. I don't have that Interior Ministry ID for nothing, whatever you say. The gypsy has pictures of you and little girls—not nice pictures, but interesting. You amaze me, boss; you get your cock up and forget everything you were ever taught about there being surveillance cameras in rooms. I also have a shot of you with your rich Austrian friend, you two eyeing the little girls with their pants pulled down and the gypsy grinning. You two look like buyers at a horse auction. Gypsies haven't changed their ways, selling little girls with rickets or spavined horses. Later I saw your Austrian going into UST&D. Now that is an interesting bank, more employees than I can understand. What do you think, is there anything there at UST&D for us? I mean, if they are a Ukrainian laundry like everyone says, can we shake them down?"

Giorgi liked the way this young man's mind worked; open, ruthless, opportunistic, willing to take, but willing to share.

"Don't know anything, best not to. Out of our department. Central Bank and Finance Ministry responsibility."

"Okay, but now do you object if I blow away Vasil? I mean now that I have those photographs of you damn near killing the little girls? That and the fact they prove you have the smallest cock this side of a chicken house?"

Giorgi paused but his voice was surprisingly without anger. "You be careful what you say about a senior officer or I'll export you back to Turkey in a box. As for the photos, screw you. Print them up as glossies and sell them to tourists for all I care. But don't overplay your hand. I need you, but not enough to be your life insurance." The look he gave to Mustafa was educational. Mustafa took the instruction.

"Sorry, Giorgi. Just trying."

"I know, boys will be boys. Just hope you live long enough to become a man. But now it's time to go to work. We meet with the department head tomorrow. Have you summarized the tapes we have on the British meet you translated between the MI6 man, their commercial attaché here and our Bulgarian Air fellow they're pumping on privatization plans? BA obviously wants to be sure Lufthansa, KLM and Air France don't have a shot at ownership. If it were me, I'd want my worst enemy to buy Bulgarian Air. They're still flying those Tupelovs that dissolve when exposed to air."

A chastened Mustafa answered. "Yes, and I've summarized the tapes on my translation of the French Ambassador with our Finance Minister on their little ploy to have Crédit Lyonnais trade shares with our Tourism Development Bank, one for one; Bulgaria gets .0001% of Lyonnais partnership shares and therefore liability for all its troubles, and France gets 20% of our tourism development loan profits in a safe bank supervised by IMF."

"Not so stupid. Well, to show the bosses I've been working I have the tape abstract from my translation with the U.S. CIA station chief and our air force procurement chief. The Americans want to secure IBM as lead supplier for any new NATO-financed communications system our air force installs. Money and of course a chance to bug the basic software for our entire military air command commo network. Or crash it all on command. What the hell, all I can do is put the warning in my report to C&PI to pass over to military intelligence."

Mustafa shook his head. "How dumb can these foreign embassy bastards be? Nobody comes here speaking Bulgarian, we translate even top secret stuff, otherwise they'd be talking to themselves. And they don't have a clue who we are or where the stuff goes."

"Now Mustafa, be kind," Giorgi was grinning. "We, ITS are a free-enterprise, absolutely trustworthy, confidential private translation service. Each intelligence service in Sofia using us has had the Interior Ministry people check us innocent civilians out from our childhood's up, Mustafa, even a boy bugger-er like you."

Mustafa looked up angrily.

Giorgi went on in a relaxed way, "Yes, Mustafa. I also have photographs. And here what you do, not what I do, is a felony, so we must be kind to one another, yes?"

Mustafa just stared at his boss.

"Anyway each of these so-called spy and financial crime intelligence services, each station chief exiled to this poor, dirty inconsequential little country of ours, has to make his or her way as best they can. Now we both know that ordinarily Bulgaria is first assignment as so called "chief" for somebody either on the way up or forever cast in limbo. That means he or she is also, but for clerks or real juniors, the only intelligence person in that embassy and, for that matter, between here and Bucharest. Those poor children are responsible for intelligence on drugs, finance, politics, and no doubt weather reporting all at once. And so, to find a nice clean outfit they go to our Interior Ministry which, sheerly out of the courtesy of the new NATO, they hope, brotherhood, EU, they hope, community, does backgrounds—and, lo and behold, tells them what nice children we are."

Mustafa nodded. He knew that much.

"What a surprise, eh? You and I and Vassili and Vanya and the rest come out absolutely non-political, non-criminal, trustworthy as English Boy Scouts. Interior guarantees it. And there we are. And there they are. And every week we summarize for C&PI damn near the whole of Western embassy confidential local transactions of interest. Interior doesn't need, and can't afford, to gather more foreign intelligence than that. The six of us really are the stay-at-home CIA for Bulgaria—and we don't even have to pay the price of the bugs in their embassy wall, only the cheap ones on their phones."

"Yeah, we should get raises."

"We might do that for ourselves. Think about it. Any embassy using us which might have an interest in any other embassy which uses us could, just maybe, buy into what we are doing. As long as they don't know we are doing it to them. An exclusive of course, with every assurance that we would never do *that* to them. But we could promise, cross our hearts, to be really exclusive to the one that paid us the most. Germans, I think. We could offer it to the Americans since they like to spend money. But the Germans are more reliable. And they're the major investors here. They still like that sphere of influence notion, but then what once-imperial power doesn't? Poor Brits, can't afford it. Think about that, eh?"

"Sure wouldn't want C&PI to know about it."

"Well, I think maybe we'd want to cut one or two of our bosses in on it. Protection from above. As the American slang has it, a shade tree, an umbrella."

Mustafa was thinking, "I don't see that we can't screw a couple at once, take the money to be exclusive but what they don't know—which is a whole lot right now anyway—won't hurt us. Realpolitik, Boss. The Americans hate the French; they would love to know how the French are trying to screw everybody in NATO, which they are. The Germans don't trust the Russians, the Israelis spy on everyone. Everyone wants the latest on the Russians, whom no one trusts, especially not with that plutonium and those old missiles for sale. The Brits would like to stay in the game out of habit and pride. Giorgi, there's a fortune to be made. Not counting, I still say, maybe UST&D, if they're laundering."

George stroked his chin. "There is a problem, Mustafa, a very serious problem. If we make the offer not even the Americans would be stupid enough not to see who we are, that we are doing it to them."

"Yeah, I guess maybe. And so?"

"We solve the problem by walking a different path. We tell the embassies that have requirements levied upon them for any kind of intelligence, and these days we see it is mostly commercial after all, that we have access to totally different sources, that we're branching out through our relatives into private security doing 'investment protection as preventive industrial espionage.' Call it that and it's a capitalist virtue. Or a public health one, like vaccinations. For each client we phony up a no-name list of repairmen, you know—roofs, elevators, broken windows, painters, floor tiles, coffee machine service people, whom we tell them we own. Urge them to check out their own contractors to be sure no other embassy is doing that for them; say we can do it or better, more objective for their own protection, and let Interior Ministry help. Then we bring them a little good stuff from our translations and they're hooked. Pay on a piece basis, they're in control after they hear it. They won't stiff us because their foreign office people don't have the imagination. And they do know if they stiff us that is the end of the information flow. We beg them to check results against price. We turn all the little station chiefs into cost/benefit heroes back home. Like telling the Germans, for example, about the U.S. computer ploy with our air force. Or telling the French about the Brits wanting Bulgarian Air. Every week there will be some tidbits for somebody. A business manager's dream. And they will love us. Furthermore, we guarantee they will never suspect ITS, us personally as a fraud or penetration, because we insist that they ask Interior to monitor our security company, to check out the sources we tell the station chiefs we are using, deploying, all those relatives and friends. We are so open and above board, Mustafa, our very goodness gives me pains of joy."

"They ask the wrong people in our Ministry, the goody-goodies in our Ministry learn what we're doing, and we're dead meat," said Mustafa glumly.

"No, no. That's why we cut some chiefs at Interior into the game. They tell embassies that Interior has this new security company monitoring capability. Why not? I know an American advisor has already recommended it. Good idea; half the security companies here are *mafiya* anyway. Let our Interior lads blackmark a few semi-retired thieves working as embassy janitors, parking space guards, whatever. So our lads in Interior volunteer the replacement service—and how coincidental! Nobody else ever knows. Everybody in the embassies and the Ministry is happy. By the good Saint Rila, how the money rolls in."

But Giorgi knew Vasil once again would be a problem, especially since he was friends with the Brits and the Yankees; spied on them, sure, but he was fundamentally their friend. Vasil, who had gone to those Cambridge economic crime seminars and had come back with religion, might think it dirty pool to sell the embassies out one to another on a grand con scheme. No matter that he was duping them all for Mother Bulgaria. An honest man in your own shop was a real pain. Vasil had a convoluted mind. Giorgi repeated what Mustafa had diagnosed earlier. "You're right though, Vasil is a problem."

"I told you so, Boss. So we do something about it?"

"Maybe, only maybe. I have to take it under advisement."

They looked at each other appraisingly, nothing more said until Mustafa spoke.

"I may have something else for us, Boss."

"Yes, Mustafa?" Giorgi's facial muscles relaxed.

"About that Austrian of yours. The gypsy told me he was importing little girls into Vienna for your friend's friends' hobbies. I don't care, but I think this might be the same guy who worked with some of the big boys in the red days."

Giorgi looked up, "I don't know anything about it. How does it happen that you do?"

"The gypsy pimp told me—well, the fact is I squeezed him a little, had one of the Interior toughs work him over a bit. That's how I got him to photograph you playing with the little girls. I let the gypsy know he was my source from now on or he would be speaking only to his Roumeli ancestors in the cemetery."

"Finish your sentence, Mustafa. A translator doesn't lose his words."

"Right, well, he'd already met your Austrian, whatever you might have thought to the contrary. A few years back the Austrian came with the old red government's senior financial deputy to find some high-level pimps. Seems the pimps in Sofia have a business association to keep the girls in line, pay percentages the same, pay off cops, black-list the girls too drunk to work, that sort of thing. Wanted a bunch of high-class clean whores for a weekend meeting at a fancy government dacha, some pre-Communist millionaire's estate of course, down near Plovdiv. Lots of estates down near that beautiful old city."

"Yes?"

"Odd. Insisted that none of the girls speak any European language but Bulgarian or Russian. Some hookers are educated women who've been forced to make their living on a bed. They know some languages, French or German for sure, English as the red regime loosened up. Anyway, it was no go for cosmopolitans."

Giorgi was intent, "What else did you learn?"

"Only that when some of the girls came back, the pimps beat the shit out of a few of those who were holding back on the big tips they got. The girls said it was a very fancy affair. Lots of big shots there. The Austrian they recognized. The major player was a fat guy with official bodyguards, chauffeur, two-limo entourage, the works. After the fat foreigner arrived the language changed from French or German, they had a translator there for some, to English. Fat guy was big man for the weekend. One of the girls who screwed him said he might be Jewish. He took them on three at a time but only weirdo stuff, they said. Happens when guys get older." Mustafa paused to look at Giorgi. "With others I suppose they're born kinky."

Giorgi ignored the remark, asking only "Jewish?"

"Just a hunch. Those days in the 90s when the reds were in power, if you were a rich visitor to Bulgaria and not a Russian bigwig, you know, an authority, *nomenklatura*, people figured you had to be German or American or Jewish. Anyway the fat man wouldn't eat the pâté after he inquired and learned it was pork, or that's how it seemed to the girl."

Giorgi sarcastically said, "Mustafa, you're not Jewish and you don't eat pork."

"I don't get driven around in limousines and pal around with European bankers, either."

Giorgi grunted acknowledgement, then asked, "Did the girls pick up on what went on?"

"No, just recognized the languages. But obviously something important was going on, with those bigwigs, foreigners, imported food, whores, even French champagne. The government reds were spending lots of other people's money. They wouldn't have done that unless it was about politics, or money to be made."

"And so?" Giorgi scrutinized Mustafa.

"I just had a feeling about it, Boss. If we could pick up on it, now the reds are supposedly out, we might learn something worth a few dollars. You know, buried bodies, secret treaties, whatever. I thought maybe you'd like to know."

"Thanks, but I don't hear anything that tells me there is anything more to know. Of course some deal was being made. Like selling the fat man another piece of Bulgaria, maybe the Austrian banks buying in, maybe selling little girls for foreign export to both the fat man and that Austrian son of a bitch." Giorgi was annoyed. "That son of a bitch, let him play games with me again about not knowing Sofia and the pimps and he'll have one serious traffic accident."

"So that's it, Boss?"

"Yeah, you've got work to do. So do I."

For Giorgi, however, that was not quite it. He had some serious thinking to do. The last time he translated at Saborno Street for the CIA, one of the new President's people was there. An accounting type, with thick glasses, very serious. A democrat. Honest-looking. The new Bulgarian scene, at least for a little while. Giorgi had disliked him on sight. The no-name messenger was bleating to the station chief that a Bulgarian Treasury audit came up $12 billion short out of what should have been on deposit in national pension funds, agricultural exports income, the State health insurance fund. The cupboard was nearly bare. The reds had taken it before they were toppled and left town. Not Bulgarian currency, mind you, but dollars, real money.

The President's man, his Treasury assistant with him, explained. "The money has to have been laundered somewhere. Nobody knows how, where, or who has it now. The President himself has ordered the economic police in the Ministry to look. They say finding it is impossible, and if not impossible, more expensive than the government can afford. We called in one of those big Western accounting firms that has offices here. The head, a Bulgarian, agreed."

Giorgi had thought at the time, how convenient. How much did the reds pay for that accounting opinion? In any event, the President's boy went on to say that all the suspect ministers had disappeared abroad. He admitted some honest red former officials remained. What the hell, Giorgi had thought while translating this, only the honest ones dared to stay. Or wanted to. Who the hell else would live here if they could afford Monaco?

Their presence here did testify, the President's man was sure, to their not having known what was going on—the former Central Bank chief for example, or the senior economic advisors to the Council of Ministers. Giorgi was only the translator, his profession disallowed an interjection, but he could imagine situations where a well-protected guilty guy could stay in Bulgaria after all, planning further looting with privatization going on, or for that matter plotting a return to power. Giorgi knew that in Bulgaria it was inevitable power would change hands, and devil take the hindmost. At that point the Bulgarian had raised his hands, damn near squeaking. "Empty pantry, fat mice have skipped away. Would America please help?" Giorgi had been disgusted to hear a Bulgarian official plead like that.

The station chief promised to "bring it to my superiors' attention." How many years would that take, Giorgi had wondered. The station chief said something about an international financial investigations group that would be good for the job, once Washington "looked into the problem." Washington would do that, no doubt with the speed of a Russian-built farm tractor.

Giorgi did not need the CIA to remember that during 1994 and 1995 there was no bread because Bulgaria's wheat got shipped out to Serbia, Montenegro, the Baltics, and Poland. The whole country damn near starved. Which had led the rebellion of January 1997 and the fall of the reds. "Bastards," thought Giorgi, for his own family had almost no health insurance now, his parents no pension. They lived with him and his sister and her husband and two kids, all in one apartment, because of that. The public had been told at first that the funds "appeared depleted" because of inflation, accounting problems, and bank failures after all, some twenty or so out of thirty banks had gone under in two years, but now Giorgi knew the government knew. Big time theft.

"Bastards!" Giorgi recognized some inconsistency in his anger. He had been one of the strongest reds in the Ministry, and even now maintained, massaged, discreet friendships with red leaders both overt and mafiya. "One never knows," he reminded himself, "just when the tide could turn." That for sure included red tides, and any coming red one, just like those on ocean beaches, could well be deadly.

Giorgi wondered which officials in the Ministry had been involved. Some had to have been, since no posh meeting like that could have taken place without Interior Ministry conniving. They ran things in the old days. Someone big inside had to be on the take. The red Interior Minister himself might not have known, and probably didn't, since Giorgi knew he lived on scraps now. But some clever Ministry group was in on it. It was a small club, the Interior Ministry, even if some members had others killed. He knew them all, in and out of power. He knew no one senior in the Ministry had moved abroad. Yet. Giorgi nodded to himself with satisfaction. "Some people in Sofia are sitting on a big overseas nest egg. And they know who else was involved—maybe also where all the money landed." It was such a brilliant insight he spoke it aloud. "And all I have to do now is find who's here with the fat Swiss nest egg, making plans to be big again."

Giorgi, whose meeting with Mustafa had been in the inner office, certain Mustafa had left by now, got on the telephone. That it might be, no doubt was bugged, did not worry him. All senior Bulgarians, democracy or no, treated any telephone as the enemy's ear. All telephone speak was doublespeak.

"*Zyenaida*, Jeanette dear, some information please. ITS is going to do some translating on a big job for the Austrian Embassy." He would enter appointments in the book to document that invention. These days the Ministry was such a *schlamperei* no one would ever check up. "One guest, I'm told, is an Austrian banker named Brody, and perhaps there will be another even more distinguished; I'm not sure, try South African or Israeli. I'm guessing your Directorate gave them VIP treatment at the airport in 1994 and or 95. Limos, escorts, the works. Both important men then and now. You know how it is with bigwigs. If you get the names, I'll pull the dossiers. We want to treat them right. We'll pay for your putting clerks on the file search to get it done right away. And of course, sweetie, there'll be twenty-five dollars American for you in it. And oh yes, the file will show who ordered the VIP treatment, and who in the Ministry approved. I'll want to tell them, if they are still around, how hard we're working to please. You know that we here at ITS are a capitalist service industry. 'Smile all the time at clients,' that's the American advice to us dour Bulgarians. So sweetie, I want you to smile too, and so I'll make it fifty dollars for enough information to allow our best service." That fifty dollars would be half a month's salary for Jeanette, the file chief at the Border police. And she would be smart enough to know that where fifty dollars was, there would be more if she didn't blab or ask questions. Her loyalty and discretion were unquestionable—until, of course, somebody offered her more or put her on the hot seat.

He leaned back in his chair, smiling, talking out loud to himself rather more loudly than he might have wished, "Not bad, a fifty-dollar down payment on a piece of twelve billion dollars." He burped in satisfaction.

Vasil, returning from lunch, entered the dreary foyer. The lift of course was broken. Vasil trudged up the dingy stairwell. The treads, limestone once, were dark with the ground-in dirt of decades. When he reached the third floor, its corridor walls yellowed over time and, windowless, without even a memory of sunlight, there seated on a decrepit rattan chair was Russian-fathered Igor, the hallway guard. Those of you who remember your Moscow hotels, and Bulgarian ones if yours has been an odd tourism or darker mission with such poor cover, will recall that each floor had its watch-bird. Igor was now one of these, the epoch itself gone but Igor remaining.

Igor was one of the *moutri*, a class of mindless and brutal thugs, made husky by wrestling, whose like had for so many years been the muscle, the intimidators, and occasionally—only the smarter ones and Igor did not qualify—"mechanics" for the mafiya bosses. Igor's muscle had gone to fat, and his luck looked going downhill as well, but for Giorgi's corporate patronage support. Giorgi, Vasil knew well, was neither the loyal nor the nostalgic type. Igor still had a few rough tricks, a bounce or three for some suspicious visitor down the stairwell, and, since in Bulgaria no one ever knows what is to come, a bomb or two left in him. There was no love lost between them, Vasil and Igor. Neither acknowledged the other. Outranked by Vasil, Igor could only pretend sleep while Vasil moved to open the door of the ITS office. Noticing a dropped pen on the floor which he stooped to pick up, Vasil had not entered or opened wide the door. Still outside he had heard the conversation at a point where it was said, "Vasil is a problem." The door slightly ajar, he listened to the two men. He wondered how long the conversation had gone on. He realized he had become for them a very big problem indeed. And then when Mustafa went to his own office, he heard the telephone call and the figure of twelve billion dollars, followed by the burp. Giorgi's desk faced the outer office and outer door. Most Bulgarians had heard rumors, read some wildly speculative articles as to missing monies, those government funds, and about maybe billions of banking assets gone missing. No layman and so far no one in government could tell which was which. Twelve billion dollars! It could be that much. "My, oh my," Vasil said to himself, not out loud at all.

Very quietly he closed the heavy but quiet door. Then, noisily, pretending to have trouble with the key card and cursing, he entered, comrade to comrade, sauntering through the outer office to the table in the inner office where Mustafa and Giorgi had been talking. Vasil, the others, were all smiles, all good cheer. Ah, to be among friends like these.

Giorgi, in the best of moods, for he appreciated opportunities to be enjoyed as well as pleasures past, calling to Mustafa to join, poured out three glasses of raki. "To the good things, and *nazdravye,* bottoms up!"

Glasses clinked. Vasil, moving a conversational pawn forward, put a philosophical question casually. Such intellectual gambits are common among Bulgars, a thoughtful people, and when educated, well read in Plato, Leibnitz, Kant and always Hegel. "Giorgi, you seem so happy, you should be happy because you are bright and you are boss. But consider the dialectic, good and evil coexisting and the difficulty, if there is no God as the reds claim, of achieving higher resolution. Can resolution be achieved only on the material-political plane? And allowing good and evil, Giorgi, where evil is an abstraction and cannot thereby be only material, although the material must be its instrument, well, do you ever think about the nature of evil? What portion of the material harbors evil?"

Giorgi, responding seriously, nodded. "Yes, Vasil, I do."

"Well?"

"I agree with your implication. It is an evil world. We are all evil, all of us.

Only the others are much worse. Hegel had too much hope in God, Mind and solutions. We can say that now the Marxists are gone. I have a second cousin with whom I discuss these matters. He is a monk who follows Rila. A hermit, no less. And still a *bogomil* at heart. God is good, but not that God who made us evil. I know more than most that the flesh is evil, as is what we create. And as if there is not enough evil in this world, all of us have much more of evil we can learn."

Giorgi drained his glass, smiled, and with the others went off to work, to learn.

6

"Senator?"

"Yes, Rayburn."

"Another cable for you. They're keeping the radio officer busy."

The Senator did not look up. He fed the paper through the code descrambler, a purring little machine by his side, and began to read. He turned to his servant. "Bring me a Chivas and some smoked salmon. Don't forget the paprika and capers. Be sure the bread's thin. Whole wheat. Butter it for me."

"Yes, Senator. Anything else, Senator?"

Senator Cranmer was reading. He did not reply. The muffled baritone hum of the engines might soothe a man capable of enjoying the luxury, the miracle of flight. The new Falcon 50—richly appointed though nothing showy like the pricier Gulf stream V, often favored by corporate money types—was both his and not his. His because his company had bought it. Not his because the company was registered in the Bahamas. Other senators preferred to save money flying Air Force planes, but each flight was a matter of public record, and opponents, come election time, typically claimed abuse. Junkets. Most on the Hill preferred, if the truth be known—which would be rare in Washington—their travel to be paid for by corporate or other special-interest groups. Not on the public record, if anyone could help it. But when the President was not to be caught shoplifting, or some other earth-shaking peccadillo, and the press therefore idle, such flights came more easily to public attention. And the opposition come election time would shout, "Captive of special interests." And of course, "Junkets."

Royston Cranmer was the only senator who regularly flew at his own expense, an expense concealed through offshore banks, trusts and companies, which in turn owned shares in, Luxembourg holding companies, which in turn held shares in corporations X, Y and Z, all profitable, most immense, and many worldwide, with one exception. Senator Cranmer had no holdings which by law and SEC (Securities and Exchange Commission) regulations could be traced to his multiple company selves. The senator liked privacy and he liked money. He was honest up to the point where it interfered with either. But he was always careful. And a bit theatrical; to avoid recognition he would wear disguises, practice avoiding surveillance, have his staff arrange alibi meetings, and the like. He deluded himself. It was not that he failed to escape recognition, it was that even though he was an extremely important figure in Washington, one of the most powerful on the Hill, the press corps did not give a damn where he, or any other members of Congress, spent their weekends, unless a nude photo, preferably showing sexual perversion, might come out of it. Or a bribe changing hands. All members of Congress, and most all royalty, prime ministers, or chief executives had become sensitive to these journalistic priorities. Senator Cranmer need not worry. He was a prude, sober-sided and too rich to be interested, these days, in vulgar improprieties.

"Rayburn." The senator had finished reading the cable. He fed it into the shredder, also within reach. He had not touched the drink or food.

"Yes, Senator?"

"Bring me the file marked "holdings" from the safe. The safe is open, but if I even get a hint you're looking at the papers, you're fired." He spoke as a businessman would, no menace, no ego, matter-of-factly.

No chance. Rayburn was sensible enough to fully appreciate his high pay and weekend travel as the senator's butler *cum* valet. They flew to sparkling cities, stayed in opulent hotels. They lived in Georgetown during the week, in a large elegant house on Dumbarton Street. There were servants to do the work and help Mrs. Cranmer host the many parties. Life on Dumbarton Street was not a bad ticket either. At parties Rayburn simply announced guests, most of them with names he recognized from the newspapers; after the maid had let them in Rayburn handed her their coats and made sure the waiters saw to keeping the glasses full. Waiters took care of the canapes. These were cocktail parties. The Cranmers did not entertain at dinners at home. "Cushy," he'd told his admiring wife. Rayburn could not care less about the senator's files, visitors or interests, or indeed the senator's introverted, cold, disdainful personality. "Screw him," was what Rayburn would say to his delightful new wife on his allotted one day off. They had things to do not concerned with politics. His wife Carabella, from Barbados, was gorgeous. She was twenty years younger than he, a buxom, milk-chocolate-skinned delight, with a smile that would light the sea from Kingston to Aruba.

If Rayburn had any interest in the Cranmers' life, private or public, it was in the occasional seance that Mrs. Cranmer held. Dark rooms, a turbaned mystic, creepy music, the whole nine yards. Mrs. Senator Cranmer was a bit nuts about the psychic. The senator, humorless and serious as an abstinent preacher, humored her but paid her little mind.

This weekend he was on his way from his country home in Virginia to New York City. He tried to get away from the Hill Thursday evenings, and would usually be off on personal business late Friday. No one objected to his schedule, for who was to gainsay a senator who was Vice Chairman of the Banking Committee, had seats on Foreign Relations, Commerce, Judiciary and Budget, and chaired the Crime Committee? All of these were his choice; he had more seniority than all but a few antique Southerners, enough to take his pick. Were it not for the President and those older senators, Royston Cranmer might rule the country, insofar as an obstreperous autonomous republic's public could be ruled at all. It was a matter in which the senator had no further interest. Years ago he had thrown his hat in the ring to run for President, but had lost right out of the starting gate when his party's convention had rejected him on the first voting ballot. It was not even close. He was bitter and forgave none involved, but was too intelligent to bother with any difficult vengeance. He had turned to things that suited his new resolve. In doing so he had accumulated enough information, and political markers to ruin Fortune 500 corporations and politicians across the land. Such incentives were useful in place, not in destruction. He was an operator, not General Grant marching to the sea.

It was as he had feared. He closed the company holdings file. The dull gray dog-eared cardboard cover gave no hint that it was the most private and potentially dangerous, to himself first of all, document in his possession.

"Rayburn."

"Yes, Senator."

"Tell the pilots to refuel and set their course for," the Senator paused, "London."

7

Claire was astonished that she slept so well that first night of captivity. Depressed and frightened, yes, but except for awakening in the wee hours with her stomach in knots, she slept. She was still jet-lagged, for she had had only one night at the Palais Schwartzenburg before her abduction. Would her absence signal anything there? She had pondered it, but could not be hopeful. The staff had probably not noticed at all. Here in her luxurious prison there were some old English-language books in the room. The lights worked. The bathroom, marble again, had towels and toilet paper. One of her captors—wiry, not bad-looking but for a tough, cruel mouth and shining ferret eyes, darkly Slavic, wearing gray gloves—silently, had brought rather good meals into the room while another stood in the doorway, a pistol at the ready. Dinner last night, breakfast, lunch and now again dinner time. She heard steps in the hall outside, the door opening.

A new one. The other two followed respectfully behind him. The one always with the pistol in his hand. But this one, square. Short. Heavy. Black hair. Noisy breathing. Smoking a cigarette. Expensive black suit. Red silk tie. Alligator shoes with brass rings on their tasseled laces. Styled black hair still oily, newly barbered and shaved. He smelled strongly of cologne. He pointed aggressively at her, then at an antique chair with worn, once-rich brocade covering. He gestured toward it. She sat as if he had cast a spell. Her heart was beating hard. He had cast a spell. Fear.

He plumped himself down, drew deeply on the cigarette, gave her a look which she had only seen in films recalling the evil enemy in James Bond movies. The very look made her perspire, grow hot and then shiver with cold chills. His was the professional interrogator's inspection of her as, yes, utterly helpless. The man with the pistol pointed casually at her smiled for the first time, not at her, but at the event. She knew instinctively that he was anticipating his pleasure in giving pain.

Square, for what else could she call him, looked at her steadily for, what? a minute? Five? She was drifting in sheer terror. She anchored herself by attending to her heartbeat. Likely a hundred beats a minute. But by counting she focused on herself, not the scene Square had set of virtual brutality.

"You," said Square. His voice was deep. Baritone in the former KGB choir. He encouraged her mind to wander. Square singing Gregorian chants in the Lubyanka.

"You. Pay attention." He nodded to the wiry one who walked over to her chair and, without warning, slapped her face so hard she and the chair almost overturned. She was reeling. No one had ever hit her before, other than in women's soccer at college. She gasped.

"I told you, pay attention." He examined her as if she were a fish in a tank. "There need be no more violence, indeed you can go home from here any time. You are not stupid. We know who you are. Now we want to know what you know that we do not that concerns our affairs. I am not going to play clever games with you. I am an honest person. I can also be more unpleasant than you could ever imagine. I can shred your flesh for example, blind you, rape you with unkind instruments. Just as you read in your history books, or imagined about fiends as a child. We can do those things to you. And enjoy doing them very much, very much indeed. And then just let un-quietly, no not unquietly at all, let die what little is left of you. Do you understand?"

She did. She nodded.

"We know you are here from IFinCIG. 'Network,' we call it, so do you. We know you were CIA. We know something about why you are here. We know you are a spoiled and ill-tempered woman with an important father."

Claire's thoughts, not his words, interrupted him. Spoiled and ill-tempered, odd, she didn't know people who thought of her that way, who *had* these people been learning about her from? Yes, why hadn't she asked that so obvious question before: one day in Vienna and she gets kidnapped. Who had the informant been? She realized she was not truly spellbound, her questioning mind because it *was* questioning was hers after all, not this snake's fascinated bird. "I am no bird," she repeated to herself. "Yes, that's it, my mantra," and she would focus on it, it could be strength. And if she could make a good guess about their source, inside somewhere or thieves or electronic surveillance somewhere, that was also something in her power.

Square caught her at it. "So, we surprise you, but don't be surprised. We know so very much and no, you don't like our knowing about how bad a temper you have. Here you are, a choice to live or die, and you can only think about being insulted, caught out in your petty little character, eh?"

She stared at him coldly. Square was no mind reader after all. He had got her entirely wrong. Good.

"We also know you're here to find a Mr. Brody. We would like to find him too. Child prostitution we understand. Poor taste, but an inconsequential business. So moral of you. And such a waste of your resources. And back in California your people will be looking for a drug runner named Mr. C. These people, what they do, are of no interest to us. But others you may know about may be, not because you have that knowledge, but because your government does; that could trouble us. So in your preparation what else did you learn about Vienna, those of us near here in Europe? And what papers did you bring? We looked in your room and couldn't find any. When you were apprehended you had no briefcase. You have not been to your embassy. We appreciate information might be there as cables, but not so quickly. And," he smiled, "not so likely. And so, we start these questions. What and who are you looking for in Vienna, in Europe? And who else is looking?"

Claire was surprised. They knew of Brody and Mr. C and child prostitution and seemed not to care. Could they be so clever as to have set this whole thing up just as disinformation, to let her loose believing Brody and C were inconsequential? "Unlikely such luck," she told herself, "my unconscious mind wants an ice cream cone, fat chance of turning me loose. Claire, you are obsessed, 'fat' again."

Square had his snake eyes on her. The pistol swayed toward her. The other man walked casually toward her, his fist poised to hit her again. She noticed he'd put a new glove over his hand. Its knuckle side looked odd. As he came closer he calmly showed her the back of his glove close up. It was a composition material of some sort, rougher than coarse sandpaper, like something you'd use for getting grit off the bottom of a stubborn frying pan. A 'knuckle duster' didn't they used to call them? Not quite brass knuckles, but that was the idea. My God, he was intentionally going to abrade, to mutilate her face.

In this interim of time—had it stopped?—she felt amazingly clear in her thinking. So far she had learned from them, more so far than they from her: Square knew the content of IFFY cables to and from embassies, or at least some from what must be electronic surveillance. If IFFY was as careful about its codes as its library books, no wonder. With the former KGB, GRU now gone private with those NSA-like capabilities they had, not surprising. And Square and Company were here working, were worried about IFFY penetration, to know if IFFY knew what Square knew, about something and no doubt a very big something. Including, but more than Brody and C, she asked herself? Heavens!

Brody et *Cie* yes, it could be, yes why not?; could "C" have meant "cie", the French abbreviation for compagnie, company, as in English "Co." or "Incorporated." How easy for an American team and those Polish informants, none thinking of or in French, to have made such a mistake. Square and Cie, or Brody et Cie, any of them, if one of their businesses was drugs, cocaine, if they had French and American associates to enjoy a double entendre, a pun, yes, use C for cocaine and for Cie as company.

It does make a kind of sense, she was reflecting, but Square here isn't the kind of intellect to play with words; he would have some smarter partners, or bosses. Would they be, she allowed her mind to race, a conglomerate as international as these thoughts suggested? Polish known because of the snitching lawyers, American and French implied, and if cocaine, for sure with the U.S. the biggest market. Austrian because Brody was here, or had been. Russian as the surveillance capability, she had jumped to the conclusion and Square's style strongly indicated this; but other groups than Russian too if Jonesy, and everything she had read, were correct. And child prostitution, Square's worries about what else? Well, Brody and his banking, the Polish lawyers guaranteed it, all would require a corporately diversified "Cie." The new New class, and rich enough to afford the old-world luxury building she was in as their sometimes town house, now her prison.

"You are about to say?" suggested Square.

"You know everything I know and a whole lot more. There are no papers because two names don't require me to carry a book with me. I was to go to the Austrian police and ask them to work with me to find Brody. You can verify that if you have somebody inside there, for they will have access to the letter requesting cooperation that IFFY sent via our embassy last Thursday. If anybody else is working on this, they haven't told me. Your informants should have told you since they probably know more than I do, IFFY wouldn't have sent a new person like me if they thought Brody was much."

Square nodded to the mailed glove man. Time was suspended as he approached. She waited in the pit for the pendulum, just as in Poe's story. Square smiled a bit and drew back his fist. He was being sure she saw the grinding wheel glove raised against her. She shut her eyes knowing, against her will, she had screamed. The bastards wanted her to do that.

She was lying on the floor, coming out of unconsciousness, pain coming from her cheek and her jaw, all of her face it seemed, and from the back of her whiplashed neck. As she tried to sort out her sensations, she distinguished an ache in her elbow upon which she must have crumpled, and something blocking the vision of her one eye closest to, parallel with the floor. She noted the worn Oriental carpet, too close up, from the other eye. She put her hand to her eye. Felt gooey, sticky, a bit slimy. She wiped her eye, its vision cleared. It was blood, thickened, odd how my thoughts go sidewise, like gravy thickened with arrowroot. The pain from her torn cheek was growing. A mutilated face. Pain seasoned with terror becomes much worse.

Mailed Glove was smiling. Pistol, what else could she call him, but here there was no Shakespearean farce, was resting his weapon on his crossed arm. Square was slowly shaking his head. "All so unnecessary, don't you see? And this is just the beginning, or is unless you have more sense. It does hurt a lot, doesn't it." No question, a statement. "You'll want to think about what we will do next." He nodded to the gloved man who, she was surprised, removed his dusters. He came over smiling. Pistol put down his weapon and walked toward her, holding her wrists. Was he going to help lift her up, what a gentleman, but no, he held her wrists tightly down to the floor. Smiling man knelt on her feet, spread-eagling her. His ungloved cold hands ran slowly, caressingly up the inside of her legs, slowly, slowly to her crotch. She twisted and turned but pistol man held her hands tight, the other one worked his hands, her limbs, indifferent to her struggle. Higher his hands now to her waist, gripping her panty hose, slowly pulling them down, steadily, roughly too, as his knuckles raised her belly, her legs a bit off the floor to yank her underthings off. "Oh my GOD, my GOD!" her mind was screaming. But there was no noise. Her petitioned God was kept silent within her.

Smiling man pulled her dress up to her waist. All of her below her waist was exposed and held that way, as in steel. Nothing happened but for the holding of her.

Square spoke. "You won't like what's coming next, will you? Not a bit. Rape is so humiliating. And it can be very violent; the worst is that some of your being will enjoy it, yes, that can be so. And you will not, for the rest of your life, get over the memory of either the violence or that awful animal pleasure you hated yourself for. Think how much pleasure it is giving Andrei here; how much pleasure it will give him tomorrow and as much as he wants it until you decide he's had enough. Your decision you see, all yours."

Claire was breathing so fast, her heart beating so fast, she could not have spoken.

"And so, because we do after all want you to leave here as soon as possible, as unharmed as possible, as alive as possible, we leave you now. When we come back is somewhat up to you. There is a call button on the wall next to the door which I suspect you hadn't noticed. Use it when you decide to end the trouble. Or we shall come back when *we* want to. To do what we will. But soon."

The three men left the room. She heard a lock being turned, a bolt being slid on the door. Claire was shivering, almost in spasms. She remained frozen in the moment before they departed, when Gloved man's now unmasked hand had come up the inside of her thigh once more, and it had slowly, repeatedly stroked her crotch, fingering her intimacy. He had groaned. She vomited.

8

It was 6:15 when he arrived at the Jockey Club, but he could do no better. The day had been exhausting; IFFY, DEA, main Treasury, the doctor looking over the stab wound and making the obligatory, "Take it easy and be sure to take your antibiotics" pronouncements. Barbour had lost blood, he was bandaged like a swaddled child, and the damn thing hurt. He hoped Nancy had waited for him. The place was an expensive choice for coffee but he wasn't familiar with the local watering holes anymore. It had been a long time since he had been in Washington, and had come here several times with a friend, Bidwell, who had headed the DEA. "Crusader mouse," some officers had called Bidwell when he was young and righteous. Barbour remembered a Bidwell story told to him by a furious Berkeley whore.

Bidwell, a young cop working vice, had picked her up. Con wise, she wouldn't strip, thereby denying him testimony as to any offer of pussy for pay until he proved his bona fides as a true john. At her demand he had stripped first. She figured no cop—well, no honest cop, and Berkeley's were—would go that far. Bidwell stripped but kept his socks on. "Damn him" she'd said, "he had his badge pinned inside his socks, flashed it after I'd undressed and demanded my meat market value."

"Sock it to her-Biddy," had thereafter been his new nickname on the force and even among the brethren, until he made it big along the Potomac.

Nancy was there waiting. She had an iced tea in her hand. It was about where Bidwell had sat when they were last here. An irresistible image came to Barbour's mind of an older, fatter Bidwell, stripped down to his socks sipping a drink, while in his quite pictorial imagination Nancy began to strip. "I have been away from women for too long," Barbour told himself, "much too long."

Their greeting was more prosaic. A casual kiss hello. The "glad to see you" exchange. Inquiries about the wound. His lie that it didn't hurt. Her knowing enough not to believe him. Quick reference to his day moving about government offices. Her being glad she had spent most of it catching up on sleep. The usual. They both knew they liked each other but that it would stop there. Just friends, whether or not one day they went to bed. Neither of them had that immediately on their minds, although it is unlikely that when any single man and woman meet and know there is liking, that bedtime speculations do not occur.

"You were on the plane with my second cousin Royston Cranmer? My memory of you together was right?"

"Fantastic, Nancy, yes, that's right. How can you remember?"

"It was one of those emotional occasions, everything about it scorched into my memory, like a too-hot iron on a shirt. I'd welcomed him on board and was glad to see him—rare enough, believe me. It's good to have family, ordinarily, and Royston was cutting quite a noble figure in the Senate. You know what a handsome fellow he is, cast for the role in Hollywood. Tall, poised, great shock of white hair standing at wild photogenic angles, fabulous honest blue eyes, that aquiline nose; I was proud of him. It made me feel important to be kin. And it is a good family, the Archbishop in his time was more than ordinarily decent. Regardless of what Aunt Letha thought of Royston, I believed his press. And much of it was true, he seemed to be a dedicated moral idealist. And there were rumors he was going to run for President. I was excited."

"What happened?"

"I tried to talk to him, and just in case reminded him of our cousinship. Even so he cut me off as though I were some smelly bag lady hitting him up for a dollar. More than rude, snarling. Told me to go back to my 'watering' and leave him alone. He had 'work to do.' Of course he did, heaps of it, but only a minute of familial chitchat is all I wanted. It was that hard and selfish side of him that my aunt knew too well."

Barbour looked down, stroked his chin. "I got to know that reaction of his, total rejection, maybe it was on the same flight. I don't know." He went on to say how he had himself been active in state politics, had declined an invitation to run for Congress. Cranmer had been a congressman then. Barbour was Cranmer's advisor on law enforcement and drugs. Later Cranmer had become senator during the same period Barbour had become involved as a volunteer in national politics for his party. Issues papers. That sort of thing. "Cranmer and I were still friends, I thought, until it really blew up. I didn't play to his ego. I gave him my honest view that he shouldn't run, and he was furious. I've learned since about that ego, and about his opportunism. His idealism was shallow, a self-flattering way to get public brownie points contributing further to his immensely good opinion of himself. Not unusual. I knew a piously married fundamentalist preacher once who screwed every girl in the choir and got the one who played the singing saw pregnant. Took his evangelical tent and left town."

"What do you know?" Nancy said, "same casting mold. Aunt Letha, who really knew him told, me Royston had left three wives each for the younger; a couple of other unimportant girls left pregnant, borrowed heaps of money from his rich grandmother with promises of repayment, which never happened—well, you get the picture."

Barbour nodded. "That's for sure."

"Are you still interested in him then?"

Barbour decided to be more disclosing than guarded. "In my business, where you sometimes get quite near the top of the social and power ladder looking for the bad guys, I hear him mentioned. As you know, he became bitter when he lost the Presidential race at the convention, if you can call a one -state nomination withdrawn after the first ballot even being in the race. He changed his public face into what may have been his hidden self for a long time. More focused, more calculating—more competent in the Senate, in a way, because he let his ruthlessness be known as well as his charm. You might think a bit like Lyndon Johnson maybe, but not as earnest or genuine. Lies were nothing to either of them. But unlike LBJ, Cranmer lost interest in politics except for staying in office as a means to his new interest, money. He's pursued two jobs at once ever since he turned sour.

"Two jobs at once—senator and grand master of international banking. He heads both the Banking Committee and the Crime Committee, is on the Judiciary and the Appropriations committees. On the Hill that's real power. He uses it to push any legislation that helps big banks who will in turn help him. And what I hear is that help includes hidden roles advising boards of directors for overseas-headquartered banks. They scratch his back. I have heard of one instance, and I trust the source, where a Swiss bank was selling off a failed major corporation whose debt they held. The bank knew the company's hidden assets were a lot more than were shown on the public book—you know how frail the reporting laws for corporations are in Europe, and there was collusion between some of the corporate directors and the bank to sell out the stockholders. Cranmer got the tip to buy the stock. Got to be worth millions within a few years."

"What had he done for them?"

"Put the kibosh on a SEC, Comptroller of the Currency investigation of the portfolio management operations in their offices in New York and Chicago.

Introduced a special 'probable cause' and 'no fishing expedition' bill to restrict Federal investigation of foreign banks that are only officed, not licensed to do traditional customer banking in The States. It was a protective godsend for a slew of foreign-headquartered outfits. Cranmer called in some serious markers to get the bill passed."

"So?"

"He had to have been paid off."

"And he'll never get caught out as long as he does it in the big boys' club and by sophisticated rules?"

"If he keeps the action overseas, and doesn't let vanity take over, that's so. But people can get so full of themselves they take more risks. Miscalculate. Go beyond safe greed to taste more excitement. For example, I knew a big insurance executive who at about age forty turned into a major cocaine dealer. He already had his private jet, got close with the Colombians, made a few million more that he didn't really need, had a ball. Crime is fun as well as profitable, maybe as much fun as the money is, for most people. Maybe working the edge is more normal than not. Think of a respectable churchgoing married man with kids, shacking up with a gorgeous glamorous nightclub singer and thinking no one will find out. Maybe a lot of us have a dark side that longs to be a dramatic and secret player, go for the high pleasure risk, or enjoy the con game where you beat the suckers."

"Do you really think many people do it? I mean respectable people going into the dirty money game, as you suspect Royston did?"

"As far as I know, not usually. After all, you only know what you read in the papers. For the rest, life goes on in the dark money big-business economy in the dozens of billions of dollars—daily, and comfortably."

"And my cousin?"

"We may never know. It's just that some of the signs are there. New wealth," Barbour smiled, "beyond, I gather, what he failed to return to your rich grandmother, or made as a businessman before he went to Congress. New alliances with foreign bankers, foreign real estate companies investing in the U.S., and running through protective legislation with no real evidence of oversize campaign contributions in return."

"How do you know?"

He took a moment during her question to become aware that when she was intense, as she was now, she became quite a good-looking woman. It had been boredom, perhaps depression he had seen on the airplane, or here when she greeted him with some uncertainty or tension that raised havoc with her beauty. As with many women who prefers honest looks to face paint.

He grinned as he confessed. "Your cousin pissed me off and I don't like him. So as a personal hobby I have been looking at records, filings and, when occasion arises as in Montreal, or more importantly last year in London with a banker in potential judicial distress, offering a little to get a little. Just like Cranmer, just like the world. And so, like Mr. Unnamed of the once-famous London Bank of You Guess which went under last year with some billions gone bye-bye, their Mr. Unnamed is unindicted. Perhaps in gratitude for my small and calculating kindness—he was only a minor player, so there was no great miscarriage of justice—this banker gave me to believe that the good senator probably got paid once again several million in pre-crash shares, including an offshore subsidiary, happily and profitably unknown as such, and thereby overlooked by receivers in the bankruptcy proceedings."

Barbour continued. "This one is a damn near identical replay of the 'no fishing,' 'probable cause' bill he wrote earlier, which protected foreign banks and restricted even trying investigations overseas by the Feds. Of course it's to Cranmer's advantage not to write to broad bills; this way, each time he does a legislative favor he can get paid off. This time the *quid pro quo* was a bill exempting independently incorporated U.S. assets from bankruptcy proceedings when financed only by bank loans from foreign failed banks who had no share ownership. All perfectly okay, the rationale being to protect U.S. workers and shareholders from loss. But the point is when there is any information of failed disclosure as to concealed conflict of interest in share ownership, the kind of thing that we saw so much in the U.S. savings and loan frauds, here it denied SEC and IRS expeditions abroad to seek to identify asset holders behind foreign and offshore listed company ownership. Here and in the future it denies possible identification of board members of the You-Guess-It-Bank. The good senator and who else knows are recipients, and thus beneficiaries, of the bank loan's made to some front corporation that they hold abroad."

Barbour stopped and shook his head. "But then I'm only guessing. Hanged if I really know. It's just that each time I have a case with big money, big banks, big men, lots of across-the-border shenanigans through cut-out companies, haven banks and the like, I keep smelling the air for our good friend, your cousin. One day I will not only sniff him, I will find him out."

"This case you're on now?"

"No idea if there even is a case. From what I have, I doubt it. IFFY," for he had explained to her, perhaps a bit vaguely, his connection, "may just be doing its politically correct duty—which is to posture and protect its own ass."

9

Cranmer checked in at the Dorchester where he was well known, his status and heavy tipping fully respected. He made a few telephone calls to set up meetings the day after next. In the meantime he would give himself a treat and return as old boys do to his school, in this instance Jesus College, Cambridge. He had spent but a year there as a postgraduate, taking a certificate in international studies. He had known then that his career would be political and fancied someday it might be international. Being President one day had always been a hidden ambition. Cambridge, for all its miserable weather, had been his joy as a graduate student. He had since given his college a great deal of money. There were contingent negotiations in progress whereby his college might soon make him an Honorary Fellow. High worldly rank and very large contributions do call an Oxbridge college's attention to practical, rather than academics, definitions of excellence. No wonder that upon the Senator's telephoning the Master, a guestroom was made available for the senator the next night.

A limousine brought him to the Chimney Entrance about eleven in the morning. The porter, also carefully instructed, carried bags to the suite of rooms, which were old, worn and inelegant in the domestically masochistic English collegiate tradition. Old boys, and new ones coming up, minded not at all. Pride and display, taste and wealth, were external trappings; gratification of richer tastes were to be found in the dons' common rooms, and at high table. Aesthetic supremacy ruled in antiquities, decorations, wine and food there; and more so did aesthetics, and yes, even for Cranmer a hint of spirituality, in the chapel. But Jesus College, even in its religious presentation, was not uncomplicated by other joys and appetites. Its history too informed its present. Once a twelfth-century convent, notorious for the elasticity of its nun' morals, it had been founded as Jesus College in 1496. But the good times were hard to suppress. Why, only last week a don from the theological faculty and a town tart had disported themselves for a somewhat noisy night in his College rooms. Only polite silence, and of course confidential insider gossip, ensued.

Jesus College's Gothic buildings had, beginning in the twelfth century, served as a nunnery. It was the convent of St Radegund. The nunnery protested Ely's presiding Bishop John Alcock was too close to the university. What he meant was that the nuns were too close to the students, or at least sufficiently close to be changing one habit, for another. The good for the bad so to speak. Those of you who have run bordellos know the problems: personnel mostly, winesack girls, finger scratching feuds, jackanapes for customers, as well as the ecopolitics of mordita and the skim. So what should have been, under good management, an holy, and wholly profitable whorehouse declined into a state of profitless hedonism. A well-run diocese could have none of that.

One does make that leap of faith to affirm that Bishop Alcock was more distressed at the frolic than at the cathouse convent's growing debt. However, those of you who sport a jaundiced eye will remember from your own business, city government, or university, that even the very pious, when owners become salaried or winning investors, can overlook a bit of mischief, say constructive cooking of the books for a few million quid, when, overall, the bottom line is pleasing. However pleasing may have been their bottoms and their lines, the nuns' bottom lines seemed not.

Even today sermons as the fine art of homiletics, dwell on continuing marginal risks which can arise when people have fun for its own sake, complicated these days and then when the moral envelope is pushed so far that, essentially, cash might also flow in. Call that the "St Radegund dilemma," how to diversify and maximize pleasure and cash without getting caught. The Bishop of Ely, chastiser at least of nuns, and no, there is no knowledge of simultaneous fondness for leather and chains, but nevertheless in founding Jesus College, used censorious language. "Sin" was no doubt thundered about when sweeping the holy bawds, those sanctified strumpets, those good time sweet tart mothers more prone than superior, away. Whether his was a placating move, if, for example, his wife had caught the right revered with one of the girls, both pants down and panting, one does not guess. Clerical history is not without its scandals, and history generally, its chroniclers often guessing wrongly, has turned on events a good deal less consequential.

In contrast to the St Radegund frolic, a lot of people make money without having any fun. Call this "Calvin's delight." That is nowhere called a sin, but it can be an unholy waste of time, at least if those out making that hard living would prefer bed, beer and good cheer to the incessant ring of a cash register and the tedium of carting money off to the bank. But more and more people these days find a middle ground which is destructionist, only and optimizingly functional, i.e., without concern with values, the anchoring morality of a tribe or culture, because the magicians of materialism have made values situational, integrity a PR term, and "morality" a cultural antique. The pragmatist's mantra—"It is all relative."

It is a fundamental failure of modern criminologists that they dwell on the sour side of etiology. Psychopathology, poverty, impulsivity, bad examples. True sometimes no doubt, but it is also quite possible that most of the people out there making dirty money positively enjoy being crooked. There is a tingle to it, a high, and to exceed at selfishness is to enjoy that success as well. If your mother told you that selfish people are miserable, and that only the good are rewarded, your old lady, God rest her soul, had a dead fish for a brain. But then, the religious message to us all being one of kindness, so do most of the rest of us. The good nuns of Radegund, giving of themselves, fully so to speak, were similarly denied, so is the talk from the pulpit, their eternal reward. (One must qualify that; the lodger's list in heaven is unavailable on the Internet.) As the proverb has it, "no good deed goes unpunished."

The Bishop of Ely suppressed the good times at Radegund's, now Jesus College. The College dons have been ever since, trying to get their jollies via the side door; i.e., to remain respectable, while at the same time enjoying more than just tutorials, lively fantasy about the co-eds and the musty lusty aroma of carousings yet lingering in their medieval corridors. Freud called it "sublimation," as for example in describing sex as nothing but the sublimation of the baseball instinct (in the UK, read "the cricket instinct"). If nothing else, Cambridge dons have learned over ten centuries to sublimate, or at least, not get caught. The cases of notorious Cambridge-spawned spies getting caught, Philby for instance, demonstrate that sex and politics are different, whatever contemporary newspapers suggest to the contrary. But deceit is attractive, as the very nature of perfidious Albion reminds. It is a delicacy over which one lingers.

It should come then as a matter of pride and historical continuity, not surprise, that beginning in 1984, Jesus College once again turned to the heady brew of sin. Specifically, it was that consequential as well as delectable criminal sin where, as always in public one avowal is like the preacher with a pornography collection or the Inquisitor screwing the witch, denouncing that which excites. Unexcited was the respected lecturer in economics, Dr. Gavin Garrity, who had been an original organizer. He liked his field but was not selling spice to the conference trade. The Symposium itself; all content echoes of Ambrose Bierce in his *Devil" Dictionary* defining piracy as "commerce without its folly-swaddles, just as God made it."

The nuns of Radegund, God blessing but not as blessed, should be given credit as historical quasi founders not simply of the College but also of its Symposia. Unlike most cases discussed, or indeed examples among delegates attending—some in the Nigerian and Ukrainian governmental delegations outstanding—the nuns at least gave value for coin. Using that criteria your friendly neighborhood drug dealer is a more honest businessman than many an American insurance company.

College old boys often returned, attending the lectures, enjoying splendid meals in the ancient and ornate hall, drinking in the din of the immensely popular bar on F staircase. Some come back as Lords, Chief Justices, (CJs), DGs, CCs, and PMs from here and there to give after-dinner speeches. Some did that and learned new tricks as well. One of these had been the Honorable Royston Cranmer. Already a senator, he was as well received as any man of fame, money and power in the banking world might be. All colleges see bequests writ in the faces of new boys just coming up, and why not? It is "the way of the world as it was when" Congreve titles his play, and indeed it is yet so. Congreve, an old boy himself of Trinity College, would have been a splendid speaker. Crime is best approached with some sense of comedy—lest we cry.

As for Cranmer, no regular registrant, he had first visited in 1994. He sat on a panel discussing crime in international banking, a subject about which he professed insufficient knowledge, except for praising the U.S. Senate bills to prevent and control it—which, he was proud to say, he had legislated. He shared the panel with Dr. Gavin Garrity, who expounded on the banks of once Soviet, once CIS eastern Europe, including those dozens that were fly-by-night havens and those important in Moscow, the owners of which were at high risk of takeover bids exercised by "torpedoes." Russians use the American word not for the naval weapon but the killer, where in Russia the weapon is typically a Kalashnikov. Gavin had been estimating boodle, decrying the unpaid taxes that forced Russia to run the government from borrowings rather than income. Like everyone reading the papers, he had counted bankers' bodies as well as boodle, of which there were many and much. If there were a law of economic development about this, it was the only "law" Gavin had found operative in these recent wild West, devil-take-the-hindmost, free-enterprise years in Moscow. So spoke the professor.

When discussing international banking, the senator, did expound on and roundly decry the obvious: for example, failures in due diligence; collusion with central banks or auditors; falsified balance sheets, and looting of funds hidden in secret accounts. Except in Switzerland, which has secret courts as well as accounts, foreign holders who were unsophisticated financial felons themselves could not make themselves known, and thus had no recourse but hatred. The good Senator touched upon lots of other tricks as virtuously condemning as only a knowledgeable player could be.

It was in the bar, after the interminable after-dinner speeches, one his own, that Senator Cranmer was introduced by the good Dr. Garrity to a senior official of the Bulgarian Finance Ministry. That was in 1994. The man was a Communist, which did not deny him either the knowledge or pleasure of an imagination that would exploit the intricacies of the international banking system. What he lacked were international—read "western and trusted"—means. Sofia in its red-star days was hardly connected to the world except through funerals, the product of KGB-directed Interior Ministry assassination squads. (Remember those notorious umbrella killings in London? There were many others not so well noticed.)

Materially, there were Bulgarian liquid and convertible assets to be had, but assuming their governmentally-arranged disappearance, no assured money laundry was in place for their secret transit and safe reinvestment in the west under entirely new private ownership. Such investments were to be Western-managed, of course. No Communist was nutty enough to trust what he had stolen fair and square to transit through his own Eastern bloc financial system. "Those mafiya? Never!" And by the 1990s no Communist in power, was mad enough to fail to see democratic forecasts written on the fallen brick of the Berlin wall. The way to transform oneself from a Communist bureaucrat to a millionaire could only be, in that time before the Bloc fell, to hurry the stolen monies, or goods convertible to money, out secretly and reinvest them in the solid and safe havens of Western financial centers. No, not Asia, not Central Europe, not the Caribbean of the warm beaches, and under no circumstances the collapsing Soviet bloc. With great care in the selection of front men, straw men, Geneva, New York, and London became the final stops for laundered big money wanting the guarantee of joyful profit realized in honest democracies with judicial protection. Latvia, Cyprus, Austria were way stations.

The Bulgarian official was discreet, suspicious, enterprising. So was Cranmer. The two suspected they had much in common. Unspoken comfort. One item of their common interest was Sir Alfred Means, megacapitalist extraordinaire, probably from directorships, investments, some majority share holdings, South African gold. Indonesian timber. North American pension fund and health care management, banks, UK insurance, Luxembourg trusts, German chemicals. EU spread import brokerage. Israeli munitions. Austrian publishing and Panamanian shipping. Agricultural sales and futures so multinationally spread that their very company headquarters had no fixable place nor nationality, just a dynamic network, which also described Sir Alfred himself. To describe him also required words such as abhorred, loathed, abominated, detested, cursed; and traits such as obnoxious, megomaniacal, flamboyant, unscrupulous, brilliant, amoral. Sir Alfred, one sees, was not exactly adored.

One exception might be his exclusive sailing clubs, well-appointed luxurious settings. His sporting donations were appreciated. It was widely rumored that yacht club managers provided him, for pleasure while sailing (it was quite an old-fashioned kind of rumor) with young "white slaves" abducted from among the population of foreign girls touring, say Capetown, the Virgin Islands or Paris. Only rumors, who could say? Of restauranteurs he was beloved, a free-spending glutton—or "gourmet," of course, when said by a restauranteur publicly. He was corpulent, but not beyond measure, for his was a 48-inch waist on a 5-foot-7 man. Art traders, particularly those most unscrupulous themselves—it is said no honest dealer is wealthy—also welcomed him. His collection of stolen masters and smuggled national treasures was nonpareil. No matter that he was hated, expressed egregious lust for food and young women; he was rich, and for that, and for his ability to indulge himself to the very limits of the flesh, he was in some ways very much admired.

Cranmer knew Sir Alfred because of the banking connection. Tellingly, the Bulgarian admired him by reputation. His name and skills, the latter rumored to be varied and open to very high offers—which is the world the way the authorities in the Eastern bloc practiced it anyway, was for Mr. Bulgarian Finance possibly just the thing for certain tasks he had in mind. How excellent that the senator, himself charming when he wished, and as an old boy in the famous bar on F staircase at Jesus College, was more than happy to make the introduction. The senator too struck Mr. Finance—"call me Todor" and "yes, pleased to do so"—as flexible, one authority to another. The price for this kindness in making the introduction was yet to be discussed.

They agreed they must meet again, in Cambridge perhaps, or London for greater convenience. Cards were exchanged; the Bulgarian would be "in touch soon." Cranmer in turn would learn when Sir Alfred, who was often in the UK in any event, would be available.

"This Cambridge, it is such a delightfully impractical place," Todor of

Finance had said smiling, watching an Asian central banker, an African justice minister, and a likewise Asian national police chief walking near, deep in conversation. Finance was much pleased with prospects and his little irony, for after all the pedestrians so observed had much in common, little of it honest.

"Yes," had replied the senator, assessing what might be his best play in this new Bulgarian and "Alfredian" game.

"All of us absent-minded academics, da?" Todor of Finance was chuckling. His open-mouthed grin revealed crude Russian dentistry, his gold-capped, overly large teeth. It reminded the senator of the movie 'Jaws.'

The senator nodded, began to walk away without further speech. His departure was but a step toward other arrivals, consistent with that their unspoken but understood agreement. It was then the summer of 1994. More understandings, whose wording was not always distinct, would be reached. These would have far-reaching effects, not the least on the fat man himself.

Now, some years later, sitting at high table on the Master's honored left, the senator, handsome and affable as must a Master also be, was—despite the shock of the cable received little more than a day before while in flight—feeling confident. The Master in his lodge had served the senator an 18-year-old Macallan single-malt scotch whisky. His palate had been pleased by the Haut-Brion '84 with the shrimp starter, and then the pheasant had been accompanied by a Baron Pichon Longueville '78.

The senator's confidence? A man of action acts. That was why he had made calls to London and elsewhere not from his room but from the Green Park tube station. Things were in motion. Partners elsewhere were also in action. Lips would be sealed and papers made to go away. Layerings for money in the pipeline would be elaborated, altered. A few of the partners as principals would soon be meeting for a damage control review. To date, in spite of Warsaw and possibly Vienna, because of Paris, Sofia, Geneva, London, New York—Moscow was always dark with the winter of uncertainty and instability but that was taken into account—the business of this world was carrying on. The senator had always admired St. Paul's ambiguous term, "The Prince of this World." Why not? If the senator himself had once been denied the Presidency, he would yet become such a prince, or Prince. Cranmer, like Faust, disdained long spoons when supping with Lucifer. It's good to be cozy with a fellow who can get you what you want.

10

Nothing at all was happening. Nothing. Solitary confinement in a silk chamber awaiting demons and doom. Claire was alternatively shivering and feverish, sore throat, the flu plus fright. "Not a good day," she said out loud. "No good days in sight." This one was almost past; through the steel shutters, too narrow for vision but slits wide enough to tell night from day, it was dusk.

No Messrs. Pistol or Gloves—she shuddered and the flesh of her womanhood revulsed—and no Square, either. Nor any breakfast nor lunch. Water enough from the bathroom washbasin. She was too sick to be hungry. A shower in the bathroom, she'd wondered if letting it run and run to flood the floor would bring helpful notice, but this was a private house, she knew that. It would only bring a beating. She was already cowed. What a quick revision in her view of herself as cocky, tough. "Know thyself"—was it Aristotle? Well, she was learning and liked neither the process nor the Claire revealed. Fever and the flu were no help. She remembered, was she delirious? a famous old text on "true tales of Thuggee about the East Indian criminal caste and their goddess of murder, Kali." Its title was *No Friend for Travelers*. Vienna Thuggee, and no friend here. It was psychological warfare, and it was working. Once again she cried, for the third time in a decade, for she prided herself on her self-control, on being "sensible." The recent occasion had been here in this room when she had first realized her helplessness. The other tears were long ago in Cambridge when Gavin Garrity was lost to her love.

She heard the key being inserted, Square entered, with Pistol behind him and Gloves with a smile. Conditioned response; she recalled the smile that had replaced his earlier stolid stare while he enjoyed yesterday's fingering foreplay of the rape she knew was to come. She sat, her mind woozy, in the silk upholstered chair. She had just enough time to lean forward before she threw up.

The smile disappeared. Both men were repulsed by the smell and sight of her vomit, as indeed was she. Gloves put the dinner tray down on the floor. It appeared they had intended to begin starvation; one piece of toast, cold cabbage, nothing more. About that she could not at this moment care less.

Square appeared in the doorway. "I must leave you, Agent Dubois, for a few days. Something more urgent than you. The men here will look after you, one way or another." He smiled in contemplation of evil. But then, he had not smelled the vomit. "By the time I return you will be very hungry, tired, and perhaps more than over-used." He nodded toward Gloves, who wheeled in front of the door a cart on which stood a small sound system. Gloves put on a disc which yielded screeching sounds of chalk on blackboard, women's screams, gunshots, awful thuds. Were these memorabilia of Square's work in Lubyanka? "This will keep you company at night, the noise. And it will anticipate Andrei here, who will enjoy your body in his own special ways. Nikolai, perhaps, as well. I have given them a pleasure schedule. The suspense is interesting, yes? You may of course prevent their little delights, all of this discomfort, by cooperating. Would you like to do that now?"

"I told you that you know more than I do." She wondered why this monster, with all his interrogation skills, could not tell that she was telling the truth. "Please believe me. Check your data. You seem to know everything. You'll see it's true." The fever, the fear, the nausea, the terror and revulsion she felt, could he not sense them by contagion?

"Ah, my dear woman, you will be obstinate. You will also reconsider. If you do that before I return, for instance when Andrei comes for you, there is a signal. Just tell them, for they have no English, 'yes' four times. When I return I will expect your 'yes' to be cooperation. If you have lied, even I shudder to think of how the torture will go. Two days, then, or three or four. Be waiting, fearful, be hungry, be sleepless, think of Andrei bursting inside your every rupturing orifice, and when you say 'yes' repeatedly—be sure you mean it."

There was a look of savagery on Square's face that would have made Attila at the kill seem the compassionate Christ by comparison.

They left. This time she made it, staggering, to the bathroom before vomiting.

11

Belonging to the Athenaeum Club, upon a time at least, was the finest thing in the world. Less so now perhaps, but still one place where distinguished old boys gather round. Not all the members egregiously famous, some no doubt badly behaved, but discreetly so, it was expected. Trollope, Macaulay, Thackeray, Burton, and Dickens; bishops and archbishops; Speakers of the House, Governors General, were immediately elected without the (once), sixteen-year wait—it is not too bad a place. And the food, once the dread of London, is now splendid. Some interlopers would yet attempt the blackball barricades, earning the distasteful characterization—here we rely on Anthony Lejeune, the authority on London clubs, quoting an anonymous worried member: "All the little crawlers and parasites and gentility-hunters, from all corners of London, set out upon the creep; and they crept in at the windows, and they crept down the steps and they crept in unseen at the doors, and they crept in under the bishops' sleeves, in peer's pockets and they were blown by the winds of chance."

Sir Peter Dixon had once and was now temporarily again directing the Yard. He had once been a presence in MI6, and was a practical scholar. It was rumored he spoke Turkish as well as read Coptic, and had done Classics at Cambridge but somehow earned a degree from Tokyo. What was public about him was his watercoloring hobby, and a show or two in the best galleries, a review in the *Times* and surprisingly respectful of a Tory, in the *Independent* and the *Guardian*. One keeps in mind the Brits can be as reserved about great talents and achievements as about the horrendous episodes in their lives. Antecedents in England are intentionally murky. For someone who likes stable ground it can be infuriating when histories, individual and political, are intentionally and silently convoluted. One who had recently met Sir Peter, assessing him from the record, would not be on stable ground.

Sir Peter's guest for lunch was Ambassador George Dubois. He was in London for a meeting and rest from Kiev. Another guest was one of the few American members, Dr. Quincy Adams. They were seated in the ancient leather chairs of the morning room. Old, old friends, and the time now should have been for the joy of it. The sherry was no help, for they had all become anxious indeed.

Oddly enough, the question had first been posed in pleasure by Quincy, who had come to know Claire through her parents, as had Sir Peter. The ties were old; politics, intelligence, the interplay of these with other international issues such as crime, drugs, policing. These linked them together, along with the cold war and the part each had played in that, publicly silent but well known to each other and to the losing side, were the normal policy and newspaper fare of the 60s, 70s, and 80s.

"Not as much change as might be expected," Quincy had been saying to Peter while they had waited for George to arrive. "The issues, well at least ours, are still crime and drugs, but expanded now to diversified contraband and mischief." Old friends look at each other in comfort, but wise friends make assessments as well. Dr. Adams was, Sir Peter could see, in fine shape. Thin and in electric trim, about five-ten, one could take him for fifty or sixty or seventy. His china-blue eyes misleadingly seemed sweetly innocent; his hair was rust but also white; he wore a dark gray suit and one of his predictable neckties, Liberty or Sulka or Harvey and Hudson, flowering out from his vest.

"Eastern Europe still requires attending to," Sir Peter had replied, "and woe to us politically if it destabilizes any further. The mafiya empires there bode no good." Sir Peter was also in good form. Six feet tall well-carried portliness, a cane when he walked (a sword-cane, in fact, legal by special license). There was more than a dash of style, sometimes a blasé Noel Coward touch to him, contrasted with an impressive imperial roar when the lion in him was roused, or reminding others of where he stood in the rigid English hierarchy. Military once, obviously, and commanding then and now. Thin nose, jutting chin, not yet jowls but they could come, penetrating hazel eyes, hair somewhere between brown and sand and gray, and eyebrows so bushy and red that they were awnings for his face. The man had Scot in him, that was for sure. And the lairds' taste for all things good in, mostly, moderation.

They had been talking further about the historical mess that began wherever the Russian boundary was and the Russian dissatisfactions with that, when Ambassador Dubois was announced by the porter, a woman of all things (my oh my, how the Athenaeum had changed). The Ambassador clearly was at home here. Short, showing bridled power and confidence, yet walking with a quiet grace, courtesy and a "I shall seek not to disturb" sign in his measured gait. Aging, blondish hair, age itself also uncertain as it is in men and women of health and success. But himself no child, and his look told you no fool. Nothing was missed by these brown eyes so ordinary one knew they weren't.

Now the three of them had their drinks, and Quincy was saying, "Claire wrote me from Washington a week or so back saying she hoped to be in Europe and expected to run over soon to London. 'We'll have a reunion, I so much want to see all of my friends', she said 'Perhaps I can get Beulah down from Scotland and we can have a party.' I really expected to see her right away, not because she was, as it were, too revealing to say when exactly or where she was to be posted, but by sending it Federal Express quite obviously she wanted me to know she was coming immediately. I suspect she may have been putting on too much of the secrecy bit, but you know Claire, she does like drama, spicing the story up a bit, and in her new job would err on the side of confidences. She so much wants to do well at whatever she's up to."

Yes, they agreed that was so.

"And so, George, how fine it is, and so what brings your daughter across the pond? When she's about she is a magnet for parties. I can hardly wait."

"Yes, George," Sir Peter interposed, "Claire wrote Susan and me, and express mail as well. My wife and I have been expecting her here momentarily. Thought we'd have a party of course. My, but she does like champagne. Not a word yet though—a bit odd, since the tone of it was that she'd be in London right away. What is she doing now, George? I mean if you can say." Old Discretion was not about to push; he'd known well enough she'd been with "the cigar factory" as the Agency was once known, and she'd written most of her friends some weeks ago that she planned to move to IFinCIG or, as they called it in London, "the Network."

Ambassador Dubois, the puzzled expression on his face becoming worried, replied, "Actually I don't really know when she was to take up the IFFY, that is Network, job. About now I should think, but she didn't give me an exact date. The appointment was firm, of that I am sure. And she was excited about it. There's nothing really hush-hush about working for IFFY, as we call it, except as with all serious criminal investigations, when gathering preliminary intelligence on what may be a case, one doesn't telegraph suspicions to suspects. And with IFFY the diplomatic niceties about who gets access to what confidential records can be difficult. Believe me, I know. I've been in the middle of such cases."

The ambassador went on, "I do know in general where she was headed because she called and told me. No security breach on her part. Her new boss, or at least the chap who fills that slot when she came aboard—she described him as a prissy idiot named Jones—told her there was no spooky stuff at IFFY. And no mention of undercover. So she could tell me, she said, in confidence, but as I say I think she's being too careful about what I presume is her first, and precipitously quick, overseas assignment, without breaking the regs. Fair enough. There can be no blowback." The Ambassador was pleased at his daughter's cautions. She could be as tough-minded as they came, and think like a lawyer when it suited her.

"In any event she took the trouble to use a secure line. Well, you never know, but the communication people try, and I myself sometimes think it's secure, encrypted, scramble and all that. She telephoned from the Ukraine desk at State in D.C. No reason not to tell you two rogues in confidence that she was to head for Vienna. She was rather discouraged about whether it might not be a wild goose chase. And she admitted—Claire is very honest about what she doesn't know—that she didn't know a thing about what she was to do. She was to wait for some more senior fellow to meet her. And she was to be there by day before yesterday, said she'd get a signal off to me from our Embassy there. At this level the State Department is family. Ron Owen is our ambassador there; thank goodness it's not one of those miserable political patronage appointments." Both of his friends nodded knowingly at that. Career diplomats loathed the often brash, ignorant, sometimes red-necked party donors that money-hungry and culturally insensitive Presidents could reward by naming them to posts abroad. "Ron has known her since she was a child. Anyway, I left Kiev via Frankfurt yesterday afternoon. No signal."

"So where then?" asked Lord Peter.

"Right here is where I expected her, since she said she'd try to make a London stop either on the way over or come back over for the weekend. You know Claire, always her own boss, and optimistic as hell that nothing about work should interfere with a party. Or even better, work should *be* a party. She's right most of the time. Anyway that explains the express mail. And, you know me, it explains one reason I was eager to come to London right now."

"But?" asked Dr. Adams.

"But blank," replied the Ambassador frowning down at his glass. "She'd have left a message for me with our embassy here, either with the secretary to the ambassador—a political appointee out of Mississippi, you know," he said with wry disapproval, "or with the duty officer if she called after hours or weekends. No one has heard 'boo'."

Sir Peter said, "Before we begin to worry, good heavens there are so many reasons Claire might actually be having to work in Vienna, much as she'd prefer to set her own schedule. She is junior, you know. As a realist I can't imagine any supervisor letting her off on her own so soon after arriving on assignment."

Dr. Adams grinned, "Well, we all know she's bullheaded, could charm a Persian rug merchant into giving away a free Nain, is her own autonomous republic, and well, probably because she's with the government she's even *more* intent upon being independent. No offense, George, but in an earlier talk with me, we met where the hell was it, Paris? she said she didn't give beans about the civil service or a career in government—on the contrary. Frankly I can see her simply quitting on the spot if some idiot supervisor told her to do something that made no sense."

Her father smiled agreement. Oh yes, he did know his Claire.

Sir Peter's eyebrows went up in mock shock. "Consider this civil servant overruled. We are used to tamer staff in this, I confess it, sterner or more authoritarian sceptered isle. And in view of what we all know about Claire, and yet have to be a bit worried about nevertheless, I propose we take a course of action. Right?"

"Right." The three had already mapped it out. After all, they had worked together before, and were used not just to talking action but using power.

"First," Ambassador Dubois began, "I'll have our people here quick cable the embassy in Vienna. Have they seen her? The same to Washington. And of course Kiev. I'd like to ask the Vienna people to query the Austrian police, but even if they get agreement on secrecy, there's no guarantee. It could really foul up her work if the wrong people, and they can be police, get the wind up. That will have to wait until we raise the level of this alert."

"In turn," Sir Peter said, "I call the head of Network U.S.A. to ask him, on behalf of the Yard and our 'ongoing urgent investigation,' if Claire Dubois has in fact come on board officially, and where she is, or is supposed to be, at this moment. And I tell him that he must advise me immediately. Or..." his face conveyed imperial confidence, for in such men the Empire yet lives to rule... "he is in trouble." Sir Peter went on, "There are a few things in civil service one can count on . One is that in the Foreign Service the first and perhaps the only serious duty is to serve the perfect martini. The other is that if a man senior to you with known connections commands one to 'advise me now, or else...' the junior chap, and Network is a junior Treasury agency I do know, will leave burn marks on the carpet, his rubber heels smoking, as he speeds to do what his superior bids."

It was Dr. Adams' turn. "I once knew well a competent but obsessive Mr. Hashimoto, when he was but junior in an agency which must remain unnamed, but wherein he had some call to respect me. And once to be grateful, indeed to be so grateful that I may still call upon him for anything. He had been, you see, surreptitiously marked, with an orange flag on his own 201 file, by a second-in-command Security anti-Japanese bigot in that unnamed agency. Hashimoto was to be considered a Soviet mole."

"My God," said Sir Peter, "how awful. If I understand you, no one—certainly not Mr. Hashimoto—would know why he would be fired nor ever again hired in any position requiring any security, or indeed non-security but governmental, clearance."

"Right," said Dr. Adams. "But though it is not to discuss here, we should always keep in mind the secret violence that paranoiacs and self-serving conspirators can do under cover of secrecy, including the destruction of the good by the bad."

The others nodded. Each had his own reasons to know what wrongs went unrighted. Mr. Hashimoto had indeed been lucky to find an honest champion. "What happened afterwards?" Ambassador Dubois asked of Dr. Adams.

"A good outcome. Mr. Hashimoto changed agencies, his record unblemished, and rose up in ranks through ambition, energy, single-mindedness—and, by dint of being so compulsively boring, being able to attend speedily to minutiae so trivially hateful that no one but a Cray mainframe computer could compete with him. He is so orderly that the very wobble of the earth in its orbit troubles him. He keeps a gyroscope on his desk to assure him of a stable point, and dreams of the day when he may own an atomic, thus exact, wristwatch. He now heads Personnel in the U.S. Civil Service, doing, as I hear, an amazingly good job. He will have access to everyone and everything that bears on records, including those poor drones, the equivalents of Dickens' Bob Cratchit, who enter the accounts of lives—the very Doomsday Book of those who work for the government. That includes the wheres and whens of work, and access via the reciprocal-favors network to specialized office clerks to learn the "this very minute" of travel vouchers and cash for travel allowances issued, even airline reservations made by an agency staff and not the staffer. And if necessary, (though not in Claire's case), false names used, what disguise out of the wardrobe and other such, for after all, there is a charge and authorization for each wherein the clerk exercises authority."

"A dreadful tomb of the nether world you describe, Quincy! Shades bearing quills and parchment and the hopeless thirst, if I recall Homer's Tiresias, for red blood," said Sir Peter.

"And computer systems which, at three billion dollars, as with our tax agency the IRS, should but do not work," added Dr. Adams. They laughed briefly as they went in to lunch early, to accommodate the time difference between London and Washington for telephone call. Ambassador Dubois was already making his from the U.S. Embassy on Grosvenor Square before coming in for lunch. The club lunch gammon on the silver trolley would prove excellent, as always was the claret, and their confidence in solving the mystery of Claire's whereabouts was restored. They agreed to put all other appointments aside and to meet again in the Club's drawing room for tea at five o'clock each to report.

"I have some troublesome non-news," said Ambassador Dubois. "No embassy has any word. And without my urging or cautions, Ron in Vienna did circumspectly check all police and hospital reports. Nothing. If she is in Europe, she is not letting me know."

Quincy spoke. "Curious. And troubling. Dr. Hashimoto, who now has a Ph.D. in Public Administration, reports that Claire Dubois' 201 file, and other expected ones, show on a name check in the 'non-current employees' files of our unnamed Agency. He has not, in the short time available, been able to order direct inspection, but 'has no reason,' I quote, to imagine that anything strange is going on there. She left three months ago, 'unblemished,' as Hashimoto said to me meaningfully. He is working on the other name file checks, but one uses the word routine. One wonders about the FBI master clearance file."

Dr. Adams turned to the Ambassador, "George, I hate to ask, but Hashimoto said we must consider it. Could Claire have invented anything here, for example her IFFY assignment? We know Claire is inventive as hell. What could she be doing privately that might make her want everyone to think she was coming here for IFFY? A search for sunken treasure or the Lost Dutchman mine, an elopement, a wild affair? She's your daughter. You know her best. For myself, were I to take that romantic tack, I'd look for her in Paris. She loves that city. Can you think of anything at all that might trigger this, well, impulse for anonymity?"

The Ambassador was distressed. "No Quincy, it's devastating. But no, we all know she's as straight an arrow as ever was made. She wouldn't have invented a mission to Vienna if she were off to Paris on a lark. She hasn't lied to me since the time when she was fourteen, when she and a girlfriend sneaked out to a slumber party after her grades had made us put her under house arrest. She knows I don't care what she does as long as she's happy. No, something is wrong. And so, what did your Hashimoto say about the FBI master clearance file in which, I gather, she doesn't appear?"

Dr. Adams, who had known a girl or two in his day and was still enjoying his day, allowed a father's vision might err. Claire was fully capable of an adult slumber party in Paris but he didn't see her lying about getting laid. That almost decided, he answered his friend George. "First off, he says the FBI is as sloppy on files for those not in the Bureau as it was, maybe is, in its labs. 'Big show, all blow' is what he said. He wouldn't expect better. But he will make a physical inspection on his own Civil Service computer files, he calls them his "gold standard," and the physical paper that backs them all up. But his computers are down and it will be an hour or two before the paper file is on his desk. You can imagine how embarrassed he is about his computer's being down. Chagrined. Nevertheless he guarantees that his gold standard files will be in service pronto. And he's going to get to the various travel and cash disbursement clerks in IFFY if they haven't already done it for us, which means for you, Peter. I am to call him in three hours—that will be three P.M. Washington time. He was going to take the afternoon off to go sailing, but says now he'll just provision his day-sailer for a later sail while he waits for his will to be done in the office. He is one angry obsessive. There will be a junior head or two on his desk when I call. He promises to be back by three o'clock with the answers to our questions."

Sir Peter was not pleased. "Confirms my non-information. Network's boss is out of the country. I was referred to Mr. Nameless Mumble in Personnel. I must say I was not impressed with him. But he did call me after a routine file check. Same as Hashimoto. Claire's name is that of a current Network employee. He has never met her. Jones is her immediate boss and has taken time off. Good heavens, Quincy, Hashimoto going for a sail, Jones off, and now all this..." Sir Peter was furious. "This vacuous Mumble, all the while saying 'it isn't my job to do this'! Yet said he would, I quote, 'hope to find something.' I told him to look for travel orders, cash allowance disbursement orders, anything on Vienna. Seems the files are a mess. He says they all just exist in temporary quarters, with cardboard boxes in the halls. I'm to call him back, Quincy." Sir Peter was not quite apoplectic as he turned to his friend, his voice plaintive now, "Doesn't *anything* work in Washington?"

"It has been said, Peter, that the less work our government does the safer we are as citizens. But yes, they work, it works, and most folks do it well. Today is, we all know that, bad luck for the moment. I suspect we all have dinner engagements but we can't let go on this one. What do you propose? George, can we both call you somewhere just after seven to tell you what we learn?"

"Good God, yes. I'm at a reception at the International Bank for Reconstruction and Development, Director Bosch hosting, in their VIP bar. I'll alert them to wait for your calls. And," he looked at them almost beseechingly, "if anything seems badly wrong, might I call on you to meet again with me later this evening, after our dinners perhaps? At the Embassy perhaps? I'll see to it they stay awake for us."

Of course they would. But also of course, "George, it will sort itself out, it's not time yet to worry."

At 7:10 P.M. it was time, according to Sir Peter and Dr. Adams, to be puzzled, fretful and yes, worried, but a worry waiting for its substance. And therefore time to meet immediately, whether at the Yard or the Embassy. But by seven-thirty, while they were on their way to the Grosvenor Square, Ambassador Dubois was sure he could tell them that whatever false scents the others had followed, there was nothing to worry about at all—well, at least probably not.

The Mississippi businessman whose patronage appointment was at the top of the heap, U.S. ambassador to the Court of St. James, arose as they came in. He was dining privately in the Embassy with his secretary. He was a big man in a white cowboy hat, eating barbecued pork ribs with his fingers, and drinking beer with dinner. He had tucked his napkin in as a bib. Obviously he was not quite what the Court of St. James required. As they came in, he had just finished dinner in his private conference room, the security bubble chamber visible through a glass panel next door. Ambassador Dubois knew that Mr. Mississippi used the bubble and the red phone inside only to call his friends back home, mostly exchanging dirty jokes. One colleague told Dubois one of Mississippi's favorite themes was to chortle over "them dirt-poor Foreign Service career fellows who try so hard but don't get nowhere. The truth of it is, well hell, if they're so college smart, why ain't they rich and appointed here in sweet St. James like me? Supercilious uppity bastards." Mississippi handed his colleague a yellow cable envelope, his fingers leaving gooey Cajun sauce on it.

"I figure, George, this is what you were waitin' for. Me, I got a heavy appointment, so I'll leave you fellas to make yourselves t'home here."

Dubois fumbled the letter open, read it with great relief, reporting, "Kiev received an urgent pouch, a letter for me from Claire. I had them open it. You were right, Quincy, she's in Paris. Somebody named Harry, and no mission to Vienna. She's been diverted, it sounds to me as if fully by Harry, except she says, for 'some work with Paris banks on an interesting laundry problem.' I'm damned relieved but embarrassed to have you both come away from your dinners just to hear good news. But I grant you it's not like her. Oh well, an unmarried daughter is bound to have her flings."

"Well," said Dr. Adams, "I hope it stays good news when you hear mine. In any event I'm having dinner at the Groucho in Soho with the most wonderful woman I will ever want to meet, and can return in a jiffy. But now the strange news. Hashimoto wasn't in his office. The place had shaped up. His secretary told me he had Dubois' files on his desk and a computer print out, the systems all go. But he hadn't returned. In all her years with him this, she said had never happened. She'd even called the police to get hospital accident reports. Nothing."

"What next, then?"

"I told her, in very un-Adams language, to get her sweet fanny down to his boat dock as fast as she and her security officers could. Call the Arlington police and get them there too. People have heart attacks, and maybe Hashimoto was putting on weight as well as years. But I don't like it one bit. I told her if she learned anything to call me here immediately."

Sir Peter understood that worrying time was now. "The empty-headed Mumble at Network got me while I was still at the Yard. I had a reception to attend at Marlborough House but was—well, to put it bluntly, too ill at ease to go until I'd heard. Now see what you think of what I heard. Mumbles sounded terribly upset, almost out of control I would say. States his file clerks made a big mistake. No Claire Dubois ever had an IFFY appointment. No Dubois works for them now. No Dubois under any true or cover name or alias has been sent by them anywhere. He has no record that she exists and it is, I quote, 'not my problem, period.' The impudent bastard told me if I didn't like it I could take it up with the IFFY Second who just returned to command, or to my Foreign Minister or the P.M. and let them knock on Washington doors. As he hung up on me I heard him screaming at someone. I will not repeat the language I overheard."

A perplexed group of friends. Quincy volunteered first, "Well, the *prima facie* rational account is that Hashimoto's question was to the point. Claire, as her very letter testifies, is off on a romantic jaunt to Paris. After all, we know that she never liked the Agency nor even government employment very much. We all know if she met a stupid enough employer, and the idiot you talked to fits the bill perfectly, she'd walk out. And so she did. She will be calling us all soon. Although, I do admit, it's all quite unclear and unClaire."

"It doesn't account for Mumbles," Quincy. "Not one bit. I know my civil servants world round, and this one was, well, 'going bonkers' is the word. Deep trouble in Network-land, Quincy, George, deep trouble—and somehow Claire is involved. Or," Sir Peter paused thoughtfully, "someone with her name. It's the file after all, isn't it? That's what set Network off. Let's assume we know Claire as we do. Let's even assume she is in Paris, which we safely can, for she says so. But her file is explosive. What the hell did she do to them? Or what was done in her name? Would you say these are reasonable questions?"

They would.

The secretary to the Ambassador to the Court of St. James, who was beautiful if one likes faces made of cold marble, witless but ever so well made-up, and vain with a challenging air of come-hither, was working overtime on orders and not liking it. She walked, if a mix of undulating allure and vague disdain can be called that, carrying a sealed envelope. "From the communications room, sir." She addressed Ambassador Dubois. "A telephone message for one of your guests, Dr. Adams." Her tone bordered on the impertinent, but then Dubois was, neither her ambassador nor, more to the point and unlike Mr. Mississippi, her after-hours lover. So these like all others, men, must undoubtedly lust after her. Insult, temptation and offhandedness were good for them, she believed, regardless of their rank. She handed the envelope to the ambassador, who had overlooked her charade entirely, then handed the message to his friend Quincy who, a divorced bachelor after all, had not. Quincy Adams' anger blossomed like a gasoline-fueled fire, but was suppressed.

Dr. Adams read, read again. His handsome face turned pale, the muscles taut over his already prominent New England cheekbones, patrician facial bones set above well-formed lips. He looked up, his shocked, eyes holding the others cold. "Hashimoto was found dead in the river, floating downstream from his boat. Heart attack is the initial verdict. No prior cardiac history. No sign of foul play. All in broad daylight but no witnesses."

Three friends, one a loving father, pondered it again. Foul play—and where was Claire?

12

Barbour knew but disliked Sofia. Not as bad as Moscow, or East Berlin before the thaw, but full of remembrances. Potholes. Trams jammed like Indian trains. Buildings unpainted. Parks in disrepair. The elevator in the U.S. Embassy, itself a tenement, broke down regularly. Surly, slovenly police sitting in closed circles on park benches. A sparkling-eyed new, young, and middle-aged elite dreaming of prosperity and democracy but having no idea, day to day, how to cooperate, plan, build legislation, communicate in trust and as teams. Not that there was enough investment money to power a tax system which might have worked as the engine for change.

In the meantime traffic police in front of the Justice Ministry stopped cars for shake-downs and people with any enemies at all were reluctant to put keys in their cars' ignition, for when that gelatinate explosive kicked in, one went up not forward, and in bloody shreds. St. Peter used micro-diameter mesh netting to collect your pieces.

Barbour had waited impatiently for the immigration line to shorten. Stone-faced officers who could read no language but their own or Russian spent long minutes inspecting foreign passports. Americans, Canadians, and Brits, having waited to reach the window, were waved back to a corner kiosk to pay a "visa" fee, tit for tat it was said, for visa charges these nations imposed on Bulgarian applicants. Official passports (Barbour chose not to show his) were exempt. The first time Barbour had paid his twenty dollars, handing her fifty—dollars were more in demand than the local lev—the woman had given him already yellowing, locally printed counterfeit bills in change. Welcome to Bulgaria.

"Welcome to Bulgaria, my friend." Vasil was waiting outside the customs exit door. He rushed forward to embrace Barbour about whom his father had known, shall we say professionally? and whom he had now met both in Cambridge at the symposia and here twice in Sofia. Their friendship had been immediate. Vasil—who well knew whom he worked for; what he did was a great joke between them—was one of the new democrats. If need be he would sacrifice his life at the barricades. Always, in these countries, the images of democracy at the barricades: shades of the Paris Commune, Prague Spring, Yeltsin in Moscow, the overthrow of Communism in Sofia in January 1997. "Christ," thought Barbour with some bitterness, "if only Americans could remember what the price of democracy, as opposed to TV sets, grass and fancy coiffeurs, was." Bulgaria was Thomas Paine's dream. Here people had actually been willing, in this century, to fight for the rights of man.

Barbour returned the bear hug, stood holding his young friend to check for wear and tear, joy, nutrition. The quality of a suit; shoes worn out or still presentable? the look in the eyes—sad but pretending better? Or in fact happy because good things actually were happening? In Sofia a look told a lot. Vasil looked sad and happy, poor but getting by, his shoes in fact newish; but predominant now was joy in seeing a friend who, by his presence, represented the West and better days, perhaps, to come.

They walked from the airport building to his car. Vasil mentioned he could hardly afford his creaking old Lada. "I don't drive it with the lights on because that runs down the battery...We can talk here but when you take cabs, mind what you say. Who knows, even now that we're a democracy, who is listening and what the next year will bring politically?" But always among friends it is the close things that are most important to know about. So they exchanged news of family, health, Barbour's failed loves and Vassili's glowing love for wife Natasha and three children. Somehow the recent weather always slipped in, as though in a reunion one was painting a backdrop for the events that took center stage. And repeatedly, because words always fail, the two men slapped one another on the arm, gripping hands again and again, saying, "How good it is to see you"—"How fine you look"—"I am so glad that you, I, am here"—Yes and again yes, and it was wonderful, truly so.

Most people who are poor or low in economic self-regard will, being embarrassed, not invite those who are wealthier to their house. Not so in Bulgaria; all the good people had been poor for a long time, and few could afford to go to restaurants. Now many bad guys and some good ones had presentable housing; but for true friendship, friends came to dinner at home, where raki and an extravaganza of home-cooked food replaced square footage as a basis for rating a good time. The rich of the world still have much to learn.

Vasil drove Barbour to his hotel, the Sofia across from Parliament, so he could check in. With two sets of in-laws, an out-of-work brother, a wife, and three kids in four rooms, he could not offer his friend a place to sleep, but dinner was damn sure ready. And a beaming wife Natasha and jumping bean kids for a welcome. The brother and in-laws had courteously disappeared. A family evening. They would talk about work at breakfast, at lunch, at dinner the next day. Barbour had entered the country prepared to offer, if challenged, a dubious, casual, daringly provocative cover. His work in Montreal had generated it: a salesman for small arms, a buyer for wholesale computer game programs. Bulgaria had been a piracy capital for the latter—raided and closed down, the government had said. But then so had said the Chinese with $100 billion in continuing piracy production ("ITP" for intellectual property and counterfeit Adidas, Hermes, Lanvin as that).

"What the hell, Vasil, I'm here to see you on my way to Vienna for work, some wild-goose chase. So while I'm here, if anyone bites, I'll see what I learn." In this last year Barbour had been learning a lot about small arms sales. Not as much publicity punch for IFFY as plutonium or missiles for Iran, but a good steady trade for small-time bad guys satisfied with a world-wide income of maybe a few hundred million, much more if you rightly counted automatic rifles as small arms. The boys were selling to "guerillas" in Sri Lanka, Chiapas, Congo, Sedan, Nagaland, Kashmir, "but Vasil, today's guerilla is tomorrow's triumphant democratic party. It's not quite all relative, but you can argue the case, and you may be right."

Vasil grinned. "I'm arguing the case for your having another raki and beer, one after the other like we do here; and less than six or eight means you don't even intend to celebrate."

More grins, more raki, a great deal of recollection of Vasil's father, who had been in the foreign directory of the Ministry when it was a near arm of the KGB, about how Barbour had once met him in Geneva, which had been a spooks' convention hall. He recalled that Dulles himself had served there. Barbour had tried to recruit Vasil's father, not seriously nor by any means unkindly, but Vassili Sr. had been loyal. A mistake, it turned out; Andropov when KGB head, Gorbachev serving loyally under him, had had Vassili Sr executed for no known reason other than Byzantine pique.

"I have hated Gorbachev ever since," Vasil affirmed angrily. "A saint, maybe for perestroika and all it led to, but a devil before he was a saint. He was one of those who had my father killed." Such experiences can determine the ideologies of sons. No wonder Vasil Jr. was a democrat.

More raki, more beer, more laughter and finally it was time to go home. Barbour remembered enough Russian, and a bit of German; the cab driver did his best, but delivered him nevertheless to spend the night in the wrong but, what the hell, Bulgaria Hotel. Barbour was too tired to fuss.

Lunch began the serious business, for at breakfast the fare—cheese, sweet rolls, dolma, meats, dreadful coffee—all seemed flavored with raki aldehydes, but thank goodness, not filtered through headache. Over a long lunch at the Crimea, at a remote table, Vasil had reviewed events, the palpable threat from Giorgi and Mustafa, the story of that secret Plovdiv weekend.

"I may need your help," Vasil was saying, "a quick visa from your Embassy and, forgive me for asking, enough money for me to fly to, say, London temporarily. I can't protect myself. In the Ministry one never knows who's still red, who's mafiya, who's opportunistic, who owns whom, and who Giorgi, or Mustafa might hire off the streets to kill me."

"I'll do my part. By tonight you'll have travellers' checks enough for London and a stay there. Come to me in America if need be, and I'll put in a word with the Embassy. The ambassador is a fabulous woman. For the rest, well, good and bad."

"I will give you something in return, Lee, right now. Something you can use in your work, something good for this country if you can find out where the money has gone. I believe about twelve billion dollars' worth."

"Wow, that *is* real money."

"It was our country's entire pension and health fund, plus all the agricultural export income from a few years ago. Plus, no doubt, sale of the doorknobs off the Parliament building by the worst among the reds. Understand many of them in that 92-96 government were quite decent—wrong, but decent. None of us yet knows who the senior thieves really were but for what I have heard in the office as Giorgi talks, or as he talks to Jeanette, the central files woman whom he pays for everything. For sure someone senior in the Finance Ministry; it has to be his equal in the Central Bank, I suspect likewise in the Prime Minister's office, but the only names I have are foreigners who attended the meeting I just told you about."

"You have your own bug in your own office and on his phone?" Barbour knew the drill and smiled.

Vasil nodded, "Sure. It's my business, simple tradecraft. And it's my country and its money, and me alive or dead. I have a family, Lee, all of these to support and protect.

Anyway I'd like to team with you on this one, no word to anyone here about my part please—not your ambassador, or the 'drugs and thugs' attaché, or anyone, okay?"

"Of course."

"I know you'll have to tell Washington Network something if you want to be diverted from whatever it is in Vienna, but I think twelve billion is worth it. Finger Giorgi, be my guest, and Mustafa, and Vanya no doubt. Warn your Western embassies that they are in the translated information resale business, industrial espionage in twelve tongues so to speak, but keep me out of it there too, okay?"

"Of course." Barbour had worked with vulnerable colleagues before, and informants, and had seen them die betrayed or caught out on their own home ground. The modern mafiyosa were far quicker on the trigger than the old spooks who, after all, had to clear everything through headquarters. He turned to his friend, held his arm reassuringly. "Let's figure on getting these bastards, okay?"

Vasil smiled. "Okay." He was a very brave man.

"Now who have you got at the umpteen-billion-dollar Plovdiv meeting?"

"I think it's a good make. Jeanette, the files chief, ran files for incoming bigwigs; their airport welcoming committee, bodyguards, limousines, the works, all for matches. About eight heavily laid-on trips in over six years, and the same crowd. The Finance man ordering them was always Mihailov; his wife's father was Traicho Kostov by the way, a red leader whom the reds, brothers to brother, executed first off. In 1949 they say one hundred thousand were sent to gulags. Killing him saved Traicho the trip. One of Todor Mihailov's regular guests was an Austrian listed as a banker, who used to be a good-times buddy of Giorgi. Brody is the name. Giorgi, for reasons too ugly to discuss, knows that Brody is also a European importer, and taster of the goods, of Bulgarian, Roumanian, Ukrainian girls, big and little—all slaves sold into prostitution. What a pair of bastards. He has a passport in the name of Westley Evangelov Frederich Brody. How does that moniker grab you?"

Vasil, who loved colloquial English, delighted in slang. Barbour couldn't bring himself to tell him that "moniker" was an AKA convict's name, even if romantically derived from (maybe) "monarch," as in king of thieves, or "monogram," and had gone out of parlance years ago. Barbour responded, "Well, if you're going to invent a name that works in five cultures and suggests as many different fathers, great." Barbour was excited. "Any other names to hook on the regular guests of Finance executive Mihailov?"

Vasil shook his head. "No, they really worked to keep the other ones anonymous. It was as though by listing 'Brody' it marked the event, the group, the VIP treatment. They came in by private jet, were met on the tarmac by a limo, never signed anything or had a passport stamp on the way through. But Jeanette found a note from Mihailov in the file on the occasion of the first visit in 1993. There were copies to Interior, Foreign Affairs, and Finance saying, "Mr. Brody's boss is to be shown every possible courtesy. No one is to inquire after his name. He is to be referred to as 'The Visitor.' English is his international language, so I order that the best English translators with the very highest clearances serve him while he is with us. Any offense to The Visitor, and the culprits will answer to me, and the gulag."

"That's it?"

"That's it, but for a note that could only have incidentally been put in the files. Giorgi's Jeanette is a file nut, the kind that saves rubber bands and paper clips even after they're broken. She read Giorgi the note filed under Finance Ministry VIP Visitors 1993. 'A tailor is to be at The Visitor's service. He wants made one of the brown tweed nomenklatura winter overcoats from the Slava mill.'" Vasil interjected, "As you know, we have always made lovely textiles. The Slava woolen mill is still first class. Anyway," Vasil was reading his note to himself, "'short and extra large in the arms and body. Extra large waist. Silk lining. Immediate tailoring. No mistakes. Tailor to be at the Ministry guest house at ten A.M.' So we have a short fat man as Mr. Very Important Visitor."

"Looks like that. And English *speaking*. Note it does not say he is English. Inference is, he's not. Fat, fancy tastes, private jet, speaks English and launders billions with his banker boy Brody. Tell me, were your reserves in dollars?"

"Had to be dollars to be. Levs were never worth a damn and couldn't be traded. Central Bank would have handled it. Probably credits in dollar accounts held in Switzerland against Central Bank gold. Bulgaria followed the Nazi lead in using the Swiss banks. We Bulgarians have been sweet on the German business for most of this century. And you tell me who wasn't sweet on the Swiss banks? And since Bulgaria has a strong German influence from way back to 1900, I'd guess it was a German-speaking bank to hold our dollar-converted or gold-backed government reserves. So I say Switzerland."

Barbour countered, "But Austria also speaks German. By the 1960s their banks were on solid footing. And unlike Switzerland, which even by the 1970s was worrying the worst of the baddies by negotiating an exchange-of-information treaty on criminal matters with the U.S., and however crooked the Swiss banks were and some still are, I think the Austrians by 1990 could be foreseen—by those with private bankers there willing to work the edge—as a safer haven for the big bad boy. They want an ever bigger piece of the six trillion dollars that the Basle Committee of BIS estimates is private money held very privately offshore. Tax free. No awkward questions about origins or intents. A private banker who knows something of what his criminal or despotic thieving client is about, who ignores the European Commission rules about due diligence, can make a heap of money. More risk for him, more charges to the client. In Europe, The Swiss, Austrian, and Luxembourgeois bankers still play the black game."

"And until recently, the majority of banks here in Bulgaria were doing it too. Cost us immense losses, including confidence. I wonder if the Fat Visitor was into that too?" Vasil mused.

But Barbour was concentrating on the case at hand. "With Finance Ministry, and Central Bank people working with him, all any of them would need was conniving. After all, the government kept the books."

Vasil said knowledgeably, "As many sets as convenient, and with no public access anyway, they could invent the figures—but for knowing what there was real to steal."

Barbour was still thinking about the porky man. "You know what? I bet The Fat Visitor speaks German. Better not to brag about it right after the war and no reason to use it much in big business, since English is the transactions language anyway."

"Do you suspect he's a native German?" asked Vasil.

"Somehow, no," responded Barbour, weighing the possibilities. "The Germans have been very clean since the war—politically, attitudinally, commercially. I think for a dirty money deal this big, for which you needed a Western-connected master-mind, you'd want a crooked tycoon, but one essentially without a country. A true international wheeler-dealer can't afford to have any national loyalties. Or pay taxes to anybody when he can help it. Wherever the action is, that's his home. No, I'll wager The Visitor is a real cosmopolitan. He can't be French because they're too stuck-up about their language to elect English for a meeting in Bulgaria, even if all that emphasis on English, just as the whores reported it, could well have been a cover, a pose so as not to reveal another nationality. The girls wouldn't have caught an accent. But The Visitor, to be facile, must have gone to a school where English was taught. And depending on his age during the war, that couldn't have been anywhere in Continental Europe. But he might have been a refugee kid in England, Canada, Switzerland, the U.S., South Africa, even India."

"You know more about that sort of thing than I do. Here in Bulgaria we were kept to being provincial."

"I'm only guessing, don't credit me with more. But I'm not guessing when

I tell you, Vasil, you have given us the gold key to the outer vault. You see the only damn name I have in Vienna on this, I thought it was some idiot snark hunt, was Brody. No initials. Now for me he's a whiff of the real big time, thanks to you. Some finks in Warsaw trying to save their ass rolled over on him, gave up his..." Barbour paused and switched verbal gears for kindness' sake, "gave up that moniker, obviously thinking he was nobody. Or at least they weren't bringing on big-time wrath. So the Warsaw lawyers hadn't made him as anything, which meant they didn't know anything about him but his name. I bet they ran across it accidentally, and fed it to IFFY as a sweet in a con game. I know damn well Network in Washington thinks he's nobody, but they're CYA, covering their ass, by sending me to check, me and some damn greenhorn woman with three days' experience in a Washington office."

Vasil was shocked. "Brody's Vienna is hardly a safe environment for any greenhorn woman, as you say, up against mafiya and their *avotoritet*, authority bosses. Vienna isn't Moscow, not a violent place, but like here you never know who's paying whom. Money buys a lot of harm."

Barbour nodded. A new and unpleasant wrinkle. "A girl like that, all sweet-sixteen and playing detective, might just call every Brody in the phone book asking, 'Are you a big crook?' I exaggerate; she's probably drinking café *schlag*, whipped cream all over her nose, watching the Lippizaner stallions do stunts, and wondering how to get tickets to the opera. Even so, if this job is as big as your information tells us, you and I both need a grown-up partner." Barbour pressed his lips. "So yeah, Vasil, you give us all a maybe way in, that's Brody, and right away Headquarters has given us the wrong way out, this amateur Dubois and a ready-made cockup."

"I wish I had something more for us to go on, but I don't. On the other hand, if you want a wild hunch—not on this at all, but just intuition, put this in your notes in case if anything else big and bad on money ever breaks in Sofia, and there are too many people whom I can't account for working in what I suspect has been a dirty bank anyway. As you know, with IMF and the World Bank in here, the obviously dirty is cleaned up. We're not like Poland with brass-plate banks, or Latvia with pass-throughs, but something funny is going on, I think."

"Sure, shoot." Barbour took out his notebook. "Can I write it down for future reference?"

"Lee, my friend, please, you have forgotten that we may still be what we were, may still become the past again in the future. What if you get hit by a car? What happens when they put it together? By now someone will have seen us together and made it an official record. No matter as long as we are a democracy, but tomorrow democracy may be gone, and that official entry will still be there, and maybe those people in that bank helping run things again." Vasil gestured a knife across his own throat.

Barbour blushed. He had been stupid. "I apologize. Each day I must learn my kindergarten lessons over. May I know the bank?"

"Ukrainian-Sofia Trust and Development Bank, UST&D. Rich, clean, new-built, pure on the outside. But our Central Bank inspection system is so new, with so few resources; and IMF can't help because UST&D is private. Who knows who really owns it, whatever the filing papers say? Who knows what they really do, whatever you can see going on in the regular offices and the lobby?" It is always the big question in Bulgaria: "Who knows?" But better that than the plaintive, helpless question—so Russian, still, echoing down from Lenin: 'What is to be done?'"

"Well, my question is, What is to be done about my taking you out to dinner? Does it still need to be our private business, or can I invite your wife, any friends you want to bring?" Both understood that Barbour must be the one to be host; no Bulgarian in the mid-public sector could afford restaurant hospitality.

"Yes, my wife of course. That's quite good of you. And what about you? When you were here last there was that clothes designer, Sonya. Lovely lady." Vasil paused. "I believe you were close?"

Barbour considered indeed it had been so. "But friend, as you know the moon rises, the moon falls, and so I have learned she's engaged. A friendship to be memorialized through Christmas cards. The fate of a divorced man terrified of remarriage. I have no one to invite for dinner." There was more sadness visible on his face than he would have wished. There are many ways a man can fail; the easiest is with women.

"Before I go back to the office I do have a serious question for you, my friend. You know how we Slavs like the philosophical ones. You were much younger than my father of course, but you were both in the same business in those cold war days; on different sides of course, and his was wrong. But Bulgarians don't get to choose what country rules them, ever. What my father did was still patriotic, never for or about money. And I know that must have been true for you too. Ideals, even wrong ideals, can be gripping, at least until you see they are totally false and cruel as Communism was for us. My father came to hate it, as you know, but it was an honorable hatred. Like I hope my own was and is. My father died, as you also know, watching all the Soviet bloc become free-market pirates. Bulgaria is on its way to that. It troubles me." Vasil hesitated.

"Go on," Barbour encouraged his friend.

"Well, right now my only business, embassy or anywhere else, is about money. Yours too—IFFY and all of it. No ideals anymore. No ideals even if we're the good guys. Old spies, young spies, cops, all of us, more and more we are in the money game, right side or wrong, but that's it. Grubby. We've been retrofitted to be practical. No ideals. No dreams. Wherever we are we play the police game, the intelligence game, the diplomatic one, all the same. All playing Monopoly: pass 'Go' and collect wealth and boredom. Tell you the truth, Lee, I don't think what we have on our minds is much different from Mihailov, Brody, or the Fat Man."

Barbour nodded slowly. He had never been able to get excited about big business, clean or dirty. Vasil was only partly right, but after all Vasil was twenty-five years his junior and not yet cynical. And he was being a narrow philosopher. Selling little girls, stealing the health and pension fund of a whole country, or having Crystal Man throw a knife at you was, in anybody's book, nasty stuff. He reminded Vasil of that. And Barbour began smiling again, a little of the felt grubbiness removed, his friend—the son of a man who in another day without those deadly red "ideals" could have been his friend as well, smiled again too.

"Now, about the dinner you're buying." Vasil could be in a good mood now for several reasons. "Shall I invite someone for you? My wife has some vivacious friends who would be delighted. Marrying an American is a great catch for a Bulgarian girl. So many want passports, Disneyland and Cadillacs. But yes, Natasha's friends also want democracy and it is here still, you and Thomas Paine, my friend, are quite right, a fine ideal."

Both men laughed. Natasha might well find an English-speaking friend without designs and committed to democracy. After all, they were fighting for it here. But, to be practical, as Vasil had said, since Barbour was leaving tomorrow Vasil's wife must be sure to warn his date it was unlikely there would be a Barbour or a Cadillac in her future. What *was* in Vasil's and Barbour's future was, on the other hand, not ascertainable. But that death stalked Vasil was certain.

13

He was, initially, the FAA's problem; that is, they had to write up the initial report. After being arrested *de facto* on an airplane, *de jure* under Federal law, he was physically transported from Dulles Airport to Linton Detention in Virgina to be held prior to mandatory hearing on attempted murder. A Federal public defender was apppointed, bond set at $250,000, and he was transferred back to the Linton facility until trial. Barbour had been cut by the thrown blade. Crystal Man was coming down from what was just that, a crystal methamphetamine high, with maybe some ecstasy (MDMA), plus a line or fifty of coke, mixed in. He had enough stuff in his pockets—pills, pellets, packets, crystals, ampules, envelopes, glass pipes, weed, red devils, and yellow jackets (no needles, was he health-conscious?), to supply all the freaks in sweet River City—or wherever.

Crystal Man was coming down, screaming all the way. His orange jail suit was decorated at the wrists and ankles with chains all the way. Being hustled out of any honored authority's presence all the way. A simple high-pitched refrain, "fuck you all," all the way.

Until he became thoughtful under interrogation, his public defender sick of him. That godawful stink was now improved but for the smell of his sweat, for the wardens had thrown him, not entirely delicately, into the basement "shower" not generally shown to visitors, where they'd washed him around the walls a few rounds with a fire hose. Jailers are scream-, insult-, and stink-aversive folks. Paternalistic, they know—like masters of boys' schools—that a cold shower will do a heap of good when spirits are either too high or unclean. Stinkie was thus cleanly burnished and only half unconscious when the fire hose finished with him. Not a mark on him but those glistening rosy abrasions. That was the trick—and not to let them drown. A time back Linton had a heck of a time explaining how an ever-so-well-washed inmate had drowned on his jail cell cot. Or at least was found there like that.

So, on Crystal Man, there were just some bright abrasions. "He musta fell." the guard wrote in the jail log. Lots of unruly lads in the Linton Detention Facility fell their first unruly days there before finding their way around. Like lots of boys, they soon became shower-aversive. Interrogation led nowhere. Fingerprints would lead to a name when the FBI could find time to plug in the cord on its computerized scanners. They were probably all too busy posing for the national cameras taking credit for some local police department's good work. Anybody who thinks that law enforcement works with speed on a crossed-jurisdiction, already jailed, no-crisis case has got another think coming. If it requires FBI help, unless the electricity is on, think slowly.

"Crystal Man," Barbour's name for him, was as good as any for the Feds and Linton; the file showed the IFinCIG interest and Barbour as their man. Crystal Man, clean and calm as any furious paranoid plotting murder could be, was now into abstractions. "He was a goddamned Arab terrorist and the FBI," distracted. He raged, then became "Shit, you fuckers stole my agent's badge, I'll hang your asses for that!" Crystal Man had put his hand in the it-ain't-there direction of the no pockets in an orange jail suit, gave an I-hate-you look to the detective, and another to his own lawyer lady. "Shit, you're one of them too. I can smell you all a mile away." That concluded his defense.

Pressed, he snarled, "I'm dry. Gimme something, you fuckers."

Three officers were present, a police detective doing the interrogation and two facility guards (screws), not because they enjoyed his company, but his violence was known and feared. The few times a woman public defender had been hit by a defendant, hell there was an attempted rape on one just last month here at Linton, it looked kinda bad. Not in the papers, it never got that far, but wardens are a pain and even a screw is sensitive to being suspended without pay. It spoke well for Linton that no screw was ever caught trying to rape a public defender in the facility. Inmates maybe, defenders no. They might think about it maybe, but get caught, never. All in all a fine, squared-away place. Anyway, when a cigarette was proposed by a guard to soothe and encourage him to speak, the defendant showed pique.

"Cigarette? What are you, a fuckin' fairy? You got to have some crack in here somewhere, I know you sell it. I know them Arab terrorists too. I know something, bet on it. They got plans."

The officers asked the public defender, pretty please, to excuse herself while they straightened the man out on his political correctness. The polite word to use when inadvisedly calling a maybe homophobe screw a "queer" or, as they say in the UK, a "poofter," was "gay." It was entirely improper that a defendant's lawyer would accede to such a request. She did so smiling. She would by this time happily have plea-bargained him up to Murder One With Special Circumstances, i.e., the death penalty.

When she returned, whatever her client had learned about politeness during her absence, he wasn't telling nobody. Seemed like he had a whole lot of trouble talking. "Speech impediment," one screw said. "Yeah," said the lady lawyer. "I'd say."

They all called it a day.

IFinCIG, represented by one "Doc" Dolan, with no friendly mien on the telephone, had insisted on their own interview with Crystal Man—"right now." That meant as soon as Dolan could get there, having arrived that morning at headquarters to learn, not easily, that his friend Barbour had been there and gone, heading toward Vienna to meet new agent Dubois on the Brody case, as it was now called. To Dolan, having been briefed by Jones but also by McLaughlin whom he did respect, the case seemed on its face to be insignificant. The cable transcript was garbled but for Brody and C, about whom not even allegations had been made. "Of interest perhaps," had been the exact language. The tipsters in Warsaw were unknown. The U.S. Embassy had no record except of the cable, not even a copy. IFFY's original Warsaw-Baltic team was on its own difficult assignment somewhere unreachable east or west of the Don, no doubt flowing unquietly uphill.

It had been Jones of course, no chief at all but a middle-level something, who had sent Dubois off, then sent Barbour orders to follow. Jones feared only one thing. If he didn't respond officially to Warsaw he might err. If he did send them off and nothing was there he had done his duty; Dubois and Barbour would have failed in theirs. Dolan had seen that immediately. It was almost as an afterthought that Jones mentioned to Dolan the attack on Lee Barbour on the D.C.-bound aircraft.

"Unrelated, my good man, absolutely unrelated. The assailant was drunk, or on drugs or something. Nothing to link him. Don't get into a stew about it."

"Let me see Barbour's report to you, *now*!"

Who was senior to whom was as uncertain as everything else in IFFY during these transitional days, but Dolan's tone was emphatically senior, whereas a calculating Jones had as many lies to give to his country as might be convenient.

"I think McLaughlin has it," replied Jones. McLaughlin was senior, having returned to post.

McLaughlin had heard nothing about it. He loathed Jones as much as

Dolan did. They learned that Jones had taken a few days off, nice weather and all that, just when Barbour had been in town. Barbour had hand-delivered his report of the airplane incident to Jones' desk. Jones, who at State had learned to mix martinis and to put work papers in the outbox unread, hadn't seen it until a few minutes before Dolan came in. Indeed, that reading had been an accident, unstated but obvious. Jones had wanted to change the date of his next official travel to Paris. The outbox held his instructions to the travel office down the hall in IFFY. What a surprise, he'd shuffled Barbour's report on top of it. When he heard Dolan was back in town he scanned it. And now all this silly fuss.

In fact, it was more than a fuss. McLaughlin told Personnel to file a "request for suspension" report on Jones. Most unusual. Almost nothing in government gets punished except initiative and originality.

It was when McLaughlin was in Personnel that the deputy there, having a great pile of paper on her desk as the excuse, but in fact tremulous because she realized the disaster could be blamed on Personnel, reluctantly handed the red-stamped URGENT AND SECRET, EYES ONLY letter from Hashimoto, Deputy Chief of all Civil Service, to H.G. McLaughlin, Acting H.Q. Chief, IFinCIG, etc.

McLaughlin read it twice, handed it to Dolan. "This is trouble—big as it gets. Doc, come talk to me about this (Dolan had some kind of doctorate; in government nobody cared much if or what). You know the Chief is on Travel. Obviously I'm Acting. The disaster is mine. If it's mine it's ours. You're the only sane and senior man here. So here, read it."

The letter read:

"You are advised that the agent hired by IFinCIG under the name of Claire Dubois has been identified (true name) Greta Liebowitz. Liebowitz is known to be a member of a Russian mafiya (Grivchenko Moscow-Kiev-Baltics) group, reputedly heavily staffed by former KGB people. She is believed to have been assigned to penetrate the CIA, where she was employed for eighteen months before resigning and seeking employment, on a favored-transfer basis, to IFinCIG. Liebowitz formerly ran a prostitute export business from the Eastern bloc before being promoted to finance. Intelligence estimates that she was groomed for IFinCIG by gaining CIA bona fides. As we know, financial crime is the major activity of many former Soviet officials. CIA is a secondary source these days for such information. Intelligence advises that her IFinCIG penetration was intended to place her in a position to provide intelligence to Grivchenko management (who are believed not to have any U.S. ties).

"Our records are not now on line and so do not indicate how long she has been on IFinCIG staff. IFinCIG Personnel may be presumed to have made serious, perhaps criminal, errors in not accessing our own Civil Service Intelligence Section data—as here cited—prior to clearing and hiring her. All responsible IFinCIG management may expect to be investigated for negligence. I myself will recommend FBI criminal investigation for collusion, possible conspiracy, and national security violations. YOU MAY EXPECT THAT FORMAL ACTION TO INITIATE SUSPENSIONS WILL BE FORTHCOMING.

"Under no circumstances is this EYES ONLY TOP NATIONAL SECURITY matter to go beyond IFinCIG management and the FBI or CIA personnel to be involved in the investigation. I repeat: Claire Dubois, whose last known authenticated employment was in a New York publishing house and whose present whereabouts is unknown, has never been a CIA or IFinCIG employee. Greta Liebowitz must be presumed to have photographed and transmitted to her employers all accessible IFinCIG files dealing with your Eastern European financial crime investigations. If she is on station have her arrested immediately. Our agency will be filing a formal complaint with the FBI today."

McLaughlin and Dolan were dumbfounded. However brave he was, McLaughlin would have been a lunatic not to be frightened. This was beyond the usual shark-tank politics of Washington. Hashimoto, whom he did not know personally but who was known to him by reputation, he received a Presidential award as civil servant of the year. He played no politics and pulled no punches—nor should he. McLaughlin, himself an honorable man, could find no fault with Hashimoto's response.

"Sweet Jesus." said McLaughlin. "And my horoscope today in the *Times* only said I would have 'surprising news.' Yeah."

Dolan asked if his friend and boss had ever met Greta Liebowitz, AKA Claire Dubois. "Never. Never heard of her. Where have I been? Where has *she* been? How long?" He picked up the phone to his secretary. "Get Smith from Personnel and Jones in here on the double."

"You ever meet her?" McLaughlin inquired of Dolan.

"No, I was here until about ten days ago but no one told me about her. Somewhere along the line I sent a cable to my old buddy Lee Barbour in Montreal, telling him, courtesy of that idiot Jones, that he was to head to Vienna. Yes, that was the first time I heard of her, his new assistant, Dubois, blessed be her name. I had a quickie liaison assignment in the Bahamas, a short trip to milk a banking snitch in Panama, back yesterday. The usual baddies there—Noriega never dies. Never met her...She's a new hire. At least that part's good news."

Jones and Ms. Smith arrived. Jones was tra-la-la, but Smith knew somone's nuts, or in her case ovaries, might fry.

McLaughlin was gang boss now. "You, Ms. Smith, what procedures did you follow when you hired Dubois?"

"Sir, I didn't hire her. Never met her. I think she was processed by—" she referred to some notes in her hand, making sure they were hidden, like cards in poker. And for good reason, since the paper was blank, "I see, sir, that she was processed by Evelyn Klein. Ms. Klein has left us since then, sir. Yes, she handled the entire processing."

McLaughlin, not new to government, gave her the fish eye.

Smith, intending to stay in government, gave him a "you can't catch me" stare right back. By the time anyone got to this, even if it were an hour from now, the whole matter would have Evelyn Klein's name on it. And what couldn't, wouldn't; that is, those papers would be "somewhere in those awful temporary paper file cabinets, sir." As for Klein, poor affirmative-action hire, she had been on board a month, and pregnant longer. She'd gone because her husband had gotten a job elsewhere. She would have no recollection of Dubois. But now that senior tits were in the ringer, what did that matter? Smith would defend Klein nobly. No criminal fault in being in Personnel only a month and not knowing what to do and then forgetting names. Not that Smith would forget Dubois, now, never. That little bitch. Hadn't trusted her in the first place. But she had full clearances, everything peachy in (all the) forms, all stamped "approved" by somebody. There was the Agency transmittal itself, and her father was an ambassador. She had her story ready for screening, it wasn't Personnel's fault that the Agency hired more Russian moles than it did people. They should have gardeners do Personnel screening; they'd be better at muckraking. Do their recruiting directly in Moscow, or Tel Aviv. A good line. Stick the other bastard. It would save her ass. Yes, the fix was going in.

Jones of course affirmed that he had suspected Dubois-Liebowitz all along. Not that he knew what she—he presumed with some certainty that she was in fact female—was suspected of. McLaughlin had simply referred to "an inadequate screening" and "negative information in her history." Okay, Jones would also be vague. "I sent her to Vienna because it was no case at all. Still, I couldn't be the one to decide that; after all, it was Warsaw that sent the information and you, sir," he looked pointedly at McLaughlin, now nominated as Culprit in Chief. "You, sir were away, there was no one officially Acting. I had no adverse information on Ms. Dubois-Liebowitz. Nor indeed do I now," he stared pointedly, "none at all. I exercised my responsibilities for the good of IFinCIG and the country, sir." Translated silently: "You were away, you fry for it. I just sit in my permanent civil-servant's chair. Worst case, I go back to State and fix martinis." Fix number two was solidly in.

McLaughlin realized a tight box had just been made for him. He did not like the fit. He was impolitic, crude, very un-PC in saying it: "You are both shits." He did not care that Ms. Smith might try to make a sex discrimination case of it, but, McLaughlin knew, she would try that ploy only if Personnel files could prove she was lying about her lack of knowledge about Dubois-Liebowitz. "You are," he said to Ms. Smith, "a particularly obnoxious bitch." These are not the words of which federal management promotions are made. But then some days even the best of us, and McLaughlin was one of those, are driven, when all else has failed, to honesty.

He sent them away, warning that no word of the fiasco was to get out. None. "Just tell the truth as we know it. If anyone asks, Claire Dubois has never and does not, work for IFFY."

That was the word that Ms. Smith delivered to the staff of the Personnel department people when she gathered them around her important self. "Dubois never worked here. There is no Dubois in, for, at, or around IFFY. A big mistake over names. Typos, misfilings, whatever. Got it?"

"But I—" began Mr. Swobo in confusion, mumbling as he always did.

"You *what*?" Ms. Smith turned on him with the fury she had dared not release on McLaughlin. "What, what, *what*?" she screamed.

Mumbles Swobo could barely get it out; she could barely make it out. "We had a call just a while ago from the Commander of Scotland Yard asking about Dubois. I looked in her file. Nothing wrong. Told him so. He told me to check travel documents, cash disbursements, that sort of thing. Very intent he was. Very commanding. And the secretary in the Director's Office had transferred him to me, telling me to cooperate."

Open-mouthed, Ms. Smith was more than a little panicked now. Scotland Yard already. How big was this Dubois thing going to get?

"*You let Scotland Yard tell you what do*?" The register was high, the volume was mighty, the face was twitching. Ms. Smith could see Pain coming. She knew Dubois: whatever had happened, hard to imagine, the government hired damn near anyone given these group rights, any high school diploma would do, a murderess maybe? Whatever Dubois had done, someone *must* have checked with Civil Service. But Smith was the supervisor. Someone would fry, and McLaughlin wanted it to be her. She had to get to the Dubois file. Klein was a short name. Any personnel supervisor who couldn't forge that couldn't last. It was practically in the job specs. What could be in that file?

"I said I'd call him back," mumbled Mumbles Swobo.

"Then you damn well call him back! Tell him there's no Dubois—not now, not ever, and *no*!"

That was when the call to Sir Peter in London was made. That was when Smith marched out of the room. That was when, Ms. Smith gone, Mr. Swobo lost his mumble. As he hung up on Sir Peter, to him high and mighty and certainly scary, the words Swobo screamed at the absent Ms. Smith's surprised even himself. And he had learned a lot of them during his little stay at San Quentin Prison, that bide-a-while-by-the-Bay. Even a mumbler can fake a history, see to switching prints, and get a good secure job in government.

"Big. Very big. But about what?" Dolan, street-wise, con-wise and otherwise not stupid, had no idea. Why not talk to yourself—who else in this business, besides Barbour and McLaughlin can you trust? By the time he reached Linton his agenda was clear. Barbour's assailant was going to sing.

Crystal Man was skinny, pale, still strung out. A little guy jittering. Bags under his eyes it would take a porter to carry. Crystal Man's body was shaking, his head ached, his mouth was dry, his intestines were twisting, his mind was switching on and off. The "on" switch meant the unmerry-go-round was whirling. He needed those downers. Now.

Dolan showed his badge, folded his arms, and leaned back in the wooden chair. He looked at Crystal Man across the wooden table in the barren room and said gently, "You tried to kill a Federal agent out of my agency. His report said you tried to swipe his papers. You obviously have an interest in his work, and maybe in his being dead. I have an interest in your work, and maybe in your being dead. Maybe soon. This is a nice quiet room. I am a nice quiet man. You are known to be very noisy. People outside will not be bothered no matter how noisy you get. Now, direct your noise constructively. Who hired you to do what to Mr. Barbour, and why?"

Crystal Man suppressed his usual "fuck you" greeting. When coming down hard off uppers and a mix of psychedelic whatevers plus grass, a man loses his confidence. "I need something, man, need it bad. Just one red devil, man, please. I got to warn you I don't know nothing about these terrorists. I lied earlier about that. But please, man, I'm going to shake apart."

Dolan considered the matter. He got up, went to the door, knocked, as it opened asked a guard for something, waited, got something from the guard, brought it in, showed it palm up. It had taken barely two minutes. Linton is a well-supplied facility. One cop to another, you do what works. Two red devils and two yellow jackets, enough to waste a normal brain for hours. Kill a baby, maybe. On Dolan's face was the inquiring negotiator's look: You scratch my back, I scratch yours.

"Here. Look. Barbiturates. No use our being enemies, because if we are I am going to beat you to a pulp. Now, talk to me sweetly. You keep thinking about these goodies. You can make it out of this room okay."

No contest for Crystal Man. He spilled. "I got me a little record here and there. Burglary mostly, with some drug beefs around and about. A few assaults—but only, you understand, in self-defense. I'm a little guy. People want to hurt you. When things are not going so well, no bread. I got to get other work. Legit nearly. I'm hip, Man. I advertise. *Bay Guardian*, Las Vegas Strip throw-aways. Chicago *Sun. Post-Dispatch*. Hell, I've gone national. I use the Personals."

"I just say," he recited it, 'Difficult sensitive assignments undertaken. Discretion Cheaper than a PI. No license to lose. Phone contact only.' I give an accommodation number. Phone booth in one or another flophouse, bar, or strip joint run by friends. Keep switching which one I use. Anybody shows up physically by the phone, he's had to trace it and my friend says I just stayed there a while and I've gone. He doesn't know me. I piece the friends off every time I get a job. Check it out, man, you'll see. I been doing it for years. Newspaper classifieds, hell, they'll print anything. Only once a curious prosecutor investigated—in San Francisco. Had to hand it to him, on the look-out like that. Conscientious."

"You use some big words," said Dolan. "Go to school somewhere once?"

Crystal Man was hesitant. "Yeah, I did."

"Blow it?"

"Yeah. My folks were schoolteachers. I wanted to be one too. But I got too involved with chemistry. Yeah, I blew it."

Dolan had, as good interviewers do—if and when the guy in the chair across is human—established a bond.

"I'm sorry about that," he told the shaker. "You can con me into putting a good word in for you if you give me what I want." A pause. Crystal Man nodded. "And so, the phone call?"

"And so my accommodation number this time is in Reno. My Reno friend calls me in San Francisco with this 702 prefix number to call. And the guy there gives me a 212 number to call. And he gives me an 011431 number to call, which costs me more money. And then I am told a patriot worries about an Arab terrorist on an airplane, gives me the flight and a description, says he is carrying plans to bomb the White House. Says it is my patriotic duty to see what the plans say. Or lift them. And for my trouble there's a round-trip plane ticket. They offer me a sliding scale. If I get the plans I get $4 K. If I get a look and remember something they like to hear, I get $2500. If I get zilch I keep the $750, free ride and Merry Christmas. Ticket up front, $750 up front, I mean a business-class ticket, man, that's thousands! Of course that's where the terrorist was sitting. Expressed me my ticket, with a New York postmark, to Reno and my friend expressed it to me in San Francisco. Gave me a good description. Recent, I could tell. Arab was wearing the suit they described. Man, I never got near that kind of class before. I dressed all up for that plane ride like some left-over Berkeley hippie." He paused. "Which I guess I am. Put on a hippie haute couture show, I did. Shit, the buyer has to be crazy rich to take a chance like that. But he's in luck, I'm an honest man. You see that, don't you?"

Dolan could see that in his own odd way, he was. Dolan, a softie, knew that when it was over he'd get nothing and give away the barbiturates. It was just going to work out like that.

"And so I take the job. How couldn't I? It's right up my line. When I get to Washington, to Dulles Airport, I'm to call a number and if I scored the paper I say 'A,' only a memorizing look I say 'B,' and if nothing I don't call. Man, those people are full of trust. Anyway I know the gig. Public phone at the other end. What they got is someone watching the phone with a little parabolic—picks it up, lets it dangle and he can hear what I say. Some cut-out paid like I am who knows nothing would meet me. And somebody nastier is watching him. Typical gig for careful clients."

"So?"

"So nothing. I saw one name on Mr. Barbour's paper, 'Brody' it was, then he made me, gave me a wrench and a knee in the groin that still hurts, and pissed me off. So I lost my temper and threw the blade at him. Maybe I was a little high, so what?" He paused, looked ashamed, and said defensively, "Bastard made me, hurt me, provoked me and now look where I am. 750 bucks, a trip to nowhere, no way I'm not going to serve time, and shit, Officer, will you please give me those downers?"

Doc Dolan gave him the pills. Whoever had set this one up was a very careful group: it had to be a group with all of those numbers, readers, watchers. Rich men. And women too, of course, like Greta. Warsaw, Moscow, Vienna, Washington; a New York area code; lots of people, lots of money, lots of very big worries on their part. Worried about IFFY, about Barbour, whoever knew about Vienna. Who told them? Liebowitz, of course. Well, she was the best guess. And so, there he was driving back to Washington, sorry he wasn't going to be in Vienna with his buddy Lee Barbour who, with a little luck—good or bad, depending on how careful he was—might find Greta or

Brody or Grivchenko…or all their friends including, the way things were going, Attila himself.

When Dolan got back to McLaughlin's office he learned that McLaughlin in some desperation, in order to learn what the hell the "intelligence" source was or pretended to be, had put in a call to Hashimoto. McLaughlin had been in Washington too long to be awed by a Boy Scout's word. It could be used to dignify nonsense or a schemer's planted items; or it could mask a "source" that was an astrologer, a Chitral shaman, or, contrariwise and most respected, a final weighty report from the Company's secret wise men, the National Board of Estimates itself. He had demanded to speak to Hashimoto himself. Hashimoto, an old hand, was certain not to have been relying on the silly sources, not for a memo like that. But McLaughlin had hoped to worm out of him which of the heavy sources had interested itself in IFFY's turf.

It could not be the FBI for sure, and the CIA was a lightweight; these days it was behind in most games. McLaughlin pondered it; there were simply no other agencies who were likely to be sources for Hashimoto's shocker. Interpol, however well run as a coordinating bureau, was in essence a big international filing cabinet. The DEA was good but they would not have played a secrecy game with IFFY, nor been a Civil Service clandestine source. They would have been on the horn yelling loudly about their find. And so who? Then McLaughlin hit on it. Somebody in Moscow had wanted to burn Liebowitz, and thus put the news out about a competitor of the Grivchenko group. McLaughlin's best guess was a manipulating source eastwards. But if so, how was it that Hashimoto had trusted them? Never, not unless a Western embassy in Moscow, maybe Kiev or the Baltics, had authenticated the report. Even so, how had they proven their bona fides whether via an unquestionable source or to Hashimoto's face? That was McLaughlin's question. It wasn't by postcard for sure. If not, a Western embassy authentication, it could have been an accidental find by IMF, World Bank, or a confidence-betraying snitch in one of the big international accounting firms with a Moscow client. The Big Five, the Five Sisters, that might be the right number now, all did bookkeeping in Eastern Europe. Big time. Weird books, with weird numbers in them.

It would take one of these to get Hashimoto's confidence. No fool, he would not go off half-cocked. But McLaughlin must know who was competing with, and might one day again be recruited for, IFFY's work. All that was in his mind while the Dubois-AKA-Liebowitz roof came tumbling down on IFFY.

"But what, just say remotely, what *if* Hashimoto had reacted too soon? Had been fed a line from a paper mill, what used to be called a 'black' source? Been played for a fool?" He was talking to himself out loud now. "Damn it," he slammed his fist on his desk, "I have to know what his source is!"

McLaughlin kept muttering to himself between threats, arguments and pleas as he fought his telephonic way through Civil Service walls of silence to reach Hashimoto, which was itself more than strange. The balloon was up over there as well. What kind of a day *was* this?

He plowed his way through assistants, deputy chiefs, a special public relations man, and finally a conversationally-inclined chief detective of the D.C. police who was smart enough to realize that any one as insistent as McLaughlin and as heavyweight on the Mall as McLaughlin, might have answers as well as questions. That was how the detective learned about the Liebowitz-Greta-alias-Dubois letter, a copy of which was nowhere to be found in the Dubois file on top of Hashimoto's desk nor, in his neat out basket. "That's really odd," he said to McLaughlin. The cop called in Hashimoto's distraught secretary, who knew nothing about the letter either. That *was*, he opined, "also odd."

The prominence of the Dubois file on Hashimoto's desk was naturally of interest to the police. In ascertaining why that was, indeed why a police investigator and not Hashimoto was sitting in his office chair, McLaughlin learned that Hashimoto had been found floating in the Potomac. He had immediately told Doc Dolan, solemnly, with suspicion, with further unease.

Too many other civil servants in possession of interesting knowledge, or strange careers, had gone for that particular dip for any old hand to buy the heart-attack story as a certainty. A "maybe," sure. But not this time. Not this story. And the chief detective sitting there by the phone in Hashimoto's office lent some credence to skepticism. And speculation.

"Blown away, no doubt."

"No doubt, but elegantly, expensively. I don't see Greta as we know her having that skill. Whorehouse accounting gone export and big-time, okay, but Hashimoto was fancy work."

"And behind it, muscle and plans."

"Or as we used to say in my old shop, Greta's recent shop, sometime back, 'Plans'."

"Someone besides you," Dolan was looking at McLaughlin, "must have wanted that intelligence source as well. Someone who fingered Greta, for instance—payback time."

"Or someone who knew the source and made sure Hashimoto wouldn't be around to discuss it. The other side doing damage control here, maybe."

"Maybe."

"Maybe" was where, thoroughly uneasy, they had to leave it.

14

Doc Dolan and "Mac" McLaughlin showed up at the IFFY building, "the barrio," as they called it, early next morning. They wanted to look through the Dubois file, had left a message with Smith at the end of the preceding day telling her to get it all together and leave it on McLaughlin's desk. He was so pissed at her he wasn't going to use names anymore. Maybe the tight box he was in would fit her better.

The file looked just fine. Greta was somewhere between better-than-okay-looking and maybe better than that. It was grainy shot without definition—poorer quality than expected in a 201. The file had been handled a lot for one so new, that much they did learn; she'd been hired two weeks ago, came on board a week later. Vienna orders authorized by Jones shipped her out after three days on duty, no training beyond a couple of seminars.

"Lousy photo. Odd."

"File's been handled a lot. Odd."

"Jones shipped her out as soon as she showed up, no training except what she learned at the Agency and knew from civilian life, that is, if she had been Dubois."

"And if Jones didn't know she was Liebowitz. But if Liebowitz was to get our files copied for Grivchenko and company, and if Jones was her sponsor—understand I only speculate—she'd want to stick around longer."

"Unless she already got everything she wanted out of the files, courtesy of our usual sloppy security, and it was time to say byebye."

"Yeah."

"And everything is so ship-shape. Even the Civil Service security check access is ship-shape, which Hashimoto said hadn't been done. Now that is also odd."

"Not like Hashimoto's shop."

"Not a bit."

"Weirder and weirder. Either Hashimoto or his shop made a mistake, or somebody's erased their computer access log so it looks like IFFY Personnel blew it."

"Which gets Smith off the hook."

"So do, to some extent, the processing signatures in here. All signed Klein. And no approval forms signed by Smith, which means Klein didn't bother to get routine sign off by her Supervisor Smith."

"Unless Smith pulled her signed approval form out of the file last night and shredded it. And, for that matter, put Klein's name on anything Smith herself may actually have signed."

"Yeah, that too. Do we go for questioned document authentication on that yet? Just in case? If she did it Smith is burned, even though Civil Service sign-off is in here. Ironic."

"Unless Smith faked the Civil Service access and sign-off, which would clear up the question of Hashimoto not knowing what was happening in his own system."

"Yeah, that makes sense. So we call the Bureau for document authentication on everything with Klein's name on it in the file."

"We'll look mean-spirited if Smith comes out clean."

"Yeah, but I am mean-spirited," McLaughlin meant it.

"What if, given the size of this mess, we ask the Bureau to check over the whole file? A guy has to wonder how Greta and the Grivchenko boys got her this far. Sooner or later the Bureau, the Agency, and Civil Service will have to work on that anyway."

"Right. Give the whole file to the Bureau, and they can take an extra look at that lousy photograph. Everyone will want some clear prints when the 'WANTED' bulletins go out, after the embarrassment is over."

"And Greta is back in Moscow."

"She is probably already there."

McLaughlin's secretary had activated the "urgent pick up" buzzer. McLaughlin picked up the phone. It was the DEA who obviously knew nothing of IFFY's problems, although by now everybody who could read a morning paper back page knew that Hashimoto had had "an apparent heart attack." The Washington press had a regular section for obits of senior Government officials. Dolan had read it on the way in on the Metro. The reports indicated no suspicion on the part of the police. Okay, the police were playing it cool.

"DEA are coming over. Want to talk to us about Mr. C out in California."

"I forgot about him. Or maybe the way this case is going, he'll turn out to be Mrs. B in Florida."

It is difficult to meet a DEA man a drug dealer likes, or a cop dislikes, or with whom an ambassador is comfortable. However rough-hewn and street smart they may be, the higher up you get in management the more diluted good stuff becomes. Added the lateral transfers from the Bureau, "gray suits," political appointees from state law enforcement—typically nephews of governors whom a President wants to please—and you get "silly suits." Or folks with what Greene called the "icy sliver of ambition in their hearts." The oppressed real agents on the street called them, with disdain, "suits."

In McLaughlin's office now was a real man from California DEA, and two "suits."

Suit Number One said, "We got the signal courtesy of you, Director McLaughlin, (who noted the flattery), relayed from your Warsaw people via the U.S. Embassy. We didn't get more than a name, a place, and a tie-in with some Austrian banker, which we further presume implies money laundering. But we are told that so far it is not an IFinCIG case. Is that all correct?"

McLaughlin nodded. He wore a suit, a good one in fact, but he would never be a "suit." "We do, however, have a senior agent on his way to Vienna now."

Both suits nodded their approval. "We came over for two reasons. One is that we generally know about big dealers in California, and the name, or alias, whatever it is, of 'Mr. C' doesn't mean much. Isn't that right, Alan?" He turned just a bit patronizingly to the less well-dressed, clearly subordinate man.

"That's right, sir. Assume statistically maybe five, six million Californians use a little dope now and then, mostly grass. Mostly younger folk. A lot of it is grown there; it brings income to the poorer northern counties. Kind of like Mexico, but white and richer. It is not our major priority. 'C' generally means cocaine although it can also refer to a C-note, a hundred-dollar bill, which is the major currency that dealers have around. Well, maybe half a million Californians have smoked crack not too long ago. I'm guessing, but I don't think that many are current. Anyway crack smokers are mostly black. My personal view is that blacks get a raw deal in the criminal justice system, which differentiates between smoking crack and white folks' powdered coke. There are proportionately more arrests for crack, more convictions, much higher penalties. The blacks are poorer, more exposed to arrest, and less well defended by public prosecutors when they're defended at all."

Alan, who was glossy black, was daring anyone in the room to take him on. No one did, certainly not his bosses, who were on their best behavior. As for

Dolan and McLaughlin, Alan was testing them. He had, as good street cops do, established right off who was who. Not whom. And Dolan knew he was, right, at least about cocaine law, right. Not a word between them yet, and they were already friends.

Suit Number One, schoolteacherish, "But I asked about our knowledge of Mr. C, Alan."

It was truth time. Alan turned to Suit Number One. In America, the first name and how it is used is what the "hmmmm" is to England, or "tu" and "Du" are on the Continent. "Yes, *Herman*," Alan replied. "I will answer you."

There was a pause that turned two suits to fury and, because here in official company they could not play boss to a black (who knew damn well what he was about) felt their cocks be seen to shrivel thereby. Dolan loved it.

Satisfied with the havoc, Alan went on, "We rely on a Stanford professor, who was actually once a narc like me, who did a big study. For every seven users there's a regular dealer, although income is stratified, fewer and fewer as you near the top. Truth is, we have no idea in hell who all is dealing." He smiled at we-know-it-all Herman. "But the big guys we do tend to know. And no little guy unless he's a runner carrying cash, is going to be known to anyone in Austria. Period. And so, *Herman*," he underlined, "we have maybe a thousand guys, and a few women, who are going to make the, say five hundred thousand or so year above expenses which is worth the cost of setting up laundering. We know almost all of those people. And until yesterday, when I got called here to Washington, I never heard of a pipeline between California and Austria, and nothing about any 'Mr. C.'"

McLaughlin—it was his turf—had the right to chair. Turning to Alan he asked, "Sir, I don't think I got your last name, but what miserably little we know says Mr. C operates in, perhaps out of, Malome. That town is famous as a murder capital with rates once higher than D.C.'s. But it's tiny; I read maybe 25,000 people. Surely if a big-time dealer were there in any shape or form the local police and your people would have heard of him?"

"Grossman, sir, my father was Jewish, that's my last name, Mr. McLaughlin." He smiled. "We *should* know, but it's vanity to say we do. But I'll tell you this, we will get something going. I've already telephoned to a detective there, someone you yourself might know, sir, since he was once with the Department of Justice, the old bureau of Narcotics and Dangerous Drugs and no doubt other agencies as well. Markowitz is his name, Stanley Markowitz. He's retired to the pleasures of simple violence there. I asked him if he would please get on to Mr. C."

Dolan interjected, happy at the thought, "I know Stanley. He's good friends with Lee Barbour who's the man on his way to Vienna right now. I think Lee visited him recently. They worked together here in D.C. before the good Lord saw fit to bring a Presidential plague on their and many other houses." Grossman and Dolan grinned at each other. McLaughlin wanted to grin too, but as ranking officer could not. The two suits clearly did not find the slur on a former President funny. They had worked for him. Hell, they had admired him.

Suit Number Two, a cold chill in his voice, was peremptory, "I told you we came here for *two* reasons. The inadequate information IFFY has supplied us on this case is one. The other, to which I regret you didn't take the time to attend, is that our office has been in cable contact with the U.S. Embassy in Warsaw about the firm of attorneys; Balinski, Konopnika and something, who were the original source of the information. Snitched on clients, I gather, in return for prosecutorial consideration." Suit Number Two, a tall and thin man, provided a theatrical pause which worked, for all were attentive.

"The building which housed the firm was destroyed by fire. 'Defective wiring, no arson' was the fire department's finding. Nevertheless, seven people are dead. These include Balinksi and Konopnika, who were the sources. Naturally their files were burned. A bit of bad luck, I'd say."

It was a silent room, some wondering about "luck."

Suit Number Two, pleased, went on, "When we received that news we naturally communicated with the U.S. Embassy in Vienna to see what kind of a line they could get on the other person identified by the Warsaw sources—Brody, a banker, no first name or address. The return cable is based on the embassy queries via their Vienna police and banking liaison, and oh yes, we've ordered DEA in Bonn/Berlin, which is covering Vienna right now, to get down there for a further look-see. In any event, the cable reads as follows:

"Anton Brody is the only Vienna Brody identified as in banking. He is well known, a politically respected private banker with many Eastern European clients and banking investments. He is politically active and influential. He is on the board of directors of many firms, including a major South African gold mining company. He has pioneered hydroponics for produce production in joint ventures with some major Middle Eastern players, and built a major fertilizer plant in Bulgaria as a joint venture with Rhein Chemish AG. A few of his Middle Eastern partners were reportedly 'innocently'—Suit paused here to give the paper in his hand the fisheye—"involved in BCCI."

Suit One stopped again to remind the others that BCCI referred to a world class international banking scandal run out of Pakistan, Saudi Arabia, and the

Gulf States but with lots of London, Washington and other western help. Washington bigwigs, including lawyers and Senators were implicated, then exonerated. No cop ever believes a "not guilty" finding is anything but a miscarriage of justice.

Suit Number Two went on reading: "Brody has been married and divorced four times; some of these were messy. His most recent wife is suing him, alleging he molested her two young daughters, his stepdaughters. The Austrian police, privately, do not put much credence in the charges. His bank, Brody AG but also Brody et Cie, for there is a Paris branch, has been contacted. There are corresponding banks over the world including, I might add, a small new bank in San Francisco." He paused. Cops like him draw conclusions about conspiracies from names being in the same phone book. "Anyway Mr. Brody, who travels widely on business, is abroad. His private secretary will not say where. There is no criminal action of any kind pending against him and so no pressure can be brought to bear.'"

It was Suit Number One's turn. His tone was acid. "Now, that's not much to go on, is it? It doesn't seem to us," Tweedle Dum's gesture included Tweedle Dee, "that short of something massive, Vienna is going to get you much, and Warsaw gets you only the ashes. Let the Poles sift them if they want to. We concentrate on California, Mr. C and the drug business, which is our business anyway."

McLaughlin ignored him, saying grimly, "'He that kindled the fire shall surely make restitution.'" Exodus 22:6."

"'Let them be cast into the fire; into deep pits, that they rise not up again.' Psalm 140: 10," intoned Grossman.

Dolan searched his memory. " 'The Lord will come with fire, and with his chariots like a whirlwind.'"

"Amen," said Grossman.

"Amen, brother," said Dolan; McLaughlin, nodding, repeated, "Amen."

The two suits were irritable and puzzled. Suit One asked, "What's with you people, a damned tent revival?"

What Suit Number One had disliked, of course, was the others' immediate fellowship; their intensity about vengeance; and their implicit rejection, indeed mockery, of what the Suits had said, and who they were. It would not be the first time that lifelong enemies and friends were made in the course of a management meeting.

McLaughlin, who had the rank and rancor, retorted, "First, even some policemen base the law on morality and the morality, forgive the lack of sophistication, even on religion. And second, you assholes don't tell this agency where we do our work." It was not McLaughlin's subtle week.

The Suits stared at him coldly. "Well, Mr. McLaughlin, we do decide where *we* work as well as what evangelical Alan is going to see to—and that is finding Mr. C out there in Schrecksville within the week. When we find him, we'll decide whether to let you or maybe the Bureau instead have anything we get on his European money laundering connection. Understood, Alan?"

They were trying to pull Grossman's plug. The street cop in him was outgunned by rank. He had no race card to play this round. He replied in a matter-of-fact manner.

"The town, sir, is called Malome, and if 'C' has never come to attention in all these years, it's going to take more than a week to find him. And as an outsider I sure as hell can't do it. You have to look at a town from the very deep inside to get to somebody as smart and invisible as Mr. C. As usual, the local cops are best placed. We assist, do undercover, provide buy money, and big guns later if needed. If we already have Markowitz on thc ground, we're all in luck. But he's going to have to get the leads, lean on people, turn them, get snitches. No snitch, no Mr. C. After that the hard work starts. Not a week, sir, no."

"We'll see, Alan—and we'll be evaluating your performance, be sure of that. Our office runs on results."

Grossman bit his lip to keep from saying, "If you two are the results, we're all in deep trouble." Which of course they were.

McLaughlin, who had intended to tell them obliquely required, of a possible tie-in between Brody and C and Hashimoto's death decided against it. These suits had no imaginations, nor could they be trusted. But then, seeing what was happening, not many people could be. He ushered them out of the office.

It was as he reflected on all this that McLaughlin suddenly glimpsed the startling possibility. "Doc, my ears had missed the possible double-entendre while that bloody DEA deputy director was reading the cable. 'Brody et Cie' could be 'Brody' and 'C.' Anybody along the way who was thinking of cocaine or hundred-dollar bills, and they are not always related, could have added the 'Mr.'"

Dolan was disgusted with himself. "What an idiot! I missed it. Of course."

"So, if not 'Mr. C,' then a Brody bank related, maybe laundry *company* in California."

"Yeah, could be."

"Yeah, anything in this case 'could be.'"

The two men parted, both with other work to do, agreeing to meet for lunch.

Later, over lunch, McLaughlin began. "I'm drafting a cable to Barbour for when he hits Vienna, with a copy via Sofia embassy if he hasn't left there yet, telling him our, or his, Dubois is Russian mafiya, Grivchenko financier, ex whore-in-chief *cum* penetrating mole cum deep embarrassment Greta Liebowitz, to look for and look out."

Doc looked quizzical. "That widens the loop. Remember Hashimoto's memo instructed us to keep it on a need-to-know, eyes-only, basis, and the like. I agree Barbour has got to know, but if there's blowback on the inevitable top-level investigation coming up, somebody looking for scalps is going to ask you why you widened the loop."

"Doc, you know I can't let Barbour believe his junior partner is loyal when she's in fact working for the other side. Whatever they learn as a team, Grivchenko's Moscow boys will get; and if that isn't protective intelligence for them, nothing is. If they're in any way aligned with whatever it is honest Brody is up to, they'll block us. Or use what we learn to get to a competitor's operation first, Moscow style, which is with AK-47s. At best she'll wreck our game, at worst put a shiv in Barbour on her way out. Doc, you're not really asking me to do that just to protect my ass?"

"Yes, I am asking you. For your sake. It's the Washington way. Won't be the first time a field man or an investigation has been sacrificed in a CYA move."

"I don't believe you can mean that, Doc. You're his friend."

"Oh no, I can't let him be played the fool. But you see, you got the memo; you're under the gun as Acting Director. Smith is covered; as Acting, you're not. So, we never had this conversation. Tear up the cable you're writing."

McLaughlin was shocked, getting angry; soon would *really* explode. Doc grinned at him. "Mac, I already sent a cable, Sofia and Vienna. Under my authorization, not yours. If the ship goes down over this, I drown before you."

McLaughlin, no sentimental man, bit his lip. "Doc, if anyone doesn't know the Washington game, it's you. God bless you."

15

Before he left Sofia, recollecting the fine dinner they had had, Barbour had splurged, taking Vasil, his wife Natasha, and his own date Neda to the Hotel Intercontinental for dinner. Dinner, with musicians playing and at U.S.-plus prices, added up to a two-month's salary for Vasil. This next morning he and Vasil had breakfast—again the Intercontinental. The Sofia Hotel breakfast, a bizarre effort, soggy rolls, appetizers left over from dinner, coffee mixed with lime, chicory, and sulfur—was always a disaster.

Vasil was serious. "Did you hear a boom in the night last night?"

Barbour thought about it and wasn't sure. Somewhere perhaps, through muffled walls and sleep, a boom. Any visitor to Sofia might hear the night so punctuated. Not often, but possible.

"Like a bomb?"

"Yes." Vasil was now very solemn. "I leave my car somewhere near my house, but change the plates fairly often. Like to think it would make it harder to ID, but that's silly, anybody following me knows. As you know it's an old car. No poor man drives a new one, nor even a rich man if he can't afford a twenty-four-hour guarded garage as well. The advantage of an old wreck of a car is that they're less interesting to thieves. One takes the windshield wipers into the house at night. One loses tires overnight of course, and engine parts if they pry the locked hood up, but that's just Sofia. If you have anything valuable you have to be rich enough to have someone with guns protect it. The rest of us, even if we have guns, just keep getting burglarized. But I'm wandering, my friend. The news is that last night some stupid thief tried to steal my car; that or the 'engineer' putting in the bomb in was careless. It blew up around two o'clock."

"My Lord!" Barbour was shocked. No phony tough-guy look, nor feeling. He remained in his heart an innocent, capable always of being surprised.

Vasil squeezed his friend's hand over the elegantly set breakfast table. "I never drive it to work, but had planned to take the family to my wife's mother in the country this weekend. We would have all died. You see there's no very good way to detect a small plastique under the car wired to the distributor from underneath, or at least not for me because I'm a rotten mechanic. I don't know which wires are to start the car, and which to end me. I had a colleague in our Central Service for Combatting Organized Crime who was on to something big in the mafiya, probably inside the Ministry as well. A good mechanic, he always pulled up the hood in the morning to inspect for new wires on the starter. Never found any. But one morning when he pulled up the hood, the bomb went off. They'd watched his routine. Bulgarians are fatalistic, Lee, can't help it, *bogomil* and Slavic, inward migration, Muslim Turks, Russian hopelessness à la Oblomovism. It kills us politically, it kills us personally; paralysis, not sloth. I will never bother to look for wires in my next car. Not that I can afford one. It's just that from now on my family stays in the apartment until I have started the some-day car." Vasil was depressed.

"Sweet Jesus," Barbour put a strong hand on his friend's arm. Sometimes strength as well as affection flows in this way.

"I'm going to the Alexander Nevski Cathedral now, dear friend, to thank God for my and my family's life. Come with me. You don't need to pray if that sort of thing bothers you. So many Anglo-Saxons are removed from religion. But I ask you to come anyway. I am a bit shaken. I need God and a friend. Maybe there you can thank God that you could buy me this expensive breakfast this morning instead of having to send more expensive funeral flowers. Okay?"

The Alexander Nevski Cathedral is Sofia's biggest. It is headquarters for the Metropolitan who, during the red and pink years, was alleged to be paid by the Communists in power. Red halos for any saints there. Hammer and sickle perched on top of the cross, or so it seemed. Many democrats go there only for the music. For worship they go to the "blue" cathedral some blocks away, one whose priests had refused money from the reds and were supported by the impoverished but idealistic congregation.

Vasil, nevertheless, wanted to pray in a place where, at ten A.M., the choir would be singing; singing, Barbour knew, those formidably beautiful Gregorian chants. Underneath the Nevski is also great beauty. In the vaulted crypt is a collection of exquisite ancient ikons, a museum both of art history and the living spirit. The Orthodox believe in the ikon as epiphany. Here, despite all the red payments, the history of priests fighting one another on the front steps over political matters, no one really questions that God is present, and listens to prayers.

Vasil lit tapers and prayed. Barbour, a prosaic and passion-free Protestant, also lit tapers and prayed. He was no less intense than Vasil in his thanks and implorings.

Afterwards, Vasil had to leave. "I must translate for German intelligence in their embassy. No doubt," he said cynically, "they are hiring some patriotic Bulgarian Air Force captain to help them penetrate those French commercial efforts which right now are trying to secure an air force contract with us for some special communication computers. I tell you this just in case you want to pass it along to your chap on Saborna Street, who is equally interested in that and the German proposal for a joint venture with the Dutch in a new pharmaceutical plant. You see how it goes? And of course you know *where* it goes." The exchange allowed them laughter, cynicism and a kind of evidence that Vasil valued his friendship more than his "grubby" work. He also knew that Barbour would not "pass it along." They held the same views.

"Spooks as business gooks," Barbour said.

"Grubby," repeated Vasil.

"If you find out anything more, and you need me, reach me at the Intercontinental or the American Embassy by note in Vienna. In a pinch, the embassy here, as you so very well know, has an overworked attaché who handles 'drugs and thugs,' and there is the CIA station chief whose local mission is economic crime. Whether the Agency talks to IFinCIG in Washington on any given day depends on the turf politics of the moment. They try hard, but there are no guarantees. A field man can send it in, but a desk man in Langley can make sure it stays dead. Like I said, no guarantees."

Vasil nodded. "None in life," and walked away.

It was ten A.M. and the ikon museum had opened, as had the shop next to it which sold wonderful replicas of old ikons made by modern artist copyists. This trip Barbour had just enough time to buy one, rush it to the cultural museum down the street to be stamped for export as modern not antique—Bulgaria and Russia both had lost much of their national treasures by KGB art smuggling abroad over the years—and to pick up his packed bags at his hotel one street away.

A gentle-featured older woman, French, the assistant who presided in this quiet gallery, diffidently offered in French to help him should he have questions. "Merci, Madame," he said. "*Vous etes le bienvenu*" came her courteous reply.

A middle-aged man came into the retail area from an administrative office. He smiled at Barbour and offered, in English, to handle the ikon payment and himself run down the street to get export approval. His sport coat was open. As he leaned over Barbour saw a shoulder holster, with what looked like a 38 automatic, secured under the armpit.

"Interesting, a museum director carrying a weapon."

"Oh yes, a necessity. We've had several robbery attempts over the last few months. By Bulgarian standards, we take in a lot of money."

"In God's house, in the Church museum, with ikons breathing the spirit of the saints, can robbers invade?" This one was new to Barbour, although his friend Markowitz had told him that in his ugly town of Malome ("mal homme" came to mind) a priest in the Catholic church, one known for distributing food and other charity, had been killed in his tumbledown rectory just for the Sunday service collection-box proceeds. Markowitz had told him, at their last meeting just a few weeks ago, that a strange young man deeply connected to local crime, whose name he said was "Rooster," had called him to finger the killer. "Most unusual," Markowitz had said. Whether Malome or Sofia, God and his people needed protection.

As Barbour handed over three hundred and fifty dollars in cash—almost no retail transactions in Sofia involve credit cards or checks—a distinctly non-artistic, non-tourist type sauntered into the ikon display. He was thin, dirty, with a ragged beard but wearing a beret that hinted at some self-image, nervous and yet an aggressive look. But no glance at all toward the gentle, elderly French gallery assistant; instead he looked insistently away from her.

Barbour could see it coming. So could the museum director. Barbour was unarmed. Both the others were armed. Beret eyed the cash on the desk: three hundred and fifty dollars was half a year's pay for a police inspector. He moved too slowly, too dramatically, if that was his intent, for his gun. Barbour ducked, and Beret was taken by surprise as the museum director took his weapon out and leveled. Beret fired anyway. The poorly aimed bullet went downward through the wood of the ikon of St. Clement that Barbour still held in his hand. The responding fire from the director went straight through Beret's, torso, and Beret crashed to the floor. The pale old woman sat on the floor in stunned silence. The museum director returned his weapon to the holster, looking with frightened concern at Barbour, now rising unhurt from his crouch. The bullet had splintered a hole through the palm of St. Clement of Ochridski, a copy of a 14th-century ikon. The Saint's palm, fourth finger touching the thumb, was directly in front of his heart. The color of one of the wood splinters was deep red, although the pigments were more burnt umber and ochre hues. It looked as if he were bleeding.

The bullet had missed Barbour's groin by scant inches.

"You are all right?" queried the director.

"Yeah," sighed Barbour, without pretending not to be badly shaken. "It's been a noisy day for the bad guys in Sofia." The director could not understand allusion.

The director inspected the damaged ikon. "It can be repaired," he said. He was staring at the red of the wood splinter from the area of the Saint's palm. "It does look like blood, doesn't it?"

"Yes."

"A kind of miracle, perhaps?"

"As with his Son, so with his Saint perhaps, God sheds His blood with us," murmured Barbour, surprising himself by sounding suspiciously reverent—he hoped not fatuously so.

"If you wish we will repair it for you; the artist who did it is quite competent, and it will be our gift to you. Can you return in a few days?"

"Not for a few weeks, perhaps a month, but yes, I would appreciate that. I'll come back for it. But do keep the red splinter where it is—unrepaired, obvious. Right now, and on any tomorrow, I'll be glad for more miracles. I think today I can count three."

The director looked up as a contingent of policemen, four patrolmen now in the first response wave, came in noisily. Their drawn automatics waving were theatrically, exuberantly dangerous. Their uniforms were shabby; none had his necktie neatly knotted; one was unshaven, another looked sick or terribly hung over. The director had no time to wonder to what the American Federal policeman—Barbour had shown him his badge—had been referring when talking about his "three miracles." Barbour suggested softly—his French was not elegant—to the elderly, bitterly sobbing assistant that she discontinue wiping the dead young man's forehead, though ever so loving was her touch, in order not to disturb the crime scene.

She looked at Barbour with immense and shaking sadness. God himself, and this was his house, would cry looking at this woman. She murmured, leaning close over the corpse, her hand on its hand, "Il est mon fils."

A day of miracles, of beauty, of God and of monstrously stupid tragedy. Barbour, after rather brusque and disinterested police questions translated by the director, gave his hotel as his address, but did not tell them he was checking out—they would have kept him pointlessly, almost ritually in Sofia, he knew—and went back upstairs to the cathedral, silent now but for the shuffle of a few worshippers. It was emptied of its glorious music and the earlier throng.

Barbour lit four tapers: for the son, the mother, for the director, to whom he knew the shock of having killed another would soon come, and in special thanks one for St. Clement Ochridski. A casual Protestant, he was again reflecting, can be moved to do surprising things, indeed they felt awesome, on a day like this.

The Austrian Airlines plane arrived, one time zone earlier, in a gloomy Vienna afternoon. He immediately took a cab to the Intercontinental where he had been advised by Dolan, in that early cable to Montreal, he was to meet his field trainee, partner, whatever they thought she was. He was broodingly angry, his emotional gyroscope out of whack after the morning's events. Overreaction perhaps, but he was by now furious that he would be babysitting an IFFY idiocy; not her, perhaps, she might be a fine person, but the very idea of sending out an untrained agent bothered him. Jones should be drawn and quartered and fed back to the State Department himself, martini pickled in cocktail-hour hors-d'oeuvres-sized-pieces.

It was, as in Sofia, an almost elegant hotel. The receptionist was gushingly welcoming. No, there was no Miss Dubois in the hotel, but she had left a message for him a few days ago. Summoning the porter to take him, and his two light bags to his room, the receptionist handed him two envelopes. One was in a woman's hand. The other was official, from the U.S. Embassy. Barbour opened the Embassy letter first.

He had no intention of stopping by the U.S. Embassy. "What the hell could they want; it could wait," he muttered. He was in a foul mood. Killings, attempted killings, weeping mothers of dead sons who came in to make their rebellious, insulting, deadly, post-adolescent, misery-ridden statement in mom's workplace, itself a church, made foul moods. In any event IFinCIG field agents, well, the ones with initiative, used embassies only as an intended speedy, post office. Or when they were in the old Eastern bloc and had a hankering for peanut butter or salsa, they used its commissary.

Once in his room, having washed and taken a diet cola from the wet bar, he opened the woman's letter, from Dubois of course. She had written in a strong but feminine, well-formed and graceful hand, with here and there a baroque scroll or an emphatic crossed T sweeping skyward at the end stroke of each sentence. A good hand; he liked it.

Dear Mr. Barbour,

Welcome. I look forward very much to meeting you, and working with you. I realize you can hardly have the same expectations of me, and I apologize for my raw recruit status. It is exciting for me I admit, but I am ill qualified to be much help. I will do whatever chores you can entrust to my hands. I don't know exactly when you are to arrive; no one told me when I left. But I promise to check with the concierge at my hotel, the Palais Schwarzenberg (I have stayed there with my parents, when with them as a girl, on their version of a chaperoned Boswell's tour for me) every morning and every afternoon for your arrival note. And I will make no plans for any lunch or dinner that cannot be cancelled so as to be with you, ever so dutifully, once you arrive.

I would, however, be very grateful if this coming weekend or the next, you could see your way to letting me pop over to London, for my father will be there briefly. I have written to him, though not about where I am. (Jones told me it was a dark secret, though I can't see how that can be, when my passport is in my true name and I check into hotels. I shall tell you later, regrettably, more of what I think of him. Sorry if that's undiplomatic, but might as well get things off to a truthful start.) (My, that is a long and dangling sentence, again, sorry.) But I wrote saying I would try, pending your permission and what our work requires, to get to London even if just overnight, while he is there. (I don't know if you know, but he is with our State Department in Kiev, which is awkward to get to and from.) He is my favorite father, i.e., I would really like to get to see him, for it's been a while.

Anyway I look forward to lunch with you today (if you arrive A.M., or dinner tonight if it's P.M.) and work as soon as you say we start. And where. And how.

Respectfully,
Claire Dubois.

"Well, well. Not what I gloomily expected, a set of very nice, open touches, that." Underplayed. He had been told her father was an ambassador, but she had been careful not to play the card. She had put it all in personal terms that delighted him. How fine she was, not a tightly-wound bureaucrat. And the final touch, "respectfully," setting a tone, like the rest of it, of modesty—no "we women are boss now" aggressiveness. Yes, he would look forward to dinner tonight and beginning work, even after Sofia, damned serious business. Perhaps she was in her hotel at the moment. Her being there, as the literate Boswell allusion to the grand tour, probably also told him she was rich. Ah well, a girl can't help a thing like that. Barbour liked women who dressed well, and money made that easier. Taste, style, courtesy come from the heart, perhaps to be embellished by education, but an adequate pocketbook allows appearances to become more like one's imagination thereof. Barbour smiled. The original line, profound and pessimistic, had been Thomas Hardy's but my, how thoughts of well-dressed women did alter it.

He rang the Schwarzenberg.

Yes, Miss Dubois was registered. No, her room did not answer. A bit indiscreet for a concierge to intervene in the receptionist's formal response, but André of the Schwarzenberg, like the famous Victor had been at the Ritz, does homework on his clients and is sensitive to their needs. In this instance, however, André was uneasily balanced between discretion and growing concern. On the telephoniste's signal Barbour's picked up the phone.

"Excuse me, sir. This is André, the concierge. Are you a friend of Miss Dubois?"

No, he was not, but he had just arrived from America and would like to reach her as soon as possible. Her note to him had said she would be available to meet with him on a matter of mutual interest today.

"She has not been in," he hesitated; yes he would allow a further tear in the cloak of aloofness, "are you sure, sir, that she was expecting you today?"

"She has been expecting me over the last several days. We are to be working together. Her note to me at my hotel advises me she awaits my arrival."

"Ah, well, yes of course. Sir, may I be so impolite as to ask your name?"

It was unusual but not necessarily impolite, particularly if she had left a message for him with Andre. "I'm Mr. Lee Barbour of Washington, D.C. Has she left a message for me today?"

"No, not exactly. Again I conduct myself quite incorrectly, in terms of form, sir, but would you be able to come over here at your convenience?"

"Yes, of course. Is there something wrong?"

"That is just it, Herr Barbour. I, we are a bit, well, let me say, confused. I would be grateful if you could come over. It may prove helpful if I could get your opinion on a matter."

He would be there right away. And while telling the taxi driver, "Vite, s'il vous plaît, schnell bitte," he found himself feeling very uneasy indeed. In the cab he opened the Embassy note. From the secretary to the Commercial Attaché. "Agent Barbour. We have two sealed cables awaiting you. Pick them up as soon as you can."

What the hell was it about the small fry in State that made them incapable of saying "please" or "at your convenience" to people unimportant in their power hierarchy? Barbour was annoyed, feeling tired, in Sofia it had been an eventful day. He was no longer that young. A couple of emotional murder situations tired him out. So did any airplane journey out of Sofia with its pointless exit forms and hostile customs, emmigration stares, its departure lounge, with hard chairs all the charm of a cinder-block latrine. Yes he was beat. And worried. The U. S. Embassy could wait.

The Schwarzenberg was most surely not "commercial." Andre was surely most welcoming, indeed inviting him to retire to a paneled room off the lobby, for this was, "I hope you will understand, Herr Barbour, possibly a delicate matter. A drink, Herr Barbour, or some coffee, tea?"

Barbour looked at his watch; 4:30 P.M. He would have tea. It was brought shortly, an elegant service as expected. André was, for a man whose life's work it was to handle delicate matters, clearly not at ease for all his finery of tails, dark red velvet vest, striped trousers, perfect hair style, shoes shined to brilliance.

"Herr Barbour, again I apologize for being so rude, but would you be so kind, sir, as to show me some identification? A terrible intrusion, sir, I realize. But I emphasize the delicacy here."

Barbour showed him a black official U.S. passport. This was no secret mission, and indeed IFFY had none. He was more than willing to hand to André his IFinCIG Senior Agent ID. André was much relieved.

"Now, what's going on?" Barbour asked.

"Miss Dubois had reserved with us. Her parents have stayed with us from time to time. Do you know Ambassador Dubois?" No, Barbour did not. "A distinguished diplomat, most certainly. We looked forward to extending every courtesy to Miss Dubois. Our records show she was with us with her parents some years ago, when she was perhaps of college age. Yes, a refined family to be sure. She arrived around noon a few days ago. We made every effort to assure her comfort; one of our better rooms, flowers, a fine Mosel, fruit, a note from the manager, the things an hotel does for its respected guests. She dined with us for luncheon, an endive, walnut and orange salad, our trout specialty, a bright Heuringer, that Austrian spring wine—perfect for one just arrived having a light lunch, attentive to our local wines. Miss Dubois knows her palate. And, a rather resplendent dessert, ah we are proud of those, coffee and an open sauterne, an 83 Barsac. All, well but for the large Sachertorte, the pastry cook was instructed to be generous as to size, all fitting for a tired traveller."

Barbour was becoming impatient, and more worried, but Andre's story would flow in the time it must.

"Yes, you are right. I see what you are thinking, and yes, we reviewed carefully her order lest something there might have displeased. But no, the waiters say she was in a fine mood, tired of course, but very courteous, and she ate all of the Sachertorte, finished her wine, retired to her room. There is some uncertainty about when she went out; we have a new clerk who may not prove to be up to our standard, he recalls only that she checked for messages." Andre was frowning, pressing his lips together. "The best estimate is that she went out at about 4:30. She had rested and bathed, the chambermaids who prepare the rooms for retiring do remember that. Her suitcases were unpacked, her clothes are hanging in her closet. She made no phone calls but to the telephoniste asking if she had any messages. She was obviously expecting someone. That, Herr Barbour, is why we hoped you might shed some light on the mystery, indeed our concern, for she is after all a young woman in I hope romantic Vienna, and she is very pretty, as you know."

"I've never met her. But what, please, is the mystery?" Barbour in fact had little doubt, but hoped strongly to be wrong. These people had been as meticulous as the police in checking the record.

"She has never returned, Herr Barbour. In an hotel such as this, one does not intrude, one does not ask, one knows one's guests have lives to lead. She is young, indeed lovely if pneumatic; perhaps she was here to meet a young man, we thought. But still, not to return for a change of clothes? No, that *does not happen*. We did discreetly inquire as to pedestrian accidents, even hospitalizations. Nothing. And so you see, Herr Barbour, might you know anything to relieve our concerns?"

"Hardly. André, I appreciate your excellence in this. Since she was to meet me immediately upon whatever day I arrived, I regret my plans were not quite firm, nor could I communicate with her. She was to wait here for me, for we do have some joint business. Obviously something quite unfortunate has occurred. I have no idea what."

That was not quite so, after what Barbour had learned in Sofia. Brody, the fat man, the Finance officials, the sale of little girls, and twelve billion dollars missing, all seemed to point to Vienna. As exclamation point, the attempted murder of Vasil. That was easily attributable to Giorgi and Mustafa protecting one of their crooked enterprises, one of which was trying to get a piece of the twelve billion dollars. Carrion hunting carrion. Business propositions back and forth, as blackmail and extortion may be called. Until one side or another became really annoyed. While less immediately relevant to Claire Dubois's disappearance, the bombing attempt did tell one about how this bunch conducted business.

"It is probably necessary to call the police," said Andre unhappily.

"Yes, I think so. But before you do, would you please wait until I make a telephone call? There was some mail for me at the American Embassy. It is conceivable that Miss Dubois had to leave urgently and someone is sending me a cable to say that." It was a long shot, but now those two cables might be important. Andre handed him the telephone in the simple but luxurious private reception room. "Shall I dial for you?"

Yes, a first-class concierge would know all the embassy numbers, the airlines, the call girls, and so on. "Please."

The voice mail in English and German announced the Embassy was closed. If an emergency, a number to call was given. Barbour gave it to André. André dialed, redialed. "The duty officer's announcement says to leave a message and he will return the call."

"Give me the telephone, please." Barbour had had it. "Vienna duty officer. Get your ass in gear. This is IFinCIG Senior Agent Barbour just arrived in Vienna. I have two sealed cables waiting for me there. We, and I mean *you* as well as me and some important other people, have big troubles. Big ones. Leave a message with André, the concierge at the Palais Schwartzenberg, as soon as you pick this up. Put the cables, sealed I said, in the hands of the marine guard. Tell him I will come by to pick them up sometime this evening. The cables may bear on our problem. And no, it won't wait until morning and yes, I will show the marine guard my ID, and I will sign for them, and my hotel is the Intercontinental. Sometime late this evening you can reach me there if I am not here at the Schwartzenburg. Oh yes—tell the guard to check all of your incoming no-pass guest signatures over the last four days. Look for Claire Dubois, and yes, that *is* the Ambassador's daughter and an IFinCIG agent due now in Vienna. Let me know exactly when she signed in and with whom she met in the Embassy. Thank you very much." Barbour's infuriated tone was hardly that thankful.

"André, have you interviewed any of your staff, doormen for example, to see if they have a recollection of Miss Dubois—obviously they would have to be given a description—getting into a cab, being picked up by a car? Or the telephone reception, do they have any record or memory of her getting any calls?"

"No, Herr Barbour. Until now and your confirmation of our concern, that would have been precipitous. Even the very best of staff, given some idea that a problem, possibly a scandal has occurred, cannot be entirely trusted to keep it to themselves. The newspapers, Herr Barbour, pay for news about our guests, and there will always be a delinquent in service who, if the bribe is large enough, will report irregularities. For us to indicate that Miss Dubois is in fact missing—well, her father is important; one would not now rule out kidnapping, as you certainly must yourself be thinking. But if we are wrong, if there is some indelicacy only, Miss Dubois suffers. Her parents would hear of this should the press hear of it, and it would be very bad publicity for an hotel which is not known for scandal, invading privacy, or insofar as we can, allowing any indignities upon our honored guests."

Barbour could have no quarrel with any of it. "Would you mind introducing me as, say, her 'friend' who has just come from America hoping to meet her, that is sufficiently vague and romantic, so I may ask the clerks, doormen and so forth? You could ask them to cooperate, reminding them—switch to German so they will think you are telling them the real situation—that affairs of the heart don't always go smoothly, but the hotel has no objection to my inquiries. And of course I will give them a tip."

"I will do that, yes. Happily. No tip is necessary, Herr Barbour."

"In Austria, André, a tip and a wink, in an affair of the heart, are always necessary."

André was relieved that Herr Barbour understood both discretion and reality.

"If my Embassy mail sheds no light on her disappearance, I will call in the police. I must do that. But the hotel is protected, for it is my decision as her, well, either colleague or employer, and not yours. Yes?"

Yes, indeed. "We are very grateful for your understanding and assistance. Wouldn't you be our guest for your stay in Vienna?" André paused, "For however long that might be? This is, was, her hotel. She will expect you here. She will return here. You can leave messages for anyone at the Intercontintental. Please, Herr Barbour, and you can assist us should difficult matters arise with respect to publicity."

Barbour sighed. They were already figuring her dead and how to spin the news. But yes, it was a generous as well as helpful offer. He would move here in the morning. Nor was it painful that the good life in Vienna, as here represented, was a good deal better than the commercial one.

Sometimes luck happens. The duty doorman this afternoon had had the same shift a few days ago when Claire had gone out that afternoon. The man himself resplendent in gold and black and braid, could understand Barbour's pursuit. "A very lovely woman. One notices such women."

"I leave my post at five P.M.. I get here at seven A.M. for the day shift. I change and walk to the tram. I see our guest in front of Bally Shoes. She is talking to two well-dressed gentlemen who were driving—well, at the moment, standing beside—a luxurious Mercedes. A 600 V12, black. This year's model. I admire good cars, you see. That model is the best car in the world. A beautiful woman talking to welldressed young men in downtown Vienna is not so special. They assist her into their car. She must know them. I am sure of that, for I assure you there was no disagreeableness. Maybe a spoiled woman; two, three rich men; a woman who appreciates what a 600 V12 represents, and is," he smirked, "probably willing to please to be close to that much wealth."

The insulting, foul-thinking bastard. But what he had said confirmed Barbour's worst fears. A snatch in broad daylight. Cool hoods, and no doubt a gun in her back. "Was there any identification on the car you remember, or anything special about the men?"

"I was not interested. It was not my business." His face contradicted the statement.

Barbour took the cue, handed the doorman another twenty dollars worth of schillings. "Please, make it your business now." The doorman smiled in derision, a beggar daring to jeer his patron because the patron was in need. "I know it was a private vehicle because it had private license plates. I don't remember numbers; I am not," said scornfully, "an arithmetic teacher, but it seemed a local plate, surely Austrian; I think Vienna. There was also another man in the back seat of the car. I saw a head. I think he wore a hat—I would expect a Homburg—and was smoking a cigar. That's the way men who own such cars go about."

"Nothing else?" Barbour held out another 260 schillings in his hand, but did not give it to the man. Let this needling son of a bitch sing and reach for it.

"Well, perhaps. It depends. You see my father was a *gantier*, *Handschumacher*, glove maker. Only the very best in gloves. I was walking by quite closely; actually, I could hear the men speaking very softly to her. I didn't hear the woman speak. One of the men was wearing very expensive gray kid gloves, with an unusual sewn design, a floret, on the back. Doeskin. Light gray doeskin. I noticed that. The two men on the sidewalk were foreigners."

"Foreigners?"

"Of course." The doorman was arrogantly confident. "In Vienna we have millions of tourists. At the hotel we get the most discriminating, of course. I know as I open a limousine door for a guest, before they speak, what is his nationality. For a Frenchman I can tell a Parisian from a Marseillais; for Americans whether they are Texas or New York. Clothes, mannerism, and speech certainly. I'm quite good at it. These men, I heard them faintly. The Schwartzenburg these days gets a rich Russian trade. Their politicians go to the Imperial on the Ringstrasse. None of them are high class. New rich. Rude. I despise them even as they tip too much, bad-mannered fools. These men with the American woman had those high cheekbones, Mongols. You know everything East of Silesia is Asia. These men were Russians, or very close."

Barbour gave him his schillings. "A few more questions, please. Could this have been a rental car?"

The man shook his head. "We rent the best cars available for our guests, but a Mercedes 600 V12 isn't available for rental. That is absolutely certain."

"Is there any special district in Vienna where very rich Russians might live? Something with expensive houses to show off?"

"One never knows tastes. There are a number of mafiya who have bought property here, usually flamboyant big houses, old palaces if they can get them. But they have no taste and the sellers make fools of them. Sell them fancy old barns without good heating, old plumbing, outdated kitchens no civilized European would have. These Russians don't know the difference. After all that's what they grew up with. Outhouses. Pigs really. Rich pigs." Barbour realized the old Austrian habit of denigrating stereotypes was in play. A bad character this one, but good now that he was speaking naturally.

"You said 'mafiya.' Do you really believe these fellows were mafiya? I don't mean just the word one uses for any Russian businessman these days."

"You're wrong. Every Russian who has come here rich, who still works in the East and keeps a house and a few women here, is mafiya. The old Russian nobility used to live here after the Revolution. Their children are poor unless someone marries them for a dead title. Or they marry some hemophiliac Hapsburg who's made good in business. All stupid. No, I'm certain they were mafiya. There are no other kind here with those cars, those clothes, a kind of peasant uneasiness at being here in civilization." The doorman was enjoying his impudence. "That lovely woman André tells me you are in love with? You will have to be very rich to compete. After all, she went with them. She did not wait here for you."

Insolence, effrontery, but Barbour had to let it pass. The doorman was too big for his boots and Barbour knew it because of the allusion to the overtipping. His own secured, the doorman now felt he could afford to be contemptuous, test the situation's limits. Barbour remembered there were more Nazis per capita here in Austria than in Germany during Hitler's era. This fellow would have loved it then. Barbour kept cool for the last question.

"Where in Vienna would a man with a taste for expensive gloves like those you saw go to buy them? And are they only made here or are they, say Parisian, Italian?"

"Ah, you might do well to buy yourself a pair; perhaps then your young lady might look at you, but then again..." It was the nastiest sort of sneer.

It took considerable control for Barbour to let that pass. "And so, where do I buy just that pair of gloves?"

"Your first trip to Vienna obviously," the doorman nodded disdainfully, generating the vision of one more peasant riding into town on a cart sucking a straw. "You buy them at Knize. My father's company sells only to them. Even these Mongols know enough to buy them here. The shop is at #1 Gaben, in the Inner Ring."

"Thank you, you've been a big help." There was no point in ending it otherwise until the man asked, "Mein Herr, you have only given me a small tip for such valuable information. Are you that poor?"

He saw only Barbour's back as Barbour reentered the hotel, strode up to the magnificently attired André at the concierge's great mahogany and marble desk, and allowed himself a small explosion. "Your doorman was very helpful but for too large a price. And exceedingly, intolerably rude. If you ever think of firing him, please don't hesitate."

André, quick at cost/benefit analyses and guest assessment, well understood that the hotel would be relying rather more on Barbour to prevent a public scandal than on the doorman, about whom complaints had already been made for his ethnically-tinged insolence. It was also the case that while the feelings that this master concierge displayed so fully in the lobby—solicitude outrage, fawning, mastery, satisfaction over a guest's pleasure—were theatrical, André in this instance felt genuine gratitude for the American's reassuring presence, and his in fact likeability. A five-star hotel concierge in Austria who even for a moment gives up the ingratiating, dramatic fraud is a better man than expected. Barbour had not even thought about the constellation. He rather liked André.

"Consider it done, Herr Barbour. Consider it done. And we thank you for your intervention."

Maybe the day which had gone so very badly so far in Vienna, with the ugly news that Claire had been kidnapped at gunpoint by mafiya—for he had no doubt the doorman had pegged them right—would get better. Getting the doorman fired was a step in the right direction. Getting to work on finding Claire was the real right direction. Barbour no longer harbored hope the

Embassy mail would be relevant. And he had best get there, wherever it was, fast. Even so it was too late to introduce himself to the police detective "Untersuchens Bureau" head with whom this rescue must be done. IFFY would routinely have advised the police, and indeed the Foreign Ministry, of his and Claire's pending arrival, asking for routine police and Finance authority's cooperation. That was not always easy to come by in a financial crime investigation. But a kidnapping? The locals would be on it like gangbusters.

He knew what they must do on the morrow: run all the Mercedes 600s in their vehicle registry, every address and name. One could not be sure it would show anything Russian. Indeed it was unlikely, since no doubt for laundered money, straw men and phony companies would be their fronts. Check for property taxes in the wealthier neighborhoods to see if house ownership matched names on the Mercedes 600s. Run all immigration, visa, police foreign residence permit information on Russians. Again, hope for matches. Hope for police willingness to share, without the usual secretive fuss and legalities, what their organized crime and ethnic crimes bureaus knew about Russian bad guys in Vienna. Again, cross-match names or, if they had an intelligence software program, bust out all of the business and social networks, chains of acquaintance and finance. With real luck, the car and the trio, gloves and Homburg hat *et al.,* might already be under investigation. That depended on more than luck, for with that much money involved, the risk of the fix being in was always high. A well-connected banker, a police executive with lax morals and extravagant tastes—the Western countries were by no means immune to greed bugs, corruption virus, and power above the law. In the meantime, whatever the local scene, his second stop in the morning would be working out the labor, with utter discretion from the police, for kidnappers anywhere are good at killing captives. Item numero uno was a visit to Knize to inquire about a Russian customer who might have purchased expensive, rosette-embroidered gray doeskin gloves.

There was not much else Barbour could do now. André was off his 10 to 6 shift. He had arranged that Barbour could check Claire's room, just in case she had made a note of anything which might prove useful. He insisted he be accompanied by an assistant manager. Barbour was ill at ease violating the privacy of this young woman who had come so enthusiastically, as her letter reminded him, to work with him. Damn that fool Jones for exposing a novice to such danger.

He looked about the room, found expensive clothes in very good taste, some extravagant hats which surprised him because women these days rarely wore them—hers were dramatic—purses all empty, a briefcase waiting for work, now empty but for letters with return postage in Scotland and, via State, the U.S. Embassy in Kiev. These would be personal. He could not bring himself to snoop through them. Nothing special amongst the toiletries but a half-empty bottle of ibuprofen. He guessed she had headaches or painful menstrual periods. There were also some diazepam, perhaps she had trouble sleeping, and a mysterious, for him, collection of dainty brushes and colorings, all for madamoiselle's toilette. He liked the person who chose such clothes. He was embarrassed to know so much, uninvited, about her. He hoped he would be able to be embarrassed in her presence quite soon. Hers was not a funeral he wished to attend.

Shortly after entering the elegant, crystal-chandeliered dining room, for he was in no hurry to return to the Intercontinental, a tuxedo-attired waiter brought him a telephone. A who-the-hell-are-you? grumpy voice introduced the embassy duty officer. Background laughter, clinking glasses made it evident his was no military kind of duty, where the officer stays overnight on post. Grumpy had been remarkably slow to answer his beeper, not that what he had to say made much difference.

"No, you can't pick up your cables from the Marine. You have to come by during working hours to sign the log in the cable office just like anyone else." Barbour said something unflattering and also something important. In reply, "I don't give a damn who or what your trouble is, it isn't mine, and I don't care whose father is an ambassador, and so if you want your messages, you can damn well come by here in the morning. Oh, and one more thing, Senior Agent Barbour." Barbour wondered what the hell did this idiot who seemed to have a bit of a drunken slur in his speech, have to be sarcastic about. "The mail clerk says you have an express letter from California. And the Marine register shows no entries by any Dubois. Okay? Now, I'm at an important diplomatic party and I hope this answers all your questions." Grumpy hung up.

16

"You're a lousy mechanic and you could have gotten both of our asses in a sling." Giorgi glared at a chastened Mustafa.

It was the daylight after the bombing attempt on Vasil. Vasil had not come into the office, nor, presumed Giorgi, would they see much more of him. Vasil had enough juice at the Ministry to get away with calling in to ITS for his assignments. After this stupidity of Mustafa's—stupid because he failed—neither of these opponents would want to see the other. No matter if Giorgi and Mustafa denied it. No matter if Vasil made no mention of it. It was not easy to face a man whom you had tried to kill, knowing he knew, and in addition despised you for incompetence. And now Giorgi and Mustafa would have to watch themselves everywhere. Vasil was no cream puff. His father had been in wet affairs and some of the blood had rubbed off. No, it was not a good situation. Giorgi wondered what idiot he could innocently entice into starting his own car each morning. Either that or take the stinking crowded trams to work.

The telephone rang. It was Jeanette, the Ministry's file head. "I have two hundred dollars in American new bills' worth of information for you."

"Two hundred dollars!" Giorgi screamed angrily. "I have already paid you a fortune. You get no more."

"Fine, you get no information. And maybe I tell someone what you have been asking me to do. Very improper. My duty is to report anyone who tries to get denied access. And I will tell them you offered a bribe."

"Jeanette, I will kill you."

"Not easy to do from a prison cell, little brother."

"All right, all right. What do you have for me? I am willing to negotiate."

"What I have for you is my palm open waiting to be paid. I have already negotiated. Threaten me again and it will cost you more than three hundred dollars, which is the new price."

Giorgi, overweight, underexercised, overimbibed, and with an already red nose underwent a scarlet generalization. His face, his neck, his ears turned bright red. But aside from that he controlled himself. "I must read it to know if it's worth half a year's salary," he told her.

"Half a year of *my* salary, not yours. Besides, we all know that with your tricks you're bringing in much more. Don't lie about it. It's common knowledge except for Internal Affairs who, these days, want people to be clean. Pay me as you read. And I won't tell IA."

"Okay, okay. I'm busy at lunch. How about after work? I'll come by the corner at General Gurko and Sixth-September Streets at seven o'clock. Pick you up there, okay?"

Her voice went from sullen to dulcet. "Okay sweetie, bring the cash."

Giorgi did not mind splurging on liquor, food, or other good living, including the gypsy for little girls. He was warm-hearted as a host—when the payoff from the meal would bring more than its costs. He was generous with little bribes, but this, this was—after all, he was a man of some sensibilities, ridiculous! But Jeanette was tough as nails, had been in the Ministry long enough to have something on everyone, and in fact be liked by everyone because after all that is how anyone intelligent survived. If she wanted to, just as she had threatened, she could hang him out to dry. He had the three hundred dollars with him. Picked her up. Stopped the car on Vasil Levski Boulevard next to the park, and handed her the crisp large American currency as she handed him photocopies of hand-written notes once attached, one had to surmise from the paper-clip rust marks, to a printed document. All the papers, only one had a year dating and that was 1995, referred to the upcoming August twenty-sixth arrival of the important Visitor, along with "our friend Banker Brody." There was an authorization signature by Deputy Finance Minister, in such a scribble it was unreadable, and a counter-authorization, very interesting that, by Undersecretary of the Interior, S. Burmov. Giorgi knew Burmov to be the lackluster nephew and political appointee of the then deputy prime minister. Giorgi scorned him. The fellow didn't know beans about Ministry work, but this signature told him he knew a few beans about making money. "Not so stupid as I thought," muttered Giorgi.

Also most interesting, though still not three hundred dollars worth of anything, was a reference to providing suitable transportation to the airport to greet the arriving visitors. "Pick up 'G.'" (for Gospodeen?) Dobri N, no last name, at the "executive" entrance to the Central Bank. Hmmmm indeed. I'll get that within the day; there are not so many Dobri Ns among the Central Bank big shots. If he were still here in Sofia, he was meat for Giorgi's table. If he had gone abroad, as was most likely, well, one would be bribing clerks to find his old files, records of any accounts over which he had authority.

But now the main course. He could smell it coming right off the notes as he read them enthusiastically to Jeanette, who of course knew them, but was glad Giorgi was pleased. She had her own thoughts about where this all might come out for her. Jeanette—this Zenaidya had been his girlfriend once, a lousy piece of ass but then they all were until Giorgi had discovered the gypsy's secret—Jeanette was nodding now, a knowing grin. She waved the banknotes in front of him and yes, yes, agreed Giorgi, she had been right, it was worth it. A chunk of twelve billion dollars worth if he played it right.

Someone had slipped. It always happened. That was what had made Giorgi so optimistic in the first place. And reminded him that once he was into them, there would be nothing in writing except his deposit receipts under some respectable-sounding company name in some respectable bank in, perhaps—actually he would need advice on this—Cyprus. Why not Cyprus indeed? Giorgi was reading, he was always a slow reader, a few teachers had said not very bright. Giorgi found comprehension easier if he sounded out the words. Some words! This was the part that was the real gravy. Some clever fellow in the cabal had written it. Some other equally clever fellow—or girl, what did it matter?—had dutifully filed it under, for it was so flagged, the "Attention: S. Burmov: Special Visitors' file."

A simple message, he sounded the words out slowly, his lips smacking with their good taste, as with a fine pilsner beer. Good things for Giorgi merged; food, sex, drink, money, sometimes blood. Simple things for a man proud of his peasant stock. A pleasure soup.

"Under no circumstances is anyone to speak or write the name of the Special Visitor, Sir Alfred Means. No one is to ask at any time for his (South African, no doubt others) passport, or any other identification. I have advised him that should messages arrive for him care of this Ministry from the pertinent bank on Guernsey, they should be addressed to his code name 'Gold,' care of me here. By order of S. Burmov."

"Thank you, you genius of a conspirator," Giorgi said happily. "And," he was beaming with good will, "thank you, Jeanette." He was tempted to tip her another one hundred dollars, but that was imprudent. She might think she could make a habit of hitting him up. "Thank God," Giorgi told himself, "she has no idea what this whole thing is about. But I know what it's about and I can smell the trail." He smacked his lips. Perhaps a trip to the gypsy tonight. To celebrate.

"And thank you too, you clever conspirator," Vasil said, putting down the earphones. He had done his translation for the Germans who were, of course, engaged in government industrial espionage against the French. Yet spies must have employment and espionage empires must be sustained; somewhere along the way, if national business interests are protected (one's own) or destroyed (the other fellow's), so much the better. But government spies are graded on showing activity, not outcome, so they don't care much.

On the other hand, Vasil today was grading government spy Giorgi and his sidekick Mustafa on outcome. Yes, a very businesslike point to take. They had produced a bomb to kill him. It had failed to work. Take away points for competence and achievement. The bomb also worked adversely, because it had annoyed Vasil. "Giorgi, Mustafa, you lose another point." And now Vasil was going to make a competing investment. With luck, those two would lose several more points. The goal of this game was to put the other fellow out of business.

Vasil's bug on Giorgi's office phone, and the one on the house too—after all the great tape reels were there for the using, in the basement of the telephone company, courtesy of the Ministry's installation from the moment the Russians had come to power—had proved useful. That recording had provided the information on Giorgi's meeting coming up with Jeanette. That provided Vasil with time and reason to tamper with Giorgi's car. No bomb. That would have been counterproductive and, at a personal level, wrong. Killing followed in the wet affairs business his father had been in, done, been done in by, working for the Sixth Department.

Productive tampering. A bug in the car, a position locator underneath the frame of the expensive Volkswagen in Bulgaria, and behind them a few cars, close enough to listen. An absolute stroke of luck that Giorgi had read Jeanette's find, and so slowly, aloud. Vasil had expected only hints, prepared to see what Giorgi did with the papers so that Vasil could get at them later. But now the whole thing was a present. He had, he grinned, struck "Gold." "Yes, Sir Alfred, gold." An interesting, timely set of disclosures for which, as Giorgi had thanked S. Burmov for his idiocy, Vasil thanked Giorgi for his carelessness. Giorgi and Mustafa were lousy bomb mechanics, showed no counterespionage tradecraft at all. Giorgi lost another point. They were adding up. Free-enterprise performance measures, he realized, were not such a bad thing. Yes, put the other fellow out of business.

The question was whether the embryonic team of Vasil and IFinCIG, the Network could compete with, or indeed at this end piggyback on, the work of

Giorgi and whomever he might enlist as governmentally higher up co-conspirators, for he must do that for access and survival. They would undoubtedly try to cheat each other, but that was expected, and some losses were part of business costs. Being "clever" in Bulgaria translated as not being caught napping while putting a hood over the other fellow's eyes. He knew he had to get through to Barbour right away.

Vasil had an idea of the trail to follow. First, identify Dobri N. Not difficult. How many senior Central Bank D.N. officials could there have been before democracy? One. Ask IFinCIG, already an occasional presence to assist, to work on this, just as he and Barbour had discussed. IFinCIG were in and out, unrelated to Barbour's tasks, working on the Multigroup criminal organization. For this job they would need to enlist the government effort, identify honest people in the Central Bank, work with the organized crime control people in the Ministry, with outside accountants to help. Finding the old files was the big job. Finding some clerk who had been paid off but not enough, who would finger exactly what the big boys had done. They would start by looking at the accounts Dobri N. controlled. They would look for documents purporting to authorize branches of Central Bank holdings of Finance Ministry funds sent abroad as dollar-, mark-, or-pound-denominated pension fund investments. Look for money sent abroad as collateral in support of letters of credit for government purchases of whatever—probably hospital supplies and medicines, but could be any kind of equipment, perhaps also bank-secured short-term loans ostensibly to be repaid to Bulgaria with high interest. And billings to Finance from abroad during this period for consulting, insuring, and accounting services.

The exit route—Vasil was no expert but it would seem normal laundering given the personnel now identified—to something Brody controlled out of his Austrian bank. That would take work in Vienna and no doubt elsewhere. Maybe he had a brass plate in Cyprus, thence maybe another paper cut out, thence Guernsey; by then the monies would have been well washed in secrecy jurisdictions. In Guernsey the money would be transformed yet again, Proteus as profits, perhaps co-mingled in Guernsey with Sir Alfred's own corporate investments, or client's monies, or pension funds for companies around the world. Out of those distributions then would have been the final one. Dividing up the loot and wheeeeee!—off for its enjoyment and investment in London, New York or Zurich, under good trustworthy company names or strawman fiduciaries. If companies, their directors would be unnamed, sitting on offshore secret paper, whereas in real life onshore, the owners and beneficiaries would seem ever so innocent. For immediate cash they would typically "borrow" from a fronting bank to get their own money in return. After all, if you had retired to an EU country, or the U.S., you, an honest citizen, didn't want to look like you cheated on your taxes. Be happy, be comfortable, self-satisfied, safe.

At this very moment Giorgi was working out a map very much like Vasil's. He was thinking of the Important Visitor, his big guiding-hand broker's fee, and his banker boy who would supervise the actual transfers, bank to bank to bank. Oh yes, Brody—that chinless, lying pedophile, exporting sweet young Bulgarian tail abroad. Oh my, yes, Giorgi knew *him* well. Obviously the various ministerial deputies had to trust both of the foreigners completely with their, well it really was the taxpayers,' looted twelve billion dollars. Crazy. How dare a Bulgarian thief trust a foreign banker who's been helping him steal? Giorgi was outraged. These Government people had been unforgivably trusting. Or else they were sure they had sufficiently frightened the foreigners. How do you believe you can frighten one of the world's richest men, a "Sir" no less? Or a conniving Austrian? Or whoever else was in on the deal? How much might have Sir Alfred, Anton Brody, and no doubt other lawyers, bankers, advisors feeding at the Bulgarian trough, all helping the embezzlement, transfer, laundering, reinvesting, beyond their 25% or so—how much more had they skimmed while doing the laundering? One had to worry about that. Even Giorgi, heading for that same trough, had to worry how much of *his* money had been skimmed. "Miserable double-crossing thieves."

The only thing crooks can do about treachery is what mafiya always do when contracts are violated. Outside the law there are no lawyers to call on. So they put out another kind of "contract." They kill each other. Giorgi grinned knowledgeably. In some ways, in fact anywhere probably, that was so much easier than dealing with lawyers. He'd begun to recollect that Dobri in the Central Bank, still around and living well, was in fact their head lawyer. "*Dobrui den* (good day), Dobri N." made a nice little rhyme; I'll get to him right off, a little sweet persuasion, shakedown, where are those accounts really, some nice place like Florida? Arizona? Majorca? Dobri would authorize signatures and then...All Bulgarian school kids read Shakespeare. "Yeah," remembering Prince Hal, thought Giorgi, "yeah, first we kill all the lawyers—and why not?" Giorgi poured himself a large raki. He was in a splendid mood.

17

He lived very well, this cosmopolitan Budapest-born Genevois. He owned a hand-crafted Aston-Martin. One of a kind, his kind, subdued ostentation, rich. His were the best Havana cigars. Napolean brandy that was, unlike most, not counterfeit; it poured like maple syrup and had been, as he told his friends when they complimented him, stolen by him from the nectar cellars of the very gods. Sandor dressed well; elegantly, in fact. Handsome still in his 70s; the photograph of him on the Bosendorfer grand piano in his luxurious apartment, as a Hussar Captain before World War I, showed movie-star quality.

Anyone who met him when he was on his good behavior, and there were defining constraints as to when he was good, testified to his exquisite old-world Hapsburg charm, even though he was Swiss. Swiss by a rich marriage to be sure, that his wife was ugly had never bothered him, for she was loyal while he was a complete *roué*. Nevertheless he was non-Genevois, although authentically, comfortably, reliably, punctually and completely dishonestly Swiss. Not that he must always appear Swiss. If need be, for a confidant's sake, or a look at a major investment property, or a vacation with some young mistress, he might become German. Or South African. Or Belgian, Austrian, *und so weiter*. His parents had had homes in Vienna and Budapest, spent summers in the Italian Dolomites. His father's mistresses had been in Paris, Berlin, Trieste. Sandor's introduction to sex had been with one of those mistresses, a gift from his father of a Paris weekend at age seventeen. A glorious beginning. His father had managed his own life well. Sandor managed with greater finesse, but much less honor.

Sandor managed other people's money. European money. South American money. These days, Slavic money. Money which must have no memory of itself. Money which must not speak. Money which had very important owners, owners who relied on Sandor to make them even richer than they were. He supervised, managed well Swiss and other portfolios. Everything tax free. Everything secret. Free from troublesome questions. For Sandor any kind of question but for rates of return, market risk, or his own commission, was troubling. His being a good lawyer helped. Opportunity arises in the intricacies of Swiss law. Sandor got on well with Swiss officialdom. They knew how things worked, all properly, punctually, righteously. *Richtig*. Foreign officials often did not. How surprised they were when Swiss courts, guided by Sandor's subtlety in law, might decree that the foreign officials had improperly sought to question a Swiss fiduciary, gain bank account information and in doing so violate Swiss law. Foreign officials had been known to have personal liability costs assessed. Petulant notes had been delivered from Bern to their own capitals. Once or twice a foreign official had been held in jail. Switzerland is an autonomous country, and guarded well what it loves best: treasure. One must be fair. Swiss like bratwurst too, and clean streets, and—contrary to prejudice—can have a fine sense of humor. Sandor had often laughed. Until recent laws penetrated bank secrecy, forcing the return of bank-stolen gold, Sandor and his friends had laughed confidently. They were more furtive now. But the Aston-Martin hummed along happily. Secrets can be within secrets. Disclsure was not yet the national rule.

But given these unfortunate changes in banking law, with diligence duties, treaties and commissions and radical parlimentarians disturbing the safety of treasures, the accounts Sandor supervised were being renamed, shuffled around the world through haven banks and offshore companies, massively reconfigured. The more delicate accounts—should there be due diligence inquiry, demands from new democracies or tyrants for the return of monies accumulated by, say, a Marcos or a Shah or any of a dozen African "Presidents," most Mexican ones, Southeast Asian men of consequence—all such booty would already have found secure residence elsewhere. Regrettably, Sandor cursed his countrymen, the Swiss body politic was losing its nerve. It had already lost unknown amounts of the two trillion dollars privately, secretly held in, but now creeping anxiously away from, its banks. Think of these francs, Swiss Francs, dollars, pounds, marks, pesos as alive but nervously amnesiac, looking behind them, always fearful of policemen, taxmen, family lawyers, thieves, angry divorced wives. Think of this so-anxious money, its owners if not also nervous, then arrogantly disdainful. Thus they presented Sandor with the task to reassure, provide profitable refuge, be masterful, be deferential, and not himself ever, *ever*, to be caught stealing what was theirs.

A dusty looking man of about sixty with whom Sandor had been dealing these last ten years or so, a man who wore black suits, black neckties, black-rimmed glasses, black Borsalino felt hats, whose whole being bespoke quiet, being a shadow himself, others for whom he worked invisible in his shadow, this quiet thin man was here in the office in Sandor's apartment. So was a young man, wise beyond his years, a scholar albeit practical. He was an expert in the new wealth that a new decade in the east of Europe had brought into Sandor's care. More correctly, he was expert about and in the eyes of those in power in Russia, its near-abroad and former satellites who were accumulating power and with it, money.

Neither man cared to have a name. Whatever passport they carried today would not be genuine. Sandor thought of the one who brought him others' money from Europe and America as, understandably, the Shadow. The Shadow also brought orders for European transactions from a particularly consequential American political figure. Sometimes Sandor thought that person might be a President, or a cabinet secretary. He was unquestionably eminent and powerful. One could tell that from the Shadow's respect.

Sandor read avariciously. If it was a senator, Sandor thought he might know who his mysterious client might be. A man who longed forever more power, but denied it, would have in its place, wealth. Whoever the American was, he was, in the terminology of his *confrères*, colleagues, a Partner. The Slavic East was embracing free enterprise and its terminology, but not yet the laws of commerce ordinarily governing these. Sandor also was a Partner, a position of high trust and high but unwhispered praise. Sandor put little faith in honorifics or his Partners. They were, like him, in a special business. That was hardly a guarantee of any law abided.

The other, whom Sandor believed lived in Ireland, was known as The Advisor. He advised in many languages. He saw to the special distribution of payments due from honest recipients to their origins and exporters in the East. When their shipments of steel, gold, oil, gas, timber, agricultural/fisheries products such as wheat or herring or caviar, occasionally art treasures, arrived in Western Europe or the Middle East, occasionally the Americas, the Advisor saw to it that payments were, in the course of dispatch or transit, made so as to favor the authorities who ran those companies. Their "favor" saw to it that payments were in part rerouted to secret Western bank accounts over which recipients had powers in fact but were, on their public paper face, held by straw men. These were impenetrable companies. Sandor could be a straw man, among his many other facilitating or commanding roles.

The Advisor also assisted in the reception of "difficult export monetary instruments."

That was a euphemism, of course. The task was transformation of public monies into private. Non-transparently, as the IMF would say. Or taxation in reverse one might say, or wealth redistribution. Selective welfare payments, the state to citizens of a sort. What belonged to a national treasury, central bank, or national pension or health fund, indeed even foreign loans themselves once in the recipient's hands, or monies set aside for any foreign purchase, these were the mines which were worked. Sandor's work, considered in this simile, was that of a mining broker. So too was the Advisor. Any extractable asset, denominated in a stable world currency—in practice, dollars, the new euro, pounds, or deutschmarks—could be refined and reshaped. The miners were typically government officials, heads of state enterprises, anyone with export powers over goods or trading currencies in the third world or the Eastern bloc.

This afternoon it was impossible for Sandor to be charming. He had nothing to sell or lie about, and had no intention of buying what had been set before him. The questions were troublesome indeed. He could well become his bad self, a fount of ugliness. Evil many would say. The gist of it was this: Anton Brody was their lesser colleague. He only supervised, had not designed nor run a major mine sluice so to speak, but was mearly a conveyor belt for assets extracted from rich veins tapped in producing honest lands, and thence conveyed into Austria. Sometimes the assets had already partly been processed by dubious banks in Poland or Latvia, Belarus, the Ukraine or Moldavia, and thence to Anton's Austrian resource refineries, thence further westward to respectable investment and profitability. But Anton had been required to disappear as the result of an unpleasantness. Bad news.

Anton, who was in fact a cousin to Sandor on the poorer and less bright side of the family, only avoided being a ne'er-do-well because the Partners needed him. In that connection, they had arranged business structures and a bank for him. They bailed him out of minor difficulties. They told him little and did not encourage his guessing. In return they received loyalty, fawning respect, and his dutiful travel companionship for important people visiting lands where mining of riches was occurring. There a Partner might defer to Anton as senior clerk to provide off-the-shelf company names, brass-plate bank account names and numbers, the names of fiduciaries stretching from the Isle of Man, Guernsey, to Montserrat, Vanuatu and Nauru. This was the geography of lesser pirate islands.

Anton had other duties. A major one was to put his signature on documents he was not allowed to read, and to accept as account books for his bank one set in reserve with storybook entries. In this fiction Anton was a more central figure than he might imagine. And a good thing he had no imagination of that sort. The entries told of billions being washed, thus establishing his guilt and, more important, providing a fanciful dead end for investigators looking for monies that were never there and were shown to be booked onward in other banks, under other names, all likewise misleading.

Useful Anton. Anton, as with the second set of the ledger "books about billions," was being held in reserve as a scapegoat. *Pharmakos*, the goat tied outside the walls of Athens, upon whom the wild animals would prey. A sacrifice to take away the sins of the city so that its inhabitants might suffer no bludgeoning from the gods. Such a goat enjoyed one security: he must be protected until his owners decided the time of metamorphosis, from Anton to scapegoat, was nigh. Toward this end the Eastern partners saw to his safety, a fact of which Anton, never clever, was unaware. The Partners assured his mothering surveillance and, in situations of any potential danger, his bodyguarding by those lads with the high cheekbones and Slavic accents. Of anyone in Vienna or Sofia, on a dark street in bad neighborhoods, off to gambling or a bordello, Anton was safest from a mugging.

Now this last week, after the crisis of Warsaw revelations, they saw to his sudden departure to a country dacha somewhere in the East. One called Square, a Partner himself, had even left the comforts of his Vienna mansion to see to Anton's pleasant journey. They had no reason to make it otherwise; thus unprotesting, for Anton did so want to please, journey. Poor Anton, no Sofia for the moment. He would have to make do with little Ukrainian girls imported to Moscow for service. Again, of course, there would be photographs for the file. Useful Anton, useful photographs of Anton should he think of balking.

"An even more painful matter," the Advisor was speaking, "is raised by our auditors going over the transmittals from the Isle of man to Panama to Curacao to Anguilla to Guernsey. The Austrian connection is, as you know, window dressing, inserted only as fiction on the books. As you know, funds management becomes the responsibility of Sir Alfred. The monies are well placed. We all know that exact amounts in dealings like this are fictions. One suffers bookkeeping carelessness, normal minor skims along the way, currency fluctuations, invested asset value changes, legitimate bank charges, exchange costs, negative interest when in transit through Switzerland, more so the normal exaggeration by clients' imagination. Certainly the twelve billion dollars bandied about in Bulgaria is ridiculous. Eight billion perhaps could have been realized *in toto*, before distribution." He paused. The "could" told them a reason for his frown.

"Sir Alfred," the Advisor turned to Shadow, "brilliantly designed and supervised the work setting up routes, facilitation, transmittals, transformations, etc. We all know he is a genius at that. If history ever allows for truth, he will hold a place in the annals of finance as perhaps one of the greatest," he looked for an agreeable word, " 'manipulators' of all time. Recall now, all fees and costs were to total an undemanding, indeed modest 35% of the corpus, $2.8 billion before costs or profit distribution to any Partner.

"Perhaps only Sir Alfred of anyone in this world can provide us such opaque, beyond accounting reach, respectable origins for major funds as we have in this Bulgarian coup. His non-SA African mines, gold and diamond—with some South African exports co-mingled to escape SA taxation—the Indonesian timber, the Panamanian shipping, all are perfect, because their income is so massive and nation-of-origin tax and accounting requirements are non-existent, but for bribes, to claim as the income sources for the Bulgarian assets once laundered. Sir Alfred of course has no doubt guided his holdings so as to provide for sources such as these, where no numbers but the company's own exist in contradiction, or for investigation. His other holdings, pension fund management portfolios in the billions, lend themselves equally well as concealing placement vehicles, although these are not essential to us. Sandor here invests equal sums. I do know that much of the money was intended for investment in the U.S. as the world's largest market, four times greater than London and Tokyo combined, and of course Europe second."

The other two men in the room knew all this, but allowed the Advisor his way. He resumed, "Now, coming to the crunch. Sir Alfred agreed upon 40%, or roughly $1 billion, $100 million, as his share. I have been reasonably diligent in employing well-placed members of his own accounting staff in his Guernsey bank where the master transaction records for the Bulgarian funds are kept. And of course we pay for reports from our own people in all of the transit banks. When dealing with a man of Sir Alfred's reputation, one must protect oneself. And indeed, as we know, from one another." The other two men frowned. It was true of course, watchbirds watching watchbirds; one could survive no other way. But only an Irishman or American would be so crude as to say it. "Sir Alfred has been skimming. A billion dollars plus has not been enough for him. He has betrayed our, the other Partners', the Bulgarians' trust. He has, to put it crudely, stolen four hundred million dollars which—need I emphasize it?—comes out of all of our pockets. Who knows of what other mischief he is capable? Further treachery...perhaps even informing on us, should the benefit be great. As they say in argot, the fat man might sing."

The Shadow said in his ever-so-soft-voice, "Regrettable." Even his accent was incapable of identification.

Sandor, his voice not soft at all, said, "Unconscionable!"

The Advisor said, "He is ultra-powerful. None of us are of any real consequence to him. Our recriminations will be unheeded. He has always been first among the Partners. In view of this reality, I have suborned the deputy manager of his Guernsey bank, who will assist us in retrieving the money."

"Can we manage that under Sir Alfred's very nose?" The black and dusty-looking man was frightened.

"Oh yes, but only when his nose is very cold. We shall recoup most of Sir Alfred's original share, less a considerable bonus to his Guernsey banking staff, and some in other places as well, once Sir Alfred is dead."

Ah...

Ah...

The Advisor resumed. "Death comes. Arranging it sooner than nature intended should not be too difficult. With your approval, I will advise the two Partners temporarily working out of the UST&D Bank in Sofia of this state of affairs." He turned to the shadow figure. "The permission of," he paused, searching for the right word, "your master, and of our Vienna partner now with Anton, is also required. The Paris partner should also approve. For this little group to continue successfully, we must be careful that each Partner," he continued with such care that all could imagine the word 'Partner' capitalized, "be careful not to exclude those central to any one operation. We must all anticipate vibrations when such a heavy man as Sir Alfred falls. But afterwards he will no longer betray us, nor be able to sing."

The man of shadow and dust, who gave one the sense that he was about to evanesce from wherever he stood, interrupted. "I believe there is another Partner active in this operation, one far away. He liaises, I am not fully privy, with Latvia, the Baltics-St. Petersburg associates. Keep in mind how the Riga port facilities are assuming great importance for contraband. The Northerner also liaises with—well, the one," he smiled at the Advisor, "you call my 'master.' "My master," again a smile; there was some secret joke inside the shadow, "refers to the latter as 'running the dark kingdom.'"

Those in the room looked quizzical. The Shadow elaborated.

"The U.S. is a moral country you know. Righteous. Pentecostal Holy Spirit. Evangelical radio and television stations. Such a vocal morality requires a very active Devil. Sin on toast. And so there is the Devil—distasteful, offensive, not thoroughly part of the split national character. Drugs, prostitutes, child-killing automatic weapons, pornography, vulgarity, pederast priests, egregiously shabby Presidents, the daily illuminated part of the American soul. In an image-conscious country, the Devil wins hands down on appearances. As we know, the U.S. constitutes an immense market, 50% of the world's cocaine consumption, for example; I presume that of heroin to be even more. And so there is a Partner who serves that market. He hides himself well, right in the middle of vice. Since the Warsaw event, along with Brody, the police know his alias: Mr. C."

The others nodded. "And so, if you will allow me, I shall advise the Northerner and his importing colleague, Mr. C, as well."

There was assent.

The Advisor resumed. "The partners temporarily in Bulgaria can call upon resources there for a job like this. We cannot afford a bad name. Clients over the world trust us to take only our commission. Our risk is low, theirs is high. We kill the golden goose otherwise. Nothing like a public lesson to assure clients, potential clients, Partners, that we are conscientious. Watchful. And vengeful. Taking out Sir Arthur will chill potential adventuresomeness in smaller men."

They deferred to the Advisor. Despite his youth he had become a personal confidant to Presidents as well as the secret police, central bank heads and military chiefs of staff of several Eastern exporting nations, thus of the protectors of the Partners' clientele. He was wise in the ways of banking, and obviously in recruiting informants, and now, this had surprised them, was cold, practical, ruthless. Yea and verily, thought the dusty, shadowy man, who liked his Shakespeare, and gadzooks. The Advisor, who had been nominated by his "master" as a Partner not too long ago, was working out well.

Sandor, who dressed warmly, in cashmere sweaters and usually tweed sport coats during the day, felt a chill. Additional, warming work on some of the accounts entrusted to him was in order. In the meantime he lent his approval to what he must.

18

Barbour had checked out of the Intercontinental at seven A.M., taken a cab to the Schwarzenberg to check in and have breakfast, called the central police station at eight, and the American embassy four minutes later. Major Hans Kohler, of the Serious Personal Crimes Section, would be in at eight-thirty. Barbour had asked that the already transmitted IFinCIG introduction be on the Major's desk and that an emergency appointment be made with him for eight thirty-one. Such punctuality, not a Viennese characteristic, would underline the gravity of his visit.

The American embassy operator said offices would open at 9 o'clock. Barbour protested that someone must be there now who could get him into the message center to sign the receipt log. The receptionist—in American embassies these were usually local hires; Barbour could readily detect her accent—was trying to be helpful. "The only official actually in, sir, is Ambassador Owen, who arrives around eight, as does his secretary. But other staff who might help you come in later."

"May I speak to the ambassador then? It's urgent. Tell his secretary it's Senior Agent Barbour of IFinCIG, Washington. I may have messages for me there relevant to an emergency. Tell the secretary, damn it, that the duty officer would not get them for me last night."

He was put on hold more minutes than he wanted to wait before the receptionist replied. "I'm sorry, sir, but the secretary says the ambassador is busy. Please come by at nine when regular staff can assist you."

Barbour fumed. He had no way of knowing that the U.S. Ambassador to Austria, Ron Owen, knew Claire as a family friend to Ambassador Dubois, or that Ambassador Dubois had been on the telephone to him from London rather desperately asking for any news of Claire. Of course Ambassador Owen had offered all assistance. If only Barbour had been more explicit. If only the secretary, always protective of her boss—Barbour had found her disagreeably off-putting, which was indeed her intent—had sought more information about what was "urgent." If only. All of us do so review history as it should have been, wishfully revisionistic, anticipating how it sometimes unfolds catastrophically.

As for Barbour, finding Claire Dubois had priority over wasting precious, perhaps life-saving time to run a message-retrieving errand. To get to police headquarters on the Schottenring in time he must leave now.

Major Klaus Kummering of the Federal Police was welcoming and cordial. Handshakes, coffee, all that. When Barbour told him of the kidnapping of Claire Dubois he was immediately and seriously professional. But also carefully exact. "You cannot be sure she was kidnapped. That is your interpretation of the doorman's observations, your own mission, her letter, and the like. There is no ransom letter, no corroborating information. We have found no bodies recently. We cannot exclude that what the doorman presumed and told you was a voluntary entry into the auto was, in fact, accurate."

Barbour acknowledged that the Major had a point. And Barbour knew he himself was already too emotionally involved. He had considered that possibility not at all, given what seemed to him overwhelming contrary evidence. Was this embarrassing proof of overinvolvement with a woman he had never met? Or was it typical European police caution, even resistance, showing the American whose turf he was on? Barbour's face flushed; he was getting angry. He must not show it. He reviewed once again that contrary evidence for the Major, showed him Dubois' note to him, explained what he could about the fiscal crime investigation which was his mission, and the events pertaining to that in Warsaw and Sofia. He could not give details of these, or names. Nor could he report what he did not yet know, namely what Dolan and McLaughlin in Washington had learned about the deaths in Warsaw, or Hashimoto's in Washington. What details he knew, derived from Vasil in Sofia, must wait at least a while for the organized and fiscal crime bureaus of the Federal police, and then only after he had established their ability and willingness under their rules, those of Austrian law, to cooperate.

None of this had been worked out in advance, as in other cases it might have been, through the foreign ministries involved, or via Interpol representatives. Barbour knew from long experience that the legal and financial access, and inter-governmental foreign ministry communications, could be sticky. With some luck there would be help from someone here in Headquarters assigned as IFFY liaison. In the meantime, for Barbour, the kidnapping was unquestionable. Obviously for the Major there was some doubt—understandable, given what evidence he had. Even so, Barbour outlined what he thought were the compelling immediate steps.

"Yes, Agent Barbour, of course, I am willing to proceed with inquiries along just those lines. Prudent, obligatory, just in case it is as you fear. We will immediately begin internal file reviews with respect to criminal cases past and pending involving Russians and other mafiya to whom Vienna has become, unfortunately, a shopping center, contraband transport route, and comfortable vacation home. They have caused some trouble here. Do understand, however, I cannot make you privy to this file content. You have at the moment no formal legal or police status here except as liaison, due to our courtesy under the various financial-crimes agreements our government may—I say only 'may,'—have with yours. As you surely know, you may carry no weapon, conduct no investigation, interview no Austrian citizen, without judicial authority specifically granted upon diplomatic request and overseen by us. Do you comprehend that?" The Major's was definitely one of those exact, repulsive, "Me Tarzan, you chimpanzee" policy statements for which some historically Germanic police officials, especially the more old-fashioned, rule-ridden, and procedure-obsessed, were notorious. Major Kummering was already notorious in Barbour's book. They were also known, since theirs were based on Napoleonic code rather than Anglo-Saxon common law, for the magnitude of police powers they could exercise, and from which there was no appeal.

"I would like very much to work with you, Major, directly in the field on this case. Dubois is my partner, a U.S. Federal agent; our governments do have treaties respecting cooperation. I am sure you can understand, official to official and man to man."

"Of course I can, Agent Barbour. Of course. Please do not misunderstand. I tell you the rules. But man to man we can be somewhat flexible. But cautious. I do not forget that our Miss Dubois may have been on personal business, not your government's, business, at least until she had news of your arrival. In any event there is little to be done until we run all of those files, cross-check names—you know, the fundamentals, the tedium first. Our computers are fast enough. Clerks are less so. No more than an hour or two, since there's a good deal of clerical checking involved. Do not worry, Agent Barbour, your missing Miss has priority." He called in a junior officer and barked out orders. Whether the military salute in response was a show for the visitor or the way they actually did business around here, Barbour could not guess. "Now, if you have a photograph of her we will distribute that to all police, immigration at once, *nicht wahr*?"

It was embarrassing that he did not. The major gave him a raised eyebrow. "You do at least have a physical description of her?" There was a hint of sarcasm in the tone. "Yes." At least he had that. Barbour had gotten it from André had used it to be sure of a match between the woman the doorman had seen and Dubois in fact. And of course he had written it out to bring along. Discerning André the concierge was an excellent observer. After all he would wish to assess his guests, anticipate their lifestyle needs and, not inconsequentially, tips. Watches, for example spoke volumes as to wealth. So did tailors, or *haute couture*. Andre's written description: "Blonde, blue-eyed, typically English, rosy-cheeked clear complexion, about 30, height about 5'4", weight about 135, last seen wearing a blue straw narrow-brimmed hat, dark blue silk suit, ivory silk blouse patterned in golden bumble bees, a golden bee pin on the jacket to anchor the Hermès crisp silk scarf streaked with blues, grays and gold; handbag black, probably Hermès; black patent leather low-heeled shoes, a gold Piaget wristwatch, small gold hoop earrings." The note paper-clipped to the description had said, "Your assistant, Herr Barbour, has excellent taste. A fine woman. I do hope you find her soon." Barbour did not include this latter personal item with the paper he handed Major Kummering.

"Major, we should immediately get over to Knize to see if clerks there have any recollection of or information about the young Russian who wears those individualistic, expensive, Vienna-made gray gloves. Remember, the doorman recognized them as work of the glove-making firm where his father works. If the customer has an account, we'll be in luck."

"Agent Barbour. I understand your eagerness. But we must have a foundation first, be thorough at the start. The file checks, auto, warrants, visas, outgoing flight manifests; a check with our ethnic crime people for after all the tough men, the doorman described do stand out in a *gemutlich* city like Vienna. This business with the Russians can take on diplomatic overtones—for example, we had a personal assault involving the son of the commercial attache a few weeks ago. You can't imagine the headaches. And you realize that I myself cannot be certain, no, not at all certain, that Miss Dubois was kidnapped. I must act only as if she might have been. If it is her at all. Doormen can be wrong. I must use caution. To go to a famous store such as Knize, well in Vienna in those higher circles everyone knows everyone, that will let, your expression is it? the chicken out of the bag. And maybe no one stole a chicken at all, a '*poule*' maybe..."

Barbour, all of his relatives said quick tempers were a family trait, was about to blow. "Major, a woman's life is at stake. Time is of the essence. And you sit here wanting us to stall on what could be our only quick lead in. And," he glared at the Major, "she is no *poule*, no whore."

"Patience and temperance, my impetuous American friend. Thoroughness, prudence, correctness. Good police work gathers everything in. If indeed it was your associate, Agent Barbour, and if she was kidnapped, she will not be harmed. They will want something—if not money, something. You describe her as new to your Agency. She has certainly not information to give them if that's it. If they didn't want something, were unwilling to wait for it, we would have had a body dumped into the River Dauna Kanal. The major shrugged. "That's seems to be the fashionable place to dump bodies these days. We have had four so far this year."

"Major. I'm going to my Embassy now. I'm going to tell them about your prudence, your caution, your perfectly proper file search, your doubts, and your obvious gutless procrastination. And to remind them that Miss Dubois is an American Federal officer, the daughter of our Ambassador to the Ukraine, and an important visitor to Austria whose life does not seem as important to you as it should be."

Major Kummering was not used to challenge or insult. After all, he *was* a major.

"Disobedience, impudence," were words he wanted to say. His face was turning red, a fine contrast to the deep green of his uniform jacket which was reminiscent of the Austrian national hunting suit for men. "I am doing all that I properly can, Agent Barbour. I regret your personal feelings are interfering with your professional judgement. I too will be in touch with my superiors." The tension between the two men was high enough that if a fly had landed on a biceps, one of them would have let go with a punch.

"Right, Major, you do just that. And expect a brand-new diplomatic problem on your hands. My advice is make sure your computers are plugged in. I'll be back at noon, Major. I will expect your full cooperation. And if you do find Miss Dubois' body in your river, don't plan on a long police career. Or," Barbour was menacing, "ever being able to walk again."

Barbour realized he should have kept his cool. Thank heavens he had the sense not to say he would stop by Knize men's store on his way to the embassy. Technically unlawful now given the Major's stance; he himself could be arrested, but he could not care less. A number of swear words came to mind.

"I'm looking for a very special pair of men's doeskin gray gloves, preferably with a flowery pattern of some sort on them. My lady friend saw them on a gentleman and liked them very much. Something for the evening and a dark suit or formal wear. The man told her, she believes she got it right, that the gloves are made right here in Vienna and one can buy them here. Is that so?"

"Oh yes, Mein Herr. Exactly. A distinctive glove, in the very best of taste. Here."

They walked to a counter. Drawers behind it were pulled out. Gray doeskin gloves in various patterns, and astonishing prices beginning at 2300 schillings—about $175—were there. One drawer held gloves with a rosette sewn on the back of the hand. "Ah, these are exactly what she said he wore."

"Excellent. Yes, in perfect taste. Would you like to try them on?"

"Yes, thank you." A pair fitted. As if casually, "My lady friend said the man who told her about Knize was quite unusual. Thin, Russian I guess, very intense-looking, well dressed, 'handsome,' she said. I can't help being a little jealous, but she said she would like for us to buy him a coffee. He suggested the Imperial, Dommayer, Frauenhuber—we don't know them ourselves, and this fellow had an accent, said he wasn't a regular. So we almost set it up and just then the man's limousine pulled up and he rushed away without our getting his name or setting up a time. Do you know whom he might be? I know Joanna, my lady friend, would be pleased. Although frankly, I don't particularly care."

The clerk pondered. "Well, I don't know. We have cards for our better customers. Perhaps, well perhaps, someone might know him."

Barbour recognized this hesitant hint for a gratuity. "She would be so pleased. Here, let me express my gratitude for your help." He pulled 650 schillings (about $50) from his wallet and handed it to him discreetly. The clerk sauntered off, spoke to a colleague in the same section, and disappeared through a door, returning in a few minutes. "We do not like to invade the privacy of our customers, monsieur, but if you are sure that your lady friend made a coffee-house date then there can be no impropriety. Yes?"

"Of course not, oh certainly not."

"We have one foreigner who comes in not too often, then again, often enough. Excellent taste. A quiet person, yes, I should say intense-looking, very. I can understand why your lady was…attracted. Intense men, excitement in that for a woman, yes, although I must say—I shouldn't say, but he seemed standoffish, serious-looking. May I be frank? A bit sinister. Are you sure you want your lady friend to have coffee with him? Well, that's her affair…" He giggled a bit at the obvious pun, not intended lewdly but still a bit out of line. Barbour was getting a streak of these, it seemed.

"Anyway it may be that the man is," he read from a scribbled note, "Andrei Rastropovich. My goodness, he must be related to the great musician. That accounts for his good taste. I fear there's no telephone, but for the purposes of our sending out announcements of occasional sales and new arrivals, his mailing address—I checked and it's the same as on our master mailing list, you know even Knize's these days has to keep up with the times by advertising—yes, it's Musiker's Allee #12, how appropriate for a Rastropovich, in Laxenburg. That's a little town to the south, the Hapsburg court went there in the summers. A number of fine private houses, late 1700s, early 1800s, nobles of the time. And ah, Herr...? "Baedeker," replied Barbour. "Oh, a good name too; well, you'll find Laxenburg easily enough. Ah, Herr Baedeker, you understand I'm sure, I must ask that you please don't mention that Knize's gave you his name. But the Imperial for coffee, only the best people go there and well, you seem so nice, Herr Baedeker...discreet, I should think..." This with a grimace and a wink.

Barbour took the cue and gave him another 650 schillings more, saying, "Yes, I think that is best, on my part as well, and so, well, this inquiry was never made, eh? We both know how these matters of the heart can be delicate." This time from the clerk, a knowing grin. Pleased with himself that he wasn't born yesterday. He guessed that Herr Baedeker himself had a romantic eye for Gospodeen Rastropovich. Matters of the heart indeed. Ah, these rich tourists. And himself one hundred dollars richer for playing queer cupid.

The embassy Marine guard was spit and polish, tough and courteous. Barbour was admitted after a call to the cable/mail clerk, given a photo tag for his neck, escorted through the fine building to a nondescript basement office. There he showed his ID and picked up two cables, one from D.C., one from London, both via State, plus an Express letter with Stanley Markowitz' San Francisco return address on it. What the hell, Barbour wondered, might all these be?

London first. "Jesu Christi!" Ambassador Dubois in London wrote from our embassy there. His daughter Claire was missing. He had been told by Ambassador Owen, who had called IFFY, that Senior Agent Barbour was to arrive to become partner and field supervisor for his daughter, and would Agent Barbour for the love of God—hardly a customary ambassadorial tone—do *everything* he could to locate Claire if she had ever arrived in Vienna, etc. There was a possibility, for things were a bit confused and information was contradictory, that she had in fact gone to Paris. In which case, his apologies as an over-concerned father. Barbour would please call immediately on Ambassador Owen, to whom Ambassador Dubois had spoken, who would drop everything for him, who had promised all cooperation, etc etc. Background: Claire had telephoned saying she was being sent by IFinCIG to Vienna, had hoped she might pop over to London, if Barbour allowed, one of the two next weekends for a much-desired brief reunion, Kiev being chancy for air travel. Barbour was to call him immediately, please, care of London Embassy, with any information. Foremost, had she arrived in Vienna? Was she safe?

The second cable was from IFinCIG via Main Treasury via State—as top secret as IFFY could pretend to. "McLaughlin sends warm greetings, Dolan likewise. Shit has hit the fan. Claire Dubois a mafiya plant. True name Greta Liebowitz, member of (Gen) Grivchenko Moscow and elsewhere mafiya. Ex whoreperson, whore-export management, now senior mafiya finance made mole into IFFY via CIA made good. We look worse than bad. No Dubois ever entered Govt to work for the CIA or IFFY. Unlikely she is in Vienna, probably stole all of our files she could eat. If in Vienna, so close to where her buddies work, look out. Buddies dangerous, no doubt. Whatever Brody represents in Vienna is big business for her bad boys. All Warsaw lawyer informants—they say accidental fire, I know arson—are dead. Worse, Hashimoto of our Civil Service, who uncovered Dubois as Greta's alias and cover, sent out the orange alert, ended up as a floater in the Potomac. Heart attack they say, but autopsy not complete. We make it murder. His original letter cannot be found. His intelligence source for the make cannot be identified now that Hashimoto is dead. Utter confusion. Did mafiya competition finger Greta? Did original intelligence source fix Hashimoto to retrieve protective cover? FBI is working on document authentication. New and as deeply troubling an idea: was the Hashimoto letter, not Dubois, the ringer after all? Nobody here but Jones remembers Dubois and he, in fact all Personnel, are CYA. Lots of asses will hang high. Be sure yours isn't one. Burn this cable. We sat over the clerk while he dispatched it and got his, all file copies. Be sure boys at your end don't keep one. So no indictable message from Garcia—remember the Maine and all that; it got blowed up like we can—is to go unshredded. May our reputations be so lucky.

Write home to mother when you have solved all our problems. Oh yes, Brody and Mr. C may be Brody et Cie. Ain't it fun?"

Barbour grinned, but only momentarily. Obviously Dolan and McLaughlin had both been drunk by the time they got this off; so no doubt had been the code clerk. In a mess like this it was the only way to be. "Oh yes, oh what fun," thought Barbour. Goddamn, Major Kummering might be right. The lovely AKA Dubois may have set them all up and gone off with her buddies, laughing all the way.

But somehow, Barbour didn't think so. Not with that charming, informal letter she had written to him; not with those clothes, which no Greta-out-of-Moscow would have had; not with Dubois having called her father saying she was coming here. And fathers know a beloved daughter's voice and ways. Someone, somewhere, was killing a lot of people, going to a whole lot of work—one piece of which was to get rid of Claire Dubois, as file content, as presence. Someone, no doubt with a Russian name and it had to be some IFFY mole as well, who else God only knows? it could be the Major for that matter, was trying to put in the fix by design, resulting in the spontaneous unraveling of what had begun as, well he had thought so himself, a "pointless" investigation. Vasil's Sofia information pointed to tying it all in to the twelve billion dollars; to Brody, one of the world's richest, most slippery men; to Sir Alfred himself; and now to John Does in Vienna, surely Moscow, self-evidently Sofia, Warsaw, and, he'd bet, Washington, D.C. Guns, capabilities for electronic surveillance of U.S. Government communications, and their own secure commo, both of which meant old or new KGB, GRU involvement for capabilities for Federal agency penetration. No doubt unlimited rent-a-thugs available. Man, this is *big*. Barbour realized it now.

Last was the letter from his buddy Markowitz, still stomping out crime in Malome. "Mal homme," indeed. He had seen him in San Francisco on his detour from Montreal to D.C. to here. Markowitz knew nothing of Barbour's Vienna. With old buddies there's no holding out when talking about current work, but when time is short, work commentary may not come first. Had he mentioned Mr. C? Barbour didn't remember. He did remember telling Stan that he was being sent on a wild-goose chase with no facts at all to support it. Mostly they had serious dining and drinking to do. Now Markowitz' letter wrote:

"Dear Lee,

> Just a quickie in case it has any bearing. DEA called me for help finding a Mr. C right here in Malome. Nobody but a barkeep has heard of him. But if there is one he is BIG. Invisible nevertheless. The point is that your friend and mine Senator Cranmer, the "Chummer," has an improper interest in an ongoing investigation which he has no right to know about. No doubt some sycophant suit in DEA was his source. But in your drunken cups you did hiccup a name or two. Brody and I thought it was 'Brody et Cie" as in, "and Co." or 'incorporated' and now, guess what? We may have a case together 8,000 miles apart. And is the Chummer looking for good press, or what? Watch your ass. Next dinner is on me. How about the old Flytrap? Keep me informed, never by any government commo. But you already know better than that. Postcards are more secure. Don't forget your favorite California charity begins with buying me a drink. (Signed) Stan"

Well, well, well. A world flying apart, a world coming together. It was time, on the double, to see Ambassador Owen.

"Agent Barbour, I am delighted. Do sit down." To the secretary, "Coffee and rolls, please." To Barbour, "My friend George Dubois is worried sick. So am I. Claire is damn near as close to me as my own daughter. What the hell is going on here? Any idea?"

A field man makes his own decisions, which is why headquarters desk people and section chiefs have gray hair. It is also why, if they are not too ambitious, the desk men wish they, too, were back in the field, top secret be damned. Barbour showed McLaughlin's cable to Ambassador Owen. A distinguished, gentle-looking man, brown eyes, a trim 5 foot 9, tailored brown herringbone suit and gold Cosmos Club necktie, he read it and whistled. "Holy Mother of God! Didn't anybody in IFFY ever get a look at Claire? A single glance would have told them it was her—or not her. What does the personnel file photo look like?"

"I don't know, sir, but you'll see McLaughlin says the FBI is authenticating documents. I read that to mean the letter and the personnel files could all be ringers."

"So somebody got to the files?"

"Could be, sir. After all it smells like they got to Hashimoto, and he was the master of the files."

"What do you think? Was the woman who came here a few days ago Claire Dubois or the gangster Greta?"

"Do you know Claire's handwriting, sir?"

"Yes, I most certainly do. She's a loyal correspondent, in fact she loves to write letters. She and my wife trade all kinds of personal news."

"Is this her handwriting, her letter, sir?" Barbour handed over the note he had received at the Intercontinental.

The Ambassador looked it over. "No question at all, Agent Barbour. This is Claire's handwriting, her manner of writing, her personality. Not a Greta in a carload. No possibility. None!" He slammed his fist on the table. "What the hell are these mobsters up to? Or those lunatics in Washington?"

Barbour gave him a studied look, spoke slowly. "Going on what you say, sir, plus the rest of it as I read it all, I should say that some mafiya group has decided that by tampering with the personnel files and killing Hashimoto—we don't yet know why, but it must be about the files—they could convince us that Claire Dubois is an infiltrator. Then when she was kidnapped we would believe she had never been the real Claire in the first place, so we wouldn't look for her. Bad luck for them that her father knew she was coming here. Bad luck for them that you and I have connected. Bad luck for them that McLaughlin, on reflecting, isn't buying it all. But the worst luck is Claire's. She was the one exposed, the one they could get to, the one they could—" he sought a gentle word but knew it was a euphemism, "well, lean on."

"Why would they do that? The poor girl has only been with IFFY a few days. She can't know anything."

"But they don't know that sir. Obviously. They don't know how much Warsaw spilled. But what they do know tells us they monitor our cable traffic; they have plants inside IFFY and Lord knows where else. They knew about Claire coming here, presumably about me; by inference about our knowledge of Brody—I suppose everything else that I got in that lamentably thin packet. That would mean 'C' as well, whether he's Mr. C or Cie, as in compagnie, or both. What they just don't know is how much we are on to other things that are terribly important to them. Which, of course, *we* don't know.

"What they really don't know is how screwed up we are, how novices like Claire can get sent innocently into the fire just because some damn bureaucrat wants to protect his rear. They can't imagine, sir, how stupid we are and how so much of all this is accident. They'd laugh at how little we know. But they have shot themselves in the foot with all the blood they've shed. Now that we can infer their file penetration, we know something very big is going on. The mob has brought on just what it feared: our full-scale interest." Barbour was thinking of Vasil, Brody, the fat man and especially the twelve billion dollars. It all connected.

Barbour trusted the ambassador enough to state his guess. "I suspect, sir, on the basis of what I've just learned in Bulgaria, that Brody was laundering money for the reds there, that some very important Westerners are involved, and that they are protecting their fannies and twelve billion dollars of looted Bulgarian government monies. How's that for a big-buck conspiracy worth kidnapping and killing for?"

Ambassador Owen could only say "Wow," and again, "Holy Mother of God." He blanched. "We've got to get to Claire as fast as we can."

"Yes, sir. But I'm not at all sure about the cooperation we'll get from the Austrian Federal Police, especially Major Kummering there, who's acting, I must say understandably from his point of view, all correctness, procedure, caution. And he may be dirty himself, just maybe. Can you push one of them to get the Austrian top brass moving?"

"I can try."

"Shall we just wait for that, or shall we make like cowboys in Indian country and go in after Claire ourselves?"

"You think you know where she is?" The ambassador was amazed. Barbour told him of his visit to Knize.

"What do you think, Agent Barbour?"

"If you want to know the truth, I think they may have killed her already. They are certainly never going to turn her loose. If she's alive, it's by the grace of God. If, sir, you'll push on the official front for Austrian police action, with your permission sir, what I propose to do right now is entirely illegal and portends a potential diplomatic incident. It may be violent, and if it goes wrong it will make snazzy reading in the press. As for the action, if it backfires, well, a spin-doctor, or getting the Austrian police to back us up pronto, or the truth *may* save us. The last is always least likely. Alternatively Sir, you will at the very least receive a reprimand, maybe early retirement, and possibly a criminal indictment."

The two men statred at each other, judging, knowing how much was at stake on such short acquaintance.

"Good. We have to risk it. What's your plan?"

"If you approve, sir, we recruit two Marine guard volunteers. The Marines wear civvies and carry no wallets. Report them AWOL the moment we all go out the door. Authorize, but not in writing, weapons from the Marine armory. Deny you ever met me. Swear your secretary to the same. Tell the rest of the guard to keep their traps shut and pray."

"And please, the moment I get out the door, close out my room at the Intercontinental, pick up my gear, and tell anybody asking that you have no idea where I am. One discreet exception: please cable—and keep in mind I think yours out of here but for Agency are all decrypted by KGB mafiya—a note of reassurance to Ambassador Dubois, something like, 'I hope soon to be able to send a case of delightful Heuringer.' If that is all okay by you, I will lead a little expedition to Laxenburg and the street of our musicians."

The ambassador, who had officered in Vietnam, and Barbour, who had done Korea and Vietnam, agreed it was all a peachy-keen idea. It was almost difficult to persuade the ambassador not to come along himself. But somebody had to stay at the embassy to prepare for cover-up, deniability—in other words, to lie eloquently. After all, what else are ambassadors for?

19

"General Bratislav, sir." Deferent but confident as befits the Technician in Charge, an exceedingly responsible position.

"Yes?" A voice to be respected, which sometimes cultivates irritability.

"It has been nearly a week, sir. Is it your view that following our records penetration things have gone well?"

Bratislav turned to his two companions. Both were Partners as well, the nervous one and Sergei, who fancied himself the modern counterpart of the original Dr. Faustus of Stauffen. He would occasionally confide that he considered himself master of the ether, of the ionosphere, of all waves and impulses—all those man-managed energies by which distance was informed—and about which his colleagues were misinformed.

"What do you think?"

The nervous one: "I am never sure. One hopes. The Dubois woman is securely ours, but because our Vienna colleague has departed temporarily, she has yet to enjoy her final round of interrogation. On the basis of his work so far, he suspects she knows nothing more than our original intercept yielded. There is no one with more experience in his sort of work. It is possible that we are fortunate. All of the trouble with the file penetration negating a relief effort, any alarm over her but for IFinCIG's own embarrassment would have been worth it. Yes, damage control may have been sufficient. Our project, our group would seem secure, but for..."

Sergei interrupted, "I have talked to him myself since he brought Brody back to Moscow. He's much more confident than that. You worry too much. He's sure she doesn't know anything. The Warsaw lawyers revealed no more, and probably knew less than we feared. IFinCIG is clueless. DEA will no doubt pursue, what is our American Partner's theatrical term for Brody et Cie, the invented name, 'C'? *Si*, as the Spanish say," Sergei was in an ebulliant mood, "the 'ruler of the dark empire.' Do you know the American *Star Wars* films?

Marvelous. Darth Vader, that's the image." Sergei burst out laughing, not chortles but booms.

The huge and sterile windowless computer, computation and strategy room inside the UST&D bank, which was lavish by Sofia standards, resounded to his mirth. A number of white-coated technicians, analysts at gray steel desks, operators at rows of computers turned with worried looks. The very room's existence was secret. The work and people within it were clandestine. Any emotion, any revelation was secret, as indeed it had been in remembered Soviet days, when no truth was ever spoken. And here was a Partner roaring with laughter. It was frightening. It was encouraging. Things must be going well. Capitalism did encourage good moods and free expression. Glasnost. Perestroika. Profits! Imagine!

A white-coated clerk, wearing rubber-soled shoes like all staff members in the room did, came silently over to the Chief Technician. He carried a yellow envelope of the sort used for urgent transmissions received. In the free market world all business was urgent. In the UST&D world of the Partners, "urgent" was likely more so.

The Chief Technician handed the envelope to General Bratislav. "The senior American Network agent assigned to Vienna has arrived, and has been advised by Network to his embassy in a most informal text that Claire Dubois is Greta Liebowitz. There was an earlier transmission out of London to Vienna, unusual since they rarely use an urgent channel. It came in last night, but the monitoring computer's descrambling program was down, and so was its hard drive. No reason to believe it had anything to do with the captive, but we should be alert." The voice was confident.

"How can we be alert when we don't know to *what*?" The nervous voice again, an always edgy man, but then, these men were all working the edges.

"Oh, for God's sake, *relax*." Sergei was immune to nervous contagion. The nervous Partner was always like that. "I am," he reminded him, "an expert in these matters, master of the ether and all that, remember?"

The tense voice, now moved to sarcasm and thus the better mood that hostility brings such men, said, "Oh yes, reminds me of alchemist Faust, 'master of the wind and waters, master of earth and fire."

"And what's wrong with that?"

"He almost lost himself, after the deal, to the Devil. Dicey ploy."

"Ah, but think of our colleague who rules the dark empire; he may *be* the Devil. So, if one is old-fashioned about it, might we."

They all laughed at that one; even the Chief Technician grew brave enough to join in democratically with the three Partners whom he admired so much. The work here was so much more exciting than the career in poisons that he had given up.

It was nine-thirty in the morning. Computers were humming. Tight whispers among the workers. The Partners each at a desk in the adjoining, well decorated Management Room, usually redolent of cigar smoke. Two more messages arrived for management. The first was a Washington follow-up, confirming that the coroner had found Hashimoto's death be to a coronary attack. The nervous man who had been supervising Plans for that operation out of this room some days before, along with the General, allowed himself a rare smile.

"You might break a jaw smiling like that," joshed General Bratislav. "What's the good news?"

"I like competence. Congratulations to you and the Sea Scouts who did the job on Hashimoto. It was a ballet. Perfect moves perfecting death."

The Master of the Ether, hearing, pulled out a celebratory cigar. "So, the civil service man had a heart attack and fell off his sailboat." He chuckled.

"So, he didn't know how to swim."

There was a chorus of chuckles. They repeated in unison, clapping, "So, he didn't know how to swim!" Ah, to mourn the loss. Ah, the tragedy of it. Ah and oh my, the morning was going well.

The next message was to the General. Delivery was systematized by message clerks either by specialty of the Partner, or by serial rotation.

"Well, speaking of the Devil, and coincidentally the Sea Scouts, some disturbing but in fact good news. The fat man," his very voice was scowling, "has screwed us out of four hundred million dollars. Personally, I suspected the bastard would try to take more. But it's been arranged in Guernsey that we can not only get that back, but most of the fat man's original share—or at least," he paused, doing a quick calculation, "One hundred million dollars plus—for each partner."

Nerves said acidly, "Not possible. He's too well situated. No, it's dangerous to even think about it."

Sergei's beetle brows were plowing into the top of his nose. "Come on, I'm sure Geneva and the Advisor are good at their figures, but do you really mean to say the fat man's own Guernsey bank is so wired in our favor that we can pull it all out from under his nose, no matter where he's stashed his portion?"

The General held up his hand, "Remember, I said again 'Sea Scouts'—and no, we can only do it when the fat man is dead. Then his staff will play ball. Then, then, then. You understand now?"

Ah...

Ah...

They set about organizing a meeting with the old head of the Sixth Department. His boys were just back from Washington. A fat bonus was soon in their hands, deposited safely enough by first making the usual laundering round-the-world tour, this one via Cyprus, Nevis, and the Seychelles to land in comfy London. They were delighted with the idea of a plane ride, helicopter ride, rubber boat with silenced jet engines, wetsuit and snorkel to their fellow soon to be swimmer, probably digitalis for this portly one, and then, yes the Chief Technician's Master's degree in the University of Sofia had been, would be again much appreciated.

The recipe was as he had recited it. Use a bowl of harmless, healthy common Oriental take-out restaurant seaweed soup, leaving the cardboard carton in the galley. Let the same seaweed soup be found in the stomach by the medical examiner. The swimmer is understandably reluctant to enjoy his soup. But he is induced to swallow as the syringe with the soup is pushed, always so very gently, just like you'd push a pill down a dog's throat, leaving no marks, by four strong men with rubber-gloved hands, one pressing the ultra pain spot so that a man's mouth must open. It all happens so quickly, open and shut so to speak, right down his gullet. The scouts have added that millimicron worth of lab-cultured Limu, and no coroner yet has ever found it. Hold the darling tight, it only takes a minute, then over the side and off he goes for a swim.

There was no hurry about the fat man's sport. He owned a passenger line and might one day go aboard. He sailed often out of his yacht club in Nice. He had a swimming pool in his ostentatious mansion outside of J'berg, and one in England, and one on Majorca. No shortage of attractions for a bathing, sailing fat man and the surveillance team who were now on him night and day. Trailing carefully behind his bodyguards, but well ahead of them in technology. Their Russian-military-developed Global Navigation Satellite System, signals encrypted of course reported the exact position of his every vehicle, usually a Bentley or a Lamborghini; he only used a Rolls when the mood was upon him. A well-bribed upstairs maid had inserted into each right shoe heel—an expense for he had 200-some pairs—a tiny device that announced the wearer's location to a second receiver in surveillant's hands a few blocks away.

There was no more hurry than the urge to get your collective hands on a billion and a half dollars. The fat man obliged. One evening he went on a lovely sail off Port Elizabeth, South Africa. In a lovely, well-crewed, (seven including the chef), ocean sailer. A lovely dolly with him in the sack at bedtime, which was whenever he got the urge—less often now that he was fatter and older. A well-paid dolly to take him on a midnight stroll on deck. And so the Sea Scouts took Sir Alfred for a swim. As they swam away from his bobbing not-yet corpse—fat is as almost as good as cork for buoyancy when you're are not face down—most of the Sea Scouts were grinning. But one Sea Scout was actually vindictive. "Fat bastard, try to screw us Bulgarians, will you? Takes some doing!"

The well-paid dolly, her money of course in an account far far away, would of course be questioned intensely by the police. Dollies get rattled. Dollies slip their tongues. Dollies are not cool enough, when the cops start leaning, not to blow the whole game. Men and women who are wise to the world, knowing the unreliability of dollies, anticipate these problems.

Poor Dolly. She had been exposed to typhoid just before putting out to sea. Doctors cure people. The visiting team gave those doctors something to do. A careful team wants to be sure that to health authorities the typhoid can be traced, be understandable. When Dolly breaks out with fever, headache, abdominal pain, cough, aching bones and, what ho! the lab test shows bacilli in stool and urine, Dolly gets rushed to hospital, too sick for any interview, no matter how much police curiosity there is as to why the fat man had a heart attack. Dolly, of course, had told them she was sleeping, didn't even know he'd gone on deck.

When Dolly gets a diagnosis, for typhoid is very worrisome in a squalor-ridden place like South Africa, urgent public health routines are followed. One looks for contaminated fluids or a carrier, infected or otherwise. One doesn't think to look for, nor would one ever find, a visiting team dosing Dolly's coffee with typhoid bacilli, courtesy of a Russian research laboratory's bacteriological warfare stock, still maintained. Nor would the good public health doctor know that there had been some thoughtful epidemiological "salting" going on. For instance, Plans involved surveilling the heavy-drinking yacht's mate, before, during, and after, though he didn't know it, a visit to his favorite bar. A source! Just as epidemiology requires, there it is. The ship's mate is found to have been infected from polluted water right there in that crummy Capetown, at his favorite bar.

Dolly, feverish and rushed to hospital, no police interviews please, this is a potentially deadly disease, was, bless the competent medical staff, to receive the proper therapy. Telltale rose spots had appeared, and a host of other symptoms: prostration, bradycardia, splenomegaly, leukopenia, intestinal bleeding, that sort of thing. Regrettably for the patient, who would have otherwise lived, the prescribed capsules from the J'berg hospital pharmacy, so carefully administered by Dolly's nurses, had been replaced by some containing colored powdered sugar. This was not, as often happens in cost-conscious health insurance programs that substitute a poorer medicine for a more expensive one, just another cost-saving move. To the contrary, the hospital pharmacist was well paid indeed. Pity poor Dolly, who never got to be browbeaten by those curious police.

"That part went damn well, but it was expensive!"

"Hell yes, it was expensive!" thundered the Paris Partner in reply. He had flown to South Africa to supervise. The locals had welcomed one of Europe's most successful, famous investors. As with many Europeans he was buying up fine residential estates deserted by departing Afrikaaners and original English whose optimism about the new democracy was moderated by knowing the risks, in Capetown for example, of getting robbed, raped and/or killed. Genial General Bratislav, under false papers, came in also to supervise, ostensibly separately.

"Documents, travel, training, pay for ten men, one woman, two safe houses, however many bribes, equipment, warehousing, trucks, a couple of million pounds before all was said and done. With all of that the Russians might get Afghanistan back again—if they wanted it."

"You are entirely right." Loudly said to the accompaniment of clapping and knee-slapping.

"And complicated? Ridiculously complicated."

"Yes!" Some cheers accompanied this.

"And risky, very risky."

"Yes, yes, yes!" Accompanying laughter.

"And a conspiracy! Imagine involving strangers, amateurs, not our own people tested over time. Every moment possible exposure, utter confusion. Can you imagine the father of Bulgarian conspiracies, Rakovski, or even a child like Raskolnikov, coming to South Africa expecting to succeed?"

"No, no, even though it is their, *our* life's blood, not to be done with any sophistication in a place like Africa. Never."

"Right!" Other voices shouted, "Never, never."

"And to trust, however well planned, to trust anyone there at all! That hospital pharmacist, for instance. Yes, we know he never met his controls, was surveilled, was a reliable liar and thief, as you learned—at some expense mind you—from his record and revoked licenses. Well bribed yes, transported and located abroad yes, but expensive again. Still I grant that to have him substitute inert powders in a few dozen different medicines' stocks in the pharmacy, so he would not know which patient was the target, now that was actually clever. Imagine what surprises spread through that hospital when no medicines seemed to work, eh? An untreatable typhoid epidemic, so it seems. I grant it was an original and amusing approach, but again, high risk."

"Yes. Yes, I agree, perfectly dreadful. And without compunction, without remorse if you want to add that in. And even more difficult, we had five contingency plans every step of the way, each one of them more risky. We might have had to kill four or five people, ten maybe, who could say, who could care? Such things can't be helped."

The Parisian threw his hands up in the air. "How terrible, eh?" He and his companions were sobbing with laughter. One had fallen down and beat his fists on the floor in paroxysms of laughter.

"The fat man couldn't swim! What do you know, another man overboard and the fat man just couldn't swim!"

"Nor sing, never inform on anyone at all."

Shades of an earlier celebration in Sofia. Hands clapping, all in unison, the refrain, "The fat man couldn't swim! Can't sing!" Drunks tend to be repetitive.

"Terrible, eh?"

"Yes, terrible. Think of it. Total, total success, daring, brilliance, and now the Partners each more than, it turns out, about one hundred million dollars richer. On the lips of the smart half of the world, sardonic, 'Don't go swimming with Bulgarians!' The stupid half of the world just asked, 'How could it happen? Everything to live for and the rich old fool falls off his boat!' The smart money knows we did it. A lesson to anyone thinking to rip us off. My God, business will come in as if we were selling money at a discount!"

Cheers. Laughter, tears running down a cheek or two, and cries of, "Champagne, raki, more champagne, more raki, more vodka, more armagnac, more, more, more!"

The two Partners who had flown from J'berg to Cairo, joined by a third, were now hugely, gloriously, ever so splendidly drunk. In a suite in the Semiramis Hotel, Cairo, at a thousand dollars a day, a magnificant, luxurious suite, cushioned from unwanted sound, unwanted anything, the only right words for such a gloriously right moment were "More, more, more! And then more!" Which, of course, is what the Partners were all about.

20

Giorgi had no trouble finding Dobri N, now a retired red, as the present government intended most to be. He lived in a pleasant villa on the lower slopes of Vitosha Mountain. A good, indeed wealthy, neighborhood as long as one ignored the potholed roads. Diplomats and the new businessmen, including mafiya, lived here, which no ordinary civil servants could afford. Doctors, for example worked for the government at fifty dollars, or as hospital chiefs-directors, for a hundred dollars a month.

Why would Mr. N stay here in Sofia where he was vulnerable if his share of the loot, surely enough on which to retire, was abroad? Giorgi, asking himself that, realized he also knew the answer. Bulgarians liked Bulgaria. Abroad they were nobodies. Who ever heard of Bulgaria? Who but Bulgarians here spoke the language? Giorgi, thinking proudly of his own family, back to the old *bogomils*, knew the feeling. Your own people, your own place, the only place where being a Bulgarian was important to anybody. People put up with a lot to belong somewhere.

And Mr. N was old now, probably arthritic, too old to learn another language, maybe too old to find a new way to a new grocery store, accept strange foods in it. Screw it up as he had as a red—and he had—here was his Bulgaria, his ancestral home. With access to plenty of money to be reimported home from some haven abroad, say by an unsuspecting daughter, Mr. N would not want. Be Prince of Vitosha Mountain, so to speak. Giorgi, thinking about it, wondered if—when he himself had extorted some of those exiled dollars from Mr. N, or swilled at the trough abroad of red Finance executive Todor Mihailov—would he himself not just want to stay on as another prince of Vitosha Mountain?

Giorgi knew he had insufficient juice, Interior Ministry or not. His running a translation service would throw no fear into a comfortable ex-central bank executive who obviously had a clean enough record to escape immediate jail-ing. Or so Dobri N would think. No, Giorgi needed senior juice on this one. Nor was he so greedy and stupid as to fail to understand that share-the-(others')-wealth was a requirement for some kinds of success. He had duked in his boss' boss, BB so to speak, the deputy director of C&PI in the Ministry. He was high enough to provide cover, credentials and pretty good cemetery maps, both literal and figurative, as to where bodies were buried. A crook of course, one surviving well from having been a red executive in the same Ministry. Policemen stay, governments change. The same with spies. The Ministry such as it was, was still peopled with old hands.

"A recipe for success," Director BB had said, upon hearing about billions stashed abroad and Dobri N a sitting duck here in Sofia, waiting to be persuaded to quack. Yes, a recipe for success. DBB approved. Translator Giorgi was amused. "DBB," indeed. In German those were the initials of the Deutsches Bundes Bahn, the German federal railroad. Fast trains. With DBB aboard, Giorgi was sure he was on the fast track.

"A preliminary investigation. Sound about right?"

"Sounds right. If anybody gets the wind up, we say we're worried that people in the Service with jurisdiction—the Central Service for Combatting Organized Crime, or the Enforcement Branch in Finance—are tainted; there have been rumors of Multigroup mafiya, so here we are—public-spirited investigators, working free overtime to see if there is anything to a rumor we heard. No evidence mind you, no allegations, just a hint from a barstool, that Mr. N might know something that would help the government locate some missing money."

"Right. Virtue and a good alibi all the way."

They called Mr. N Giorgi, as junior explained that he was acting as assistant to his senior, BB. He courteously explained that the Interior Ministry needed Mr. N's assistance in a minor matter. Might they meet him for a drink at some quiet tavern near his home? There were several fancy eateries in that area, and no shortage of velvet barstools. Mr. N, they knew, no longer having cover in the government, had no choice. Cordially dissembling, they set up a meeting.

Dobri N, punctual, well but informally dressed, well groomed, was not exactly the cat that ate the canary. His hands trembled. He had feared such a day. *He* might be the canary. Giorgi, he liked playing with words, greeted him, "*Dobrui den*, Dobri N!" (*Dobrui den* in Bulgarian and Russian means "good day.") Both sharks smiled at the now-old man. They showed him their Interior Ministry credentials. For a red out of power these were much more frightening than for a modern youth who thought little about the Sixth Department, or those old furnaces in the police station, or the one hundred thousand sent to gulag or death in 1949. Dobri N, station master himself for some of that red railway to hell, had long understood that the new government, despite promises of being a government of "reconciliation," would get around to serious vengeance as soon as it felt itself powerful enough. That was, after all, the Bulgarian way. The history of political promises was just that. Dobri N, dominated by memories, still lived in the old days, dominated by fear.

"Beautiful," thought Giorgi, who understood the old man immediately. "This canary will sing."

"Beautiful," thought BB, who understood nothing so well as a fellow red, a fellow bureaucrat, the beauty of his own power, and old Dobri N's powerlessness. "I am about to get rich."

A dance, a waltz, a minuet, the familiar steps: of course "I know nothing," of course "I have heard of nothing like that," of course "I'm sure you have checked all my financial records here and found nothing improper," and, more desperately, a plaintive protest, "I have done nothing wrong here." They all knew that 'here' was the operative word. Giorgi got tired of dancing, they all knew what was coming anyway. Who, when faced with implacable police, believes that any words will save him? Mr. N fell silent.

"Mr. N, it's all a pile of shit what you're telling us. We have it from Todor Mihailov himself, who's decided to cooperate informally—notice the emphasis on 'informally'—with us. He gave you away. He gave away Brody. He gave away Sir Alfred Means. That fact might tell you something about us. It should. It should tell you it's time for you to be generous. We want some of the action. It's that simple. And we want more than Mihailov gave us. You can guess we know he's lying to us about where his own hunk of the stolen money is, and who in the ministries, in your bank, and others beside you and Burmov were in on this. Deal well with us and we can arrange that all of this nastiness can be made to go away. Alternatively, you yourself will certainly go away."

The old man shivered, said nothing.

"You do remember those endless betrayals, those gulag islands, those police furnaces, those massacres, those cold dark cells underground with nothing but the rats and the smell of your own death approaching. You do remember them, yes?"

The old man, his white hair thinning so that one could see beads of sweat on his balding scalp, felt his own trembling rise, like a storm moving from the ocean, to become tremors, then a shaking so violent he could not stand. The two police officials moved to hold him. Not gently, you understand, but in a tavern with others watching one must appear solicitous. Plainclothes police always look what they are. Bulgarians remember what they were. The other drinkers in the tavern gave them bitter looks. Yes, Giorgi and the DBB must appear helpful to an old man. At the same time they made sure Mr. N felt the vicious fingers stab into, crush, his old, weak muscles. Yes, the whole of the old man's body remembered many things. Things done. Things he had done, had ordered done.

Their voices were soothing. "Understand, we are not vindictive. Not like some in the present government. No, we are not political. No recriminations. What's over is over except," a pause, a smile now, "all of us know that what was over may always come back. But not in time to help you, Mr. N. No, so you just tell us the whole story. Who has what stashed where, who has what on whom. After all, in the Central Bank you must have known where those government monies were being sent, laundered. For these nice stories, we want you to know we'll be gracious, capable of accepting your thanks for all you are doing for us. Money, Mr. N, U.S. one-hundred-dollar bills. New. Next week for each of us, five thousand of them for a start. And tomorrow, since this is not the place, we shall bring our private tape recorders and enjoy the stories you have to tell."

The old man had so deteriorated in strength during this meeting that he could neither stand nor walk nor drive his car. They helped him to his new BMW. They all knew where *that* came from. Giorgi drove it behind the DBB as DBB drove the old man to his villa in the government sedan they were using. They helped him to the door. A maid answered. She looked frightened and bewildered. "He just needs some rest, Miss, it seems he heard something about the old days that shocked him deeply. Poor devil, but we're quite sure," BB repeated, "quite sure that by the time we come by here tomorrow at four o'clock, he will be feeling much, much better."

"Four o'clock then, Mr. N?"

The old man's now palsied head shook enough in an up-and-down direction, as opposed to simply shaking randomly. They could see he understood.

He did. At four the next day when they arrived at the villa, an ambulance and local police patrol car were pulling away, beginning their siren ride. An old Volkswagen with a caduceus on it was parked nearby. The maid explained that her employer had had a heart attack. The doctor had said it was very serious, that he might not live.

Luck was not running with Giorgi and the DBB. But BB, who had a network of resources at a level considerably greater than Giorgi's, realized that with a little effort he himself could find Todor Mihailov wherever he might be abroad. BB and a few unpleasant friends would then make a call—whereever he was.

Giorgi was unnecessary to that visit. BB knew the lower-ranked Giorgi well, too well. He knew Giorgi was a greedy, unscrupulous man, ugly to look at, too intelligent for his own good perhaps. His reputation for sordid sexuality was known. Unlike himself, or so BB tended to think, Giorgi was a scoundrel—a scoundrel who now expected BB to share the wealth. Hardly. BB by himself, or with a simple thug or two, would have no trouble working over Dobri N's family. The usual. Midnight arrest. Slap them around. If a girl, well, a little molestation, or if she were pretty rather more; yes, much more than that. One got the idea across. One of them would know where they went to get the hidden money. BB, who was respectable enough in appearance, travelled easily abroad. Not Giorgi, he was a slob.

The next morning when Giorgi turned the key to his car's ignition, the only thing Giorgi heard was an electrical sputter. The bomb shards got to his brain before the sound of the blast. In the former Communist East, free enterprise continues to arrive, sometimes with a bang. Competition is keen among entrepreneurs. Some win, some lose.

Mustafa got a telephone call when he arrived at the ITS office, telling the news of Giorgi's assassination. He blanched. "That son of a bitch, Vasil." Mustafa was sure of it. "And I'm next, by the Prophet he will get me next."

That day two embassies went without translation services. Giorgi was unavoidably absent, so to speak. Mustafa left for a visit of unknown length to cousins in Turkey.

21

Vasil knew he must get to Barbour that information secured from the audio surveillance on Giorgi. These were the leads IFFY must have if it was to assist the Bulgarian government. The "if" in IFFY and that government was whether IFFY had the money to do anything at all, for no U.S. interests were involved unless one could say the fiscal health of Bulgaria was a philanthropic interest.

Vasil had seen too much simply to walk into a Bulgarian government office with his information. "Hell," he thought to himself, "I probably couldn't even get in the door." Once in, he might be faced with another crook, another Giorgi trying to cut himself in on the deal; or a slovenly lazy bureaucrat; or simply a rain of insults because Vasil was a mere Interior Ministry translator. The old ways of Balkan and red dictatorial management styles were still in place.

Vasil knew it without even thinking about it. Without the contacts, the relative power, or the independence of a Barbour or his like to front for him, armed only with the dynamite report fuse burning in his hand, Vasil was at risk. With any delicate matter, shocking news, or valuable asset, one works best through friends. In Bulgaria as in Whitehall or Washington, friends made things work, scratched each others' backs, covered each others' ass.

"Damn!" Vasil thought, "I don't have the network."

Barbour, Vasil's key, was worrisomely missing. Vasil had telephoned the Hotel Intercontinental in Vienna from the Intercontinental in Sofia. A telephone booth. He assumed his call was piped to several governments' ears. And unquestionably, embassy lines were bugged inside and out. What did he learn? Barbour had checked out two days before. Vasil called the U.S. Embassy in Vienna. The switchboard had not heard of Special Agent Barbour. "Who else might?" Vasil asked himself. Well, Barbour had said, "send a sterilized message." That meant going through the embassy mailroom. Clerks in any embassy get paid to be the eyes of other embassies, Vasil knew that well enough. That was part of his job. No, no letters, even if cheaper.

Two international calls were costing him money at the Western rate, thanks to the cashier's surcharge. Since he had to pay that hotel cashier, the calls were also calling attention to himself. Any diligent cop or spy could check up. His casual disguise, moustache, wig, might work to protect him from being identified, but he could not prolong his presence in the elegant lobby where he felt so out of place. Even the two calls meant Natasha would have to scrimp on the food budget this week because of his 'No, no letters' decree. He asked the Vienna embassy receptionist for the ambassador's office. Vasil, familiar with embassies in Sofia, could not imagine the degree of greater formality in an embassy in Vienna. He erred, too, in presuming Barbour more important than he was, and so Vasil asked for "the ambassador," and mentioned Barbour.

It was sheer luck that Ambassador Owen's private secretary at least perked up her ears while lying.

"No, no Special Agent Barbour has seen the ambassador. I have no idea who he is. Who are you?"

Downcast, Vasil could only say, "A friend. If you ever see him, tell him a Bulgarian friend needs to talk to him immediately. It's important."

She hung up on him. She rather liked being rude. On the other hand, she knew she had almost muffed things earlier. This Barbour case was too hot for her not to report the call to Ambassador Owen.

"Mr. Ambassador," she called through on the intercom, "Someone with a Slavic accent saying he was calling from Bulgaria asked for Mr. Barbour."

Ron Owen sat up straight. Anything touching on Barbour was consequential. Something with a Slavic accent had to be hot. Even if a mafiya call, something. Something hot. If from Bulgaria, meaning the twelve billion dollars that was likely the key to this whole thing, as Barbour had told him, the call was boiling hot.

"Put him through immediately."

"I can't, sir. You told me I was not to acknowledge any knowledge of Barbour. I told the caller we had never heard of Barbour."

"Oh, sweet Jesus!" Ron Owen could hardly believe she had been so stupid.

"Did you get a name, a call-back number at least?" Once he asked the question he realized no one in this game was giving out identification over the listening cables.

"No sir, he said he was a friend. Nothing more."

"Christ, why, *why* didn't you put him through?"

"I just told you, your orders. If I put him through it would reveal interest on your part. Implicate you, sir."

"Oh, good thinking, Gladys," the ambassador was sarcastic, furious. "Really clever. So if someone had information in this situation which looks like igniting World War II and one half, you just decided that I shouldn't have it, right? You like to leave me wondering what someone in Bulgaria might have for us on this case, a case where I'm getting cables daily from the Secretary. Right, Gladys? You don't even *ask* me, you just like being the righteous goddess of fools?"

"Hardly, sir, but those were your orders." Her voice vacillated among the wavelengths of snippy, acid, frightened, hostile. She calculated. Her fanny was covered. She could indulge herself in hostility which, in any event, she liked best. Next to vengeance. Personnel investigators don't appreciate ambassadors calling secretaries "fools."

"Mr. Ambassador, don't blame me for your orders. I remind you, there is a harassment complaint procedure."

The Ron Owen volcano erupted. Welshmen, even four American generations removed, can be like that. "Gladys, I'm reminding you I'm your boss, that there are requests for transfer forms in Personnel downstairs, and that if tomorrow morning you don't have one filled out on my desk, I will have one filled out, along with a 'totally unsatisfactory' rating for your file. And so, Gladys, goodbye."

Gladys, in the office outside, let her mouth drop so wide open she could have caught not just flies, but buzzards in it.

If wishes could be winged, the ambassador would have had them there, carrying her dead body off.

The rejected Vasil mixed depression with desperation. "Should I go to the CIA station chief?" That young man for whom he translated, for whom he had no feelings good or bad, was, in fact, the whole "station." He was COS (Chief of Station) for the first time anywhere. He was trying hard. But if Bulgarian history proves that a Bulgarian cannot deal with or forecast his country's paroxysms, how was a nice young man from America to do so? If the Ministry of Interior was not sure who was and was not mafiya, how could an American college graduate, selected for his squeaky-clean personal history, trained at best to play with plastique and pass notes via holes in tree trunks, who spoke only kitchen-quick immersion-course Bulgarian, who had never met a gangster or indeed a cop in his life, how could that man discerningly report on the mixed Russian, Bulgarian, Belarus, Chechen mafiya in Sofia? That man who had never even considered who his translator was, or where the summaries of everything translated went, or, on good stuff, the full tapes recorded on that nice necktieclasp wire worn by Vasil, were delivered? No, Vasil could not go to the naive young supposed-to-be spy. In the Balkans babies are born wiser than this man would die. "Governments are ridiculous!" Vasil fumed.

That was his last expressive gesture for several days. It is, as with Oblomov in Russian literature, a Bulgarian condition. "Regressive fatalism," the political scientists and diplomats call it. Under the crushing emotional impact of his lost link to Barbour, thus of energy and hope, faced with the uncontrollable whimsy of assassinations, the success of Sir Alfred and the rest, his government's disarray, other crime hardly controlled, poverty such that his two phone calls to Vienna actually meant that his family would have less to eat at home this week, it was too much; Vasil ceased to rule himself. For the moment he didn't even look to see if there were translations scheduled; Vanya now was in charge of that. He went home, took Natasha to bed, got up in time to greet the children coming home, drank far too much raki, and could not remember what it was he had wanted to do this day.

Only the next day, somewhat hung over and back in ITS, did he learn of Giorgi's assassination and Mustafa's escape. Making connections does not mean one gets the wires placed right. Vasil presumed that Mustafa and Giorgi had gotten into a serious fuss. They had after all threatened each other with exposure and blackmail. It was a perhaps a silly partnership of those two sinister clowns to try to find and extort money from the highly placed thieves of Bulgaria's stolen billions. And so? Mustafa had assassinated Giorgi, fled and good riddance. And so? Vasil no longer cared.

22

It had been conceived as a three-man rescue and relief mission to Laxenburg. The embassy Marine contingent, quite small, was commanded by a master sergeant who had received a call from the Ambassador. "You understand, you have never received this telephone call?"

"Yes, sir."

"Okay, now are you willing to recruit two volunteers and dispatch them on an illegal mission fraught with political and personal danger, about which I shall deny any and all knowledge if things go sour? The volunteers are to be listed by you as AWOL the minute they are out the door. You are to equip them with personal weapons and grenades, all of which makes your role illegal unless you can arrange to make it look like they were stolen from the armory, in which case you will be severely reprimanded if any of this comes out. Which is likely. There will be shooting, I fear. Your marines may get arrested by the police or killed by mafiya, in which events the embassy would disown them—but perhaps not their corpses."

"That's quite a sales talk you have there, Ambassador, sir."

"The only icing on the cake is that they are to serve with an American Senior Agent to rescue a pretty young woman who is a Federal officer kidnapped by Russian hoodlums and who, if she is not already dead, will—if this mission doesn't succeed—soon be dead. Understand the parameters?"

"Yes and no, sir. I don't know what a 'parameter' is, but I can see what you're asking, sir."

The Marine master sergeant was of a type. The Corps, as with the choice of Dalai Lamas, selected them, one looks at it fatalistically at birth, but as honorable killers rather than saints. It cast their iron into molds, rolled and annealed them in steel mills, direct-wired their brains to fog horns for voices, internally connected their amygdala-center for anger in the brain to the triggers of elaborate weapons, formed their bodies into athletes with permanent nettles under their hair-shirt loincloths to assure exceedingly irritable alertness, taught them sly cunning by master Byzantine monks, tatooed the flag on their gluteus maximus, permeated them with the sin of Pride, made their loyalty mindless, their vocabulary weak, and their humor when drunk legendary. The Corps assured they would be first in and last out with respect to wars and virgins, and tested this product not only on every battlefield in which American had fought—Tripoli to Bosnia—but gave it a final challenge by telling them to act like gentlemen when receiving calls like this from Ambassadors.

"Good." The Ambassador waited.

"I can't ask any of my men to volunteer for anything as out of line as that, Sir. And I can't order them to either."

"Oh." Severe disappointment was in the voice. The Ambassador realized he might have to go with Barbour himself. At his age he was not the help Barbour deserved.

"However, sir, in view of the fine opportunities you've outlined, I will do it myself, sir. Hate to miss a chance to get marked AWOL, reprimanded, jailed, killed, or rescue a lady, sir."

"I thank you, Sergeant." The Ambassador's voice could not hide his emotion. "The woman is the daughter of a best friend, a colleague in the Department. I've known her since she was a child. Her name is Claire Dubois. Except for the one-in-a-million chance that I'm all wrong and she is someone named Greta, who is a mafiya agent herself."

"Yes, sir. I..." The sergeant paused. "I would like to understand, sir, but maybe it's best not to. Your last remark kind of leaves a man wondering, sir."

"I appreciate that. In any event, you have never talked to me, and what you are about to do I know nothing about. We all invisibly appreciate what you're doing. Agent Barbour will be around in say, twenty minutes. He has to rent a car. I propose you get your car, load it surreptitiously with the weapons you need, all concealed in boxes, tarps, etc., and drive around the back alley. I'll tell Barbour to drive by there where you can transfer the boxes. Maybe get a highly visible case of soda pop from the commissary, hot dogs and mustard, talk picnic when you get the stuff into his car, just in case folks are watching. I'll repay you personally for your costs, if you live. Right now, change into civvies, leave your wallet behind, and be sure you two are rigged with enough firepower to make certain that we all get even. And yes, if we get away with this unskinned, I'll put you in for a special merit citation."

"Thank you, sir, but actually what I'm looking forward to is the action, sir. A little breaking loose, if you get my meaning."

Ambassador Owen did indeed get the meaning. He'd often wanted to break loose himself.

The map showed Laxenburg. A little market town, lovely old buildings on the way, and itself old and new, including a collection of beautiful 17th and 18th century palatial summer homes of the Hapsburg nobility and merchant followers of the court. Not just your ordinary peasant village. Barbour and the sergeant drove by way of reconnaissance in ever-narrowing rings around Musicker Allee. It was a short street as shown on the map, and as they drove by one end, was seen to be a mix of old palace/mansions, a small shop or two, even an old barn still in use—cows were slowly being herded in. The fancier houses, those old Hapsburg court mansions, were difficult to see behind trees, high walls, ancient high gates. The walled gardens were an advantage; once inside one might not attract attention. That depended of course on the inevitable security cameras, and possibly the heat, vibration and motion detectors which any sensible mafiyosa would have installed.

There was no back alley. The big houses backed up to just as large old buildings on the street parallel, Dichter (poet) Weg. Another tree-lined, elegant street in the same mode, this one perpendicular to the musicians' and poets' ways, the one they were driving slowly along now, was Maler (painter) Weg. The Hapsburg court had clearly emphasized the arts. "Well," said Barbour, "let's see how creatively artful we can get."

They had binoculars and night vision scopes, but nothing by which to assess the type and placement of security devices. A jump over the high wall and into the garden invited alarms, camera surveillance, the full clamor.

"You see those cows down there?" asked the sergeant.

"Yeah."

"I grew up on a farm. I like cows."

"Yeah?"

"If that farmer has got a tractor, he's got to have one in that barn, I can damn near hear it. If that tractor accidentally bumped into the gate at #12, if he had a load of hay on one of the small wagons these Bauer around here use, given a little help those cows would sure go for that hay. And if the tractor and the hay are in the garden at #12, and those cows get to moving around a lot, say we get a billy goat or a horse in there with a burr under his blanket to get him dancing a bit and spook those cows, every damn surveillance device except on the doors, windows and inside is going to go nuts. If nothing else, it will bring the goons inside outdoors to take a look. Maybe we get into a beef with the farmer. Lots of distraction, and we get to see what the goons look like. See if they meet your description. Maybe we even get a cow in the house. Sure does arouse a householder's interest to have a bunch of cows parading around on his Oriental carpets."

"You have any particularly good way to interest an Austrian farmer in all that?"

"Maybe. My family went to Ohio in the 1820s as German farmers. Godly folk, helped found a town, one of those utopian communities, lots of them in those land-grant days, New Hope, New Harmony, New Concord, hell, even Free Love. Lots of city names too—New Paris, New Antioch, New Jerusalem, New Matamoras. Well, I think maybe mine founded a New Laxenburg. Catholic of course, wouldn't you say?"

Barbour was puzzled. "If you say so."

"Yeah, seems to me it's so. I speak German you know, down the family line. Now if I can find out this farmer's name, and here I am out of a Laxenburg line, we're bound to be cousins some way or another. Let's go ask who owns those cows, looked to me like Swiss Browns for milk, maybe the white and red ones are Landstater for beef. Two breeds were going into that barn."

The sergeant was dressed in casual civvies, blue jeans and a plaid shirt. Going into battle one need not be dressy these days. He gave Barbour the once-over.

"Buddy, it seems to me you got some Austrian ancestry, wouldn't you say? Little farm town somewhere, maybe? I heard tell they had a lot of cows up in Scharding on the Inn, across from Bavaria, not far from Passau. Yeah, you can look German. What do you think their name was?"

"Whose?"

"Your great-great-great-grandparents for Chrissakes, the ones who went to America from Shärding, that has an umlaut in it by the way, sound it like 'sure' and as if you were sing-song Swedish."

"Schmidt?"

"No, no zip to it. You ever use a German alias?"

"Yesterday, Baedeker."

"Good enough. Prussian-sounding, but the ne'er-do-wells came south. Printers, I think they were, thus the guidebooks. Yours, the poor branch, not too bright, got your many-greats grandmother all knocked up and had to come across the Inn. Set up a bookshop. Remember they were Catholic, most folks here are, your folks hated Luther. That'll get you lots of points. Hey, you ever herded an unwilling cow?"

"Nope."

"Get right up behind it fast, lift its tail straight up from the asshole, twist it around tight and hold on, stay feet close in so it can't kick you, push ahead with your hips while twisting, and with a little luck we can get it inside the Rastropovich front door there in a jiffy. But just so we stay like farmers, don't mind carrying your automatic rifle, grenades and .45 in a gunnysack with straw spilling out, hauled over your shoulder. What do you say, Herr Baedeker, cowboy?"

"Why not, pardner?"

In perfect soft south German, no pretense at dialect, the sergeant got out of the car wearing a puzzled American tourist face. The plaid shirt looked the part, so did the cheap camera hung around his neck. This man planned his campaigns. Gracefully bowing, speaking in courtly "gnadiges Frauen" German, he stopped two old ladies passing by. Both were dressed in traditional Austrian costumes, dirndl skirts, embroidered black jackets and roses handwoven on their black scarves.

"Kuhe" "Bauer" "Amerikanischer" "Alt Stamm" were words Barbour heard in passing. The old ladies jabbered like blue jays in a bird seed mill, "Yah, yah, *Herr Bieber sicher, Musicker Allee zwolf," unt so weider*. The two men had to resist being taken to Herr Bieber by the arm, for they had a few other things to arrange first. Even so, they now had introductions from local old friends, Frau Wipplinger and Frau Puschbaum, on whom they had promised to pay a call once they met the sergeant's long-lost maybe-cousin Bieber. Frau Wipplinger pointed to her fine old house, 45 Maler Strasse, the one with the rich red geraniums blooming in the window boxes. It was half a block down. That was where they were to pay the elder women a call. Conditional of course upon their, and Claire's, living through the next hours.

Some things are too easy. You think, and Barbour was thinking it, the devil is there simplifying it all so that when you get where you thought you were going, it isn't—it's him and a hail of bullets instead. Farmer Bieber, suspicious, homely, smoking a pipe, eyes like black beads hiding in the fat, leather trousers, leather Austrian jacket with horns in the lapel, all stinking of three hundred years of manure, just glared. They were as welcome as plague in the nursery. Until Sergeant Bieber began to chatter. Yakkity-yak, all good cheer and innocence, as an American come abroad for the first time, all this way to look for family.

Barbour watched farmer Bieber's sour look turning sick and acid, suspicious, lip curling, pipe puffing. Until Sergeant Bieber mentioned the family name, their founding New Laxenberg, Ohio, their being Catholic, and his family being rich. Oh my, what a few of the right words can do.

They would so much appreciate a chance to look around the farmyard. Could his old grandfather on his deathbed, with memories still of Austria (no matter that this was 180 years off as to dates) write? Could he send presents? A numismatist, granddaddy collected silver dollars, and Bohemian Joachimstalers, and best of all Austrian thalers with Empress Maria Teresa's portrait engraved, bless her still-adored majesty and those days, weren't they Herr Bieber, when Austria was truly great, yes? *nicht wahr*? Yah and yah and of course Herr Bieber, swelling with pride, knew those days of glory. "Of course, I knew you would, and, well, Granddaddy would love to send some thalers," etc. etc., now evolved into Nevada silver-mined, San Francisco-minted dollars, to start an old Laxenburg family collection. Herr Bieber, curator.

"Yah, yah" and in German, "Yah, that might just work out."

"Here, Herr Baedeker," Sergeant Bieber explained his friends' lineage and family shame, "happen to have a C note on you?"

"Yeah."

The sergeant passed the crisp new hundred over to his new cousin the farmer. "To show sincerity, maybe to let me drive your tractor, let Baedeker here just be with your cows. I know, it's crazy Herr Bieber Vetter (cousin), but we're back at last, back to the soil of our homeland. And with family." Barbour quipped to himself "and singing Hearts and Flowers." The sergeant in an aside, "Herr Baedeker, slip him another two, three if you have them, C-notes, I'm going to warn him there might be some damages, a fence maybe, I'm telling him you never herded a cow, and I haven't driven a tractor for years." Barbour was looking in his wallet for Mr. C, in multiples.

"*Verrucht, ganz verrucht*," (quite crazy) said the stolid farmer, no pain on his face as he pushed three C-notes into a worn leather vest pocket. "*Viel Spas* (have fun), afterwards come in the house and we'll have some beer." Now that *is* trust. He went into the old stone farmhouse, barn attached, to begin the beer. Even the sergeant, obviously a con man out of Jersey City, shook his head in surprise. The cows, out of their routine, were milling about indifferently.

What followed was a mix between Laurel and Hardy, a Destruction Derby managed by cows, and Civil War General Sherman's unrecorded Cattle Drive to the Sea. Number 12 was next door. Eight cows readily followed the tractor, its small towed cart filled with hay, to its imposing heavily locked gate. The sergeant put the tractor (made by Mercedes Benz—clearly his new cousin was no pauper) into low gear and pushed. The gates were intended to open outward but experienced a crashing new destiny. The sergeant drove the tractor into the yard, singing yippeeyi; yippeeiyay; cows followed the yodeling cowboy over this new Chisholm Trail. Austria, meet Dodge City. Barbour, gingerly trying the tail-twist-and-push trick, persuaded one cow to join. Soon the other eight came along and, following them, another twelve or fifteen from the barnyard next door.

If this was a battle plan, Sun Tzu, Napoleon, Von Clausewitz, and Eisenhower would not have been pleased. Spontaneous Confederate generals such as "Swamp Fox" Mosby or Jeb Stewart would have applauded. General Patton would have loved it best. The truth is, and both men knew it, there was no battle plan, only as Barbour phrased it afterward, "invention, opportunity, foolhardy daring, necessity, and stupidity. Mostly luck." A lot of battles have been won with less. For serious ones you need more.

For the moment it was a circus. The cows just loved that garden, fertilizing as they chomped. From the activated house buzzers were buzzing, whoeep-whoeep-whoeep sirens went off, spotlights erratically moved back and forth, but the roses were too good, the lilac better, the berry bushes best, for any placid Biebersleek cow to be scared off. There were maybe twenty, shoving and pushing to munch the goodies. Meanwhile, the sergeant kept the front yard active throwing out additional hay, letting the tractor rev up ready for a go at the massive steel, obviously newly-installed front doors of the house.

Barbour, giving the high sign, did the circumference of the house. Three stories, maybe twenty-five rooms, an unused back entrance, old stables to the rear, back garden an overgrown mess, paint peeling from the door jambs and window frames, there was one item of great interest. All of the windows had old-fashioned European drop-down horizontal high-security steel shutters. All were open, as is normally the case when a house is occupied. Except one window on the second floor, south side, was shuttered. Only that one window. "If I were keeping a prisoner," thought Barbour, "it would have to be in that room with the shutters down." Alternatively in the basement, but about that region the outside of the house offered no clues save an ancient rusted iron coal-slide door that proved immovable.

There was, of course, one little question in their minds. Were the people here in fact the ones holding a woman captive? One haberdashery clerk's information was all they had, not a lot to go on. If they were wrong, someone was going to owe some refined Russian violinist, pianist maybe, a big explanation. And a bigger check for insult, landscaping, new front gates.

The front door opened as the sergeant had the tractor facing it. As Barbour came around from the side of the house two men in white turtleneck sweaters and dark slacks, came out. Trimly athletic, with high cheekbones, black eyes, and if one needed a clincher, both were holding menacing AK-47s. Their stance told their intentions: they were going to shoot somewhere out of furious, excited but uncomprehending compulsion. Would it be the cows, the tractor, Sergeant Bieber on the tractor seat? The billy goat who had just wandered in to join the crowd? They did not see Barbour at the corner, so he was not an option. Their big problem was that the whole scene was a circus. The billy goat now climbing into the trailer of the tractor wearing an accidental hat of marigolds added to it. From the *mafiya* standpoint, first and foremost there was nobody shooting at them, just this yodeling farmer on this tractor with his cows all seeming to have gone nuts in their front yard. The thugs had done their share of gunfighting, plenty of *ubrat, uryt, prishit* (wasting a guy ="tidying up" someone, killing="burying" a guy, blowing away="sewing up" a mug) but was that what this ungulate invasion was? Moscow city boys, isolated in an Austrian safe house, a little high on coke and vodka at the moment, they took too long to figure a diversion for what it was.

Barbour had dropped his gun in its gunnysack on the ground, already had strapped on his pistol, hung a few grenades on his belt, and because the goons on the top of the steps were so utterly confused, had time to level the gun and get off a few short bursts—not directly at vital organs, but very close across their bow. One hoodlum lost the tip of his nose, another his weapon, and a piece of finger, as some slugs tore into the AK 47 and part of the hand gripping it. The one with slug-surgery on his nose, blood spurting, was now sure this was an unfriendly visit. In pain and anger he let loose a nowhere burst. Not a cow was hit. Some damage to starlings in a tree maybe, but before a second burst, Barbour had put maybe five, seven rounds into his legs. The fellow decided to fall over on his face, skidding down the front steps. Barbour noticed he was wearing gloves.

The sergeant revved the tractor and rolled it, wheels intentionally passing on either side of the prostrate wounded man, up the stairs and through the steel double-front doors into the house. On the way, the sergeant slammed a few rounds into the bandit's automatic weapon lying on the ground. The tractor was moving ahead; right behind was the bleeding gloved mobster whose bullet-battered AK-47 had tumbled off the top steps into the bushes alongside. The other man was running into the house. Turning, he saw he had no doors left to close, and no weapon with which to shoot the driver. A knife yes, but not useful while being chased by a rather unpleasant-looking machine. The man hightailed it down a hall toward the back of the house. No doubt, as both Barbour and the Sergeant realized, to get more weapons.

So far no one else had appeared from inside the house to join the defense. That was a good sign. There were no other signs to read. The firing had started a miniature stampede but when it ceased, the cows, sensible Bieberbrushed critters, turned their attention to flowers, sweet leaves and hay.

The cows and the rest of the Pickle Family Circus behind them, Barbour and the sergeant, moved cautiously, weapons ready, through the house. Barbour realized that if Claire were here, she was hostage material. He'd damn well get upstairs to that south-facing shuttered room. If Claire were Greta, the closed shutters made no sense. But if a woman with a gun firing came at them, they had solved one mystery; it was Greta Liebowitz after all.

The sergeant would sweep the ground floor. He'd seen some house-to-house combat and moved appropriately, pausing, listening, sudden rushes, never assuming his back was safe. Barbour on the first floor heard screeching sounds and soft screams upstairs, unsettling but not seeming quite human. Mechanical. But who could tell? This was not a good sign. Not at all. Once on the second floor he was doubly cautious, but although he had had police training years before, was rightly insecure about his close combat skills. His trigger finger was very tight, his mouth dry, his heart racing, and if at this moment he had a word for himself it was, "coward."

He must try each door on the south side hall. As he moved toward that hall, testing, opening doors on the way, two messy lived-in bedrooms suggested this was where the minders slept. The noises, scratch, shriek, scream increased. He opened the first door on the south hall. Inside was a well-furnished bedroom, no evidence of current use. Outside the second door in the hallway was a steel surgical cart. On it a sound system with speakers turned toward the door. That was the source of the chalkboard scratching sounds, the female screams. It could only be there as an intimidation, fear torture, sleep deprivation device. Its volume was turned much too low to be fierce. Barbour suspected the thugs, probably contrary to someone's instruction, had turned it down so as not themselves to be bothered by it. That door at which the speakers were aimed should be a prisoner's room, locked. And it was. The door to the third room along this hall opened easily and was a furnished but stately unoccupied bed-sitting room.

Barbour wanted to do a full circuit of this square floor but feared to. If the bloody-nosed man came back to seize the hostage, it could be immediately. His back to the wall, Barbour, not too loudly for he did not wish to announce his presence to the enemy, asked, "Anyone in there?"

No reply. She could be sleeping or afraid. Or not hear his voice against the damn audio torture disc. "What the hell. Out with it," he told himself. He turned off the sound system, kept his M-16, fully automatic, at the ready, and shouted, "Hey Claire, are you in there? This is Barbour."

A feeble woman's voice replied. A voice sick, tired, in pain, perhaps weakened by hunger. "Oh, thank God you're here. Thank God."

He would never find the keys. "Stand way the hell back from this door against the wall that separates your room from this hall."

He pulled out the ancient 45 which still seemed to be dress issue for some embassy marines, blew three shots into the lock, watched it disintegrate, opened the door, and there God bless her was, it must be, Claire. Or if not, Greta in equally bad shape. She wore a robe which must have been forty years old—no doubt something left in the closet. She was pale, with fever-blue eyes. She had a nasty face wound, a seriously abraded cheek which was beginning to develop scabs. There were some thumping large black and blue marks on her chin and forehead, wrists likewise, and she was barefoot. "Are you Claire Dubois?"

"Yes, what's left of me." She managed a grin. The whole world of Barbour's worry lightened.

He beckoned her toward him. She moved slowly. He stayed at the door, M-16 swinging from side to side, because with all the noise he had made, if the thug on the loose wanted to find him, he would know where to look.

"Find your shoes. Get a sweater or put a blanket over you, whatever. We're going to get you out of here."

She was wobbly. He put his arm around her waist supporting her, liking the way she felt. Womanly. She was toughing it. No whimpers. Tried to joke about his name being on her dance card for the rest of this Viennese ball. His heart went out to her. When this was over he himself might allow himself to cry on her behalf. The poor damn woman. She had taken a great deal of abuse he hated to think of how much and what. There was no chance this woman was any Greta mafiyosa. She clung to him as they reached the great front stairway. With his holding her, one arm on his M-16, they were, he realized, sitting ducks for any rearmed stalking thug. Unless the yodeling marine cowboy had gotten him first. Below was silence. They walked down the stairs very slowly.

23

Even mafiya can be unlucky. All that meanness, all those plans, a house full of weapons, money, drugs enough for kicks, vodka enough for months, and magnificent food, even champagne—for when Square was in residence, it was nothing but the best for him and his friends, and some Partners as well. The girls were selected from the loveliest of high-class whores, who came in to serve a man in everything he needed: in the kitchen as cooks; serving table for the assembled male company; and in bed, as imaginative as acrobats, and as pleasing as their high pay required. And believe it, a great deal was required.

The armory, for it was that and loaded for bear, was in an old pantry off the huge kitchen. They'd locked it yesterday because the Austrian maid came in every other day, a local woman, fat, trusted in no respect. The two thugs kept their personal weapons in the drawers of their bedroom bureaus when the woman was here. She was not allowed on the second floor because of the prisoner. The third floor was unused except for the big parties when friends came roaring aboard. For maid's days, good sense necessitated they lock up the armory. They also locked up the silver, the china, the linens, you name it. Anybody out of Moscow knows everyone is a thief.

Pistol, for it was he whose nose had been shortened by a slug, too angry to be in pain, and too professional to be afraid. A *patsany* (mafiya soldier, warrior) with as many hits to his credit as anyone his age in Moscow, he believed he had no reason to be afraid of these farmers whose surprise attack, and he was embarrassed about *that* success, had taken advantage. Both cowboys, he had no idea where they were from, were rotten shots. If they had not been he and Andrei would both be dead. They'd been sitting ducks. Neither of the cowboys, as Pistol's mind registered the action play by play, had hit his target. Andrei was shot only in the legs, and then the tractor driver missed him when he aimed to finish him off by driving over him, missing again when he fired to get the AK-

47 on the ground but not hitting Andrei. The other one, firing at him from the corner, missed him entirely but for this damn bleeding nose. Jerks. Cowherders.

He locked the kitchen door behind him, reached the pantry, and reached for his keys. That was when the panic hit him. His keys were in his room upstairs. Holy Mother, Blessed Virgin. Fuck! In the rush of alarms he had grabbed his AK-47 but left his pistol, never his weapon of choice, upstairs. All he had was his knife. Plus those here in the kitchen. Pistol was good with a knife. Against the farmers, well, he smiled. If only he could get them one at a time from behind. Child's play.

He moved slowly, listening, toward the locked kitchen door. About to open it, he thought he heard, yes, he heard a movement just outside it. Saw the door handle turn, the door softly being pushed and, because locked, unyielding. Not so good. Maybe the farmer would let it go. Maybe not. Maybe best move just behind the door so that if the farmer entered he could grab him, slash his throat from behind, making the man's automatic—it had looked like an M16 but Pistol was not a weapons buff and could not be sure—completely useless. Pistol grinned. He *liked* slashing throats. It was so much more personal than bullets, than *na grochnut*, to bang.

People make mistakes. The sergeant would no more move into a locked room, yeah, some kind of hint there, with an half-opened door behind him than, well, think of something terrible like becoming a civilian. As a precaution against killing someone who didn't deserve it, he shouted in German and in English, "Anybody in there?" No answer. "Hey!" loudly. No reply. Himself close to the door he could just hear the breathing, ever so slight a sound, inside to the left, where a person would stand just behind an expected half-open door. The sergeant said to himself, "Well, that does kind of clinch it." He let loose a straight-on shredding blast from his M16 to shatter the handle, lock, and then up, down and sideways, most of the ordinary wooden door. As expected, no slumping body. The breathing, after all, had been immediately to the left. He kicked the remains of the door hard. Only the furthermost left upright portion with the hinges on it, maybe six inches across, made it to the wall behind.

His playmate must have stepped further back. No, not a good time to enter, since the man there would have the advantage, assuming any weapon or indeed a good leap. Ordinarily, say sitting at home reading a good book, the sergeant would have preferred not to do it; he was a murderous man only when aroused. He feinted with an attention-getting blast, he could see nothing there but sinks and cabinets, to the right wall of the kitchen, then pushed his weapon around the corner where the remains of hinge and door still hung and let go, up, down and sideways, a serious round of fire. As he did so he felt the sting, looked down and saw the knife. It had buried itself in the back of his left hand, which held the carbine stock. The sergeant didn't like the fellow who had done that at all. He raked the inner left wall behind the door, the whole wall of the kitchen wall perpendicular to it, and listening, heard the last wheezes, saw the blood running on the old linoleum to the doorjamb. Very cautiously, with another rake of fire for good measure, this one right on the floor to the left, Sergeant recently Bieber but né Erwin, poked in his head and was gratified, deeply gratified. The son of a bitch, or what was left of him after maybe twenty-five rounds had done some serious meat chopping, was seriously dead.

Barbour, asking Claire to lean against the wall at the bottom of the staircase, yelled out the $64 question—maybe $10,000 now with contest inflation. "You okay, Sergeant?" No answer would have meant not only was he not okay, but maybe the thug was. Important question, important answer.

From down the hall, way to the back, came, "Yeah, semper fi all the way." Sergeant now Erwin again was strolling down the hall, M16 over his shoulder, a bloody knife stuck as a prize in his belt, and a very bloody kitchen towel wrapped around his left hand. "Paraphrasing Pogo, buddy, we have met the enemy and he wasn't us." There were introductions, smiles, a bit of triumph all around.

They moved toward the front door, not without caution, for who knows? to see farmer Bieber standing where the gates had been, shotgun leveled at them. His eyes, however were darting round about the large front garden. In German, "15, 16, 17, 18, 19, 20, yah gut. *Und* the billy goat. *Und* the tractor," even if a bit airborne in mid front door, the small wagon behind it on the steps, not visibly the worse for wear. "*Gut*." And in German, "Cows are fine, goat is fine, tractor looks okay, but you were badly noisy." He lowered the shotgun to his side. With a downward patting stroke farmer Bieber motioned to Barbour, who absent-mindedly held the M16 in his hand, to lower the weapon. Farmer Bieber then walked—one would say with amazing confidence, given the cows milling, the billy goat now climbing a tree, the gunfire just now and the wounded man lying bleeding on the walkway—toward the front door. Passing the wounded thug, Bieber leaned down, rather brusquely pulled his hair to lift up the man's head and see his face, and with something less than tenderness dropped the head, thudding to the ground. "*Gut, gut*."

In the meantime, the sergeant, neat farm boy he once had been, slowly backed the tractor and tow down the steps, around the wounded thug, over the crumpled steel gates, and quick turned it back into its home barnyard. The cows, still munching on garden luxuries, had no intention of following. Farmer Bieber waited for his new-found, well maybe, Ohio cousin to return. It was only a few minutes, the sergeant and the tractor were both quick.

In German, Bieber explained to the sergeant who translated as necessary to Barbour and Claire, "I hated these people. Rich damn *mafiya*, dirty Russian foreigners, and everyone in the neighborhood knew it. I caught them one day stealing two chickens and a whole ten-liter canister of my fresh dairy milk. I came out with my shotgun. They pointed that," Bieber gestured toward the AK-47, "and told me in rotten German that they would kill me and my whole family if I squawked. I'm no coward but I knew they meant it. And so, every few days they walk into my barn, barnyard, take what they want; chickens, eggs, a goose twice, milk. Thank goodness my wife is fat and my daughter has moved away. Bastards. I was just hoping you'd be the fellows to show them what for. I wasn't sure, but with a crazy story like you had, I had a hunch."

He was smiling broadly. He reached into his worn leather vest pocket, pulled out the three hundred-dollar bills, and returned them. "I owe you, not you me," he said. "Now come, I'd say let's have that beer, lots of beer, and dinner too, but," he was looking at Claire, "this lady seems badly hurt. My wife would gladly look after her, but I think she may need a doctor or a hospital, don't you think?"

They all agreed. They were walking toward Musicker Allee when a black Mercedes began to turn in the driveway before being halted by the broken gates. There were three men inside, one square-jawed, and none looking anything but mafiya. Farmer Bieber quickly whistled, a herder's kissing sound with his lips, and moved his astonishingly responsive cattle in a throng toward the car, into the open gate space, thus blocking the view from the car as well as eliminating any chance of the men leaving it, stuck now in the midst of the herd.

"More of the neighbors," said farmer Bieber, "and not at all nice people. Look, I can get out with and behind my cows but I think you'd better go around back. I know you don't want a firefight with that sick lady with you. Go around the side. There's a big old stable at the back, used to have carriages for the nobility that lived here, then horses and buggies. Inside the stable three stalls down there's a door that goes through the wall at back into neighbor Janggle's garden. They're very old. Please don't bother them—all that shooting—they'll already be terribly frightened. You two with your guns and that wounded lady would be too much. You can't get from the Janggle's back into my place easily. If you can find your way I'd shelter you, but I don't think it's safe.

"Those mafiya will look in my barn and house for sure, not for long because everyone around here has called the police, but we have no Laxenburg city police—well, one constable but he'll be in hiding after all this noise. He's a coward, drinks too much, is only good for girls and dancing. The serious police have to come from Vienna, which is why you haven't seen them by now. Nor am I sure the police will be so happy with you; that man there on the ground with the bullet wounds who's fainted, I think shooting him might be considered a little bit illegal, especially on his own property, even if his AK 47 is illegal. But then so are your American M16s. And those grenades," he looked at those hanging on their belts, "even if they are for killing fish, no, the police won't believe it, no matter how stupid they are.

"Lord knows what you left in the house, but I did hear the shooting and now I see only one mafiya, not two, so I have my idea. Well, if I were you—unless you are somehow already approved by the police, I doubt that, and you know I don't care who you are"—he smiled at the sergeant, "maybe even some kind of cousin, but that was too convenient. But seeing that you have saved this poor beautiful woman here, I think I can guess you came to do that. Anyway I would lay low for a while. She will be all right in hospital but you'd need a car, and right now yours is in sight of the Russians where they would see you."

The sergeant was no good at plans for retreat, nor was Barbour. They were set to pondering. Claire leaned heavily against Barbour, who had not taken his arm from around her waist. "Problems," they agreed.

"There is a retired doctor near here," continued Bieber, "who keeps a little clinic in his house to see his old patients—Dr. Wipplinger, who lives near here on Maler Strasse. An old friend, I'll call him to tell him you're an American cousin whose friend's girlfriend has had a bad fall. But you'll have to leave those weapons somewhere."

They interrupted to remind Farmer Bieber they already knew Frau Wipplinger and she had shown them where her house was.

"*Gut, gut*. Nice old people."

The sergeant paused, some mischief on his mind. "Herr Cousin Bieber. when you call Frau Wipplinger to say I'm your cousin, better tell them something."

"Yah? What?"

"Well, the Biebers have been in America a long time. Lots of intermarriage there. Tell her I'm part red Indian, Shawnee, a descendant of chiefs Blue Jacket and Little Turtle who fought General Mad Anthony Wayne in Ohio. She'll have read the Winnatou stories, she'll love it."

Bieber looked at his mixed-blood no-way cousin curiously.

"And tell her I'm part Jewish, on grandmother's grandfather's side."

"*Gott in Himmel*!" Bieber was stunned. "You know how anti-Semitic Austrians were, maybe some even still are. You my cousin, part a Jew?"

"Yeah, Cousin, why not? It'll be good for her. I liked the old lady. You know, you Austrians have a lot of World War II penance to do, Hail Marys, that sort of thing. I just bet that she'll see this is her chance for atonement, especially since we are all going to have to live with them in hiding. And besides I have some wonderful red Indian stories to tell. Some of them are maybe even true."

Farmer Bieber was readjusting his head. Games had been played with, on, in it. He sighed, "Yah, Cousin, whatever you say. This will be a day little old Laxenburg won't soon forget." He paused, scratching the ground with his boot like an old horse. "Ah, what the devil, Cousin. You play the family games. Me, now, I have to be practical. You've got to get rid of your guns, as I said. I tell you what, stuff them under the pile of old saddle blankets, other ancient junk on the floor of the tackroom in that old stable in back. Don't let the rats there bite you. When the mafiya leave—and the Vienna police will see to that—I'll come get your guns. I'll put them in my barn safely. I will keep them for you. Here is my card with telephone number. Call if you need anything, call me to tell you how you are. You can trust me.

"And yes, I want to hear your red Indian stories. I myself read Karl Marx. I know he wrote them all while sitting in some German jail, all about Old Shatterhand, Winnetou. So here you are, a red Indian you say. Tecumseh's child? Next Sitting Bull will be my cousin too, and Geronimo, eh? Oh well, when I tell my wife she'll love it. Now you need to know something about my side of the family. My son is that cowardly girl-chasing constable I told you about. But oh my, how that boy can sing and play the accordion! And his girlfriend of the moment is a Tamil gypsy fortuneteller, her coin earrings reach to her shoulders, can you imagine that happening, like you are happening, to a respectable Laxenburg Bieber? *Gott in Himmel*. But she did tell me last week, oh my how she stared into that crystal ball, that my cows would get into some neighbor's garden. When you two arrived, I already knew something interesting was going to happen. Why else would I have let you play, eh?"

This was one very nice Bieber. And not so dumb or slow when he needed to be quick. Waving goodbye, ducking next to the side of a cow on the far left side of the gates as he headed to his barnyard next door, he would easily elude the Russians who were stuck, furious, no doubt cursing, cow-blind to the world, inside their car. A herd of cows is not likely to be budged by pushing from the inside of a car door. Along the side of the house, could they have seen them, two musketeers and a limping blonde woman headed toward the tumbledown stables in the back. In there they would find a groom's old brown smock there for Claire to wear, a place to stash their munitions—and Bieber was right—rats almost big enough to carry the dry and fraying saddles hung on the tackroom wall. Through it all Claire was tough as nails. For all her pain she hobbled gamely.

There was an alley behind the houses on Maler Strasse. It was this route, happily narrow with garbage cans and piles of other rubbish so that fugitives could successfully slink, they took to the Wipplinger house. As with Musicker Allee, back walls had back gates. Number 45 could be identifed, once Barbour had boosted the sergeant so that his head could see over the top of the high wall, by its geraniums in window boxes at the rear of the large, old wood-and-stucco house,with its red-tile roof; traditional Austrian village architecture. On Maler Strasse itself, as all about, policc sircns, ambulance sirens, fire engines, howling dogs, mooing cattle, billy goats baahing, and no doubt ambulances. If cats were daytime singers they, too, would have joined in this excitement, this din. "We'll remember this, buddy, as the old Laxenburg Stomp."

A wisecrack did not confidence make. If the Wipplingers did not take kindly to this sweaty, messy, gunpowder-fragrant, let-down-after-the-party exhausted American duo, with the battered and clearly ill gun moll Claire hobbling along, this night and many others would be spent in Austrian jails. With quite a bill building up on a rented car, happily under the name of Riskin. (With a conspiratorial tip from Ambassador Owen, who confessed he didn't like him either, about where the man's office was, Barbour had called upon the attaché Riskin, who had proven to be such an unhelpful duty officer. Having worked once with pickpockets, learned "the scissors and the bump" Barbour had stolen the man's wallet to use at Vienna Hertz.) No one ever looks at driver's-license pictures, especially when the photo is a bit smeared with pastry. Barbour had had a gooey rich cream and chocolate Viennese pastry in his hand when he went in to Hertz. He left Attaché Riskin's credit card on deposit as well. "What the hell," Barbour had said to himself, "if you're going to go outlaw, go full-bore." Besides, the pastry was delicious.

As they entered the heavy but surprisingly unlocked back gate, they realized that everything depended on the Wipplingers and what Farmer Bieber had told them on the phone. There were no police armored vehicles in the backyard nor machine guns mounted in the windows, a good sign. They knocked at the back door as a police cruiser with sirens blasting, searching for them no doubt, careened down the alley they had left just in time.

The gray-haired Frau Wipplinger, about sevent-five, wearing steel-framed glasses, probably not a bit over 5' 2", had run; they had heard her sprinting to answer their knock. She was marvelously excited, her inquisitive blue eyes gleaming. Her English was excellent. "This is such fun! Herr Bieber told me everything. You killed the Russian gangsters, you saved his cows and chickens, you are American spies, the one of you with the plaid shirt," she nodded at the sergeant, "had family who came from Laxenburg to America to fight Indians but your grandfather married one instead. And, oh I cannot imagine it, somebody else married somebody else to make a Jewish connection for Herr Bieber! That's so funny. You can't imagine. He'll brag to everyone about it to prove he's no longer a Nazi. He was one of those brown-shirted little—may I swear in front of you?" They nodded yes, wondering how frightfully vulgar this gentle old lady might be. "A Nazi brown-shirted little *jerk*, that's what he was. A real," she paused, "my grand nephew who lives in Nashville teaches me English naughty words, a real nerd. A vulgar little boy. But time, democracy, a good wife, children growing up tolerant, and then there were those war crimes trials as reminders, all these were good for his character. Now he's going to go bragging that he helped a red Indian Jew kill Russian gangsters! He'll be showing us the bow and arrow, or some such. I've never heard him so happy as he was a few minutes ago. And oh yes, he's my second cousin, but everybody in Laxenburg is some kind of cousin. Not that," she gave Sergeant Erwin a penetrating look, "I think for a *minute* that you're any kind of cousin to anyone in this town. But what does it matter? You've killed those awful Russians who were frightening Herr Bieber and his wife to death, and now if we don't hide you, just like the good Dutch did for Anne Frank, those awful Vienna police will throw you in prison for the rest of your lives. No, we won't let that happen!"

She stopped. "Oh dear Lord forgive me, that's dreadful of me." She rushed up to Claire and hugged her. "You poor dear, here you are beaten and starved by the gangsters, and I haven't taken you in to my husband, who has been setting up his clinic to look after you. And you two boys look a positive fright. You," she looked at Barbour, and suddenly her eyes grew moist, "you remind me of my brother who was killed in the war at Stalingrad. Ah, ah, do forgive me, this is just not an ordinary day for me, well not for anybody in Laxenburg, I suppose. I guess I have forgotten how to act."

She led them inside, slowly walked Claire to the front of the house where old Doctor Wipplinger had his clinic in his home, took the two "boys" upstairs, told them to bathe, showed them the back room where they would sleep. "It used to be my son's, but he's married now and lives in Salzburg." Pointing down the hall to where she had "fixed up ever so nicely" a guest room for Claire, she reminded them to keep the draperies closed at all times so neighbors couldn't see them and added, My Lord, she had forgotten they hadn't eaten all day. "I have a little something cooking. Sauerbraten, dumplings, beet salad, strudel, a good strong kirsch. Your lady, Claire is it? I'll serve her dinner in bed. She has to rest for a few days. I'm afraid we can't risk taking her to a plastic surgeon in hospital, but Klaus, my husband, has a friend, a specialist, who'll come over here to see what he can do about her face. The poor girl! Those awful Russian gangsters! We're all so glad you killed them. But now, what's the phrase the American movies have? You'll have to 'lay low.' Yes, now, no nonsense boys, do what I say."

They were too tired, too grateful, too wise to give her any nonsense. For now they would wash up, enjoy the clean clothes laid out on the bed, sleep, eat and then wonder what one did when (a) an AWOL Marine master sergeant turned felony fugitive, and (b) a Senior Agent stole a wallet, procured a rental car using stolen documents, and (a & b) both found themselves no doubt wanted for murder. Perhaps the ambassador could fix it so that somewhere under Austria's quite harsh Napoleonic law, saving a kidnapped woman and shooting in self-defense might be construed as extenuating, if not justifying, circumstances. Both knew Ambassador Owen would hear it all over the radio, see it in the press, watch it on CNN with the rest of the world, and do his diplomatic damnedest. With Claire's father on the team with him, there would be lots of U.S. clout to bail their poor asses out of the mess they were immensely proud to have gotten into, then emerged from, with Claire alive.

In the meantime, for however long it might be, they must stay hidden. God bless farmer Bieber and the Wipplingers! When they visited Claire in her room their gratitude was multiplied. She was pale as a ghost, with a great bandage on her cheek, one on her forehead, some on her elbows, and one foot up, suggesting under the blankets a sprained ankle on ice—but smiling. It was time soon to get acquainted under circumstances other than a hail of gunfire. Frau Wipplinger, nurse and châtelaine in charge, had given permission for them all to gather round for wine together, including the doctor himself: red-cheeked, white-haired, a plump advertisement for the "before" photographs for slimming products. Not a bad hideout.

They watched CNN that evening. World news. Big news. Them. Shootout in Laxenburg. No witnesses. Federal police initially held three Russians found at the scene of the crime. The Russian Embassy protested and one, the commercial attaché, was released with apologies. Two others also released. Two unidentified men had been found shot. One had multiple bullet wounds in the leg, but the cause of death an assassination-style bullet through the back of the head. The other had been shredded with automatic rifle gunfire. Initial ballistics tests suggested a Russian AK-47.

Further, there were indications a woman had been living in the house. Police would not release any information as to her possible nationality or identity. Speculation had arisen that she was a member of the mafiya who had successfully fled, perhaps kidnapped by the unknown assailants who had gunned down the two Russians. Russia lodged a major diplomatic protest with Austria. Austrian police indicated they had strong leads as to who the assailants were. A source who spoke on condition of anonymity said the American CIA were suspected. Another anonymous source said the murdered Russians were investigators looking into possible Austrian ties to Russian drug smuggling. Killers were believed to be Austrian drug dealers. The mayor of Laxenburg told of UFOs seen recently in the region. Etc., etc., etc.

"Can you boys tell us what of that is true?"

Barbour replied, "We can't tell you what we don't know, unlike reporters who, as we see there, are happy to tell the world what they don't know they know. First, we aren't CIA. Vetter Bieber there, born Erwin, is a U.S. Marine. I'm a Federal agent who investigates international financial crimes—mafiya for example. Second, as you know, the Russians who were killed and those arrested were mafiya. Third, we did not kill the man with the gunshot wounds in his legs; the Russians in a Mercedes that was coming in the gate, though Farmer Bieber's cows stopped them, must have executed him. It's an old mafiya way of saying thank you and shut up. Also, the other man we did kill, but not by using a Russian AK-47. That is either bad reporting or the police giving out disinformation, I've no idea why, unless the Austrian government is inventing a defense against the Russian protests, or setting up the Russians they had to release, or some other kind of fix is being put in."

"Fix?" Doctor Wipplinger had not heard the word.

"Manipulating evidence and facts to hide something, to set someone up, some kind of cunning at work. Nice if it were on our side, which remotely it might be." He knew that Ambassador Owen must be making frequent trips to the Austrian Foreign Ministry, most certainly to remind them that their Federal police (a) had not provided an emergency response to the kidnapping of an American Federal agent; (b) would have had responsibility for her death had not Americans (unspecified, but obviously known to all insiders) saved her at great risk and with no backup; (c) had not cooperated with a

Federal agent in spite of a mutual cooperation agreement, (d) could well expect a major U.S. protest on these and more counts unless they cleaned up their *schlamperei* (slothful, indifferent) act and provided a police investigation that would clear the Americans involved, so that when they came forward, as the Ambassador was sure they would given satisfactory assurances, they would be more likely to receive medals than life sentences in prison. This Barbour surmised, knowing Ambassador Owen. He might equally have guessed that a set of cables from the State Department, courtesy of "smoothie" Dubois and his cronies, had reinforced Owen's message.

Barbour found out later that it was not a happy time for Major Kummering, particularly when the independent investigators assigned to his case found (a) inexplicable deposits in his personal bank account, which proved to be at a private bank, Brody et Cie, where secret accounts were also suspected; and (b) he had given no orders whatsoever to follow up on the information that Agent Barbour had given him. Indeed the Major denied, huffing and puffing, that Agent Barbour had ever been to see him. "Never!" Unfortunately, a police lieutenant, a file clerk, a secretary who had found the American to be "rather handsome", and a telephone operator's call log showed the Major to be somewhat less than truthful. He was put on suspension and his home telephone tapped. The public prosecutor would be indicting him, but not before the Russian section of the Federal Police Organized Crime Bureau had time to make some inquiries. Telephone company records of his calls from home were seized, and odd they proved to be, showing calls to Moscow, Talinn, Warsaw; twice Pakistan; lots to Warsaw, and California—lots of calls to California. And travel to Warsaw, too, as well as the East, and Germany, and Paris. "So many relatives," the peripatetic Major had explained to the investigators, "so much to see in the world." "Odd," they replied, "that there is no record of your ever having paid for the tickets or informed your superiors of your travel plans." Lest the Major prefer balmier climates, or leave without notice, he was watched. The real questions remained: Who else in the Federal service was compromised? Who was this stupid Major Kummering working for? And just how much criminality had been going under the protection of the Major and his conspirators higher up?

A phrase that Barbour often used seemed apt. "You never know. You just never know what just plain folks may be up to."

Frau Wipplinger had bustled about with duvet, lavender sachets, flower-embroidered pillowcases on the freshly plumped pillows, new magazines in

French to make Claire's room. It was as homey as could be, a fine place for the rest that, after all Claire truly needed. Now for that rest they must leave her. But before they departed, Claire asked Barbour and the sergeant to her bedside.

Weak though she was, she squeezed their hands in thanks, and asked them to lean down so she could give them each a kiss. Having done so, she said to Barbour, "Mind if we do that again?" Courtly here in Austria, the home of gallantry, he allowed as how he did not mind. This time the kiss, right there in front of God, Wipplingers, and an idiot TV announcer selling vacation trips to Moscow, was on the lips. It suggested there might be a tomorrow.

24

Most English gentlemen have several clubs; their attendance at one or another depends on the lecture, the wines to be tasted, or preference for a mood or a food. In the case of the Caledonian Club tonight in Knightsbridge, it was the range of single malts and the excellence of the smoked salmon and roast beef. Tonight Ambassador Dubois was the grateful host. As an ambassador with Scottish friends, a Scots devolutionist movie star as sponsor, and a wee bit of Stuart in him, being elected to membership had been easy. Easy too to be ordering doubles, one need not specify "neat" here of Macallan, for to celebrate Claire's safety was worthy of the best. Well, almost the best, for a 25-year-old Macallan might cost twelve pounds a dram, and that is beyond a Scotsman's tolerance. No, it was the 12-year-old. No insult to Claire, understand, but respect to thrift.

They had all seen CNN and read the local papers. The London tabloids, a lunatic match for those at a U.S. grocery checkout stand, had made most of the "Wild West shootout" in Laxenburg. One good authority reported that MI6 was at war with the new Russian security services, with thirty or so killed on each side At stake was the "massive secret Russian electronic surveillance site in Laxenburg," etc. One tabloid headline read, "Is this the start of World War III?" Pundits weighed in: "Stocks of weapons-grade plutonium in transit to Iran are stored behind the facade of a quaint Austrian village. Dozens of villagers have died of radiation poisoning. Fear that military raid released a nuclear waste cloud." Or again, "From a reliable source, Austrian neo-Nazi right in secret pact with Russian Communists to undermine EU and NATO, U.S. Green Berets secretly invaded their headquarters in quaint Austrian village where, significantly, Hitler was born." Etc. etc.

Quincy Adams, summarizing for the three of them, for Sir Peter was the third, said sarcastically, "Without the press's deep insights, one would hardly know what was going on."

Happily they did know a bit better. George Dubois's friend Ron Owen, more sensitive now to Eastern electronic surveillance capabilities than before, had retreated to the old ways—the mail, albeit express—to write to George care of the U.S. Embassy, for Ambassador Owen had elected to stay in London rather than return to Kiev while his daughter was still missing. He described the success of "expeditionary forces,"including the reluctance of certain Austrian officials to assist and assured his friend that "your most precious treasure is no doubt safe, although apparently still with the expeditionary force, whose emergence must await a change in the official Austrian position—which is that murder has been committed and those responsible charged."

It was to the latter that they had addressed themselves. Sir Peter, who had gone to school at Oxford with the present Foreign Minister, told his friends he had managed to get the Foreign Office to send a private communiqué assuring that "the British Government would most forcibly demand of the Austrian Government a strict adherence to international law guaranteeing the safety of NATO and EU member government officials"—a reminder that Claire Dubois, since she had been travelling with an official passport, had the right to diplomatic protection, not police indifference. Appended, for such confidential communiqués always have attachments, was a private note, Foreign Minister to Foreign Minister: "Her Majesty's Government is appalled to have learned through our private channels that the Austrian Government takes no responsibility for the operation of protected Russian mafiya on its territory, criminals who made attempts on the lives of legitimately present Western officials." Read that as saying, "You bastards, our boys had to go in because your cops were corrupt and willing to sacrifice our officials' lives."

Of course, the most confidential of diplomatic exchanges is made public any time an interest is better served by public outcry. The Foreign Minister thereby let it be known that Britain was prepared to open the matter before not only the Parliament in Strasbourg (which some in the Cabinet quietly muttered would be the first time that august body had ever addressed a matter of any consequence), but also the European Commission in Brussels. As if Britain had not made enough trouble over Maaastricht and the euro.

Quincy Adams, more informal as Americans are, had undertaken simply to write a private note to the wife of the Austrian chancellor who had once been—long ago when he was working darkly in Vienna—his mistress. "Darling. Get your husband to see straight on this one. The Russians otherwise will have the collective Austrian behind. And if our boys who saved the day and the girl don't get out unscathed, be prepared to find Washington and Brussels collectively hanging the same Austrian behind from the UN flagpole. (signed) Love and sweet memories, Quincy." His note combined all the niceties of bluff, old markers called in, blackmail, and in fact good advice.

"Remedial action," said Sir Peter.

"A much-needed intervention," intoned George Dubois.

"A friendly reminder," Quincy added.

"A toast to Claire, her rescuers, diplomacy and the ability of the Austrian Government to get its head out of the anatomical dark place where it seems to have been inserted."

"Here, here," by which they also meant the waiter should return with another round of drink. After which, feeling the world was in good hands—their own—they repaired upstairs to the no doubt best smoked salmon in London.

25

The IFFY Director was still on vacation, and would see to it that he didn't return until his Second, the ever-reliable Mac, had cleaned up, buried, burned, done whatever he had to do to eradicate the mess. It was bad enough when the Director had heard about Dubois being the malevolent impostor Liebowitz, thus leaving IFFY with mafiya mud on its face. Equally as bad when Hashimoto got his. Whatever the coroner said, the cop establishment believed Hashimoto had been blown away. Soon every reporter in the world would be digging, and one of them would find out that Claire Dubois was really Greta Liebowitz. Somebody already could have learned who made a sane inference from the IFFY telephone log, Personnel's bloopers, and what Mac had reported by telephone he had learned through a rather hostile interrogation of Mumbles Swobo. Conclusion: Sir Peter Dixon, Acting Head of Scotland Yard, knew more of this Greta-to-Dubois mess than he did, and did so many days ago, before IFFY had an inkling. "What the hell," the Director asked himself, "has Scotland Yard got going on this case?" The Director, not an intrepid fellow, buried his head in his hands.

His wife was used to that. She loathed him for it but played the wife well. "May I get you an aspirin, dear?"

"Yes, darling, please, make it three." As she brought them she knew this was one of those days when she wished the little white tablets were arsenic.

The Director was feeling sorry for himself. And frightened. And angry. Everybody knew everything but him. All he got was the static. And when the Dubois-Liebowitz-Hashimoto thing got out, the Director might just as well stay on vacation for he would certainly be fired: this kind of thing required blood for blood. He was a former President's hold-over political appointee in any event. Expendable, especially so by the new administration. "Expendable," he said to himself gloomily, "or worse. I might be indicted for criminal negligence, violating national security, whatever."

Now, via CNN in his living room, wrecking the Director's happy vacation bungalow in Hawaii, came the news from Laxenburg. Barbour of course—Crusader Mouse, as cops called such righteous loners. Who else could it have been? He had gone to private war, along with some unknown but equally loony avenger, to snatch, that is how the Director read it from the mail sent on by his office, yes to kidnap a goddamned Russian mafiya agent, Greta Liebowitz. In this vendetta, Barbour and Co. versus the mafiya world, he and his Schwarzenegger Terminator #2 had killed Lord knows how many Russians. Lovely implications for IFFY's treaty negotiations going on with Russia, established with Austria, expanding in the European Community. "Oh yes, indeed. A total disaster. Just yummy," said the Director grimly, lifting his head from his mothering hands. He asked his wife to fix him another mai-tai to go with the rice krispies, for it was only breakfast time. "Mac's mess," he muttered. "Yes, dear," she responsed soothingly, inwardly bitter, wishing she had married someone less wimpy. She secretly poured a stiff one for herself. If this was a vacation in paradise, she would make her next reservations for hell.

He had sworn he wouldn't, but he couldn't help himself. His speech was only slightly slurred by the three mai-tai's slurred when he called Mac at IFFY in Washington. "Where do we stand goddamn it?"

"In the mud, head down, with swamp tigers pulling our boots off," replied his second. Mac was never too good at reassurance. Dolan, in the room with him, found the image too vivid for comfort.

"Was it Barbour?"

"He hasn't been good enough to send us photographs of himself in Laxenburg posing next to a row of his kills strung up like coyotes, but who else? Who else but our Lone Ranger?"

"And who was in it with him?"

"For all we know, Martians."

"What does the embassy in Vienna say?"

"They don't know him. I suspect they'd deny they were in Vienna. He did get our cables, plus some mail, the contents of which they don't know, and then he blew town—no doubt to blow up Laxenburg and get the girl out."

"Did he get her?"

"Well, nobody said they found her body, so we think so."

"What's he going to do with—"

Mac interrupted his boss, "Don't assume this is a secure line, so let's not use names, okay?"

"Okay." The boss wasn't a bit happy about that and asked instead, "So, all in all, where do we stand on the Brody case?"

"*Stand*? Free fall, boss, free fall with no parachute. Brody has disappeared. Austrian Federal police won't cooperate on anything. Like I say, our own embassy doesn't talk to us. Barbour has disappeared off the face of the earth, a fugitive; he'll be hiding out in Libya next. All the Warsaw tipsters are dead. No cable transmission records anywhere. And if Barbour and the woman he retrieved aren't safe—and I'll explain that second possibility some other day when the FBI comes back from vacation to finish their document integrity analysis—we will have more hell to pay from more government agencies than the taxpayer ever knew he was supporting."

"Christ!"

"Make every day a Sunday, boss. Go to church, pray, ask for absolution, make miracles."

"So we have nothing, and the world is crashing down around our heads?"

"Nope, we got one thing left, and that is Mr. C, if there is one separate from Brody *et Cie*, boss, which is French for 'incorporated,' and if he—if it is a *he*—is in California operating out of a place called Malome. And as for the tip, boss, it doesn't matter if this telephone line isn't secure, because the guys with black hats got it all originally, and knew it all anyway. So at the moment, C in Malome, Californ-i-ay is all we got, our only way back into some giant operation in Austria and Eastern Europe(sic). He, Mr. C, is our only route back to Barbour, Warsaw, and Greta whoever, as well as Hashimoto's killer, whoever eliminated all the Warsaw finks, what big money is protecting itself from—essentially, boss, *us*. This C, and for all we know that could just stand for 'C' as in hundred-dollar bills stuffed in a crock of cocaine profits, like 'C' for cocaine itself, all of that. But the tip had a 'Mr.' in front of it, just like Brody had an 'et Cie' with it, and in Malome, California, there's no known action with C for money and C for cocaine. Understand?"

"Yeah." The boss, no artist with words, understood these homonyms by the confusion they caused him.

"So?"

"So, boss, we've got choices. We have no jurisdiction for IFFY Stateside unless we have evidence of money laundering. DEA does have jurisdiction and we've met one field man of theirs, a black guy named Grossman, who while covering most of California DEA, was told to find Mr. C. Grossman tells me it's a near-impossibility unless you work long and hard from the inside. Fortunately we do, in a way, already have a man inside, an old friend of Barbour's who's gone native, works as a detective there. DEA seems to trust him. Grossman will, so we have to. That's our team, boss: Grossman as backup in the big city, and the kindness of an ex-Federal officer who, if we say pretty please and suck a little DEA you-know-what, *may* get us to a Russian mafiya ring that killed a bunch of folks. And some obvious international associates, since Mr. C in California working with Brody in Vienna and people getting bumped off in Warsaw and Washington does not suggest we are dealing with provincial, or in any way nice people."

"Okay, you handle it, Mac. I'm extending my leave until this case is solved and I can come take credit for it." He laughed congenially. Ho, ho, ho.

Mac McLaughlin at the other end did not laugh. Extending his leave was exactly what the boss would do. Unless they were fired which, right now, seemed to be as good a bet as Tuesday following Monday with the calendar proving it in front of you.

McLaughlin called in Doc Dolan. Together in the room they telephoned Suit Number One at DEA, had a few extra helpings of humble pie shoved down their throats, and were told that DEA had "suddenly been tasked with other priorities, thank you." Further, California Group Supervisor Grossman—who should not be expecting a promotion any time soon after his D.C. performance—nevertheless still had the responsibility for finding Mr. C, if there was such a fellow, which, given what had been happening to IFFY's reputation lately, seemed unlikely. No, DEA would not be sending anyone in to Malome. No, Grossman would get no further resources to search for Mr. C.

"So boys," Suit Number One cool cat concluded, "Grossman tells me you have a friend in Malome, and that town does need friends. Your Agent Barbour, who was going to Vienna, wherever he is now I wonder—do you think he was the guy that started the war in Laxenburg we've been reading about? Barbour has a buddy, Markowitz. Two of a kind, both of them got out of Washington just before their asses were going to be hung high. Fine crew you got—oh yeah, just fine. So what you got now is Markowitz, Malome, Mr. C, and you ain't got us. Just like you ain't got any of them in fact." He burped noisily into the phone. "What goes around comes around, eh? So toodle-ooo, boys. Let me hear when you've made the case of the century." They could hear him and Suit Number Two chortling in the background as the receiver was replaced.

"Doc, get going to Malome. Call Markowitz and tell him you come as a beggar. Remember what Grossman said: you've got to work a town like that from the deep inside. Whole new ball of wax. We can't even give Markowitz a salary, but we can maybe get him an expense account, pay a consulting fee. Tell him straight we're desperate. Anything." Mac paused, shaking his head, thinking of Barbour and Laxenburg. "Tell him almost anything goes."

Doc Dolan was on the plane from Washington to Malome that evening. A hard day already behind him, he cramped into the required sardine position that economy class imposes. Three glasses of Scotch under his belt, a teetotaling stewardess giving him the fish eye for it, he snoozed. The attendant poked him awake with a food tray, prepared by the looks of it, by the retired cook for punishment row at Sing Sing. Tired, muddled, he wasn't sure whether he was talking to himself, or the Scotch and his drifting mind were talking to him. Disjointed, broken phrases and images floated through his consciousness. "Malheureusement, malevole, malefice, malefique, Malomemme." He nodded a yes. "A whole bag of Frenchified furies found summarized . . . and in Malome, trouble here we come." Doc had in fact spent student years in Paris. How he wished the plane were heading there now.

He poked at the dead dinner. It poked back. A couple of glasses of red wine greased his way back into sleep, but it turned nightmarish. He awakened in sick panic, depressed. This was not his nature. It came from outside him. He recalled a closing line from a poem by Baudelaire, "Inject my venom, O my sister." But this dream had been worse than anything by Baudelaire, although the martyred woman of his dream also became, as in the poem, headless. It was a horror beyond any Freudian insight Doc had of himself, or the pieces of the day's brain work that make up, so the more cold-blooded experts say, a dream. Doc was sweating; he wondered if he were becoming feverish and hallucinating. But no, there was a link to the day. Mac's image of a head upside-down in a swamp, with a tiger chewing at the boots. That was half-funny this morning, but this dream just now? A young Asian woman, naked and alive, her head being held down and forced into in a halved wooden fifty-gallon barrel, the sort nurseries sold for planting. There were other atrocities going on that he wouldn't seek to summon. The barrel had been filled with soupy, freshly poured cement. She was forced in—yes, the atrocities were returning, he fought them, spluttering. That image would never leave him, nor any other part of the Rooster's tale, that trail to C, in Malome. Not ever . . .

26

They had agreed to meet outside the baggage pickup. Markowitz made it easy by driving a Malome black-and-white. The police car, unwashed in weeks, had a battered fender and the wiper blade on the passenger side was missing.

"Welcome to Malome and we aren't even near there yet," Markowitz had said, nodding to the dirty windshield where a blade might have been.

"Yeah, I can see." What Dolan saw told him almost everything about Malome that he had not dreamed about earlier.

"The local jolly pranksters rolled a grenade under this buggy on patrol last week, but it didn't go off. Thank God most of the hoodlums are stupid and the guys who sell them mean stuff are crooks."

"Yeah," nodded Dolan.

They had shaken hands on the sidewalk, Markowitz taking one of his two bags without a word. How things are done means a lot. They were glad now to meet, not only because they shared a friendship with Barbour and both knew Washington and the streets, but because the signals told them at a glance that working together would be okay. In bad spots, cops needed each other. The cops' club is a club like no other except that which forms on the front lines in warfare. Holding nothing back, Doc had told the whole story.

"So we either find Mr. C, if there is one, and get him to lead us all the way to Europe, or other places, or all asses in IFFY hang high. And maybe others, since we already have a number of dead bodies, just counting those in Washington, Austria, Warsaw. Who knows what we'd find in places where no one has looked."

"I've started. No leads but what the barkeep said, if he wasn't jiving us. I don't have any best bet, I have only one bet to rely on and that is this patrol officer Stein, who in turn says he may have one snitch, well both more and less than a snitch, Black kid, well maybe more than a kid, name of Rooster."

"Stein turn him?"

"No, nobody turns anybody worth turning in Malome. No deal we can offer is as good as the money they can make, or as certain as getting killed for finking. The streets always outbid us. No, this Rooster is thinking about life, maybe. A smart kid with one hell of a rap sheet, but Stein says he's 'reflecting.' That's the word Stein uses. Says the kid spells it out slowly, unsure. And so I have to tell you up front what Stein tells me, which is that Malome, Rooster, and C if he's there, are different than anything you or I or Barbour ever worked before. No leverage. Their rules. All ugly. No suits.

"We sit and we listen and we pray that Rooster comes to tell us slowly, slowly, a story. That's all we got on our side, ears to listen to Rooster, because Stein says the kid may think himself into doing us all some good. No one knows. There's no other way. I'm a new boy; I don't know the town. So many of my brother cops are low-life dirty I can't trust any of them. Stein, I trust. More than that, Stein I like. Friends. Stein says maybe someday soon we can trust Rooster, but first he has to remake himself and then trust us. I don't count on it. So we sit back and let Rooster talk to us, and be damn lucky he's not like the rest of the hoods out there whose only relationship with a cop is a gun, a blade, a heap of lies and fast leap over the back fence."

"I'm not a sit-back type. Listener maybe, if the story's good, but patience, no, it's not my thing. My job is to make things happen."

Markowitz, driving maybe seventy-five in the rattling junk heap, steering wheel loose, not sure both front wheels were going the same direction in this wreck of a black and white, looked at Dolan. He was reminded of his own Washington days, his own vanity then, the sense of a man feeling big, bringing himself from Washington as power into town, having his finger on the red nuke button. And it was all such horseshit, all of it. Not Dolan's fault. He had been a Dolan himself once, relying on the naiveté of the innocents in the safe towns in which he walked. Well, Malome was not one of them. He asked Dolan, "Ever read Nietzsche?"

"No."

Dolan, who did have a decent Ph.D., had learned to hide it, for Washington did not forgive intelligence or literacy. He was not quite sure how to respond. Nietzsche in this old patrol car hurtling toward the slums of hell? What was with this guy? When in doubt, play stupid. Cops, by Act of Society, are not supposed to be well read.

Markowitz paid no heed, "German guy. Nazis liked him but he was better than that. Said there is a universal need for power, need to create its appearances, an intoxication."

"So?"

"So, avoid intoxication. It can get you killed here. Neither of us are in Washington. It never existed. We're going to work together, I don't know how long, maybe you're only a fireman. But remember I'm here not because anybody told me to, but because I said 'yes.' Maybe you were lucky enough to make it your choice too. But here it's a different ball game. You work Malome, purge the power-drunk dreams. First you go to church, temple, whatever, and clean it all out, so if you go, you die clean. Conrad Aiken, remember his poetry about attitudes, those lines? 'Have out our hearts, confess our blood, our foulness and our virtue, I have known such sunsets of despair as god himself might weep of a Sunday'."

Doc was very tired. It was now two a.m., Washington time. He had been in Washington too long. Maybe the heartland was the strength and he was himself the weakness. What the hell, let it all hang out.

"My mother used to read Tagore. I sneaked looks at it when I was a kid. Remember a line or two. 'Where is my dwelling place? In the dreams of the Impotent comes my answer.' Stanley, believe me, I have no hard-on for power."

Markowitz nodded. "I'm not your rabbi, but better that way. There's always a faster gun, and you never know what sweet smiling face is going to be the one to kill you. Some folks in Malome smile once in a while. Not a whole lot. I once met a poet named Gavin Ewart in Cambridge, and yeah, I know you wouldn't expect me even to know where it is. We had a few drinks together in his room at Jesus College. I was there for a symposium. He wasn't. All kinds of people were there. For instance I remember a senator I didn't like much, and a Bulgarian name of Vasil whom on the other hand I'd like as a brother. He and Barbour got close. As for the senator, Barbour hates his guts. Anyway, I keep in mind Ewart's lines, well, quoting fairly close, 'It's on a Victorian page you will find the innocent purity of the child/but don't believe it/ Evil's a card that's wild.' Oh yeah, another line from Ewart, 'The sadists are always waiting, the police, everyone fixed in a squad/are tempted to go for the beating up, like Oxford dons in a squad'."

Doc Dolan yawned. "Everybody in Malome like you?"

"Oh yeah, basically. Just natural, like Dostoyevsky said. 'Being human is a burden for all of us, a disgrace, and so we invent the impossible idealized man.' Or like Lord Chesterfield. 'We are all the same everywhere, we just look different'."

"They really said that?"

"No, but something close. I always whittle a little on quotations. Nobody ever knows."

"Yeah," Dolan paused. "Where do I sleep tonight?"

"Stein is putting you up. He lives near Malome. Nobody on the force lives in that town; we can't take a chance on it. They'd kill you coming out the door, do a drive-by on your kids playing on the lawn, or nail your windows closed and burn your house to the ground with you inside. A little neighborhood dispute among drug dealers last week and they did that—burned alive nine people in a family. You can see why houses don't sell at a premium. I live farther away than Stein and have a little honey warming up at home this week, one whom I'd rather not introduce to anybody good-looking. Anyway, it depends on how long you want to stay. A couple of miles away there are some decent motels, but housekeeping apartments are expensive. Depends on your per diem. Don't worry about it just yet. Just worry about this guy Rooster, his character and his story. And yeah, when in Malome as any kind of a cop, worry about staying alive. Actually I don't want you to surface as a cop. Play it cool, undercover. No major moves, just hanging out while we try to figure it. Okay?" It was a kind of order. Markowitz was taking charge, which was what he had to do. Markowitz repeated, "Okay by you?"

Doc Dolan grunted. He had heard and agreed, but was too tired to care.

Officer Stein pulled up his patrol car near Robbie's Club, stopped Rooster who was headed somewhere in a hurry, and shook him down. All for a sidewalk show. Their inaudible conversation was about setting up a meet. Not in town. They agreed Stein would appear to bust Rooster, same place, noonish. Rough him into the patrol car for show, then drive off to a white man's restaurant Stein liked, maybe ten miles away. No one from Malome, no cops from anywhere dined there. Rooster's choice. "Yeah, sure, man," he said, going through some kind of brooding 're flek shun,' as he spelled it out, acting superficially indifferent. "No way he's that cool inside," Stein told himself while pulling away from the curb, his siren on for a 246 (shooting at inhabited dwelling) call was coming in. "What happens tomorrow at lunchtime is going to change his life."

"Shit man, if I am going to talk to you at all, I talk in front of anybody I want, as many brothers as I want, and nobody is going to fuss. 'Cause those brothers know I ain't so stupid as to be seen with you cops unless I am top pig, so to speak. And to use the old—" he sounded it out slowly, "'vur-nac-u-lar,' it's good for my rep, man. You order the beer when I say, even for the whole house if I say, and the brothers know who is boss nigger: me."

Stein, who had no make at all on this cat, could only say, "Hey man, please, I'm not using Department buy money. And yeah, I do have a little information shopping kitty courtesy of Detective Markowitz whom you met, will meet, but not more than one round of beer for the house. Oh my, my mother would be so ashamed. She hates to encourage drinking."

Some time ago Officer Stein had decided that the personal, honest, even sentimental touch would work best with this puzzling cat Rooster who had, in fact, taken some kind of shine to him. Big brother stuff maybe, black on white and no shades of gray. Rooster, brighter by far than one would expect, a still-young gangster, older in this town by virtue of living to the age of twenty-two, was going through some kind of change that would even allow the possibility of conversation, however general, about what was really going on in Malome. The cops got the emergency calls, sometimes two hundred a day. They got to meet every shooting victim in town and all the dumb gangsters still standing around afterwards picking their noses. But Mr. C? anything big? No way. You don't attend board meetings of Bigtime Crime United while doing fifty miles an hour down a potholed street on your way to a killing, in a squad car just as likely as not to blow a tire on the way. With, once in a while, somebody shooting at you so the sound you heard was not a tire blowing.

Fact is, it was Rooster who had approached Stein on the street the day after that evening at Robbie's Club saying—shades of community policing that never, ever happened—that he would "like a chance to shoot the shit, man. You're the Man, maybe you got some fresh views on things."

Stein leaped to a "Yes." He would have anyway, but man, would he like to get Rooster working an inside track! Who was, where was, Mr. C? Some big Fed named Doc Dolan was coming to town on this, treating it as heavy business. He was going to team with a guy who had already had a quick visit from a DEA supervisor whom Markowitz had known earlier "as a youngster, when he was assigned to work Mexican drug intelligence with me."

Stein had met the guy, Grossman, and liked him. And had heard him say to both of them, "Look guys, I'm desperate. The suits in Headquarters want to put IFFY on the wrong side of a Senate Crime Committee investigation table. Roast their ass, maybe get some criminal indictments. Not that the suits know, but they can smell blood after the Hashimoto killing (which Grossman had then described). And there is some private war in Austria that DEA knows damn well was started by one of your IFFY guys, you know anybody named Barbour?" At this point Markowitz had interrupted to explain their friendship and ask for details.

"The word according to the suits is that Barbour killed a half-dozen Russians mafiya over some Russian broad—screwing her maybe, but who knows? Understand me, there isn't a fact in a carload here. Nobody knows really, but in Washington you publish newspapers because your source has better rumors than the other guy. And no question, Barbour is in hiding. Nobody can find the broad. The Austrian government is screaming for his ass. They claim some MI6 agent was in on it with him. Big protests diplomatically, and I mean *big*. FBI, on the other hand, says it was a joint MI6 and CIA operation. FBI will do anything to make the Agency look bad, and they are not above planting evidence, as we all know. FBI sent a team to Vienna to help the Austrians. They couldn't do that without the President himself, it's that big, so he's authorizing it all the time he's disclaiming any knowledge of U.S. involvement. Meanwhile, the Brits are playing it cool. The *Post* is full of London sources saying the Brits are leaning on the Austrians. The biggest rumor is of a Scotland Yard involvement, with Austrians maybe dirty. The Austrian police put one of their agents in a box and are now trying to get us to take a fall for it. If all of this confuses you, you're right. But back to basics, Mr. C is right here in River City, or so all the intelligence (such as it is) tells us. He is somehow tied in with Austria, Hashimoto, a bunch of folks who got dead in Warsaw, and again—just yesterday now—some assassination in Sofia."

Stein, whose political world until today had been as provincial as any nineteenth-century peasant, was awestruck. Markowitz knew the game, as did the younger DEA man. He knew most of it had to be nonsense. But it was a story so big, with enough dead men in it, that a river of political blood would flow in Washington and maybe elsewhere. The suits in every agency concerned, the already named IFFY, DEA, FBI, CIA and inevitably the Department of State, overseas of Scotland Yard, the Foreign and Home Offices, inevitably Austria's Federal Police, and, Foreign and Justice Ministries, were positioning themselves. "Draw blood or die bleeding" was the Washington rule at the agency head level.

"And so?" Markowitz asked, looking sympathetically at Grossman, who replied, "So the suits are using this to hang me out to dry. 'Twisting in the wind,' as Mr. N. used to say. To make IFFY look bad, they don't want anybody to find Mr. C. To make sure of that they have taken seven senior agents, can you imagine? seven guys out of my central office here in California, on 'emergency assignment,' they say. Then they tell me it's up to me to 'assist' the Malome police, 'local jurisdiction' they have decreed, to find C. On my head, on my head alone. And I don't have anybody to send in for undercover. All my best black agents were in that seven." It took no psychologist to see that Grossman was depressed.

"And?" Markowitz, who knew the game, knew more was coming. "The Bureau? The Senate Crime Committee?"

"Yeah, them too. Bureau had the courtesy to call me and wish me, I quote, 'Have a good day. Don't scream for help from us. We're busy.' Obviously they've teamed with DEA's suits on this one against IFFY, and will try to pin something on the Agency. And that asshole assistant to Cranmer who heads the Crime Committee was on me just yesterday, talking about their 'forthcoming investigation in which you had best begin cooperating now.' Dirty pool, of course. They can't ask for ongoing investigation material except on the QT, but they're pushing me to tell them whatever I learn as you learn it up front, unprotected, which makes me a public source whenever it's convenient for them to name me. And so I get fired for it just as the suits want. And behind it of course, if I did give them anything that comes out of here, Mr. C will read it in the papers and be booking his travel arrangements the morning before off to Dominica to get a new, non-extradictable fifty-thousand-dollar Dominican nationality, with passport to match. He'll spend a while on a Caribbean beach buying or growing a beard, and re-emerge a new man. No doubt his criminal business as usual, whatever it is, will go on all the while. Now, is that a picture?"

It was, they agreed, a picture. One compelling enough to lead Officer Stein, a cynic but not an atheist, to offer up a small prayer of thanks to the dear Lord, who on so many days seemed absent from the violent streets of Malome. He arranged an off-duty meet for that very evening among the four: Markowitz, Dolan, Rooster, and himself. Stein would not make any paper on it. Officers who were already dirty could read it and make everyone bloody weep. The Chief, who was not dirty but had his head so far up his ass it would take him three years before he could see daylight at the very fastest rate of extraction, could only mess things up. As he had everything else.

Stein, huge, intense, Wagnerian, a belly to match any Ring-singing baritone, was happy. He had a hunch about Rooster, this tough, charming, crooked, lying, appealing, whatever he was young man working on a new vocabulary of big white man's words, sounding them out as he did, like "re-flek-shun." Whatever else, the kid was independent, unusual, and changing in some right direction. Stein was a professional cop. Tough. Guarded. Suspicious. Cynical. Extremely dangerous when annoyed, as for example when being shot at, he was underneath his tough exterior a cream puff. Remember his habit of sending flowers anonymously to mothers of any kid killed in Malome? Don't tell anyone, but two-hundred ninety pounds of Stein had been known to cry, privately of course, when some poor kid in Malome got blown away.

"Andy," he asked himself, "what's wrong with you? Liking this felonious, slick-tongued kid, fifteen years old going on sixty who would maybe get himself shot? He answered himself, "You've got to hope for something, and that there is a God who cares. Besides, we need the little bastard."

27

For some days Frau Doctor Wipplinger brought the newspapers. A born conspirator herself, having more fun than she had imagined possible, happily felonious in concealing such dramatic fugitives—although they were in fact delightful to have as guests, and it had been a long time since she had such enthusiastic children to cook for. The Frau Doctor drove into downtown Vienna to buy them, so not to attract notice at the local news stand. The *Herald Tribune*, the *Times*, the local Austrian press. All of them covered the raging story. It was too good for the press to let it go away, and too hot to go away by itself. There were too many opportunities in it for it not to be fed by politicians, reformers, fascists, communists, liberals, conservatives. For anyone able to manipulate the press or find a TV media ear, an invented new piece was an axe, a fulcrum, vengeance: the sheer malevolent excitement of important liars being believed.

For the European public the Laxenburg incident was more fun than the Olympics, a Tom Clancy, or President Clinton claiming that having oral sex is equivalent to hardly ever having met the girl. The story somewhere was real. Was opportunity for righteous nationalist outrage. "Austria invaded by Anglo-American spy killer squad." For the sentimental, "Mysterious kidnapped woman still missing." For the salacious, "Russian *mafiya* have tortured and raped missing captive." For those lovers of intrigue wisely suspicious of governments, "CIA, MI6 deny involvement in Laxenburg death squad raid said by Austrian ministerial source to conceal U.S. and British government conspiracy to topple present Russian premier." For the communists, always strong: "Government uses Laxenburg incident to foment anti-Russian mania." For the police reformers, "Highest anonymous source says Federal police rotten to the core: Austrian Justice Ministry creates 'ghost squad' on Scotland Yard model."

It was this last article, in a local English-language paper aping *The European*, an international newspaper, that attracted the fugitive threesome's attention most. In 1998 a secret anti-corruption or "a ghost" squad had found two hundred fifty Scotland Yard officers, including ranks up to commander, entirely dirty. It was the worst scandal in British police history, involving protection of drug dealers and armed robbers and offshore bank accounts full of protection money paid out. The three of them hiding out here in Laxenburg hoped this report of a ghost-squad-equivalent hunting corruption on the Federal Police was true. Whoever was with and behind Major Kummering was framing them with a barrage of lying leaks and accusations, and had set up a reward of $100,000 for their capture, depiciting them as "persons believed to be American, perhaps British government agents, a Russian turncoat female agent may be involved. All are armed and extremely dangerous." One sector of the Russian Government ministry had announced its own reward fund, $25,000. No "believed to be" nonsense in that: just that old-fashioned Western "Wanted Dead or Alive," right there in print.

Well, there was nothing for it. They had to take a chance. Frau Doctor Wipplinger was quite willing to drive to Vienna someday soon and park her car near the U. S. Embassy, with Claire hiding under a blanket on the back seat. Claire was not officially wanted; so far no precise description of her had yet appeared in the press. Surely IFFY would not do it, given the likelihood in their minds that she was Greta Liebowitz. But you can never know who knows what, and it would be best for Claire to be disguised. Some cop surely had been in touch with André the concierge and all police would likely have seen a sketch of the woman never officially, never kidnapped, rescued in Laxenburg, the woman who might be an American agent, or who might be a mafiya one. But blonde Claire could readily become brunette by home dyes that Frau Wipplinger could get at any cosmetics counter.

The risk to Claire was high, since her sketch had likely been circulated among Austrian police watching the U.S. Embassy. There was also risk of her being held up or even denied admission at that great electronic door controlled by the Marine guards. With the political situation so tense, and the usual agitators trying to whip up anti-American demonstrations, the Embassy would be on full alert. They would want complete documents from anyone seeking entrance, and Claire had none to show. A delay getting in would allow waiting Austrian police chance to pounce. No police department anywhere has a problem in inventing charges; certainly not in an incident of this magnitude. And Austria, once and recently fascist, gave its police considerable power.

Alternatively, Sergeant "Injun Joe Bieber," as they now called him, could try it. The Marine guard would recognize him, let him in, and if the Ambassador had handled it well, no one outside the embassy would know he was missing. But one loose mouth, one "did you notice who hasn't been seen around here?" comment to the Austrian police by, say, one of the many Austrian employees in the embassy, would guarantee the sergeant's arrest before he made it near the U.S. door.

They were half-good plans at best. In the meantime, life here was damn near beautiful. The sergeant entertained them all with stories; truth was never of the essence. Six hours a day the Herr Doctor, ever so fine a side-whiskered loden-coated gentleman, taught Barbour intensive German. Claire was getting much better. They had decided against the risk of a plastic surgeon, for her healing—according to the good Doctor, and all agreed—was proceeding remarkably. Scabs, not scars, appeared on her cheeks and these blemishes grew less visible day by day. But there would be no run to Vienna for her until her cheeks were shining again, and that would require many more days at least. Barbour read and rested as if in a grand hotel. The Wipplingers loved them like their own children, and these new children reciprocated. The good farmer, Herr Bieber passed by one day to call on his "cousin" and was suddenly in on the secret. Surreptitiously he brought fresh farm produce to his Wipplinger cousins. Life in hiding had never been so good. Best yet, rippling energies underlay it all for Claire and Lee. Quizzical looks, the brush of a hand—no words yet, the two were falling in love.

But with a little bad luck, intergovernmental negotiations now underway could undermine their escape plans. Sir Peter Dixon was lunching with Quincy, this time at the Saville Club. Ambassador Dubois was back in Kiev, happy in the knowledge that his daughter, whatever her voluntary status as a fugitive for the sake of her rescuers, was safe. The Austrian government had secretly conveyed such knowledge of Barbour and Claire as Major Kummering had, in return for future consideration, made known. The Major was officially suspended. He was in fact under investigation of a most serious kind: the pivotal point in a battle within the Justice Ministry and the Federal police between a few powerful people who were protecting him (and thus themselves) and the remainder, who were appalled at the extent of the corruption, *mafiya* involvement within the ministries, and their collusion with banks such as Brody's, which was crumbling. Major Kummering was, at least for a little while, protected by the honest chiefs as well as the dishonest ones. For reasons of political damage control, even the most honest of high officials wanted the mess cleaned up before the press knew of it. Democratic capitals are the same over the world. However innocent he may be, no politician wants to be caught at the helm of a corrupt and sinking ship.

"Our government," Sir Peter was saying, "is excruciatingly sick of the Austrians who are denying it all while their investigation is underway. Threatening to make a major diplomatic furor over it. They seem willing to claim publicly that the other men in Laxenburg were British agents. The Austrians are coming to believe their own media rumor-mongers. Behind it is a struggle in Austrian politics over whether or not to move to NATO and within the EU to crack down on their haven banks. There were, we must remember, more Nazis per capita in Austria than in Germany at the *Anschluss*. And today Austria is the only country in the world that still has the hammer and sickle, held by the Hapsburg eagle's claws, on its flag. The Austrians like being cozy with the East."

"Can't treat the hives successfully if the patient in reality also has German measles," said Quincy.

"Privately, the Austrian Prime Minister assures us he agrees perfectly and asks that we tolerate temporary delays—'internal tempestuosity,' he calls it. He guarantees the safety of our people if we can get them in safely, a matter he unfortunately can't guarantee because he says they don't know yet which of their police are dirty." He paused, reflecting.

Quincy took up the theme. "For reasons anyone who knows what happened recently in your own Yard will understand, or for that matter, our New Orleans."

Sir Peter reddened a bit. "I daresay. And so it proceeds more slowly than we anticipated, but good will out."

"If the good don't get shot before goodwill has its way."

Sir Peter pressed his lips together. "Righto," Sir Peter. "And now," he asked, "what do you hear from your side of the pond?"

"Much of the same," responded Adams. "Agencies against agencies mostly, with the old State Department guard preferring to wring their precious hands and cry, 'oh my oh my.' Thanks to George and his friends, the tough guys are pushing the Austrians. Our Treasury Secretary, under whom IFFY is placed, is leading the charge. The Attorney General, who heads the Bureau and DEA, has been lobbied. She has her own troubles and needs their support in some hard cases—not always objective matters, you understand. Under their persuasion she would just as soon let the Austrians have their way, and sacrifice Barbour as a renegade who can reflect on his purported sins for the rest of his life in an Austrian jail. The Russians are split in half as always. One half is putting heavy pressure on State on behalf of their own mafiya authorities, lobbying from within the Kremlin and the private banks. The other half, reformers and modernists, are screaming at the Austrians and us to shoot every mafiya on sight, pin hero medals on our people and Claire."

"Austrian Parliamentarians have their noses out of joint because of the clamor. That's sheer embarrassment, a potential public relations disaster for them," continued Adams, "because they know now that Major Kummering, and no doubt some of his superiors, are tied in with the Russians. The last thing they want is to see anything made public. An American senior enforcement agent on trial in Vienna? They'd retire all their judges before letting it happen! Can you imagine Claire Dubois coming forth in a courtroom to tell all? Hardly! The Parliament hopes they both stay out of sight until after the next elections. If we'd agree to bring them in quietly, the Austrians would go for it. I have assurances to that effect in an exquisitely worded private letter from a certain woman married to the Chancellor. Discretion, you see—ours and political. That's what any Chancellor's wife appreciates. You will admit it is a very sophisticated channel."

Sir Peter nodded, "Indeed, Noel Cowardice if you will allow allusion and pun."

Quincy did so with a chuckle. "Indeed they beg we arrange it all quietly. They want it all swept under the rug until they can clean up their police and banks. It will take months, if not years, of course."

"But we can't guarantee silence. Claire particularly would be too principled for it in spite of her short time with the spooks. Barbour is probably too jaded to care; after all, he's done a good deal to be mum about from what I hear of his record. It's all moot anyway. Ron Owen—you remember our ambassador there—says no one has the foggiest idea where our kids are. He knows they'll get in touch when they can, but the headlines don't encourage their taking chances. As it is now, an Austrian policeman could shoot either of them on sight and get off the hook, no matter what the Prime Minister or Chancellor assures us of privately. And some of their crooked cops would like to do just that."

"Delicate and appalling."

"Yes, appalling and delicate."

"We both push where we can, right?"

"Right."

"And hope for the best."

"Right. Hope for the best."

At least the claret had been splendid. The pheasant a bit dry but adequate. The trifle off the cart was heavy. Food at the Saville could be unreliable. Claret never anything but excellent. Atmosphere, men only except on Friday dinner, politically incorrect but for two stuffy old chaps, they'd admit to that, their preference. The gender bar in some of his clubs was not a matter Quincy enjoyed arguing whenever it came up with his current love, whomever she might be. On the other hand, if Claire or those like her were being nominated for membership, even at his all-male favorite club, the Athenaeum, Quincy would argue the feminist side. Prejudices are so inconsistent.

28

Rooster was not what Dolan expected. Thinner, shorter, more nervous, no wisecracking hostile veneer, instead doing his best to be courteous. He seemed intent upon making something work. Dolan, who had read more about street hoods than he had experienced them, was suspicious. Rooster was neatly dressed: a clean white shirt, black Levi jeans, not the expected Adidas or other fashionable jogging shoe. His hair was African-American curly, but without hip-dude arrangement. A quick glance told Dolan that if the kid was packing a gun, it could only be strapped to his ankle. It seemed unlikely but, he asked himself, what did he know about ego, anxiety, or security necessities for a young man from Malome?

Unlike Division Director Dolan, who was ill at ease, Officers Stein and Markowitz were relaxed, easy in their manner with Rooster. No familiarity mind you, no pretense at friendship, but just taking things as they went,wherever that might be. The restaurant, Rudolfo's, had deep crescent-shaped booths with dark red leather backs so high no conversations could be overheard. Markowitz had chosen it. People who had private things to say and who looked for seafood salads or steaks came here. No push, no shove. Lunch could last past dinner and dinner past midnight. Rudolfo, who owned it, was the maître d': a fellow with wavy white hair and a fine Italian tailored suit, soft voice, gracious manners, appreciated privacy. Guaranteed it. All on the up and up mind you, including, maybe especially, the prices. Markowitz, who liked to know about where he was doing important dining, a meet, had run the record on Rudolfo. A long time ago, he had spent some time for penance up the river, old-fashioned young hood mafia stuff. But for years now Rudolfo had been clean—not just respectable, but savvy. Maturity, so Markowitz believed, was a great gift, however achieved.

Stein was Rooster's connection to anyone here, to anything that any of these three servants of the establishment represented, symbolized, knew about.

All of that was a world removed from Rooster. An anthropologist might understand how tenuous a bridge this luncheon table was between two worlds. Officer Stein, closest to Rooster's world, would run the interview. It turned out that "instructive monologue" could be the only characterization.

"I told Detective Markowitz here, and Mr. Dolan, who is in from Washington, that you have only agreed to meet them. You tell us as much as you want and no more. It is all off the record. No one is wired. No pressure. One promise: your name stays out of it once we leave this room. If you decide you want to give us information leading us to Mr. C, we will pay you. Damn well in fact; it's only taxpayer's money, so take it at fifty dollars an hour if you want, and a thousand-dollar bonus if we get to C. We know you're not anybody's snitch. A mapmaker maybe, that's what I'd say we need."

Markowitz nodded. "I'd say we need you to be a talking camera. If you like poetry as I do, I'd say we need a bard of sorts, who tells a history of everything, a catalog of people and events, the where, what, who, and how come."

Rooster stayed silent. He was just watching them, appraising. Dolan was annoyed at Markowitz for the fancy talk. "Bard, my ass," he muttered. "Look Rooster, maybe this is off to a slow start. What the hell is a 'bard' anyway, and who cares?"

Rooster looked at Dolan hard. "If you don't know Mr. Dolan, I'd say you did not get a good," Rooster paused, struggling with the longer word, "ed-u-cation."

Dolan turned beet red. He had come here to learn. It was beginning.

"I apologize."

"Yeah," said Rooster. "You see I'm going back to school and I'm trying myself to get an ed-u-cation. But that's for telling later. Where do you want me to start?" His first hint of a smile was for Officer Stein.

"The works, Rooster. Begin like in the Bible as though it were the first day in the first place. Who you are, how you got to be, and what Malome is like from your camera eye. Lead us as slowly as you want, so we can understand, to wherever you can—Mr. C, we hope."

Rooster nodded. "I 'preciate that. I told you before I want to take it very slow. Each step I got to weigh where I am going by seeing where I have been. I'm not promising anything. Any time I look around in my story and don't like where it's taking me, I quit. I ain't easy about this you know, this where am I going stuff and being here with you honkies. Eldridge, dead now, used to say 'pigs'. I don't anymore. But Malome is a place where you get dead real easy. Each step as I talk to you about what Malome is, who's doing what, what happens, where I come from, I got to have in my mind looking at the graveyard from the coffin, bottom up."

The three men nodded. The film, minus the singing bard, had begun.

"First about Malome. Not much in our town, not really. Not on its face. Drugs sure, crack, cocaine, PCP, heroin, lots of drunks for that's where a junkie or crack head goes when he gets burned out, that sort of thing. Some grass, but just recreational, local smoke, no profit in it. Chop shops, sure—chop up a couple thousand cars a year, sell the parts. Unless, of course, it's some fancy rig like a Jaguar, a ragtop red Mazda, or a new Cadillac. Those just pass by, to get the registration numbers off, turn a hot car cool, so to speak. Ship them out in truck trailers to Mexico, big SAFEWAY GROCERIES sign on the trailer. Near the border they just drive them over and collect the big bucks. No pesos, only dollars in this trade. This town works hard for its money. There's more than you think out there, than when you're just looking at this downcast town. Money, dirty money, this is where it begins.

"Not from the whores though, those are mostly trades: pussy for crack, trading a suck on a cock for a suck on a crack pipe. No big deal. Those women are all on dope. Makes them ugly by the time they're 24. Nobody in his right mind would touch one; they all have AIDS, the clap and ten other," again Rooster was slow with the big words that he was clearly trying to learn to use, "put-ri-fy-ing diseases no other town has even invented yet. But the guys who score that stuff ain't in their right minds no way. Heads up their ass, snow up their nose, needles up their veins. Only out-of-towners touch those girls, or the down-and-outers here. Local folks don't have to pay for poontang. Easy come, easy go, that's the way it is. And money so dirty it's just got to be washed."

"Town ain't without theater though, like an old Clint Eastwood spaghetti-western movie. Like the other day when an out of town gang was coming in. One thing Malome stands for and that is local control, from the city council down. One hour after the word come in, we had one hundred, maybe two hundred shooters out there on the street with their Uzis, Mack 10s, AK47s, Glock 17s. That's guns enough to tell you just why we call them the 'arsenal' gang.

"Everybody wears the same things down to his shoes, black leather coat, never mind that it's summer, one of those wool hats, the kind you can pull down over your face but still see through if you want to be anonymous. Yes, I'm learning those words, some I have to spell out, a-n-o-n-i-m-u-s. Like I told you I'm going to junior college now, learning about words. And money. Anyway those shooter dudes don't bother pulling those caps down. Know why? Tell you a story.

"About three months ago there was a dispute between this white guy come in here to buy himself a little crack, driving a Mercedes in here no less, that man he *born* to lose, and Bernard. Bernard is a retailer, works for Boomer who works for Slash who works—tthat's what I believe but no one knows and anyone who knows don't say and anyone who did say is chopped meat the day he said it—but you ast me and all right, my first giant step with you guys, he may work for Mr. C himself. Your Mr. C. Listen up. You see, when Mr. C don't want you to see Mr. C, then you are very very dead, which is where, as of this real good fancy lunch, I am more than halfway to."

Rooster paused. There was no way his facial muscles, so obviously used to showing nothing, could not now show something: Fear. Depression. Resolve. The three very serious men watching suddenly understood what he was saying, what he was doing, very well. Dolan sucked in his breath. Markowitz tapped the table. Stein moved his huge hand to cover Rooster's skinny one compassionately. He caught himself just in time.

Rooster resumed. "Anyway, Bernard is a skinny little homeboy who carries a 9mm pistol and has an Uzi strapped to the fire hydrant next to where he sells. Homeboy and the honky are doing the deal; white boy has the car window down, homeboy is standing on the curb. 'Hey man,' says Bernard, who has half the cash, the white boy what *he* thinks is half the crack—folks don't trust each other a whole bunch on a street deal. 'Hey man, don't you fuck with me you motherfucker, you only give me half of the half, I mean motherfucker, you tryin' to slice me, huh?'

"Well, now, of course Bernard—his mother called him that because she thought it was such a refined-sounding name—he knew the hundred dollars in his hand was right, but he had no intention whatsoever of completing the transaction, 'cept his own way. Quick and dirty. That white boy he began to protest and he see—well hand it to him for being smart enough to see that Bernard, ole sweet name, was reaching real quick under his jacket. If a man don't have an itch in his armpit, the only other reason he reach up there is he has got to have a shoulder holster. Which is what Bernard had whether or not his armpit itched. The honky has got that M car spinning rubber so hard it lay down a cloud of smoke. And he was off while sweet-name smiling Bernard's laying eight lead ones at that car. Oh, poor little Bernie, fifteen years old and still can't shoot worth diddley. Maybe five lead ones into the car, two into the sky and, well, shit man, everybody can't be on it all the time, one hits this little kid down the street. Little bastard shouldn't been out there on his bike anyway, not this time of evening when the street belong to the dealers. Every mama and brother on the street will be nice and quiet, like, 'No officer, little Bernie he ran out of the house when he heard all that shooting is going down. Not my sweet Bernie, he wasn't on the street that day, no sir.'

"Oh well, this little side story I can't go on telling it. The little kid flops over, the cops and ambulances all over the place, Bernard is back in his house like he was never away from the TV set, and believe me ain't no one in this neighborhood crazy enough to have seen anything. But for that damn Mexican just moved in. You cops you collar him, tell him they're arresting him as material witness, and this idiot he start bleating like a sheep on my great-granddaddy's Carolina farm. 'Si, Mr. Policeman, I see him do it.' And he points right down toward where Bernard is inside watching TV. 'You come with us and make the ID,' says the cop, some white guy almost as big as you, Officer Stein, maybe six-foot-three, weighing two hundred fifty-some and very unfriendly. Sirens, cops, you'd think it was the police fraternal ball game so many swarming around.

"Bernard was out the back door and ready to go to Zassu's house—that's not her real name but everybody calls her that—when he gets to thinking that dumb Mexican is going to be a witness against him in what could be a trial. Around here there are no trials because there are no witnesses. And there are no witnesses because everybody but this Mexican knows they're dead meat, maybe their whole family dead meat, road kill, if they see anything. Way up the line it's Mr. C who see to that.

"'Son of a bitch,' Bernie says to himself, and changes course, goes into little Malcolm's garage where he's got a 9mm sniper rifle sitting there on top of a box of grenades. Bought the grenades just last week from Hiram's Liquors, which has a back room just full of stuff stolen from the U.S. of A. Army.

"'Sure like to launch that grenade right into all of them,' thinks Bernard but declines, knowing his throwing arm is no good at all. Hand it to the boy. It's getting dark now, nine-ish on a summer night, and he shinnies himself up a tree onto a roof and sights right into the middle of those six squad cars where one fat white cop is about to put that protesting Mexican, by this time screaming cusses, into custody. Don't pay to open your mouth, even the Mexican knew that by now.

"'You history, man,' Bernard says and, lying there flat on the roof, he pulls that trigger twice and damn, better shot than I'd ever thought, that Mexican is all gizzard dumpin' out onto the street. You should have seen the face on that fat cop. We were all in our houses of course, watching TV so to speak, but looking out our windows and see that fat cop's face, like a kid who'd dropped his hot-day ice cream cone onto the street. No offense meant, Officer Stein, but I mean, this cop was mad. I mean, man, that cop was furious.

"Anyway, I don't want to string this one out but I had to tell you why home-boys on this street don't worry too much about," Rooster looked pained, he seemed to know it was the wrong spelling, "a-n-o-n-y-m-a-t-y. Damn. I have got to learn spelling. The other side of that is why you never heard of Mr. C because he stays a-non-y-mus just that way. That's got to be on my mind. And frankly it should be on yours."

He stared a message at the three older men. They received it. Reflexively Markowitz laid a reassuring hand on his jacket where it covered his 9mm in its shoulder holster.

Rooster resumed. "Anyway, the detective—another big white guy with a face like prunes and a butt like a beer barrel—next day he finds, can you believe it? another witness. Mrs. Kay, the old woman whose kid Bernard shot, had, so she told the cops, they all old grateful ears, actually seen Bernard blow away the spic. Lying I imagine, but people forget they're Christian, get spiteful. So she made Bernard on the roof as the shooter.

"'Bernard,' Boomer told him, he was taking it easy in Lou Anne's place because she was another one of his girls. 'Bernard,' says Boomer in a voice you listen respectfully to, because Boomer is meaner than snakeshit on a razor, and kills just for practice, or when there isn't anything good on TV. '*Bernard*.'

"'Yessir.'

"'Mrs. Kay, she done snitched on you, and she has said she is going to go to court to be sure you get that little green gas chamber on the way to the sky. Understand?'

"'So,' and here Boomer put his face right into Bernard's face, could have bit his nose off and on a less kindly day he might have. 'You teach Mrs. Kay and all those nosy neighbors a lesson, right?'"

"'Yessir.' Bernard shivered so hard piss ran down his pants.

"Next morning about six-thirty a.m., ten, maybe twelve shooters, long black coats, they line up in front of her house just as that woman comes into her living room turning on the lights. Boom, boom, and rat-a-tat-bang. All the lights they go out, including hers, unless, maybe so, the gates to paradise are illuminated.

"Which is why, when the lesson finally gets home to the neighbors, shooters don't usually bother to pull those caps down over their faces. And you never will hear of Mr. C 'cause who needs a mask for a-non-y-ma-t-y?

"And that white boy in the Mercury with those bullet holes? Now that ofay was dumber than donkey doo. Two cars, all full of snot-nosed white boys—no Mercedes this time—come cruising down the street looking for, of all people, Bernard. Talk about timing. Live carcasses for the shooters. Three white boys dead, one wished he were dead on the way to the hospital when he learned the bullet was in his spine, he'd never-walk-again, and the others got away. And two of Bernard's shooters also on their way to wherever dead shooters go. Bernard, he was one of them. You should have heard his mother hooting and crying and wailing about her sweet little baby, he never done any wrong, and oh how could the world be so cruel, and oh how the government did it. You got to know Bernard's mother used to deal coke and H out the house herself until the arthritis got her and the man she lives with is a pimp and a gaffler. A gaffler sells phony rock cocaine. You sell gaffle only to unarmed kids.

"Tonight I go see Purple Willie again, maybe even see his Cynthia who works the back room. She is no whore, no way, as Purple Willie says, she is an amenity, a-m-e-n-i-ty. Willie's right, says I can't spell for shit. What for he make me feel worse than I do? I am, believe me, trying to learn. I am working on it."

It was then that Markowitz realized Rooster had been a stutterer, that bigger words might still be triggers for a stutter. That was why he did them so slowly. Not just the spelling. He wondered if the kid, this already world-in-age old man, was also dyslexic. It would explain even more about the word troubles.

Rooster was still at his tale. "Purple Willie's place looks like a house, it's got people in it like a house, it's got cars around it like a house. But it ain't no house. Not with one hundred fifty cars and two hundred people inside and maybe 7,000 square feet it ain't. And Cynthia and Celeste as amenities. Purple Willie and I'll B Frank, no shit that's his name, it's their gambling house. Craps, roulette, poker, slots, baby keno, that kind of thing. I know there's a big safe in the floor under the Chinese rug. There's a bloodstain on it won't come out. Open only weekends, Sunday opens at noon to accommodate the after-church crowd. Used to be open for cards only on Thursday nights but too damn many people got shot. This town goes crazy on Thursday, nobody knows why. And last night was Thursday. But I had got a summons I couldn't refuse, because I run for Purple Willie and Frank and it is the most sweet-assed job in town.

"Their office is upstairs, maybe twenty feet by fifteen, a tiny mahogany bar in the corner with some Wild Turkey, Hennessy, and Sloe Gin bottles on the mirrored top, half-open bottle of Budweiser, big teak-looking desk, maybe two file cabinets all fancy wood, a velveteen rose-colored couch—in case one of the bosses is tired or wants some quick nookie—or is dozing on Qualude or Valium if the coke gets stringing him out too tight, a leather recliner, three really crummy wood chairs, and a computer. Frank is crazy about computers.

"Last night Frank did not look too crazy about the two white guys there in the office. One looked like George Raft from one of those TV re-runs. He was wearing a white suit, linen I'd say, gladrag stuff with a red and purple tie, diamond tie pin, soft Italian pigskin leather shoes. Fellow with him was his muscle, big as a Samoan or damn near but dressed in black pin stripe, black shoes, dark glasses. The white suit reminded me of the Rev. Goodfellow down at the Universal Baptist Church, black suit looked like a 300-pound undertaker who churned up his own trade, my e-co-nom-ics teacher calls it, I like that, a 'vertical industry,' especially if he owns the cemetery too."

Markowitz felt proud as a teacher might when Rooster managed 'vertical industry without slowing down. I'll bet, he thought to himself, the kid is getting more confident with us.

"'Hear that, dude?' they say to me. Willie and Frank been sending me to that junior college where I take accounting and business e-c-o-n-o-m-i-c-s. I have, they say, a 'future.' That's more than Bernard had, not that him or any of those punks around him give a shit whether they are alive or dead, in fact whether anybody but their own family is alive or dead."

Rooster paused and looked shy. "You know, even the simple words I got trouble with. For instance how do you spell 'shit' anyway, two 't's or one? I can't seem to get it right and when I put it in a paper at the college they just cross it out like they don't know how to read."

Officer Stein replied, "It hardly matters, Rooster. You got bigger things to think about."

Rooster nodded okay, resumed his tale. "Willie is looking at me. 'Rooster,' he says, 'Mr. Furbo is here.' He look at white suit and white suit look at him and Frank with one of those 'you nigger' looks, then does the same for me. No matter what, white people in charge have that 'you nigger' stare. If I get an opening one day I am gonna kill white suit, a nice burst one night from behind some bushes into his skinny white back. He won't 'you nigger' me anymore, the motherfucker. And the big undertaker goes with him. I think I will get me some help for that job." Rooster stopped, embarrassed. "I don't mean you white guys are like that. But most are."

Dolan, trying to recover from his earlier stupidity, was the first to say it. "Yeah, I know. I apologize for all of us."

Stein knew that Dolan lived too far away from the real world. Liberals read somewhere that they are supposed to apologize like that. Stein lived in a mostly black world and had no apologies to make. He only apologized when he made a mistake. Racism was not one of his mistakes. He had a flash of anger.

"Speak for yourself, Mr. Dolan. I don't apologize for what I never did." He looked at Rooster. "But I can damn well say there are too many people of any color who are a real pain in the ass."

Rooster nodded acknowledgements, looked at Dolan. "I 'preciate what you said. What Officer Stein said too. Different folks got different strokes. I'm being honest with you." And indeed he was.

He resumed his story. "'Rooster,' Frank say, 'Mr. Furbo here wants to talk to you about some changes in our business. You're getting some new responsibilities.' Furbo, old in the eyes, stares at me like I'm only black pigshit. 'Asshole, talk to me,' he says. I shrug my shoulders. What the hell I gonna say to him? 'Asshole,' he repeats, "where do you take the money each Monday after Frank there totes up the tally?'

"'Take it like I'm told. Blade, Snake, and Moffat.' I don't tell him, I figure he knows anyway that they're always with me on the way out and in the car, each with a weapon and a sawed-off strapped to their legs—they be with me each step. So far nobody come up against us. I carry it, maybe $20,000 or so each Monday but for Easter, when we close because Willie's father is a pastor. We go to that big grocery the Arab runs in the city. He gives me a receipt and after that I dunno. I guess it works. If he screwed us we'd kill him and he knows it.

"Furbo turned to Purple Willie, 'He screwing you?'

"Frank answered, 'Don't think so. He takes twenty five percent commission. The money goes into his grocery chain account—him and his relatives got maybe twenty of those Arab mom-and-pop stores plus the two big everything stores—then the Arab writes a check to A-Plus Food Wholesalers for the seventy five percent. Willie and I *are* A-Plus. The Arab has an accountant who gives us receipts every December, couple hundred dates over the year, showing we bought from factories, importers and that sort of crap. He gives us purchase orders too. Good accountant. Nobody wants the IRS on your ass so we do an honest tax form showing our operating costs—bookkeepers, warehousemen, that sort of crap, of course none of them exist any more than the factories do—and our profit. Last year that was $863,000 we got into A-Plus, less all receipted and phony payroll costs. He even depreciates the warehouse we don't have and the delivery trucks that ain't there. Maybe $73,000 profit left and we pay a total tax of maybe, look here,' Frank shuffled some papers on the desk, '. . .$29,000.' Frank looked as proud as a pimp with a new pink Cadillac. Actually Frank once *had* been a pimp. Anyhow Furbo tilted his head, scowled at me to prove he was thinking, lit a cigarette."

Rooster stopped to explain. "I've stopped smoking—a kid like me, who wants a future if what we're doing here doesn't get me killed, ain't going to catch lung cancer. Anyway Furbo shrugged his shoulders at me and said, 'You there, asshole, they tell me you're a college boy. What do you think of the deal?'

"I'm thinking to myself, All right you cocksuckin' motherfuckin' shit, I'll tell you that I *can* think. I tell him it's a good service. The Arabs don't have to file Treasury Reporting forms on currency bank deposits because they got an exempt business—groceries. Their accountant does all the work and A-Plus is straight up honest because it pays taxes. It's only been working for a year and a half but it looks good. If the IRS wants to pay a call on A-Plus, the Arab has a deal with a real supplier, a relative of course, Damascus Grocery Wholesalers, who do have trucks and buildings and an office inside with A-Plus on the door. And the same accountant does A-Plus and Damascus. Says we don't have a thing to worry about, a perfect store. I say it's worth the money—twenty five percent is high but we got a lot in it. My bosses here take about $830,000, with all actual overhead paid out of the cash as they go along, and that includes a big piece to local politicians. No one has ever told me how much, but it has to be about $100,000. The police chief ain't on the take but he looks the other way because the politicians told him to look for another job if he don't. And that chief couldn't ever *get* another job except maybe security guard at six bucks an hour."

Rooster looked at Officer Stein, daring him to respond.

Stein, who unlike Rooster was not putting his life on the line, could hardly justify a diplomatic lie. "Right on, but I don't know anybody who'd hire a door shaker that stupid."

Rooster went on. "So Furbo rocks back on his expensive heels; I could see the shine on the backs. All he says is, 'You're right, kid.'" Rooster was hesitant again; Markowitz could feel him straining to control the stutter and to get the spelling right. At these forced moments the kid was miserable but brave, plunging into the word. "The back of his shoes, l-a-m-i-n-a-t-e-d. See, go to college, learn big words, make yourself a fortune. Anyway, Furbo is going on this time staring at the ceiling, 'But, Asshole,' Furbo had forgotten his 'you nigger' look because now he *was* thinking, 'Now do your bosses here, who have invited me out of Nevada just to consult on these matters, *know* they have $730,000 left in the bank?'

"Frank and Willie, they turned their heads sidewise looking at this wiseass. Willie spoke loudly, a big man, a big voice. 'We know it cause we got it in the bank, thass why we knows it. We get statements and when we write checks they's good, no rubber to 'em.'

"'You ever see that bank, Willie?'

"It was I'll B Frank who did not look real good, kinda like he had a pain in his stomach. He gave Furbo a cross between a fish eye and a sick eye, and said,

'The Arab set up the account. The bank is in Chicago. It is U.S. of A. Government, FDIC- insured, good as gold. But I never seen it. Here, look at the statements. Real address, real returned checks, real statements.'

"Furbo ran hard eyes onto the soft paper of the documents. Surprising it didn't furrow with those steel-plow eyes of his. 'My, my,' he said softly. 'I do believe your bank is good. And so, when the Arab decides to clean out your account, he's got good money to go back to Cyprus with.'

"My bosses were not happy," said Rooster.

"'How,' asked Willie, 'can he write a check on our account?'"

"'Ever see the signature card? After all it was the Arab who set up the account and ordinarily a fellow who does that has his name on the signature card, right? Can you prove he doesn't?' We all shook our stupid heads. 'No.'"

"'How do you know he'd go to Cyprus?' I asked Furbo.

"'Nobody as smart as this big-nose A-rab,' he drew out the word in disdain, 'wants to go to Syria to live. Cyprus, though, is real nice, close to home and away from dictators and real tax collectors who'll burn a whole city down if collections go slim. And besides. I know this particular A-rab.'

"'You *know* him?' I asked."

Rooster explained to the three cops. "Understand now I'm trying hard to be ghetto tough, do the ghetto stuff. In the ghetto you had better be grown up. I carry a gun. I screw women. I snort coke, but just for show. I have shot people. A lot of show-off in that too. I go to college to learn something. But I am only twenty two, short, and sometimes my voice squeaks. I hate being short. I hate my voice. I hate moments like when the white man make me feel shitty."

Rooster went on. "Furbo liked surprising us. The shit smiled. 'In my business, Rooster, I am supposed to know people like the Arab. Believe me, he has his name on that signature card. He will one day soon retire, after first telling you that you need more Federal deposit insurance coverage so that you have to use more banks. It is good advice, but a couple of the next banks he will get you will be in Vanuatu or Montserrat or Warsaw, Poland. The insurance is all his and your money will go on a nice island vacation. And it's even legal, as if anybody cares. The Arab is, after all, an owner of A-Plus. He probably provides the same service to twenty other operations. When he decides to split he will be very, very rich.'

"Frank, looking a little less tough now than ordinary, and ordinarily he was one tough SOB, nodded and said, 'I presume we pull all of our money out now before he gets it?'

"Furbo shrugged. 'You got time. And you can't open an A-Plus company account until your accountant gets a DBA (Doing Business As) and all that crap. Right now you can't afford to lose the accountant and the store, or some store. You got to have a laundry. Now if you want to pay a little less than twenty five percent commission, get a good store and accountant, get some advice on how to improve the play here in your shop, my colleagues and I can arrange that.' Furbo looked at Muscles, 'Dimples' he called him, 'We can do that, can't we?'

"'Dimples?' I am beginning to learn that in this world anything can happen. A pro wrestler of a hit man called 'Dimples'! So Dimples yawned, moved his frame on the chair, making the floor creak, started picking his nose, said, 'Yeah, boss, just like you say.'

"Furbo asked my bosses, 'What kind of players you get in here, I mean who are they, locals or outsiders too?'

"Purple Willie, he jiggled in his recliner chair. When Willie jiggles, two hundred eighty pounds of fat jiggle and you feel the air around your head like a jet plane shaking its wings at you. 'No white players going to come into this town at night, hardly in the daytime. Good reason. Players here are bigger drug dealers, bigger pimps, store owners, other local businessmen, some preachers, most all the politicians and the mayor regular, ordinary working folk lookin for a good time, the chop shop auto wreckers and yeah, a couple of regulars, blacks from out of town somewhere, but they play and do not speak. Serious men, serious gamblers. Lose big, sometimes win big. Everybody gets along, has a good time, know we is straight and our wheels, cards, machines, they is all straight. I mean we get five percent to ten percent on the play depending, but the rest is travellin' money goin' back and forth to the players. My boys, aside from Rooster here, Blade, Snake, and Moffat, they always lookin out for keeping the peace, crush a few heads now and then to insure local tran-quil-ity.' Willie he nodded at me then, 'That's a Rooster word,' he said smiling. 'Blade killed a customer a few months back by accident crushin him too hard but nobody worries over that sort of thing. We keep a good house and Celeste, Cynthia, they keep folks happy too. We don't make money off the girls, they is a kind of loss leader like the city stores advertise, you want to bring the folks in and keep them happy.'

"Skinny Furbo, muscled tight as a gymnast, you could tell he'd come up the hard way too, gazing at the ceiling thinking—first time myself I saw the stain where rain had come through—said, 'Well, not hard to expand the business if we limousine the rich white local players in, hire couple white bodyguards maybe to make them feel good, be sure nobody ever gets hurt out here. Got to redecorate, though, make it classy, add a food service, spiff up this office, make them feel it's racy, a little dangerous, exciting, black class. Yeah, this should be "The Black Class Club." Just stay where we are, keep the politicians greased, keep the cops chasing fleas, and you, thus us, are going to double the loot.'

"'Loot?' I'll Be Frank ain't strong on vo-cab-u-larry."

"'Money,' I told them, 'as in stolen money.'

"'We ain't stealin money,' Frank bleated out.

"'Just a word, Frank. A term of art, so to speak,' I told them.

"Furbo he stared at me surprised, so did the undertaker who even took his finger out of his nose. Furbo smiled again, said, 'You're good, kid. The Rooster,' he tells them all, 'is good.'

"You understand I was happy as a clam to hear him say that, but hated myself for it. Any self-respecting black kid ought to hate himself when he looks for praise from a son of a bitch white gangster. The day I used to think I'd feel most good was when I'd get to meet Mr. C, have him give me a nod. That's to arrive at the top.

"Anyway, Furbo turned to Willie and Frank, 'Well, you want our services or don't you? You got any problem with the Arab that we can't solve?'

"Willie and Frank did not, as my farming granddad used to say, come into town ridin a hay wagon suckin' on a straw. They're not gangsters but nobody pushes them, not even big timers. Furbo and the undertaker could be going home in bodybags anytime they wanted it. Blade was in the office next door with his 9mm pointed at them through a hole, invisible behind one of those Mexican black velvet nude paintings behind the bar. Talk business, talk tough. But I could tell from their faces that Furbo and the mob sounded okay to them.

"Then Frank, oh my he was a dapper ragtime dresser in those violet-black threads, asked, 'What's your percent, do you do the accounting, do you cover our ass with the IRS, do we get a bank account with only us owning it, are you stupid enough to think you could move in on us in a town where we own the shooters, and how are we going to trust you?' He threw the questions out rapid-fire.

"Furbo was as relaxed as your friendly personal banker, like the ads say, only the only time my folks went to a bank they couldn't get a loan even though they both had jobs."

Rooster turned to his listeners. "Don't you see, black money ain't ever as good as white money for bankers. The terrible thing is, you see, you can't ever cure yourself of being black. It's a disease others put on you, one you're born with, like some eternal voodoo. Son of a bitch, don't you see being black is a voodoo curse?"

For three tough men the air was moist with their own sadness for Rooster, for any and all black men who felt as he did, and for themselves too who had to know it was true.

Rooster shrugged, went on. "And so here was Furbo being friendly because he could see we had a good thing goin' here. Furbo then continued, 'Twenty percent plus is our rate, and we provide you gaming equipment to upgrade your place at no cost. Your gain is our gain. Yes, we do the accounting and you never have to file with the IRS, except for any personal income you want to report if you decide to invest in some front business. And we do the Let's-Pretend loan so you can account for the purchase monies. And yes, you get your own bank account, yours only, all offshore and uninspected—Aruba, Bahamas, you name where you want to vacation. You get spending money as you need it through us as Let's-Pretend loans out of your own account offshore, so you never need pay it back. And no, we ain't stupid enough to throw weight around in anybody else's town, certainly not a murder capital like this. We know you can off us anytime. Keep in mind our boys will come meatchop your asses in turn, but us all being dead is no way to make money. Which is a lesson that these street gangster friends of Rooster here ought to learn but won't. So much for your morality lesson from your reverend father Furbo. As for trust, we make money off of each other. To keep that going you got to keep the trust, which is the name of the game. And we know we will kill each other if someone throws dirty dice. Greed and death equal trust. Agreed?'

"Frank and Willie pondered it but seemed to agree. Dimples, the undertaker, was staring at Furbo perplexed. It was the first time he spoke. 'Christ, boss, I didn't know you was a priest.'"

"I could see that Dimples was kind of slow, not wrapped too tight as they say; his elevator never made it to the top floor. Furbo just looked at him long and low, shook his head, and then, in what was an amazingly personal moment confessed, 'But my mom did want me to be a priest and God rest her sweet soul, I disappointed her. I went to Sing Sing instead of seminary.'

"It was this, the combination of piety and prison in Furbo that made Willie and Frank trust him and the mob, more than anything he'd said. They looked at each other and nodded. 'It is,' said Frank, 'a done deal. You draw up the agreements, Mr. Furbo, and our lawyer will review them.' Then Furbo shook their hands, and said, looking at me, 'I want the Rooster here to keep working for you, and if not you, then us.'

"Purple Willie beamed at me, 'You see, Rooster, everybody they getting to see what a talent you got.' Made me feel real good.

"Fine Threads Frank, who never had given me much of a think, no bad time ever, remained his usual indifferent self. But then almost everybody in this town is at his very best when he's indifferent, because if they aren't the only other thing they got to show you is pain.

"Dimples got himself up from the chair. He moved damn quick for a big man and there was nothing slow about his eyes either—like someone working for the Secret Service guarding the President. They were high-speed, get-to-know-you-fast eyes. And his hand was always underneath his lapel, like hand on his heart pledging allegiance, or like when we were real young, promising 'cross my heart and hope to die.' For Dimples and his kind that reads more simply, 'cross me and die.' Fact is of course he was just keeping his hand close to his gun.

"So Furbo ends it saying, 'We'll talk next week. That will be your last week with the Arab. Then we move the A-Plus money. We don't use this phone here *ever*. I'll send a runner down. Rooster, you meet Jamie. . .' He wrote on a piece of paper a place, a time, a man's description, and an emergency number to dial if something went wrong: 'Just say one word *no* into the phone. We'll get to you, Rooster, as the cut-out. Got a phone at home?' I did and gave him the number.

"'Don't,' Furbo said, 'tell anybody, not even your Mom, that you ever saw us or what we arranged here today. Right?'

"I nodded. Right.

"Dimples shark-stared at me and drew his hand across this throat. The stupid SOB, thinking he could scare me. Furbo was off my hit list now but Dimples, if he ever got in my way, was road kill. In Malome, my town, he better walk real easy or he die, and maybe even then he die just because that is how things go out here.

"'Rooster,' Furbo was at the door now, 'you come with me, I got a few questions to ask you. Maybe you can even ask me some.' We looked at Willie and Frank, who were surprised, suspicious. 'Don't worry, it's nothing to do with our business. Remember, we trust each other.'

"And right then, maybe ten o'clock last night, that old reverend Furbo put on such a ben-ev-o-lent smile you knew how he would have looked had he been a priest—smooth, man, smooth. Sell you heaven easy. Shame maybe he didn't go that route. Behind him came Dimples in his black suit, top of his sumo-wrestler head nearly scratching the door frame. Dimples looked at Willie and Frank and real slow drew his cutting hand sideways across his throat. He just loves that gesture. Some shitasses just got to have the last word."

Officer Stein commented, "Yeah, got people like that at every level, but then, well. . .?" His voice ended in a question mark.

Rooster paused. "No, man, I got to go. Got to think on this. I'm gettin in deeper with everything I tell you. Now you already promised you'd keep me out. One thing more right now, promise me you won't make any move on Purple Willie's place or Furbo."

Markowitz replied, "You know it yourself. We couldn't even try. Whoever in the town Council isn't getting paid off by Willie and Frank, goes there to gamble. Since somehow they're sure to win, that's the same as getting paid off. Everyone on the force knows about the place. It's untouchable. It's got the Chief's blessing, enjoys his blindness."

Rooster nodded. "Yeah, good."

Doc Dolan asked, "So what's next?"

"I'll tell you when I know myself. When I make up my mind, I'll call one of you—you give a telephone number at home. If I decide to meet with you all again I'll take the bus into Palm City, the Rodeo Shopping Mall there, that's only twenty minutes from Malome. I'll meet whichever one of you wants to in front of Bloomingdale's. *If* I decide. I ain't playing you guys, I just don't know. Safe enough meeting there. Nobody from Malome goes to the Mall. It's too rich for our blood. Just like Palm City itself right across the river from Malome. Man, that river is wider than the Mississippi for keeping people apart. But I used to go to the Mall anyway. I have a map of the Mall pinned on the wall at home, like a treasure map. First time I came home from the Rodeo Mall, maybe I was eight, did my first shoplifting, and man was I close to getting caught, a black kid they just know he's in there to steal even if he ain't. Man, they follow you around, they watch you.

"Anyway after I saw the Mall I thought that was what heaven would be like, except in heaven I'd have the money to buy stuff. And in heaven I wouldn't be black, and small and have trouble reading, speaking the big words. Wouldn't have no sign of that stutter you catch me doing. That's what heaven was for me as a kid."

Markowitz ventured a sympathetic question. "What would it be like now, Rooster?"

Rooster looked depressed. He spoke slowly. "Wouldn't be no different. No different at all."

Rooster had been seated at the open end of the restaurant's circular leather booth. He stood up and looked at the three men. Took a deep breath. "I never had a talk with anybody white about anything serious before. I don't like it. Makes me uneasy, feel stupid. Talking to a bunch of cops about how I feel, let alone even mentioning Mr. C. . . No, I don't like it. Don't plan on my calling you."

Markowitz replied, "I'm honored you've told us what you have, Rooster. Really honored for that much trust. I agree maybe you shouldn't meet us again. But now, in exchange, let me tell you something serious about me I don't ever talk about, not to people black or white."

Rooster shrugged. The other men were equally ill at ease. The quick exchange of intimacies is not cop style.

"I was in love with a black girl once. Really in love. She loved me. She was an A student all through college. Her parents liked me; her father was a janitor. Mine was an artist. We were seniors. We talked about marriage. It was an accident, but I made a baby with her. She said we should get married. I told her to get an abortion, that I wouldn't marry her. I didn't have the guts to marry a beautiful black girl who loved me and to bring up a mixed-race baby. It was the weakest, worst thing I ever did in my life. If there is a heaven and I don't get into it, that will be why. So Rooster, if you don't ever want to talk to me again knowing this, not putting your life in the hands of a guy who wouldn't marry a black girl, you'd be doing the right thing. Believe me, the right thing."

Stein and Dolan were stunned. Stunned at the story being told, stunned at Markowitz possibly wrecking their investigation. Rooster stared at him, still standing. After a time he spoke.

"I 'preciate you'd tell me. Yeah, we all do miserable things. You want to know why I was, am, a hoodlum, a runner, a thief, a shooter, maybe a killer, now heading up to money laundering and the big-time rackets?"

Markowitz said, "Please."

"Cause there ain't no heaven up there so glorious that I'm going to be rich and white and tall and strong and not stutter and know all the big words. Not any place that good, anywhere. I've got to make it down here all on my own. Nothing to lose because I don't have anything. I came to you guys because I was thinking maybe, just *maybe*, I could turn it all around, make my own heaven in your big money a lot closer than me to that heaven world. But I'd do better faster, easier, more at home like, if Mr. C, like some dark angel ever took notice of me. Furbo is only a step on the way up. Mr. C, his kind, his money, his operations, are a kid like me's best road. He's a hero. Ain't no white cop can be a hero like that. With you, remember I had no start like some black kids, not even Head Start, it's all the hard way. Being a money launderer was just about the finest thing I could think of, and I tell you true."

Markowitz picked up on it. "Was?"

"Yeah, Malome, Willie, the guns, the dope, Furbo, Mr. C if I ever meet him, I already know, they all make me feel dirty. Unclean. No matter where I am, I don't fit. Dirty as a hoodlum with my own kind of gangsters, but across the line I'm black and a failure before I start. I'll never shop in Rodeo Mall feeling I belong there. I'm closer to you, Detective Markowitz, than you think. I don't mingle. I don't blend. I don't fit. If you hadn't told me your story, well maybe you wouldn't have seen me again. Fuck it. What does it matter what happens to me? You go catch your gangsters. What does that matter either? Right now moving the money, that's what it's all about. That's how you guys make your living. All righteous. You got pensions, respect, badges, you feel real good about putting some bad guy like me or Furbo or Mr. C away. You need us. We're all just making a living like you, but we're starting from a harder place. You can be righteous as you want while the poor and honest ghetto suckers starve. Like I say, maybe I should go with Mr. C and the big money.

"It's the same street we're on, just different sidewalks. Your way, my way, it's all about money. Anyway I'll meet you tomorrow at ten in the morning in front of Bloomingdale's."

It was four o'clock. It had been a long lunch. A considerably disturbed trio of white men drove Markowitz' car away from Rudolfo's. In front of them they saw Rooster sedately driving, of all things, a modest, muffled motor scooter.

Stein had been going over it, and now he was in a heat. "A lot of what Rooster said is downright crap. The usual 'it ain't my fault, I been shat on' excuse. The African-American hood's violin playing hearts and flowers. 'I go kill somebody and it's your ofay fault.' 'I launder money, get rich, and you aren't supposed to notice it's theft, tax evasion, betrayal of trust, and incentive for every greedy drug-dealing, whore-mongering son of a bitch in the world to go for your throat.' As usual, 'it's not the law it's me that matters.'"

Doc nodded agreement.

Markowitz turned angrily toward Stein. "A lot of what he said is true. Sure, not for every person of color, but for those still stranded at the bottom, and Malome is the bottom of the bottom, no question, that's the way it is. The old motto, 'Make your way as best you can in this land of opportunity'? He's doing it. *We're* doing it. The way you talk, it's as if human misery doesn't matter at all."

Doc nodded again in agreement. But he was angry, too. In fact, they were all angry. And yet somehow they were all in agreement. They just weren't sure about what.

29

Vasil stayed in bed for three days. Natasha was sexy, beautiful, and loving, but that was not the reason why. He had given up. He felt himself one man against the world—not just the Bulgarian world, but the American world too. No Barbour, no Vienna Ambassador, nothing but his knowledge of Giorgi, Sir Alfred, the red thieves and how twelve billion dollars must have disappeared. But no one cared. Now he too was unable to care.

Natasha knew Bulgarian men. All their women did. Their wisdom told them that the end of the world took longer to arrive than Oblomovism—that Russian model for all Slavic relapse into sloth—or her Vasil here, hopeless in bed, assumed. She knew he had to get back to work or face being disciplined. Not fired, because of his father, her family, his own happily fashionable politics protected him against that.

As for her knowledge of the situation? He had told her about Giorgi, about everything. Wives of spies know much of what their husbands do, no matter what the security rules say. Secrecy is a family affair. Wives of cops know much less; there is no intriguing code of secrecy to be broken, then shared. Less intricacy, less ideology. Cops' wives are unhappier.

But this time she had heard the same story from the Ministry investigators who had called the house for Vasil. She had told them Vasil was ill.

"Give him our best," they had said, "no need to bother him really. Tell him the Turk did it."

How easy for everybody that Mustafa had killed Giorgi and fled! His name went out on the wanted lists. Interpol got it. Istanbul, too, but despite agreements, Mustafa would not be extradited. He had Turkish juice. The fact that a 'wanted' notice went to Interpol showed how far Westernization, trust had proceeded. In the old red days, Interpol in Lyon, or in Paris, would never have received word of any Soviet bloc crime that bore a whiff of anything political. Fair trade, too, for in the old days Interpol in Paris had collaborated with the Nazis.

Natasha had tried to get him interested again in life. In, for example, what interested her—gossip.

"Darling, you'll never guess whom I met at the Oasis Supermarket today."

No response. But even an ordinary husband might have remained silent.

"Svetla was shopping. She'd been to Moscow, you know how much money they have. Anyway her sister is married to a sister of that Russian general who is in town from time to time. You know, Sergei Bratislav. Well, she flew Bulgarian Air and you know how those old Topolov planes shake apart each time they take off? They were forced down in Budapest to reglue the engines on the wings. Or some such. Right there at the airport in the lounge was Mrs. Bratislav. Oh, they had such a good visit."

Silence.

"Really, the Bratislavs are doing so well. He's *mafiya* of course, but after all it's family, so what does it matter? Anyway, she told her Sergei had had such a good time on vacation. Brought her—I don't mean Svetla's sister but Sergei's wife—a real antique alabaster tear vase from Cairo. He was in South Africa last week, sunning I suppose but also something about real estate, and brought her some gorgeous Zulu tribal cloth. Brilliant patterns and colors, she said. Darling, wouldn't you like us to go to Cairo someday when we can afford it?"

"Yeah," was the sour response from the bedroom.

When the groceries were put away, Natasha came breezily into the bedroom.

"Here, darling, the morning papers." She brought in both Bulgarian and the local English language ones that had accumulated. He was sitting up in bed drinking coffee, eating well. Natasha was a good cook. Not everything, for instance breakfast in bed, is incompatible with the inertia of Oblomovism.

Vasil, leafing through the press, whistled. "Holy Saint John!"

"What, dear?"

"Sir Alfred Means drowned off the coast of South Africa. Fell off his yacht on a moonlit night. Left his girl friend in bed to take a stroll, she said. A heart attack," he paused, "or so they say."

Vasil's father had been a Sea Scout Master in the Sixth Department, in the clandestine murders called "wet affairs," for a while. Vasil knew a lot about people who couldn't swim. He knew enough from his wire in Giorgi's car to know that Sir Alfred would not have been a spontaneous midnight swimmer. The Sea Scouts' M.O. (*modus operandi*) was written all over this one.

"The Sea Scouts. you think?" Natasha guessed immediately.

"Who else?"

"Why?" She knew that too, but wanted him to be energized again—it was a jump-starting question. Vasil was already gulping his coffee, a good sign. He would be grabbing his clothes soon enough.

Vasil explained. "The fat man went for a swim. He was a principal in stealing twelve billion dollars of the people's money."

Not that the Sea Scouts were avengers of the people. Nobody who had lived under the Communists believed there were any "people"—except the poor and tyrannized in whose name so many who weren't "the people" became rich. No, "the people" couldn't afford assassins. Even their violent deaths were inexpensive. "The people" died in camps or from illnesses like malnutrition, alcoholism, pneumonia—illnesses preventable by care only money could buy.

"Obviously he was skimming and took too much. Like any of them would. Someone caught him out. He got too confident." Vasil chuckled. "So the world's biggest man didn't think a poor Bulgarian could do anything about his stealing from us, eh? Well, we're not that helpless, are we?" He smiled broadly and reached for his old robe hanging from the post on his side of the old bed.

Vasil, at the moment, was one proud Bulgarian. So was Natasha. Both were delighted at Bulgarian vengeance against the foreigner. No matter who or why; it mattered only that those so often stomped upon could stomp back.

"Did you read the Vienna news, honey?"

"No, what?" She turned to the inside pages of papers running over two days. "Here, honey. Read it."

The stories were headlined as Bulgarian papers and English tabloids are wont to do. Historians could worry about truth. Papers need sales. People who buy them want entertainment. Truth is for universities to worry about.

"Look at this one: NEAR-WAR NEAR VIENNA. FIRE FIGHT WITH U.S. AND BRITISH PARATROOPERS KILLS RUSSIAN DIPLOMATIC MAFIYA."

"And this one, honey!" "NEAR-BREAK IN DIPLOMATIC RELATIONS BETWEEN AUSTRIA AND THE U.S. OVER AUSTRIAN MANHUNT FOR U.S. GREEN BERETS. RUSSIA SIDES WITH AUSTRIA, THREATENS TO USE NUCLEAR WEAPONS. BRITAIN MOBILIZING TROOPS. BRUSSELS, EU PARALYZED. BULGARIA TO OFFER TROOPS TO NATO IN RETURN FOR PACT."

"Hey, Nash, listen." "SECRET SOURCE FINGERS AUSTRIAN POLICE BIGWIGS AS RUSSIAN MAFIYA HIRELINGS. AMERICAN AVENGERS FACE MASSACRE AFTER WIPING OUT MAFIYA WEAPONS STOCKPILE. RUSSIAN PREMIER THREATENS RETALIATION AGAINST U.S."

Vasil, whose own agency paper mills—like all intelligence agencies—had churned out lies by the gross, nevertheless saw a truth behind all this. His name was Barbour. No wonder he had been out of touch. Vasil's grin was so broad it could have swallowed the Balkans.

And then it hit him. General Bratislav, on the board of directors of that beautiful new bank, the UST&D, had been visiting South Africa—and my, what a coincidence, he's there when the fat man goes for a not-quite-swim. Holy St. John!

"Honey, get me my good suit. I'm going to see the American ambassador, whether she wants to see me or not. I have got some news for her."

Natasha, pleased with herself and the man she loved, fetched his clothes.

The Bulgarian in him preferred something more devious, for the truth in Bulgaria is the last resort, to be used only when all else has failed. But given the security, status, and scheduling barriers to seeing the most important ambassador in Sofia, of whom all Bulgaria was singing her praise, he had no choice. On the other hand, what he would tell the American Chief of Station was more congenially deceptive. He called the young man who was Chief of Station. Sooner or later the ambassador would tell him some of Vasil's story anyway. It was up to her how much.

"Ernest, Vasil here. We don't have a translation date today but something has come to my attention as a personal security matter that must, I emphasize *must*, be brought to your ambassador's attention immediately."

Ernest, as Vasil anticipated, said, "You tell me and I'll see the right people get it."

Bluff. "I'll tell you only in front of the ambassador herself. And you should know better than to trust the phone."

"You'll tell me and I'll tell her. The phone line is secure." Vasil had a scene in his mind of two children going, "nyah-nyah-nyah, your father's moustache." As for the secure line, where had this child gone to school? He should see those dozens of firehose-sized reels of cable behind the locked door in the telephone company basements.

"*Ernest*. This one goes my way. Either you get me in the door and get brownie points for shepherding the boy with the important news, or you get to explain to Washington why your ambassador is going to return home in a coffin."

Ernest met him at the door of the unpainted, tenement-like embassy. He had two security men and the commander of the Marine guard battalion along. The elevator was broken again. They walked the five flights to the ambassador's unpretentious office. All four walked in with him. Ernest introduced him as his private-sector translator.

"Madame Ambassador, my pleasure."

"And mine. My colleague here," she nodded toward Ernest, who was wearing his fierce, in-defense-of-God-and country look, "tells me that there is an urgent security matter." Her tone was calm and businesslike. She was appraising Vasil.

"An urgent matter, yes, Madame Ambassador, but my acquaintance," he nodded toward Ernest, "may not quite have understood its nature."

The security men and the Marine frowned suspiciously. Ernest began to splutter. "I heard you explicitly say the ambassador's life is in danger!"

"When you run the tapes you will not hear those exact words. But no matter, it's up to the ambassador to decide whether my visit here is worth her time."

She bristled. "I don't like being misled. What you have to say, Mr. Stambolov, had better be good."

"I must say it in private. You, Madame, will decide who else is to hear."

She was not pleased; it smelled of a time-wasting, manipulative ploy. Yet Vasil's sincerity, confident presence, and contagious urgency were apparent. Fact was, she didn't think much of Ernest herself. She nodded to the head of her security group.

"Frank, you stay. Go sit down over by the wall there. Keep an eye on us. But shut your ears. Okay?"

"Yes, Madame Ambassador." Frank took a watchful place in a far chair. Ernest stalked out the door in a fit of pique, humiliated and furious. For the others there was no issue. The ambassador is always boss.

She looked at Vasil with disapproving curiosity. "All right. Get on with it."

"I have three things to tell you. But first, I apologize for the security ruse. It was the only way I could get to see you without being blocked by Ernest, and it was something unrevealing made up for the people tapping the telephone."

Her eyebrows went up. More distrust of her visitor, but again balanced by her intuition that he was not lying. Quite a pretty woman, it was clear she would be animated when playing ambassador didn't impose its formal mask.

"Ernest assures me, as do my security people, that it's a secure line. And how could a commercial translator like yourself know anything?"

"Madame will forgive me." He began to reach for the ID in his inside coat pocket, but was stopped by a very alert and intimidating Frank pointing a large-caliber automatic at his head.

Vasil was unperturbed. "You will remember that I went through a metal detector on the way in. However, to assure you, if I put my coat on that chair, will you get my wallet from the inside pocket?"

Frank kept his pistol pointing at Vasil while searching through his coat.

"Okay," he said to his boss, "he's not packing. It's his wallet."

"Please, pull out my ID card which you'll find inside a second lining. You can feel where it is. It's not visible."

Frank did as instructed, found the hidden ID, read it, and frowned more deeply.

The ambassador said, "Frank, give it to me."

She studied it. "Ministry of the Interior? But Ernest said you were a commercial translator." She was now disturbed.

"That perspicacity—or lack thereof—Madame, is why I wanted Ernest out of the room."

"How long has Bulgarian intelligence been doing translations for our CIA station here?"

Vasil's eyes twinkled. "From the beginning, Madame. From the time the Agency stopped sending trained Bulgarian speakers."

She contemplated that bit of history wryly, sighed. "Yes, that sounds right. Oh, my. Am I correct in presuming that you wear a transmitter?"

"Not ordinarily, Madame. There's little of importance that I translate. Commercial interests; industrial espionage as nations do it these days; and what Ernest is trying to learn about our mafiya—how the old reds are involved in it, how some present officials are also involved. Nothing unexpected. The same interests that our Ministry has, essentially, but naturally as Bulgarians we're a few light years ahead of him. I write up a summary and submit it. Wearing a wire that might be found could prove embarrassing."

"I see. And so why do you tell me all this, obviously to the detriment of your government's ability to continue these activities?"

"The moment speaks for itself. You didn't trust me before and now you do. I had to give you something to earn that. Besides you have no one else to translate and you don't want an issue to arise with our struggling democratic government. It means no harm. It does what Bulgaria has always done badly, tries to protect its interests from bigger powers. The issue is beside the point here, but we don't want to become an EU or American satellite any more than we wanted to be German or Russian. It is our fate, until perhaps now, to be a satellite."

"I know."

"And by showing you my credentials I allow you to guess what everyone else in Sofia knows, except those in the Western embassies: that Ernest is naive. It's not entirely bad. It allows Bulgarians to sense a small triumph over giants.

But Ernest nevertheless is not terribly clever. You will want to bear that in mind. It's in our interest that America be clever. The Russian bear is not tamed. He can become violent at any time. Most of us think he will. Then we will need you, NATO, to be quite clever and powerful."

"I know."

"And so, Madame, you might wish to continue Ernest's use of me. I regret this mostly irrelevant conversation which I think we should both forget until a Bulgarian speaker arrives from the States. It causes no embarrassment to continue, nothing said outside, as things are. Only if there is anything important that Ernest wants to say with a Bulgarian, you can ask me to delete it from my report."

"You're offering to be a double agent?" Surprise, scorn, distrust, amusement. "And in doing so, you ask me to conspire with Bulgaria against my own government? A tall order, Mr. Stambolov."

"No, not at all." He was polite but offended. "You should understand, Madame; I'm offering to continue being a gentleman and to avoid embarrassment within the Embassy here."

"Ah, I apologize," she said, and she meant it. "And I thank you. As for keeping up appearances, I will do what managers in sensitive situations always do: I shall kick it upstairs for a decision back in Washington. Isn't that what you would do?"

"If I had a rational administrative structure above me, yes. But I agree that serves all of your ends. I would appreciate, however, not being identified as the source of your knowledge. Wait a day or two, Madame, until one of our papers carries the same common information by one of our more sarcastic columnists."

"You can assure me such an article will appear?"

"I can predict it likely, that's all. After all, the death of Giorgi so far hardly reported, is a news peg. I know a reporter or two. In any event, if no helpful source article for you to cite appears, you must of course go ahead and, as you say, kick it upstairs. I will guarantee no translations by me in the interim so that you cannot be accused of failing to stop the practice. But, again, please don't identify me as your source. I would join Giorgi dead—or be the first prisoner to reopen the gulags."

"Fair enough. Decent, after all. What I tell the Undersecretary about how I learned of this little bag of tricks, and Ernest's perspicacity, makes no difference. *Quid pro quo* once again. You are a sophisticated man, Mr. Stombolov. I might add I recognize yours as an honored family name."

"Not always lucky in politics," he replied, smiling.

She did admire his savoir-faire; all so neatly packaged. Appreciating him at one level did not mean believing him at all levels. Many conversations leading to defined trusts are like that. But about Ernest, well, Vasil would make a better station chief than he, if one were a little loose about the rules. Inside she was laughing about that. Relations between the Station and the ambassador were often strained. Ambassadors had to put up with so much. When she bucked this problem upstairs everyone in State would be hooting with laughter. Her face remained carefully noncommittal.

"And so, what is it we are really to talk about?"

"First, you are aware of the current crisis in Vienna, Madame, concerning alleged official Americans and British killing Russians? The fact that those doing the shooting cannot be found?"

"How could I not be aware?"

"I don't know if your people there know who the American was, perhaps they do, but if not I can probably tell you. He is a close friend of mine. A senior agent for your IFinCIG. Lee Barbour."

She wrote that down. "And?"

"Your IFinCIG , and the Brits, South Africans, Israelis, Interpol will want to know that Sir Alfred Means... do you know the name?"

"Who doesn't? Filthy rich and drowned. And it's rumored he's someone's secret agent."

"Not ours."

In this game one gave a little when given a little. It was called, "tossing and trading bones."

"Next?" She was a bit imperious.

"No 'next,' Madame, until you can assure me of your trust."

"You joke, Gospodeen. This is Bulgaria. We are having an intimate conversation. No one trusts anyone. Yet somehow we seem to. Do you think me a liar or a fool?"

"Neither, Madame Ambassador."

"But," she smiled, "we might have certain agreements."

"Vraiment, Madame, et j'en suis content."

"I'll damn betcha we can both make that happiness short-lived."

This time Vasil grinned. He did so enjoy the American idioms. "Yeah, but why screw up a good thing?"

Madame Ambassador chortled undiplomatically. This guy, whatever his angle, was interesting.

He told her. The works. The twelve billion dollars, about which she knew in general, and how it flew. Which no one not in on the flight knew. Sir Alfred; how the fat man could not swim, and how that had likely come to pass. The new insight, General Bratislav and, so clear now, the UST&D Bank.

"My boss, Giorgi,was assassinated," he told her. "Stupidly I thought it was Mustafa from our office who did it; they were after all both trying to take a bite out of the billions. I was crazy. I see that. If the Ministry investigators think the Turk did it, something must be wrong. Too easy. Too convenient."

"You think something more conspiratorial then, something more sinister?" she asked.

"Death in Sofia in this crowd is always easy to come by. Easy to push under the rug as well. There is always a conspiracy."

They parted on that note. He pondered it as he walked from the Embassy to the now nearly inoperative ITS offices. What was the extent of the conspiracy this time? Who benefits?

30

Madame Ambassador prepared her own cable, to be scrambled for sure, but her own personal cryptographic slug still to be used as well. She had received the call from State telling her that the Senate Crime Committee had, upon the vote of the full Senate, expanded its investigations to Vienna and Sofia because of the State Department's, this was the resolution as drafted by the senator no doubt, "utterly inept handling of the frightful and unresolved Vienna incident with its portents for disaster in relationships with Russia and Austria."

Madame Ambassador was not new to Eastern games, nor to new players appearing, others disappearing, as new rules were being made. "Chinese baseball," as the Taoist philospher Siu called it, "just like American baseball except that any player can move the bases anywhere at any time."

In this game, here, the stakes had become much higher. State was a target; so was her friend Ron in Vienna. The wording made it clear she might be a target too, for reasons quite beyond her. How the Senate Crime Committee included Sofia in that Vienna crisis she had no idea, except for Vasil Stambolov's astonishing report, indeed his trust, from which inferences, or alternative attribution to typical Balkan fantasies, could be derived.

The matter was bigger than she had conceived. It was being *made* big. Who would benefit? Talk of diplomatic problems was being fed by newspaper headlines about war. Idiotic. Of course the newspapers benefited. European politicians were taking up the hue and cry, each pursuing interests, or wraiths, down different alleys. Publicity in it for them, but a slippery slope. The worst case of that was the most important and unpredictable visible player, the Russian premier. He was too new in office, too much subject to fierce factions in Moscow, to play it cool. He had not paid attention to the incident soon enough. The old Communists, the new military, the apparatchiks and *mafiya* authorities were pouring on the heat. The premier, unseasoned, felt compelled to take a jingoistic stand. That fed the fires and made problems not there before. "The poor idiot," she mused to herself. She knew from experience; in politics you learn the hard way or go belly-up trying. In general she liked the Russians. But not when they began to beat the war drums. Hardly.

She learned from the State Department's embassy-circulated daily *Intelligence Bulletin* that the Austrian government, being savaged by their own right-wing party piling up gains at the polls, was being forced to intransigent wrong-headedness. Behind the scenes Washington knew the Austrians wanted the whole mess to go away, to get on with cleaning up their own shameful mafiya-involved police. A trusted London source, a "distinguished American" as the report described him, with a personal channel to the Austrian Chancellor guaranteed that. But the unyielding anti-American public stance was being forced on the Austrian government by its opposition, who smelled an issue that could bring the government down if enough lies were believed. That accounted for much that one read in the press.

By now even if no one knew who, it was accepted that Americans with some kind of official status had been in the shootout. That announcement had come from the Austrian police. And everyone accepted that the dead were Russian mafiya, some or all of whom—no one had said how many dead there were—carried diplomatic passports. "Hardly a surprise," she said to herself.

Most surprising to her were events back home. Senator Cranmer's Crime Committee, inviting Senate's Foreign Affairs Committee, other political raiding and scalping parties to join, had come down heavily on the side of the noisiest anti American Austrians. Those were the fascist far right, once-Nazi, once-Communist—they were damn near all the same now. A bizarre alliance. Those Austrian politicians were the ones also denying any Russian mafiya or related police corruption in this "Vienna Incident," as it had come to be called. She knew it intuitively. "The far right are protecting the crooks," as usual. Extreme politics was linked to organized crime, money laundering, the works. "So what," she asked herself the rhetorical question, "is new?"

Cranmer and his allies in the Senate must be supporting the bad guys of central and Eastern Europe. Ironic, the Crime Committee, and its head Cranmer also on the Banking Committee, both committees mandated to protect the public from crime, fraud, and unstable markets, were doing the opposite, at least as far as Europe was concerned. "Why? Who benefits at home?" As she asked, she knew.

Cranmer and company were using the Vienna Incident to aim at the President himself. The shots at how State was handling it, at failures in Vienna and this blast at Sofia too, were means to get at the Chief Executive. Embarrass and discredit the President. That was really it, and it was nothing new in American politics. State was always expendable to the Congress when there were Presidential scalps to hang. Insofar as the publicly unidentified official American shooters—those "loose cannons," "death squads," "out-of-control hit men" were the Congressional epithets—belonged to Justice (DEA, FBI) or the Defense Department. Congress would have a go at them as well. But Foggy Bottom was always the juicier target. Only because of Vasil did she know it was Barbour out of IFFY, which was part, of all things, of the Treasury Department. Poor Treasury if that news got out before an honest account did. They had no horde of congressional PR people to defend them.

"Howling at the Executive!"

It had hit her. "Of course! Cranmer is setting himself to try to run a second time for the presidency! Why didn't I see that right away?" A natural for any unscrupulous politician. That adjective, in her view, included about one third of the Senate and half the House. "What a constituency for Cranmer to develop!" Just as in Austria, where appeal to the far right and the far left—always hostile to the idea of government—meant votes, in America appeal to the wealthy and the middle class as the critics of adventurism abroad translated also into votes. The U.S. was doing well; most Americans were confident and comfortable. The status quo was just fine. And Cranmer was arguing that a wildly interventionist President, his departments out of control, who engaged in "outlaw barbaric imperialism"—that was one quote the *Bulletin* had carried—was "bringing shame and danger to the Republic." And the liberal intellectuals, who were always being shot at by conservative scholars plus the cadre of America-haters, the Americans who always said "them" not "us"—would love those words,too.

Senator Cranmer, she realized—respected, already well known, unquestionably connected to the big money, and, as Crime Committee Chair, "protector of the people from crime," as he often characterized his role—would be formidable riding this issue into the Oval Office. Providing the flappable new Russian premier did not let off a rusty missile that blew everyone off the map. "And so Cranmer will have to begin Russia bashing as well." Not because of the reality of the mafiya, but because the inexperienced premier was making offensive noises and playing into a candidate's hands, a ready-made issue. Worse, the premier might be fool enough to have to prove he meant them. If the Vienna Incident—and now only she and a few others knew its Siamese twin on the way, her own twelve-billion dollar Sofia Source for it—could not be set right immediately and damage control instituted politically, Cranmer's Presidential course could be irreversible.

And at the moment it was already very dangerous. It was already disturbing the peace of Europe. Russia was the wild card, Austria the joker. World War I had begun with an Austrian Duke in Sarajevo, right next door to Sofia. The Balkans was where players had their stacked decks hidden. She would have to find some aces. And some allies.

At the moment Vasil Stambolov, of the Bulgarian police/intelligence/translation services, seemed one of those. He was touchingly frank, coldly realistic, intensely purposeful, a lone player in his Ministry, and a gentleman. He was also a gentleman with a dagger in his pocket, for he could compromise her by any revelation about their meeting, about not blowing the whistle on the Ministry penetration immediately, or on Vasil himself. She could kill Ernest for getting her in that spot. The cable she was preparing was to a dear friend, Ron Owen, in Vienna. There was no question that, given the ruckus, Ron was in need of allies. Following Vasil's warning that there was no secure communication, her cable kept that in mind.

"Ron. How fine that our interests continue to be getting closer. I thank you for your congratulatory birthday letter and yes, I am older, wiser and realize that even if I had billions, whether ten, twelve or more, nothing is as important as having old friends, good recipes, or, as my husband says, a good barbour. I understand my husband's favorite is near Vienna. Right now I am indulging an inherent dislike for ambitious senators. Wars start so easily when people throw firecrackers into ammunition dumps. I have also learned through a friend, who speaks of accidents, that at our ages even yachting is dangerous. We must be careful. One of us should visit the other this next week. I cook, you buy the beer."

As her secretary left to carry the cable draft to the commo room, the Ambassador, robust ordinarily, felt exhausted. So much happening, exploding, and no real sense to it. She had three social events on her calendar tonight. All essential appearances, and all equally ridiculous. She was going to go home to rest instead. Maybe not come in tomorrow. For the first time in years take sick leave. She thought of Goncharov's *Oblomov*. With all her Slavic Foreign Service years she could never come to be sympathetic to that essentially lazy, irresponsible, parasitic lout Oblomov, or all those contemporaries she had met who were too much like him. But Oblomovism was contagious. "This place imprints you," she mused. Vapors and emanations permeating like damp in an English house. No one who walks in a swamp can keep her feet dry. . . . Or, she thought of the Okefenokee swamp and the wonderful old Pogo comic strips, "avoid the alligators." "Lordy, I am tired."

31

As Vasil walked toward what he knew were the deserted offices of ITS, he pondered. If it were a conspiracy, and shame on him for failing to see the obvious right away, who other than Mustafa would have done in Giorgi? Who stood to gain? What had they been doing? That was easy: looking to take a bite out of twelve billion dollars. He reviewed the car bug revelations; Giorgi being told by Jeanette of local identities; a red deputy minister of finance, name not picked up by the bug; of Burmov, the D.D. of Interior back then, whom Vasil knew had emigrated Lord knows where, and the Central Bank's Dobri N, the N easy enough to identify.

Vasil did just that and learned, upon arriving at N's villa that afternoon, that Dobri N had left not just the country but this earth, for as custom dictated on the front door were a memorial poster and photograph of the deceased. "A foreigner wanting to invest in Bulgaria ought to invest in cemeteries," Vasil said to himself. A big new business. He rang the door anyway, thinking he might as well see if the family knew anything, and how the man had, or was supposed to have, died.

The maid, in mourning black, opened the door. He showed her his Interior Ministry ID.

She stared at it too long, then looked up at him accusingly. A thin, tiny, homely woman, her face was contorted with despair and her voice vibrated with an old woman's anger.

"You haven't done enough harm here? You have the courage, the cruelty to come back? What more hurt can you give?"

No ordinary person, even in this new democracy, spoke that imprudently to an Interior Ministry senior officer. Vasil comprehended the degree of her pain and thus her indifference to cautious good sense. As to the "you" and the "hurt," it was obvious that some of his more loathsome colleagues had been here before him. Vasil, who was genuinely sympathetic, was able to get the old woman talking. One Interior "you," by her description, was indeed Giorgi. The other, from the maid's excellent memory, could only be BB, the boss of Giorgi's boss, and thus third in command in the Ministry.

"Yes, of course," Vasil said to himself. BB invited in on the scheme would be Giorgi's umbrella, his access to records; his powers of intimidation, travel, permission to take time off from ITS to pursue the money. Yes, BB of course. Vasil knew BB to be as dirty as an abandoned hound dog rummaging in the bloody rubbish of an abattoir. Indeed BB had been the same in his earlier red-ruled, red-ruling life. Vasil knew about that work. "Bad news BB" was a real son of a bitch.

It took no great insight to guess who might have arranged Giorgi's fatal exit. When BB had the leads he needed to take his bite of the twelve billion dollars, Giorgi was a natural for the bye-bye trip to the great beyond. But with Dobri N dead, where would BB's own search take him? He would be digging for names and addresses of the wealthy absconded. Or if Giorgi had any earlier success in investigation, BB would have a name or two already. Maybe getting information by interrogation, torture of course, was how Dobri N had died. He asked the maid what she knew of the death.

"Heart attack after the two men visited him. He came home with them from the tavern with a palsy that never stopped. He was so upset that he couldn't speak or stand up. The daughter called the doctor who was here just as comrade Director had the heart attack. He grabbed his chest, fell over. Nothing the doctor could do. The ambulance was too late. The comrade Director died within minutes."

"Do you think your master confided in them before he died?"

She didn't know. But one man had come back the next day and done great harm to Katherine, Dobri N's daughter.

"Where is she now, the daughter?"

Fear again in the maid's eyes. Terrible fear. He reassured her.

"No, I won't hurt you or her. You can see I'm not like those terrible men. I hate them as you do. Please, it may help others if I can find those two criminals. Please tell me where the comrade Director's . . ." Vasil paused. 'Comrade' was a usage that belonged to the past, but her life years had been used up in that red and the Nazi past. Fear had been its staple. He continued, "where The Director's daughter might be. She might want to hear my apology on behalf of the Ministry. Perhaps with her help I can find the bad men."

The maid pointed him up the stairs. "By the dear God, promise me you will help her, please." The old eyes were crying.

The maid followed him into a bedroom where a woman, perhaps fifty years old, lay in bed. Bandaged all about the face, her arm in a splint, only one eye visible through the swathing, Vasil knew her hurt was BB's work. It was known throughout the Ministry what he had done in the old days, and now it seemed he was starting it again, on his own, in these new democratic days. Vasil was repulsed. He approached ever so quietly, that one tearing beaten eye watching him fearfully. He told her of his sorrow for her pain, and the wrong done her and her family. He explained why he had come—initially to learn whom "those criminals from the old days of government" had wanted to find through her father, but now, compellingly, to find out "Why have they hurt you?"

Slowly, painfully, her bruised lips formed the words.

"I don't know what they learned from Father. I think nothing. That is why not 'they' but only one man, the tall one with terrible teeth, awful breath and half an ear"—now Vasil knew for certain it was BB—"why he beat me until I told him where he could probably find, among my father's things, the address of Todor Mihailov."

"Ah." Vasil remembered Mihailov now, a senior in the days of the reds in the Ministry of Finance, and one whom he had mentioned to Barbour when Barbour was in Sofia. "Shame on me," Vasil reprimanded himself, "forgetful at my age." Of course Mihailov was a name to add to the circle of thieves.

"Did you know Todor Mihailov yourself?"

"No. Father mentioned him as a colleague back in the old days. He never came here. They were not social friends, just worked together in the financial matters of government."

Vasil did not tell her what he surmised was their real interest in working together. He asked, "Do you yourself know where Mr. Mihailov might live now?"

"In America, I think. Near the capital. Father mentioned it once. Is there a city called Virginia? I believe Mr. Mihailov had come into money."

"And your father, did he seem to come into money?"

The one sad, hurt eye looked at him accusingly. "My father is dead. He died of fear, fear of those people from your Ministry. They killed him. Beat me so badly I couldn't go to his funeral. As in the old days from my village, our relatives dressed him for his journey. He is a traveller now. His guardian angel will be with him. He will be crossing the great river to Hades. His relatives will have put a coin in his hand to pay his passage. Yes," she hissed at him, "yes, he has come into money—the coin in his hand for the ferryman to Hades. Good he has that money, otherwise he cannot cross to Hades and he becomes a vampire. That's money for you, isn't it? Coming into money as you say, eh?" Her voice shook with helpless fury, drawing strength from her anger. "Get out! *Now*!"

Vasil held his ground. He had to. "Please, I'll go immediately, but may I know if you have told the regular police about this assault?"

"Does the chicken complain to the fox about weasels? Do you think me mad?"

"No, but understand, these are new days. The police aren't political now. They'll do what they can. They will conduct an honest investigation. Bring charges. Press for punishment. That's the law now."

"Your police will do all that against an important man in their own Ministry? Do it for the sake of a dead Communist and his useless daughter? As rabbits will pursue wolves?" She pursed her hurting lips, and would have spat at him if she could. "You guarantee that, I suppose, do you? That justice, you who are so idealistic but so much less important than any of them?"

Vasil felt abashed, depressed, angry at her truth.

"No, I can't guarantee it. I can say it's likely, but in this life, now, there are no such guarantees."

The bruised and knowing eye blinked its sad knowledge. A wounded Cyclops, it stared at him. Her fury spent, she was breathing hard. Vasil felt humiliated, shifted about uneasily, searching for something to give.

"May I help you in any way? May I get a doctor for you?"

"My father's doctor, he's my doctor, and attends to me. He says I'll be all right. So no, isn't it obvious that you can do nothing for me?"

The wounded Cyclops continued to stare at him, her one eye holding him fast like a binding curse. He felt magic in her eyes: the evil eye which all villagers still knew. He could not help but stare back at her, conscious of her irregular blinking like some morse-coded message to which he had no key. Yes, there was a message. They stared at each other until she broke the silence. Her weak voice, words mouthed slowly through those swollen lips, was a monotone. She was the village priestess of the supernatural; she was Cyclops become Cassandra, portending doom.

"You and the other rabbits come to avenge my father, eh? Hardly. Not against the Devil himself. I can smell the evil. Smell it close to you yourself, do you now? Look at you, just a craven boy, that's what you are!" The rattle of her hate was now that of an old *bogomil* believer, herself village witch as well, faith and counterfaith coexisting. The venom in her was speaking: "You, you liar, you can't even do anything to save yourself!" She cackled. "You'll see that soon enough!"

He could not say why he feared her, why he believed her, but he did.

Suddenly, arms flailing, she shrieked, "I told you to go."

Vasil left. He was trembling.

32

It was good to have meetings in Paris. A light-hearted city, never short on beauty or pleasures. The Paris partner dabbled in industrial real estate all over the world, but his portfolio belonged to Paris. And his heart belonged to his portfolio.

His major holding was a closely held munitions and military aircraft industry. The very name of these sleek jets, with nuclear missile capability from which commercial space ventures now derived, was the pride of all France and the source of billions from sales abroad. The Parisian was too light-hearted a fellow to have created any of this wealth and glory himself. He was an *n*th descendant generation owner, one of whom no one of his family in his youth had been very proud. At the time of the Revolution the family smithy had begun to make pistols. Its initial contribution to *liberté*, *égalité*, and *fraternité* had been—not entirely without self-interest but understandably popular—the killing of tax collectors. Three generations later, the smithy had industrialized to produce those small arms so praised for excellence in the Franco-Prussian war, those excellent arms so unlike French organization, generals or good sense in that sàme war France lost. Not all Frenchmen, however, lost; for that war had been the making of the family's fortunes.

The Parisian partner, a spoiled son, by becoming ever more arrogant, intransigent, vain, and grandiose, displayed the very characteristics of Napoleon III against the Germans, to which the son added a tendency to be dissolute. Thus the family forecasts proved true but for one saving grace: the Parisian partner turned out to be cunning and unscrupulous in business. He acquired, not lost—wealth and bad habits.

"Very convenient indeed, as usual, and as usual we thank you." The Advisor, speaking to the Parisian, was sipping a barrel-blessed armagnac. He spoke in that melody of the Irish, an happy man.

"How very useful, so many billions routed so circuitously for your munitions, so many embargoes circumvented thanks to nests of companies nested within nests of companies, to chameleon bills of lading, ships renamed and repainted en route, crews replaced at sea, government-approved destinations as diaphanously immaterial as ports painted on silkscreen, all those millions of tons of magical munitions, moving by prestidigitation. No serious bank is but pleased with these so properly sourced millions, our pieces of Sir Alfred's billions being soundly reinvested."

Shadow spoke. He was abstemious generally, but on this occasion he was enjoying an armagnac so rich it was dark as amber and poured like syrup.

"Properly sourced, oh my yes," laughed the General, "nothing more proper than a war, although most of them are not very well run these days. In Africa this last trip when we were doing that rather nice bit of work," he paused, smiling, as glasses were raised in congratulation, "every day I read of those slobs, those ruffian rampaging bandits that call themselves soldiers, running amok, wasting perfectly good munitions—killing children, women, often their own officers. The last is unforgivable. Rabble, downright rabble. For myself, as a military man, I like to see fine munitions used, well, to show off their best. A *real* war, like my father generaled at Stalingrad. Slaughtering Germans, now that is the right use for the kind of weapons you make. *Nazdroveye*!" His vodka glass was a white-bottoms toast to the Parisian.

Macho generals bored Sandor, who knew armagnac, knew that one and was drinking it as well.

"I drink to this particularly pleasant occasion where we celebrate over a hundred million dollars to each of us, partners from Sir Alfred's, shall we say, somewhat reluctant largesse." He held up his glass, which tilted dangerously. Sandor was at rather a tipsy angle himself.

"To the Advisor who arranged it, and very well indeed—since once into the fat man's Guernsey banks, he found he could steal more for us than just the fat man's piece of Bulgaria." He lifted his glass to the Irishman, who was softly humming. The Irishman, his eyes a benign blue and a child's smile on his face, returned the gesture, kept on singing a soft Celtic tune.

The general, still tan from South Africa and Cairo, boomed out—for the umpteenth time that liquid evening—another window-shaking "*Nazdroveye*!" And to our Parisian colleague, memories of sailing off the Cape, a brilliant caper, a brilliant coroner's report, our brilliant Sea Scouts, our own brilliance, yes!" Gold-filled teeth glinted under the crystal candelabrum. "And to memories of the cool-skinned Nubian women of Cairo. To our pieces of the fat man.

We're eating the best part, eh? Better than the sharks had off his blubber in the Indian Ocean."

They were all a bit, or more, drunk. "I like your place here." Sandor was looking about an exquisite salon decorated in the style of Louis Seize, and all of the furnishings the real McLouis. Marble floors, deep satin cushions, Oriental vases, silk Nain carpets. On the pale orchid-colored wall hung a David, a Caravaggio. It was elegance as only the French do, innately.

The Parisian gestured self-deprecatingly. "Not mine—good Lord, I couldn't have a meeting like this at home, my wife would kill me. No, I have this for one of my mistresses, a countess who enjoys this view of le Tour Eiffel and the park below." All present looking could see the tower behind the trees. "The Seventh Arrondissement isn't quite as fashionable as it used to be, but this Rue de Buenos Ayres apartment, with three bedrooms and the servants quarters below, will do. Indeed the countess will do. Almost anything, some nights anything you ask!"

Bellows, guffaws, fantasies, but only the General was slavering at the mouth. The Parisian was simply a king, enumerating his holdings.

"Get yourself countesses, my friends—not by birth, but by marriage. The nobility, well in France it's only on paper, want beautiful women. They find young ones, train them well. Once they know their way around, the smarter women ditch their thin-blooded noble has-beens for real men. They keep the title, keep the money, and enter in the marketplace of sumptuous flesh. Shop around, colleagues; there are no bargains, but some lovely finds." He winked but he was so drunk that one droopy eyelid could hardly reopen. The voluble Parisian chattered on expansively.

"I keep another one in the First Arrondissement, Place Vendôme; it's close enough to the Opéra to walk. Or ride," he grinned, "—her, of course. Oh, she is a wild one."

Chortling, chuckling, tongues moving over their lips, the Partners were feasting in advance. They knew the Parisian had made certain arrangements for them once the meeting was over. Delectable arrangements.

The Parisian was riding his own bragging horse now. He shouted, draining the liquor in one gulp, "And another one on the Rue Alfred Dehodencq in the Twelfth Arrondissement."

This time there were cheers. Even Shadow was heard to say a mild but approving, "Very good." He had been invited to celebrate his master's wealth; yet his own portion, not niggardly, was numbered also in millions.

The Parisian had to tell them, "And the newest, a young, and oh-so-tender," he showed his teeth and bit loudly, imagining what gorgeous pink flesh he was biting, "Ukrainian girl, thanks to the General here. I've installed her like a queen also, in the sixteenth, in Neuilly. Can you imagine, A Ukrainian girl just out of the haystack presiding over Amiral de Joinville in Neuilly? She'll have the old men there drooling after her like dogs, like dogs, I tell you" He poured from a bottle of champagne icing in a silver bucket into a crystal glass, set down the armagnac, and shouted a toast: "To the girls!"

The General roared his response, his grin as wide as the Volga, "No, I tell you, to us drooling dogs!"

The ordinarily self-contained Advisor had tears of laughter in his eyes. Irish eyes were smiling.

"I hope there's no real business to which we have to attend," said the Parisian, "although I suppose one of you has to assess the Vienna Incident. The press loves a stir like that, and so do I. The *Premier Ministre* has ordered increased production of armaments, but can't quite make up his mind whether to offer an alliance to Russia. Can you imagine on behalf of the bloody Hapsburg Austrians just to thumb his nose at Britain and America? The EU can't survive such nonsense. I think my country's policies are so amusing." The Parisian leaned back. The light shone on the satin lapels on his purple velvet dinner jacket, his extra large black silk bow tie beginning to droop a little. "France is a delinquent child in a constant international snit, a spoiler, an irritant, a four-year-old. You should have seen what *The Economist,* and indeed the Russians, had to say about us. I love it. Oh, how those armaments orders pour in."

Sandor was not so happy. "Stability is best for business. The markets don't like this Incident nonsense, nor do I. General," he turned to Bratislav, "I recall that you, Warsaw, Vienna, and the Sofia partner, the Banker, were running whatever led up to Vienna, yes?"

Bratislav, in no mood to have a drunken revelry turn serious, was dismissive. "You Swiss have no imagination. It was all damage control in case the Warsaw lawyer fools had leaked something that might lead back to us personally. You understand, to *us.* So, with very considerable help from his American 'client', as he calls the Partner," he gestured toward Shadow, "our Partner there, we stopped any trouble from happening. As it turned out, the Americans didn't learn anything at all from the Warsaw fools, but for identifying that sidecar idiot Brody and some drug stupidity involving the company, Cie, in America—which, I gather, moves like a ghost, invisibly. So, no worry. It's all rather funny really."

"Amuse me, General." The Irishman had stopped his soft singing and grown serious. "Exactly what's so funny about the whole world focusing on—I don't even know what it was, but somehow American and they say British, commandos killing some thugs working for Square? It's exposed our Austrian police friends to investigation, and no matter what the Austrian posture is, the government there will have to get down to the truth of it; we don't have enough influence to stop it. How did it get so out of hand? What happened?"

The General's eyes narrowed, "If I tell you it's funny, then believe me, it's funny. We took care of any danger immediately. Immediately, I tell you. What's humorous is that it's all over a woman. This damn fool American IFinCIG agent went looking for a new hire, an American woman agent that Square had kidnapped to interrogate the day after she arrived in Vienna to meet her senior field man. Fellow named Barbour, as if that matters. Somewhere he picked up someone to go raiding with him. Two musketeers—and all for one woman! With her then, there you are; the two musketeers whom Square's people and our Austrian police friends tell us are in hiding. Our police friends will kill them if they ever show themselves."

"In the meantime it's all going our way. The American Senate, or some of them anyway, are as bad as the French, siding with the Austrians. Denouncing their own ambassadors in Vienna and, I must say it is an accident, Sofia. No one knows about the Bulgarian source. A freak shot from Capitol Hill, no more than that. The Senate clamor takes the heat off our Austrian police friends; so for us, business as usual. I think we will want to move more of our export control operations to Tallinn however, and less through central Europe, until it cools off.

"As for Russia, I assure you, our Partner the Oligarch in Moscow has told me himself that the Duma, and that President we have now, are simply making noises. Nothing is going to happen. The truth is, the President knows he's been a fool. The Oligarch has scolded him like a child. The child has gone to bed, and pulled the covers over his head until it all goes away. Oblomov again. Even Lenin, God rest his soul, was known to do that. There's going to be no war, I guarantee it. I'm one of the generals that would lead it, and so I know."

"General," Sandor asked in his soft voice, menace always hidden behind its silken timbre, "have you ever been wrong?"

The provocation shocked the group into a moment of sobriety. The general said nothing as he marshalled such thoughts as were not soluble in alcohol. The others waited for his perhaps quite dangerous rage. But instead a sad, gentle look brushed across his heavy, weather-beaten, crude-featured face.

Finally he responded to his Partner's question. "Yes, Sandor, I have been seriously wrong. Most recently in voting for the invasion of Afghanistan. Earlier, as a boy, I was so confident in my father, the general at Stalingrad, that I delayed in sending him a filial letter. He was killed before he received it. I have never forgiven myself or gotten over missing him. There, Sandor: some serious errors. As for the silly President Russia now has, he is not serious enough to fool anyone, certainly not our own Partner, the Oligarch. Are you satisfied, my exact, not-quite-genuinely-Swiss friend?"

Silence all around. The Partners did not expect one another to be so human—either as vulnerable or as personally honest. The unpredictable Russian could be, they now saw, a most uncomfortable man to drink with.

The General carried on as if he had said nothing extraordinary. He was still responding to the Advisor. "You know what's in my secret dispatches? Orders to find food, housing, and clothing for our troops. Spare parts for junk equipment. Shades of the siege of Leningrad. That's all. Our army has become ridiculous. No war. And there's going to be no road that leads to any of the Partners, none. The musketeers had better stay hidden for years—or, if their embassy can find them, let them be brought in secretly and flown back home in a stealthcraft where they will damn well want to keep their mouths shut. It was all a romance, a cowboy rescue. Let the romance end happily, on some quiet farm in Ohio or some such. There is no threat. They are of no concern to us. Now, does that reassure you?"

Even men of the world want reassurance, especially when the mood has been celebration. A man cannot worry about every contingency all of the time. Especially when he has been dining and drinking well and soon more entertainment will be at hand. It was only the Advisor, fey as the Irish are which means never quite in tune with others' worlds, who asked, "But why did the Senate mention Sofia?"

"Maybe they want to take an inspection tour to the Black Sea resorts." The General would, in a moment, be very angry. The Irishman was not that interested in the question.

"And no one knows who the other musketeer was—I mean, the commando?"

"No."

"And the woman agent, do you know who she is?"

"Of course, everything we did in Washington depended on that. And the kidnapping in Vienna. All of the operations that Sergei ran out of Sofia to penetrate the computers, which led the Sea Scouts to kill the civil service man in Washington, all that required we know who she is."

"Yes, of course. Sorry, I'm a little drunk. It was your operation. And it was beautifully done, General. I don't mean to carp."

The General, assuaged, gulped his vodka. His voice was low, almost as if he were talking to himself. "Stupid woman anyway, that IFinCIG agent—utterly naive. Square would have killed her soon enough, but the cowboys did save her. She'll want to notify her father and that's how our Austrian friends will locate them. Sergei keeps superb electronic surveillance on the embassy in Kiev. Just kill them to make things neat."

The Advisor, still drinking and unused to it, had barely grasped what was said. "Her father, you say. Do you mean he's an ambassador?"

"Yes, that's what makes the surveillance so easy."

"His name?"

"Dubois, he has quite a reputation. They call him 'the Smoothie.' Can you imagine, he's worked out permanent U.S. naval operations with the Ukrainians off the Crimea. Talk about tweaking the nose of our Russian bear! We could sink them all in a minute, but Dubois is putting something of a necklace around the Russian throat. I think maybe someone will kill him someday." The general was dozing off.

"Dubois," mused the Advisor, frowning, those innocent blue eyes trying to focus. "I have heard that name somewhere. I wonder—no, but somewhere though." He took another sip of armagnac as his mind drifted to another land. He was thinking of the past, the little people, the heroes of the Tain, of Cuchulainn, the greatest hero—so wild only Ireland could have made such a man. 'Mad rattling his shields, a tornado of dark blood rising high in the air from the center of his skull, so great was his fury as he rode into battle.' The Advisor had wanted to be Cuchulainn. Dizzy now with the search for memories personal and racial, he wondered for a moment how he had lost his way to become, of all things, an economist warrior only in a banknote world.

Shadow, who had had the least to drink, felt the responsibility of this group as a business meeting. In response to the Parisian's question he began seriously.

"Well, as further business I must tell you that Todor Mihailov, who was one of them who got the money in the first place, before Sir Alfred and that silly Austrian sideshow Brody moved it, complains he's frightened. The daughter of one of the original reds called him. I gather she was safely circumspect on the phone, to tell our contact that 'a Sofia vulture is on the way to Virginia' to shake down Mihailov. I think the daughter must have told the vulture where Todor Mihailov lives, and now is worried for her own hide. What a betrayal of her father—dead, she said now, old Dobri N. What won't people do for money!"

The General was surprised. "I didn't know you had been in Bulgaria. I'm working out of there now. Miserable place. How did you come to know Dobri N?"

"I didn't. I just know he was one of the originals." Shadow hiccoughed, "I don't usually drink. I'm getting maudlin. Of course I don't know if she betrayed her father. I just suppose she did. What else do people do?"

No cheers for that wisdom. The Partners knew what people did.

"What do we do about Mihailov? Who does it?"

"Let the vulture eat him. He knows nothing about any of us, nothing about the Partnership. We know him, but he doesn't know us. That's an operational definition of power. What do we care?" The General had had his say.

Shadow sobered up enough to say, "It's my client's territory, the eastern United States. The West, you know, is much more crude. That's managed, as we all know, by another Partner, although territories do overlap. Not like us, really, only my client knows him personally, that mysterious C. In any event, may I have your consent to advise my client about Mihailov and the vulture? Let the Partner decide what to do."

They were pleased to consent. Whatever that American Partner or his client did, they had benefited from his work immensely, and they knew he would do it thoroughly.

The General was ten or so peppered (vodkas with beer chasers) into drunkenness. Sucked lemon slices were thrown on the marble floor beside him, along with a piece of chocolate candy that had slid from his greasy fingers. Two lemon slices littered a nearby silk Esfahan carpet.

"Good work the Partners do, all of us, all of them." His speech was slowed, slurring; he had smeared some of an after-dinner petit four on his Chardin necktie. "Who are they all, I wonder? I know Warsaw; Square, of course, in Vienna, the Oligarch in Moscow, the Banker who works with me these days in Sofia, Sergei in and out of Moscow, the Northerner in Tallinn who runs the Russian exports—for the rest, well, I wonder, how many of us are there?"

They looked with no great curiosity, and some congenial stupor, at one another. The Advisor, deep in his Celtic cups, an important memory of Cuchulainn dominating, shrugged his shoulders. "We could be, I suppose, any number at all. There are so many like us, aren't there? I mean—well, our number is legion in a way, isn't it?"

"But not with respect to particulars. People have names. Partners have names," one protested.

One replied, a bit thick-tongued. "We don't know all their names, though, do we? Nor do we want to. Nor even as here, ours. Our business is anonymous business; companies, banks, trusts, fiduciaries, straw men, corporate aliases, organized, yet amorphous at the same time; fluid and unidentifiable, but also well structured, nothing more real. That's how we've done so well. That's the secret isn't it?"

Another remarked, "There are so many secrets, aren't there, isn't that *the* secret?"

"Almost anyone is a possible Partner. Think about it: the sharks that ate the fat man are our Partners, aren't they? They take as big a piece as they can get, grow sleek, stay fat. No one knows their names either, except that they're out there waiting for more. One doesn't know where they really are. They swim together when that works, eat one another if that works better. Eat any fat man they can. Now, I ask you, think about the sharks; doesn't that sum it up?"

Those who were still able to listen nodded. They all needed a little sleep before the arrival of those svelte, pneumatic, so skilled and willing "delectable arrangements" the Parisian had thoughtfully provided. So they nodded "yes" for the coming pleasures of the flesh, and "yes" for the sharks, "yes" to what happened to the fat man, and "yes" to good life. That about summed it up.

33

From the pickup point in front of Bloomingdale's, Markowitz drove Rooster to a new rendezvous—his own house. The others would be arriving shortly. "Now this," Markowitz said to himself, "is an act either of extreme trust, or dangerous stupidity." For any cop in Malome to show any citizen of that town, let alone one of its competent hoods, where he lived, was certifiable madness. "Never mind, all humanity is a throw of the dice," he said to himself. Einstein, and Moses, and Jesus, and some others claimed there were rules that God had made. If so, half of Malome had never heard of them, except maybe the law of gravity. Shoot a bullet and it eventually falls down. Markowitz, a split-brain theist/atheist, tended to think that God—at least the Old Testament sort—saw to mechanical physics and had maybe a hand in quantum mechanics. But given chaos theory and lotteries, He was as likely to be a victim as to be the designer. Markowitz' religious friends were appalled. Markowitz thought about it. "I bet if I talked it over with Rooster, the kid would agree."

Once again the four of them—Rooster; Markowitz, their host, who had made the coffee; Officer Stein, who brought three dozen mixed gooey donuts (what would the others eat?); and Doc Dolan, who brought luncheon sandwiches, gathered, this time around the kitchen table. It was not the same kind of a meet that cops usually had—turning and squeezing a snitch, debriefing or instructing a regular informant, setting up a lying bad guy for a fall. None of that.

If there was a conspiracy, it was getting to be a foursome. Each of the four had reservations, suspicions, and memories of how wrong it could be to trust—whether in love, business, the weather forecast, crime, virtue, or a bad guy's promises to go straight. Maybe the difference was this Rooster, who made no promises and said straight out he hadn't made up his mind. None of them knew what to make of the Rooster, of his personal intensity, his appealing uncertainty, his discombobulatingly objective reporting, this Rooster in metamorphosis to no one knew what or where. Not, Markowitz hoped, Kafka's cautionary tale of a man turning into a giant insect before his final deterioration.

What held the four together was surely the Rooster, with his street talk, his story-telling eloquence—"the Rooster's Tale," as the three cops termed the last session. The tale was juxtaposed to the boy-man telling it, for the hero—so to speak—who figured in it was not the same as the teller. Perhaps it was that the tale was about itself in transition, none of "the butler did it" stuff. Markowitz thought about it; Rooster's tale the movement itself. The end to come proving rules and mechanical physics? Quantum probabilities only in criminology? Or chaos theory and who the hell knew, God included, what had been an initial condition leading to whatever transitory moment the end was defined as being? Sure as hell, if the tale led to Mr. C, that was enough for the cop in him. Even the California papers were carrying the news of the Vienna Incident, a cops and robbers incident with neither in sight, drum beating by the Russians, and the stock market way down as the scare caught on. "Lee Barbour, when he sets out to do a righteous job—man, does he bring on the whirlwind." Markowitz had seen Barbour do it before. Their having had their asses fired out of Washington had been an example.

"Well, Rooster, what happened, what's happening, what will happen?" Stein asked through donut-powdered lips.

"Well, let me tell you about the other night a while back—no, a ways back, and what happened after."

Rooster put down his coffee cup, finished a donut, and wiped his mouth with deliberation on a surprisingly scarlet paper napkin. "Tell you how it came down. We—that was Furbo, Dimples, and me—were in the mostly-empty parking lot next to the soon-to-be Classy Black Club. Right now it was still just that run-down scrambled around big house, paint peeling, roof leaking so good that the money run in. Big storm of money every weekend. Mind you now, a dude doing well in this town has got to own both work wheels *and* show wheels. Use the work wheels around town, specially if you're carrying dope so that if the narcs seize the car what they get is (a) only junk and (b) junk stolen off someone else so that it has got to be turned back to the owner, not the motherfuckin narcs." He looked at Doc Dolan, and added, apologizing, "Sorry if I offend."

"I ain't no narc," commented the Doc, "and I'm thick-skinned, anyway. You go right ahead."

Rooster nodded, picked up the rhythm. "So out of habit, since most dudes doing well are also doing dope one way or another, expect to see junk wheels belonging to those of us doing business any night. Purple Willie had an '87 Toyota sedan as his wreck; Frank a '68 crushed-door Chevy; more junk belonged to Blade, Snake, and Moffat. Oh yeah—a junk car don't mean the engine don't work. Keep that thriving just in case events require a speedy departure, and yeah, I can spell it out, d-e-p-a-r-t-u-r-e, essential, as in *now*," he grinned, "like I say, need to hurry.

"So this eight-mile-long shiny white Cadillac with the-one way mobster windows in it looked outstanding, man, outstanding. Some antsy fucker works for Furbo inside at the wheel. He had an old Ingram Parabellum XI on the top of his dash. Had to be an emotional thing, like to an old dog to still carry around that kind of weapon. Probably he'd killed his first ten playmates with it so it was a memento, or maybe like Linus in the 'Peanuts' comic strip, a security blanket. I liked that Charlie Brown. Every time Lucy gets him to kick that football and Charlie he is up in the air and falls on his head, I know just how he feels. Anyway, even a Parabellum is better than a slingshot. You understand how, in this town at a late hour, a white guy sitting in any car is going to carry action close to his finger. Fact is he was safer here than he thought except for the real losers, crackheads, that sort. Willie and Frank paid for neighborly relations with the local gangsters and what they couldn't buy they had Blade or Snake or Moffat blow away. Respect is the name of the game.

"Cars are important. So a well-doing dude will have at least one classy car for driving with style—like with a woman, or making a call, or when the boys all go someplace. You guys have seen it. Gold Mercedes are big, so are white Rolls and, this year, that big Lincoln Town Car, any color. Now you got to drive these in this town once in a while just to show people you are arrived, glad rags with wheels. But push your luck any and someone with an envious eye, that voodoo eye, will put a round of semi-automatic fire into it just to prove you aren't the big man you thought you were. Homeboys have low levels of tolerance and high, I mean high im-pul-si-vi-ty, and some are real bad just because being mean is the way they are.

"Some of them are real niggers. Don't be surprised, a black man—you don't want me to say 'African American' to show I'm hip, do you?—I might use that word in the same way. It comes down to him being him once and meaning no fucking good, or being a shining-up, bending-down Uncle Tom, or maybe all white teeth and chatter but inside his motor ain't running, not even plugged in. What you ofays call 'correct political thought' reserves 'nigger' now for black folks to use, like here, because for everybody else it isn't dainty and marks you as the bigoted motherfucker you probably are anyway. So who cares about a word anyway?

"'Rooster,' Furbo asks me as we stand outside the car, 'how does a company man expand business, improve relations in a war-zone town like this? I mean now we are tied to yesterday's no name but today's Classy Black Club, where else do we go? Any other action here?'

"I told him about the wrecking yards working as stolen car trans-shippers and chop shops, getting parts to sell to junkyards or car dealerships. When I told him they were lucky to clear $750 profit on a car, so that their income needed high-volume turnover of stolen cars, he spit. 'Too much trouble and exposure for too little,' was what he said. I agreed.

"I could tell he didn't know the drug trade around here which was, according to what any of us in town figured, worth maybe a couple thousand dollars income per citizen. That's statistics, same as saying 'per capita' as they say. It only means that that's about how to figure how much drug income comes into a town like this. "Or at least," Rooster let loose one of those silent meaningful looks around the table, "on the street-sale, low-level wholesale surface.

"Now obviously only a few guys make the big money, but lots of folks are connected in a family way really; families here can share things, you know. But as little as I knew then of how the big money worked, I couldn't see how Furbo's company could tie in unless they were supplying wholesale out of Europe and to something bigger than Malome on the streets. You all know it. The Mexicans in town bring in the Mexican brown heroin and some of the cocaine. The biggest dealers are black, and where they bought, except from bigger wholesalers, I didn't know. We had maybe fifteen big dealers—all low-profile in that they lived down-home lives, same kind of small, middle-class suburban ranch-style house my folks and I live in, nothing shiny on the outside.

"Now that's not the only place they live. Playtime is something else and they have fancy apartments and fancy women in the big city and, who knows, maybe places far away. Paris, I don't know, I wouldn't know anything about that. I never been more than fifteen miles from home, and that's to the junior college. But I don't really think any black dude from here wants to go far, not Paris or even New York. Any fellow working out of this town, no matter how big a wholesaler he is—well, there is that one exception I'll be coming to—is just a homeboy at heart. He is going to know he is out of place anywhere that is not black, poor, sick, fucked-up, shot-up, and home. Home is here where the family lives, where you know everybody. Paris is a crazy idea. Maybe a real big dealer from here has been all the way to Southern California.

"Those customers come into town—white, rich, they been to Paris maybe, but when it comes to what really matters to them rich fuckers, getting their dope connection, we're more to them than their mothers, their daddies or their itty-bitty blonde sisters. You gotta understand this town is like a belly button cord, u-m-b-i-l-l-y-c-a-l—see, I can spell—for lots of folks. O-m-p-h-a-l-o-s, like my professor said. Center of the universe. And that means, however poor we look on the outside, and believe me we is a poor town, tired mule- shit poor, a lot of money comes through here. A whole lot.

"Until Mr. Furbo showed up I had never really thought how much or—but for my own knowing the Arab and where that one million dollars goes—how the rest of it gets blessed, which is to say gets out of town, from black into white. I hate that about language. Understand? When it's dirty it's black, it's here and it's me. When it's blessed it is gone from here, it's clean, it's white, and everybody loves it. Black is bad, white is good, no way anywhere you escape it. The whole linguistic world is motherfucking racist. I hate it. One day I'm going to do something big. These days I start by getting rich.

"Furbo was rockin' back, waiting for me to say something else. Okay, so I'd give him a little suck. 'You know this town is essentially one big drug store, so to speak.'

"'Yes, Rooster, I could figure that.' It was not quite sarcastic, but I guess even big gangsters like Furbo don't want to look like shit-eating idiots.

"Well, so that's where the big money is, that's all." And, I added, "just bein' a white gangster doesn't mean you know fly piss about black crime. I tell you, man, you don't even want to *think* about moving in on the big money, no matter how much muscle you got. Not even if it's smarter than Dimples and their elevators *do* go to the top floor.

"Furbo he nods, says, 'Yeah, I knew that before. What I don't know is whether any of the big dealers here need help finding laundries and accountants. I mean, Rooster, do they *really* know how to move all that money and keep their tits out of the DEA and Treasury wringer?'

"I shrugged my shoulders, told him true. I don't know. I'm just studying sophomore economics; I ain't got no money to launder, and sure enough I ain't got no reason to ask anyone big who it is might do his banking.

"It was then it came to me out of somewhere, nowhere, a name I'd heard, the name you guys heard, but I realized I'd really heard it. So I said to Furbo, "'Someone big like Mr. C.'

"This perked up Furbo. He rocked back on his heels again, this time securing his back against that long shiny limo of his. I didn't know, and still don't know, how much he knew. Furbo is one cool cat, man, cool.

"I told him back then, you understand I was making it up as I went along, but if a man wants to look big he's got to be seen movin around with big men. If you're bullshitting someone, why not the biggest bull pattie you heard of? So I say, 'Yeah, he's the biggest man, the richest man in town. Everybody knows it. Untouchable. Doesn't hold drugs himself, doesn't personally move drugs, does have the warehouses, but I don't know if they're in town. He's like a ghost but sure does get the money. Sells only to wholesalers, the main men, all over the West. Beyond it, maybe. Beyond that I don't know anything.' I can lie to anybody so good they'll never dig. Furbo may be a smart mafioso but he got no special ears to screen out my kind of lyin'. I'm proud of it, you know."

The men around the table, chomping donuts and drinking coffee, knew that all right. Why bother to answer?

Rooster continued, sure of his audience. "So Furbo says to me, 'About this Mr. C, the main man. Like to find out something more, maybe?'

"I say, 'Like I'd like to be burned alive. No way I go lookin for Mr. C. I got parents to help, I got two kids of my own already I sometimes give the mothers some help too. I ain't dying for you, Mr. Furbo, no fucking way.'

"'Not asking you to, Rooster. I am just going to write you a letter from me to Mr. C and ask you either to give it to him or put it in his mailbox or, if that scares you, give it to one of his lieutenants to deliver.' Furbo is looking at me like on a dare, son of a bitch had figured out I might be lying. Testing me? Mocking me? I don't know, but maybe on to my bullshit somehow.

"'But you, Rooster, you are our new man in this town. If Mr. C is interested in what my people can do for him, he gets in touch with you.' Now you guys know that I know by now that when Furbo says 'his people' he is talking some very tough people from New Jersey and Chicago through L.A. and Vegas, those wops making alliances I hear with the Mexicans and, I heard it on the radio, Russians coming out here to do business. Serious people I do understand. So Furbo, he goes on to say, 'I guarantee you'll have C's respect for that, and since there will be money in it for him, he isn't going to want to shoot his bank connection. Make sense?'

"'Yes and no and maybe.' The idea of even meeting Mr. C made me feel good. Scared me shitless too. Like meeting Moses and thinking maybe he'll smile or maybe not, but that tablet's hanging over your head.

"Furbo sat in the back seat of the limo; you see we were talkin in his car. I was up front with this muscle with the Parabellum. I saw there was a TV and bar back there, and some silk rope. I didn't like that. Whether it was for kidnap-rape or kidnap-murder, I have never liked to see rope in the back seat of a one-way window glass car. You think maybe I am on the way to becoming middle class and squeamish? No way José. Not good—you got to stay ghetto-mean and ghetto-don't-care to survive in this town.

"I didn't know what the hell to do. I had to try something. I went down to the grocery where they have this copy machine. I made ten copies of Furbo's letter to Mr. C. Figured I'd give them to the ten meanest, hard-assed, best-dressed black dudes in town and hope one of them had heard of C. What else could I do? I didn't know nothin.' 'Shoot an arrow into the air' I heard somewhere, maybe it comes down on the skull you want.

"One of the homeboys I gave the letter to was Slash. His name tells you he commands respect. I told him it was from a big white gangster from out of town who might be my new boss. People don't communicate by letter in this town. No wonder Slash spit and was about to tear it up. Looked like he wanted to tear me up too, but looking mean as tiger turds is part of how a man *be* out here. Look soft, man, die soon. Slash knew I had to be lyin anyway, but a good lie to him meant there might just be some real action in the bushes behind it. A real good lie is worth payin' 'tenshun to, a man asks, what's behind that he go to such trouble to hide it?

"I tell Slash, 'My new boss says there may be money to be made by Mr. C. Why don't you just deliver it?' I was surprised how uppity I'd become just overnight, not as scared as I would have been, actually felt like I never felt before, I mean real businesslike, like maybe I got something to tell, not just get told. Somehow that must have got across to Slash. 'All right, asshole, we'll see,' he says.

"I am never sorry to see Slash leave. He gives me the creeps. One ear and part of his cheek are missing, that's why they call him 'Slash.' The doctors had cobbled up some kind of lip on his left side for him—you can always tell by which side of the face is sliced what was the handedness of the other razor man—but the two half lips looked like reefers and made Slash talk like he was always chewing a pencil and the splinters from it were sticking.

"'Right, asshole,' I say right back at him, yeah, j-a-u-n-t-i-l-l-y, I spelled that out myself, I mean that is taking a chance, turning who's who around. Risk. A boss hood like Slash hates it most specially when a man he pees on is saying he can't pee on him any more. You could just see it going through Slash's mind: shoot me, slash me with his blade, maybe razor, cuss me out or just live with change. You see it was worth life or death to me to get on top somewhere, somehow and now." Rooster looked around the table. "You understand? M-o-m-e-n-t-u-s."

The three men understood. Any boy who becomes a real man understands. Gutless people never understand.

Rooster went on, "I could just see Slash putting his mind back in his brain at a different angle. I could see him ask hisself: Who's backing this little turd up? Is there something in the letter worthwhile to Mr. C, so Rooster made dead by Slash would be inconvenient not simply to Rooster but to Mr. C and therefore, oh so true, for Slash? All in neon letters on his pock-skin forehead—you see, Slash has some kind of skin disease. He stinks even upwind. Anyway, his printout about what to do had given him too many options; as Frank would say, his system crashed. Slash stopped looking mean, looked confused and just walked away, that letter in hand. Looked tired. Maybe just like the rest of us here, you tired of living the day after you was born.

"Boomer come by the house. My sister Thelma—she's fifteen now—was in the bedroom screwing some guy I didn't know. You could hear them thumping. Thelma always is one to make a racket when she screws. It's a noisy house. The folks probably don't like it, but there're so many things go wrong in a parent's life that fighting with your otherwise good-natured daughter over how much, who, and where she screws ain't worth the trouble. And when Thelma got a present, which she did once in a while, she would give it to the folks. She's a nice kid, Thelma. I remember when we were little the old lady caught us playing with each other, you know, showing each other. Kid sex. Just lookin'. Man, I mean that old woman threw one God-thundering righteous lesson into us kids. Generally I try to please the folks. And yeah, we're Christian if you were to ask, but not enough. The town divides itself. The Christians and then us. We all know who each other is. In Malome the real Christians, lots of them, are really good-church going people. Maybe I should be, but I ain't like that. As you guys know.

"So Boomer asks me how I met anyone from Nevada, from "Exceptional Inc.," so as to be delivering a letter from someone signing himself G.E. Smith. I knew I was to keep quiet about the deal between the club and Furbo, and obviously Furbo was keeping his real name to himself. Not that the whole town wouldn't know in a few weeks when they saw the club being redecorated, then whites in a limo coming in to gamble at the same tables with them, but what people learn is up to them, not up to me. I ain't no teacher and I ain't no snitch. So I just told Boomer that Willie and Frank had introduced me when someone out of Nevada was in the club and this guy had asked me to run for him.

"You could have knocked me over with a feather. I had hit gold. *Boomer,* of all people! I never figured he knew snot, but he just say, 'I got a message for you, Rooster. Come down from Mr. C. I'm to tell you that Mr. C might be interested.

Asks you to tell me how Nevada can do business for Mr. C? And you better be able to answer—hear, boy?'

"Now anybody who calls me or any other black man 'boy' is like calling him 'coon' or 'burrhead,' or any other plantation word worse than 'nigger.' I'm twenty-two, a college boy—means something different when you use it that way—working for Nevada. That's what I am calling Furbo and his people now. Movin' up I am, on my way into the laundry business, and I don't take shit from Boomer.

"'Don't call me boy,' I tell him. We're standing on the front lawn. Right then Boomer and I are standing off serious. You stand like that—think of it as a kind of stance or dance of p-r-o-v-o-c-a-t-i-o-n—and it's like blowing a bugle, I mean everybody knows that something rough is going down. No never mind that it's night; everybody sees. Boomer's even dumber than Slash, which means when you put your face in his like I just done he had no options. He started to reach toward his belt under the suede jacket. Now, I had this guy standing at the side of the house—I had told him to go out there and wait when I saw Boomer coming up the walk, I never had liked Boomer much . . ."

Rooster stopped and looked at the three cops. "All right, now this is that moment of truth. I tell you what really happened and you got a duty to go arrest who did it, and I think maybe you, Officer Stein, know what I'm leading up to, that's your duty. But this is someone close to me and no way am I going to finger him, no way. He was doin' it for me in my self-defense. So this is your moment of truth too. You tell me you got to be lawful and we are finished talking. Understand? No more. We go our ways. Or you decide to keep it to yourselves, and I keep on talking—including telling you who trashed Boomer to save my ass. I could be sly-like and not say, but like I say: it's truth time. Which means you got to violate your duty to keep me talkin about Mr. C. You commit a felony doin' that. So you get closer to bein' like me while I, not joshin' you anymore, get maybe closer to that honesty you say you're about. What's it goin' to be?"

Stein, Dolan, and Markowitz sat thinking how the kid was roping them in, implicating them in this conspiracy. Anytime he sang on them, they could face prison, although in truth it was not likely because any cop who had informants, any spy who had agents in place, made it his business to know what they did and protect them. Symbiotic, so to speak. Anybody else who knew the handler man's business respected how it is done. But there was always the risk of a scheming asshole in your own outfit using it to do you in.

Doc Dolan spoke first. "My orders regarding getting to Mr. C say that almost anything goes."

"I have none, just the California Penal Code Section #32, Accessory," said Markowitz.

"Who's got the Boomer case?" Stein asked Markowitz.

"Ordway Lewis."

"A no-good, slimy crook himself. Hell, I don't care if Lewis never makes a collar. Whoever took out Boomer did us all a big favor," said Stein.

"Right." The three men looked at one another. It was Dolan who spoke their minds. "Okay, Rooster, you're on."

"My brother Beauregard took him out. I had him standing by the side of the house to cover me if Boomer looked to blow me away. Which Boomer was about to do. Beauregard is seventeen, and tougher than I'll ever be. Renowned as a shooter. People hire him to do just that, hire him from places fifty miles away. Hell, he's been farther away trashing people than most of the people on this block have ever been for vacation.

"Anyway, two shots and bye-bye Boomer. Nobody saw who did it, truly. Mothers out front with their itty bitty kids, kids on their bikes, even the postman walking his beat, all looked—but there was nobody to see but Boomer shitting his dying man's pants. Bullet through the spinal cord will do that every time. A smelly way to die. People out there on the street saw I didn't do it, couldn't know who did. I didn't even walk away as the siren gang pulled up. And Beauregard he came out of the house wearing a towel around him, all wet from the shower. We was one clean family. Cooperative with the police? You never saw such cooperation. 'Yes, officer' this, 'No, sir' that. I mean we were real good niggers and those white cops, beggin' your pardon gentlemen, your buddies loved us for it. Ate it up. There was one black sergeant there. That brother was very good at his work. He didn't even bother to talk to us. Knew damn well what had happened. Knew what Boomer did, knew my brother and me, knew what no one ever saw or would ever see—and knew that there would never be a trial. The sergeant didn't even bother to take out his notebook, just looked at us in disgust. He drove off leaving the fire department paramedics to hose the blood off the lawn. In his place I suppose I'd have been pissed off too."

"And then what?" asked Dolan.

"Well you know it don't take five minutes for everybody to know what went down, look. Boomer went down, boom. Whoever sent him, he knows right away Boom hasn't delivered whatever message there was. So guess what? Not twenty minutes later I get a telephone call from Slash.

"Hit gold again. 'Mr. C is goin' to see you in one hour.' No hello, no please, no goodbye, and I can tell you from me, no refusal. I just say, 'I ain't got no idea where to go.'

"'Don't you never mind about that. Someone he comin' to get you. And you better be gettable, understand?'

"I do understand. I wait. Black man I don't know comes by in a set of work wheels, old green Pontiac maybe fifteen years old. Engine hums though, you can hear that. He sits me in the back seat, tells me to cover my head with some hood he gives me, and off we go—maybe a twenty five minute drive. Now I know there ain't no place in Malome twenty minutes from another, and I can tell when a man be drivin' round different blocks just to get you off track. No matter to me. So it's real late by the time we pull up to a driveway, an electric garage door opens, and he says to take the hood off my head. There's a big dude standing by the car, with an AR cradled pointing right at me. He had walkman earmuffs on. I could tell he was listenin to the watchers. You know any serious operation out here, or just sellin crack, everybody has watchers posted a block away every direction.

"I figure they had watchers out to see if I had brought company—you know, someone, well, like you guys, followin' me. Hard to believe Mr. C was so crazy as to believe I was *that* crazy. But you be that crazy out here, and you stay alive making money. Nobody asked me inside the whatever it was, house or building or whatever. Nobody came outside. The man with the AR I didn't know, real light skin and straight haired meaning maybe one-fifth black blood behind him just pointed me to stay in the back seat. We all wait, nobody say nothin, for maybe twenty minutes. Just to be sure no one was tailin me. Mr. C, if he was even there, obviously intends to live a long time.

"So we start drivin again. I got that hood on but back seat is dark. No one next to me, just like I got a chauffeur. I scratch my nose a couple times and jiggle it up sideways so I can halfway see. We drive past the junkyards and nurseries, past the abandoned railway yard and that sagging abandoned steel fabrication plant way down on Simmons Street. Finally we came to a warehouse it looks like."

Rooster looked at the men at the table, at the coffee, the donuts. "I know, I should say 'appeared to be'. My college English teacher is always on me to say it right. I get talking fast like now and I forget. But I got to remind myself how to talk so I can leave this low-class 'you're stupid' black talk behind me. 'Patois,' I like that word. 'Ebonics' as a special language, my ass. I just don't know how to talk. I keep moving in and out, old worlds and new, and neither at this point worth shit. It's the hope keeps me going; the hope I'm different from almost everybody I ever met. The hope I'm going to make it. Fat chance, huh?"

He didn't even wait for a word of reassurance and obviously wouldn't have believed it if they offered it. Rooster went on with his story.

"There was a big sliding steel door next to that old rusting railway track. It's back a dirty pothole road aways from Simmons. Hard to see much. Late at night and no streetlights; the driver douses the car lights and uses an electric entry signal. Big steel warehouse too and when that sliding door closed behind me it sounded just like a heavy jailhouse door. Furbo isn't the only one to know a cell. Out here hardly any black man hasn't known a jail cell. Kind of a nursery maybe. But sure don't learn anything leads to big money, like laundering. Inside that big big room were some people. Surprised me, not all black. Two or three white guys, two Mexicans, two Asians. Couple guns on a table but nothing, well, military about it. Room had lots of boxes, wooden chairs that didn't look real well-used, but as if the business, if there were any, either wasn't here or was just passing through. In a way it looked like something in a movie set, so, well artificial. For instance, the cement floor was too clean, too scrubbed. I didn't like what I thought about that though, why they would have cleaned up that cement floor so much. That strong janitor soap smell. Hurt my nose almost. I'm gettin scared again. They goin to process me in this meat plant, I wonder?

"There's this really good-lookin black dude, pomade, medium hair styled classy, wears a pale red silk sport shirt, gray trousers, Italian leather shoes on his feet. He's maybe six feet, slim, athletic. Sharp, nearly a white man's nose. High forehead. Nothing I could read on that face but power and being a real cool cat. His eyes are so bland and empty I couldn't be sure they were there. That is an unsettling vision. His voice was businesslike. Nobody else so much as murmured.

"'So, homeboy,'—unlike 'boy' that is no insult, just means he knows I'm local—'you run for this Nevada company, and you blow away our Boomer right on your front lawn. You represent maybe "the Force" on Star Wars, do you? I mean you are playing a very heavy role for a kid. Very heavy. What's Nevada going to do for me? The letter said to ask you.' He stood there waiting, very still. Like some panther.

"I figure I either give him a college paper on money laundering economics or go out of here in a body bag. I knew that much. All I knew was what I'd done with the Arab and what Nevada had proposed. What Nevada said they could 'offer' laundries anywhere; offshore banks, CPA accounting to cool the IRS, washed loans for clean front investments, and all on a commission; no partnerships required.

"'Mob, I presume?' Mr. C asked me.

"He spoke white English, not this town's blackman's lingo. Is this here the big man lookin after local business, doing a site inspection? Why bother, tote up all the drug money, chop shop money in town and it may be a few maybe even ten, twenty million, but that gets shared out in thousands of hands. Not that much by the time someone at the top gets it. Malome had to be a drop in the bucket. Unless some really big operation went on in this warehouse or ran out of it. Not impossible as I thought about it; big place, that staff hanging around so to speak, no one would ever guess the building was used much. Malome is damn near next to two international airports, only a few miles from a major seaport. Maybe it did figure, his using it. Malome as some kind of warehousing or operations center.

"I answered his question about the Mob. 'I think so, yeah.'

"Mr. C shrugged, I mean not that he had introduced himself but it had to be him. 'The Mob's going down, we're coming up.' He looked at me. 'Black power through white and brown powders, wouldn't you say, kid?'

"I shrugged. 'Maybe.' It didn't strike me that Mr. C was a political person. He spoke too white, dressed too fine to worry about black power. He already had power. Why struggle for it for someone else? Not a man like this. He kept looking at me with those eyes I couldn't really locate in his head, but could only feel.

"'Does a man like me need you, kid, to deal with Nevada?' he asked.

"I felt clammy. I could see me in that coroner's body bag. But why even try lying when Mr. C knew the score anyway?

"'No,' I said.

"'You're too modest, kid. The letter said we go through you.'

"I'm sure I looked as stupid as I felt. I know Furbo had said that to me but I sure didn't expect it to be anything but jive. But Furbo had written it. Even so, there's nothin real that's paper but for money. So here I was, self-promoted to where my big mouth had put me by talking to Slash. Killing Boomer had been something else. I was just mad at being called 'boy' and my brother had done the work.

"So I told him, 'You're too big to need me, Mr. C, or even Nevada. You can teach them economics.'

"One thing, life or death, I wasn't going to be any nigger shining him up. I meant it. Maybe he is what I want to be, a model they call it, but I ain't going to be a shiny ass nigger for anybody. No matter how big a man he is."

Rooster looked hard at the men around the table. His was a general message. It was received. He went on.

"Mr. C is being thoughtful. He said to me, now mind you this whole time no one else even whispers; I'm like in the center of an all around stage. 'Temporary and fortuitous perhaps,' he was rubbing his chin now with a long ebony cigarette holder. Some white slinky guy in a blue suit comes running up to him with a gold cigarette lighter. Fawny toads.

"'You frowning, kid. You got a name?'

"'Rooster,' I tell him.

"'And the frown? You don't like what's coming down business-wise?'

"'Not that.' And suddenly I thought, what the hell, he could see through me anyway, no bullshit at all. 'I hate the smell of cigarette smoke. You shouldn't be smoking. Not good for you. It causes cancer.' I could just feel everyone in the room break into a cold sweat when I said that. But hell, if I was going to die, do it honest. I meant it. I hate cigarettes.

"'She-e-it,' Mr. C strung out the word like he was some street kid. He's just shaking his head grinning. 'I do declare, you, Rooster are very much like my mother. And damn if he didn't put out the cigarette in an ashtray. I watched that. Clean and neat, Mr. C.

"'Now, on a need to know basis, Rooster, you need to know from nothing about what I do or how I do it. But fate has a way and you found your way here and for a moment or two maybe Nevada will help. Come with me, Rooster, and we will talk to my accountant about some untoward events of the past few weeks. And I shall see just how smart you can invent your ambitious self to be.'

"I tell you, I was dumbfounded. He was treating me with respect.

"We walked away from that too-clean sanitized room; antiseptic fumes were hurting my nose so I was glad. We walked through a little door, steel bolted and no easy pry-through, into a business office. Very efficient, computers, telephones, little cubbyholes for the people who weren't there, fax machines, all kinds of stuff. It could have been Standard Oil. There was just one guy working, but consider, by now it's ten at night. I'm introduced to the accountant, glasses, small check gray suit, nervous, just like you expect, mousy, too. He was Asian. He didn't get up. That struck me. Mr. C pointed me to a wooden chair. He took one of the same kind for himself. He talked.

"'Before I tell you, Rooster, you know the rules. You snitch and you die. You work for Nevada, fine, but you also work for me, and you do not try to work both ends of the street. You are our connection and maybe you know why we can use Nevada for a little while until we put one tiny misplaced piece of the local operation back in shape. Any ideas what happened?'

"'Only if I guess right. I never heard of you before this week.' I had to cover myself on that slip so I lay it off on Furbo, but I'm thinking, and there has been some street talk about I didn't know who at the time.

"'What do they say on the streets?' Mr. C was real interested. Stared at me like someone buying fish in the market.

"'Newspapers have some of it, too.' I fended off, not wanting to commit.

"'Fine, now tell us what they say.'

"'Somebody around is here wholesaling dope big time laundering through a realty outfit in South City, Asians running it, doing well. Somebody set up with them to invest for some big mamas out of Hong Kong. By now I know a couple of ways to wash the cash or make bucks from somebody else's clean washed money. Figure you're a big time realtor; juice off a title company so you get yourself a looks-clean title to some big property. Maybe use a cut out of an offshore bank—never your own name of course—which lends out of the laundry. But it's real money, reinvested. Just maybe the title has a trick or two. Smarten it up, you con some high flyers whose money is maybe not their own. Stolen, drugs, fraud, who cares. You do them the favor of letting them carry a high interest second mortgage on your property. They make big bucks until you stick it to them. Maybe a title problem so they don't have a real second. Or you pay city hall to threaten to blow the whistle on their money, like the Feds are going to breathe on them for forfeiture. You look clean of course. But you got a couple of real big, I mean millions of dollars, buildings. All out of money you washed through the offshore, or conned out of those smart fellows who lend to you on that second. Lots of ways, but the street says that's what happened through those realtors using the Hong Kong and offshore laundry. And ain't nobody who used hot money for the mortgage gonna sue. Try to kill you, sure, but you figure that and blow them away first. Or the realtors if they decide to run a skim. I even know how to do it making it look good to the Internal Revenooers.'

"'Now exactly what happened with you, Mr. C, I am not sure. Cause it did go real sour. Whether you were on top of it all the way in and out of Hong Kong and South City so there should have been no surprises but for someone freaking out with greed, or you were not quite on top of it as good as you maybe thought, with those brainy Asian realtors figuring from the start they were more clever than you. Anyway they stiffed you. In any event something went down where you got turned from boss con, laundryman and property owner, into first sucker. You blew it and you didn't have to. Want to know any more?'

"Mr. C crossed his legs, crossed his arms, reached for but did not take a cigarette, a nod to me, and says, 'Rooster, begin.' So I told him how a very complicated laundering scheme turned fraud could have gone down maybe five, ten ways. Whichever way it had to be good for lots of millions, because the property somebody ended up owning, no doubt C and company, are big buildings downtown worth, what, maybe thirty million dollars and then their income.

"Mr. C he smiles at me and says, 'You guess it right again, Rooster, it is C and company or, as I call it using the French, 'C et Cie.' Anyway, carry on.'"

Rooster turned to the cops. "You want the scenarios, they really are a little complicated like I told him, or just the d-e-n-o-u-m-e-n-t?"

They already knew he was smart. They elected not to hear how smart. Dolan, who knew financial crime inside out, realized that Rooster might be beyond him in devising a laundry incorporating fraud. "Just cut to the ending, Mr. Banker," said Dolan. "I might not be able to keep up." Not snide, it was a respectful remark.

"Mr. C liked my college paper. He flickered his tongue over his lips, eyelids half-closed over the eyes I couldn't find. 'And one of those complicated fifty million-dollar schemes, Rooster, is what you think we did, in spite of the fact that none of that could possibly be in anybody's newspaper?'

"'I got no idea what you did. I just imagine what you can do, should you want, that's all.'

"'And is there anything that the street says it's sure somebody did do?' Mr. C, he's looking at me real close.

"I tell him straight, 'Yeah. When the Chinese realtor got scared and made a move to go to the cops to snitch, you had him iced. The newspapers liked that. Car with driver comes to curb in front of big realty firm. Black dude well dressed and polite comes in and asks for Mr. Lee. Mr. Lee's secretary asks who wants him and why. Black dude politely says he had a big payment to make. Lee gets called, comes out. Black dude asks: 'You Mr. Lee?' Mr. Lee says, 'Yeah.' Black dude pulls out his cannon and blows away Mr. Lee's head, which splatters, ruins the new office wallpaper. Black dude scares the office staff shitless by firing a few rounds in their general direction, legs it to his car, wheels spin. Car is gone. Black dude, car, never found. That was a year ago. Newspapers and the street says somebody did all that, Mr. C, but the street never knew who was that smart. Now maybe I know it's C et Cie that smart."

Rooster turned to his attentive audience, "Mr. C, he stared at me. I know, I do that to people. Sometimes I sound like I know what I'm talking about and say it well, next time I'm a black patois ghetto idiot no English speaker can understand." He looked at the men around the table. "Right?"

They had noticed it.

"Mr. C is still talking to me. He says, 'I'll tell you something, Rooster, any big firm that relies on just one supplier, whatever the service, is in trouble. Unless it is for public utilities. For instance, I had already forgotten Boomer, who, in any event, handled nothing but local good will, since in a business like this you have to get local support. There's no other reason I'd supply jellybeans to the streets of this town. Good will only, Rooster, is my twenty-million-dollar contribution to the local economy. There are twenty hoodlums to replace Boomer, and every one of them can be dead by this date next year. You agree?'

"I couldn't take issue with that.

"'It's not that you need to know, but I want you to know. Mr. Chang here can fill in the details. First, we need someone as bright and streetwise as you are because last week we had, in another office, another icing. This time he was my man iced. Competitors or a jealous wife or a bookie tired of waiting to be paid. That's what they want me to believe. Not on their life. Anyway my man Parker was a pro in moving dope and money, and now maybe a new business, girls from the Ukraine, and the usual higher-grade weapons for a very select market. Until he's replaced, these local operations, the ones I provide for the big western metropolitan areas, and the big money militia dingbats in Idaho and Arizona, are half strangled. You're not ready for it yet, Rooster, but you and Chang are going to have to fill that gap, which is to oversee the European connections. I can use Nevada Inc. for a little while, but cool-cat-black and mob-white is not my favorite color scheme for currency business. Do you comprehend?'

"Suddenly he grins and asks me, 'I mean, man, bro, you dig this shit?' I'll tell you, Mr. C has a sense of humor and he can win a man over.

"'Rooster,' he was saying, but man it was late and I was getting bushed. Mr C never drooped an eyelid. 'You listen up to a business question now. I told you Boomer handled nothing but local good will. What do you think of that?'

"'What do you mean, "good will"? He had to be turning maybe, I dunno, half a million, two million a year over to you up the ladder through Slash.'

"'Chicken feed, Rooster. He thought he was selling drugs to street dealers like you used to do, but what he was really selling was my good name in this town. This is my headquarters although I myself am, happily, an absentee slumlord. I want to keep the locals happy. Since maybe one quarter of the people in this town are dopers, and most everybody who drives in is a doper, I let some profit trickle down. I'm king here, kid, King C. Feudal, Rooster, and one thing the king gets is some mighty fine whompin. The girls come to you begging for it, but sometimes I go looking. Once in a while I want a homegirl. I whomped your sister a while back, went over her real good. Gave her a present, she was so tasty. Your old man was so pleased to have the connection, he knows my money not my name, he's been bowing to me on the street ever since."

Rooster's hand was trembling. "Until he said that to me I might have worked for him, aimed to be like him, but he was bragging to me about his power, pissing on my dad, making Thelma out as a whore and she's not; she can just have her head turned by a handsome dude with money. He did all that to make me eat it. That's when I saw his other side. I know, Malome is that kind of place. This was when I saw he was stupid. His ego made him stupid and nasty as rattlesnake shit. Hadn't been for that I wouldn't be here talking to you, spilling my guts. You see I do want money, I do want to be a big man, I would in fact like to launder money, but if you get to be like that, no surprise really, that's how Slash and Boomer would be if they were on top, well, that's not where I want to be."

The three cops of one sort or another refrained from lengthy comment. This man-kid was so moving, so straight, what could fellows with an easy life, coming from easy childhoods like theirs have to say? Only a little.

"I'm proud of you," said Dolan.

"More power to you," said Stein.

"Thank you," said Markowitz. "I wish I could be sure I had as much guts, sense and honesty as you do, Rooster. Whenever a crunch comes I'll be thinking of you as a guy who knows what's right."

Rooster looked at Markowitz in astonishment. It might have been a tear came to his eye.

Rooster rushed back into the telling. He was not a boy-man who wanted to be seen with tears in his eyes. "Anyway, Mr. C has now gotten to explain all this 'good will' to me.

"'All the guns in this town, Rooster, you think they fly in here on their own wings? You think Herman's Liquor Store got that armory in back on Herman's own? No way. You look at those manufacturers' labels and if you read Russian you read "Kalashnikov." That's a Michael Kalashnikov toy, the AK-47 you see on the streets everywhere, AK for "avtomat," K for Michael, and 47 for the year it came out. When importing became illegal my company got them in and sold them. Keep in mind, the good people who import vodka do not bring us these goodies. I do, and from a long way away and a whole bunch of people getting paid to do it. Billions, when all is said and spent, Rooster, not profit always, but always investments. Watch the money roll in. I have my eye on you.'

"Then he reaches in his coat pocket, pulls out an envelope, shakes out the white powder on a paper and shapes it into lines, and sniffs himself a line or two of coke. I mean I have seen a lot of people use stuff, done it myself, but what was he trying to prove? Didn't seem sensible and I told him so. 'Mr. C, cigarettes are bad enough, but snorting coke, eleven at night, it'll wreck your brain.'

"He was already feeling the high, smiling. 'I know, Rooster, but a big man has got to get through a day. You know that; my Lord, if anybody knows that it's a scrawny little work-scurrying hoodlum like you. But,' he shrugs his shoulders and gets that white-powder oh-so-high beam on his face, oh I've seen that before, 'I got to get up for the next day and this day's work, and play ain't done.'

"I just shook my head. I *did* feel like his mother. He's there playing his fingers on the table like it was a piano, coke piano, I've seen that too. And then he says, 'Rooster, I'm a little high but I am clear and I feel like talking. I don't know why but you strike me as a kid I can talk to, who maybe understands.'

"What can I do but nod, like some jack in the box with a spring neck running down?

"'Tell you, Rooster, it's a good life and it's a bad life and it's better with a little of this white man's powder. Makes a king feel like an emperor. You want a line?'

"'No.'

"'Well, I do. Couple of lines. Maybe lots of lines of coke to sniff. You see my father he was a dentist, lived well but he had no vision, no imagination. So I had to develop it for myself. So I went off to a fancy school, practiced my English accent, moved ahead. One head, two roads.'

"What the hell can I say? I ain't no psychologist. I ask myself, is this great man coming apart? So he runs on, 'You see, Rooster, unlike my father, I have always wanted to be a king. A king, that's what I said. If you only knew, Rooster, knew how rich I was, man, beyond your silly-ass street dreams. . . . I sniff a little of this and I'm there on the throne sooner, that's all.'

"I just looked at him. What could I say? He was getting higher by the minute, sniffing and snorting, oh I had seen all of that before. My Lord, am I his priest or something?

"He says, 'I got a secret, Rooster. There are two of us going to be kings, the white guy of course is going to be the real king, but I am coming close. Rooster, you know what?'

"I didn't know what. Hell, I didn't know diddley.

"'I've got a partner, Rooster. I got me a bunch of partners all over. Big men. Princes. One, back East, is so big you'd fall over if I told you his name. This guy's aiming to be President. He's got it fixed. Bankers, the press, the lefties and the righties in the bag; don't give a damn in between. Yes, Rooster my new man, my partner is going to be President, and we are on the way. I've got it fixed, too. I'm going to be a cabinet secretary and we are going to rule the world.'

"I didn't exactly like the sound of that, but he's all full of himself now and just talking away. 'I'm king of the poor, Rooster, and all their dirty pleasures, since that's all they know and can pay for. King of the slums, the dealers, of under the bridges where the homeless fogheads sleep. King of the dark lands, Rooster—the Darth Vader of more of America than you can imagine.'

"'So better off folks get better strokes. Yuppie chumps and who cares? My market is basic goodies for basic folks. Like here in Malome, my people are outfitted, loaded for bear, and I sure don't mean the churchy ones. Basic violence, basic sin, basic greed—which I sell as gambling and fenced goods. Stuff for real desires.' Mr. C grinned, the way sharks grin or hawks look at rabbits, or a man with hobnailed jackboots looks who's getting set to really kick some ass. 'In that kind of merchandise, Rooster, and in the magic trick of turning the dirty money white, with the taxman no wiser, that, kid, is where the money is.'

"So know—since in this business you belong to me and you do not ever forget it, soul brother—I am going to put you next to who is going to put you next to the South City Currency Exchange, who do some of my wash for me, and my Pakistani who does my heroin importing through his people in Germany and Latvia and points eastward. Why, do you ask? Because my good man was iced and they think I do not know why or who, but I do. I know it was the South City Currency people out of their big airport office where our laundry goes. It is only a part of our laundering operation, but as I told you, diversification is essential, so they're worldwide. These people give us credit in Germany at their *cambios*, their exchange banks there, for each dollar we give them here, so that the money itself doesn't move. Since there are two sets of books at that big airport, it doesn't even get counted by Uncle Sam and is thus an unbeatable laundry. And so on from Berlin to Warsaw to Moscow. And if we are buying goods, and don't want to use the usual offshore import-export cut outs, the same money buys the stuff that, these days, comes out via the Baltics. And lots of Russian money that I invest comes through Latvia. Trivia question: how much of Russian export goes out through the Baltic countries?'

"I didn't know.

"'Counting St Petersburg, forty five percent. Most of which has a *mafiya* stamp on it saying, in effect, paid off. With regard to this current matter, my current Balfours, that's the exchange accountant, tells me we were not paying him in full, and I mean hundreds of thousands of dollars in full, which monies were supposed to be in our credit account there. And so my now deceased associate was going to give me the full book on all of this when he, and the books he was going to show me, left this world. You, Rooster, are going to take care of the currency exchange people as my new bookkeeper. You compare Chang's record of deposits with theirs, then with the chief accountant up there, and then you are going to work your way into their confidence so that you are the back-up man to Chang. That should lead to some drama, some public ceremony. If you get the goods on him, along with Chang, we may have ourselves an execution, Rooster, and just like when Shakespeare was shaking and shagging about, it has got to have its delighted audience. No good having executions unless the people who ought to know about them know about them. Right? Just like the judges, we have a law of deterrence.'

"'My company's law is that vengeance is deterrence. It works. I am maybe as rich as any man in the West, barring the top twenty. Rich is like being whitey. I have his accent and his suits, Rooster. I have his education. No, I have a much better education in fact. But I want his money, his position, his house, his women and his power. That is what my business is all about. Just catching up, Rooster, just catching up. Oh yes—and having fun doing it.'"

Rooster looked at the three older men. "So you see, here is your Mr. C working right here in River City, just like your bosses told you. I can't help liking some of the man, and yeah, admire him. Love that money. But not the brutal stuff. Do the flimflam, sure no problem, and that's what I can do. Arrange dirty money into clean. But not the ugly. No. Sure as hell I don't like his insulting me by telling me he was whomping Thelma and turned my old man into a nigger. Once I ask myself if I really want to be like Mr. C, I am really asking, am I cut out for his kind of work? A 'C and Cie' kind of ego? Do I want to be king? And we all know once you even ask that question in Malome, you are character-wise, attitude-wise, not fit to survive here. Even so, my mind ain't made up."

"What comes next, Rooster? And keep in mind whatever it is, we want you to survive." Markowitz meant it. So did the other two, more than tough-cop macho veneer would admit. Markowitz had become their spokesman for tenderness.

"I show up tonight again. Furbo first, then probably Mr. C. Mr. 'In Between,' as the old song said. But I see now mostly I do what Mr. C wants and send the business that fits to Furbo's people."

Markowitz respectfully asked, "When do you think we can move on Mr. C, Rooster?"

"Well, you got nothin at all on him now. He's not the type to welcome a social call, if you knew where he was when, which is unlikely. He'll have a dozen lawyers, so when you do bust him you won't get to talk to him anyway. All you can hope for is to get probable cause which right now you don't know 'causes' what, get a warrant, break into that warehouse without his having notice—which means no one on the town council or your own department knows anything about what you are doing, that means Dolan here has to do it at the Federal level, and get to the right files which show you those European connections which you tell me you are after in the first place."

The kid, as they already knew, was no dumbbell.

Markowitz, having heard Rooster tell of the man who would be king, but first President, and not forgetting that call from the Senate Crime Committee's Council chaired by the good Senator Cranmer, added, "Thanks to you, Rooster, and your very accurate recall and reporting, we also have an interest in the American connection."

Doc Dolan, who knew exactly what Markowitz was referring to, who knew a barrel of worms when he heard the slithering, who knew what could happen to an agent at any level who went after the powerful on the Hill, shook his head.

"Count me out, brother. My wife and family want me at work and feeding them. Don't think I haven't heard the rumors about who might want to run for President again, who is stirring the jingoism, pacifism, internationalism, isolationism, I'll-have-State-Department's-behind-and-broiling-thus-you-Mr.-current President's mulligan stew. Just count me out."

Markowitz had already done that a long time ago. Doc Dolan was too much of a bureaucratic type ever to be a maverick political hero, however good he would likely be as a policing partner.

"Never counted you in, brother." Then, turning to Rooster, he asked, "so where does your strategy leave us?"

"You know damn well. With me doing the work. Your man undercover with C and Cie, and me being very careful, because Mr. C isn't hankering after that kind of new assistant, neither are Furbo's people."

That they knew. "You sure you want to go ahead?" asked Markowitz.

"No, I'm not sure at all. Do you think I'm nuts?"

"By three this afternoon I will have a bank account in Palm City set up in your name with five thousand Federal dollars in it. That help with your decision?" It was Dolan, of course, speaking.

"I promise to keep you in donuts, buddy," grinned Officer Stein, holding a chocolate nut one out to Rooster.

"Take your time, Rooster, your being safe comes first."

Rooster made up his mind. "Okay, you guys are the best con artists I ever did see. Okay, I'll do it. But I need someone watching my ass." He surveyed the three. "Since Officer Stein here is hardly invisible, and Detective Markowitz hardly unknown in Malome, that makes you, Agent Assistant Deputy Director Dolan, my undercover backup. But not dressed like you are. There's only one kind of white man out here who can be obvious and not suspect, and they are all so down and out that Malome is all they can afford. Be a junkie, be a junkie matured into a drunk, or be a cokehead so burned out in the head his lights are all out. You decide. I'll call the detective at his house here, or try to slip you a note on the street," he gestured to Dolan, "to tell you when and where we next meet."

Markowitz smiled. Rooster had become their new lieutenant. It was a pleasure to see him at work.

34

The Wipplingers were so pleased to have their, well almost, children at home that they could have kept them there forever. That trio had rarely had the chance to regress so guiltlessly into idleness, language lessons, books, fattening Austrian food, wines, philosophical talk. Claire and Barbour each day found themselves more attracted to each other. Neither clearly admitted it to themselves but they suspected it was love. Neither would rush it but each felt it would work out. Things were looking mighty fine, if you ignored reality. Claire's wounds, for example, still wore scars but hers was healing skin, and there were no longer great scabs on her cheek and chin.

It was time for Frau Wipplinger's drive with Claire to Vienna. It would be best for their composure that they not think about the content of the daily press which was in froth and frenzy over the Vienna Incident. As the press goes so follow these days the Parliament, presidents, and the people. Posturing, threats, prospects of war were more entertaining each day. Oh my, how the media money rolled in.

The sergeant wrote a cryptic note for Claire to give to the Marine guard in the hopes of facilitating her admission, yet without giving away the show should the note fall into Austrian hands. In essence it listed the first names of all EMs who were in the Embassy squad and might have gate duty, used some explicit sergeantly-imperative language saying, "Let her in pronto, you blankety-blanks . . . and closed, "Semper Fi."

Barbour also wrote a note, for whatever staffer would also be gatekeeper. "Ron, you know her anyway, but, yes, it's her." It was signed, "Yes, it's me."

It worked like a charm. Claire, upon showing the notes and uttering the words, "I'm Claire Dubois, whose kidnap began the Incident," was surrounded by Marines at the foyer and rushed in to see her friend from adolescent days, Ambassador Ron Owen.

Hugs and kisses, so many "Oh my, how glad I am to see you's" were exchanged. Then the story was told. The first action was a telephone call to the embassy in Kiev. Claire could hear the gladness in her father's voice, knew well that he could hear the sobs of relief catching in her throat. No matter if their talk was monitored; it was no surprise to Square and Company that she was somewhere safe, and that her report would be a nuisance they could now silence only with great difficulty. But, where there was a will there might be a way.

"What do we do now?" Barbour and "Injun Joe," as the wild bunch at Wipplinger's had come to call the sergeant, must be brought in from the cold. And without identifying the Wipplingers as their safe house owners.

"We did work out a communications system," Claire said. She explained the midnight semaphore signal they had arranged and the pick-up site at the alley corner two blocks down.

"And I do have a visitor coming tomorrow," said Ambassador Owen, "who'll help us put the facts together: an old friend who is now our Madame Ambassador in Sofia. She flies up tomorrow. I'll tell you what she seems to have learned." And he did.

Washington governmental offices, when the cabled news was received, were delighted. Now perhaps, with a first-hand account from the woman soon to be labeled the "Helen of Troy for Laxenburg," the hostile Austrian apologists could be rocked back irrefutably. "But only if," as the wise men in State's council rooms opined, "the woman stays alive."

"Quite so," said Sir Peter to Quincy as they lunched at the Athenaeum, for Dubois had telephoned Sir Peter on getting the news, "quite so. All kinds of people are bent on eliminating her. Lots of strangling hands are reaching out to silence Claire and her liberators. How then, as LeCarré used to put it, to bring them in from the cold?"

"Ah yes," Quincy sighed, "not easily. The Austrians will have to provide police protection and safe passage. And the bad cops will kill them. Maximum security all the way to embassy, airport and safe haven here. I see the opposition's scenario as working in one of two ways: making the murder venture look as if it were done by the American and British governments being blamed by the demagogues for the Incident in the first place; or alternatively, letting the rogues among the Austrian police shoot them down, claiming they were escaping felons. So look for bad lads wearing British or American military uniforms, or impostors carrying FBI, CIA, MI6 identification and letting the press know they're there—fake intercepts, insider tips, some such ploy, or just a swarm of cop-blue uniforms carrying automatic rifles as they keep the peace. There'll be police and mafiya surveillance of course of every official who leaves the U.S. Embassy."

"But perhaps not the British embassy? After all, the Austrian police well know the lead liberator is American and Claire is in the American embassy. How does that sound?"

"Very much like the 'special relationship' of cousins across the sea still working."

"Righto, well, let's get cracking on it."

They did. Vienna did. MI6 did. An elderly Anglican cleric entered the British Embassy in Vienna the next day. He was so arthritic he used a cane. He left a few hours later. A taxi picked him up delivering him to the English Church. At evensong service a young man was with the emerging parishioners. Circuitously he went to the airport to return to London whence he had two days before come. Liaison was in place, with no eavesdroppers the wiser.

Later that same evening a TV service van left Vienna, direction Laxenburg. Its contents included a remarkable stock of weapons and emergency medical supplies, as well as surveillance audio. Some minutes behind the van followed an unmarked Austrian police BMW whose senior police occupants had been selected by the Chancellor's own trusted Interior Minister. Behind them, spaced another ten minutes, a police van with a dozen, you can be sure, politically-screened SWAT officers, armed to the teeth. The convoy to Laxenburg had begun.

Once in a while luck runs the right way. No hostile surveillance of the three-car caravan was detected visually or by audio. The police helicopter a mile to the rear saw no unusual traffic activity. Its pilot and crew had also been hand picked. Woe to the Ministerial and police general hands that made any error in screening for loyalty, honesty and competence tonight. The clerical BMW van drove slowly past 45 Maler Strasse at exactly 10:15 that evening. A blue masked light shone toward the house from the front seat. The light flashed three times. The BMW drove on, did a circuit around the block, returned at exactly 10:25. At 45 Maler Strasse a window shade was pulled up, showing a lamp with a blue shade in the window. The window shade stayed up until the TV van made a pass by at 10:35. One red masked light from its front seat shone pin-pointedly at the open window. The shade was pulled down. The pickup maneuver was underway.

Two men walked through the back yard, out through the alley gate they remembered so well, down the alley in a direction opposite to Farmer Bieber and his neighbors, and two blocks further to the alley intersecting with Schubert Strasse. Frau and Herr Dr. Wipplinger had scouted the place, reported a good collection of garbage cans and bushes and no immediate street light. The BMW cruised by slowly, flashed blue four times, saw an immediate return blue signal twice. The TV repair van and the police van pulled up behind to give cover. The BMW back door opened, Barbour and the sergeant leaped in, greetings were exchanged, and the entourage sped off. The helicopter moved in overhead and ahead to scout. A Federal radio channel not in ordinary use was to be used only to warn or report of emergencies for which, to be sure, all aboard were prepared, armed and ready. It was almost anticlimactic, as the Sergeant said as they neared the steel garage rear service gate of the embassy, now flanked by four heavily armed fatigue clad marines at the ready.

"A piece of cake."

"With lead icing?" Barbour was first to spot the muzzle flash from an automatic weapon as it spat at them. Easy inference after the fact: someone on a hostile stakeout had spotted the four Marines not ordinarily stationed, and certainly not at almost midnight, at the daylight-use-only vehicular service entrance. Clearly, someone was being brought in. But the ambush crowd had not figured on the firepower, a 30-caliber machine gun in the TV truck, nor a fully ready SWAT team right behind them. The BMW was lightly armored, but that was good enough to get its passengers into the compound before heavy slugs took out the rear tires. The SWAT-plus-Marine team took out the bushwhackers in less than five bloody minutes. SWAT teams live for—and are prepared to but have no intention of dying at—moments like this. Adrenaline highs, epinephrine rush, the sweet music of rat-a-tat-tat go boom, and guess what? You there in the upstairs window are, whoops, just like in the shoot-em-up bang-bang movies, falling out dead. Splat. The SWAT guys love it. A couple were wounded, which only makes the story better. They get medals and tales with which to enthrall their grandchildren one day. Never, never underestimate how much SWAT teams love drilling a real live, now real dead, enemy.

The two men in the BMW, dressed now as police supervisors, both had been given armored vests and the change of clothes upon entering the vehicle at Schubert Strasse, made it into the embassy unscathed. Well, just scathed enough to write home about. Barbour had a crease in his arm, Sergeant Injun Joe caught one sliding sidewise on his gluteus maximus. Nothing better than a hero with just a little blood to show for it. The sergeant would get a Purple Heart.

This time the Austrian police would be, the euphemism is, "reconstituted." As with Scotland Yard in 1998 after the Ghost Squad discoveries. As in New Orleans in 1977-78, when cops were found to have murdered witnesses. As in Denver, sometime earlier, when cops were found running burglary rings. As in Malome, where at one time a third of the police force was under grand jury investigation for such minor peccadilloes as brutality, theft from evidence cabinets, cocaine use and sales, deputy chiefs forcing sex on women patrolpersons—just the ordinary stuff that cops do when the watchbird is not watching them closely enough. Or the watchbird is a bad guy.

"But why try to kill Barbour and the sergeant when Claire was safely in? After all, she is the informant respecting the mafiya."

The Interior Minister and the police Major General had demanded an immediate meeting with the three tired heroes. Ambassador Owen was likewise exhausted. The Austrian top brass were edgy and unpleasant for they had an immense area, mostly of their own ass, to cover. The ambassador did not have to agree to it, but had a before and after strategy in his mind. After all, the Austrians had brought all of this on themselves. In any event they had to promise total confidentiality, to use the interview only as a basis for their investigations. Napoleonic law allows a lot of opportunistic bends in the legal road. They entered the room essentially hostile, as powerful people with a lot to hide can do when seeking to intimidate.

Protocol required they begin with Ambassador Owen who was at his formal, prevaricating best. "The reports are not in. This meeting is a courtesy only." Claire was declared too ill to be interviewed.

It was Agent Barbour's turn to answer questions. He played it cool.

"Claire couldn't testify to what went on between me and Major Kummering, nor could his staff, who only saw us together. I am the only one who can state that Kummering vetoed immediate action to find Claire and forbade me to investigate on my own. I accuse the Major of obstruction of justice. My bet is that if you check his telephone log immediately after my visit to Federal Police Headquarters there will be some interesting people contacted—all mafiya. Damn lucky he didn't figure Injun Joe and I would be out there to Laxenburg so fast, or he would have had a brigade-size defense in place and Claire would have been dead before we arrived. Slow and sloppy."

The General, the Minister had their own script. Coldly they set out facts.

"Your ambushers tonight were seven in number. All in mufti but three were Federal officers, one a lieutenant working under Major Kummering. The others were Russian irregulars. No ID, but we had their pictures. Now we have their dental charts. A rather neat package. Two lived, and with interrogation under either lots of morphine or none at all—forgive us but we are not feeling caring at the moment—will spill all. Major Kummering is already about to roll over on his superiors. We suspect he was in direct liaison with the sorrier side of the Russian Embassy here. None of his superiors had any knowledge of his disloyalty. None! CNN has asked for the rights to interview you with substantial cash up front, but Austrian TV will get to you first. As I understand your statements, there is no doubt the Russian mafiya kidnapped and tortured Miss Dubois; that Dubois is an American Federal enforcement officer; that you, Agent Barbour, with an otherwise unknown aka 'Injun Joe' set out to rescue Miss Dubois because, you claim, the Federal Police under Major Kummering would offer no assistance; that you were fired upon first in Laxenburg; that you claim Miss Dubois was held captive there at risk of imminent death; that you two men deny killing both of the captors there, if either; that you did identify a Russian Embassy car coming into the driveway of #12 Musicker Alle; that you allege at least one of the captors was killed by Russians in that car, one of whom we know was a diplomat; that Agent Dubois states a man she calls 'Square' was in charge of her captors and ordered her torture and interrogation and may be assumed to have been in touch with the Russians who arrived at #12, etc. Is that substantially correct?"

"Yes."

"Is that substantially what you would relate on television should, as we understand it, CNN ask you for an interview and your superiors allow it?"

"Yes." Barbour was uneasy. They were being handled as suspects.

"And if they ask you, who can corroborate?"

"There was a farm next door. Whoever the farmer was, he must have heard it all. We borrowed his cows and tractor as a screen, a Trojan cow so to speak—not that we bothered to ask him—to get close to #12 Musicker Allee."

"His name?"

"No idea. We needed his cows and tractor. He had to hear the shooting. We never saw him." It was Barbour speaking to cover Farmer Bieber's involvement.

"And where did you hide out all that time? You got food, we must presume good medical care for Miss Dubois, and someone washed your clothes, at the very least. What will you say when they ask you that?" The officials were now prosecutors. The Americans were not pleased.

The man identified only as "Injun Joe" replied. That his disguise was courtesy of the CIA wardroom officer could not be guessed. The russet skin and the long braid down his back graced with a pigeon feather were particularly artful. His own (Ohio) mother would not have wanted to recognize him.

"Now, you fellows understand I was just passing by. Heard the banshees howling. Can't let down a Yank. Man, the tour director never told me Vienna would be like this. But now you fellows, let me help you with your questions." The sergeant's Texas twang was pure delight. So was the look on the two high officials' faces as they were addressed as "you fellows" or "partner." But the sergeant never missed a line when on stage, as Barbour remembered from Laxenburg.

"Now hear, you boys know that sweet little Alpine Blick Hotel down there in Laxenburg? It backs up to the creek, you know, the arroyo with water in it. Damnedest thing. We were hustling along after the getaway from the Russian reinforcements and went by the back of the place in the alley. There was this Canadian couple bitching about how boring the place was. I cleaned the gunpowder off my face and sauntered in, telling them my new friend Barbour here and I were looking for a poker game. I have to confess, I'm not an entirely honest person. My mother was a gypsy, you know. Taught me bad ways. My father, well, I never knew him. I hate to tell you what my mother did for a living to support us. So maybe it's not so terribly bad that I use my own deck of cards. I hate chance after a childhood like that. Terrible. My priest will have me saying Hail Marys for eternity.

"We played up in the couple's room. I told them Lee's sister was with us, told them she'd gotten in a fight with her husband who'd hit her, that he'd amscrayed from the hotel before the cops got him. We asked if they'd let her rest while we played. They were drinking schnapps and were about three sheets to the wind themselves. We played; I won. Barbour had a few good cards himself. We won enough to pay for the other room in their hotel suite. Nice people. We played cards, kept them from getting bored. I told them about my childhood on the Arapaho Indian Reservation up near Hudson Bay, how us Arapaho hunted polar bear and tamed penguins. Thank God they were Chinese Canadians from Vancouver and didn't know the difference. You want to know where we stayed? That's where."

All of this entertainment Injun Joe provided for free on TV.

The police general, eyes as black and hard as granite, cold as Siberian winter, began in a most unpleasant tone, "You . . ."

He was interrupted. "Just call me Injun Joe, General, that's what the Ambassador here calls me, right, Ambassador? I'm an affirmative-action tourist you know, they had to take me. Didn't want to, wanted me stuck back on that reservation. Everybody on the tour bus knew I wasn't quite right in the head. But you see, I *am* trying."

Ambassador Owen was stifling his laughter, but the tears of it were perilously close to streaming down his face. Not good on camera, but he had to blow his nose or burst.

The Interior Minister cut off the General. Both were furious. "Impertinence! You will tell the truth or we will impound your tourist visa and have you out of this country by nightfall. *Verstehen Zie*?"

Injun Joe looked at Ron Owen. "Gee, fellows, I don't think you can do that as long as I'm here on embassy soil, ain't that right, Mr. Ambassador? And besides, I'm doing like you asked and cooperating. Rough me up and I suspect the Ambassador here and these other good folks are going to have a second think about who's charged with what around here. I mean, you just put that in your peace pipe and smoke it, if you see what I mean."

A face turned purple is a harmonious color for a pompous general wearing a dark gray uniform, but he would not have elected it.

"Anyway, now that's settled, just keep in mind I'm just poor ol' Injun Joe, a little weak in the head maybe, but aiming to please. Call me by my first name, Mr. Minister, makes me more down-home and comfortable."

The Minister was beginning to understand what Vienna's own Dr. Freud had meant when talking about death wishes. Thanatos was here today.

"So," he demanded, "nevertheless, you stick to this story about where you were while in hiding?"

"Of course, Mr. Minister, I couldn't tell a lie."

He was fuming. "Then how in *Himmel* did you get away from there?"

"Same way the Canadians did, sir. Us Arapaho, we got us a mystery dance, we call on Coyote Spirit and Joking Uncle. This big coyote comes up when we really need him, saddled, ready to go. Singing Yippee-y, Yippee-yay all the way. And there's Joking Uncle, he and Coyote are gods of course, riding up behind him with a string of ready horses, hell, they're outfitted so fancy they got English saddles, like he always does when his Indian children are in trouble. The Canadians were glad to get out. Couldn't pay their hotel bill, I'd won so much off them. We all just rode those horses out of that hotel toward Vienna. Then your captains in their police car saw us and took us into the embassy here, General. That's when it got nasty, General. Way I hear it your own damn police officers—I know the press can prove it if I tell them the truth—tried to kill us, and your own cops were part of that ambush. Now General, and Mr. Minister, is that any way to run a police force? I ask you. You can maybe understand why I ain't real pleasant with you folks. Why, Kimosabe—that there's Indian talk for 'blood brother comrade' they could have killed Ambassador Owen here himself. Ambassador?"

The sergeant, aka Injun Joe, turned to Ambassador Owen the most innocent of faces, making sure that any hidden cameras caught a full-figure shot of the butt-swaddling bandage running from around his waist down to his thigh. Battle casualty stuff. He'd worked on that prop with the embassy nurse a bit earlier. And once again to the Ambassador, "Don't you want to tell them, Kimosabe, how you're part Indian, too?"

Injun Joe's turned out to be one hell of a way to take control of an unfriendly interrogation. Especially when Barbour began to speak ski-trail German, the grammar of which was undecipherable.

The good news: CNN got hold of the tape which the Austrian officials had secretly filmed of the interrogation. Now, this had been very bad manners. The police officials had presumed that the large black button on the end of a small briefcase camera held by an unimposing aide standing behind the general during the interrogation would not be noticed. Barbour made the device immediately, as did the American security man on the way in. He, in turn, had signaled the sergeant and the ambassador. Yes, it had been bad form. Visitors like that get what they ask for. In this instance CNN was told, on the QT of course, that there was a film. One should not be astonished at what five thousand dollars in local currency will do for a poor peasant clerk who works in the Federal photo lab downtown. He gave CNN a copy. When CNN saw it they didn't even bother with a follow-up filming effort. They did give the surreptitious film to an Austrian sister station bent on embarrassing the government. It did.

It was not in a fully private conversation Ambassador Owen suggested to the television producer that his people needed a little more time to prepare for real coverage. The official Austrian tape, illegally and discourteously made, the Ambassador allowed, although his comment was off the record, was an embarrassment that could be remedied. "If you folks know what I mean." And CNN did.

Two days later, the script was ready. Claire, made up to be a bit more bruised than she really was, appeared before the cameras to read a statement describing her assignment, her kidnapping, beating, brutal interrogation, and near-rape. The description of Glove's hand on her pudendum was pruriently gross enough, delivered with the genuine force of Claire's revulsion, as to horrify, and, one must assume titillate—to ensure, in fact, that many hundreds of millions of viewers followed every detail of the Vienna Incident. One must keep in mind that, given the world media furor, and titillation aside, it was by no means clear to the public that war—Russia vs. the Anglo nations, with Austria's side unclear—might still not break out.

Claire told how she had seen only "Square" and the two captors, now dead. She did not mention Brody or Mr. C. When she had reviewed her statement, she was herself ashamed at how little she had known, or learned since, about the events that had so nearly cost her her life. Face flushed with pleasure as she read that portion, she did warmly thank Agent Barbour and his "companion." To divert attention from the State Department's, the Ambassador's, and the Marines' roles, the sergeant's affiliation would remain secret. In a sweetly innocent admission, she closed her statement by sentimentally confessing, "I have come to be particularly fond of Agent Barbour."

"Darlings," commented the CNN producer, who was talking shop to colleagues after viewing the material, "whatever we didn't get out of Dubois by way of blood-and-guts firefight reporting we got in spades with that love interest angle. Play it for all it's worth: 'Daring love comes to Federal agent—heroic rescue while the bullets flew.' Darlings, this here is fucking yummy footage. If that sweetheart Claire doesn't get a book offer out of this, I don't know my publishing. Shit, darlings, can't you see the low-road *National Enquirer* now? 'Rumor of pregnancy in Federal agent raped by Russian mafiya'? Oh darlings, don't we love the news business?"

Lee Barbour was not way savvy to the workings of a news director's mind but neither was he unmindful of the makings—and effects—of a good tale, well told and well spiced. He did what he could, zigging and zagging where he must, never forgetting that the goal was to swing world opinion toward the truth. He told the camera, with appealing intensity, of the desperate search for Claire before she could be killed; the suspicious and sinister lack of interest of "some high officers" of the Austrian police; the charge of the Holstein cow brigade in Laxenburg, the use of the stolen tractor as a tank; the finding of the wounded but still beautiful Claire; and then the firefight and escape from the black limousine full of Russian mafiya—as well as the Russians' murder of their own wounded man.

"Great stuff, darlings," enthused the news director. "Elliot Ness in Austria. Somebody's got to put this guy under contract. Who cares how much of it he invented or lied about? This is *news* as it should be. And both these Fedcats look divine on camera. Cool, darlings, cool. I want them reporting from the front lines if this thing does bust out into a war. Imagine the ratings, darlings—gangbusters!"

His staff loathed him but they did grin at the idea of that much coverage. And he was right, the Lee-and-Claire-Act was *big*.

Next on the show was presented the panel of interviewers: those eminent pundits, an Austrian deputy premier, a fiery American congressman whose name had been bandied about as possible vice President for Senator Cranmer's Presidential run; big-name reporters. All were assembled via satellite connection to question Barbour and Claire, then to pontificate. The Vienna Incident was, after all, Big News: full of portents, sharp edges to be honed, and scandals for the raking. And it could still—or so said the analysts—lead to war. As the questions came, Barbour was in charming control.

"Yes, sir. I asked Major Kummering for immediate assistance because I had every reason to believe Agent Dubois had been kidnapped. The Major insisted on following routine procedures; he forbade me to intervene; and he was entirely uninterested, if not downright uncooperative, in rescuing Ms. Dubois. That is not how most policemen respond to news that anyone, let alone a Federal agent, has disappeared after being forced into a limousine."

Barbour went on to recount the doorman's testimony, the concierge's concerns, the contents of the note he had received from Claire assuring Barbour she would be waiting for his call. Barbour put the question to the panel, but in fact to the viewing audience: "Ladies, gentlemen, if you were in this situation, where you had powerful reasons to suspect your colleague or friend were in danger, would you not do your best to find and rescue her?"

There were no nay-sayers. Barbour repeated, elaborated, the events of the rescue. The media were calling it the "Siege at Laxenburg."

"No, sir," he reported to a reporter on the panel, "I cannot tell you how I learned agent Dubois was held at 12 Musicker Allee. That information will come out at the criminal trial."

"No, Sir," he explained to the German Federal Prosecutor on the panel, "to my knowledge, sir, neither of the mafiya captors was more than disabled by us. I am certain that the man with the wounded leg was killed by one of the Russians in the car with diplomatic plates."

"No, sir," was his response to a question from the Russian Ambassador to Britain, "I'm not at liberty to divulge the identity of my siege companion, nor his nationality other than Red Indian. He said Arapaho, did he not?" Barbour was rather pleased with this. "That will be up to officials from his country when they've had a full report. I will say this, you mustn't assume that my companion's mission was at all the same as mine. Coincidences happen, you know." Again he was pleased with the implication it might be an Apache agent from

Oz sent to Laxenburg to find—who could be sure by now?—the yellow brick road.

"No, sir," answered Barbour in response to the American Congressman on the panel, whom he detested just by association with Cranmer, "I can't comment on what you tell me are the inflammatory remarks of the Russian premier, because I didn't hear them. I can't make that kind of, well, your characterization seems to me 'inflammatory,' too. I'm sure that when the Russian government has had a chance to review the full reports, they'll clean up their mess. After all, we don't even know that the official diplomatic passports found on the Laxenburg mafiya kidnappers are genuine. If they are, well, I'm sure the Russian Government will want to send off to jail whomever in their Foreign Ministry is dirty and has been providing that cover. So you see, sir, I'm fairly optimistic that the Russian government will be cool-headed and ready to move against these, well, vicious scumbags. By implication, however, and contrary to what I've been told of your own position, sir, I don't think anyone on our side or theirs should be beating the war drums. The Vienna Incident can be contained, and should be—in spite of your own party's political interests. Sir." Barbour wiped out all those pseudo respectful "sirs" of his, with one malicious, lingering "up-yours" grin. But . . . gentlemanly.

The Congressman could have killed Barbour, but not right there in front of maybe one hundred fifty million TV viewers. Later, maybe. Anonymously. Not for attribution.

All in all, the TV program went well. New mysteries had been introduced, the U.S. position asserted; Austria embarrassed; the Russians implicated as a mafiya trust; and the Siege of Laxenburg had entered history as a real-life James Bond chapter, with entertainment had by all. In London, Quincy and Sir Peter, watching, applauded through it all. In Kiev, Ambassador Dubois was a proud father. On a scale of one to ten he gave Lee Barbour, whom he realized with delight might become a son-in-law, eleven points for his ability to charm, to con, to keep his cool, and—for a man who was obviously irreverent autonomous—to play the game. Richelieu with a mid-Atlantic accent and a gun. George Dubois told himself to look around in the State Department to see if there were a senior spot open, and an Assistant Undersecretary who was game enough to hire his possible son-in-law for it. Barbour was a talented, civilized man with exactly the guts and savvy the Department needed, even if he might not be able to mix a perfect martini. George guessed the lad's drink would be Talisker single malt. Or maybe Macallan.

35

The next day, Madame Ambassador from Sofia arrived in time for lunch at noon in Ambassador Owen's private dining room. Barbour and Claire were there. It was a joyous day: shared vibrations, old friendships, family ties; relief, and undeniably an electric romance was sparking between Lee and Claire. Never did four people get along better.

"Sophie," Ron asked, "tell us what you can."

"Your friend Vasil, Lee, has been invaluable and courageous. He told me about you as the likely John Wayne or Prince Valiant of—what did they call it on the TV show? The Siege of Laxenburg. He told me about how the missing twelve billion dollars went bye-bye, or at least how Messrs. Burmov, the former Deputy Minister, and an Assistant Interior Ministry Director whom he calls BB, in Interior are involved, as well as Dobri N from the Central Bank. Who, by the way, is now dead, as I learned from Vasil's telephone call last night.; I gave him my home phone numbers, which tells you how much I really trust him. Also involved is Todor Mihailov, who was, I gather, a director or deputy in the red Finance Ministry and is now richly settled in Virginia," she paused. "And one of you, do pray tell me why a major Bulgarian immigrant thief would bed down so cozily close to all that law enforcement investigative power in Washington? Think about that, will you? Who's his host, his protector? What is he doing there besides learning to ride to hounds and spending his part of some billions?"

They reviewed other players, now identified as part of the game. That included whoever owned the UST&D Bank in Sofia and no doubt at least some of its board members, most of whom one presumed to be Ukrainian and Russian.

"Then there was Bratislav, whose South African trip happened to coincide with the date of fat man's swim. And what Vasil has said of the Sea Scouts makes him part of their 'wet affairs' and . . ."

"Hey," exclaimed Barbour. "That's just the way Hashimoto of Civil Service died; he had a 'sailing accident and heart attack.' And it was he who started the mess, who identified Claire as really being Greta Liebowitz, *mafiya* moll *extraordinaire* and . . ."

"I was? Why didn't anyone tell me? Who did that, how, why?" Claire interrupted, sputtering with surprise and indignation.

Neither Ron Owen nor Sophie had heard of it either, so Barbour explained as best he could—which was but superficial knowledge and inference. "So someone accessed all those secret personnel records, including the Agency's Personnel ones, but also certainly IFFY and Civil Service, to recreate Claire as a Russian infiltrated mafiya mole. My own instructions in Vienna were to watch out for her as that, which of course meant that if she really were a Greta, she would probably not show."

"Which meant that if the kidnapping had gone off smoothly—if you, Lee, hadn't pursued Claire so, well, I was going to say *passionately*—Ambassador Sophie smiled warmly, "no one would have missed Claire for weeks, maybe months."

"Absolutely," chimed in Ron. "Her father, George, told me about the letters he was getting from Paris, letters telling of her new lover there, all of that, and all appearing to be in her handwriting. George said her friend Beulah in Scotland received similar letters. Somebody was going to a great deal of trouble to deconstruct Claire as ever having been Agency or IFFY."

"Which means an immense intelligence capability for computer penetration, mail cover, communications surveillance, ordinary burglary, and agents around the world—including at least one in IFFY itself."

"But who would do that, or want to? Only a KGB-GRU or current Russian Security Services, unless MI6 or the Agency has turned totally sour. Taking the most likely possibility, it means this bunch engineering the Vienna Incident *must* include some of the most powerful and skilled old KGB technology and spy master hands, now turned commercial."

"And hand in hand with the bankers and the old mafiya thugs, some seniors in government."

"Which of course is the story of post-glasnost Russia, the Ukraine, Belarus, Latvia, and you name it. The land of the Oligarchs, as we all have come to know them."

It was Claire's turn. "But why go to all that trouble to kidnap, interrogate, and then—obviously kill me? I'm the new girl on the block, with only one week in IFFY! I don't know *anything*."

Barbour replied, "But, obviously, they didn't know that you didn't know.

After all, you were sent here to Vienna with the name Brody et Cie to pursue, as I did. Do you remember the very first incident in this whole story, which was the burned-out hippie I called Crystal Man trying to get his hands on my IFFY package, way back when I was traveling to Washington from San Francisco? Someone hired this jerk, using enough cutouts to make a million donut holes, to find out what was in my mission package. They must have known from surveillance, and maybe from inside, who we were, where we were going, about the Warsaw tips, and since it was up front, about Brody and whoever 'C' or 'Cie' is in California."

"Did you know that the whole Warsaw law office group, from bosses down to clerks, was killed in an arson fire?" Ron asked Barbour the question, because there were so many bits and pieces of information that one had and another did not.

"No, no I had no idea. That means the outfit we're up against has a Warsaw branch, just as Brody means a Vienna branch; and just as Sir Alfred being with Brody in Sofia—as Vasil told us—means they were laundering through a worldwide net. Sir Alfred's, as we know, on its own covered Europe, South Africa, and no doubt every useful offshore haven the devil ever visited. And of course there is Square. He is now no doubt safely and unextradictably in Moscow, probably with his crony Brody and the very mysterious Mr. C, or Cie, in California. *He* ought to know a great deal about it all, simply because it is so very odd that an underworld figure, which is what I make him to be, stars in the top of this very rich and ugly company. And so far he is the only American. Given our role in the world, including crime, that doesn't quite make sense."

Madame Ambassador Sophie was relatively unfamiliar with the world of high-stakes, high-finance money laundering. She asked, "As a best guess, where would you think a high-powered operation like this, if Sir Alfred was its measure, would have senior people?"

"As a banking and investment system, coupled with incidental thug muscle, plus the usual accountants, lawyers, and paper pushers? Beyond where we already know, I'd guess London, Geneva, Luxembourg, with correspondents in Panama, maybe Mexico, Cyprus; someone big in the Baltics because of their export role for so much of Russia's resources, and representative firms in the usual havens from Guernsey across to Nauru. Istanbul seems to be moving right up as a center. Latvia, of course, where big billions of suitcase rubles go right into the banking system for exchange, no questions asked. This outfit will have a Riga man, although he could handle Tallinn also. It depends on the resources, the industries being looted, whose taxes are being evaded—in

Russia, for example, that means almost all of them—what contraband is favored; the development plans of management; and the accident of where the buddies' network blossoms, that is, where you live and where your friends are."

"But nothing, well, operational in the U.S.?"

"That's odd, isn't it? Except for C nothing points there, and if C's into drugs, street guns, and whores, he's just a downscale diversification. But who got him in, who does he know? That's what's really important. Even for a conglomerate, an aggregate of convenience, there should be the equivalent of a board of directors, an executive director. And since the U.S. foremost and London second is where maybe three-quarters of the value of all the world's securities are traded, that's where power is. Where power is, is where decisions are made—and where the money ends up. We may never find them, but I'd bet your bottom dollar, Madame Ambassador, that's where they are."

"Sophie, please."

"Sophie, my wager is that somebody in the U.S., and also the U.K., is on the Board. Who knows? If he's a Darth Vader genius, it could be Mr. C after all."

"Odd you use that Star Wars image. It came to my mind, too," said Claire "although since I love Tolkien I suppose one could refer to him as the Dark Lord of Mordor."

Madame Ambassador Sophie responded, "I don't think he deserves praise for a Tolkien character's imagination. For all I know Mr. C in his world is not so utterly different from us in ours, except that he's forgotten altruism, is unscrupulous, and is a menace to community—a pragmatist without morals or love. He's two-dimensional then, with no richness of any personal kind except money. But we too need money. Lord knows I wish I had millions of it to spend on behalf of Bulgaria."

Barbour considered and spoke. "The members of that group all want to eat of the lotus without losing their grasp. But they are captives nevertheless, like Midas."

Ambassador Ron leaned back. Such philosophizing bored him but, having just had a raise himself, he was no hypocrite. "Ah yes, perhaps the lotus, better than eating a bank vault, to be sure. Remember Tennyson? 'There is sweet music here that softer falls/Than petals from blown roses on the grass ... music that brings sweet sleep down from the blissful skies.' Blissful, you see, Lee? Old man C is looking for bliss. So am I. My club in New York is the Lotos, spelled with an 'o'. It honors bliss, and we have some walloping good times."

Barbour grinned. "You see, I told you so! The power guys come out of New York."

Ambassador Owen felt not one whit guilty. He liked the Big Apple.

Sophie said, "Let's get back to business. I take that to be, in part, beyond getting the Austrians straightened out, World War III prevented; getting a handle on the twelve billion dollars the Bulgarian government so badly needs returned; and formalizing what we know about where and who the bad guys in this particular show may be."

Yes, they all agreed that was what they were about. But at that moment Ambassador Owen's secretary knocked and entered.

"There's an urgent message for Miss Dubois. The caller said she was to be given it right away."

"That urgent?"

"'As urgent as life itself,' the caller said, but then he had an Irish accent, and they're all eloquent, aren't they? If not fey."

She handed a note to Claire, who read it—a mix of pain, puzzlement, pleasure crossing her face. She looked up and said, "An old friend from Cambridge saw me on the CNN show, Professor Garrity. He congratulates me on my being alive, reminds me that years ago he warned me of crime in Moscow, says that as soon as possible he must see me to tell me something urgently important, and asks me to remember Noisui in the *Tain*."

"Who and why?" asked Barbour, for the lover in him was not pleased. Claire's reaction was visibly intense, and Garrity was clearly not just a professorial acquaintance. Claire was no poker face. Who was this man of whom he had never heard, who could intrude and so easily command her attention during a meeting as important as this one? Barbour flushed with a jealousy of which he felt obscurely ashamed.

Claire was confused by her own reaction, both to Gavin's mysterious message and her reaction to the once-lover who had been so cold just last year at the Cambridge symposium where he'd spoken, and yes, where he'd introduced her to Senator Cranmer, who'd helped her get the IFFY job. She found herself biting her lip and thinking somewhat defensively. She knew that whatever she said to Barbour would not come across as it should. After all, she'd never yet had reason or duty to mention Gavin to him. So, one might call it diplomatically but it was wilier than that, she answered the content, not the meaning of his question, for she did not know herself what message Gavin had disguised.

She took a breath and answered, "The *Tain* is an Homeric epic of Ireland, perhaps more than two thousand years old. In it there's Derdrui, who's engaged to a king she loathes. She runs off with a prince, Noisui, but they're caught and Noisui is killed. Derdrui is forced to marry the king. There's lovely poetry there as she mourns Noisui; she never smiles again. Finally she kills herself. I don't know really, most of it's about kings, and battles, and the tragedy of loss, and the power of women. I suppose that Gavin," she caught herself as she used his first name, surprised that she was embarrassed, trying to be guileful but not very good at it, "I suppose Professor Garrity's trying to tell me something."

Barbour flushed, "About your being with me? Who is this guy anyway?" He was suddenly angry, without knowing—well, admitting—why. All lovers will come to this, to jealousy leaping up, to the exercise of felt rights of possession that are not yet granted.

Claire couldn't handle it face on. "He's no one special." Women's lies are like spring hats; they fit the color of the moment. "He was a professor of mine at Cambridge years ago, that's all; an economist specializing in Eastern Europe. Even then he knew how it was going to come apart with crime. He's famous by now, but typical in a way—though an economist, he never really cared about money, just research and books. Anyway, I'm flattered he's glad I'm alive, and pleased he's still concerned." Claire, in one sensible moment of anchoring, reached across and held Barbour's hand. He relaxed. Through the ages a man's hand strongly clasped has always been the quickest path for a woman's fib to reach belief.

"Please excuse me," she said, "I'm going to call him back. Maybe he has some light to shed on all this. Lord knows he's studied it all enough." She brushed out of the room. All three of them pretended to not be as puzzled as they really were. It was Sophie who came to the heart of it. After all, she did feel a bit motherly about the two, and worried out loud.

"Aposematic, I wonder. The *Tain* and Derdrui's fate as the oracular aposematic?"

Neither man knew what she meant. Sophie explained, "Is this professor the man who would not be king but oracle? I feel—well, Claire made it clear in telling the tale, that there's an ominous portent there. *Aposematic*, a great word because nobody uses it, I do want to show it off—it comes from biology, but means a warning, like the rattle of a rattlesnake, just shown or heard. Garrity, who obviously is Irish, draws from some particular cultural store we don't know about. I'm not at all sure Claire doesn't. But she's just told us Derdrui and her runaway lover, both die at the hands of the powerful." Sophie was thoughtful. "I read as much of Eastern European economics as I can. I vaguely recall an article in *Foreign Affairs Quarterly* by a Garrity some years ago. It was very good. It worries me in a way that the man does know what he's talking about. I'm sorry, Lee, it's not my business, but as a woman I'm quite sure Claire knows

Professor Garrity rather better than she admits."

Barbour was glum.

Claire returned perhaps ten minutes later. She was flustered. "He says he has to see me. He was all very mysterious, but kept reminding me of the *Tain*. Obviously he thinks telephones aren't secure. Right now he's chairing a conference in Strasbourg at the European Parliament. Maybe he's a member, or it's an expert committee; I don't know. I told him I could meet him tomorrow in Geneva. It's midway between, and an easy flight for us both."

Barbour was angry now, exercising those lover's rights not even discussed, let alone granted. "All right, I'll go with you. I don't like any of this at all."

Whatever it had been before, the group of four had become intimates now, with reference to love, fear, and jealousy, as well as to criminal violence and international politics.

"I do understand, Lee, and I appreciate it. But Gavin," she paused, allowing her first partial confession, "yes, I did know him on a first-name basis at Cambridge. But it was so long ago. Gavin said it's very, very delicate. He used the word 'minefield.' I think he knows something that can help us. Lord knows after all that research on Russian economics, with all the powerful and sleazy people he's met doing it, it wouldn't be a surprise. Frankly I think it's Gavin that's in danger, not me. Maybe what I know can help him. Maybe in some other way the Russians are threatening him. Look, I just can't let an old friend, who may be in real trouble, well—twist in the wind."

Barbour looked at her in pain and anger. "So you quote that great sentimentalist Richard Nixon and his thugs to imagine our professor is Noisui and you are, or were, Derdrui? Deirdre, if we're modern?"

Claire's face was sad. "You must understand, Lee, it was all a long time ago. It's been over for years. And yes, his pet name for me was Deirdre, but no, he was never a Noisui. Frankly however much I admired him, I think there was always too much caution in him. He was no fierce *Tain* king Cuchulainn *cum* Achilles, trained to war by three women—hardly. Fact is, he was scared silly of his wife. So was I, frankly. Both of us for good reason. Will it help if I tell you all she threatened to kill him and his children? Her name was Medea, and she *was* from Georgia, what was Colchis in the days of Jason and the Golden Fleece. She's probably still ferocious."

"So, kidnapped in Vienna, under siege in Laxenburg, and now to be killed by an insanely jealous wife in Geneva? Is that the scenario?" Barbour couldn't help but be sarcastic, bitter. Nor could the two ambassadors looking on be anything but embarrassed. It was suddenly too intimate and yes, there were portents of danger. Whence was less clear.

Barbour looked at Ron Owen. "I suppose there's no good reason she can't leave the Embassy? You trust the Austrian police to be under enough control by now to have the good guys arresting the bad guys, instead of trying to assassinate us like they did a couple of nights ago when we broke in here? I suppose if they try, it can only be out of pique since we've told all on CNN, and no doubt you and Washington, London too I'd guess, have been working like hell to get the Austrians into line?"

Ron Owen nodded. "Yep, as far as I know, the good guys won the last three shootouts. You and your unmentionable—except here in this room—Sergeant Erwin in Laxenburg, you two on CNN winning by a knockout yesterday, and from what I learned from the Austrian Foreign Ministry this morning, all of the above, gave the Austrian Government freedom and public reason to move against at least the dirty cops so far identified, and to let loose some telling political blasts at the opposition left and right. You should see the morning papers. Black into white. Jubilation of righteousness and all that. The Foreign Ministry told me this morning, that's all I can tell you, you're all free to move about. No criminal charges, maybe someday a public apology. Who knows, Lee? You and Injun Joe Erwin, Claire and the Wipplingers, once it's safe, will get a secret medal from the Austrians." The Ambassador smiled. "Or so I have it on very good authority. I hear tell the Chancellor's wife has a particularly warm spot in her heart for Americans."

There would be nothing more on that from Ambassador Owen. He was now all official discretion, the sphinx of Vienna so to speak. Not that Ron Owen hadn't heard unofficially just how it was that the State Department had been so *fully* informed of the Austrian government's situation and intentions throughout the crisis. His mind wandered back to the time when he had known Quincy Adams in Washington, Quincy now resident guru in a major London political think tank not entirely unallied to the Foreign Ministry and the Home Office. But then in London no useful private institution was out of the Establishment loop. England was a tribal society made up of gentlemen who kept in touch. As for Quincy, that devil had always been a lady's man, but to be still carrying on something with the Chancellor's wife—well, now that was *savoir faire*.

The meeting ended, summarizing. Barbour would come to Sofia soon, to explore with Ambassador Sophie such connections as they might muster to get Vasil out of Bulgaria.

"I think I can find a string that might pull Vasil to the FBI Academy," she said, "if the FBI plays ball. Not that quickie outfit they have in Hungary, but the real thing, in Quantico. Or maybe Treasury can lean on Interpol in Lille, France, to get Vasil there. I can surely arrange—worst comes to worst but good for us, for sure—for him to be appointed Security Liaison between the Interior Ministry and my own Embassy." She was thinking of the next bunch of American aid money coming in. "Strings on loans and aid, monies not yet received, are notoriously successful bargaining chips."

"But we're still missing a lot of names, aren't we? Probably some of the biggest, when it comes to the Bulgarian caper. I have no idea where or how we can look further, unless maybe the Bulgarians lean on the UST&D Bank to add a few." Ron Owen was reflecting.

"No chance, Ron," commented Sophie. "I can pull strings at Vasil's level, but UST&D is an outfit that's been built into thc Bulgarian financial woodwork for eight digging-in-deep years. No chance, with all the opposition and uncertainty, that the government is going to take on that institution. Its assets probably are greater than the government's own. It's connected into every nook and cranny, including the dirty ones. And since they do give development loans, private ones that the European Bank for Reconstruction and Development won't make, UST&D owns a lot of paper and people. Frankly, give it credit, it's playing an important role in financing Bulgarian development. Real investments, even if some of it is bound to be dirty Russian, Ukrainian, Belarus money looking for clean income. Whoever the bad guys in it are—and I have to presume at least the major executives, some of them on the Board—no one is going to touch them."

"I hope we haven't forgotten," it was Barbour speaking, "Mr. C, or Cie and C, as it and he may be. If he really is in California, and yesterday I heard IFFY had sent a friend of mine in management named Dolan out there for a real push, just as it seemed when we began and especially now that Brody is bye-bye, C may be our only way of opening the remaining sealed pages in the book. Another American connection as I told you almost has to be there in New York, and again someone big in London. People managing the major money. It will be billions upon billions."

"There's no one we can lean on except Tudor Mihailov, who may be our sitting duck right there at home in old Virginee. So that's all we have after all. As for finding Mr. C, my morning's Washington IFFY cable from my good-guy boss Mac McLaughlin, tells me that DEA has abandoned interest in C out of sheer bureaucratic venom. But they've found one of his haunts, anyway: Malome, California, one time-murder capital of America. I was there just last month it so happens, with one of my best friends from uglier Washington days who's retired, if you can call it that, to become a detective. So we have Dolan and my friend Markowitz pulling out all the stops to find a ghost. And for what it's worth, and minding our steps because he sure as hell has to have powerful protection or be the biggest idiot this side of *Mad Magazine*, to find one Todor Mihailov, the original billion-dollar thief."

The group broke up with hugs all around, well wishes and fingers crossed, see-you-soons and knew they would, Sofia and Vienna most likely within the month, and for Claire beyond Geneva for a day, her father in Kiev or, preferably, London. Ron, too, had London in mind, and Quincy Adams' and, better there than Kiev, George Dubois and Sir Peter Dixon, of whom he'd heard but not met. For Sophie, London was unlikely, but Washington was easily called. And so they agreed, since IFFY after all and State were there, it might be Washington where next they met.

Claire, who was maintaining many silences now in her internal disarray, knew it would not be Washington for long. Every time she looked in the mirror at her still-blemished cheek she thought of the Jonesys, how ready they all had been to believe that she was Greta Liebowitz. For God's sake, how could they? It was so insulting. And in their hurry to cover their fannies, they'd sent her off so unprepared, although she had been stupid too, it was true, to Vienna and considerable pain and almost death.

"I will," she said to herself, "be sure that all the clowns I see in the future are in the circus. No matter if it disappoints Daddy, I've had it up the gazebo with bureaucracy."

Her thoughts, a muddle and a passion, returned to Lee Barbour. He was in the bureaucracy temporarily recalled on his own terms. What did he plan for his life? Did he really want her to be part of whatever they might or might not be able to make together? What did she want? Before this meeting she had been quite sure it was Lee Barbour. But if so, why had she so outrageously sabotaged everything with him just now? Gracelessly yes, and embarrassingly yes all of a muddle, just because Gavin Garrity, old love, cold love, almost nasty when last they met in Cambridge, cowardly in fact, and pussy-whipped by Medea, except for the fact that Medea's vengeance was no fantasy, just because "Professor Garrity" had called.

"What's happening to me?" It came to her only in patches and pieces, not as her calculating brain working but rising up from the reptilian old brain, the deep-down limbic in us all. She had read about that, where sex and fear and smells and anger and hormones assembled and set forth, with never a chance for mind to know about it until afterwards.

"No," she thought, "I certainly don't love Gavin Garrity. If anything, I dislike the bastard. But it was his note and the fear in his voice, just like when we were lovers and Medea really was going to kill his children and us if she found out. It was contagious, then, his fear of her, and its contagion is infecting me now."

Since the kidnapping, and Laxenburg, and coming into the embassy in a hail of bullets, she wasn't as good at handling fear as before. But then she'd never been really afraid before. Fear climbed directly into the nostrils of that olfactory-connected reptile brain, down deep in her skull. She could smell it, his smell, Medea's smell, Square's and Glove's and Pistol's smells. Her own smell, too, and no perfume of woman to it—she was *afraid*. And what he had said to Deirdre was ominous; that was why she was going to Geneva. "And yes, I think maybe Lee Barbour is King Garrity's Noisui. Or does Garrity think himself, oh that great Irish 'himself', to be Noisui, whom somehow in this mess of evil money Garrity thinks his Deirdre-Derdrui is somehow stupidly going to get him killed? What is it that's going through my mind?" She almost screamed it, "Get this snake-brain fear out of me!"

For this very evening, Barbour had booked a luxurious double room through André at the Schwarzenburg. After their stolen intimacies at the Wipplingers, limited out of respect for decorum, the sensibilities of their host, and not wanting to flaunt anything in front of the sergeant either, there had been last night, after the CNN drama, an agreement: that Claire and he would celebrate togetherness, intimately, privately, tonight. He had, after one bad marriage so long ago which had gone on for far too long, never thought he might again—but yes, he might again, and might this night have proposed. He loved her. He had thought it ran both ways. It didn't look like it now. Grown men do cry, and for honesty's sake should cry, but they try not to. He only half succeeded. His eyes were burning. Depression covered him like a clinging cold fog.

He had been too upset to be anything but awkward with her as they left the room. Business and discretion had impelled the two ambassadors to hurry out of the luncheon conference room, out of Ron's office, to somewhere else in the building. They had left the office to the ill-omened, disrupted lovebirds. Barbour was so damned angry and hurt, but he didn't want her to leave. He had to talk to her. "But what the hell can I say?" he wondered.

"Aposematic," Barbour said to Claire, "meaning, so Sophie tells me, your old friend Gavin, she says the word is used in biology for markings or warnings. So he's our rattlesnake rattling, right?" Lovers can be so foolish in what they say.

She bristled, but what else is a woman to do when she's angry with herself and has a truth she will not tell?

She glared at him. "Gavin is an old friend and he's frightened about something that has something maybe to do with this whole mess. Lee, you know that. Now, please don't make a fuss. He's nothing to me. That was over a long time ago."

"Which is why you go to Geneva the minute he whistles for you, his sweet Deirdre, right?"

"No!" she shouted it. He had gestured for them to sit down on the great dark red leather sofa in Ron's office, even gestured a question toward the bar should she like a glass of wine. She stood angrily, stiffly, against him as in an opposing wind.

What she might have said, she didn't. What he should have said at this moment, he couldn't. Until finally, he asked, "Well, I suppose that finishes our plans for a first private night together, doesn't it?"

"I suppose it does." Both voices were full of conditionals, dares, defenses, pleas. Voices waiting for self-imposed wreckage of dreams.

"Well?"

"Lee, I just don't know." What a stupid moment it was, somewhere within her she knew, to reject this man.

"Call me when you find out." Inside himself he knew his was the idiotic male ego, set hard in challenge. He wanted to say, "Please, I love you." He didn't have the strength, or weakness, to be that open. He'd been hurt. He was angry. And this Garrity was his natural enemy.

That night, his first away from siege and embassy captivity, Lee stayed in the mass-produced, sterile pseudo-luxury of the Intercontinental. He kept his automatic under his pillow, but it was not danger that made him unable to sleep.

That night Claire also failed to be able to sleep in the guest room within the embassy, where she had been for the several nights before, though none as miserable as this one. The next morning Sergeant Erwin, no longer Injun Joe, and a companion Marine, both in civvies but with illegally concealed side arms, drove her to the airport for the plane to Geneva. Ambassador Owen kissed his friend's child, now a woman, good-bye for the day. He did it with misgivings stemming from more sources than he could identify, but surely her row with Barbour, whom he liked very much, was one. An antsy Cambridge professor full of Irish stories scaring the poor girl into an emergency meeting seemed a poor reason to the Ambassador for troubling, it seemed, an ideal relationship. He took Barbour's view of it. Claire had been silly and stupid.

Sophie had left on the seven-thirty a.m. plane for Sofia. She arose too early to see any of them for a goodbye. Of all of them she had the most sensitive ear for oracles telling of epic tales, of Deirdres and Noisuis. An old hand at crises and alarums, she had slept, but with nightmares. She felt so tired. Oblomovism again? The Vienna Incident, the Sofia Source, the fat man who couldn't swim, and now the famous Irish professor, expert in the mess that was Russian economics, himself obviously once Claire's lover, himself so Irishly full of tales and strong yet with the power to beckon her, himself with an at least once murderous wife named Medea. "The doomed house of Jason?" she asked herself, "or maybe Iago whispering to Desdemona, not to Othello? Life follows art. Villainy follows everywhere."

She decided she would invite Vasil and his wife to dinner. It was not done of course, the high and the low over a meal; the ambassador herself would cook. But with Barbour whom she had much admired not available, and this mess clearly going to keep Sofia, the city, hot with intrigue and sometimes deadly, the politics of it sly worms speaking in double tongues, she needed another honest man and true, pleasant and honorable, yet expert on villainy just to check her readings. Nothing sensitive, nothing indiscreet, just general readings of the Bulgarian compass. That compass was so easily guided to false north by lies, by evil, by its ancient-running *Bogomil* curse.

"As for Junior," (her term now for Ernest, who ran the two-room "Station" behind its special locked steel doors inside her building), "I'll see if I can't find a good strong string to pull him home. How good it would be to get someone like Barbour as Chief of Station!" Too bad he quit the cigar factory so long ago, and but for his temporary duty voluntary recall to IFFY, had turned his back on bureaucracy as well. Out loud she said, "But, oh I so surely do understand."

36

The CNN broadcast had attracted viewers. In Sir Peter's apartment overlooking the Thames, across from the MI5 building, Peter, Quincy, and other friends gathered. They thoroughly enjoyed the crafted performances. There was applause—and a quiet reminder to each other that however well things were progressing, surprises might loom ahead.

Quincy told Peter of his recent private mail from Vienna. The Chancellor had enclosed a brief note in the same envelope that carried his wife's letter to Quincy. Quincy was not at all sure that she knew of the insert. Her note, warm and brief, thanked him for his patience, his role, and his faith in Austria during its crisis. The Chancellor expressed his appreciation for being such a friend to both himself, "although without introductions," and "over the years" to his beloved and most helpful wife. And also, during the crisis, for Quincy's playing his middleman role, "advising your patient friends in Washington of our realities." Now *there* in message and manner at multiple levels, was *savoir faire*. "That girl has married well," he said to himself. "God bless them both." He lit a cigar in complete satisfaction. Austria was for the moment in excellent hands.

In Washington Senator Cranmer, together with those seniors on his staff for his not yet launched campaign, watched the Vienna show. He himself was a professional producer of theater—all senators were—who now watched a competing show. Well done, Vienna. It would be more than a minor setback if international crisis upon which Cranmer's campaign would depend were indeed calmed, but other cards remained up his sleeve. A man who very much wants to be President, supported by powerful interest groups, electable time and again to the Senate, is not to be counted out because a few pros in Vienna have scripted things well. Nothing truly disastrous to his cause had emerged.

Cranmer's possible running mate, the congressman whom Barbour had baited, had looked the very fool and thereby guaranteed himself not to be Vice President on the ticket. Learning that was useful in itself, and came at no cost to the Senator. It was the future that mattered. There were phone calls, plans to be made. No one expected becoming President to be easy.

In Virginia, Todor Mihailov had found himself amused. A free press, or rather an imaginative, manipulative, mindlessly entertaining Fourth estate, was rather fun to watch. Nothing in Vienna that he had seen was cause for concern. Stupid Russians, they had brought it on themselves. Stupid Austrians, they had always been that way. The Americans were making it on sheer bravado, but after all they were rich and powerful—which was, in part, why he had come here. He had not given up being a Bulgarian. Never. Pride was his. Bulgaria made its alliances with the strong. When there was no choice, it succumbed to them. Roman, Byzantine, Mongol, Turk; briefly and northerly incursions by Vlad the Impaler; then, in force Nazis, Russians. In Todor's view, democracy, America and the European Community were also invaders to be accommodated and manipulated. Nowhere in that history had been a major solo alliance with the Austro-Hungarians. But CNN from Vienna brought waltzes to mind. Todor had a new young mistress. He bade her play some Strauss in honor of the dance, and of the world, which he had made into fools. Todor was not aware that outside, even now entering the manicured lawns of his estate, well-trained men clad in black had inconvenienced his guards by slitting their throats. Todor should not have been playing Strauss, but Saint-Saëns' *Dance Macabre*, that *Dance of Death*.

In Moscow the Oligarch, the pre-eminent one of several, called in the premier. An unpleasant scene ensued after which a chastened premier, having overestimated his powers, did as he was bid. He recorded for television—there were cameras and staff always at the ready in the Kremlin—a speech that once again rattled sabers. Austrians, Americans, British, even Hottentots, if he had been ordered to name them as well, were perfidious! All the powers were plotting against Mother Russia! Shades of the paranoid rhetoric of the past. Russia would not have its diplomats in Vienna pilloried and suspected, some of them murdered by Americans and their British allies. Russia, a great power always, home of the Slavs and the Patriarchy of the Church, economically one of the Group of Eight after all, demanded respect—at any cost. In a voice that was not entirely convincing he ordered initial mobilization, a military alert.

The Oligarch, who handled such mechanics himself lest the children in office screw up, dispatched a formal message to the general staff. This mobilization was "for show only, you understand." The premier, not entirely sure what he should do but being patched through to the always reliable General Bratislav, could only awkwardly repeat, his heart not in it, the thrust of his television speech. Bratislav had already had his coded e-mail as to which theater the Oligarch intended. There was no reason to spoil an evening of love-making because this nervous puppet was on the phone. Bratislav said only, "Yes, premier," and "yes, premier." It was difficult to appear to talk seriously on the phone, while laughing at the puppet premier and foreplaying vigorous love, but he and the Bulgarian girl managed it.

In Kiev a happy father looked forward to arranging a visit with his daughter soon in London. He had enjoyed the staging of the CNN interviews; he knew from Ron that Claire had been made up to look a bit more damaged than she was; the more he reflected, the more pleased he was with the idea of Barbour as son-in-law. In the meantime, there was bothersome news of Russian fleet maneuvers off the Crimea. It was now owned by the Ukraine, but the status of naval bases and forces there was a bit dicey. That the U.S. Mediterranean fleet had staged joint naval war games with the Ukrainians, with the Russian navy looking on, left out and thoroughly displeased, had exaggerated the tension. News of the threatening speech by the Russian premier, so much in the tradition of the old Soviets rather than of a new and democratic Russia, reminded him, everyone, that the Russian military, paranoid Slavic ideological card could be put in play by anyone clever enough to steal the deck. There were many such thieves in authority to play that game.

In Malome, California, another scene was set, another dance begun.

37

Markowitz and Stein wished Dolan luck. Over the telephone, the DEA's Alan Grossman, who was stuck in the big city charged with managing a Headquarters-sabotaged office, wished them the same. Apologetically.

Dolan had been a street cop once, a long time ago. It was his first job out of college, before he went back to get his Ph.D. Probably he'd done it before he'd begun to shave. Happily it was in an upper-class town. The big job was to be polite, and issue traffic tickets only to nonresidents. Oh yes, he'd had other relevant experience. Undercover? He'd done that financial detective style in the big time. Covert? Yeah, for a few years with the Agency during that difficult period when it wasn't certain that anything but high tech and magazine subscriptions were needed for intelligence gathering; when the analysts were kings, and it had hired its first ten slick PR agents. It needed them badly. Still did.

His communications system with Markowitz and Stein was set up. Small cell phones here and there about town hidden in garbage cans deeper than the homeless searching them for food would go. You could do that by putting them under the can. Use the same spots for drops, if need be. Only five devices on his soon-to-be-stinking person: mike, transmitter and tiny receiver under his filthy shirt, his 9-mm automatic likewise. And a near-useless, in his view, .32 in an ankle holster, under his likewise ragged high wool socks. Not even a bulletproof vest. He felt damn near naked, except in the shopping cart that his homeless self would be pushing, were a sawed-off shotgun and an Uzi, both wrapped in filthy burlap sacks.

"With these I take on the world, eh?"

"Right, buddy." said Markowitz, giving him a warm grip about the shoulder. "With those you are Rooster's one and only immediate set of eyes and ears behind that lad's very exposed back. This is only a little town, two miles across from dead bodies north and south, east and west. One of us will be on your solo frequency 24 hours a day. The chief got his marching orders about our twelve-hour shifts, seven days a week from the Federal prosecutor in the City via the county manager who controls half the Police Department's budget. He told the chief chump there was a very hush-hush tip to the effect that a federal witness living here under the witness protection program was being gang-hunted by the Bloods out of L.A. Our names were given him, the prosecutor tells him, as 'trustworthy,' we were the angels going to be assigned, 'period' he said. The PD, in recognition of its supportive services, would have four thousand a week put in its kitty for discretionary use; that's to be handed directly to the Chief for his 'narcotic fund' slush bucket for each week we are pulled off other duties. Chief loved it. Dislikes us both anyway, and loves the money. He'll tell everyone he can, of course. They're all Crips first, and doubting that, think Hispanics and maybe the Lobo gang; they won't envy either of us a bit working eighty four hours a week and, in their view, very likely to get shot for our troubles. A big funeral and quiet cheers, and IFFY at least got the money through a savvy prosecutor. So all, you see, is well with the world."

Dolan knew this was his duty. He liked Rooster a lot, and was excited by a field assignment right down and dirty in the nitty-gritty after so long playing mostly the accounting heavy in overseas banks. He had only one problem. "It scares me shitless."

"Bravo, brother." said Patrolman Andy Stein. "It do that to us all. Welcome to the club." It *was* a club. Dolan was honored, as a real man is, to be in it.

"Besides surveilling Rooster, what the hell do I do all day? I mean just sitting next to garbage cans isn't enough. Besides, I should be taking notes or something, don't you think?"

"You literary types," Markowitz grinned. "But yeah, why not? You can be an ex-writer-turned-drunk. Ex-writers write; folks around will get used to it, and know for sure you're loony. For sure nobody out here writes, especially not sitting on curbstones with a bottle of cheap booze for inspiration. Yeah, what the hell? Stuff your rolling office in here." He gestured toward the shopping cart whose motley contents had been hand-selected after a drug bust in a homeless encampment under a nearby bridge. "Stuff it with notebooks, somebody's old school exams, paper and second-hand ball points galore. Gives you an image; nutty, harmless, cooty old coot."

We have Dolan's narrative, begun that first day:

Imagine me—a honky, amateur, scared-shitless, half a cop, and that by pretense, playing undercover whiz-bang in this black, Hispanic, Filipino, Samoan town. Like sending a non-German-speaking fresh Sandhurst lieutenant to a Junkers general staff meeting wearing green whiskers and a swagger stick for disguise. It was not that I recommended myself for the job. But my fate's not as bad as Markowitz' here. Poor bastard, I am beginning to like the guy. He doesn't know I know his history but I made sure I got it before I came here. Markowitz fell foul of two senior bureaucrats in his Bureau and his ass hung high. Still does. There is certain justice in this work world, as we all know: do well, and your punishment will be swift and certain. They wanted him dead because he caught their hand in the narcotics buy money to the tune of $283,437.83. His criminal complaint is filed, Internal Audit is working on the case, God is in his heaven, and Markowitz and his buddy in that same whistle-blowing caper, not counting some more serious stuff which is only rumored, will never enjoy justice. There ain't any.

And so here I scribble, sitting on a curbstone outside the gambling joint where I have seen little Mr. R go in. To keep alive here *and* do my work, thanks to the helpful ideas of Markowitz and Stein, I souse my utterly filthy clothes with whiskey, lunch and dinner drippings dribbling down. I have to keep up the sour smell of being a drunk. I do daily poor man's nickel buys of such rock cocaine and free base as are consistent with my story. Reputation building? Well, if anyone asks I tell them I'm a once rich and famous writer who did a little time in the nut house; I admit that ideas about which end is up are not entirely clear in my head. My ex-wife got all the money. Most men will sympathize with that; so do the whores. Everybody in Malome understands losing and taking money.

I tell them—already now a few winos, youngest of the street kids, a coke head or two have asked—that I am trying to make the grade as a novice pickpocket. Amazing, even though I'm sitting down on the curb their hands go right to their stash. Socks, wallets hung under their shirt, one guy keeps his bills in his hash pouch. Amazing what giving of a little confidence will get you by way of insight.

None of this will keep me or Mr R alive except for some street smarts I've got to learn fast, and that firepower which I keep handy. I am, let's face it, not cut out for this. Too many hours in offices. And here I am in Malome. I feel odd, and scared as I write you. And yes, I am writing to you, Doreen, wife of mine, because I must focus on something personal and lovely. I know you hate my being a cop here. It scares you too. But I had to do it, my love. Everything is on the line respecting Mr. C. As you read, even hints of World War III from overseas, as C is part of the key to the war-mongering.

The job I do is odd enough, or has the odds against it, an odds-bodkins cop if you enjoy Willie the Bard. Quoting him, I "would fain die a dry death." No, not as a scared "Tempest" sailor, but around here I am learning in a hurry that a dry death is one where the blood stays inside, not bleeding all over. Or one is not dumped heavy into the water. The Bay is near here and, methinks, forsooth and all that, it receives a lot of fish food dumped in the a.m. off the bridge. Chum for little sharks, crabs, striped bass maybe.

Environmentally sound, wouldn't you say? Other people call the dumping structure a bridge, but from what I hear, it's a convenient disposal facility for murderers.

Malome is "underclass"—a census sociologists' word. I have a Harvard friend, David, who on occasion wears a green velvet dinner jacket that belonged to his grand-uncle back in England who was Lord something or other. David's uncle invites him to their fancy manor house across the pond for some weeks in the summer. David looks at zebras there. That side of the family is heavily into zebras. The place is, as we Americans say, a zoo.

David says I am not to use the word "underclass," because it implies that the people defined by our U.S. Census as "underclass" do actually exist. "Common usage, but implicitly wrong, prejudicial," says David. "It implies they are not as good as the rest of us. It implies," David says—and he uses a fine Harvard English—"that they are criminal, lowdown, dirty, diseased, depressed, inept, unemployed, uneducated, on welfare, and hopeless."

"Right on, David," I say, balking only at the "hopeless," since some of the folks I know here are aiming for, and may get, the brass ring. Mr. C seems to have not a brass but a gold ring. Not everybody who rubs underclass shoulders, or noses, is what he seems. Out of the underclass, come big big bucks it seems, and from what we hear, world-class connections.

David, as you know, Doreen, finds me revolting. A bigot. I don't know. Am I? I know you agree with David. But Malome *is* a miserable town, as defined by the quality of life of the people who live here. That's my private opinion. The houses aren't bad, better than most in New Haven that I've seen. Streets are paved; sewers work; there are not enough street lights, it's true, but plenty of liquor stores. Lot of good people live here. Behind bars, of course—not jail-cell ones, but bars they put up on their own windows in order to live through the night. People don't go walking in the evenings, as you might guess. Unless they're drug dealers, and even they move in company.

"Cat feet," I call them, as I come across them in their favorite park of an evening. Carl Sandburg's fog. They don't walk, they float; they drift along like ground fog. Creep, yes, but it's creepy. Their feet don't touch the ground. A patrol car comes toward them and, floating, there seems no hurry but it's really fast after all, they disappear.

You might call this town the regional adult amusement park, something akin to what Boston set aside for an "adult entertainment" zone. Dandy. The favorite game, again I don't deny that I am a cynic, now after just a day on the curbstone, and in fact a very depressed one, is "bump 'em." You remember that from the days when you were a kid and went to amusement parks or to carnivals. Little electric cars with all-around rubber bumpers and all of us little bastards, yes, me too, shouted with glee as we revved up that five-mile-an-hour Maserati and rammed our little girlfriends as hard as we could. Remember later, Doreen, we did some ramming in bed. We were all too young, you and me, to realize that kind of childhood carnival ramming is sublimation. I loved her so I hit her, so to speak. Our kind of "bump 'em" here is a variant, like yellow sparrows in the Galapagos, or some such, evolving. Our "bump 'em" here is "bump 'em off." A good game and all that. In consequence, the only really classy business building in town is the mortuary. It's an ill wind, etc.

This town is famous for its violence rate. The newspapers credited us two years ago with two guys killed per 1,000 residents, and another 50 per 1,000 badly damaged. That was a national record. Shows you can't even be a shooter these days without knowing your Guinness records.

Baseball and violence, the two great American sports. Ice hockey is when those two sports get married. In baseball you got umpires, half blind, I grant you, who keep score. Out here homicide statistics are articles of faith. No problem counting the bodies you find, although I have heard arguments within the police department as to whether he's "ours" or "theirs" when the body stretches over a two-city boundary. And there was this time last year when the chief, getting embarrassed about the homicide rate, although it sure was no fault of his, claimed that in an incident where two guys shot each other simultaneously, it was, I quote, "one shooting."

Maybe yes, maybe no, but it tells you what every citizen needs to know about police crime stats. The shootings of course, among adults, are about money. For the gang kids it's more like play. When we find Mr. C it's going to be about whose laws rule.

Sitting on the curb here, just waiting for Rooster, or "Kid R," as I've come to think of him, across the street, I will be tangential. But informative. If this town weren't so close to a first-class hospital's trauma room, the murder rate would double just because of distance and emergency room staff's lesser competence. Same as it would go up if it weren't for the public health nurses in this town who, as home visitors, sterilize and bandage some of the unreported wounds and keep the patient pumped up with antibiotics.

Illegal as hell for a nurse to do that; the law says gunshot and stab wounds have to be reported. But she knows the victims won't, and if she does then she gets killed, and then the families she visits get no more medical care. All lawlessness is not selfish, as any cop bending the rules knows. And most cops bend the rules every day. Think no evil of us though, sometimes it's necessary. Doreen, remember last year when your brother was driving drunk and the cop kindly drove him home, no jail and no ticket? Give a big hand for the cop as curbstone magistrate.

I figure a fellow as visible and vulnerable as me can figure to be mugged maybe two, three times a day out here, and ripped off in almost every drug transaction. I have reduced that expected rate, a phrase epidemiological statisticians enjoy, to about zero by successful crime fighting. A national model? You bet. I have this one day threatened to shoot, by actual count, seven greedy people. No bluff. They see me pull the gun. I hold it a bit unsteady for theater's sake, but they can stare right down the barrel. Their Star Trek wormhole.

I have to be careful not to kill anybody, which is a kind of morality. Self-control and a loud voice keep me from getting busted, then exposed, and Mr. R with no one to cover his back. It is already leading to a live-and-let-die standoff between me and the local young ones, whereas no savvy older gangsters out here would have bothered with me in the first place. If I have to I will shoot as many somebodies as I must. I like you, Doreen, and want to come home to you walking with all parts intact and ready to give you the greeting that missing you so deserves.

It's been a couple of days now. I'm an accepted dangerous drunken friendly scribbling one-more-local freak. And Mr. R, bustling all the time, I do have to move this cart high speed sometimes, seems to be doing just fine.

"How you doing, Rusty?" I always greet people jolly like. Rusty is one of the better looking high flyers in town, dyed red hair straightened, nice tits, enticing saunter. Hangs on the arm of middle level dealers, chop-shop mechanics, once in a while a fancier dude short on his regular stable. We're friends, insofar as that is possible here. She thinks I'm a voyeur, really "auditeur." I pay her to tell me in great detail of her sexual encounters. Since for her these are theater anyway, she doesn't mind, particularly since the pay is good. Doreen, don't get upset, for along this casual chaste way she's gotten used to telling me who, what they do; where they live; who comes along for the ride, yes, pun intended; whether the money is running or not; and thus, lo and behold, she is an intelligence source. I am only a dirty old man who chuckles and slobbers, but I am good-natured to her. I would like nothing better than to find Mr. C before Mr. R does.

That's for his sake. I have electronics to call for backup and am more heavily armed. When I flash a Federal badge, should that glorious moment come, Mr. C will pause. On the other hand, he'll blow Kid R away like slapping a fly.

Today Rusty's walking on by me. On her way to, not from, work. Maybe around five o'clock tonight I'll learn more. She's auditioning, she tells me, for Purple Willie to work the back room of his newly remodeled and quite sparkling Classy Black Club.

Desegregation. White players are now bussed in for the action, just like black kids are bussed out of town for school. Purple Willie and Frank have teamed up with the mob. Rusty does have eyes and ears as well as what's between her legs, which apparatus is interesting to one 'Dimples' who comes down from Nevada, and on her, from time to time. Dimples works for Mr. Smith; yeah, I know, sure, and is keeping a slow eye on things. Low self-esteem. He hypes himself by talking too much to Rusty to whom, poor dear, he has taken a fancy. His fortune cookie forecasts a short span.

"Got a minute, Bo?"

"Hell yes, I got hours. Judge gave me years once but I figured he was too generous with my time. So I left," was what I replied. Out here that's a joke.

Miguel was the fellow who had hailed me. He lives in an apartment off Coleridge, full of illegals living ten to a room. Poor bastards. Kids all over the place. There's a man who OD'd dying on the ground; kids bouncing the soccer balls right over him. Cops come swinging in in black and whites, red lights like tiger eyes. They're chasing a knifer on an aggravated assault, I should say so, 245 in the California code, call. Junkie woman on the nod drops her purse full of paraphernalia and a knife. Cops don't have time to stop. Little Salvadoran kid—his T-shirts says, "I [heart design] El Salvador"—picks stuff up for her. Other kids keep bouncing their raggedy balls, throwing their worn broken jacks while the running cops try to get through them. No kid breaks a beat. Cops are well behaved. "Please, kid, out of my way," or "Hey, *muchacho, vamos por favor*." Hot pursuit through the courtyard kindergarten. I'm really happy when I see cops well behaved, doing their job. Sorry to say they missed the knifer, who disappeared somewhere into this tenement. All this writing while I wait for what might happen to get us to Mr. C. People are crazy if they think the crime fiction gets it at all right. Mostly it's waiting, hoping, recovering from one more screw up. Most of the time, on-the-job crime fighting is like watching a TV set when it's turned off. When it's big money crime, Mr. C as we're told, it's like reading

IRS and CPA manuals over and over.

You understand, Doreen, we love each other, but even you and I get bored.

Miguel is moving up now, a middling retailer of heroin, a little crack on the side, but with his sweet smile and savvy he's going to do well. Not a bad guy, all in all. You live with people, you see how it is to be savagely poor, and this uppity business of "I" versus "them" becomes a permeable boundary. Consider it. Miguel brings me one-pound burritos because he's sorry I'm a down-and-out drunk and cokehead. And he has given me money. Held, he thought, my drunken head in his lap. Do that out here? Miguel in another time, another place, would have been preaching in a little adobe church, eligible for sainthood. No justice for Miguel when he gets caught. Circumstances are destiny.

I wonder how Mr. C got started? Bigger question now is where he, or we, end up.

And the "Bo?" That's my street name out here already. Good name. Locals have a lot of little Beauregards running around. For me it harkens back to my father's time and his idols, Woodie Guthrie, and Paul Robeson, singing about the Great Depresssion and the "hobo," thus placating this "Bo," the poor miserable wandering bindlestiffs. "Bo" Dolan, how does that grab you, honey? Don't tell your folks.

I'll tell you something. I would never bust Miguel on any drug charge. Fact is, I wish no one would be busted on drug charges alone. It's stupid. My soapbox speaks out against violence and thieves, not poor depressed bastards killing themselves, or silly kids playing with dope. Health insurance is what they need. Counseling. Families. And no horseshit education campaigns.

Miguel was talking to me. "I got a proposition for you, Bo. Money in it, and I figure you could use some." He gave me a wink, a gentle co-conspirator so as not to look like it was charity. If the guys I have worked for and with in Washington were as sensitive as Miguel to how others feel, this dope-dealer government would be a better scene. How's that for honky hearsay? And yes, Darling, maybe curb sitting gets me loonier than I thought.

"I just want you to sit in on a little deal that's coming down tonight. I know you're good with your *chica pistola* and so I want some insurance, just in case. Corner Gwendolyn and Russell Streets, *siete horas. Bueno*?"

"You know I'm not a gun for hire, Miguel. I only do self-defense."

"*Sí, yo* savvy, but just insurance, *seguridad, amigo, contra peligro*. Hey, you are *mi amigo*, no?"

What the hell, why not? Kid R is safe in the gambling house doing books for Mr. C and the various Smiths and Joneses, probably using the phone as frequently as a bookie. I've got to look ready to move if I'm to gain trust. Somebody's trust leads maybe to Mr. C. I work fourteen hours a day for Kid R. The reality is one has to take a piss, sleep, see what Miguel has going down. No one's life is certain. Kid R knows that. Fingers crossed.

So I agree to cover Miguel and all is well so far and I have made a better friend for it. And some more respect on the streets. People don't ask just anybody to bodyguard at deals going down. Markowitz has told me he has, in earlier reincarnations, done the same for government ministers in lesser lands, for lesser breeds than ours.

Already from somewhere I hear the whispers that I have to amplify. Whispers that from way over the great gray waters, comes big money. Whispers about the Samoan's liquor store as a laundry. I hear floating words like banks, armories, a drug network, one bright kid even said "network." I have my business images of course. Wait, wonder, listen. Most whispers are blown out of electronically amplified trumpets, typically by one crowd trying to burn another. Probably these, too. But we do know from Kid R already about the *bureau de change*, which currency exchange listed on its Treasury reporting as one of its accountants a Mr. Chesterfield Parker. Just a few days ago I learned, on one of those calls I make with my transmitter held under a pillow in the joss house where I flop with some other winos, that Mr. Parker was made very dead just a little while back. And Mr. Parker, when earlier asked on a "routine" undercover query, ostensibly by someone thinking of hiring him for a slightly smelly bit of lucrative corporate bookkeeping, said he also worked as an accountant for a chain of bars, apparently legitimate, serving mostly ghettos across the West. And one minor owner on record of the company operating those drinkeries was a Mr. Clyde King. Bonnie and Clyde? Maybe his mother was a fan. Anyway, further inquiry turned up the fact that Mr. King, officially a resident here but a drive-by look at his house finds a Lewis family living there all neat and clean is, when his name is checked by DEA and the Bureau, King with a chain of aliases long as a necklace, a name that keeps coming up as big!

Wait and listen, and keep checking with the home office, and now I have a name who has no house but about whom the whispers center. Could it be that IFFY's Mr. C, Kid R's Mister C, might better be sought as Mr. King? Lots of ego in that alias. I think it's what the detective stories call a "clue."

Mr. King, I hear from most, and none I know, unless he is Kid R's genuine Mr. C, have ever seen him, is the richest man in town by all accounts. I add that no one in Treasury, last I heard which was yesterday, have seen any of his accounts, whereas the mortician had been the last to see one of his laundry accountants, Mr. so-called Parker. Laundry?

Yes indeed, because this *bureau de change*, Balfour is the name, is suspected of providing worldwide services doing just that. Deposit one dollar here. Collect one dollar, less 10 percent service charge, anywhere in the world where the company has a *cambio*. All as postings to the credit of whatever person—in the legal sense of an entity—the depositor wants to be, create, pay off or buy from. One day I will see Mr. King's extended books and enterprises. Kid R may beat us there. After all, we all know the warehouse building where we're going to go one night. But every time Markowitz or Stein wheel by, it's empty and silent. There's no making of a search warrant on Kid R's information in front of any judge, because he does not have the standing of a "previously reliable informant." To use the jargon.

But right now . . . "Hello there, James," I say, nodding from behind my whiskey-wet, filthy whiskers to a barkeep who works at Hiram's, where, the street talk says, one can buy anything from Budweiser beer to grenades, rockets, and the hardware to launch them with. Automatic weapons, too, of course. Hiram's is not an upright joint like Stein tells me Robbie's Club is. Kid R goes into Robbie's from time to time. I follow, staggering.

"I might have the money someday," I tell Jamie, having earlier announced my grandiose interest in buying an old UK Lera L SMG, a weapon that is notoriously slow and short-ranged, but has the beauty of being almost silent. Us novice pickpockets have got to be discreet as perceived by the Jamies of this world.

"Sure, Bo, sure, just let me know." Jamie, like most folks hereabouts, is not unkind about my being a rum-dum dopefiend and notorious moocher, and he does believe—my reputation is established so far only by remarkably quick reflexes for a man my age, a quite unpleasant look on my face which I fear I come by naturally, and truly sincere gun pointing—that I shoot people accurately and readily. Someday, he thinks, I might actually be his customer. He's sort of right. When the time comes to close his place down.

"Miguel, who set up this meeting we're having?" It was almost seven p.m. We were lounging inconspicuously seated on the ground next to, behind really, some big empty crates of unknown origin in a dirt parking lot next to tattered commercial buildings doing unknown business, if even that.

Miguel shrugged. "A friend I met when I was a mule."

"No friend you know very well, I'll bet."

Miguel nodded, shifted his feet in the dust, looked worried. "A gringo customs officer who was dirty used to let mules working for the right people pass through the border. Now my mules use him. He's the one sent a note asking for this meeting for some maybe big gringo buyers who live near here. You never know."

"Right, *verdad*. One never knows."

The auto was an old model 4-door green, upscale yuppie Audi, very dusty. Two white males, maybe 30, 35, both with scruffy beards, in dress-down shirts, blue jeans, and wellington boots, got out. Both tall, good complexions behind the foliage, clear eyes, mock casual slouch marred by good muscle tone nervously triggered by, as it turned out, some kid kicking a tin can. I beckoned them to our micro-scale barrio with my finger. Miguel, for some reason—probably because they were and I was gringo, let me control the action. I pointed them to the littered ground behind a packing case. They sat down uneasily. I pressed my lips together very tightly, raised my eyes, looking at Miguel in hopes he'd get the message. He did and stayed silent.

"You guys want something?" I asked. Unlike them, I'd had practice being casual. By now I looked a real slob.

"You know why we're here," was the aggressive reply. "We are talking a big deal, ten-K maybe, if you're up to it." The blond one started reaching for his wallet like a con man ready to flash might—good theatre in bunco, but here a definite no-no. No stranger in Malome ever shows money until some kind of escrow is in effect, like two men's hands simultaneously reaching out while two armed seconds watch.

"You're fuzz." Mine wasn't even a question.

"Hell no, man, we're here to do business," the redhead protested, miffed and unsettled.

"Narc is narc and you guys smell," said I. "*Adios, muchachos.*" I got up to leave, not looking at Miguel, who was staring at his feet. I knew he wasn't carrying; nobody ever had stuff on him, it was always just stashed nearby for a sale, so even if the narcs made an arrest—illegal as hell of course in this instance with no offer of sale made, thus no probable cause—Miguel was safe. But I knew it by their taunting me that they wanted to take someone down. I rather enjoyed being a lightning rod for these dunderheads. Presumably they were wired, but not for lightning.

"No, man, please, talk to us. No narc, I swear." The blond one was pleading.

Obviously a new assignment. Wanted something better on his record for a first meet, something to brag about with the boys over bourbon when the county Narc Task Force exchanged make-believe medals, no, change that, make-believe heroes.

I gave them a look of sheer disdain and contempt, as I reached my feet. They had got off the ground to be sure I did not have that advantage over them. Watch a cop; he wants you seated, him standing, not vice versa, even in a traffic stop.

"All right, boys, philosophize for me." My tongue didn't slur once, not once I started pontificating. "Let's say you have ten thousand in marked bills on you. Let's say you just record the first buy, no bust. Do you think there's anything immoral about putting ten thousand dollars in taxpayer money into circulation buying, thus maybe raising the price of drugs?" When I am at my most moral self, even my mother loathes me; their faces outdid good old mom.

"Fuck you," said the redhead.

"And let's say," I continued, "you weren't the incompetent narc assholes you are. And say you were retailers buying ten-K of dope. Would you consider yourselves immoral as customers, or are you just like the johns who lay whores and just blame the girls, or like the automobile drivers who blame the oil companies for pollution? What do you white dope buyers say to that charge?"

"Fuck you," said the blond, also not an inventive conversationalist.

"Bye, bye, *niños*," I said, curling my hand in an itsy-bitsy wave that conveys, maybe I think you guys are queer as well as stupid, goodbye. They were clearly thinking of busting me out of sheer spite when I said, "No, boys, no bust. Your sergeant will spank you, and the DA will complain to your lieutenant. And I, poor drunk that I am, will rely on my local free poverty legal service to sue you all for false arrest. Chew on it, children, *vaya con diablo*."

Hispanics are supposed to be taciturn, that stolid Indio blood. As they stomped back to their car, Miguel was laughing so hard he had tears in his eyes.

"I owe you, *amigo*," he said. "It takes one to know one, like they say."

An odd remark, methinks. Out here you pay attention. I told him I hoped he meant one gringo to another.

"*Seguro*," said Miguel smiling, "oh sure. But I also know you're some kind of cop. Don't get me wrong. I don't mind. Some of my best friends used to be policemen. You're my friend, I know that, we have no problem. Fact is," he stared at me with utter sincerity, holding out his hand, "you are my best friend in town. But now, since we are *abierto*, open about this together, then admit I owe you. How can I pay you back?"

"I'm too old and I hope too wise to argue with a friend who's smarter than I am, Miguel. Anyone else in town think what you think?"

"I don't think so, *amigo*, you are pretty good at what you do." His voice had adopted the sing-song cadence one finds in country Mexicans. It was a bit of play on his part.

"All right, Miguel, you're on. I want to find and take Mr. King apart, bookkeeping ledger by ledger. You have any route in?"

He shuffled his feet making the dust swirl up to his belt. "Maybe. I got this cousin who lives, you know on Coleridge, my awful place. He cleans up at the warehouse Mr. King owns, south part of town. He can tell us what's there to see, although he's family and a good man and I don't want him hurt. Besides, nobody, sure not my cousin Javier, no Latino in this town, can go against Mr. King."

This was my break, totally unexpected. If it were the same warehouse Kid R had been to, invisible Mr. King and invisible Mr. C were the same. Making them visible was the next little problem. I could have hugged Miguel.

"There'll be money in it for you and Javier, and no danger. Can I meet him with you somewhere safe? I want to know who and what he sees out there and, of course, address and building plans, security system, that sort of thing."

"Sure, meet me tomorrow at ten p.m. behind the Coleridge barrio. Don't be seen coming there. And, *amigo*, Bo, I won't take your money. But Javier is very poor and his family needs it very much. I thank you for him."

In a high grass field cluttered with garbage, auto wrecks, bedsprings, old syringes—be careful this day of AIDS not to step on one—decaying tampons, condoms, empty cans and bottles, in other words the kind of park available next door to these poor devils, Miguel brought me to meet Javier. My Spanish orders beer, but not much more. I asked questions, Miguel interpreted. Javier had brought plans. I would look at them elsewhere, in the light. I now knew where the Chinese accountant worked. Would he be a tie to the also Oriental South City realty laundry, I wondered? I now knew where the locked file cabinets were. I knew that irregular shipments came in and out, all by night, unpredictable. Weeks could go by with no one in or about Mr. King's warehouse.

Javier had never seen loading or unloading. Nor contents. Heavy sliding steel doors walled off most of the building. Javier cleaned up the office once a week. There was a shredder, but he had never seen any paper left about. Mr. King liked the floors clean, the place dusted. Javier had smelled the antiseptic smells but no, he used mild cleaners like Mr. Clean. No, he had never seen blood, nor any sign of harm.

The law generally says a search warrant can be issued on a snitch's information if earlier busts have been made from his information. We were stuck. Kid R and the Warsaw source were probable cause for a transport stop if we jazzed it up a bit. So if Javier could just give me license plates, any description of vehicles, the drivers regularly used on the outgoing journey carrying whatever it was, the team could arrange surveillance and a down-the-road-and-far-away bust. Do two busts a week apart in different places. Kid R would never be involved. I could do it all without him. I was pleased with myself.

Sheer accident but I had come up with Javier, his drawings of what was where outside the locked steel doors, and proof of warehouse use. Kid R was no doubt moving on it too, but I had had the luck. My luck was his. We would never have to expose him to danger.

If we had the luck to get the signal from Javier on a busy night and the truck busts came up golden, my colleagues would be ready to go pronto, with a judge put on standby anytime of day or night so as to get a search warrant for the warehouse. A pronto bust and the staff should still be inside. Or we could stop them on the way out. DEA could do the backup and be ready for us. Grossman had promised at least that much, even on short notice. Crossed his heart and hoped no one would die. There had to be pay dirt in those files, boxes, accountants, inside Chang's head if we could find him somewhere. But two Federal busts would alert King C, wherever they occurred. He would be looking for snitches inside his ranks. Good. Let them have at each other.

I had no idea how horribly wrong I would be. Doreen, I need you. I need you and a better brain and release from memories, and very much I need forgiveness. Pray for me, Doreen, and for Rooster.

38

Eventually the Government gets things together. Social Security works; Iran-Contra did not. We beat the Axis and the Soviets hands down. Iraq is still thumbing its nose. There is a balanced budget. The debt is five, six trillion smackeroos. Al Capone was sent up to Alcatraz courtesy of Elliott Ness and the tax law. It took his own brother, not the FBI after years of trying, to catch the Unabomber. Mostly the "ten most wanted" get caught. But you get some unwanteds, like when the Feds killed mothers and kids at Waco. Government is like that—win a few, lose a few. To be fair, it has, therefore we have because we are it, won the big ones.

McLaughlin didn't want to lose this one. He was "it."

"You head up the ready room, the war room, the Vienna Incident operations room whatever you want to call it, but you damn well put together a team by tonight and you damn well get the mud off our faces by yesterday, understand? This one comes from the President himself, understand?"

McLaughlin understood. He also understood he was there alone. His boss, the "First," as he liked to be called, the presumptive chief of IFFY, was in hospital in Hawaii with a presumed heart attack. McLaughlin had seen those before; that chicken-livered SOB could bring on a cold sweat, palpitations, report pain in just the right places—left arm and chest—and wiggle just enough during the EKG to cover no fibrillations, no inverted T ways, when as the First—oh the First loved that title—started seeing trouble on the way.

Stethoscopes always came up clear, but doctors these days don't take chances if any machinery tells them a malpractice suit might be on the way. The First was a Henny Youngman, bless him, joke. "He was born at home but when his mother saw him she went to the hospital."

It had all come as a surprise.

Everyone in Washington, cabinet secretaries and heads of agencies with anything at stake at all, had seen the CNN show put on by the Vienna embassy.

Every man and woman in this bigwig crew, only one or two of them crooks and none feeble-minded—so as cabinets and agency heads go in democracies, not too bad—every one of them had thought the CNN coverage had put all the troubles to rest. Absolutely trustworthy eyewitnesses. Capital crimes committed against a federal agent. The Austrian government admitting to crooks inside, errors everywhere, and apologies. The basic data on the Sofia Source was in the hands of all who should be reading it.

This time the system really worked. "Bless it, bless them all," said the Secretary of State after seeing the show, reading the first-class criminal intelligence reports. These blessings came from a position not generally occupied by sentimentalists.

"Troubles put to rest, have them all get medals, awards, promotions, vacations, the works and whatever," the National Security Advisor had told his secretary right after the show. Then he called his boss, the President. "Troubles all put to rest."

The President's National Security Advisor was hardly referring to the little stuff like (a) criminals laundering money or (b) the Bulgarians out twelve billion dollars, or (c) Sir Alfred, who cares, shark food? or (d) Hashimoto now nobly buried in Arlington—it turned out Hashimoto had been a gung-ho infantry grunt in Vietnam—or (e) the names and probable locations of various bad guys which had come in from the Vienna and Sofia embassies straightaway and been in his morning special intelligence report. Pipsqueak IFinCIG could worry about all that. What the hell! Its very existence was anachronism after this flap in Vienna, Potomac, South African, Warsaw, Moscow, hints of Estonia, Latvia and wherever. And "You be damn sure, come next budget, that everyone who knew IFFY will be long gone and happily forgotten," ordered the Counselor, who was the man who sat next to the Man.

In PR government, if you have dead bodies and can't finger or hang the murderer, you go after the guy who found the body and made you all that trouble. Ipso facto, IFinCIG was on its way out. A lead balloon. As far as the Counselor was concerned, in the longer run the Environment, Energy, and Education departments could all go away too, but right then, that minute, he and, most importantly, his boss were happy. The Vienna Incident had been put to rest.

Until they had been made most irritable. Place in evidence the tape of that most irritable telephone call by the President's National Security Advisor and a Counselor thereto. Likewise most irritable was the Chairman of the National Committee of the President's party. One faced the President. The other faced coming elections, where Senator Cranmer was making hay out of the flaming bales of stuff being thrown at the good old U.S. of A. by the Russian premier. "I tell you he's a waffling asshole who can't go pee without the big boys telling him.

"Mobilizing his army? They can't even find it, for God's sake. Mobilizing his navy? Hell's bells, the Ukrainians own its docks! Target nukes? Half of them will blow up over their own country! God save Iceland and Tanna Touva, too. Can you imagine it? Why, shit, he and the President are scheduled to play golf at St. Andrews next week at the Group of Eight Conference. And pissant Premiersky ain't even cancelled. Uses the hot line this morning to confirm that he and the President would be in the first foursome to tee off. What the hell is going on?"

Angry pause.

"You tell me! Damn it, you tell me now! Hear?" The National Security chief then hung up on the Secretary of Defense and the Director of the CIA, both on the same conference call, before either could say, as they would have to, "I have no idea." Which he knew they would say. He had already had to say it to his boss. Which had made the Man very irritable indeed. And worried.

Senator Cranmer's campaign manager, the big boys heading the other party's National Committee, had lots of ideas. All spelled votes. No irritation, no worries at all, at least the way the polls were heading.

The Assistant Attorney General, Criminal Affairs, whose office was next door to the Attorney General himself in that high-ceilinged, long-corridored, portrait-graced main Justice building, was in turn irritable. He had been called by an irritable Attorney General, who had been called by very irritable Secretaries of State, Treasury and Defense, called by an in-over-his head Washington, D.C. chief of police under direction of the congressionally appointed District Management Poobah. A repeat autopsy of Hashimoto had come up with indications that something not at all nice had happened on that sailboat on the Potomac. If any more important bodies turned up murdered—subtly poisoned and embarrassingly undetected as such by an FBI crime lab the first time around—if any more came up floating in declared safe waters, the Secretary of the Environmental Protection Agency would be calling next.

Mac McLaughlin couldn't enjoy any irritation at all. He was supposed to *do something*. He had the same intelligence report all the chief cats and poobahs had. He knew damn well everybody had done a damn fine job, heroic, diplomatic, straight or cunning as the situation required. Nobody was publicly critical of IFFY. No one upstairs had a clue about the Greta Leibowitz hoax. Of course, anyone responsible for computer or secure personnel files knew, oh yes. Very soon, the word had come in, the FBI was going to rub someone's nose in something nasty. The preliminaries showed Hashimoto's letter to be forged. Very helpful in the investigation, very helpful in showing a foreign hand. Very helpful if you were the Civil Service and wanted to know that the old KGB-GRU, now Security Services, in Moscow could pull your chain any old time. People don't like that kind of insight. Nor that someone in IFFY had known that Claire Dubois and Lee Barbour were the agents being sent to Vienna before they even got there. Or that cables out of IFFY, and clearly some out of State, were so insecure that kids playing with the Internet must be reading them. Sure as the devil plays poker, the press was reading the transcripts now.

Nobody who's supposed to cure it sitting way down the totem pole named McLaughlin liked it. "The cure, for Chrissakes, is somewhere in Sofia or Moscow, or in better computer, security, personnel screening," his voice dropped as the conclusion became compelling, "*here*." He was saying this to his secretary. Who else could he talk to? Dolan had gone to Malome. His now Acting Third was Prissy Jonesy, who might well be the mole, and no one in Personnel could yet be trusted. For the rest, the building was nearly empty. "Our whole staff are overseas working their tails off. For Chrissakes, what am I supposed to do?"

His secretary liked him. He was a nice man. She'd help as best she could. "Drink some coffee," she said. "I'll get you some real cream."

McLaughlin put his head down on his arms on his desk. To curse quietly, not to cry. His secretary was a nice but forgetful lady. He hated coffee. His doctor had told him "no more calories, no more cholesterol." Some days just don't go well.

Markowitz was Mac's only regular Malome contact. Doc was undercover and doing, so he said, gangbusters well. Had a line, Doc had reported just last night, on a Mr. King who was Mr. C which was a gift from heaven, this King C. Who only a kid named Rooster—who wasn't even a snitch, who wasn't even sure he was going to go straight, who still had to make up his mind about life—had ever seen.

The good news, Mac knew, was how quickly the whole system had worked. Nobody on our side got killed after Hashimoto got killed. Claire was okay. Courageous SWAT-style action by a two-man, not even trained together, ad lib, pro team. No one had screwed up. Good, better and best. No one could ask for more. So what was going wrong? In the Oval Office. In the Kremlin. Hardly IFFY jurisdictions. "Maybe it's a NATO problem. Maybe UN." Mac was talking to himself when his secretary, beaming and motherly, came in. She poured coffee. Lots of cream. He drank it. You do what you can.

Immense intelligence had come in on who had done what to whom and where and why, which was for twelve billion green ones. Brilliant investigative, diplomatic police work and backup intelligence as well, from London, Sofia, Vienna, and respecting former Comrade Deputy Minister Todor Mihailov, right here in Virginia as well. And now Dolan and Rooster were zeroing in on the ghost himself, King C. From Warsaw to Malome; the system was working and not a month had gone by. King C was maybe in sight, in spite of the DEA suits who'd sabotaged it all just to spite him, yes him, Mac, and him, Dolan.

With Oval Office and AG authority behind him, Mac's first team-forming call was to Suits Numbers 1 and 2. He told their secretaries to tell them to pack their bags and prepare to spend their nights on cots in the IFFY operations room. It didn't exist. Mac told his secretary to tell the janitor to make one in a windowless storeroom. "Special quarters for our friends from DEA."

Mac didn't much care whom the Agency, the Bureau, main Treasury Enforcement sent. The Bureau of Alcohol, Tobacco, and Firearms—ATF—could tag along. The stats were they'd be okay. He told State to send someone from the Eastern European section and their Intelligence, but they knew that anyway. He gave Defense Intelligence the option, no need at all but out of courtesy. He'd filled in the round holes with round pegs but for DEA suits. He had the authority to get Grossman brought back but that was suicide. He needed Grossman backing up Malome. Mac had already gone over his authority in authorizing Grossman to send a standby team to Palm City next door to Malome. "The suits will scream," he told his secretary, whom he'd invited to have coffee with him. Someone must like the stuff. "Let 'em."

There was nothing whatsoever for the team to do. Make a lot of expensive calls learning over again what they already knew? Hope to God the lines within the U.S. between Malome, others nearby in California and the District were secure? The Russians were no longer listening but from Cuba, or so he'd been told. No scramblers anywhere near Malome. He told Markowitz, Grossman to do it all, the best they could, in rap, dialect and slang. He told the Agency to hustle their butts to get burst transmitters there and here. All for talk that didn't matter: Mac wasn't going to run anybody's field operation from Washington. No way.

"Good people doing hard work uphill know what they're about. I'll take the heat if it goes wrong. If it goes right the Secretary takes the credit," he wryly, accurately told his secretary. "IFFY, me, all of us are out the door come next budget anyway." His secretary smiled. She knew Washington. "I know," she said quietly. "Here, Mr. McLaughlin, please have some more coffee."

39

Claire knew, after all of the fatigue and stress of the last weeks, that she was not up to flying to and from Geneva in one day. She booked a room at the Beau Rivage, at which hotel she arrived from Vienna at about one p.m. She had promised to take luncheon with Gavin. His thoughtful note greeting her said he'd reserved at 1:30, having known her arrival schedule, at the Chat Botté, which was the hotel's world-class dining room. She remembered it warmly from her family and later her own travelling days.

The Maître d', Jean-Francois, greeted her with genuine warmth. In a good European hotel guests are remembered over generations. And the guests, like swallows, remember and return. He showed her to a table which overlooked the lake a few hundred yards from its becoming mother of the Rhône, immediately across the boulevard. The Lake's famous fountain was spouting froth and prisms. Gavin, dressed in an English gray herringbone suit, looking more solemn and older than she could ever expect, arose, it seemed uneasily, to greet her. Hardly, for suddenly he moved out from the rich leather banc to embrace her, a bear hug, proper kisses on the cheek to be sure, but no question, this was a man who was glad to see a woman, more than that, a woman once his own.

Claire blinked. "Good Lord, Gavin, please; a little decorum, please?" She was too overwhelmed to censure, and fact was she was glad to see him too. Not glad enough for a bear hug, but a mild embrace would have been àpropos. But a woman too remembers, and wonders.

Gavin grinned and hugged her again."Damn, am I glad to see you! You'll never imagine how much I have been worried about you! What a relief to see you on CNN, oh you poor darling, and hurt by those bastards too. You comported yourself very well, you know, my heroine you are, and still as lovely as the scent of roses on a fresh Irish breeze."

"Nothing heroic about being frightened to death and lucky enough to have some people who *are* heroic risk their lives to get you out. Very good for the character, Gavin, I now know, really *know* I'm not immortal, invulnerable or even—well, not even very resourceful. Get kidnapped, locked up, interrogated, beaten, almost shot, hidden away, not sure the police aren't going to kill you too, and well, it makes for modesty. It was my transition from adolescence to maturity, Gavin. Now I know I can and will die."

"I am so sorry, darling, but dying you'll not be doing for a long, long time. As for what happened, well if I had—" he caught himself, began again. "If I ever can help you, anything. But you know that. What happened out there was terrible. You know I know something about Russian crime, those thugs. To think you were in their hands, well, you're lucky to be alive. And I will those like them straight into hell."

"Oh, Gavin," she had begun to cry. She pulled out of his so touching embrace, took her seat across from him, saw him rather abashedly look at her. What a difference the years make; a student with an older, important lecturer as her lover is the diffident one. But now Claire was mature and, courtesy of recent events, a celebrity in her own right. Now Gavin was the uncertain one, with no claim on her, awkwardly wondering, she sensed that easily, where he might stand. Adding to her strength, she now had Barbour as love and lover, or had had him until yesterday when she had been so pigheaded and, yes, dishonest with them both.

Now she really knew why she had wanted to see Gavin. It had not just been his persuasiveness, his urgent fearful tension over the phone, what she thought had been his jeopardy. Truth was, he had been her love and, well, she wanted to compare the two men at the level of where the heart beats, the flush of pleasure comes. Evaluate herself as well by looking, now realistically, to see whether she had made a sensible choice in Gavin, was making one in Barbour. Was she even sure about Barbour after all? Danger, closeness, but was it a shipboard romance? She reached her hand across the table, took Gavin's own, squeezed it. The words "comparison shopper" flew into her mind. She was disgusted at the truth of it.

"I am glad to see you, you know."

"I'm glad to see you."

"So why did you really call?"

"I saw you on the television, learned what a frightful time you'd had, saw the handsome chap you seem rather close to, wondered how close you two really are? And I want to warn you about getting entangled with this money laundering, contraband export, really the whole business of Russia while it is still a nearly lawless, unstable place. Same for most of the CIS countries, and Latvia, not so much Estonia really, but Bulgaria as well.

Your job with IFinCIG is bound to take you to those places; hell, you damn near died learning Austria isn't safe. Claire," he gripped her hand tightly, "I want you to quit IFinCIG, it's just too dangerous. You and I both know it's a small outfit, a stepchild legislated out of the original Senate money laundering studies way back in the early 80s. You know it's not staffed or prepared to fight a war with the people in power in Eastern Europe. There are hundreds of thousands of them, hundreds of dirty banks; most of Russian industry is privatized in the service of plutocratic looters. You saw what just one banker, his Russian and Polish colleagues, and their thugs in Vienna were willing to do to get information from you, then kill you. Darling, you simply can't fight them unless the Western countries do see it as a war. Listen to the Russian premier; he's actually talking war over it. The crooks, the state itself are so interpenetrated that there's nothing you'll do that isn't political and risky. You can never be sure, no I change that, you can *mostly* be sure the police are in the pay of the bad guys. Darling, I don't want you hurt."

There was genuine pain showing in his face; it was taut with tension.

"You know a lot about it don't you, a whole lot, more than anyone said on television or in the papers." Claire was impressed, touched, it was not suspicion being voiced.

"Of course I do. I've been studying this miserable phenemenon as part of the eastern economies since before you met me. I know many, probably all of the big players in government, the big exporting state or privatized industries, and for sure most of the big bankers. They don't bother me, I'm harmless, they even consult me when it's straight economics, or politics involving the West. But Claire, you're not harmless, you're the one sheriff chasing down a million bad guys. Get too close and they'll kill you, as you learned. And they will try it again if you're still the pursuing law."

"So far IFinCIG has never lost an agent, and until the Vienna Incident one has never been shot at. We've mostly had good police cooperation wherever we went, I'm told even in Russia. Of course we're tiny but we offer a kind of service, if nothing else getting the locals to blossom into their better banking, financial, law-enforcement selves. They're by no means all bad. We've got to save them, Gavin, support by loans, enforcement assistance, IMF banking and budget guidance. World Bank, International Bank for Reconstruction and Development, the Soros Foundation. Right now it's a poor man's disorganized Marshall Plan working. But if we don't do it, I grant you I'm not sure the 'we' is me anymore, fascism can come back. The next premier who's making noises just for the sake of rhetoric—no one believes the premier there now believes a word of his threats—the next one may have a real army behind him. That's how I see it, Gavin."

"Americans are such idealists, such missionaries, out to save, sometimes I think to rule the world. Britain can't give up its basic imperialism either, for all its claims."

"Gavin, I remember you as an idealist. And you weren't cynical about my country. What's changed?"

"I was an idealist. I've learned too much, gotten older, that's all."

"Don't I recall your being a little crazy yourself in your idealism about Ireland? I remember once your praising the IRA in the time of the troubles."

He nodded thoughtfully. "Can I tell you something personal, private, not to go in your Federal agent's notebook? Really confidential, although it's about a long time ago?"

"Of course you can." She had almost said "darling."

"I couldn't tell you when you were so young, when we were lovers. I wasn't sure you could keep a secret then. You've changed a lot, Claire, impressively so. Really grown up. I trust you as a woman when I couldn't when you were an excitable girl."

"Half a thanks, Gavin. I really think I was mature even when a Cambridge student. Anyway, tell me please."

Gavin licked his lips, sipped the superb Chassagne Montrachet in the glass, nibbled at an escargot on his plate, buttered a piece of brown poppy and sesame seed roll. Deliberate tangential preparation.

"All right, when the Northern Ireland troubles were bloody, I worked for the IRA. My brother was one of them. They needed money for arms. I knew about the economics of that, had met people enough to know who could do what. I got involved in moving Irish-American contributors' money through banks, phony companies, through documenting approved 'end user' papers for arms. Got involved in learning, then helping with transshipping; small arms from France, German, Russia, ironically England, Israel, all legitimately shipped, seemingly legitimately paid for. I became one of the IRA's main resources for arms. Met some thoroughly wonderful Irish heroes, and along the way some unpleasant Libyan, Japanese, Syrian and Iranian trained terrorists. I fell into the business, and in it you meet, mostly because they want you to help them too, all those raging young, or not so young, bloodthirsty 'revolutionaries' as they call themselves. Most were just vicious, marginal savages."

"And so they all hooked into the money laundering, banking, arms industry purchases, changing bills of lading, transshipping, all those tricks, all that bloody network?"

"No and yes. The terrorists, insurgent movements here and there, civil wars, factions, all do essentially the same thing, but I wasn't part of it. What I did was for Ireland, a patriotic cause."

"For you then, Gavin, the IRA were your heroes?"

"No and yes again. Not just *my* heroes, my noble boys, but those brave ones fighting for a cause that was all of ours. A shining cause it was. I was an Irish patriot that's all, Sinn Fein member since I was a boy. How could I not be? Good God, woman, Henry the Second occupied us in the twelfth century, it's been rebellion ever since, until 1998. Think of what that bloody beast Cromwell did to Ireland, took our land, took our Church.

Think of the famines we suffered, the oppression. In 1914 the Irish Volunteers, my IRA, were secretly buying arms from Belgium and bringing them in; what I did was historical continuity. Like money itself, like a gun itself, it's only a thing, no intrinsic nature to it but its utilities. Just so then moving money, shipping weapons, using weapons has no morality but for the side you're on. My great-grandfather fought under Michael Collins in the Easter Risings. And because they fought with what they had, Ireland is free of the English after eight hundred years of real terror, English terror. I had great-uncles killed by the Black and Tans. Violence against us, and our fighting back, has been the history. I'm part of it, just as you're comfortable, hell no, it's righteous morality is part of your history." The man was getting furious.

So was Claire. "You didn't see the IRA as terrorists when they bombed buildings, killed women and children, set off car bombs on streets, in subway stations, you say that wasn't terrorism?"

"No, Claire, that was a war the way the weaker side must always fight it, by guerrilla tactics. That's what the IRA Provisionals decided in 1969 in the great split within the IRA. I saw Ulster as still our Ireland's war, and so I went with the Provisionals. And we won it. Think of those 1998 Northern Ireland elections; we changed the way Northern Ireland was ruled. The Orangemen were far more against the settlement; Sinn Fein endorsed it. Through war we brought an honorable peace. Doing what I did helped that. Don't you see, Claire?"

"I see how you see it, Gavin, but no man who is a man bombs women and children, assassinates unarmed people just because of their religion. I'm sorry, Gavin, I feel that strongly. By masterminding the whole supply system, by running all of those secret operations, you made those deaths. Gavin, doesn't that disturb you at all?"

"I'd rather it hadn't been necessary, but the English, the Orangemen made it necessary. It was their fault. You have to break the eggs to make an omelette. When your people killed the Indians, Claire, now that was evil, nothing idealistic about it; not for a cause, just bloody murder for land theft. And don't be so righteously judgmental about any of it, woman. No! You think money laundering in the fight for freedom is immoral. You condemn *en masse* those Russians who are trying for the first time in their history to become economically free men, and yes, they may be shortsighted. They export resources, the income of which doesn't get channeled to the general good, and no, no Russian pays taxes; any who can launder the unstable ruble so they can build lives for themselves and their children will do it.

"I couldn't care less. More power to them if that's what it takes to be free, have food on the table. They're all learning that capitalism you and I both believe in, Claire. It's the world as it is, and I can damn well tell you some of your biggest American corporations launder billions and your sweet little IFFY doesn't look at it at all. You've got me angry, my darling, you can be so damn rigid when the facts aren't as black and white as you think. I know some Russians doing it. They'e not all bad people. Like the Irish were, in their own way they're trying to survive. If you're an economist whose idealism is free market success, expanding economies, expanding the opportunity to create wealth, then you take a practical view of what's happening."

She was quiet for a while, attending to the main course which had arrived, tournedos with a bordelaise sauce. She sipped her wine slowly, thinking about this once lover of hers, how little she had known him after all. How admirably passionate he was, and yet, how his arguments, so very one-sided, troubled her; indeed, how angry she was about his moral relativism.

"Your idealism now then, Gavin, has no place to go except no-holds-barred free enterprise, crime and all. Is that it?"

"Don't be sarcastic with me, my sweet darling, which you still are. The answer is obviously no, although not so ringing as your righteousness. I've seen more by far than you have of this world, I grant your recent experience at the hands of thugs was terrible, so no one can be tolerant of crime against the innocent. Although I suspect a Federal agent cannot expect the people she's hunting to be entirely courteous. But in economics how you define the limits of competition, set the rules, invokes an arbitrary morality. The variable politics of idealism, really. For myself, I'm beyond the fires of youth. My core idealism argues for freedom, and no doubt I would define fewer things than you do in the business world as criminal. People enter the marketplace with open eyes, they take their chances. Some win, some don't. I support gifts of bread and soup for the losers, but no more socialism than that."

"Gavin, have you really become so unkind, so indifferent?"

"No, Claire darling, I've become realistic. Humans are what they are. In the marketplace let them have at it as long as they don't shoot bystanders, defraud through lies, counterfeit the currency or sell unlabeled dangerous products."

"But you'd let them beat the tax man and launder their money and if it came to that, kill each other?"

"I suppose so. Yes, yes I would. Ireland's free, the troubles of Belfast are over. I've had the one victory that matters. I don't have a policewoman's mentality. I'm not an Anglo-Saxon who wants a moral imperialism, whatever it is, certainly not about drugs, prostitution, or the natural competitiveness of people. Economic Darwinism I suppose, savage as it is, it's the natural design of the living world. Why shouldn't I favor what nature has produced?"

She was about to argue vehemently, but decided against it. After all, she had come to Geneva in part to see what Gavin was like, and thanks to his honesty, she had. She changed the topic.

"Gavin, over the telephone, when you called me at the embassy in Vienna, you sounded frightened. I thought you might be the one in danger. Am I totally wrong?"

"Anybody who gives people advice about how to handle their money, anybody who knows how the world really works and still after learning that doesn't withdraw totally from it into a monastery, or that non-consultant part of me which was in the University, anybody in that world is always in a kind of danger. You have to know the real rules, the Darwinian ones: either be the foremost predator, or be useful to the predator like that bird who sits on the crocodile's nose, or know when and how to keep out of the way."

"Gavin, I asked earlier if you were in danger. After all, you've been flying back and forth to Russia for years now. I remember a long time back you said you had to have bodyguards there. Are there people who would really want to hurt you?"

"Of course, anyone touching business or walking the street in Russia faces that. As with Darwin, survival choices; be on top, be armored, have a niche no one wants or understands, or be camouflaged. For myself, maybe the last two. Being an economist brings attention only if you have your theory wrong and bring on a depression. The Russians have their own economists to do that. No, don't worry about me. I was in a lot more danger running the logistics for the IRA. It's you I worry about, darling."

Claire felt ill at ease whether she pushed him away or let him squeeze her hand. "I don't think we should. Gavin, we really have moved apart. I think I am really serious about Barbour whom you saw on CNN, the man who saved my life."

Gavin Garrity was not pleased. "Your boss? Isn't he the man who single-handedly puts us on the brink of World War 2.2, maybe III if all the politicians are clowns? Barbour, the handsome fellow you were to work with to find that idiot banker Brody? Well, that's not very clever of him to allow you to have been put in harm's way for a man who isn't even in Vienna. No one who loves you would let you stay in IFinCIG. I certainly wouldn't. Claire, I know you don't know much at all about the black game you're in, but I beg of you, get out. Go back to publishing, do something with your real talents in the humanities and arts, use those tremendous social skills you have. You'e too good for government service and too precious to me to see you walking in blindly, like you did in Vienna. Don't go hunting Brodys with Barbours, please. I doubt if it's money you need, but if that is it, I've accumulated more than I know what to do with, much more. I'll give you whatever you need. Again, please," he insisted on holding her hand, gripping it tightly. His hand almost knocked over her wine glass. "Promise me!"

She stared at him. "How did you know we were looking for Brody? I thought I heard you say something earlier that passed me by, 'the banker and his Russian and Polish colleagues.' I heard you say it, but it passed me by. None of that was in the newspapers, nobody on the CNN interview talked about it. And how would you know he's not in Vienna? That he has those colleagues? Gavin, how do you know these things? And how of all people, did you, who doesn't give a hang about having money, get to be what I hear you say is rich?"

She shook her hand loose from his, in doing so knocked over her water glass, and had to suffer the embarrassment of the waiter and Jean-Francois, the maître d', come rushing over to clean up the mess and give her napkins for her dress on which some of the water had spilled. Two pieces of ice were on her lap. She had made such a clatter. Other diners close by, European in their careful disinterest, could be seen looking out of the corners of their eyes. One of them, at a table across the room but directly opposite—an exceedingly distinguished looking man of about sixty-five, accompanied by a strikingly-dressed beautiful, very sexy young woman one third his age, was not so polite as not to give Claire a disdainful glance. She'd noted the couple as she had come in to join Gavin.

She'd especially noted the slightly, well, Claire called it 'overly luscious and showing it all' display of the young woman, despite her tasteful jewelry. "Mistress material no doubt," Claire had concluded. And the older man was obviously showing her off in one of Geneva's most expensive restaurants.

As for the waterfall and clatter, Gavin was fully composed, not at all embarrassed, however much Claire might be. He reassured Claire with a laugh, thanked the maître d'hotel, glanced over unsurprised at the older man to give him the briefest of nods, the kind Europeans do when they say, "Yes, we know each other, and we know this is not an occasion where we acknowledge that."

"I tell you what, darling, your dress is damp. Let me buy you a new one right now, the hell with dessert, it's fattening anyway. Just over the bridge, a pleasant walk over the headwaters of the Rhone is haute couture, Chanel, Chloë, Jil Sander, Givenchy, Versace.

One of them has got to have a dress for you. Go on up to your room, do a quick change, and let me do something I could never do when we were younger at Cambridge."

"Damn him," she told herself, "he's still charming, gallant, loving, and mysterious, but, Claire my girl, it's *no.*" Her two brain hemispheres were in total disagreement about the man; the right found him ever delightful, the left and rational side had warning bells clanging, suspicions of the gravest kind. She'd be surprised if one side of her face wasn't smiling, the other full of appraising distrust.

"Gavin, it's very sweet but it's not right. I can't let you do it. And," she looked at him with the rational left-brain look dominant, "Gavin, you haven't told me how you came to know things that were in my document packet marked 'secret'; Brody, Warsaw, *how* are you involved in all of this?"

He had paid the check, thanked Jean-Francois, given a nod to the rich older man and, Claire knew it, the no doubt very well-kept, very well-used hussy. The hussy, whose poise was only skin deep, gave a little wave 'goodbye'. Gavin, obviously, was not unacquainted with Geneva, as if Claire now had any doubt about his worldliness.

They sat in the small, rarely used lounge across the stairs from the Chat Botté. "Gavin, please answer my questions." Her right-side brain asked the question winsomely, curiously, perhaps even a little excited by the mystery. Her left side was an angry wife, a disciplinarian mother, a police interrogator. Even Claire who owned these simultaneous traits didn't like the mix.

He smiled an Irish smile, one from the old days. He strolled his eyes not quite lasciviously over her body, let the darkness of her look not cloud the twinkle in his eyes.

"Darling, I let you know I know about Brody and his buddies so that you would see I do know something about this kind of thing. Believe me there are hundreds, thousands, from policemen to politicians to bankers to diplomats who know it all too. It's not very special, and in some circles is boringly common knowledge. Your IFinCIG is just a few light years behind, that's all. I want you to appreciate that I know what you don't, and in fact for your own safety, even for the safety of that cowboy Barbour, shouldn't go looking to learn. I'd like to be your protector, but my power is very limited. I'd like to be your advisor, but that's a role I can't play for any number of reasons. I'd like to be your lover again, Medea be hanged and we're safe from her as long as you and I begin again away from Cambridge, tonight in the Beau Rivage for instance. And I don't want to be the man who sends condolences to your father in Kiev, or sheds tears year after year on your too early tomb. Now, darling, I've said everything I should and can. That's it.

"Now, you promised over the phone to have dinner with me tonight. Au Fin Bec is a little place I like, or much better at my hotel down the street, Des Bergues. Dinner in my room. I guarantee all of the services will be satisfactory."

"Dinner of course, not in your room, Gavin, and no buying dresses for me, and as for your advice I had already decided to quit IFFY because I'm sick of incompetence and hate bureaucracy and loathe working for government and don't think I'm good enough to be a financial crimes network investigator." A weighted pause, both hemispheres of her brain signalling wildly. "Unless you let me luck into being a good investigator by telling me who you know, what they do, and what you do for them now that you and your friends are no longer killing Protestant civilians, but just careening along studying that Russian free-market rap, reggae and rock 'n' roll."

"I love you, darling, and no, not enough to sign death warrants anymore."

"I like you very much, Gavin, part of you anyway, maybe all of you no matter how much I disapprove. Maybe I can't help how I feel by way of affection, not love anymore, but I can help what I do about it. We're friends, Gavin, that's all. I know you are mixed up in this whole black game, playing the edges yourself somehow; probably because you're bored to death just being famous at Cambridge, and the Irish in you craves excitement, and being able to buy ladies fancy dresses is a lot better than being poor. I don't trust you a bit, Gavin, and shame on me for it, but it doesn't even matter. So there, that's an end to it as far as my prying, your tidbits, and any ideas you might have had about our going to bed."

"I love you, darling. Whatever you say. But . . ." he paused. He saw, Claire followed his eyes, the door of the lounge they were in was glass, the elegant silver-haired man and the expensive dolly hanging on his arm as the two exited the

Chat Botté.

"You know them, of course. It looks to me like she knows you very well."

He grinned. "Not that well. She's not my type. You are."

"Who's her charming sugar daddy, then? Don't tell me he's a mechanic in a garage."

"No, he's famous in a way Génevois are. Money manager, financial advisor, rich as Croesus, they say. Very expensive tastes. I've met him a few times, suave Central European, can't remember whence he hails but he's very respected around here. Anything else you'd like to know about the world, darling?"

"Yes, but you'll never tell me."

Gavin looked at her tenderly. "You wouldn't like the world I'd tell you about, you already haven't liked what I've told you. But let me say one thing again. I love you. Always will. Ever need me, call."

They had a pleasant dinner together later. No allusions to politics, crime, or love. He talked about what an impossibly rigid place Cambridge had become, and about Yeats. She mostly listened, but for telling him novels good and bad she'd read before coming to Vienna. They did not go to bed together. They did not have breakfast together. She got to the airport for the early Swissair flight to Vienna. She realized how very much she had learned on this trip, about herself mostly, and what was important to her. She'd learned a lot about Gavin that had helped her learn about herself. She looked forward so very much to seeing Lee Barbour. She hoped he would forgive her, for what she had done had been essential to her moving more lovingly toward him. Both of her men had depths, surprises, were heroic and cynical, were bright, had pasts about which she would never know. It was Gavin's present she would never know either, not really. On the other hand she very much wanted to know all about Lee Barbour's present, and future, because with all her womanly wiles she would seek to be central to it. It was 7:45 when she called him at the Intercontinental. Yes, he would be delighted to pick her up at the airport. One mystery less; she knew in whose room she'd propose dining tonight.

Perhaps it would be a good time to call her father in Kiev, to introduce him over the phone to Lee Barbour. She knew, oh my how she knew after today with Gavin, that electronic communications were as open to well-heeled eavesdroppers as the old telephone lines were to small-town operators at "central." But in this case, personal things so pleasant, what did that matter?

40

Me Dolan. The Kid is Rooster. The job may work out. Mr. King is Mr. C. I continue my diary, Doreen, all for you. Well yes, for my ego and some kind of history as well. We wired Rooster, the better to know what was going down. There's less risk to him if we're on line, so to speak. The numbers are better now. I have hard-nosed backup.

Grossman has got his crew, all black or Hispanic in righteously beat-up old cars, moving in and about Malome, they are all tuned to mine and Rooster's way-out frequency, a very cute electronic trick this, thus I pray not on anybody's scanner or assigned-frequency radio frequency.

Cost/benefit analysis. Modern mantra. Fact is, there's more risk to Rooster if any of King C's friends find him wired. No, not "more"—just total. He'd be dead in a minute.

Wires these days aren't as cumbersome as they used to be. Little mike, little band-aid, nice chips. But you still, for street work, best wear it on your chest to pick up what they say, what you say. Wrist watches work, too. Nothing fancy after all in that department.

We're still doing it all by the seat of our pants. One nice thing, when the Rooster is by himself he can talk to us on his mike by talking out loud to himself. That's how we are getting his narrative, and the dialogue. Right on line, dirty money put in play from the bottom up, that's what Malome gives you.

Not nearly as puffy for the Crusader Mouse cop type as running a giant sting on the border where you bust Mexico's top eight bankers, or doing a raid with the locals to surprise a bank in Cyprus; you feel real big doing that. Or putting the Caymans out of the narcotics business. That all takes buildup, years. Here we're in a hurry. Got to be, pressure is still on from the big Man on down. Papers tell me the Russian premier is still hyping up a war. And Senator Cranmer has got a campaign roast going on, the President is on the spit for Vienna. Makes me feel real big to know I'm in an outfit, IFFY, which is big and bad enough to cost a war and a presidency. Christ, Doreen, politicians will say anything, Russia or here!

I'm kind of down today, in fact. Nothing I ever do in Malome makes me feel puffed up. I feel slimy, just another dirtbag which when anybody on the street looks at me, I am. So far I haven't figured out at all why somebody as big as Mr. C, I mean we know he's connected big-time, why he would be into the down and dirty of this place, the other scumbag towns where he's king of slime, capo of crap. Must be a lot of ego there, and yeah, something insecure where even though he can climb out of here permanently, instead he spends time being big frog in the cesspond when, no question given what Rooster has told us, a man of his talent could be a big shot on Wall Street.

Right this minute, here's what's going on. King C has told Rooster to meet him at a fast food joint in South City. Weird. We thought we were looking for the invisible man, and with one pull from the hat Rooster brings him out big as an elephant. The guy actually walks in daylight, although and significantly, not in Malome. Guaranteed different ID when he's elsewhere. Side bet? He's got a Nigerian passport, a Dominican passport, a gray wig.

Rooster's been given his instructions with reference to bringing to lunch the senior accountant at the currency exchange which Rooster is using, where he travels as senior bagman for Mr. C and the gambling joint. We, well this time the Bureau did help, did a little homework on Balfour, the exchange, and guess what? We learn that uncle King C didn't tell our lad that C himself owns the building housing the local main office for the *cambio* chain in California. That landlord could meet with those tenants any time. Or maybe they're his employees but don't know it. Cute.

Balfour's biggest U.S. locations of course are international airports. Balfour, under a different name, has got to be operating currency exchanges all across Europe and South America at the very least. If Mr. C really owns a piece of Balfour, he's a global entrepreneur, so he'll be laundering for lots of folks. What a gas if he's doing it for the Mob and the whole tale told Rooster to tell Furbo about maybe using the Mob's facilities for a little while was just to shine him up. Who's taking over whom, I've got to ask?

So, big surprise, we know C ain't telling the Rooster everything. No way. Rooster's learning though. Everybody in Treasury knows how these things work. As I sit here on the curb stinking of whiskey, itching from dirt, disgusted as I see a crackhead shouting dirty talk to himself, I figure Rockefeller had it right. He had everything right, didn't he? And so God must like crooks better than cops. Moses' tablets were the clean set of books, not the real ones ruling this world. And Doreen, love, to think you call me a cynic.

I think I can see what might be happening on this meet C is setting up for Rooster, where Rooster ropes in the Balfour head accountant. We got a fact; C knows his accountant is cheating on him, wants to know who else is in on it, will most surely take out anyone doing it. Subterfuge, imagine! Mr. C wants options. One is a smart Rooster who can take over Balfour, at least here on the west coast. He also wants a witness-identifiable patsy in the wings to lure his crooked Balfour International Banque de Change accountant into letting Rooster in on the scam. Rooster is smart and con-wise. He works his way in. One day very soon he opines the accountant is till-tapping big time, opines he could make it more profitable. Stick and carrot. Mr. C writes the script, hopes the kid gets cut in on the scam. Rooster as the Undercover Kid. Mr. C draws the sociogram of who else in Balfour is doing Mr. C dirty by inventing figures in the real set of books. Serious crooks are irrascible when it comes to being robbed; it's only the slobs who don't notice it. Con men, on the other hand are amused when somebody beats them. Professional admiration.

So C has Rooster, agile, cunning, eloquent, ambitious, become his inside man. Rooster can rise and run it all. Or that other option for Mr. C: if Rooster becomes too smart, is expendable, maybe C has to move in a hurry. Let Rooster be seen running around with the accountant, let him lure a thieving fly, or the nest of them, into the web. Any blowback, any bodies found if it came to that, and Mr. C would be very sure Rooster would be the one that witnesses had seen. My guess is that Mr. C is going to give Rooster a gun, one to be borrowed by one of Mr. C's hit men, gloved of course, to do the job on the accountant, or accountants. Another Al Capone-St. Valentine's Day Massacre. Just an option, of course. I'm quite sure Mr. C has lots of options, maybe like on the stock exchange. I tell you, Doreen, I won't sell him short.

At this (later) moment Rooster has had his moment with Mr. C and has been sent undercover, so Rooster and I have much in common although at the moment his backup across the street in the big city are Grossman's DEA people. He is dressed nattily in a summer-weight wool pinstripe, white shirt, conservative tie. Since I can now retire to a quiet place to listen, I hear him on the radio I have there. He's introducing himself to someone at Balfour's main big-city retail currency exchange, situated on the ground floor of a fine office building. Upstairs, we have done our homework, Balfour's accounting offices occupy an entire floor of Mr. C's fancy building (he may own dozens for all I know, Doreen).

"My church, the South City First Methodist, is having a big-time lottery.

The tickets are free, although we would greatly appreciate a contribution, which is why my brothers and I are working this rich commercial part of town. But, as you know, the First Methodist isn't far and the Reverend Gilbert is likely well known to you."

This would be true, for the Reverend Gilbert was famous as the respectable, activist minister of a most visible downtown social service, fine singing, under-upper-middle-class, every-race, big-city church. St Paul's kind of congregation. The mayor of big city himself was on the church advisory board; so were socialites, bank Presidents. Rooster had an advance from Chang to print the lottery tickets, along with a lovely forged church stationery letter introducing Brother Rooster. The Reverend Gilbert's signature with a real phone number that would play an authenticating tape should anyone call. A whole lot of trouble. Rooster had protested to Mr. C, but Mr. C, who is not to be argued with, insisted Rooster go in cold. Get next to the chief accountant, however you do it. It would be Rooster's scenario. What a con man that kid is. C knew it all along. You know me, Doreen, I'm slower.

Rooster was working the short con at Balfour's. "Go on, just fill in your names and phone number, everyone working here do that, and maybe you'll win ten thousand dollars. Got to warn you, real low chance, but not as bad as the state lottery. On the other had, if you want to give a donation, I'll give you a receipt so it is tax-deductible, and if you don't, you still get into the lottery." Two tellers behind the bulletproof glass, one clerk visible at a desk, and a closed door behind are all there is to be seen. The place was sterile.

"Come on, now," Rooster encouraged, "give everybody a chance. Anybody working in back?" The clerk, a no-consequence, poorly-dressed maybe Vietnamese girl opened the door to the back room and called. Two people, one a good-looking Asian woman about thirty—I got these stats later and insert them now—in attractive summer-silk white, and a sour-faced gray-haired white man, heavy glasses and rumpled gray suit, came out.

Rooster is all smiles, hands the tickets through the teller's cage. "Hey, you know it's good public relations to give the boss one of these. You got a boss anywhere around?"

Yes, they did. One of them glanced upward, not indicating heaven at all. Rooster scribbled 'for the boss' on the ticket, sent it upstairs with Sour Face Man, saying he, Rooster, would wait for the boss to fill it in.

"Thank you, thank you," he is saying, taking the ticket stubs with names and addresses (these addresses he is noting allow him to identify the upstairs boss and the pretty girl who seemed in charge here downstairs). He waits expectantly for some donation. One bored-looking white teller and the very pretty Asian girl from the back room each hand him a bill. The pretty girl has given him a fiver. The others stare him down, pocketing their number stubs. "The boss takes, he doesn't give," explained Sour Face Man in a characterization which fits too many in this world.

Three days later Rooster telephoned the retail number for the Balfour Currency Exchange. It was amazing, that two stubs from there had won. The boss and the pretty girl. It had been a lucky accident for them, for when the Reverend Gilbert himself had done the drawing—"No doubt you all saw it in the newspaper photograph?" asked Rooster—the two stubs had been sticking together, thus the third prize, a fancy dinner at an expensive restaurant, you know, that's maybe $100 a plate plus the limo service, would go, magnanimously, not to one couple but to both, seeing as how those stubs had been stuck together and the First Methodist Church folk feel very strongly about honest charities. "So just choose your night, both of you winners coming with the guest of your choice. Only one thing, because we have to rent that limo, both of you choose the same night, go together even if you dine at different tables. Anytime in the next ten days, if you don't mind. I'll wait here on the line while you all decide."

After some palaver they decide on a week from Thursday. Rooster planned to rent a limo, but on clearing cursorily with Mr. C was told to steal one instead. "Don't want anyone tracing you back to us for a phony lottery. Clever, you understand, but bogus church lottery and the Methodists will be annoyed. Bad public relations. So Rooster, you have someone steal us a limo for the evening."

So it was arranged. The stretch limo was stolen late at night at the airport, and driven to Malome for a makeup job. It was an overnight spray-paint color change, white to black, at an auto-paint shop in Malome, a kind of capital for auto theft industry. Mr. C told Rooster to find three escorts tough enough to be bodyguards. "Don't want anything happening to our guest," Mr. C had said, for his focus was on his chief accountant, not the theater bit players.

Rooster invited Blade, Snake and Moffat, who, for the two hundred fifty dollars each and plus an evening's ride in a fancy black limo four banks of seats long, looked at Rooster as a big-time benefactor. Snake was busy, but the two would be enough.

Rooster explained. "I pick them up at their door wearing high-fashion fancy chauffeur's threads, you be polite as can be and see to it they be seated and treated real respectful. Royalty, that's what they are tonight. That's when I get acquainted with their boss."

He has told his crew, "Pay you that very night, and we is away for a rendezvous, r-o-n-d-a-y-v-o-o-z, see? And you each of you rents formal wear for that night. All expenses on me. We make them feel very important. I call on each guest at their very door, escort them to the car. Regal, ain't it?" Rooster bowed, hand at his waist, to show how regal he was going to be.

Rooster had every right to feel proud of himself. No better way to make an inroad than to be a gracious giver to a man who loves to take. But Rooster had been conned himself. The limo had a phone. On the way to pick up the winning guests at their respective homes, Rooster had given himself plenty of time to get there in big city traffic. The phone rings. I can hear it through Rooster's wire.

The gist of it is that Mr. C is on the phone. Changed his mind about buying the dinner, the fine evening planned in the big city. Tell the guests they are special guests at a charity ball down in Palm City. "That ritzy?" I heard Rooster exclaim. "What if they don't want to come, I mean we did promise them a dinner?" I could only hear one end of it. Rooster with his two toughs in the seat next to him isn't able to tell us, me and the DEA men, where it is he's to go, but he does say, "Blade, Moffat, the man says we bring them to where he says no matter if they want to come or not. He just raised your night's pay to one thousand dollars each. Tie them up if you have to, but nothing rougher than necessary. He says we'll find some rope in the trunk. The man plans. The man wants his accountant delivered somewhere special. Says he'll call me again in twenty minutes."

So win a charity prize to a kidnapping, which is what C had in mind all along. Cute. Rooster calls at the door of each guest. No doubt family, friends, neighbors can ID him for what is unquestionably a kidnapping, and a nasty evening at best for the accountant. For the others too, if Mr. C doesn't want witnesses, which I guarantee he won't.

In twenty minutes the car phone rings. So does all the static in California. They must be passing under power poles or in a tunnel. The ring is all we hear. None of us backup know where the hell Mr. C has told Rooster to take them. Not too bad in theory, since DEA surveillance was supposed to be behind them. Worse than too bad since the surveillance team, new to the operation, had followed the wrong limo out of the remake shop that afternoon. They couldn't know better, couldn't know what plates and new jitney numbers the makeup shop would put on, wouldn't know the right color. They followed white, not black, not knowing that in Malome black is always the important color. Look at city government, the city council. Black is all there is that counts.

The white one that DEA followed was also stolen, but what other kind of limo makes it to Malome? Preordered by a client, which is what most first-class thefts are. New plates, new grill, new brand name, also new jitney license numbers. Opaque windows like all the airport limos. The DEA crew couldn't see inside, and followed it halfway to Reno before they got the idea that, much traffic I can tell you on the air, they had it wrong, that Rooster and his guests had no back up at all. Not good. We cops pride ourselves on being so damn clever too. This mistake smelled like deadly.

One who lived, little thanks to us, told us what happened. The isolated, desolate warehouse was dark when the limo drew up after its one-hour drive from South City.

Four terrified occupants, bound and gagged, blindfolded but not battered—Snake and Moffat had bounced too many club customers, with the policy of not prejudicing their more sober or sedate return to the tables, to be brutal. As with the police arrest dictum, only that force necessary to assure compliance, Blade and Moffat escorted the two couples out of the car, left them standing now roped together as Rooster's unintended catch, and as earlier instructed in that second phone call, we had to infer it, sped off to leave the fingerprint-free limo in a major restaurant parking lot at least fifty miles away.

They liked driving the limo. They elected Sacramento, a hundred miles away. They had arranged their own expense-paid transport, from understanding friends only, back home.

A large man Rooster had not met opened Mr. C's warehouse door at the predetermined knock. Two other men he had not seen before, a total of four, again racially mixed—a ghetto black man notices race socially before anything else, given his own salient experience—stood around the nearly bare, no longer antiseptic-smelling, concrete- and steel-echoing warehouse chamber. A thin man wearing glasses, meticulously dressed, rubbing his hands nervously, limped in through the door that Rooster knew led to accountant Chang's office. One leg was shorter than the other. Limpy was a no-face kind of man.

"Take the gags out of their mouths. Loosen their ropes, keep them blindfolded, offer them cigarettes, water or whisky if they want it. We are here to treat them well so that they can be taken home as early as possible. Charlie? Your car is ready to take them home?"

Charlie's strong voice said it was. Rooster had not been to a stage play before, but he knew a con when he saw one. Had he not set up the game for tonight himself? He had seen the movies. Interrogation. Hold out hopes, set up fears, friendly interrogator, unfriendly interrogator. Typical salt-and-pepper team.

"Now, take the two irrelevant ones outside. Keep those two here." The thin man nodded toward the companions of the two Balfour employees Rooster had set up, and whose invitations had been confirmed to Rooster by Mr. C, who obviously knew them all. One was the target accountant's dyed-blonde wife, dressed for dining; plump and so frightened she could not walk without help to a chair against a far wall. The other, a handsome thin Asian man. He wore a black suit, with a flower in his lapel, could have been lover or just date to the lovely girl who had been wearing the white dress the day of the phony lottery short-con. She was trembling but held her head up, chin telling them she was tough.

The two accountants—Mr. C had said they were that, the boss cheat at Balfour and the junior Asian woman—were made reasonably comfortable in two stuffed chairs new to the warehouse chamber. With its concrete floors, metal walls, and high trussed ceilings, every noise echoed.

Limpy began setting them up, disarmingly. "We know you kept the books for Balfour International, you, Elvis, were in charge, including the airport operations and some of Balfour International insofar as transmittals came in and out from overseas. We know you kept the second set for the several laundering operations coming through. We know you are only accounting employees who did what you were told, but you were well paid because you knew it was kinky."

Anyone listening could detect a slight accent, English or Australian, in a nervous voice. He went on. "We don't know who owns Balfour or who are principals in it. They hired us through cutouts. They told us one of you is a stinking thief keeping a third set of books for himself or herself. You may not know everything, but tell us, while we are still in a friendly mood, who else is in on the scam stealing from your bosses. Tell us where you laundered that money to. Tell us where your own set of uncooked books are, so we can do what we're paid to do: get the bosses' money back. That's all we're paid to do, unless you don't cooperate . . . The thief gets fired of course, maybe moved out of the big city, but cooperate and get the money back and we don't care what happens to you.

"Don't cooperate and..." Limpy's voice was now menacing. His hands rubbed together so fast that if there had been boy scout sticks and tinder there he would have set it on fire.

The others already knew Limpy was obscene, a menace. His agitated movements were too much like jerking-off palsy. The others knew, Rooster had to know, Limpy was some kind of pervert. There was sweat on his face as he walked over to the girl, putting his index finger on her nipple, saying, "Conversation, please."

She spat at him.

He ignored her, walking to the very fat black-suited, red-tie-attired senior accountant, Elvis, of the thick glasses, little jaw, pearly teeth as befits an accountant who brushes twice a day, and an ashen face.

"Mr. Clark, I know you want to talk to me. You will beg to be allowed to talk to me. I can tell you how it can happen in a thousand ways. The easiest is that I will pay you five thousand dollars to talk and then drive you home. If through you we can get back those maybe millions you stole, it's worth it for us to pay you rather than do you harm. After all, I'm a businessman myself. And we tell no one, any more than you would. Alternatively your wife will suffer much unpleasantness, and you will soon be shrieking. Take your choice.

"And you, Camellia." He was speaking to the Asian girl, who was wearing a long dark silk dress, pearls, a pale gray silk scarf. "The same for you. Get paid now or scream later."

Limpy meant it. It was the tone of voice and anticipatory agitation that caused the chill, the goose bumps. Street violence is impulse, bravado, pride, honor, social pressure, greed, and among the experienced ones, pretended indifference. Assassinations are rational in their own way. But very few among even the bad guys torture people or get their rocks off threatening torture. Idi Amin, Caligula with a limp.

There could be no question—Rooster, however much he had been of two minds about going straight or getting rich in Mr. C's et Cie, was in over his head, and he had brought these poor bastards here. His neighborhood was civilized compared to Limpy and his friends. One knows. Rooster wished he were home watching TV with a beer in his hand, his sister, his folks nearby.

The fat accountant went for the money and spilled something of what he knew, but denied he was the main man. A gentleman, he laid it off on Camellia. "She's the brain, she set it up, she takes the skim. Always has."

Camellia gasped, called him several kinds of liar.

He snarled at her. "Camellia," he said, "knows a lot more than I do. She is smarter, they trust her more. Hell, I bet you think just because I'm older that I am in charge, I set up the scam. You ought to know better. It takes real brains and a CPA to do tricks worldwide. Hell, she's the CPA, I'm her flunky, whatever the staffing chart said. She paid me, I took a cut, sure—but salary that's all."

Limpy smiled. "Fine, okay, but just tell us the name of all your countries, all your banks, all your relatives, the numbers to your safe deposit boxes, where we get the keys, and give us on your way home a couple good samples of your signature. We do the rest. We'll take you home now."

He gestured to the others, "Go get his wife, put them in the car. Charlie, here's his ten thousand in cash, which he gets at his front door." He handed over a fat envelope. "Okay with you, Mr. Clark?" Mr. Clark nodded. Against the cinder block gray of the warehouse wall, his ashen face matched. Over against the wall, plump Mrs. Clark fainted with relief. Charlie and another white guy got them out to a car. They all heard it drive off. They wouldn't get killed until they'd been driven home, handed over the safe deposit box keys, the bank account numbers, all of it. After that, bye-bye.

Limpy turned toward Camellia. "So, Camellia, you're our girl according to what your colleague, Mr. Clark, tells us. You're smart enough to know we can't collect a penny just knowing what we already know, that the bosses have been systematically robbed. Bad faith, Camellia, bad faith, and bad business because Elvis there rolled over on you. Not a trustworthy man is he, that Mr. Clark, I mean to betray a working trust like that? Now, be sensible like Mr. Clark and go home happily with your boyfriend, or suffer a great deal and maybe die. We both know, Camellia, that no amount of money is worth even a hangnail's pain. Please, Camellia, do yourself some good and get this behind you. Don't forget we offer a reward."

Limpy sidled over to, sat on the stuffed arm of her chair. He put his hand on her leg, began moving it slowly, tender as a climbing boa constrictor, toward her crotch. He gestured to Charlie to tie her to the chair so he could play. She was writhing and started to scream. Her companion, in a chair against the wall, got up. One of the watchers kicked him in the crotch, gave him a karate chop, and watched him crumple to the ground. Limpy put his hand over Camellia's mouth. He put his lips against her ear, gave her some tongue there, saying, "You do have a choice, dear, no play and a five thousand dollar take-home payment, or I play with you lots. You can guess that I like to hurt girls, can't you?"

She managed to bite his covering hand. He drew it away bloody, slapped her hard on the face, and beckoned to Charlie to help him force her into the back room.

It was bad behavior even for Malome, and Rooster was appalled. For all its vices, on the streets there was a kind of respect for a woman—not a whole lot up front maybe, but for all the screwing, rape was uncommon. It was yet a matriarchal culture.

Rooster had a gun but could not make up his mind to try to use it. Blade and Moffat, sitting against the wall, stared blankly. Phony tough maybe, but being cool when being rough was their trade. They were empty bottles. Anyone who knew them knew that much. Rooster would have to be the Lone Ranger.

Even yelling "Hi-ho, Silver, away" and getting out with his skin by virtue of surprise fast shooting, by killing your boss's boys does not move you toward promotion. One thing on his side: Blade and Moffat wouldn't go up against him, so he just had the four in the room to deal with. Some of them might well be better shots than he was, but they were watching the sadist, ignoring the kid in the chauffeur costume. At that moment Rooster would have had to be engaged in a difficult career decision, if he hadn't got sick first. Hamlet puking. He could hear Camellia pleading, then screams, then, it took a long time, moaning, then quiet.

Charlie dragged the naked and torn, ravished and bloody body through the door along the cement floor. Limpy, nonchalant, pointed to a very large pail and some cement sacks that Rooster, Blade and Moffat, surely not the guests, had not earlier noticed. Charlie mixed and poured wet cement into a maybe-twenty gallon barrel. The fellow, Filipino maybe, who had karate-chopped Camellia's friend, helped him. Together they were pushing her head into the cement. She was still breathing, not much, but alive. She was also bare-ass naked and the bruises on her thighs and buttocks shone purple. Undignified as her bruised pudenda went upside down for all to see, a few even now to lick their tongues over. When her head went under, Rooster could hear the gurgle, see the bubbles come up the viscous wet, see one last reflexive twist as her legs kicked up and her back arched.

She was still kicking. Limpy was in the doorway watching, grinning. You could see his hard-on, behind a semen-wet fly, go limp.

If he could pull her head out, there was still a chance. She was still kicking. Rooster moved to pull his gun, a .357 Magnum, out of his shoulder holster. Four against one plus Limpy who was too stoned out of his skull to count. Wrong odds, and Rooster, naive, never was a real shooter. The gun was never out of his holster before three, five, count them, seven slugs tore into him. He had wondered if being killed hurt.

It did, but not for long enough to tell his mother about.

Charlie grinned. "Some guys just don't have what it takes. Limpy is always a test of guts, aren't you, Limpy?"

Rhetorical, Limpy was still, post-orgy, out of it. "Swab the floor, take the chair over to the dump. Put the chauffeur there in a cement hat too. And the boyfriend. Take these three stiffs once the cement is hard and throw them off the bridge. Mr. C kind of likes to hear about these head-first Olympic dives, and with the heads in concrete they won't come bobbing up months later like they can do when you only put their feet in cement."

Charlie then turned to Limpy, whose stoned, blinking, vacant vacant eyes were still on the sweet dreams pipe. He had an idiot grin. Charlie asked him, "Did you actually learn anything from her in the back room, I mean what Elvis was ratting about? I figured you were just enjoying yourself."

"Surprised me too. Toward the end. They all talk to me before the end. A real surprise.

"She really was skimming big time. Our boss has no idea. Elvis was the jerk he said he was. It was her doing it. With her father, who runs Balfour Asia. He lives in Hong Kong. She said she knows Balfour has a special office in New York, another one in Geneva. I have to think the boss knows about that. Something special she said by way of connection to Vienna and Warsaw—lots of Warsaw transmittals, she said. Toward the end they get kind of hard to understand, she wasn't talking real good, you understand; the pain gets in the way. But I take my time, I do it and I listen. Her father and some German have a special little deal going on, just like she had, screwing their partners."

"Vienna, you said, that would make him Austrian," corrected Charlie.

"All right, Austrian. Who cares, they all look alike." Limpy turned his eyes to the naked girl, lovely legs, thin back, buttocks shining in the light, her pussy dripping. "But that one was real good. And so she had a third set of books and we can get them down to the boss tomorrow, okay?"

Charlie and the others, all dull-eyed now because it had already been a late night, assented. There was mopping, carting, dragging, driving, dumping to be done. And tomorrow, thank God, only a simple break-in to get those ledgers.

41

Mr. C had been pondering the bad luck of two big busts on two major deliveries so close in time, so neatly distant in place. Wholesalers at the receiving end? Only if the DEA had connected those two disparate operations and turned separate informants from each.

Not likely. And so it was someone near him here. There were too many to consider to make it easy. Drivers, packers, muscle, like Charlie; local dealers who could have given him up on some stupid sheriff's interrogation for a minor bust, with stupid county narc surveillance following and making the cars, then busting them far away to keep away any local suspicion. His accountant, Chang? Fred, the pervert with the limp who had done so well last week pumping, pun intended, from Camellia? C shook his head with surprise. There was always something new in this business. Yes, a real surprise her father and Brody had something going on on the side. No partner likes that.

It had been a win-lose week. Mr. C didn't take pleasure in learning how stupid he'd been; Camellia, her father, and Brody, all such little people, taking the Partners for a ride.

But now, they'd go on the ride. Mr. C kept out of the other Partners' business when it wasn't his, but Sir Alfred had been his, because they had all invested trust in him. Money laundering is based on trust; Mr. C understood that full well. A little skim sure, like the rule, "an honest barkeep steals only ten percent." Fine. But Sir Alfred had been a very bad boy. Camellia and her daddy and Brody were very bad children too. Her daddy and Brody would get a spanking they would not live to remember.

Mr. C would have to tell the others. Fly to New York tomorrow. Meet with Shadow, who sat next to the man he called his Client. Mr. C wasn't nosy himself, and expected others of the Partners to respect his privacy too. "Live and let lie," was the motto.

Amazing what he had learned since prep school scholarship at Winchester in the U.K., then being an undergraduate at Princeton, going on for an M.Phil in Economics at Cambridge where he had digs in Jesus College. Lots of special people he'd met and learned from there. All a long way from Lagos, where he'd been born. "Nothing like a good education to fit a man for civilization." As Mr. C said it to himself there was more realism than irony in the thought.

"Too bad about Rooster," Mr. C was telling himself. Kid had a lot of class. He was provoked too easily to violence, one might say. In this business you have to be tolerant of quirks. Learn what matters most. Mr. C under a different name had a seat on the Board of Trustees at Princeton, and under that name the Chairmanship of the board of a very wealthy electronics company right near here. He'd used his early scam monies to invest in it. It had paid off in the millions. But this street stuff, he got a kick out of it. Two lives are more fun than one. Mr. Gladstone out of Lagos, Princeton, and Cambridge, Mr. Rich Respectable genuine Afro-American, was welcome everywhere.

And for kicks, and as it turned out rather more millions a year than he'd ever expected, milking the ghetto for every dollar they wanted to throw away. Drugs, arms, yes, and the money laundering to move it to Europe, invest through London, let the two sources of wealth feed one another. Potentiate. He said it again, "Too bad about Rooster. Just too damn sentimental, too young to keep his feelings in check."

Tomorrow Mr. Gladstone would fly in his Gulfstream V to New York. He was already wondering at which restaurant to dine. Decisions, decisions—life as a successful entrepreneur, so respected, so sought after, why he was even serving on Senator Cranmer's Election Committee as National Vice Chairman. So much to do, so much lovely time to do it in.

Before he left for New York and became Gladstone in his swank Bay city apartment, King C had to meet with Chang, his private accountant. The warehouse was their usual place. All cleaned up, safe enough at eleven p.m. in that quiet neighborhood. Mr. Chang, an alias of course, handled Mr. C's money, including Balfour abroad. They must start the damage control, recovery of whatever Brody and Balfour Asia had snuck aside.

As with the fat man, Sir Alfred, serious people have ways to get serious money back.

The Advisor must be notified. He always had good ideas. So did Chang. As Asia became more important he would become a Partner, no doubt about it.

In the meantime Mr. C sat in a strongly chlorinated smell in a contraband-filled warehouse in the debased Malome milieu at eleven p.m. Chang, too, enjoyed slumming, playing ghetto hood games, Humphrey Bogart, Fagin. They were enjoying a multi-million-dollar silence over a good cigar.

Then the whole damn warehouse seemed to explode.

"Police, police, police, open up. Search warrants. Open up."

Doreen, believe me I was the one shouting the loudest. If it hadn't been my stupidity, none of the ugliness would have happened. Of course I remembered what Rooster had told us about the warehouse. It came to my mind immediately when the limo was diverted. I had done my theatrical stagger from in front of Robbie's Club, just readying to slide into an alley to call DEA, Stein, Markowitz, for if ever there were an emergency this was it. And somebody mugged me! Must have seen the radio, seen something worth stealing from a scumbag. Or hoped for it. I had a glimpse, before I collapsed, of a couple of teenage hoods, and then boom and ke-bam!, something came crashing down on my skull. I was out, or half out, for three hours, best I can guess, since they took my watch, my guns, and the radio. Lovely Malome, I vaguely was aware that while I was lying there a couple of other homeboys came through. Two went through my pockets to see if there was anything left. The others just stepped over me. Call an ambulance, call the cops? No way. Those kids must have loved mugging a cop.

Mr. C would have been looking at that entrance room of the warehouse. He would have seen the sharpened prongs of a forklift pushing, piercing the resisting steel door.

"Sheeeyyyiiiittt." I can hear his surprise. But no panic, I am sure never any panic. Mr. C was a planful man.

Mr. C, and Mr. Chang with him, were into the secret door in the office, down into the tunnel, walking resolutely, that would be the word for a seasoned twosome like that, the several hundred feet to the tumble-down building across the street. Prudence had driven Mr. C to this arrangement when he'd purchased, via a phony company of course, the warehouse. Mr. C didn't trust life in Malome any more than anyone else. It was only much later that we found the tunnel. Only by accident that Blade and Moffat were nabbed by the highway patrol for speeding up to Sacramento in a car where the serial numbers didn't check out. Unlike their fingerprints, which did. They sang and sang, which was how we learned of the death of Rooster. Descriptions of Limpy and Charlie, the others, emerged.

Furbo incidentally. This kind of finding the police do very well. The warehouse was full of dope, guns, forensic evidence of murders. They were all charged and snitched on one another like noisy bluejay birds.

I'm only guessing about a man who might be named Gladstone. Markowitz and I flew to Washington the next day. Barbour came to meet us. He brought his fiancée, the famous fiancée Claire. We poured over intelligence reports, concentrated mostly on what Claire gave us intuitively about the moral dangers of attending Cambridge doing economics when something is unbalanced in your soul. Cambridge had nourishingly generated a different sociopathy, hatred and power lust really, with Philby and his friends, the famous five—or six or more—those famous spies for Russia in the forties, fifties. There may yet have been even more Blues, old boys who stayed at it in MI5 and MI6 betraying undetected, retiring in time for glasnost. Most disappointing for them, no doubt.

From the work of the meeting we had enough to give to criminal intelligence services in the Bureau, the Company, MI5, DEA, State, Deutsche Kriminalamt some of what they needed. Computers hummed, the analysts stayed up late. The usual network computational operation. Good software these days, very good. Sounds scientific but it is all based on one good hunch.

Claire's, for example: it came up after she had lunch with somebody she liked a lot, or at least once had, an economist named Garrity. Everything in those big computers came up blank on him but for fame in economics and lots of explicable travel to Russia as an advisor there.

So out of the possibles, and the record of those who were big at the Symposia as well, by physical description, time sequences, chains of acquaintance, whatever Garrity's role, Claire connected him as being acquainted at the Cambridge symposia with Todor Mihailov. That fellow's much-abused, obviously cruelly interrogated body was found in Virginia while we worked. Sir Alfred we knew about from Vasil to Sophie. Gladstone was an intelligence fit, a student of Garrity, with altogether too many empty spaces in his life history, but we found nothing concrete on him whatsoever. No unknown fingerprints in a Malome warehouse. No DNA on those two cigars smoked that night, for they had burned to ash. But twenty-five-dollar cigars, as determined by forensics, found in Malome, do cause speculation.

As for the others, Brody tied in from every which way—which meant only he couldn't come back to anywhere ouside the CIS without getting busted. Not to worry, he'd be killed by his own. Balfour Asia tied in nicely because after all, perverted Fred the Limp had heard it from torture-raped Camellia. For which he would die in San Quentin, and I'm damn glad for it. And we got the news on Balfour Asia et al. et Cie from Limpy Fred while he was still hoping to plea-bargain out of a death sentence. His buddy Charlie would also sit sniffing gas in the little green room at San Quentin under the "special circumstances" rule. From Sophie in Sofia, and Vasil, and Claire again, we joined others to the rich and bloody web: Bratislav, Square, all of those. Claire also had an intuition about a man she'd seen nod to Garrity in Geneva, but you can't let that kind of thing, a woman's intuition, interfere with good sense. We told her so. She didn't argue but I know she had some reservations about whose good sense was in question.

In the background, hovering, was Senator Cranmer about whom one could only have suspicions. But not the voters. With the Russian premier still babbling macho, at this moment as I write to you, Doreen, a habit now since I will be home to hug and hold you come tomorrow, I must tell you I realize it is possible that a real crook could become President. Hard to believe, my high school civics teacher would have had a stroke, but yes, Doreen, possible. Probable? Maybe even that.

Markowitz, Stein, and Bo—who is street me, your Dolan—we all miss Rooster very much. He was a man, a kid no longer, and in it for himself no longer. He turned hero in circumstances when most men turn coward. It was our fault that he died, because we were supposed to protect him. My fault because I couldn't protect the back of my skull from two—I would guess that was their number—adolescent street punks on a random prowl for bucks and kicks. No matter that DEA, and we at IFFY, got credit for the biggest-ever contraband bust ever in California. It was in the scheme of things that, like my bust on the head, it went wrong. In the scheme of things as we had envisioned them, C was our key to the partners whom political pressures pushed us to find pronto.

Everyone was wrong. Mr. C or Gladstone just walked away forever from Malome. So did the other man—Rooster had called him Chang, but names in this business are ephemeral. It was he who had smoked that other cigar. Accountants never die, they just keep adding up.

But in the scheme of things one good thing happened, at least as a battlefield death, as a hero, as a kid becoming a man. These days no one talks about it, nor let alone strives for it. Rooster's actions assured it for him in the memory of all of us involved in this black game, we who chase down those who are working the edges. To die for honor, eschewing money, to die heroic and very young, eschewing whatever power dirty money brings—that is a greatness. Over beer in Robbie's on the day we learned Rooster had been killed, three grown men cried.

42

It was worth the steamy heat of the White House Rose Garden to see Claire first, and then Barbour receive the Distinguished Federal Law Enforcement Service medals from the President. The President liked a good press more than roses; after all, few Presidents are horticulturalists. To give Claire a medal was the best PR stunt since Teddy Roosevelt had himself photographed riding up San Juan Hill during the Spanish-American War. Or at least the President hoped so. For his electioneering opponent Senator Cranmer, powered by (a) the idiocy of Russian-saber rattling over the Vienna Incident, (b) continued fussing from "elements" in the Austrian and Bulgarian, and now Polish, Estonian and Latvian parliaments as well, (c) left- and right-wingers from all around the U.S. screaming bloody murder, still pointing to those arguably identified Russians from Laxenburg, and (d) a press and public that was eating it up, was breathing polling statistics down the Executive neck.

Oh what a speech he made praising "this brave woman in Federal service who nearly lost her life, suffered privation and torture, and yet helped to bring to justice the dangerous international conspiracy of criminal entreprenueurs, profiteering terrorists (his speech writer particularly liked that) who are willing to stop at nothing to destroy the morality of nations as well as the lives and fortunes of their people." It was hardly an aside that he then announced U.S. backing for further international efforts, for NAFTA countries to join in the (1996) Council of Europe's Convention on Criminal Matters, and the further conventions on Laundering, Search, Seizure and Confiscation of the Proceeds of Crime and on Administrative Cooperation in Tax Matters; support the Vienna UN Crime and Drugs Division, also the Financial Action Task Force (FATF) linked to IFinCIG etc., etc., etc. Even the well-watered roses in the garden began to wilt. But it's the kind of thing about which every hand, however wilting of boredom, like those rose petals, had to applaud.

"Capital," said the President later referring to his speech, the press coverage, where he was and wished to stay on for another term in office, and perhaps the number of letters in the aforementioned treaty instruments. "Capital," he said again. "Give the Dubois woman another promotion," he ordered. "Capitol"—that's where he intended to live next term.

"I'm sorry, Mr. President, but she resigned from Federal Service yesterday. In private she had some very uncomplimentary things to say about bureaucracy. Sources tell us after her honeymoon she's taking a very fancy job in literature, maybe high up on the Board of the National Endowment for the Humanities. She's a mover and doer, Mr. President. I'd keep an eye on her. One day she'd be good for a National Committee post."

"Nuts to that," said the President indifferently. "See if you can keep the fact she's quitting out of the papers. It looks bad so soon after I've given her a medal. Leak the fact that she's getting married to that other fellow I gave the medal to, and wants time out for babies or something. Uh, so she quit, eh? Okay, leak it to the slimier press that she's pregnant. Humanities, eh—artsy-fartsy, eh? Turn her back on my medal, will she?

"Okay, pregnant and unmarried. That ought to do it. After all, we've got to pump this thing for all we can get out of it and we can't afford dirt on our face, no kind of dirt." He paused, then asked, "Didn't somebody tell me her father is our ambassador to Kiev?"

"Yes, sir, and no, sir. Mr. President, he's our ambassador *in* Kiev, but the embassy is *to* the Ukraine."

"Okay, okay, to hell with the details. Call him back to Washington so I can give him the National Parenting Medal because his daughter turned out so peachy-keen."

"Mr. President, there is no such medal."

"Okay, so I just created it. Let's honor the new medal's creation by giving it, one day at a time, to fifty parents, one from each state, who've had some kind of heroic child. Tear-jerking is catchy. Kid drowns saving another kid, a dog, whatever. The parents taught them selfless bravery, that kind of stuff. Play the kid angle, play the American family angle, American values, honesty, courage, how my administration stands for all the yummy stuff. Give it the works. Keep it on the front page. Damn that Cranmer."

"There is one more thing you might do, Mr. President."

"Fine, spill it. Don't just stand there thinking about it."

"Well, the two ambassadors who really did a beautiful job were Ron Owen in Vienna and that fabulous woman of ours, Sophie something or other, ambassador in Bulgaria. You know how Cranmer is riding that Vienna Incident, there's got to be something going between him and the Russian premier, the way they are playing this duet together. Well, it's the two ambassadors who really let the IFFY team do their job. They're the State Department at its best, just like Dubois is, and if we put them onstage telling it like it is, it refutes for the *n*th time all this Cranmer crap. Let the ambassadors get a medal in the Rose Garden, put them on 'Nightline,' Larry King, 'Sesame Street,' the whole enchilada. The facts, Mr. President, just as we need them: straight and manufactured to our specifications: Factual repudiation, Mr. President. Anyone in their right mind needs to know this whole Vienna Incident is a crock of *mafiya* shit."

"Right minds in the electorate I don't count on. Sometimes maybe, but they voted me in, they might vote Cranmer in. Show me a right mind in those ballots."

The senior aide rightly supressed his astonishment at what he had heard.

"So okay, get those people medals too. Bring in the Secretary of State, CIA Director, Treasury, Defense, the same cast we had for giving the medal to that damn woman who got pregnant and quit us."

"Mr. President, it is just the leak, sir. No one thinks she's really pregnant."

"Off the record, you should have brought her in here first. Then we'd see what she can really deliver. Not a bad looker, that woman."

"You never said that, sir, never. Right?"

"Said what, you idiot?"

"Right, Mr. President, absolutely right."

"So now go out and get it all done." The President paused. "I've got the angle on Cranmer now. We say he's siding with ten thousand Russian nuclear warheads aimed at us, siding with the Mafia—spell it the way people used to, damn it—trying to kidnap and kill Americans, siding with the big business and banking criminals of this world to rob the working man of what he's earned, sided with those who'd destabilize the world, give it over to gangsters and crooked politicians abroad. Yeah, that's what the son of a bitch is doing, and even if he isn't, give it the right press punch and everyone will see he's been doing just that. Damn it, I've got the angle on the SOB. See if we can't get the AG to announce an investigation, have the FBI check Cranmer's phone calls to Russia—you know, pour it on the bastard."

"Mr. President, sir, you know it's illegal to use the FBI politically. And besides, I already did. They say he's never called Russia, never even been there. He's nasty, sir, but he looks clean to them, sir, not that I've ever used them to find out, you understand that, sir?"

"Right. Don't use the FBI. Remember, I said it was illegal. And now damn it, go out and put all this together. I've got a campaign to win!"

"Yes, Mr. President."

"And mind you, see that I do win, or else I'll ask the FBI to get what they can on you."

The senior aide paled a moment. "Yes, Mr. President." And so it came to pass that power, so directed by greater power, went immediately to do as it was told.

43

Two other quieter occasions, without flashbulbs, had a ceremonial side. In England Sir Peter was present when Quincy Adams arrived, having been invited, quite a surprise, to tea with the Foreign Secretary. Protocol required that the U.S. Ambassador, ol' "Mr. Mississippi," as the Foreign Secretary also knew him but dared not say publicly, was present. A few others senior at the Yard and, ones simply presumed, MI5 and MI6 were there. Just tea, nothing formal really; just a few words of thanks from the Secretary to Sir Peter, to Quincy—referred to formally as the Honorable Dr. Adams—just quiet words of thanks for "your discreet and supportive role so very much assisting in resolving the Vienna Incident and its antecedents." And by protocol to the U.S. Ambassador, *pro forma*: "And thank you, sir, for your assistance, provided so delicately and informally that we were not made aware of it. Mr. Ambassador, the Queen is grateful for what America has done *vis-à- vis* the Russian criminal class and in resolving so fortunately the difficulties surrounding the Vienna Incident—in particular for your sensitivity to British interests in the matter. It is in the best tradition of the special relationship that has always been so much treasured between our two countries."

The ambassador, ol' Mr. Mississippi, beamed, and even refrained from being so gauche as to ask for a Jim Beam with branch water instead of tea. As for the thanks given, the ambassador wasn't even aware of what he'd done, which, as everyone else there knew all too well, was because he had done nothing. That was ever so delicately conveyed in the little kernel of words by which the Foreign Secretary indicated the English were not aware of it either. Remember that English definition again: a gentleman is one who never insults unintentionally. Only the best of civil servants can carry it off, as here so delicately that there was no insult conveyed to Mr. Mississippi. But the insult was nevertheless apparent to the others of the company with a secret appreciation of the art of language because, as they all knew, Mr. Mississippi would not comprehend any of it. The ambassador did comprehend, ever more intensely as the minutes passed, that he was sorely missing his customary five o'clock Beam and branch water and late-afternoon tussle in the hay with his, by now impatient, too-personal secretary.

As a second informal affair, the Secretary of State invited just a few Deputy Secretaries, the head of the Bureau, and the Director of the Agency; the Ambassadors to Vienna and Sofia, now returned to get their medals; Ambassador Dubois, his daughter Claire, and her fiancé Lee Barbour, to a small dinner. It was now informally known that Barbour had, as his first job in government, worked for State Department Intelligence; then, dangerously, under the auspices of the Advanced Research Projects Agency, the nature and history of which was still unknown, was pitted against Che Guevara and a man who had become Barbour's friend as well, a red guerrilla priest, the Louvain-trained Jesuit Camillo Torres.

Other news of Barbour was made known in private ways; for example, that if Humphrey had won against Nixon, Barbour would likely have headed the CIA. Markowitz was also present, which seemed unlikely at such a gathering of glittering insiders. One piece of revealing gossip, circulated via the Secretary of State—no secrecy rules violated thereby, since no such information ever circulates—that Barbour had done the work that led to the founding of IFinCIG, and had himself, with the heads of DEA and the Agency—over lunch, for where else when serious confidential matters arise in a network—founded the Bureau of Intelligence in BNDD, now become the DEA. The Secretary also let it be known, although always deniably, that Markowitz had left Washington at the boot end of a zealous Cabinet member (did that person actually represent the President, as he had claimed?) for whom Markowitz had refused to head an assassination team to work abroad—an assignment which under law was no different at all than what the Partners these days, and the KGB and Bulgarians in the old wet-affairs days, did without qualms. No honors came to Markowitz, or his often colleague Barbour for such activities or refusals; for in a world of secret deeds and private morality, a world of shadows, who could be sure which *were* in fact the honorable men, and women?

Might it be told, for example, that Markowitz, under some guise, travelled to the funeral of Camillo Torres, whom he had so intensely sought to persuade not to become a guerrilla; one of hundreds of thousands in that reciprocal dance of death, that immense silent marching column of shades across mountain and jungle?

That was why the Secretary of State, knowing that no honors ordinarily came to such extraordinary and unambitious men and women, wished to be sure that those dining knew that the two quiet men here, Barbour and Markowitz, belonged in their elite company, and were indeed entitled to their respect and gratitude, as insiders so deeply inside that insiders hadn't known.

It was, then, just another one of those spontaneous old buddies' gatherings, which just happened to be scheduled to take place in the Secretary's VIP Dining Room in Foggy Bottom. And in fact there existed in each one present a sense of familial togetherness.

Those at the top who knew, as the public did not know, just how tense and miserable the top jobs could be. They were really all good folk and had a remarkably good time, some not without a tear in their eyes at one moment or another as they realized how much they owed to one or another of their company. One might even say of each of them that they yet knew honor, patriotism, a few glories, and of course many failures.

As a matter of courtesy, Barbour invited Senator Cranmer's cousin Nancy, the airline stewardess who had been so kind when he was wounded, to lunch at the Jockey Club.

Claire of course was invited, but begged off, for she was in serious talks about her career with publishing houses in London and New York, and with the National Endowment for the Humanities in Washington. Everyone wanted her. Her book of poetry had been an immense success, and the reverberations from a prize she had received further resulted in her initiating funding for young artists, including a program of poetry readings at the Kennedy Center. Indeed a plan was going forward, so far in her own mind only, now that she was connected, for the best to be read in the Rose Garden itself. She was enjoying both admiration and celebrity.

As for Nancy, she was full of admiration for the Vienna Incident and for her now famous friend Barbour. Her news was, she said, minor. Yes, there was a man in her life whom, she said, a calculating woman might entice into marriage: an airline pilot who liked mountain climbing, parachute acrobatics, and wilderness hiking. Marriage, however, terrified him. "But," she opined, "I think he will come around."

Barbour was pleased for her, then asked after her cousin Senator Cranmer.

"Ah, that bastard! His own mother hates him more than ever, and it's all deserved. I saw him once again. My Lord, what a cold-blooded, self-satisfied schemer and posturer he is. Someone needs to bring him down before his nonsensical Presidential campaign actually succeeds. I hope you have something on him, Lee, something that reads dramatically in the headlines."

Lee regretted more than Nancy could know that he had not; suspicions do not make for press releases by honorable men. Barbour would not stoop to slander. Even so, the intelligence network software programs were humming in the Interagency Task Force even now, looking at the Partnership. Who knew, something might come up. Even brilliant schemers can make revealing mistakes.

The "wolf pack" was invited to the Cosmos Club for dinner the evening of the Rose Garden ceremonies. It was just before dinner that a top-secret printout of the interagency task force intelligence report on what had come to be called "the Partnership" was brought by two aides—one IFFY, one DEA—to the "wolf pack five." How better than "The Partnership" to describe the links and the power of those identified, suspected or, like dark matter in the universe, not understood but inferred to exist by the power of its activities? And how better to describe those who had been hunting down the Partnership than, as over perhaps a surplus of gin and tonic on their second evening in Washington, someone, no one remembered which, had said, "Hey, we *are* a kind of wolf pack, you know? I mean, it's not so shabby, that list we've tied down." And in reply from another, "Yeah, not bad. And except for Rooster, all alive and well, kicking and two out of the five engaged." It was Barbour who added, "Let's make it the 'wolf pack six,' because Vasil in Sofia deserves as much credit as any of us. So does Injun Joe Erwin as far as that goes, but nobody can take a chance on leaking his identity. The Marine Corps and our State Department are very nervous about announcing that one Marine damn near on his own, well, expedited by an ambassador, tangled with the dirty half of Russia.

"Congress or the Executive declare the wars. Sergeants are only supposed to fight them. And we also set a glass upside down in memory of Rooster, right?"

It was right, and so a crystal glass, summoned from barkeep Butch, was turned upside down in honor of their colleague who had not lived to be joined in the wolf pack. There was a moment of silence, even prayer, as they, each slightly embarrassed but doing it as though in church, made a circle around the table of their hands. A tough guy who is not also tender is only half a man.

Claire arose from her chair. It was, after all, her club and she was hostess. "And so now, formally, and to be upstanding, a toast to the wolf pack six and one half, the public half of Sergeant Injun Joe being in public eclipse. And to Rooster."

"Hear, hear!" And indeed, others in the marble-floored, elegant bar of the Cosmos Club did hear a toast made "to the wolf pack six and one half," and, so the onlookers heard it, "a rooster." Puzzling. The Cosmos Club is composed of some of the world's most distinguished persons, who by achievement in the arts, sciences, humanities, diplomacy are so recognized. (Claire's election was based partly on the prize she had received during her publishing days when she raised funds for, set up, and served on the board of a foundation whereby young writers of poetry, drama, and fiction could be published on merit, not on expected income, as commercial publishers demanded.) Indeed, in tribute to Claire, a book of her own beautiful poetry had been published commercially. Rich stuff.

"A happy Sylvia Plath, the knowledge of sorrow and despair balanced by humor, confidence and elevating beauty," one reviewer had said. Its circulation out of the Club library was active. Much brain power was assembled there in the bar lounge of the Cosmos. Even so, and however that intelligence was applied, the toast overheard by those others remained a puzzle. Wolves and roosters, a curious mix of animals.

Officer Andy Stein arose, head shaven, two hundred ninety pounds of muscle and Teutonic good cheer, though a beer belly was beginning to appear: "And to all the little cubs a wolf pack couple may care to generate. Congratulations on the engagement."

At which there was applause for Claire Dubois and Lee Barbour. And a toast of thanks returned.

There was much excited talk of what that network intelligence software had begun to display when institutions of finance, shipping, industry, and some sectors of governments and law enforcement, were set forth in red (for known control, influence or use by known Partners), in blue (institutions tied to, governed by, or influenced by suspected Partners, e.g., Garrity, Cranmer, and "Gladstone" as the public persona of Mr. C) or, in green blocks, arrows, and dotted lines, the "dark matter" partners, whose identify was inferred because of institutions, actions shown to be in Partner play (Balfour-owned or -financed activities, including banking relationships in Asia, senior Austrian, Bulgarian police, etc.)

In gray were places Partners should be found, though no search had yet begun: Tallinn, Riga, Warsaw, Geneva, Luxembourg, perhaps New York, and London. Was there a Cyprus-Baghdad person? Was Balfour Asia represented in Singapore, Istanbul, Dubai, perhaps in Hong Kong? The most interesting parts of intelligence analysis are the moments of true discovery, and those when there is the insightful intuition of the "must be," of surmise. Sleepless nights are made by unanswerable question marks.

Vasil was brought to Washington, as Ambassador Sophie's recommendation had proposed, to attend seminars in DEA, IFFY and the FBI. His first assignment, however, before these formalities, was to assist the Bureau and Virginia police who were investigating the death of Todor Mihailov. He had been advised in advance of this work while in Sofia and had done his homework there; happily, the strong and reforming power of the Interior Minister had been extended to him. Ambassador Sophie had had some carefully couched conversations with the Minister about Vasil's excellence. The translation service, ITS, had been blown following the announcement—and indeed it was a rarity in Bulgaria to make public that which was elsewhere a public matter—of the conspiracy involving Giorgi, Mustafa and Jeanette, with suspicion falling on BB and unknown others, to steal from thieves and to commit murder in doing it. Vasil was also promoted to BB's old post, to enjoy upon his return from the U.S. It would be his job to assure cooperation with the EU and other powers, with Russia as well insofar as it joined in the treaties. Its agreements with Finland would be Vasil's model to put in place with Bulgaria.

But first, preparing for Washington, Vasil reviewed all travel records of known Sofia *mafiya* and Interior Ministry personnel, some of whom in earlier days had been Sixth Department "wet affairs." As he had guessed, BB had been travelling officially with two of his cronies from earlier wet affairs for "counterpart meetings" in Belarus, Uzbekistan, Kasakhstan, Turkmenistan, and so forth. Since the latter were rated by police, business, economic, banking, and NGO authorities as among the most corrupt in the world, along with Nigeria and Pakistan, BB did indeed have "counterpart" interests there.

Vasil knew such counterparts could not be expected to be truthful about any aspect of BB's mission there, including whether or not he had ever arrived, or if upon arriving he had departed, as Vasil surmised, for a quick four-day journey to the U.S. under a different passport, and with Bulgarian thugs meeting him in, say, Washington. Their passports would no doubt have been official, since they would not speak English. His thug assistants would have been there as an active presence to persuade Todor to give up his stolen fortune to BB and the new thieves. If BB had not done the interrogation and subsequent hit, it was by now clear that the likes of Bratislav, his partner head of UST&D (still unidentified as which among the several bank directors), the people who ran Brody and the other Partners, about which Vasil now knew thanks to Ambassador Sophie, would have had equal reason, by way of damage control, to blow Todor away.

Painstaking routine investigation was likely to clear it up. If no signs of BB and his company of thugs turned up in the area, from motel and rental-car leads to Immigration Service notes, if in other words the evidence did not show a quick and crude piece of work, followed by an hasty exit out of the country, then one must assume the Partners had organized it. For theirs would not be a revealing telltale hand; it would have been carefully planned, with no need for hurriedly imported thugs.

Investigation, Vasil assisting strongly, revealed it to have been indeed a carefully arranged hit. Even so, doubt remained, perhaps BB and the Sea Scouts had become sophisticated. After all, the competitition in the commercial assassination business these days was heavy, with IRA, Chechyns, Syrians, a few fanatic Japanese, and withering old Germans all looking for the money. The Todor Mihailov work had been well done: the silent deaths of the bodyguards outside, the quiet slaughter of the girlfriend and the servant inside. All that professionally lovely work indicated high skills; no fingerprints, no rental-car or hotel records, and frankly, though the FBI hated to admit it, no leads.

Intuitively Vasil guessed that BB had set out on the task, but more skilled shooters had taken care of the actual business. Since no trace could be found of BB, at least as yet, the Partners might have sent him and his little group of friends bye-bye as well. It was a perfectly reasonable assumption; BB's knowledge was also a danger to the Partnership.

And while housecleaning at Todor's, if coming upon BB, based on intelligence Bratislav and his Partners must have found easy to come by in Sofia, why not a clean sweep?

Even Sea Scouts, come to strange waters and run by a crude fool like BB, may find themselves swimming in cement suits well off the coast of nowhere. There was no question about their efficiency. The Partners' present and future would, Vasil believed, despite the temporary instabilities, be very well assured. It was the way of the world.

Vasil's pragmatic forecast was far more valid than any Karl Marx's ideological "inevitability" in history had generated. "Futurology" with respect to economic crime was easy. Working the edges, the dark game, networks of greed and aggrandizement were always there,—past, present and future. As Evil, it was always there. Vasil and all the Bulgars had always known, for the *Bogomil* Legacy offered the wisdom of darkness as well as a glimmer of unfleshed salvation. The *Bogomil* Legacy following in the very footsteps of the Sins of Adam, constantly embellished by empire and invention, was guaranteed.

Another investigation, less weighty in that it reached no conclusions about good and evil, would succeed. McLaughlin would see to that, as would the Bureau, even though his boss had opportunely recovered from cardiac disease in time to sit beaming in the Rose Garden as his two IFFY agents were honored. The Director, wearing his favored red bow tie, had turned to McLaughlin, next to him. "My agency, my people. My God, I can't tell you how much of my own sweat went into making their mission a success. Behind them all the way I was, instrumental to their success. Damn it, the President should be giving me a medal too!"

Mac McLaughlin, sitting next to this witless, gutless source of drivel, had had it. "Look, asshole, I have your personnel records for the whole time. Witnessed documentation. Don't forget you were in charge when the files were changed to show that Dubois was really "Greta Liebowitz," the *mafiya* mole. You approved the whole of the first staff appointments, one or more of whom *works* for that gang. You and I both know that, but I know I am going to stick you with the mud if I can. We're looking at everyone who knew when and where Claire Dubois was going, and that Barbour was also on that mission. One Jones, whom you asked for out of State; one bitch Smith in Personnel who tells me, *sotto voce*, you were screwing her when you made her chief there; one poor dope Swobo, whom I can't believe even you wouldn't see was feeble-minded; and, an odd charge but Claire remembered her curious and hostile look, our so-called librarian.

"Who tells me, with her lawyer present mind you, that you made a pass at her. The only bad thing I won't attribute to you, Director, is that. Typical sexual-harassment defense and she's so damn nasty ugly I can see why pages in so many of the books in the library have curled and turned yellow—it's the sight of her. And so, in conclusion to this friendly little exchange, and because the ceremony is to begin, I summarize. I'm sick of you. I may bring charges against you. Now go fuck a duck!"

The First, as he so liked to be called, considered counter threats, then reality, then that bitch Smith who had promised she'd keep her trap shut, then how much he liked Hawaii, and then how somewhere in his chest a pain seemed to be returning. The First was not cut out for this much intemperate disrespect, nor for disputation. He would retire on sick leave, a patriot unappreciated by his country. But everyone would know *his* truth. He'd tell them he was the one who had made the Vienna Incident heroes what they were.

Markowitz stayed on in Washington. He had several reunion dinners with Barbour and Claire, and other buddies from the old days, the ceremonial one at State of course. Then came an offer from Doc Dolan, now Deputy Director, to join IFFY as his partner. That would fill the second of the two deputy directors slots. McLaughlin was now "First" since the gutless one had retired on disability. "Lucky taxpayers, right? They got rid of him and now got the three of us.

People can sleep peacefully at night. God's in his heaven, we're in our chairs. There'll be no more crime. I so decree." So Mac had said, when Markowitz came in to say he'd take the job. Mac took a bottle of Macallan out from his desk drawer by way of a toast to idiocy.

Officer Andy Stein flew back to Malome, his role known and nicely overplayed by the big-city press. Made a sensitive, good man feel good. Until he walked into the Department and was dressed down by a jealous and small-minded chief for not reporting fully on his work—notwithstanding a letter from the heads of DEA and McLaughlin of IFFY, specifically commending Stein and stating that the Department of Justice Deputy Attorney General for Criminal Affairs had ordered Stein *not* to report locally with respect to his recruiting, handling, and supporting Rooster. The chief had no grounds upon which to stand save petty, jealous, pompous hatred. Which is quite good enough for most people like him.

The next day, his first on duty, Office Stein was the first to arrive at a double murder. Two Hispanics, one of whom, Javier, interviews later revealed, had worked at Mr. C's warehouse. The other, Miguel, was his cousin. No witnesses, no clues, no motives were apparent; Mr. C's business in Malome was going on as usual. Absentee crimelords see to their interests.

Andy had a beer after duty at Robbie's Club. A new thing, for him to stay in Malome after work. He'd come to like Robbie, owed him that first tip on Mr. C, owed him Rooster's being there. Shared with him the loss of Rooster. Shared strangely and for the first time, a sense of common humanity with the club regulars. All black, some felons, many coming up to him and giving him, God forbid that it would ever have occurred before, a pat on the back; one big guy even gave him an embrace. All saying they mourned for him his loss of Rooster and thought "as fuzz go, as pigs go, Officer Stein, you are a real bad (which means much admired) dude." There was more hope that Malome might become a community of friends, not prejudices—even about stupid cops and former felons—than Officer Stein had ever experienced before. For all its troubles, even this worst of worlds might be getting better.

Barbour had been on this British Airways flight many times, but that was long ago. He'd flown out from Washington many times, but those were different times. He'd done his government-dutiful miles across worlds, sleepless and jet-lagged, a worn traveller. But this time it was different! Claire sat beside him in the wonderfully comfortable first-class seat, her father across the aisle, all on their way to London and adventures this time of their own choosing, or insofar as well-planned lives allow that. Yes, there would be Sofia again, and Warsaw and Tallinn and Riga, and this time a welcome to Moscow by a chastened premier. One stops rattling swords when rusty blades break in midair rhetorical swings. And when wiser minds in an improved economy suggest that pan—Slavism, pro-mafiyism are suicidal, partly in response to his most admired Oligarch—who, he learned, was in league with the Western capitalistic mob—well, it was time to cool Vienna; go there for *linzertorte*, not trouble making.

Barbour, at the urging of his soon-to-be father-in-law, Ambassador Dubois, with whom he got along splendidly, had accepted a consulting post in State Department Intelligence. He was free to work for others as long as no conflicts of interest were in play. While consulting he would be "guided" by SDI's boss, but as an acting senior agent in the field who would take on a problem as he saw best. He had assured them all: no more Laxenburg shoot-outs, ever. Nevertheless in his luggage this idealist had his airline-informed gun. Most of his time would be spent working for a private firm, Karlberg Associates, dealing in investigation of international economic crimes, mostly for corporations and banks, but occasionally governments. His first job was in Bulgaria, to find that still missing twelve billion dollars. That was exactly his cup of tea, and Vasil's, who would soon join him as his second. Barbour did have, after all, a head start.

Claire was taking a post in London, as senior editor in a major publishing house. Their apartment would be in London. She fancied something rather posh in Belgravia or Kensington. And why not? The family money was there to support indulgences. Her father had agreed. It was not that he expected many flights by Claire to Kiev, although surely Barbour would be visiting, but from Kiev to London, well, that was an ambassador's choice. There were London friends; no wolf pack, to be sure, but he would be meeting Claire's friend Beulah and her husband coming down from Scotland for the occasion, and all would gather around at a favorite restaurant—tiny, old, intimate Wheeler's, of Duke Street. Quincy and Sir Peter would be there. Of course there'd be talk of old times, but of new times too.

At the restaurant, Sir Peter, over a splendid wine, asked Barbour, who was unusually thoughtful, "What are you thinking about?"

Barbour smiled his gentle smile. "Frankly, Sir Peter, since I know where this next trail takes me, I wonder just when I'm going to be face to face with whichever one of the Partners is Professor Moriarty."

"My good friend," said the acting head of the Yard, "like you, I'm a Baker Street Irregular. I've been asking that question myself. Keep in mind that after Moriarty pushed Holmes over the cliff at the waterfall, Holmes nevertheless returned to triumph. A man with zest for life takes a bit of a fall as but a temporary setback. We return to new victories. We have part of one now. Think how we can bask in the pleasure of having such friends as we are and have made. And I daresay we both take some pride in having such interesting enemies yet to pursue."